THE
GRAY
HOUSE

THE
GRAY
HOUSE

MARIAM PETROSYAN

TRANSLATED BY YURI MACHKASOV

amazoncrossing 🌐

Text copyright © 2009 Mariam Petrosyan

Translation copyright © 2017 Yuri Machkasov

Previously published as Дом, в котором . . . by Гаятри/Livebook in Russia in 2009. Translated from Russian by Yuri Machkasov. First published in English by AmazonCrossing in 2017.

Published by AmazonCrossing, Seattle
www.apub.com

Amazon, the Amazon logo, and AmazonCrossing are trademarks of Amazon.com, Inc., or its affiliates.

ISBN-13: 9781503942813
ISBN-10: 1503942813

Cover design by David Drummond

Printed in the United States of America

BOOK ONE

SMOKER

THE HOUSE MALE STUDENTS

FOURTH	THIRD	SECOND
	BIRDS	RATS
—	—	—
BLIND	VULTURE	RED
SPHINX	(LIZARD)	SOLOMON
(TABAQUI)	(ANGEL)	SQUIB
BLACK	DODO	DON
HUMPBACK	HORSE*	VIKING
(NOBLE)	(BUTTERFLY)	CORPSE
LARY*	(DEAREST)	ZEBRA
ALEXANDER	GUPPY	HYBRID*
(TUBBY)	BUBBLE*	MONKEY*
(SMOKER)	BEAUTY	MICROBE*
	ELEPHANT	TERMITE*
	(FICUS)	PORCUPINE
	(SHRUB)	SUMAC
		CARRION
		RINGER*
		TINY
		WHITEBELLY
		GREENERY
		DAWDLER

AS OF BOOK ONE

SIXTH HOUNDS	FIRST PHEASANTS	LEGEND
—	—	—
POMPEY	(GIN)	(PARENTHESES): WHEELERS
CROOK	(PROFESSOR)	UNDERLINED: INSENSIBLE
(OWL)	(BITER)	
GNOME	(GHOUL)	**BOLD:** UNDER 17
SHUFFLE	(STRAW)	
LAURUS	(STICKS)	STARRED*: BANDAR-LOGS
WOOLLY	(BRICKS)	
RABBIT	(CRYBABY)	
ZIT*	(GYPS)	PHEASANT CRYBABY IS NOT THE SAME PERSON AS CRYBABY OF THE "PAST" EPISODES, WHO BECAME HORSE
TRITON	(HAMSTER)	
(SLEEPY)	KIT	
GENEPOOL*	(BOOGER)	
DEALWITHIT*	**(CUPCAKE)**	
SPLUTTER*	**(SNIFFLE)**	
(HEADLIGHT)	(PIDDLER)	
(HASTEWASTE)		
EARS		
NUTTER		
RICKSHAW		
BAGMAN		
CRAB		
(FLIPPER)		

The House sits on the outskirts of town. The neighborhood is called the Comb. The long buildings of the projects here are arranged in jagged rows, with empty cement squares between them—the intended playgrounds for the young Combers. The teeth of the comb are white. They stare with many eyes and they all look just the same. In places where they haven't sprouted yet, there are the fenced vacant lots. The piles of debris from the houses already knocked down, nesting grounds for rats and stray dogs, are much more appealing to the young Combers than the empty spaces between the teeth.

In the no-man's-land between the two worlds—that of the teeth and that of the dumps—is the House. They call it Gray House. It is old, closer in age to the dumps, the graveyards of its contemporaries. It stands alone, as the other houses shun it, and it doesn't look like a tooth, since it is not struggling upward. Three stories high, facing the highway, it too has a backyard—a narrow rectangle cordoned off by chicken wire. It was white when built. It has since become gray, and yellowish from the other side, toward the back. It is bristling with aerials; it is strewn with cables; it is raining down plaster and weeping from the cracks. Additions and sheds cling to it, along with doghouses and garbage bins, all in the back. The facade is bare and somber, just the way it is supposed to be.

Nobody likes Gray House. No one would admit it openly, but the inhabitants of the Comb would rather not have it in their neighborhood. They would rather it didn't exist at all.

SMOKER

ON CERTAIN ADVANTAGES OF
TRAINING FOOTWEAR

It all started with the red sneakers. I found them at the bottom of my bag. The personal-possessions bag, that's what it was called. Only there was never anything in it with any touch of personality. Two standard-issue towels, a bunch of handkerchiefs, and dirty laundry. Same as everyone else. All bags, all towels, socks, briefs—all identical, so that nobody would feel slighted.

It was an accident that I found them. I'd lost sight of them long ago. An old present from someone forgotten, from the previous life. Bright red, wrapped in shiny plastic, the soles striped like a candy cane. I tore open the package, ran my fingers over the flaming laces, and quickly put on the shoes. My legs looked funny. I forgot they could look like that. They acquired this unfamiliar walking feel.

That same day, after classes, Gin took me aside and said that he didn't approve of my behavior. He pointed at the sneakers and told me to take them off. I shouldn't have asked why, but I did.

"They attract attention," he said.

This was normal for Gin in terms of explanation.

"So?" I said. "So let them."

He didn't say anything. He adjusted the cord on his glasses and wheeled off. That night I received a note. Only two words: *Footwear discussion.* I was in trouble, and I knew it.

Scraping the fuzz off my cheeks I cut myself, and then broke the toothbrush glass. My reflection in the mirror looked completely terrified, but I wasn't really afraid. Well, I was, but at the same time I didn't care. I even left the sneakers on.

The assembly was held in the classroom. Someone had written *Footwear discussion* on the blackboard. Three-ring circus with clowns, except I wasn't laughing, because

I was tired of these games and the oh-so-clever people who played them, and of the place itself. So tired that I almost forgot how to laugh.

My place was at the board, so that everyone could see the subject of the discussion. Gin sat at the desk to my left sucking on his pen. To my right, Kit loudly knocked a steel ball bearing around a plastic maze until he got the reproachful looks.

"Who would like to contribute?" Gin said.

Many would. Almost all of them. To start it off, they called Gyps. The quicker to get rid of him, I guess.

We learned that everyone who tried to attract attention to himself was an egotist, a bad person, capable of anything and full of himself while at the same time completely empty inside. A jay in peacock's plumes. Gyps recited the fable of the jay. Then he recited the poem about the donkey that wound up in the lake and drowned because of its own stupidity. He also tried to sing something to the same effect, but no one was listening anymore. Gyps puffed his cheeks, started to cry, and stopped speaking. He was thanked, given a handkerchief, and shunted behind a textbook, and the floor was given to Ghoul.

Ghoul was barely audible. He never lifted his gaze, as if reading something off the surface of the table, even though there wasn't anything there except the scratched veneer. His white bangs were falling over his eyes, and he was sticking it back up with his saliva-moistened finger, but as soon as he fixed the pale strand to his forehead, it crept back over his eyes. You needed nerves of steel to look at Ghoul for long. So I didn't look at him. My nerves were in tatters already. There was no need to fray them further.

"What is it to which the person in question is trying to draw attention? It would seem that it is just his footwear. However, this is not so. By means of his footwear he is drawing attention to his legs. Therefore he is advertising his handicap, putting it in everyone's face. Therefore he is accentuating our common unfortunate condition without consulting us or soliciting our opinions. In a sense he is mocking us all . . ."

He chewed on this for quite a while. The finger traveled up and down the bridge of his nose, his eyes were getting bloodshot. Everything he could say I knew by heart—everything that was fit to be trotted out for the occasion. Every word emanating from Ghoul was just as colorless and desiccated as he was, as were his finger and the nail on that finger.

Then it was Top's turn. Basically the same speech, and about as engaging. Then Straw, Sticks, and Bricks, the triplets. The Little Pigs. They would talk all at once, cutting each other off, and this I actually watched with great interest because I had not expected them to take part in the discussion. I guess they didn't like the way I was watching them, or they got self-conscious and that only made it worse, but they ripped into me the hardest of all. They dragged out my habit of folding page corners (even though I was not the only one reading books), the fact that I had not contributed my handkerchiefs to the communal pool (even though I was not the only one with a nose), that I occupied the shower for longer than was allowed (twenty-eight minutes on average, when the norm was twenty), bumped my wheels while driving (and wheels need care!), and, finally, arrived at their main point—that I was a smoker. If you could call someone smoking one cigarette every three days a smoker.

They asked me if I knew the extent of damage caused by nicotine to the well-being of others. Of course I knew. I not only knew, I could easily give a talk on the subject, because over the last six months they'd stuffed me with enough booklets, articles, and pithy quotations on the dangers of smoking to comfortably feed a multitude. I was lectured on lung cancer. Then, separately, on cancer in general. Then on cardiovascular diseases. Then on some additional horrible ailments, which was when I stopped listening. On topics like these they could go on for hours. They would shudder, horrified, eyes lit up with excitement—like decrepit gossips discussing the latest murder or accident, drooling happily. Neat little boys in neat little shirts, so earnest and wholesome, but hidden underneath their faces were old hags, skin pitted with acid. This was not the first time I saw through to those wrinkled old crones, so it was not a surprise. They got to me so badly that I started dreaming of poisoning them with nicotine, all together and each one separately. Pity I couldn't do that. To smoke my paltry once-every-three-days cigarette I went to hide in the teachers' bathroom. Not even our own bathroom, god forbid! If I poisoned anyone or anything it could only be the cockroaches, because only the cockroaches ever ventured there.

The stoning had been going on for half an hour when Gin rapped his pen on the table and declared the footwear discussion closed. They'd just about forgotten the topic by that time, so the reminder turned out to be quite appropriate. They stared at the damned sneakers. They loathed them in silence, with dignity and with contempt for my childishness and tastelessness. Fifteen pairs of soft brown loafers against one fire-red pair of sneakers. The longer the stares continued, the brighter the shoes burned. Soon everything except them became gray and washed out.

I was just admiring them when I was told it was my turn to speak.

I don't know quite how it happened, but, for the first time in my life, I said to the Pheasants what I thought of them. I told them that this classroom and everything in it were not worth one pair of gorgeous sneakers like these. That's what I said to the Pheasants. Even to poor, cowed Top. Even to the Little Pigs. And I really felt it at that moment, because I can't stand cowards and traitors, and that's exactly who they were—cowards and traitors.

They must have thought they'd scared me so much that I'd gone crazy. Only Gin didn't look surprised.

"So now we know what you actually think," he said. He wiped his glasses and pointed his finger at the sneakers. "This was not at all about those. This was about you."

Kit was still waiting at the board, chalk in hand. But the discussion was over. I just sat there with my eyes closed until they all wheeled out. And I continued sitting like that long after they did. My tiredness was flowing out of me. I had done something out of the ordinary. I'd behaved like a normal person. I'd stopped conforming to others. And, however it all ended up, I knew I would never regret that.

I looked up at the board. It was supposed to say: *Footwear discussion. 1. Self-importance. 2. Drawing attention to collective disability. 3. Thumbing nose at collective. 4. Smoking.* Kit had managed to make at least two mistakes in every word. He could not write for sour apples, but he was the only one who could stand, so he ended up at the board for every meeting.

For the next two days no one spoke to me. They all behaved like I did not exist. I had become a ghost. On the third day of this silent treatment, Homer told me that the principal wanted to see me.

The First's counselor looked more or less like the whole group would look were they not masquerading as teenagers for some reason. Like the hag sitting inside every one of them, waiting for the next funeral. Decay, gold teeth, and failing eyes. At least he wore it all out in the open.

"The administration has been made aware already," he said, looking like a doctor giving a patient the news of an incurable disease.

He continued to sigh and nod and look at me pityingly until I started feeling like a corpse, and not a very fresh one. Once assured of the proper effect, Homer left, snuffling and groaning as he went.

I'd visited the principal's office twice before. Once when I had just come in and once when I was submitting a painting for the exposition with the idiotic theme of "I Love the World." It was the result of three days' work and I titled it *The Tree of Life.* Only when you stepped back a couple of feet from the painting could you discern that the Tree was teeming with skulls and hordes of maggots. Up close, they looked kind of like pears in among the crooked boughs. Just as I'd expected, no one inside the House noticed anything wrong. My dark sense of humor was apparently only discovered at the exposition itself, but I've never found out how it was received. Actually, it was not even a joke. My love for the world at the time looked more or less the way it did in the painting.

During my first visit to the principal's office, the worms had already started wriggling inside the worldly love, though we weren't quite ready for the skulls yet. The office was clean but still somehow untidy. It was obviously not the hub of the House, the place everything flows in or out of. More like a guards' shack at the gates. A rag doll in a festooned dress had been sitting on the sofa in the corner. It was the size of a three-year-old, Memos and notes, stuck with pushpins—on the walls, the blinds, the sofa, everywhere. But most of all I was struck by the enormous fire extinguisher over the principal's desk. It was so mesmerizing that I could not quite pay attention to the principal himself. Anyone who chose to sit under that antique fiery zeppelin must be somewhat counting on that. The only thing you could think about was that monstrosity crashing down and flattening him right there in front of your eyes. There was no space left in your head for anything else. Not a bad way of becoming invisible.

The principal was talking of the school policies then. Of the way forward. "We prefer tempering those who have already been forged." Something like that. I wasn't listening too closely. Because of the fire extinguisher. It was getting on my nerves. Everything else was as well. The doll, and the notes. *Maybe he's an amnesiac*, I kept thinking, *so this is just his way of reminding himself of everything. And when I'm gone he's going to write me up and pin that information somewhere close.*

When I tried to tune in for a while, he was just getting to the alumni. The ones who "did well for themselves." Those were the faces in the framed photos on both sides of the fire extinguisher. Irritable and mundane, all possessing trophies or diplomas that they paraded sourly before the camera. Even a photograph of some headstones would have been more fun. Perhaps they should put at least one of those up there, considering the school's mission.

It was very different this time. The fire extinguisher was still there, as were the notes on every available surface, but something had changed in the office. Something not directly related to the furniture and the missing doll. Shark was sitting under the extinguisher and going through papers. Shriveled, mottled, and shaggy, like a lichen-covered stump. His eyebrows, also shaggy and mottled, fell over his eyes like filthy icicles. There was a file in front of him. I glimpsed my own photo between two sheets of paper and realized that the file was full of me. My grades, performance reviews, snapshots from different years—all the parts of a person that could be distilled onto paper. I was partially on the desk, bound in cardboard, and partially sitting before him. If there were any difference between the flat me on the desk and the three-dimensional me in the chair, it was the red sneakers. They were no longer just footwear. They were who I was. My bravery and my folly, a bit faded after three days but still bright and beautiful like fire.

"It must have been something really serious for the boys to lose all patience with you." Shark waved a piece of paper at me. "I've got this letter here. Fifteen signatures. What's this supposed to mean?"

I shrugged. It meant whatever it meant. I wasn't about to explain about the sneakers to him. That would be ridiculous.

"Yours is the model group." The mottled icicles drooped, obscuring the eyes. "I really like that group. I cannot ignore their request, especially seeing as this is the first time they've asked such a thing. So, what do you have to say for yourself?"

I wanted to say that I was going to be happy to be rid of them as well, but decided not to. What good would my lonely voice be against fifteen of Shark's exemplary pets? Instead of offering pleas and explanations, I just studied the surroundings.

The pictures of the "well for themselves" were even more disgusting than I remembered. I imagined my own pitted, crumbling mug among them, with paintings behind me, one more hideous than the next. "He was dubbed the next Giger when he was just thirteen." It made me sick.

"Well?" Shark waved his spread-out fingers in front of me. "Are you asleep? I am asking if you understand that I have to undertake certain actions."

"Of course. I'm sorry."

That was the only thing that came to mind.

"Me too. Very sorry," Shark growled, snapping my file shut. "Sorry that you were so brainless as to manage to lose the trust of the whole group at once. Get out and get your things."

Something jumped inside me, like a toy ball on a string.

"Where are you sending me?"

He was enjoying my fear immensely. He basked in it for a while. Shuffled things around, inspected his fingernails, lit a cigarette.

"Where do you think? Another group, of course."

I smiled. "You must be joking."

It would be easier to drop a live horse into any other House group than somebody from the First. The horse would have a better chance of fitting in, size and manure notwithstanding.

I should've kept my mouth shut, but still I blurted out, "No one would have me. I'm a Pheasant."

"I've had enough of this!" Shark spat out the cigarette and smashed his fist on the desk. "What's this Pheasant stuff? Who invented all that crap?"

The papers scurried from under his fist, and the cigarette butt missed the ashtray.

I was so scared that I yelled back at him, even louder, "How should I know why they call us that? Ask those who started it! You think it's easy, remembering all those idiotic nicks? You think anyone explained to me what they mean?"

"Don't you dare raise your voice in my office!" he screamed back, leaning over the desk.

I glanced at the fire extinguisher and immediately looked back.

It was still hanging there.

Shark followed the direction of my gaze and suddenly whispered, as if taking me into confidence, "It won't. The bolts are this thick."

Then he showed me his disgusting thumb. This was so unexpected that I was stunned. I just sat there ogling him like an idiot. He was smirking. It dawned on me that he was simply bullying me. I hadn't been living in the House long enough to easily address everyone by their nicknames. You had to be pretty open minded to call someone Sniffle or Piddler to their face and not feel like a complete jerk. Now I was being told that the administration did not approve of it either. What for? Just to have a good yell and see how I'd react? And then I realized what had changed in the office since my first visit. It was Shark himself. The unassuming body hiding under the fire extinguisher had turned into a real shark. Into exactly what his name was. The nicks were given for a reason.

Shark lit up again while I was considering all this.

"I don't want to hear any more of this nonsense," he warned, fishing out the remains of the previous cigarette from my file. "Of these attempts to disparage our best group. To deprive it of its rightful status. Understood?"

"You mean you too consider the word to be an insult? But why? How is it worse than simply *Birds*? Or *Rats*? *Rats*. I think that sounds much worse than *Pheasants*."

Shark blinked at me.

"That's because you know what those who say it actually mean, correct?"

"Right," Shark said severely. "That's enough. Shut up. Now I understand why the First can't stand you."

I looked at the sneakers. Shark was much too generous toward the Pheasants' motivations, but I decided not to say so. I only asked where I was being transferred.

"I don't know yet," he lied. "I need to think about it."

No, he wasn't called Shark for nothing. He was precisely that. A blotchy, slit-mouthed fish with eyes looking in different directions. It was getting old, and the hunting was not what it once had been, which is why it was entertained by chasing after minnows like me. Of course he knew. He had even just been about to tell me, but then decided not to. Just to make me squirm. He overdid it, though, because the group didn't really matter. They all hated Pheasants. Suddenly it came to me that this might not be so bad after all. I now had a chance to escape. The First threw me out and the others were going to do the same, whether right away or not. If I really applied myself I could make it as quick as possible. Think about how much time and effort I'd spent trying to become a good Pheasant. Convincing another group that I didn't belong there would be much easier. Besides, they were all sure of it already. It was even conceivable that Shark thought so himself. This was me being expelled in a roundabout way. And afterward he could say that I wouldn't fit in anywhere, no matter how hard they tried. Because heaven forbid any blame would attach to Pheasants.

This calmed me down. Shark caught that moment of enlightenment and didn't like it.

"Go," he said with visible disgust. "Go pack your things. I am coming tomorrow at half past eight. Personally."

As I was closing the door to the principal's office behind me, I knew that he was going to be late tomorrow. An hour, maybe even two. I could see right through him now, him and his petty shark pleasures.

"The students just call it Home, succinctly combining in this word everything that our school means to them—family, comfort, care, and understanding." This was what it said in the promotional booklet. I was planning to frame it and put it on the wall once I was out of there. Black frame. Maybe even gilded. It was quite a piece of work, that booklet. Not a word of truth in it, but also not a word that was a direct lie. I don't know who had written it but he was a genius, in a sense. It was House, though, not Home. But we did succinctly combine a lot of stuff into this word. And it was quite possible that a Pheasant really was comfortable here. And that other Pheasants were a family to him. There are no Pheasants in the Outsides, so I could not say for sure, but if there were, the House would be the place they would all fervently seek out. But there aren't any, and I had a suspicion that they were created by the House itself, which meant that before getting here they all might have been normal people. A very disconcerting thought.

But back to the booklet, page three: "More than a hundred years of history and lovingly preserved tradition" are all present and accounted for. One look at the House is enough to realize that it started falling apart in the last century. There were also bricked-in fireplaces with a complex network of flues. When it was windy the walls moaned like in a medieval castle. Total immersion in history. Oh, and traditions, it's certainly right about those. The absurdity that is the House was definitely a product of several generations of not-quite-right people. Those who followed needed only to "lovingly preserve" and reinforce.

"A massive library." There was one. Game room, swimming pool, movie screen . . . all there, but each "there" came with its own little "except," and then it turned out that actually using those luxuries would be impossible, dangerous, or unpleasant. The game room belonged to Bandar-Logs. That meant no Pheasants allowed. The library was the card players'. You could wheel up there and take out a book, but you were unlikely to want to return it. Swimming pool? Under construction for the past couple of years. "And it is going to be at least two years more, the roof is leaking," as the Little Pigs had kindly clarified. Oh, they had been very kind for a while. Answering questions, showing and explaining. They were sure that they lived full and interesting lives in an uncommonly wondrous place. This had me completely floored. I shouldn't have tried to convince them otherwise, I guess. Then maybe we'd still be friends. But as it was, the kindness was soon over, together with the budding friendships, and the three almost identical signatures appeared at the bottom of the letter demanding my transfer. They had still managed to teach me a lot. Almost everything I knew about the House I had learned from them. The life of a Pheasant was not conducive to new information. To anything new, really. Life in the First was rationed minute by minute.

In the canteen, think about food. In the classroom, think about learning. At the doctor, think about health. Shared fears, of catching a cold. Shared dreams, of a mutton chop for dinner. Uniform possessions, nothing extraneous. Every gesture automatic. Four parts to the day, divided by meals—breakfast, lunch, dinner. Movies once a week, on Saturdays. Assemblies on Mondays.

"*Should we?*"

"*I could not help but notice . . .*"

"*The classroom is undoubtedly not aired out enough. It affects all of us.*"

"*That odd scratching noise . . . I am afraid it is rats after all.*"

"*Lodge a protest regarding the unsanitary condition of the premises, potentially leading to the spread of vermin . . .*"

And slogans. Endless painted slogans.

In the classroom: *When in class, think about class. Everything else—out of the way!* In the dorm: *Maintain silence, respect your roommates* and *Noise contributes to nervous disorders.*

Steel cots in neat rows. White doilies on the pillows. *Keep it clean! Cleanliness begins with your pillowcase!* White nightstands, one for each two beds. *Remember where you put your glass. Mark it with your number.* Folded towels on the headboards, numbered as well. From six to eight the radio is on. *Nothing to do? Listen to music.* All those wishing to play chess or bingo, move to the classroom. When a television was installed in the classroom, there was a drop in the number of people in the dorm after classes. The television was moved. The blue rectangle now shines in the dorm until night, which for a Pheasant begins at nine, by which time he must be in bed, pajama-clad and ready to drift off to sleep. *If you suffer from insomnia, seek medical help.*

And it all begins anew in the morning. Calisthenics, sitting up. Making your bed. *When dressing, help your neighbor and he will help you.* Ablutions. Six sinks, rust rings around the plugholes. *Wait for your turn, then be mindful of others waiting.* Distorted faces in the puddles on the tiled floor. Breakfast. Classes. Lunch break. Homework. Quiet time. And so on, ad infinitum.

As I wheeled into the dorm, it turned out that I was no longer a ghost. The First knew of the transfer, I could see it in their faces as they stared at me. There was something slightly depraved in their curiosity. As if they were planning to eat me. It was all I could do not to turn around right there at the door. I wheeled to my bed instead and looked at the TV. A woman in a checkered apron was explaining how to make honeycakes. "Take three eggs, separating the whites . . ." Such programs were very beneficial before dinner. They stimulated the appetite. By the time the bell rang I knew how honeycakes were made, how they were served, and what kind of smile you were supposed to wear when serving them. I was, however, alone in possession of this new knowledge. Everyone else was ogling me, participating in the preparation of a completely different dish.

The departure from the dorm was organized three-in-a-row, as usual, so as to be able to take positions in front of the sinks without jostling and wash hands before the meal. I did not fall in. This was duly noted, with knowing glances all around.

I began shaking at the table. I was feeling the Pheasants' stares on me. Which way would they turn once they'd had enough? But they couldn't turn away. Or maybe they really didn't know where I was being transferred.

Time stretched out into eternity.

Mashed potatoes. Carrot fritters. The fork with a bent tine. The lady in the white apron pushing the food cart, plates clanking as she goes. White walls. Deep arches of the windows.

I like the canteen. It's the oldest place in the House. Or, rather, the least changed. Windows, walls, and the cracked tiles were quite probably the same as seventy years ago. And the tiled hearth, taking up one of the walls, with the locked cast-iron door. It's beautiful. The only place where the exhortations stop, where you could tune out, look at the other groups, and imagine yourself being a non-Pheasant. That was my favorite game once. Right after I arrived. Then it got boring. And now it occurred to me that I could play it for real, that it wouldn't be a game anymore.

Mashed potatoes and carrot fritters. Tea. Bread. Butter. Our table is in black and white. White shirts, black pants. White plates on black trays. Black trays on white tablecloth. The only colors are in the faces and hair.

The next table belongs to the Second. It's the rowdiest and the most colorful. Dyed mullets, sunglasses, and beads. Thumping earphones. Rats, a cross between punks and clowns. There's no tablecloth, no knives, and the forks are chained to the table. If a day passes without one of them pitching a fit, trying to tear off his fork and stab his neighbor with it, for a Rat that day is wasted. This is purely for show. Everyone in the Second always carries a switchblade or a razor, so all that fuss with the forks is just a way of showing respect for traditions. A little entertainment for the benefit of the dining public. At the head of the table sits Red. Enormous green shades, shaved head, a rose on the cheek, and a constant stupid smirk. Rat Leader. The second one already, that I've seen. Rat Leaders don't last long.

The Third has its own show. They all wear huge bibs with kiddy designs and always lug around the pots with their favorite plants. Considering their perpetual mourning and sour countenance, this also looks like a circus, albeit a sinister one. Probably only Birds themselves are entertained by it. They grow flowers in their room, do embroidery and cross-stitching, they are the quietest and politest after us, but to even think that I might end up among them is horrifying. When I was still playing my favorite game I always skipped them over.

I suddenly have a vision, so palpably ghastly I can almost touch it.

I see myself in the dank and gloomy dorm of the Third. Ivy-covered windows let in very little light. Plants and more plants, in pots and tubs. The center of the room is occupied by the crumbling fireplace.

Birds are wielding needles, all in a row on low stools. On the mantelpiece sits Vulture, seemingly mummified and clad in moth-ridden ermine robes. He is puffing on a hookah and sending clouds of smoke our way.

From time to time one Bird or another gets up and demonstrates his handiwork to Vulture. I feel sick. Both from the heat and from the fact that my stitching looks hideous. The threads are all tangled, bunched, and tattered, I can't even find my needle in that mess, but I know that sooner or later it is going to be my turn to go and present it, and I am deathly afraid. One careless movement and my elbow upends a pot standing nearby, it jumps off and breaks into pieces. The enormous geranium falls down, clods of earth and shards of pottery everywhere.

In the middle of the carnage on the floor—a very white, very clean human skull. The lower jaw is missing. Everyone freezes. They look at me, then at the skull. I hear a disgusting cackle.

"Why yes, Smoker, you are exactly right," Vulture says, hopping down from the mantelpiece to hobble toward me. "That's our previous transfer, may he rest in peace!"

He laughs, demonstrating his unnaturally sharp, almost sharklike teeth . . .

Here I snapped out of it, because I felt my real self in the center of attention, not of Birds but of my own dear Pheasants. They were watching me with great interest. Vulture's sharp-toothed rictus withered down to Gin's lopsided grin, turning my stomach. I bent down to my fritter, hating them so much I nearly threw up. My daydream was just that, a dream. The real scavengers were sitting right here, scanning my face in search of traces of sweat, wetting their lips in anticipation. I suddenly realized that I would rather become a Bird, right this moment. Wear black, learn embroidering, dig up a hundred skulls hidden in flower pots. Anything, just to leave the First. What really upset me was that these feelings could also look from the outside like a panic attack. "That's it," I told myself, "no more games. Wait until tomorrow. Only thirteen hours left."

Once, when I was smoking in the teachers' bathroom, flinching at every sound, Sphinx came in there. I was so spooked I threw away the cigarette.

"Look at that, a Pheasant smoking!" Sphinx said, staring at the cigarette butt at his feet, starting to get soggy on the damp tiles. "Wouldn't have believed it if someone told me."

Then he laughed. Gangling, bald, armless. Eyes as green as grass. Broken nose, sarcastic mouth, always lifted at the corners. Black-gloved prosthetics.

"Got any more smokes?"

I nodded, astonished. He had actually addressed me. No one talked to Pheasants. It just was not done. I almost expected he was going to say next, "Mind if I have one?" but no such luck.

"That's nice" was all he said.

And then he left.

I hadn't assumed for a second he'd say anything to anyone about this. I was wrong.

When people started calling me Smoker a couple of days later, I did not put two and two together at first. He was not the only one who knew. The Little Pigs enlightened me again. Turns out, Sphinx had given me a new nick. Became my godfather. The House nearly collapsed, because that had never happened before. No one had ever christened a Pheasant. Much less someone like Sphinx. Above him there was only Blind, and above Blind there was only the roof and the swallows' nests.

All this made me a kind of celebrity among non-Pheasants and made all Pheasants hate me, without exception. The new nick sounded to them slightly worse than Jack the Ripper. It annoyed them. It marred their image. But they could not undo it. They didn't have the authority.

I decided not to imagine myself in the Fourth. My snitch of a godfather was there, along with crazy Noble, who'd knocked out one of my teeth when I accidentally locked wheels with him. Also Tabaqui the Jackal, who once sprayed me with some stinky crap from a canister marked *Danger*, and Lary the Bandar-Log, who coordinated all assaults of Logs on Pheasants. Imagining myself among them didn't help. I had enough trouble as it was.

I finished the soggy fritter. Drank my tea. Ate the bread and butter. Sketched out in my head two separate plans for running away. They were both utterly unworkable, but it still cheered me up. Then dinner ended.

I didn't return to the dorm. I had a smoke in the teachers' bathroom and went back to the canteen. The landing in front of it was usually empty. There weren't many places like that in the House. I parked the wheelchair by the window and stared at the darkening tops of the trees outside until the lights switched on in the hallway. They made the trees too dark. I wheeled away and started going back and forth in front of the notice boards. There wasn't anything else I could look at. I read them all again for the hundredth time and for the hundredth time found that they never changed. It was the ones behind the boards that changed, all right. They were made in marker, crayon, and paint, and they changed so quickly that those who wanted to leave a message had to paint over the old ones, wait for it to dry, and write on top. Some things were too important for the House denizens not to do properly. I didn't usually read the writings. There were too many of them, and most were too silly. But tonight I had nothing better to do. I parked the wheelchair alongside the boards and peeked into the space between them.

HUNTING SEASON IS OPEN.
SHOOTING LICENSES AS PER PRICE LIST.
THURSDAY. SQUIB.

I tried to imagine whom or what one could shoot here. Mice? Stray cats? And what with? Slingshots? I sighed and went on reading.

Scores, day bef. yesterday.
Morn. Laundry.

Astrological services. Experienced practitioner.
Cof. Daily. 6 to 7 pm.

HOW TO ACKNOWLEDGE SHORTCOMINGS.
SHALL IMPART OWN PRICELESS EXPERIENCE.
THE ENLIGHTENED ONE.

SCORES, YESTERDAY. MORN.
THRD BUFFALO LEFT OF ENTR.

Half pound of Roquefort. Cheap.
Whitebelly.

"EXPAND THE BOUNDARIES OF THE UNIVERSE!"
COF. THUR.
BAR MGR., RQST. MOON RIVER #64.
NONSTANDARD FOOTWEAR REQD.

This notice stopped me cold. I reread it. Looked above it. Looked at it again. Looked at my sneakers. Coincidence? Most likely. But I loathed going back to the dorm. I knew what "Cof." was and where it was. I also knew that I would not be welcome there, and that no sane Pheasant would ever try to get in. On the other hand, what did I have to lose? Why not expand the boundaries? I buffed the sneakers with my handkerchief a bit, to restore the luster, and wheeled off to the Coffeepot.

On the second floor, the hallway was long like a garden hose and had no windows. The only windows were in front of the canteen and on the landing. The hallway started at the stairs, was then interrupted by the anteroom to the canteen, and then went on to the other stairs. Canteen at one end, with the staff room and principal's office opposite. Then our two rooms, a disused one, the biology classroom, the abandoned bathroom that everyone called "the teachers' bathroom" and that I used as a smoking hideaway, and then the common room that had been closed for interminable renovations since before my arrival. That was all familiar territory. It ended at the lobby, a gloomy expanse at the crossroads, with windows looking out into the yard, a sofa in the middle, and a broken TV in the corner. I'd never ventured beyond it. There was an invisible boundary, and Pheasants did their best never to cross it.

I boldly crossed to the other side, went through the hallway beyond the lobby, and found myself in a different world.

It looked like an explosion in a paint shop. Several explosions. Our side had the drawings and scribbles too, but this side did not simply have them, it *was* them. Enormous, human-sized and bigger, leaping off the walls—they flowed and intertwined, scrambled on top of each other, fizzed and jumped, extended to the ceiling and shrank back. The walls on both sides swelled with murals until the corridor started to seem narrower. It was like driving through a maniac's nightmare.

The doors of the Second bristled with blue skulls, purple thunderbolts, and warning signs. It was obvious whose territory this was, so I cautiously veered toward the opposite wall. These doors could suddenly disgorge anything, from razors and bottles to whole Rats. The area was already thick with broken glass and general detritus, and this mess crunched underwheel like brittle old bones.

The door I was looking for was slightly ajar, and a good thing too or I would have missed it. *Coffee and tea only*, proclaimed the plain white sign. The rest of the door was painted in bamboo patterns, indistinguishable from the surrounding walls. I peeked in to make sure this really was the Coffeepot. A dimly lit space, lots of round tables. Chinese lanterns and Japanese origami hanging from the ceiling, horrifying masks and framed black-and-white photos on the walls. And a bar by the door, assembled from parts of lecterns and painted blue.

I pulled the door a bit wider. A bell clanked and I saw faces turn toward me. The nearest were two Hounds in collars. Farther in I could see Rats' colorful mullets. I decided not to look any more closely and wheeled to the bar.

"Sixty-four, please!" I blurted out, as the notice had said, and only then looked up.

Rabbit, plump and bucktoothed, also in a collar, was gawking at me from behind the counter.

"Say what?" he asked, astounded.

"Number sixty-four," I repeated, feeling very stupid. "Moon River."

There were sniggers at the tables.

"The Pheasant's going places!" someone shouted. "Did you hear that?"

"A Pheasant suicide!"

"No, that's a new breed. Jet Pheasant!"

"It's their king. Emperor Pheasant."

"This can't be a Pheasant. It's a changeling."

"And a sick one too, otherwise why would he want to change into a Pheasant?"

While the customers were cracking jokes at my expense, Rabbit solemnly stepped out from behind the counter, went around to my side, and stared at my feet. He studied them intently for what seemed like an eternity and finally said, "No good."

"Why not?" I whispered. "The notice said nonstandard."

"Don't know anything about any notices," Rabbit said sternly and went back to his nook. "Come on, get out of here."

I stared at the sneakers.

They no longer looked like flames. There were too few windows in the Coffeepot, and no Pheasants at all. It was a stupid thing to have done. I shouldn't have come up here to be ridiculed. The sneakers were perfectly ordinary to everyone except Pheasants. I'd somehow managed to forget about that.

"They are not standard," I said. Mostly to myself, I wasn't trying to convince anyone. Then I turned toward the door.

"Hey, Pheasant!" I heard from the farthermost table.

I wheeled around.

There, over the intricately decorated coffee cups, sat the wheelers of the Fourth. Noble, he of the fair hair and gray eyes, beautiful as an elven king, and Tabaqui the Jackal—pint-sized, frizzy-haired, and big-eared, like a lemur in a wig.

"Tell you what, Rabbit," Noble said, keeping his chilly gaze on me, "this is the first time that I've seen a Pheasant whose footwear does not adhere to what I would call a certain standard. I am surprised you didn't notice that."

"Exactly right," Tabaqui jumped in excitedly. "That's exactly what I noticed, too. And then I said to myself: He's a goner. They are going to peck him to death. Rabbit, you give him the Sixty-Four. That may just be the only bright spot he has left. Drive over here, babe! We'll have your order filled."

I was unsure whether to accept the invitation, but Hounds pulled in their legs and chairs, making a path wide enough for an elephant to drive through, so I had no choice.

Tabaqui, the one who'd called me babe, looked no more than fourteen himself. But only from a distance. Up close he might as easily have passed for thirty. He was clad in three vests, and under them he had on three different T-shirts, in green, pink, and blue, and still you were struck by how skinny he was. All three vests were equipped with multiple pockets, and all of them bulged. He was also bedecked in beads, buttons, amulets, neck pouches, pins, and little bells, all looking either very worn or slightly grubby. Noble, in his white shirt and blue chinos, appeared almost naked by comparison. Naked and squeaky clean.

"What do you need Moon River for?" Noble asked.

"Nothing much," I said honestly. "Just wanted to try it."

"Do you even know what it is?"

I shook my head. "Some sort of cocktail?"

Noble's stare filled with pity. His skin was so fair that it seemed to glow. His eyebrows and lashes were darker than the hair, and his eyes were now gray, now blue. Not even his sour scowl managed to spoil the impression. Not even the zits on his chin.

I had never met anyone else so beautiful it hurt just to look at them. Noble was the only one. About a month ago he had knocked out one of my teeth when I locked wheels with him, coming out of the canteen. I'd never seen him up close before. I hadn't even had time to think. I'd just stared and missed what he was saying. Next thing I knew the beautiful elf swung for my jaw, and that was the end of the rapture. For a week after that I tracked close to the walls, shrank from passersby, spent untold hours at the dentist's office, and couldn't sleep at night.

Of all people, Noble was the least likely to be my tablemate in the Coffeepot and, if it were up to me, the least likely to have a conversation with. But that's how it turned out. He was asking questions, I was answering them, and his damned looks started to work their magic again. It was very hard to constantly keep in mind what he really was while being so close to him. Besides, I developed a nagging feeling that this Moon River thing wasn't exactly a harmless drink. Rather, it was something I shouldn't have been drinking at all.

Just as I was fretting about it, there it was. Rabbit put the tiny cup on the table and pushed it toward me.

"This is going to be on your conscience," he warned the other wheelers.

I peeked inside the cup and saw an oily smear on the bottom. There wasn't enough there to fill a thimble.

"Wow!" I said. "So little."

Rabbit sighed loudly. He did not go away. He was standing there waiting for something.

"Money," he said finally. "Are you gonna pay?"

I panicked. I didn't have any on me.

"How much does it cost?" I asked.

Rabbit turned to Tabaqui and said, "Look, it's all your fault. I wouldn't have given him anything. He's a Pheasant, he's got no sense at all."

"Shut up," Noble said, thrusting a hundred at him. "And get lost."

Rabbit took the bill and left, but not before giving Noble a dirty look.

"Drink up," Noble said. "If you really want it."

I looked into the cup again.

"Not really. Not anymore."

"And you're right!" Tabaqui exclaimed. "What for? You don't have to, and besides, why that, all of a sudden? Have some coffee instead. And a roll."

"No. Thank you."

I was extremely embarrassed. All I wanted to do was go away as soon as I could.

"I'm sorry," I said. "I didn't know it was so expensive."

"Nonsense. So you didn't, so what? The less you know, the longer you live," Tabaqui squeaked, before suddenly screaming, "Three coffees!"

And then he spun the wheels and went spinning himself. I didn't notice how he did it, when he pushed what, but he was spinning like crazy, shedding morsels of food, beads, and other stuff, like a trash bin whirling on the end of a string. A small feather settled on my shoulder.

"No, really, thank you," I said.

The carousel stopped.

"Why not? Have you got other plans?"

"I haven't got money."

Tabaqui blinked like an owl. His hair was standing on end from all that spinning. He looked really deranged now.

"What money? It's Noble's treat. We invited you over, after all. The price is trifling, by the way."

Rabbit brought a tray with three cups of coffee, cream in a pot, and some mangled rolls. No one was listening to my protests.

"You don't have to treat me," I tried again. "I don't want anything."

"Oh, I get it," Tabaqui drawled and sat back in his wheelchair. "See, Noble? Who would want to have coffee with you after you broke his face? No one, that's who."

I felt my face flushing. Noble was drumming his fingers on the table and did not look at us.

"Why don't you go ahead and apologize," Tabaqui said. "Or he'll just go away. And you'll get what you always get. Nothing."

Noble went red. Very quickly and very visibly, as if someone had slapped his cheeks.

"Why don't you stop telling me what to do!"

Now I didn't want to just go away, I wanted to fall through the floor. That would've been faster. I turned the wheelchair around.

"I'm sorry," Noble mumbled without looking up.

I froze. My wheelchair half-turned, my head between the shoulder blades. That didn't make any sense at all. In all of my dreams of revenge, Noble never apologized. I could not imagine him doing that. I would knock out all of his teeth, fracture his jaw, make him slightly less beautiful, make him swear and spit blood, but we had never gotten as far as an apology.

"I wasn't myself that day," Noble went on. "Behaved like a total jerk. If you were to go to the Spiders I'd have problems. You have no idea how big. I couldn't sleep for two days straight. Waiting for them to come knocking. And then I figured you hadn't told anyone. I wanted to apologize but couldn't. It just wouldn't come out. It only came out today because of Jackal here."

Noble finished and finally looked at me. It was not a kind look.

I didn't say anything. What could I say? "I forgive you" would have sounded stupid. "I'll never forgive you" was even worse.

"I don't understand," I said.

"What is it you don't understand?" Tabaqui the Jackal interjected immediately. "Anything."

"But would you have some coffee with us now?" he asked coyly.

Really persistent, he was.

I wheeled back to the table and took the cup off the tray.

"This isn't right," I said. "This isn't how it goes. You are breaking the rules. No one ever apologizes to a Pheasant. No one. Not even after knocking his head off."

"Where is that written?" Tabaqui said. "I have never heard of this rule."

I shrugged. "I don't know. Same place as all the other rules, I guess. But it's there, whether written or not."

"That's rich!" Tabaqui was looking at me with what seemed almost like awe. "Look at him! He is teaching *me* the House rules. Me! The nerve!"

Noble was fiddling with the cup of Moon River, studying it.

"What do they make it from?" he asked. "What's in it?"

"I don't know," Tabaqui snorted. "Some say toadstool extract, others, Vulture's tears. I guess it is possible that Bird Daddy cries bitter green poison. Who could really tell? But it is poisonous, all right. Those of a romantic persuasion insist that it's just midnight dew collected at a full moon. But dew is unlikely to have sickened so many people. Unless it's been collected in the sock of a Bandar-Log, of course."

"Give me a bottle or something," Noble said, putting out his hand.

Tabaqui frowned.

"Want to off yourself? Get some rat poison instead. It's more certain. And much more predictable."

Noble was still waiting with his hand out.

"Oh, all right," Tabaqui grumbled, digging in his pockets. "Go ahead, drink whatever you want. Who am I to say anything? I've always been one for freedom of choice, you know."

He handed Noble a tiny vial. We observed Noble carefully transferring the contents of the cup into it.

"What about you?" Jackal turned to me. "You're awfully silent. Tell us something exciting. They say that all the recent Pheasant assemblies were dedicated to you."

I sprayed a mouthful of coffee on my shirt. "How did you know? I thought no one cared what we did."

"You thought a lot about us that is strange." Tabaqui giggled. "We strut like stuck-up peacocks, never noticing anything that's going on around us. From time to time we knock someone's head off but never notice that either. Our shoulders are heavy with the White Man's Burden and our hands are weighed down with this thick tome of House Rules and Regulations, where it is written, *Attack the weakest, kick a man when he's down, spoil what you cannot get,* and other such useful advice."

That was actually pretty close to what I thought of them, and I couldn't help smiling.

"There," Tabaqui sighed, "just as I thought. I was not far off, then. But if you had even a smidgen of tact, you wouldn't have demonstrated it so openly."

"What are those assemblies you're talking about?" Noble said and tossed a pack of Camels over to me. "I've never heard of them."

Tabaqui went momentarily speechless with indignation. I laughed.

"See! This is how you and those like you besmirch our image!" Jackal screeched and snatched the cigarettes from under my nose. "It is because of you that we are perceived as stuck-up peacocks! You have to be a complete nitwit not to know of the Pheasant assemblies. Please don't judge us by him," he said, turning to me. "He hasn't been here for more than a couple of weeks and is really quite ignorant."

"Two years and ninety days," Noble said. "And he still calls me a newbie."

Tabaqui reached over and patted his arm.

"Sorry, old man. I know this grates on you. But if you were to compare your two with my twelve, you'd understand that I have every right to call you that."

Noble scrunched up his face as if all his teeth had started aching at the same time. Tabaqui seemed to enjoy that. He even pinked up a little. He lit a cigarette and looked at me with the all-knowing smile of a veteran.

"So . . . We haven't really learned anything new except how much learning Noble has ahead of him. And still you're silent."

I shrugged. Good coffee. Funny Tabaqui. Friendly Noble. I relaxed and decided that it wouldn't be too dangerous to tell them the truth.

"They threw me out," I confessed. "By a unanimous vote. They drafted a petition to Shark and he agreed. I'm being transferred to another group."

The wheelers of the Fourth put their cups down and exchanged glances.

"Where to?" Jackal said, trembling with anticipation.

"I don't know. Shark never said. Claims it hasn't been decided yet."

"Asshole," Noble spit out. "Lives like one and will die like one."

"Now wait a minute!" Tabaqui frowned, made some quick calculations in his head, and gaped at us. "It's either us or the Third. No other way."

They exchanged glances again.

"That's what I thought too," I said.

We were silent for a while. Rabbit must have really liked saxophones. The boom-box on the counter was wailing continuously. The paper lanterns swayed in the breeze.

"So that's why you went asking for Moon River," Tabaqui mumbled. "I see now."

"Have a smoke," Noble said in a pitying voice. "Why aren't you smoking? Tabaqui, give him the cigarettes."

Jackal absently proffered me the pack. He had very long fingers, like spiders' legs. Very long and very dirty.

"Right," he said dreamily. "Either/or. Either you find out the color of Vulture's tears, or we all witness the lamentations of Lary."

"You think Vulture's going to cry?" Noble said.

"Of course. Copiously! Just like Walrus when eating the Oysters."

"You mean he'll eat me," I clarified.

"But with deep sympathy," Tabaqui said. "He in fact possesses a very gentle and tender soul."

"Thank you," I said. "Very comforting."

Jackal wasn't deaf. He sniffled and reddened a little.

"Well . . . That was by way of me exaggerating. Slightly. I like scaring people. He's actually a nice guy. A bit out of his head, but only a bit."

"Thanks a lot."

"You know what? We should invite him over to our table!" Tabaqui exclaimed suddenly. "Why not? It's a good idea. You can get to know him better, have a little talk. He'd like that."

I looked around nervously. Vulture wasn't here in the Coffeepot. I knew that for certain, but I still got scared that I might have been mistaken, or that he'd appeared while I wasn't looking, and now Jackal was going to ask him over to meet me.

"Why are you so jumpy?" Tabaqui chided me. "I told you, he's really nice. You get used to him quickly. Besides, he's not here. I meant to invite him over through Birds," he added nodding at the next table, where two of the sour-faced mourning brigade were playing cards.

"Tabaqui, stop it," Noble said. "Leave Vulture alone. Our chances to land a new one are much better than the Third's, so if you are really in a hurry go invite Blind."

Tabaqui scratched himself, fidgeted, grabbed a roll, and swallowed it whole.

"Drat," he said with a full mouth, showering himself with crumbs. "So much anxiety . . ." He picked up all the dropped pieces and stuffed them in too. "I am so anxious! How, oh how would Blind react?"

"Same as always," Noble said. "He won't. Whenever has he reacted to anything?"

"You're right," Tabaqui admitted reluctantly. "Practically never. You see"—he winked at me—"our Leader, may his Leadership days last and last, is blind as a bat and so has some trouble reacting. He usually entrusts it to Sphinx. 'Do me a favor, react for me,' he says. So poor little Sphinx ends up reacting double. Maybe that's why he went bald. It must be very tiresome, you know."

"You're saying he wasn't always bald?" Noble said.

Tabaqui sent him a withering look. "What do you mean, 'always'? Like born with it? Maybe he was born bald, but by the time I met him, Sphinx had ample hair up top, thank you very much!"

Noble said he could not imagine it. Tabaqui countered that Noble always had trouble with his imagination.

I finally lit a cigarette. Tabaqui's antics made me want to laugh out loud, but I was afraid it would sound like hysterics.

"And besides!" Tabaqui remembered suddenly. "Sphinx christened you. How could I forget? You see how nicely it all fits together? Since you are his godson, he's going to react to you like he's your loving mommy. Happy ending all around."

I seriously doubted that a bald snitch like Sphinx feeling motherly toward me looked like a happy ending, and I said so.

"Your loss," Tabaqui said crossly. "Really your loss. Sphinx would make a decent mother. Trust me."

"Right. Especially if you ask Black." Noble presented a fake smile. "There he is, by the way. Call *him* over. He can tell Smoker what kind of mother Sphinx makes."

"You're twisting my words," Jackal protested. "I never said for everyone. It goes without saying that as far as Black is concerned, Sphinx is more like a stepmother."

"An evil one," Noble said sweetly. "From those German fairy tales that make children scream at night."

Tabaqui pretended not to hear that.

"Hey! Over here, old man," he shouted, waving his arms. "We're right here! Look this way! Hello-o! I'm afraid his eyes are completely shot," he said with concern, grabbing the last of the rolls. "That's because of all those weights. Pumping iron is not as healthy as it's cracked up to be, you know. And what's more important," he continued after consuming the roll in two gulps, "he needs to watch his calorie intake. So it would be a good thing not to leave too many carbs lying around. Isn't that right, Black?"

Black, a morose fellow with a blond buzz cut, approached with a chair that he swiped on the way, placed it next to Noble, sat down, and stared at me.

"What's right?"

"That you shouldn't overeat. That you're heavy as it is."

Black said nothing. He really was heavy, but certainly not from overeating. He appeared to have been constructed that way. Then he had bulked up his muscles on various pieces of equipment and become even more imposing. A tank top left his biceps exposed, and I was studying them appreciatively while he was studying me. Tabaqui informed him that I was being transferred, and most likely to the Fourth, to them.

"Unless it's the Third, except it's not, because it's obvious that when you have a choice you always choose where there's more free space."

"So?" was the extent of Black's response. His arms looked like hams, and his blue eyes seemed unblinking.

Tabaqui was crestfallen.

"What do you mean, 'so'? You are the first to get an exclusive scoop!"

"And what am I supposed to do with it?"

"You're supposed to be astonished! Surprised, at the very least!"

"I am surprised."

Black got up, bumping a paper lantern with his head, and went to sit at an empty table two spaces over from us. There he proceeded to extract a paperback from his vest pocket and transferred his attention to it, blinking myopically.

"There," Tabaqui fumed. "And to think we were denigrating Blind's responses. Compared to Black, he is vitality incarnate!"

He was exaggerating about vitality. I'd first met Blind in the hospital wing. We were roommates. In the three days we spent there, he didn't say a single word. He also almost never stirred, so I came to regard him as just a part of the landscape. He was gaunt, but not tall, his jeans would fit a thirteen-year-old, and both of his wrists together made one of mine. Next to him I was the picture of health. I did not know who he was then, so I just figured he was being bullied a lot. And now, watching Black, I thought that if anyone looked like a Leader in the Fourth, it was certainly him, and not Blind.

"It's so weird," I said. "I don't get it."

"Yep. See, you caught it as well." Tabaqui nodded. "Of course it's weird. You look at Black, this tower of power, and even he is walking in the shadow of Blind. That's what you meant, right? He's such a commanding presence. Regal, even. Right? We're all amazed. We live side by side with him, and all day, every day, we are amazed. How come—here he is, and yet he's not the Leader? And the one who's the most amazed is Black himself. He wakes up at dawn, casts his gaze about, and inquires, 'For why?' Day after day after day."

"Can it, Tabaqui," Noble said. "That's enough."

"I am angry," Tabaqui explained, draining his coffee. "Can't abide those apathetic types."

I finished my coffee as well, along with my second cigarette. It was clearly time to go. I didn't want to, though. It was so nice in the Coffeepot. To sit here, to smoke openly, to drink coffee—which, for the denizens of the First, was a kind of mild arsenic. The only thing nagging me was the thought of Tabaqui telling someone else of my transfer. I figured I should leave before that happened. Tabaqui, in the meantime, took out a pad and started scribbling in it with a pen that formerly rested behind his ear.

"Right . . . Right . . . ," he was mumbling. "Of course . . . And don't forget this . . . Naturally. Now that is completely out of the question."

Noble was spinning the lighter on the edge of the table.

"I think I'd better go," I said.

"Just a sec." Tabaqui scribbled for a while longer, then tore out the page and handed it to me. "It's all here. The basics, at least. Study it, remember it, use it."

I stared at his chickenscratch.

"What's this?"

"A guide," Tabaqui sighed. "The essential information. Survival rules for a migrant. On top: in case of transfer to us. Underneath: to the Third."

I looked closer.

"Something about plants . . . Watches . . . And what do the linens have to do with it? Don't you get them as well?"

"We do. But it's best not to leave behind anything that bears your imprint."

"What imprint? It's not like I smear shoe polish on myself before going to bed."

Tabaqui gave me that look again—of a grizzled veteran aggrieved by much wisdom.

"Look, it's simple. Everything that's yours you take with you. Whatever you cannot take you destroy. Nothing that belonged to you must remain. What if you were to die tomorrow? Would you like a black ribbon tied to your cup, accompanied by a disgusting note along the lines of *The memory of you is forever in our hearts, O prodigal brother of ours?*"

I shuddered.

"All right. I get that. But . . . watches?"

A transferee to the Fourth is strongly advised to rid himself of any and all devices designed to measure time: wristwatches, stopwatches, alarm clocks, precision chronographs, etc. Any attempt to conceal such an item shall be immediately uncovered by the resident expert and, to prevent reoccurrences of this highly provocative behavior, the offending person shall be assigned a penance devised and approved by said expert.

For anyone being transferred to the domain of the Third, a.k.a. "the Nesting," it is advisable to acquire the following items: a set of keys (provenance unimportant), two flowerpots in good condition, no fewer than four pairs of black socks, an amulet against allergies, earplugs, a copy of The Day of the Triffids *by J. Wyndham, and an old dried plant collection.*

Irrespective of the above, anyone being transferred anywhere is advised not to leave in the quarters being vacated: clothes, linens, personal effects, items created by the person himself, and any traces of organic matter—hair, nails, saliva, semen, used bandages, Band-Aids, or handkerchiefs.

I didn't sleep that night. I listened to the breathing of those who did and stared into the darkness of the ceiling until it started lightening up and revealing familiar cracks. Then I thought that this was the last time I was seeing them and counted them all again. Then the dial of the big clock on the wall became discernible, but I purposefully avoided looking at it. This was the most unbearable night I'd ever spent in the

House. By the wake-up bell I was already half-dressed. It took me all of ten minutes to gather my things. I packed a change of underwear, pajamas, and textbooks, making sure not to take anything that was bearing a number. Just as I had suspected, Shark did not appear at the assigned time. The group left for breakfast without me. They returned and wheeled off to class, and still he hadn't come. Not at ten, not at eleven, not at twelve.

By half past twelve I had gnawed off all my fingernails, wheeled around the dorm a couple hundred times, and realized that I was going to crack soon. I took out Tabaqui's "migrant's guide," reread it, then stripped the linens off the bed. I packed them too, then gathered all tissues in the vicinity of my bed and nightstand. Stopped my watch and buried it at the bottom of the bag. Took the cigarettes out of the secret place, lit up, and started figuring out how to assemble a plant collection from materials at hand. That's when Shark arrived, with a surly Case in tow, for help with carrying, and Homer, for help with seeing off. Homer was not able to perform his duties with dignity, though. The cigarette proved too much for him. He bolted as soon as he saw it. He didn't even say good-bye. Shark ignored the cigarette but inquired what the hell did I take off the linens for.

"They're fresh," I said. "Only changed yesterday. Why use an extra set?"

He looked at me like I was mental and grumbled something about "those Pheasant tricks," even though he himself had come down on me yesterday for using the word. I told him I could leave the linens behind if it was such a big deal. He told me to shut up.

Case maneuvered my wheelchair, bumping it against the beds, and wheeled me out to the hallway, where he entrusted me into Shark's care and returned for my bag. Then Shark was rolling the wheelchair while Case was lugging the bag. We covered the familiar ground quickly and then, no matter how I tried to catch a glimpse of something identifiable, I couldn't recognize anything. It was as if all the drawings and markers had changed since last night. I missed both the Second and the Coffeepot and realized it only when we stopped in front of the door with the enormous 4 outlined on it in chalk.

THE HOUSE

INTERLUDE

The House sits on the outskirts of town. The neighborhood is called the Comb. The long buildings of the projects here are arranged in jagged rows, with empty cement squares between them—the intended playgrounds for the young Combers. The teeth of the comb are white, they stare with many eyes, and they all look just the same. In places where they haven't sprouted yet there are the fenced vacant lots. The piles of debris from the houses already knocked down, nesting grounds for rats and stray dogs, are much more appealing to the young Combers than their own backyards, the spaces between the teeth.

In the no-man's-land between the two worlds—that of the teeth and of the dumps—is the House. They call it Gray House. It is old, closer in age to the dumps, the graveyards of its contemporaries. It stands alone, as the other houses shun it, and it doesn't look like a tooth, since it is not struggling upward. Three stories high, facing the highway, it too has a backyard—a narrow rectangle cordoned off by chicken wire. It was white when built. It has since become gray, and yellowish from the other side, toward the back. It is bristling with aerials, it is strewn with cables, it is raining down plaster and weeping from the cracks. Additions and sheds cling to it, along with doghouses and garbage bins, all of it in the back. The facade is bare and somber, just the way it is supposed to be.

Nobody likes Gray House. No one would admit it openly, but the inhabitants of the Comb would rather not have it next to them. They would rather it didn't exist at all.

They approached the House on a hot August day, at the hour that chases away the shadows. A woman and a boy. The street was deserted; the sun had burned everyone away. The meager trees along the sidewalk failed to protect from its rays, as did the walls of the buildings—the melting white teeth in the blindingly blue sky. The pavement gave way under the feet. The woman's heels left small dimples in it, and the neat sequence of them followed her like the tracks of a very unusual animal.

They moved slowly: the boy because he was tired, and the woman because of the weight of the suitcase. They both wore white, both were fair-haired and seemed slightly taller than one would expect: the boy, incongruous with his age, the woman, with her femininity. She was beautiful, used to being the center of attention, but there was no one to gawk at her now, and she was glad of it. The suitcase had put a kink in her step, her white suit was crinkled from the long bus ride, her makeup blotchy from the heat. She countered all that with a proudly held head and a straight back, determined not to show how tired she was.

The boy was as like her as a smaller specimen of the human race can be like a bigger one. His hair was so fair it sometimes seemed tinged with red, he was lanky and a bit gangling, and the eyes looking out at the world were the same shade of green as his mother's. He also carried himself in the same upright manner. A white blazer was hugging his shoulders, a peculiar choice in this weather. He was dragging his feet, catching the sneakers against each other, and kept his eyes half-closed so that he could see only the bubbling gray pavement and the marks being left on it by his mother's shoes. He was thinking that even if he lost sight of her he'd still be able to find her by following the trail of those silly punctures.

The woman stopped.

The House loomed over them, bordered by emptiness on both sides, an ugly gray breach in the dazzling rows of the Comb.

"This must be the place."

The woman lowered the suitcase to the ground, took off the sunglasses, and studied the sign on the door.

"See? We got here in no time at all. No need to take a taxi, right?"

The boy nodded indifferently. He could have pointed out that it was quite a long walk, but instead he said, "Look, Mom, it must be cold to the touch. The sun can't touch it. Weird, huh?"

"Nonsense, dear," the mother brushed him off. "The sun touches everything within its reach. It's just darker than the other houses, so it looks cooler. I am going to step inside for a minute, and you just wait for me here. All right?"

She heaved the suitcase up to the fourth step and leaned it against the railing, then rang the bell and stood still. The boy sat down at the bottom of the stairs and looked away. He turned back around at the sound of the lock but could only catch a glimpse of the white skirt disappearing behind the door. The door clicked shut and he was alone.

The boy rose from the steps, went and put his cheek against the wall.

"It *is* cold," he said. "It's not within the sun's reach."

He ran a little distance off and looked at the House from there. Then glanced guiltily back at the stairs, shrugged, and started walking along the wall. He reached the end of it, looked back one more time, and turned the corner.

Another wall. He ran the length of it and stopped.

Around the next corner he saw a backyard behind a chain-link fence. It was empty and dull and just as scorching as everything around it. The House itself, however, was completely different from this side. Colorful and cheery, as if it had decided to show another face to the boy, a face that was smiling. That was not for everyone.

The boy came up against the fence, to look at that face closer and maybe even guess who was painted on the walls. He saw a rickety structure made from cardboard boxes. A playhouse covered with twigs. Its roof was decorated with a flag, now limp in the still air, and the cardboard walls were hung with pretend weapons and small bells. The hut was inhabited. He could hear voices and noises from it. Several bricks surrounded a pile of black ashes near the entrance.

They are allowed to build fires . . .

He pressed against the fence, not noticing that it was imprinting a rusty lattice on his shirt and blazer. He did not know who "they" were, but it was obvious that "they" couldn't be that old. He looked and looked until he himself was noticed through the roughly cut-out window.

"Who are you?" a slightly hoarse child's voice inquired, and then a bandana-wrapped head appeared in the hut's doorframe. "Go away. This is not a place for strangers."

"Why not?" the boy asked, intrigued.

The hut swayed and let out two inhabitants. The third stayed inside by the window. Three faces, brown and painted, were staring at him through the fence.

"He is not from those," one said to the other, nodding at the teeth of the high-rises. "He's not from around here. Look at him, just staring."

"We came by bus," the boy in the blazer explained. "And then we walked."

"So just keep walking," came the advice from beyond the fence.

He stepped back. He wasn't offended. These were strange boys. There was something not quite right about them. He wanted to understand what it was.

They, in their turn, were studying and discussing him openly.

"He must be from the North Pole," said the little one with the round head. "Look at that coat. What a moron."

"Moron yourself," the other said. "He's got no arms, that's why he's wearing it. They're leaving him with us. See?"

They exchanged glances and started giggling. The one inside the hut laughed so hard that it started swaying.

The boy in the blazer took some more steps away from them.

They continued laughing.

"Staying with us, with us!"

He turned on his heel and ran, squaring his shoulders awkwardly to prevent the blazer from flying off.

He rounded the corner and crashed straight into someone who grabbed him.

"Hey, careful! What's the matter?"

The boy shook his head. "Nothing. I'm sorry. I need to be over there. Please let me go."

But the man didn't.

"Come with me," he said. "Your mother is in my office. I was already starting to worry about what I would have to tell her if I couldn't find you."

The man belonged to the cool house. He had blue eyes and gray hair and a hooked nose, and he squinted the way people who wear glasses usually do. They went up the steps, and the man from the House picked up the suitcase. The door was ajar. He stepped aside for the boy to come in.

"Those . . . in the hut. Do they live here?" the boy asked.

"They do," the blue-eyed man said eagerly. "Have you met already?"

The boy did not answer.

He stepped inside, the House man followed him, and the door clicked shut behind them.

They lived in a room with shelves and shelves of toys, the boy and the man. The boy slept on the sofa, hugging a stuffed crocodile; the man, on a camp bed he had set up next to it. When he was alone, the boy would go out on the balcony, lie on an air mattress, and look down through the railing at the boys playing. He would sometimes stand up so they could see him too. The boys would raise their heads and smile at him. But they never asked him to join them down there. He was secretly hoping for the invitation, but it never came. Disappointed, he'd lie back again and look down from under the brim of a straw hat, taking in the high voices from below. Sometimes he'd close his eyes and imagine himself dozing off on a beach, lulled by the soft swishing of the surf. The boys' voices morphed into seagull cries. The sun was turning his legs brown. The idleness bored him.

In the evenings they would sit on the carpet, the boy and the blue-eyed man whose name was Elk, sit and listen to music and talk. They had a creaking record player and records in tattered sleeves, and the boy would study the sleeves like paintings, trying to match the images on them to the music they contained. He was never able to. The summer nights walked in through the open window. They didn't turn on the lights so as not to attract mosquitoes. Once the boy saw what looked like a rag cross the deep blue velvet of the sky. It turned out to be a bat, a mouse skeleton in a torn cape. After that he would always position himself so he could see the sky from where he was sitting.

"Why do you call yourself Elk?" the boy asked.

He was thinking of those elk who roamed the forests, with their horns lacy like oak leaves. And of deer, who were relatives to the elk but had very different horns. He'd thought about that for a long time before mustering enough courage to ask.

"It's my nick," Elk explained. "A nickname. Everyone who lives in the House has a nick, that's just the way it is here."

"I live here too now, do I have one?"

"Not yet. But you will. When they all come back and you move to one of the dorms, you'll get a nick."

"What will it be?"

"I don't know. A good one, I hope. If you're lucky."

The boy thought about possible names for himself but couldn't come up with anything. It all rested with them, those who were coming back. He wanted them to come back sooner.

"Why aren't they inviting me?" the boy asked. "Do they think I can't play with them? Or is it that they don't like me?"

"No," Elk said. "You're just new in the House. They need some time to get used to you being here. This always happens at first. Have patience."

"How much time?" the boy asked.

"Looks like you're really bored," Elk said.

The next day, when Elk came, he was not alone. With him was another boy, who never went out into the yard and had never before shown himself.

"I brought you a friend," Elk said. "He is going to live here with you, so you are not alone anymore. This is Blind. You two can do whatever you want—play, go crazy, break furniture. Just try not to fight and not to complain to me about each other. The room is all yours."

Blind never played with him, because he didn't know how. He did attend to the boy dutifully: woke him up in the morning, washed his face, combed his hair. Listened to his stories, almost never saying anything back in reply, and shadowed his every step. Not because he wanted to. He assumed that this was what Elk wanted of him. Elk's wishes were his command. Elk had only to ask, and he would have jumped off the balcony. Or the roof. Or pushed someone else off it. The armless boy was afraid of that. Elk was much more afraid. Blind was already grown up inside. A little grown-up hermit. He had long hair and a frog-like mouth always covered in red sores. He was pale as a ghost and extremely thin. He was nine. Elk was his god.

Blind's memory was full of noises, smells, and murmurs. It did not go very deep—Blind remembered nothing of his early childhood. Almost nothing. About the only thing he could fish out was the interminable sitting on the potty. There were many little boys there, and they all sat in a row on identical tin potties. The memory was a sad one and it smelled bad. He calculated later that they were forced to sit like that for no less than half an hour each time. Many of them managed to do their thing early, but they still had to remain sitting, waiting for the others. This was discipline, and they'd been receiving discipline since birth. He also remembered the yard. They walked there, each holding on to the clothes of the one in front but still tripping and falling. At the beginning and the end of this chain walked the grown-ups. If anyone stopped or deviated from the prescribed direction, a loud voice from above would restore order. His world consisted then of two types of voices. One type brought guidance from above. Another was closer and more intelligible; such voices belonged to those like himself. He did not like them either. Sometimes the loud voices disappeared. If they went missing for a long time, he and others like him would start running, jumping, falling, and bloodying their noses, and it would immediately become clear that the yard was much smaller than it seemed when they walked around it in lockstep. It became cramped, and its surface hardened and scraped their knees.

From a later time he remembered the fights. Frequent fights, for no particular reason. It could start with someone bumping someone else, and that they were doing all the time. They shoved him, he shoved back—not on purpose, it just happened—and then it was that after the first accidental shove came another, enough to knock him off his feet, or a blow that made a part of him hurt. He had decided to strike first, without waiting for the blows. Sometimes the voices from above would get angry at this, and he would be taken to another room. A punishment place. There were no tables, no chairs, no beds, just the walls. Also the ceiling, but he did not know about it then. He was not afraid of the room. Others would cry when they were locked in it. He never cried. He liked being alone. He didn't care if there were people around him or not. When he was tired he would lie down on the floor and sleep. When he was hungry he would take stashed bread crusts out of his pockets. If they kept him in this room for a long time, he would peel plaster from the walls and eat it. He liked eating it even more than bread, but the grown-ups got angry when they caught him at it, so he only allowed himself to do it when they left him alone.

He soon realized that they didn't like him. He was often singled out, punished more frequently than the other children and for things he hadn't done. He did not understand the reasons for it, but he was not surprised or angered. Nothing ever surprised him. Nothing good could ever come from the grown-ups. He established that the grown-ups were unfair, and he accepted it. When he learned to distinguish between men and women, he recognized that women behaved worse toward him than men, but left that fact without an explanation as well, just acknowledging it in the same way he acknowledged everything that surrounded him.

Then he realized he was short and weak. That was when the voices of other children started coming to him from a little higher up and their blows started hurting much worse. At about the same time, he found out that some other children could see. He did not understand what that meant. He knew that the grown-ups had some enormous advantage that allowed them to move freely beyond the boundaries of his world, but he always assumed that it had to do with their height and strength. What this "seeing" was, he could not grasp. And even when he did learn how it worked he still could not imagine it. For him "to see" meant only "to have better aim." The blows from the sighted were more painful.

Once he figured out that the stronger and the sighted had this advantage, he endeavored to become better at it himself. This was important for him. He did his best, and they started fearing him. Blind quickly understood the reason for this fear. The children were afraid not of his strength, which he did not have anyway, but of the way he carried himself. Of his calmness and unconcerned manner. Of how he was not afraid of anything. When someone hit him, he never cried, he would just get up and leave. When he hit someone, that someone usually cried, scared by his serenity. He discovered where to hit so that it hurt. This scared them too.

As he grew older, the world seemed to resent him more and more. The resentment manifested itself differently with children than with grown-ups, but eventually it grew into the wall of loneliness that surrounded him on all sides. Until Elk. The man who talked to him alone, not to him as one of many. Blind could not know that Elk had been summoned because of him. He thought that Elk picked him out from the others and loved him more than them. Elk strolled into his life as if it were his own room and upended it, rearranged and filled with himself. With his words, his laughter, his soft hands and warm voice. He brought with him many things that were unknown and unknowable to Blind, because no one cared what Blind knew and didn't know. Blind's world was limited to a couple of rooms and the yard. When other children, accompanied by the grown-ups, happily left its confines, he always stayed behind. Into the meager four corners of this world stormed Elk, filled it to the brim and made it limitless and boundless. And Blind gave his heart and soul, his whole self, to Elk forevermore.

Some would not understand or accept this, some would not even notice, but not Elk. He understood everything, and when it was time for him to go he knew he had to take Blind with him.

Blind never expected that. He knew that sooner or later Elk would have to leave, that he'd be left alone again, and that it would be terrifying. But he never imagined it could be otherwise. Then the miracle happened.

His memory preserved that day in the smallest detail, with all its smells and sounds and the warmth of the sun's rays on his face. They were walking, Blind holding Elk's hand, gripping it with all his strength, his heart fluttering like a wounded bird. They walked and walked. The sun shined, the pebbles crunched underfoot, the trucks rumbled in the distance. Never before had he walked this far. Then they climbed into a car and he had to let go of Elk's hand, so he grabbed the side of his jacket instead.

This was how they came to the House. There were a lot of children here too, and all of them were sighted. Now he knew what that really meant—that all of them had something he couldn't have. But this no longer worried him. The only important thing was the presence of Elk, the man whom he loved and who loved him.

And then it turned out that the House was alive, that it too could love. Its love was unlike anything else. It was a little scary at times, but never terrifying. Elk was god, so it followed that the place where he lived could not be a common place. It also could not cause any real harm. Elk never showed that he knew the true nature of the House; he would feign ignorance, and Blind guessed that it was a great secret that never should be spoken about. Not even with Elk himself. So he loved the House silently, loved it like no one had ever loved it before. He liked the scent of it, he liked that there was plenty of wet plaster for him to peel off the walls and eat, he liked the large yard and the captivatingly long hallways. He liked how long the traces of those who passed by hung in the air, he liked the crevices in the walls of the House, all its nooks and abandoned rooms, all its ghosts and open roads. He could do anything he wanted here. His every step had always been controlled by the grown-ups. The new place lacked that, and he was even a little uncomfortable at first, but he got used to it surprisingly quickly.

Elk, the blue-eyed catcher of little souls, went out to the porch and looked at the sky. The scorching flame was being extinguished on the horizon, but the coming evening did not promise any respite from the heat.

The boy sitting on the porch had a black eye and was also looking at the sky. "What happened?" Elk asked.

The boy grimaced.

"He said I was supposed to learn how to fight. What for? He is always silent, like he's deaf or something. So why doesn't he just stay silent, because when he speaks it's even worse. I used to think how it was so sad that he never said anything. Now I think it was better that way. I don't need his fighting lessons. He punched me in the eye for some reason. I guess he's jealous that I can see and he can't."

Elk thrust his hands in his pockets and swayed back and forth on his heels. "Does it hurt?"

"No."

The boy stood up and leaned over the railing, hanging down halfway into the yard.

"I'm sick of him. Sometimes it's like he's not right in the head. He's weird."

"That's exactly what he says about you," Elk said, holding back a smile, intently watching the dejected figure on the railing. "Do you still remember the deal we had?"

The boy pushed his feet off the floorboards and started swinging.

"I remember. No complaining, no sulking, and no grumbling. But I am not complaining and I am not sulking. I just went out for a bit of fresh air." He stopped swinging and looked up. "Elk, look! It's beautiful. The red sky. And the trees are black, like the sky burned them."

"Let's go in," Elk said. "It's even more beautiful from the balcony. Here you're a mosquito buffet."

The boy reluctantly peeled himself off the railing and followed Elk.

"And poor little Blind can't see any of it," he said with barely disguised glee. "I guess that could make him a bit edgy."

"So describe it to him," Elk said and opened the door. "He would very much like to hear about what he can't see."

"Yeah." The boy nodded. "Sure. And then he can punch me in the other eye, so that we both can't see, equally. He would very much like that too."

Two boys on the balcony were lying head to head on an air mattress amid a sea of stale popcorn and cookie crumbs. The boy in a straw hat, with the empty sleeves of the shirt tucked under his stomach, was droning in a monotone, not taking his eyes from the vivid colors of the mattress cover.

"So they are white and they move, and the edges are like somebody was tearing them or chewing them a bit. Pinkish on the bottom. Pink is kind of like red, only lighter. And they move very, very slowly, and you have to look at them for a long time to notice. There aren't that many of them now. And when there's more of them then it's not sunny anymore, and then when they turn dark they make everything dark too, and it might even rain."

The long-haired boy lifted his head and frowned.

"Don't talk about things that aren't. Describe what is now."

"All right," the boy in the hat agreed and turned over on his back. "So they're white, and pink on the bottom, and they float slowly, and it's all blue around them."

He squinted through his sun-bleached eyelashes at the smooth blue expanse of the sky, untouched by even a single cloud, and continued with a smile.

"It's so blue under them, and above them too. They are like fluffy white sheep. It's too bad you can't see how beautiful they are."

The House was empty. Or it seemed empty. Cleaners crossed its hallways every morning, leaving behind glossy trails of floor polish. Fat flies threw themselves against windowpanes in the empty dorms. Three boys, tanned almost to the point of blackness, lived in the cardboard hut in the yard. Cats went out for night hunts; they slept all through the day, curled in fuzzy balls. The House was empty, but still someone cleaned it, someone prepared the food and put it on the trays. Unseen hands swept away the dirt and aired out the stuffy rooms. The inhabitants of the cardboard hut came running into the House for water and sandwiches, leaving behind candy wrappers, blobs of gum, and dirty footprints. They were trying their best but there were too few of them, and the House was too big. The sound of their feet faded away, their cries were lost in the emptiness within the walls, and they ran back to their little encampment as soon as they could, away from the dead faceless rooms, all identical and smelling of polish. The invisible hands quickly erased the signs of their visit. There was only one room that remained alive. Those living in it were not afraid of the uninhabited House.

The boy didn't quite know what scared him on the first day when they returned. What woke him up was the din of their presence. He opened his eyes and realized that the House was full of people, that the silence—the sultry summer silence, so familiar to him now after this past month—was gone. The House creaked, slammed its doors, and rattled its windows, it was tossing musical snippets to itself through the walls, it was bubbling with life.

He pushed away the blanket and ran out on the balcony.

The yard was brimming with people. They milled around the two red-and-blue buses, they laughed, smoked, and lugged their bulging backpacks and bags from place to place. They were colorful, tanned, rowdy, and they smelled of the sea. The yard sizzled under the burning sky. He crouched down, pressed his forehead against the railing, and simply looked at them. He wanted to join them, become a part of their charmed grown-up life. He was aching to rush down—and still he didn't move. Besides, someone would have to dress him first. Finally he tore his eyes off them and went back to the room.

"Can you hear that?" Blind, sitting on the floor by the door, asked him. "Hear how much noise they're making?"

Blind held the boy's shorts for him. The boy quickly thrust his legs through the openings, one, then the other. Blind did the zipper.

"You don't like them?" the boy asked, watching his sneakers being laced.

"Why should I?" Blind pushed the boy's foot off his knee and put the other one in its place. "Why should I like them?"

The boy was barely able to wait for his blazer and refused the comb. His fair hair, grown out during the summer, remained disheveled.

"Come on, I'm going!" he blurted out. Then he ran, his feet unsteady from anticipation. The corridor, then the stairs, then the first floor. The door was being kept ajar by a striped bag. He ran out into the yard and froze.

He was surrounded by faces. The faces were unfamiliar, alien, they cut like knives. The voices—shrill, frightening. He was scared. These were not the people he'd rushed to meet. They too were browned by the sun, they laughed, they were dappled with patches of color, but they were all wrong.

He lowered himself onto the step, keeping his catlike gaze on them. A shiver ran down his spine. *So that's how they are,* he thought bitterly. *They are all assembled from little pieces. And I am one of them. I am just like them. Or will be soon. We are in a zoo. And the fence is for keeping us all in.*

There was one in a wheelchair, white like a marble statue, with snowy hair and a haggard look, and another one, nearly purple, bloated as a week-old corpse and almost as scary. This one also could not walk, and he was surrounded by girls pushing his wheelchair. The girls laughed and joked, and each had a flaw; they too were glued together from pieces. He looked at them and wanted to cry.

A tall girl with black hair, dressed in a pink shirt, came near him and stopped.

"A newbie," she said. The irises of her eyes were so dark they became indistinguishable from the blackness of the pupils.

"Yeah," he agreed sadly.

"Do you have a nick?"

He shook his head.

"Then you shall be Grasshopper." She touched his shoulder. "Your legs have little springs inside."

She saw me racing down the stairs, he thought, blushing.

"There's the one you are looking for," she added and pointed toward one of the buses.

The boy looked and saw Elk standing there with a man in black trousers and a black turtleneck. Relieved, he smiled at the girl.

"Thank you," he said. "You are right, I was looking for him."

She shrugged.

"It was an easy guess. All squirts always do. And you are a very green squirt. Remember your nick and your godmother. I am Witch."

She went up the steps and into the House. Grasshopper observed her very thoroughly but could not distinguish the little pieces.

I have a nick now, he thought and ran to meet Elk.

The soft hand descended on his shoulder; he pressed against Elk and purred contentedly. The man in black was looking sarcastically from under the bushy eyebrows.

"What's this, Elk? Another trusting soul? When did that happen?"

Elk frowned but did not answer.

"Joking," the man in black said. "I'm sorry, old man. It was just a joke."

He strolled off.

"Who was that?" Grasshopper asked quietly.

"One of the counselors. He went to the resort with the guys," Elk said distract-edly. "Black Ralph. Also R One."

"Are there others like him? Two, Three, and Four?"

"No. There aren't any. It's just that he's called that for some reason."

"He's got a silly face," Grasshopper said. "If I were him I'd grow a beard to hide behind."

Elk laughed.

"You know what?" the boy said, brushing his cheek against Elk's hand. "I too have a nick now. Wanna guess? I bet you'd never guess."

"Wouldn't even try. Something to do with flying?"

"Almost. Grasshopper." He jerked his head up, searching Elk's face. "Is it a good one?"

"Yes," Elk said, mussing his hair. "You can count yourself lucky."

Grasshopper scrunched his nose, all peeling from the sun.

"That's what I thought too."

He looked at the glued-together people around them. There were fewer now, most had gone inside the House.

"Aren't you glad they're back? You won't be so lonely now."

There was uncertainty in Elk's voice.

"I don't like them," Grasshopper said honestly. "They're old and ugly and broken. It all looked different from above, and from down here it's all messed up."

"None of them is even eighteen yet," Elk countered, visibly offended. "And why do you say they're ugly? That's not fair."

"They're freaks. Especially that one." He nodded at the purple one. "It's like he drowned long ago. You know?"

"That's Moor. Remember that nick."

Elk took a suitcase out of the pile and turned toward the House. Grasshopper kept close to him, silent as a shadow and just as unavoidable. They passed the purple one. His malicious little eyes were lost in the flowing, melting face. Grasshopper felt their gaze on his back and picked up the pace, as if spooked by it.

Did he hear what I said about him? Stupid! He's going to remember me now, me and my words.

Three of the able-bodied were smoking by the entrance. One of them, closely cropped and tall, with a fierce expression on his face, gave Elk a nod. Elk stopped. So did Grasshopper.

Around the neck of the fierce-faced, on a twisted chain, hung a monkey skull. Delicate, yellowed, with pointy teeth. The boy was mesmerized by the grown-up toy. There was some kind of mystery attached to it. Something was built into it that made the empty eye sockets glow mysteriously, even wetly. The skull seemed alive. Touching it was the only way to learn its secret, examining it closer, putting one's finger into the holes. But to look at it without understanding was just as fascinating. He did not catch what Elk and the owner of the trinket said to each other, but as he was entering the door he heard Elk say, "That was Skull. Remember him too."

Moor, Skull, and Witch the godmother, Grasshopper repeated to himself, flying up the stairs. *I must remember these three, and that unpleasant counselor in need of a beard, and the white man in the wheelchair, even though no one told me anything about him, and the day when I got a nick.*

The rooms were changing before his eyes. The taupe walls plastered with posters, the striped mattresses piled with clothes. Every bed was claimed by someone and immediately turned into a dump. Rough-sided pinecones, multicolored swimming trunks, shells and shards of coral, cups, socks, amulets, apples and apple cores. Each room acquired individuality, became different from the others.

He wandered around, awash in smells, tripped over the gutted bags and backpacks, slunk around the corners absorbing the changes. No one paid him any attention. They all had their own concerns.

There was something like a hut being built from thin planks in one of the dorms. He sat there for a while, waiting to see the result, then got bored and moved to another room. They were constructing something there too. To avoid being trampled, Grasshopper sat on a low stool by the door. The seniors were laughing, needling each other, tossing around bags and sacks, drinking something out of paper cups, then just crumpling and dropping them. The floor was strewn with the cardboard concertinas. They flattened easily and smelled of lemons. Grasshopper furtively guided them under the stool with his feet. Then a scrawny counselor with unkempt hair, resembling Lennon in his rimless glasses, came into the dorm and dragged Grasshopper out of his lair.

"You're new," he mumbled indistinctly, chewing on a toothpick. "Why aren't you in your dorm?"

The myopic eyes behind the glasses scurried like black mites.

"I don't have a dorm yet," said Grasshopper, trying to wrench his shoulder from the bony fingers gripping it.

The grip tightened.

"In which case you should find out where you are supposed to be at the moment. For a start," said the bespectacled counselor, spitting out the toothpick. "I think you will be in the Sixth. They have a spare bed. Let's go."

The counselor marched him out into the corridor. Grasshopper almost had to run to keep up with his strides. The counselor kept tugging him impatiently by the collar.

Dorm number six was located at the very end of the hallway. It was smaller than the seniors' rooms and looked gloomier because of the canvas shades over the windows. The unpacking was in full swing here as well, but the boys were his own age. Maybe a little younger or older, but only by a little. They mostly sat on the beds busily rummaging through their bags. As soon as the counselor entered, they put the bags aside and stood up.

"New one for you," he said. "You are to show and explain everything to him."

He produced a fresh toothpick and shoved it into his mouth.

"Understood?"

The boys all nodded.

The counselor nodded as well and left without looking back.

Without saying a word they surrounded him and stared at the flopping sleeves of his blazer. Grasshopper realized that they already knew everything. They had odd looks on their faces. Indifferent and mocking at the same time, as if his deformity amused them.

"You're a newbie," one of them, skinny and bug eyed, informed him. "We're going to beat you up now. And you're going to snivel and cry for your mommy. That's what always happens."

He took a step back.

They laughed. His back was pressed against the door. They approached, smiling and winking at each other.

They too were glued together.

THE HOUSE

Lary the Bandar-Log was mounting the stairway to the second floor, stomping his steel-shod boots. Horse was following him, keeping two steps back. The clatter of Horse's shoes mingled with that of Lary's, but the familiar sound—Lary so liked it in the "thundering assault" mode: ten pairs of hooves, the squeaking of leather, the jangle of buckles—was grating on him today to the point of headache. Because it wasn't real. All the clatter and sound and fury, signifying nothing that could protect them from any actual trouble. That's the Log reality. Cardboard Hells Angels. No bikes, no muscle, no true scent of the male animal. Not scaring anyone, save the pathetic Pheasants. Safety in numbers and noise. Unwrap the black leather of a wide-shouldered coat and you'll discover a skinny, pimply figure inside. Wrap it back up, hide the protruding ribs and the scrawny neck, hang some hair in front of the panicky eyes—and there's your Bandar-Log. Put ten of these together, and there's your formidable pack. The avalanche of stomping feet and wafting skin lotion. Enough to put fear into a couple of Pheasants.

Lary only realized that he was thinking aloud when Horse respectfully coughed behind him—"Wow, that's some heavy stuff, man!"—and that upset him even more.

"Hey, that's not true." Horse caught up with him. "We're not that small fry. So we don't have the heavy fists, but we know everything about everyone. He who possesses the knowledge, remember?"

Of course Lary remembered. Those were the very words he, as the head of the Bandar-Logs, had used to cheer up his compatriots. Before everything started falling apart. Before he felt the need for some cheering up himself. Then it turned out that those words were not as cheerful as they seemed. It was nice of Horse. But the worn-out words had lost their magic.

Lary kicked the trash can standing in his way. An empty sardine tin on top of it that served as an improvised ashtray flew off and clattered on the floor. He stepped into the gunk and continued on his way, scraping his heel against the wood to get off an errant piece of gum.

"I don't think we should've left just like that," Horse kept mumbling. "They'll all go to the dorms now. We'll have to pry them out of there if we want to find out anything."

"What for?" said Lary distractedly. "We know already. All the really important news. You don't have to be a Log to keep up with it."

They passed the First, slowing down as usual, but suddenly Lary felt riled up again and went into a gallop. Horse jumped and raced alongside him.

"Hey, cool it down! What's the matter?"

Lary put on the brakes so suddenly that Horse crashed into him, almost sending both of them tumbling.

"I've got my very own personal Pheasant now," Lary explained with visible disgust. "Why would I want to look at more of them? Anytime you come into the room—he's there. Wheeling around like he owns the place. Enough to drive a man bonkers."

Horse assumed a somber expression.

"Yeah, I can see that."

At the Crossroads, Lary flopped on the sofa and finally pried the gum off his heel. Horse positioned himself next to him and spread out his spindly, spidery legs. Lary shot him a sideways glance. *Am I also that skinny? Like a rake?* he thought, appalled.

Not privy to the dark musings of his friend, Horse made himself comfortable.

"He crawls like a piece of shit," Lary complained. "Like he can't do it at all. Makes me sick. Here's the question: Why do I have to look at it and suffer?"

"You had it easy," Horse sighed. "Your wheelers have always been these demons, you know. Try living in the Nesting for a while."

Lary couldn't care less about the Nesting problems. What bothered him was Horse's unwillingness to understand simple concepts and to commiserate.

"Horse," he said. "This is really easy to understand. Make an effort. See, Lary's prey can't wheel around Lary's lair."

But having said that, he started to doubt himself. *Lary's lair?* Logs were not supposed to have lairs. Because when a Log was in his lair he was no longer a Log.

"Even my zits are something special lately," Lary said, shaking his head. "Vicious buggers. All because of him. It's all nerves."

Horse grunted reverently. Lary's zits had always been special. Explosions and craters. Erupting volcanoes and smoldering calderas. Anything but regular zits. Horse was a connoisseur, he had some of his own. Alcohol pads helped a bit, lotions helped not at all, and nothing ever helped Lary because there was no remedy against direct blasts to the face. Horse eyed the calderas closest to him, did not notice any change for the worse, and decided to keep it to himself.

"Broke his face today," Lary said gloomily. "This morning."

Horse shifted expectantly.

"And?"

"And nothing." Lary shuddered with disgust. "He just took it."

"And the others?"

"Also nothing," Lary said in a markedly different tone of voice.

"And the reason?"

"He is the reason all by himself."

They fell silent. Two tall stick figures in black leather, legs crossed. The sharp toes of the boots rocking in the air. It would be difficult to tell them apart from behind if not for Horse's blond mane done in a ponytail.

"Pompey said . . . ," Horse began cautiously.

"Please don't." Lary grimaced. "Whatever it is he said, I don't want to know. We have plenty of time ahead of us to listen to it, anyway."

"What do you mean? You think he's going to pull it off? That's not certain."

Lary sighed.

"Don't try to console me. I'm already resigned to everything."

Horse pulled at his lip a couple of times.

"Damn it, Lary," he said angrily, "you have no right to think that way! How can you be so . . . unpatriotic? If I were you I would never allow myself to do that."

Lary stared at Horse.

"Are you serious? What's patriotism got to do with it? There're ten of us and more than twenty of them. Can you, like, count?"

"Sometimes one warrior is worth ten," Horse said loftily.

Lary looked at him pityingly.

"Can you count?" he asked again.

Horse didn't answer. He dug in his pockets, produced a piece of candy, and handed it to Lary. A gust of wind threw a handful of dry leaves through the open window. Horse picked up one and examined it, scratching his nose.

"Autumn," he declared, scrunching the leaf. "It's a long way until next summer. Pompey may not be one of the old ones, but you and I both know—"

"That nothing really scary can happen before the last summer," finished Lary with a faint smile. "Well, Horse, that's about the only thing keeping me afloat. Or I would've gone crazy by now."

Horse brushed the remains of the leaf off his palm.

"So hold on to that," he said plaintively.

SMOKER

OF CONCRETE AND THE INEFFABLE
PROPERTIES OF MIRRORS

The Fourth does not have a TV, starched doilies, white towels, numbered cups, watches, wall calendars, painted slogans, or any space on the walls. The walls are decorated from top to bottom with murals, shelves, and cubbyholes, and hung with bags and backpacks, pictures and posters, clothes, pans, light fixtures, and strings of garlic, chili peppers, and dried mushrooms and berries. It resembles a landfill that is trying to climb up to the ceiling. Some of its tendrils already have gained purchase there and now flutter in the drafts, rustling and clanking softly, or just hang out.

The dump is mirrored on the bottom by the giant bed, assembled from four regular ones. It is, at the same time, sleeping area, common room, and continuation of the floor for anyone who would like to cut through. I am assigned a personal zone on its surface. The other occupants are Noble, Tabaqui, Sphinx, and sometimes Blind, so my spot is tiny. To actually sleep on it requires special skills that I have not yet acquired. Those sleeping in the Fourth are routinely stepped or crawled over, or used as flat surfaces for cups and ashtrays or as convenient props for reading materials. The boombox and three lightbulbs out of a dozen are on continuously, and at any time of night someone is smoking, reading, drinking tea or coffee, taking a shower, looking for clean underwear, listening to music, or just prowling around the room. After the Pheasant "lights out" at twenty-two hundred exactly, this kind of daily routine is quite an adjustment, but I am trying to fit in. Life in the Fourth is worth any discomfort. Here everyone does whatever he wants whenever he wants, and for exactly however long he needs. There is, in fact, no counselor here. The inhabitants of the Fourth are living in a fairy tale. But it takes coming in from the First to appreciate that.

In the last three days I learned to:

> —play poker
> —play checkers
> —sleep sitting up
> —eat in the middle of the night
> —bake potatoes on a hotplate
> —smoke someone else's cigarettes
> —never ask what time it is.

I was still unable to:

> —make coffee without it boiling over
> —play the harmonica
> —crawl in a way that does not make everyone else cringe
> —stop asking stupid questions.

The fairy tale was somewhat spoiled by Lary the Bandar-Log. He could not get over my arrival in the Fourth. He was annoyed by everything. By me sitting, lying down, speaking, not speaking, eating, and especially moving around. Just one look at me made him wince in disgust.

For a couple of days he confined himself to calling me a moron and a chickenshit, then decided to break my nose for allegedly sitting on his socks. There were no socks under me, of course, but the morning was spent in explaining to various teachers the circumstances of my unfortunate fall while transferring to my wheelchair. Not one of them believed a single word of it.

The First had a ball at breakfast examining my appearance. The suspicious pill given to me by Jackal did nothing for the pain but made me so horribly drowsy that I had to skip the last class. I thought that a shower would perk me up but got only as far as the bathroom before falling asleep. Someone apparently dragged me back to the dorm.

I dreamed of Homer. With an expression of utter disgust on his face, he was whacking me with a slipper. Then I dreamed that I was a fox being smoked out of its hole by evil hunters. Just as they grabbed a hold of my tail, I woke up.

I opened my eyes and saw the corners of several pillows forming a tent over my head. There was a small hole left between them, and in it I could see a yellow kite on the ceiling looking down at me. It was capable of doing that because it had a face painted on it. Clouds of vanilla-scented smoke wafted about. I figured that those fox-themed nightmares had a foundation in reality.

I flattened the nearest pillow that was obscuring my view and saw Sphinx. He was sitting next to me, moodily studying the chessboard. There were very few pieces left on it. Most of them were now strewn around, and some were definitely under me, since I felt something small and hard poking me in several places.

"Give it up, Sphinx," said the voice of Jackal. "It's a draw if I ever saw one. You have to learn to accept the facts as they are. To maintain dignity while at the same time bowing to the inevitable."

"As soon as I need your advice I'll let you know," Sphinx said.

I dabbed at my nose. It wasn't as painful as before. Apparently the pill did work after all.

"Hey, Smoker's awake! I saw his eyes blink!" An extremely grimy little paw patted me on the cheek. "The Pheasantkind has some pluck left in it yet. Who said he was dead?"

"I don't think anyone did, except you." Sphinx leaned over me and inspected the damage. "Nobody dies over this."

"Oh, I don't know," countered invisible Tabaqui. "Pheasants, even former ones, are capable of anything. What motivates their life? What causes their death? Only they themselves know the secret."

I sat up, tired of being a bedridden patient and a topic of discussion. I couldn't quite sit straight, but my field of vision expanded significantly.

Tabaqui was clad in an orange turban, fastened with a safety pin, and a green dressing gown that looked like it could cover him twice over. He was sitting on a stack of pillows and smoking a pipe. The vanilla smoke that had tormented the fox in my dream was emanating from him. Sphinx, ramrod-straight and serene, was meditating over the board. His sharp knees were poking out of the holes ripped in his jeans. He had only one prosthetic arm attached, and his tattered shirt was exposing its workings, so he resembled a half-assembled mannequin. I could also distinguish someone's figure on the windowsill behind the drapes.

"I dreamed I was a fox," I said, fanning away the cloying smoke. "I was being smoked out of my den when I woke up."

Tabaqui transferred the pipe to the other hand and waved his index finger.

"When dealing with a dream the most important thing is to wake up in time. You seem to have managed, and I am happy for you, baby."

And he launched into one of his bizarre, mournful songs with endlessly repeating choruses that made my skin crawl. They usually extolled the virtues of wind or rain, but this one was about smoke, rippling over the ashes of some burned-out building.

The figure behind the drapes twitched and pulled the fabric tighter to try and shield itself from Jackal's dirges. The hasty movements betrayed it as Noble.

"*Ahoy, ahoy . . . Black crows over the gray smoke . . . Ahoy, ahoy . . . Nothing left, it's all gone . . .*"

Sphinx suddenly buried his face in the blanket, as if pecking it, then straightened up and jerked his head, and I saw a pack of cigarettes flying in my direction.

"There," he said. "It's good for the nerves."

"Thanks," I said, examining the pack. There were no teeth marks on it, and no traces of saliva either. I coaxed out a cigarette, caught the lighter thrown by Tabaqui, and thanked him too.

"He's so polite!" he exclaimed. "How nice!"

He started fidgeting, shaking out the folds of his dressing gown. The turban kept falling over his eyes. Finally he fished out a glass ashtray from somewhere. It was already full.

"Found it! Here you are."

He tossed it at me, even though I was close enough to just take it from his hands. It lost most of its contents in flight, and the blanket acquired a dappled trail of cigarette butts. I brushed the ash off myself and lit up.

"Where's the gratitude?" Jackal demanded.

"Thank you," I said. "For missing."

"Don't mention it," he said, visibly delighted. "Always glad to help."

The *ahoy*s resumed at double the volume.

Sphinx said that he agreed to a draw.

"Finally," a soft voice from the other side of the headboard replied. Snaking through the layers of bags hanging on the bed, a very white, very long-fingered hand worked its way up, turned the board over, and began assembling the little pieces into it.

"*Ahoy, ahoy . . . The blackened cooking pans! Ahoy, ahoy, the frame of a stuffed bear . . . It used to be a coat hanger, it did . . .*"

"Someone please shut that pervert up!" Noble begged from the window.

I couldn't pry my eyes off Blind's hand. In addition to the fingers being impossibly long and bending in ways that fingers weren't supposed to bend unless they were broken, the hand also seemed unpleasantly autonomous. It traveled to and fro, slipping on the covers from time to time, extending its feelers, almost sniffing the air. I extracted the white rook that had been digging into my backside and carefully placed it in front of the hand. The hand stopped, waved the middle antenna, cogitated, and then grabbed it with lightning speed. I startled and quickly set to producing the rest of the pieces that had dropped under my body because I had a horrible suspicion that, if I didn't, the hungry hand would just burrow in and find them. Sphinx observed me with a faint smirk on his lips.

"*Ahoy, ahoy . . . The blackened pendant! A crow would take it, bring it to its young . . . A lovely toy to bring to its young . . .*"

Noble pulled aside the curtain and flowed down. He did it a bit more noisily than usual, but still, it was all I could do not to weep from envy, looking at him.

"Stop gawking," came Tabaqui's advice. "You'll never be able to do that."

"I know. I'm just curious."

Jackal imitated a coughing fit and looked at me significantly, as if to warn me about something.

"It would be better if you weren't just curious."

I didn't have time to ask why before Noble climbed up to the communal bed. I admired the precise movements. Where Tabaqui crawled, Noble hurled himself forward. He tossed his legs in front of him and then hopped after them on his hands. It wasn't a particularly pleasant sight in itself, and would border on creepy if slowed down, but not from the point of view of a paraplegic. Besides, Noble was so fast that such deconstruction was often impossible. I was enthralled and I envied him bitterly, fully aware that this was way beyond me. I was no acrobat. Tabaqui moved just as fast, but he was half Noble's weight and he had some control over his legs, so looking at him crawl did not make me depressed.

Once on the bed, Noble stared at Jackal with a sort of vicious anticipation. It was clear that with one more *ahoy* things would get really hairy for Tabaqui.

"Why are you so jumpy today, Noble?" Tabaqui said apologetically. "That was the end of the song."

"Thank god," Noble snorted. "Or it would have been the end of you."

Tabaqui feigned shock.

"Horrible, horrible words! And because of such a trifle! Come to your senses, dearest!"

His turban settled down over one eye again. He hoisted it back up and puffed on the extinguished pipe.

The coffeepot on the floor sounded like it was about to boil. I pushed apart the backpacks and bags that were hanging on the bars of the headboard.

On the floor on the other side of the bars, Blind was sitting. His black hair fell over his white face like a curtain. The silvery eyes glowed coldly from behind it. He was smoking and looked totally limp. The hand searching for the chess pieces was almost done. It did not appear to have anything to do with him. While I was watching, it decided to return, and Blind appreciatively patted it with the other hand. I didn't dream this, it really happened.

The door slammed.

I heard a clatter of heels.

My mood crashed. This noise could only mean one thing—Lary had returned. I dropped the bags back in their place, obscuring Blind again, and tried to make myself inconspicuous. I didn't hide, of course, just froze. I wasn't exactly scared, but Lary's presence drained all energy out of me. He invariably blew up whenever I showed any signs of life.

Thin, cross eyed, and disheveled, he came up to the bed and stared at Jackal. He looked so miserable that Tabaqui choked on his pipe.

"Heavens, Lary!" he squeaked anxiously. "What happened?"

Lary's gaze was acerbic.

"Same old, same old. Which is quite enough for me."

"Oh." Tabaqui calmed down instantly and adjusted his turban. "And here's me thinking there was something we didn't know yet."

Lary grunted. It was a very expressive grunt. Blatant, even. Noble, who detested all sudden noises, asked if Lary would mind keeping it down.

"Down?" Lary demanded as if he couldn't quite believe what he was hearing. "You mean even more down? If we were any more down we'd be six feet under! We're not making waves! We are the masters of quiet! We're so quiet we're going to grow moss any day now."

"You're overreacting." Noble frowned. "And by down I meant you personally. At this particular moment."

"Oooh, I see!" Lary jumped at the opportunity. "The particular moment, that's all we care for. Only the moment, never before or after. Nothing can ever be worth anything except for the precious moment. We can't even wear watches, or someone might try to think more than two minutes ahead!"

"He wants a fight," Tabaqui explained to Noble. "A bloody massacre. He needs to fall down by the bed insensate and not have to worry about anything."

Noble paused in the careful filing of his nails and said, "This can be easily arranged."

Lary stared at the nail file and did not like the sight of it for some reason. He seemed to have second thoughts about the fight.

"I'm not overreacting," he said. "Walk the corridors like I do, you'd react the same. You have any idea what kind of atmosphere is out there right now?"

"Lary, enough," Sphinx said. "We've had it up to here with your atmosphere. Stuff it."

Lary was shaking all over, and the bed was shaking with him. I could not understand why they wouldn't just let him speak. I would've thought that could calm him down a little. It's not a pleasant experience to be sitting next to someone who's shaking from some unexplained emotion. Especially if that someone happens to be a Bandar-Log.

Alexander appeared next to the bed, an obsequious shadow in a gray sweater. He distributed cups of coffee from the tray and disappeared again. Either crouched down on the other side of the headboard or flattened against the wall. The cup was boiling hot and I turned my attention from Lary to the coffee, so it was a complete shock when he turned his to me.

The long nail of his trembling finger was pointing right at the middle of my forehead. "There! This entity here is the reason we're all knee deep in shit! And he's having coffee in bed instead of wearing a concrete suit!"

Tabaqui gasped in delight.

"Lary! Lary, what are you prattling about?" he squeaked. "What is this nonsense, my dear boy? How would you go about it? Where would you get your hands on that much concrete? Where would you mix it? And then how do you propose dunking Smoker in it? And what were you planning to do next? Flush the block down the toilet?"

"Shut up, you pipsqueak!" Lary howled. "Keep your mouth shut, just for once!"

"Or what?" Jackal wondered. "You'll call upon your Log brothers to deliver a barrel of mixed concrete and a convenient footbath? Answer me this, buddy: if you're so handy with all this stuff, how come you still can't even cook a plate of spaghetti?"

"Because . . . shove it up your ass, you freaking idiot!"

Lary's screeching swept Nanette off the locker. She landed on the table. And other things did too. Our crow liked to butcher old newspapers in her spare time, and the pieces of the newsprint puzzle flew into the air and settled down like a short, dirty blizzard. Two scraps ended up in my coffee.

Then Lary's face, with the viciously squinting left eye, was right next to mine, and then a lot of things happened at once.

The coffee scalded my hand. My shirt collar twisted and squeezed my neck. The ceiling started spinning. With it spun the yellow kite, the empty birdcage, the wooden wheel, and the last pieces of the newspaper snow. This spectacle was so sickening that I closed my eyes to avoid seeing it. Miraculously, I managed not to throw up. Then I was lying faceup on the bed, gulping saliva mixed with blood and desperately trying to hold on.

Tabaqui helped me sit up and earnestly inquired how I was feeling.

I did not answer. I brought the faces around me into focus as best I could. Lary's wasn't among them. I had no doubt that this time he did break my jaw. I couldn't hold back tears, but the pain was nothing compared to the sweet concern everyone was showing. They behaved as if something heavy had just happened to fall on me.

Tabaqui proffered another one of his miracle pills. Sphinx told Alexander to get a wet cloth. Blind appeared from behind the bed and asked if my head was still spinning. Not one of them had intervened when all of that was happening. Or even told Lary what a bastard he was. This kind of treatment made me lose all desire to talk to them or answer their questions. I tried not to meet their eyes. I crawled to the edge of the bed somehow and asked for my wheelchair. I don't think the words came out right, but Alexander immediately brought it around. Then he helped me into it.

Once in the bathroom I washed my face, trying not to press on the tender spots, and then just sat in front of the sink. I didn't want to go back. A familiar feeling. I used to have it a lot in the First, except there, no one was allowed to be by himself for long. Here nobody cared about stuff like that. Anyone was free to wander anywhere he wanted, deep into the night.

The bathroom looked exactly the same as in the First. If anything, it was even more dilapidated. More cracks in the walls. The tiles fell away in a couple of places so that the piping showed through. And each remaining tile was covered in scribbles. The marker didn't hold well, it smeared and faded, and the flowing script made the Fourth's bathroom a bizarre sight, like a place that was draining away. That was urgently trying to convey a message but couldn't because it was melting and evaporating. The writing was on the wall, but no one could read it. I tried. It was legible enough, but added up to complete nonsense. It destroyed your mood. I usually ended up reading the same one every time, the one arcing above the low sink: *Without leaving his door he knows everything under heaven. Without looking out of his window . . .* The rest of it was smeared, leaving only the very last word: *Tzu*. It drove me crazy that I found myself rereading it, and I'd even contemplated erasing it with a sponge, but something always stopped me from doing that. Besides, then I would have had to write something else in the glaringly empty space.

I wheeled over to that sink. Its edge was crusted with toothpaste, and the drain sported a clog of scum mixed with disgusting hair clippings. The hair was black. Having absorbed a large dose of this still life, I moved to the next sink. None of the wheelers in the Fourth had black hair, which meant that one of the able-bodied was carefully bending down to one of the low-hanging sinks while shaving, just to bestow the fruits of his piggishness on us. Or rather, I suspected, on me.

In came Alexander.

He brought another cup of coffee and an ashtray. Placed them on the edge of the sink. Put a cigarette and a lighter into the ashtray. The sleeves of his sweater flashed his fingers for a second; the nails were brutally gnawed off, bleeding. Then they went into hiding again. The sleeves were stretched and hung low, but he also grabbed them with the fingers from the inside to make sure no one saw his hands.

"Thanks," I said.

"Not at all," he answered from the door. And vanished.

So here were two things that I learned about him in one go. That he could talk and that he was eating himself alive.

Alexander's servility was more scary than pleasant. It brought to mind those nasty Pheasant tales of how other groups treated new arrivals. How they made them into slaves. I'd never believed them, but then I met Alexander, who seemed to have come straight out of those stories. A real person and at the same time a horror story made flesh. The way he carried himself was seriously shaking my resolve not to believe.

What did I know about the Fourth, when it came down to it? That, except for Lary, they behaved more or less normally toward me. They seemed nice, almost too nice for all those horrors attributed to them. But maybe I was exactly the reason? Who would need a slave in a wheelchair? Useless. He can barely serve himself. One who could move, now that's different. One like Alexander. Having arrived at this thought, I realized that the Pheasant poison was inside me and that I was going to die from it. But not before carrying it through the rest of my life.

That was the last straw. I looked in the mirror. At the swollen nose and the swelling jaw. Touched the bruise. Pressed it harder, locked eyes with my reflection, and suddenly burst into tears.

They came so easily that I was astonished. As if I was always on the verge of them, ready to go. I was ogling myself in the mirror, cup in hand, and crying away. To mop up the fluids that sprung out of me, it took at least a couple of feet of paper towels. I blew my nose one final time and in the mirror saw Sphinx.

Not his face, he was too tall to fit in the mirror designed for the wheelchair-bound. But even without looking at his face, it was clear that he'd been there in time for the deluge.

I didn't want to turn around, so I decided to behave like I hadn't seen him. I put down the cup and busied myself with washing. A very long and thorough washing. Finally, I wiped my face and saw that he was still standing in exactly the same place as before. Apparently he wasn't here to demonstrate discretion, so I had to pretend as if I'd just noticed he was there.

Sphinx had the same semi-assembled look, except he'd wrapped a shirt over his shoulders. The shirt clearly had been through a contentious encounter with liquid bleach at some point, and the jeans weren't much better, but taken together, the appearance was stunning. Sphinx was one of those types on whom any old rags looked presentable and expensive. I had no idea how he pulled it off.

"Does it hurt?" he asked.

"A bit."

To avoid looking him in the face, I stared at his sneakers. They were worn out, and he'd wrapped the laces around the ankles. Mine were much cooler.

"Bad enough to cry?" he continued.

Yeah. Discretion was not his strong suit.

"Of course not," I managed.

It was silly of me to have expected that he would just turn around silently and leave me alone with my embarrassment. Now he was surely going to start an inquiry into why I seemed so unhappy.

"Your coffee's getting cold," he said.

I felt the cup. It was still warm.

Whether it was because I didn't see Sphinx, who was now standing behind me so I could not see him in the mirror, or because he never did ask me anything, or because I wouldn't have known what to answer if he had, or all of it together, the dam burst again. Except now it was words gushing out of me in a flood instead of tears.

"I'm a Pheasant," I said to my puffy reflection. "A freaking Pheasant. I am for some reason not happy drinking my coffee right after a punch in the face. And you know what the funniest part is? That Lary doesn't think I'm one. Oh, he calls me a Pheasant, but he doesn't believe it himself. Or he wouldn't be doing this. No Pheasant would ever take it, he'd snitch in an instant. So on the one hand he hates me for being a Pheasant, and on the other he counts on me not being a Pheasant. Isn't that special? What if I were to wheel out of here right this moment and go to Shark's office?"

I felt my face again. The swelling was visibly spreading. By dinnertime it was going to occupy half of my face. Much to the joy of the First.

"You can put some foundation cream on it," Sphinx suggested. "It's in the cabinet to your left."

I bristled. He was so sure that I wanted to hide that shiner. Lary was too. What if I wanted to reveal it to the world? Tell everyone of the circumstances of me acquiring it and see what happened next? This was the Pheasant talking, of course, and it was scary.

"I am going to tell Shark," I said out of sheer contrariness.

Sphinx came up to the adjacent sink and sat on it. He even crossed his legs, like it was a chair. I immediately thought of the caked toothpaste and wondered if he'd still look cool with toothpaste smeared on his butt.

"Right now?" he said.

"What?"

"Are you going to tell right now?"

I didn't answer. Of course I wasn't going anywhere, but he at least could have pretended to believe me. And try to talk me out of it.

"It was a joke," I said crossly.

"Why?"

As I thought about it, he answered himself.

"Well, obviously you wanted to be talked out of it. To begin with. What else? Did you want to scare me? Possibly. But why me and not Lary? Or maybe you'd like me to stand up for you next time? Something like a covenant to protect you from him in the future? Sorry, I can't promise you that. I'm not your nanny."

I felt myself reddening from my ears all the way down to my heels. Sphinx's interpretation of my behavior turned it pathetic. And it was very accurate. I just wasn't thinking about it in those terms.

"All right," I said. "Enough."

Sphinx blinked.

"No, wait," he said. "I said I can't promise you anything, but I can go find Lary and tell him how hard it was for me to talk you out of going to Shark. He'd believe me and would never lay a finger on you again. That's all I can do. If that's something that works for you."

"It does," I said quickly. "It does work for me."

I was this close to telling him that all I'd wanted was to irk him, but stopped myself just in time. I snatched the cigarette left for me by Alexander, clicked the lighter, and took a drag so hard that my eyes almost bugged out. The wretched creature in the mirror imitated my greedy gesture, making me ashamed for him and for myself.

"Listen, Smoker, why is it that you never fight back when someone's beating you up?"

I coughed up smoke.

"Who? Me?"

"Yes, you."

The faucet behind Sphinx's back leaked, so the bottom of his shirt was getting wet. The deepening cyan color was making his eyes even more green than normal. He sat hunched up, not straight like he always did, as if trying to draw out my soul with those water-sprite eyes of his. Pull it out and then dissect it at his leisure.

"What good would that do?" I said.

"More than you can imagine."

"Sure. Lary would have a laughing fit and forget to swing his fists."

"Or be so surprised that he'd stop thinking of you as a Pheasant."

He seemed to genuinely believe in what he was saying. I couldn't even get angry at him for this.

"Sphinx, stop it," I said. "This is ridiculous. What was it I should have done? Scrape his knee?"

"You should have done whatever. Even Tubby bites when he feels threatened. And you had a cup of hot coffee right in your hand. I think it scalded you when you fell."

"So I was supposed to pour my coffee on him?"

Sphinx closed his eyes for a second.

"Better that than pouring it all over yourself."

"I see," I said and crushed the cigarette in the ashtray. It flipped over and I barely managed to grab it. "You guys crave entertainment. You'd like to see how I flap my arms at Lary, bite his finger, and douse the bed in coffee. I guess Tabaqui would even make a song about it afterward. Thank you so much for the advice, Sphinx! How can I ever repay you?"

Sphinx suddenly shot off his perch and was next to me in just a couple of steps. He was looking at me in the mirror. He had to bend down, like he was peering at someone behind a low window.

"You're welcome," he said, addressing that someone. "Don't mention it. Lary himself would have given you the same advice if he happened to be here."

His jumping startled me so much I swallowed all the curses that were ready to come out.

"Of course," I said. "He'd have nothing to lose."

Sphinx nodded. "And he'd finally be able to leave you alone. Do you know why Logs are always picking on Pheasants? Because they never fight back. Not in principle and not in practice. Just close their eyes and go wheels up without a peep. And until you stop doing that, a Pheasant will be all Lary sees when looking at you."

"You said you were going to set him straight."

Sphinx was still trying to mesmerize my reflection. The reflection that was still looking worse and worse.

"I did. And I will. Not a problem."

His tricks were making my head spin. I felt that there were three of us here.

"Sphinx, will you stop talking to the mirror?" I blurted out. "The me that's in there is all wrong!"

"Yep. You've noticed it too, haven't you?"

He turned around absentmindedly, as if he really was talking to someone else and I'd interrupted him. Then he focused on me, which was even more disconcerting. I felt a headache coming on.

"All right," he said. "Let's forget about that you, the one living in the mirror."

"Are you saying he is not me?"

"He is. But not quite. He is you seen through the lens of your image of yourself. We all look worse in the mirror than we actually are, didn't you know that?"

"I've never thought about it that way."

Suddenly it dawned on me how crazy it all sounded.

"Cut out this nonsense, Sphinx. It's not funny."

Sphinx laughed.

"It is funny," he said. "It really is. Funny how, as soon as you start to grasp something important, your first reaction is to shake it out of yourself."

"I'm not shaking out anything."

"Look over there," Sphinx said, nodding at the mirror. "What do you see?"

"A pathetic cripple with a shiner," I said darkly. "What else can I possibly see?"

"You need to keep away from mirrors for a while, Smoker. At least until you get over feeling sorry for yourself. Have a talk about this with Noble. He never looks in the mirror."

"How come?" I said in astonishment. "I wish I could see in the mirror what he sees when he looks in it."

"How do you know what he sees?"

I tried to imagine that I was Noble. Looking at myself in the mirror. Massive attack of narcissism.

"He sees something like young David Bowie. Only more beautiful. If I looked like Bowie, I'd—"

"Whine that you look like elderly Marlene Dietrich and dream of looking like Mike Tyson," Sphinx said. "That's a direct quote, so don't think I'm exaggerating. What Noble sees looking in the mirror is completely different from what you see looking at him, which is only one example of reflections behaving strangely."

"I see," I said. "Makes sense."

"It does?" Sphinx sounded surprised. "It still doesn't quite for me. Even though I spent some time researching the subject."

I was suddenly overwhelmed by desire to ask him something. Something that had been gnawing at me for a while.

"Listen, Sphinx. Alexander . . . How come he's like that? Did you just feed him to Lary? Or is that how he was when he came in?"

"How come he's like what?" Sphinx frowned.

"You know. Helpful."

"Oh man, not another one," Sphinx drawled. "What horrors did we inflict on him? We didn't. But you don't believe me, so there's no point in my telling you this."

I didn't believe him. Not for a moment.

"Why is he always cleaning up after everybody? Bringing people things? Does he like it?"

"I don't know why. I have an idea, but I don't know for sure. I know one thing, though: it's nothing to do with us."

The expression on my face must have been telling. Sphinx sighed.

"All right. I guess that's how he sees his purpose in life. His previous job was much harder. He worked as an angel, and he got really fed up with it. So now he's doing his best to prove his usefulness in any other capacity."

"Worked as a who?"

Sphinx was the last person I expected to be pulling a stunt like this. It just wasn't his style. Now, Tabaqui I would understand, that would be his area of expertise.

Sphinx wasn't about to elaborate.

"You heard me," he said. "I'm not going to say it again."

"OK," I mumbled. "Got it."

"Just observe. You'll notice that he's always trying to preempt our requests. Do something before he's asked to. He generally doesn't like it when people talk to him. Doesn't like to be personated."

"To be what now?"

"He. Doesn't. Like. Being. Noticed," Sphinx chanted. "Being talked to. Asked. Paid any attention. It annoys him."

"How do you know? Did he tell you that?"

"No. I live next to him."

Sphinx bent over and scratched his ankle with the prosthesis, like he was using a stick.

"He likes honey and walnuts. Likes seltzer, stray dogs, striped awnings, round stones, worn-out clothes, no sugar in his coffee, telescopes, and a pillow on his face when he's asleep. He doesn't like when people look him in the eye or stare at his hands. Doesn't like strong wind and flying cottonwood fluff, can't stand white clothing, lemons, and the scent of chamomile. All of that would be obvious to anyone with a working pair of eyes."

I decided not to mention that I hadn't been living in the Fourth long enough to distinguish the fine details in the most inscrutable person in the House.

"You know what, Sphinx, don't say anything to Lary. I changed my mind."

He lowered himself to the mirror again.

"Why?"

"It was all your idea. And I don't want him to think I'm a snitch."

"Really?"

Sphinx appeared suspicious of my reflection, which did in fact look unpleasant. Furtively snitchy. Confused and distrustful. And at the same time I was feeling nothing of the sort.

"Really," I said nervously. "I don't want to be a snitch, whether real or imaginary. And you promised to leave my reflection alone."

Sphinx looked back at me over his shoulder. Like he was comparing.

"I did. I am just fascinated by the contrast. Sorry. Won't happen again. So, I am not to talk to Lary? All the assurances go out the window then."

"To hell with them."

I sighed with relief. I was almost sure I was doing the right thing. And did it in the last possible moment, almost when it was already too late. It all had to do with mirror Smoker. He was a nasty character. A veteran snitch, an expert even. And my talks with Sphinx in bathrooms were becoming a nice tradition. Just him and me, surrounded by sinks and commodes. We'd have a talk, and then suddenly everything would be different. Upside down, or maybe the other way around. Somehow I sensed that there was going to be no such upheaval this time. That I managed to avoid it.

Sphinx was examining his pants, having finally noticed their sorry state.

"Lary has been asking for it anyway. Look at this mess."

"How do you know it's him?"

"Who else could it be? Thumbtacks in the sheets, gum in the shoe, toothpaste on the sink, that's right about his range. Tabaqui operates on a different level altogether. Jackal's pranks lay waste to half the House. He's not into the small stuff. So it must be Lary. See, he's just a child really."

I laughed and said, "A child that shaves."

"What's so unusual about that? A very common occurrence."

He scratched the leg again, wincing.

"What's with the scratching?" I blurted.

"Fleas. Definitely. Did they get to you yet? No? Strange."

"Fleas?" I was a bit lost. "You mean Nanette's got fleas?"

"I wish. We could hope to get rid of them then. No, it's Blind hauling them in. We can't exactly spray our Leader with pesticides, now can we? And fleas aren't even the worst of it. Sometimes he comes in covered in ticks. In the dead of winter. And not a couple, mind you, several different species at once. Have you ever extracted a tick? The trick is never to pull too abruptly, otherwise the head breaks off and stays inside."

"You must be kidding."

"Of course I am," Sphinx said gravely. "I'm the resident joker, didn't you notice?"

"Why can't you just tell someone to shut up if his questions are getting on your nerves? Why this rigmarole?"

Sphinx did not answer. He sighed, scratched his leg, and walked out. In a wet shirt and with toothpaste blobs on his butt. The toothpaste was not really visible and the dripping shirt only added coolness. So it wasn't about the clothes at all, it was about Sphinx. About his self-esteem.

I stared at my reflection.

The mirror Smoker was looking better, but still noticeably spiteful. I struck a pose. He assumed an even more idiotic stance. I guess my self-esteem still sucked.

"So what," I said. "Even Noble doesn't like himself in the mirror."

I finished the coffee that really was cold by now and wheeled back to the dorm.

THE HOUSE

INTERLUDE

The House is walls and more walls of crumbling plaster. The narrow passages of the staircases. Motes dancing around the lantern on the balcony. Pink sunrises through the gauzy curtains. Chalk dust and untidy desks. Sun dissolving in the reddish clay of the rectangle that is the backyard. Shaggy dogs dozing under the benches. Rusting pipes crisscrossing and twisting into spirals under the cracked skin of the walls. Rows of small boots with battered toes, tucked under the beds. The House is a boy disappearing into the emptiness of the hallways. The boy who is falling asleep in class, who is striped black-and-blue from endless fights. The boy of many names. Head-Over-Heels and Prancer. Grasshopper and Tail. Blind's Tail, never more than half a step behind him, treading on his shadow. To anyone who seeks to enter, the House presents its sharpest corner. Once you've bloodied yourself against it, you are allowed inside.

There were thirteen of them. Others called them "nightmare," "gang," and "ankle biters." The last of these they emphatically contested. They themselves preferred "The Pack." And, as befits a pack, it had a leader. The leader was already ten. His nick was Sportsman. He was fair-haired, rose-cheeked, blue-eyed, and taller than everyone else, except Elephant, by a full head. He slept in an adult-sized bed and didn't have any visible disfigurements or hidden diseases, no zits or fixations, he wasn't even collecting anything—in short, he had nothing that everyone else had to some extent. For the House he was too perfect.

Rex and Max, the lame twins, were just called Siamese, as they hadn't acquired separate nicks. Narrow faced, gangling, and yellow eyed, with only three legs between the two of them, as alike as two halves of one lemon, inseparable and indistinguishable, two sticky-fingered shadows with pockets full of keys and lock-picks. No door ever stopped them. Anything left unattended became theirs.

Shaggy Humpback liked marching music and dreamed of becoming a pirate. During the summer he browned almost to a crisp, became a hunched raven and a breeding ground for insects. Dogs sensed the tenderness in him from afar and rushed to partake of it. His hands smelled of dog fur and his pockets were full of bread and sausages for his four-legged friends.

Whiner and Crybaby were also inseparable like Siamese, but looked different from each other. Crybaby, with his pale bug-eyed stare, resembled a praying mantis. Whiner's deeply set little eyes made him look like a little rat. They were both dyslexic and both loved collecting things. They collected nuts, bolts and screws, pocket knives, and bottle labels, but their pride and joy was a vast collection of fingerprints.

Rabbit was an albino and possessed dark glasses tied to his ears with a string and shoes with orthopedic heels. He always knew what river flowed where. He remembered the names of cities, many of them unpronounceable, could enumerate their principal thoroughfares and inform of the best ways to get from one of them to another. He identified the major categories of national manufacturing output and the impact they had on the corresponding countries. Many considered Rabbit's knowledge useful, but hardly anyone respected him for it. His front teeth were slanted forward, making him look like a rodent. They were also the reason for his nick.

Beauty, an impossibly cute boy with very dark eyes, was ashamed of his out-of-control arms and legs and never talked. His feet carried him to where he didn't wish to go, his hands dropped things he wished to hold. He fell a lot and was covered in bruises. He was ashamed of those too.

Round-faced Hoover was crazy about his treasures. He found them everywhere. What he called treasure was everyone else's trash. In the nine years of his life, Hoover had amassed a hoard, filling a dozen secret places and one trunk, and now spent as much time each day inspecting it as searching for new precious objects.

Curly-haired Muffin was rotund and obnoxious, and liked to dress up and design pretty clothes for himself. His wardrobe took up a lot of space and annoyed his roommates. Muffin's nose struggled to peek out of his cheeks, which, in their turn, yearned to meet his shoulders. All the female teachers adored him. Their name for him was Li'l Cupid.

Crook was crooked because of a wicked disease that also made him walk sideways. His head relied on a stiff plaster collar for support. This did not prevent him from being able to run amazingly fast. Crook collected butterflies, so all through the summer, with the hunting season in full swing, he never parted with his net and specimen jars.

Elephant was enormous, shy, and retiring. He stuffed rubber toys in the pockets of his overalls and cried if left alone. Elephant's head was covered in white fuzz. He was thought of as the baby of the Pack, even though few of them came up to his chin.

Bubble wasn't quite sane, in the common opinion. Everywhere he went, he went on roller skates. His ears were open to the four winds, his bulk protected him in collisions. He called himself Wild Whirlwind and his only fear was of damaging the skates. He'd outlived seven pairs already but cried bitterly when saying farewell to each one. Under his bed he kept a box full of the busted wheels taken off his dearly departed friends.

Sportsman's Pack occupied two dorms at the very end of the hallway. The larger of those they called Stuffage. Stuffage rarely earned visits from counselors and, consequently, rarely was cleaned. Hoover's treasures, stored in the most unsuitable spots, fell out at the slightest touch. Elephant's toys, chewed to a sorry state, collected dust under the beds. The dangerous clanking collection of Whiner and Crybaby nestled on the windowsill. Sticker sets adorned the walls, fighting for space with Crook's butterflies. Muffin's clothes could not fit inside his locker and spread out onto the chairs and headboards. A stinky hamster moved in under Humpback's bed. A mysterious plant in a hanging pot took residence above the bed of Max the Siamese. The wardrobe housed their homemade weapons, which clattered like a bag of sticks every time they tumbled out.

They let the hamster out for walks. The plant dripped dirty brown water. Stickers fell off and disappeared in Hoover's secret places. No amount of cleaning could save Stuffage from accumulating stuff.

The Pack remained a pack only while it reminded everyone of itself. By means of broken windows, graffiti on the walls, mice in teachers' desks, smoking in the bathrooms. The notoriety flattered them and also separated them from their sworn enemies, the wheelers. But by far the favorite pastime of the Pack was the newbies. Mama's darlings, still smelling of the Outsides, sissies and crybabies not worthy of nicks. Newbies provided unlimited opportunities for entertainment. There was scaring them with spiders and worms. Smothering them with pillows and stuffing them into lockers. Jumping at them from behind and screaming into their ears. Putting pepper and baking soda in their food. Gluing their clothes to the chairs or just ripping off the buttons. If all else failed, there was always a good thrashing.

An equally wide assortment could be applied to the sightless, especially those who, for some reason, wanted to stand up for the newbies. Strings stretched across hallways, beds and nightstands moved, clothes painted with stupid messages. Doors barred with chairs from the inside, thumbtacks on the floor combined with carefully hidden sneakers, items disappearing and others appearing in their places. Sky was the limit if you knew how to think up such things. The Pack did.

"There! There they are! Get them!" the boys yelled, tearing down the hallway in a multicolored avalanche. Their eyes were aglow with the thrill of the hunt, their sweating hands clenched into fists by themselves.

"Gotcha!" they exclaimed once the prey was cornered.

The prey, Grasshopper and Blind, prepared to fight. But it always happened the same way, whether they prepared or not. The screaming tide of punching arms and kicking legs engulfed them, flipped them over, dragged along, and ebbed, satiated. The hunters were running away, waving the captured fragments of clothing and emitting piercing whistles. Lame Siamese struggled to keep up with the rest. Once the clatter died down, Blind got up and dusted himself off.

"Oh well," he said. "They still enjoy the advantage in numbers."

Grasshopper, his face buried in his lap, didn't say anything. Blind sat down beside him.

"Please don't," he said. "Didn't you notice there were not as many of them today? Have you managed to clobber any of them?"

"I have," Grasshopper said glumly, still not lifting his head. "But there's no use anyway."

"You only think there isn't," Blind said. He felt his cheek, which was starting to swell up, and winced. "There is too use," he said forcefully. "Max wasn't there with them, and that tells me a lot."

Grasshopper looked at him inquisitively.

"How do you know which one is which? They're identical."

"They are, their voices aren't," Blind explained. "Max must have gotten scared. Probably because of that leg of his. They're one person short now, don't you think that's significant?"

Grasshopper sighed.

"There are still too many of them for the two of us. We'll never defeat them."

Blind gave a derisive snort.

"'Never' is a long word. You seem to be fond of silly words like that for some reason. Think how we're stronger than they are. And they are only more numerous than we are. One day, when we grow up, they are going to regret ever picking on us."

"If we manage to live that long," Grasshopper said. "Which, if this continues the same way for much longer, we won't."

"You're a pessimist," Blind said resignedly.

They sat back to back without speaking. A ceiling light went on, then another. Grasshopper's ear was on fire.

"Could you feel my ear, please?" he asked. "It burns."

Blind felt for his shoulders, then his neck, and then pressed his hand against the ear. The hand was cool and soothing.

"Blind. Think of something," Grasshopper said. "While we're still alive."

"I'll try my best."

Blind was cradling the ear and thinking. Thinking of his promise to Elk. *Promise me you'll take care of him.*

All the remaining lights switched on, illuminating the hallway.

Back in the dorm, under Sportsman's guidance, the boys were installing a pan filled with water on top of the half-opened door.

"It's gonna fall down," Muffin warned. "On your own heads. Or someone else will come in before them. That's what always happens."

Muffin was sitting on his bed, nursing a finger damaged in the fight. He'd jammed it against one of the Pack, and this made his mood especially nasty.

"It won't," Sportsman assured. "We set it up solid."

Whiner jumped off the chair and flicked a sideways glance at the pan.

"Genius idea, guys! So they come in, and Blind—bang!—right in the head! And then he's like out cold, so we grab the mama's darling—bang!—down the toilet he goes!"

He cackled. Crybaby was polishing the knives by the windowsill, but squeaked enthusiastic agreement.

They went to their beds and settled in for the long wait. The pan's blue sides glistened, hanging precariously over empty space. This was fun. For everyone except Humpback. He was against the pan business, just like he'd been against the dead rat in the newbie's bed, and the dog poo in Blind's shoes before that. Humpback was a humanist. But they never listened to him.

"Let's go," Blind said and got up off the floor. "Or you'll fall asleep right here. I thought of something, except I'm not sure if it's going to work."

Grasshopper rose reluctantly, still pressing the injured ear to his shoulder. He was sure that none of what Blind thought of ever worked, hardly for anyone.

"If you thought of how we are going to go there and clean their clocks, I'd rather stay here and sleep."

Blind did not answer and started in the direction of their dorm. Grasshopper followed him, grumbling and fuming.

"I could half do with a cigarette right now," he said.

"You're too young to smoke," Blind said without turning his head.

"For how long do they usually beat up newbies?" Grasshopper caught up with him. "A dozen times? A hundred? Several months?"

"Once, maybe twice."

Grasshopper stumbled, flabbergasted.

"Once or twice? Why are they still picking on me, then? It's been forever! How am I so special?"

Blind stopped.

"You're special because you're not alone. There's two of us, and that means war. Us against them, them against us. I thought you knew."

"You mean that if not for you . . ."

"They would've accepted you long ago."

Blind wasn't joking, because he was never joking. Grasshopper searched his face for even a trace of a smile, but Blind was somber.

"So all of that is because of you?" said Grasshopper in a dead little voice.

"Yup. Took you long enough."

Blind turned around and started walking again. Grasshopper staggered along. He was the most miserable person in the whole House. And it was Elk's fault. Elk the kind, Elk the wise. Elk who gave him a friend and protector, along with an army of enemies and interminable war. He never would fit in with the boys as long as Blind was with him, and Blind was going to be with him forever, because that's what Elk wished. They would always be hated and hunted. He wanted to cry and scream, but instead he silently kept up with Blind. Because if he were to say anything against Elk, Blind would go ballistic, and that would be even worse.

Blind stopped in front of door number 10. A senior dorm. The door was painted black, with messages in red and white and splashes and splotches of paint for effect.

Blind stood and listened. Grasshopper was rereading the messages, even though he knew them all by heart.

TO EACH HIS SONG.

SPRING IS THE TIME OF HORRIBLE CHANGES.

Den of the Purple Ratter.

BEWARE. HERE BE DOG THAT BITES.

NO KNOCKING. NO ADMITTANCE.

In the House, a door into someone's dorm was not always a door. For some it could as well have been a solid wall. This was one such door, so when Blind knocked, Grasshopper gasped in shock.

"What are you doing? We're not allowed in there!"

Blind entered without even waiting for a response.

The door closed and Grasshopper crouched down next to it. He could guess why Blind would need Ancient and tried very hard not to think about it.

After some time the door opened again. The messages shifted and then moved back in their place. Grasshopper stood up. Blind leaned against the door with a mysterious smile. His unseeing eyes flowed wetly behind the half-closed eyelids.

"You're going to get an amulet," he said. "But you'll have to wait a little."

Grasshopper's heart skipped a beat and crashed down into the pit of his stomach. His knees buckled.

"Thank you." His whisper was barely audible. "Oh, thank you."

A nightlight turned toward the wall illuminated the darkened room. Ancient meditated over a tin box with an open lid. Talismans against the evil eye looked back at him through their glass pupils. Stones with holes in them; monogrammed buttons, coins, and medallions splashed with patina; dog teeth and cat teeth; fingernail-sized shards covered in Chinese characters; mysterious seeds on strings. A treasure trove such as to make young Hoover lose his senses were he ever to see it. There was a lot to choose from, but Ancient couldn't make up his mind. Finally he closed his eyes and reached out at random.

A tiny sandstone kitten. It had a human face, gouged by the long wait inside the box and repeated encounters with its other inhabitants. Ancient turned it around in his fingers, smiled, and put it on top of a scrap of suede.

To it he added a root that resembled a rat's tail, and a chip of turquoise. He admired his creation for a while, then took a drag on his cigarette and carefully dropped the accumulated ash into the middle of the tableau. Folded the corners to produce a small suede pouch and sewed up the top with thread.

"Let's hope you can bring happiness to your very green owner," he said doubt-fully, setting it aside to look for a suitable cord to hang it on.

Grasshopper lingered timidly at the door, not daring to enter. The senior was sitting on a striped mattress set directly on the floor next to a large fish tank. His hair was completely white, his face had almost the same color as the hair, and the whiteness of his fingers made it hard to distinguish the cigarette he was holding. On his face only the lips and the eyes had any color or life in them. Wine-colored eyes in the halo of white eyelashes.

"So it's you who needs an amulet?" Ancient asked. "Come in."

Grasshopper approached, tense and apprehensive, even though he knew that Ancient was not going to jump off his mattress and attack him. He couldn't, even if he wanted to.

The fish tank glowed green. It contained only two fish, two small black tri-angles. Glasses with sticky residue on their bottoms crowded the straw mat in front of the mattress.

"Lean closer," Ancient said.

Grasshopper crouched next to him and Ancient put the amulet around his neck. A small pouch of gray suede with white stitches.

"That friend of yours, very tenacious," Ancient said. "Obstinate, even. Both are commendable qualities, but they can really get on one's nerves. I never make amulets for juniors. You are lucky. You're going to serve as an exception."

Grasshopper tried to see his amulet without appearing to look at it directly.

"What's in there?" he whispered.

"Your power."

Ancient reached and tucked the amulet inside Grasshopper's shirt.

"Better this way," he said. "Less visible. Your power and your fortune. Almost as much as I gave Skull back then. So be careful. And try not to show it to anyone."

Grasshopper blinked, stunned by Ancient's words.

"Wow!" He lowered his head and looked at the harmless bump under his shirt with reverent awe. "That's too much."

"There's no such thing as too much," Ancient said with a laugh. "And besides, it's not going to come right away. Please don't imagine yourself walking out of here the next Skull. All in good time."

"Thank you."

Grasshopper felt the need to say more, but he didn't know what. He was very bad at those things. His lips formed a smile all by themselves. A silly, happy smile.

He looked at his feet, grinning widely, and just kept repeating softly: "Thank you
. . . Thank you . . ."

In his mind he was already ripping the pouch apart with Blind's fingers. *What's
inside?* Could it be another monkey skull? Or something even more wondrous?

Ancient appeared to have read his thoughts.

"An amulet cannot be opened, or it will lose all of its power. For at least two
years you are not allowed to do it. After that time, maybe. And don't say I didn't
warn you."

Grasshopper's grin disappeared.

"I'm never ever going to do that."

"Run along, then." Ancient dropped the cigarette in the glass of lemonade
and looked at his watch. "You've taken a lot of my time as it is."

Grasshopper ran out, not missing the opportunity to demonstrate to Ancient
how he could push door handles with his feet.

Blind was crouching by the door but rose to meet him.

"Well?"

"I have it," Grasshopper reported in a low whisper and stuck out his chest.
"Feel it. Under the shirt."

Blind's fingers slithered under his shirt and searched for the pouch. They tick-
led, and Grasshopper giggled and fidgeted.

"Stand still!" Blind said sternly and continued the examination. "Something
hard, made of stone," he said finally, letting go of the pouch. "Also something
dried out, like grass. The suede is too thick, I can't make out the details."

Grasshopper was hopping impatiently. He wished very much to blurt out
what it was that he now had hidden under his shirt, but did not allow himself to.
Unverifiable things like that are better kept silent. But the Great-Power-on-a-String
was egging him on. He had to rush somewhere and do something to slake the itch
in his legs, the urge to jump and fly.

"Can we go climb the big garage?" he suggested. "Or the roof, that place we
found, under the moon! Tonight is the greatest night! We can't just go and sleep!"

Blind shrugged. As far as he was concerned it was a perfectly ordinary night,
and he'd much rather sleep than scramble up to the roof, but he understood that
Grasshopper's excitement wouldn't permit them sleep. Ancient's words had to be
digested before the two of them could go back to the Pack. Ancient was great.
Blind sincerely admired what he'd heard of their conversation from behind the
door. There was no other senior in the House who could have pulled it off.

"All right," he said. "Roof it is, then."

Grasshopper gave out a shrill whistle and bounded down the hallway.

The Great Power throbbed under his shirt like a second heart, lifting him off the ground. The floorboards caught him and then tossed him back up, like a rubber mat. Grasshopper's happiness screamed and hollered. He was dancing as he ran. In his wake the dorm doors opened, letting out the indignant shushes.

Blind caught up with him only at the end of the corridor and then they were walking side by side, two boys in tattered green shirts, so very different from each other.

The Sixth was cursing them, yawning and fighting off sleep.

"I can-n-n't do it anymore," squeaked Crybaby, peeling off his socks. "And I don't wanna m-m-miss thi-i-is!"

A sock traversed the room and landed on the desk lamp.

"It's night already! How much longer?"

"Suck it in," came the curt reply from Sportsman's bed. "You waited this long, wait a bit more."

Rex the Siamese was holding his eyelids apart with his fingers. His brother was blissfully asleep, hugging his pillow.

Sportsman surveyed his enfeebled Pack.

"Wimps," he whispered. "A sorry bunch of wimps."

Muffin yawned, snapped shut the journal with sports-car stickers, and pushed it under the mattress.

"Whatever. I'm going to sleep," he announced and turned over facing the wall. "This thing is gonna fall on them anyway, even if I don't see it."

"Traitor," growled Rex the Siamese.

"Yourself," Muffin countered over his shoulder.

Sportsman sighed and inspected the remaining troops.

Just four limp, green-shirted figures, swinging their legs, each on his own bed. Plump Elephant, who was sucking his thumb, felt Sportsman's gaze on him and extracted the thumb and smiled tentatively.

"Now can I go pee-pee?" he asked.

"Damn it!" Sportsman exploded. "Can't you manage one hour without the bathroom? One needs to pee, another needs to wash his feet, and then there's watering the plant! What kind of Pack is this? You're just a load of sad sacks! All you think about is eat, sleep, and pee on schedule!"

Elephant slowly reddened; his sighs turned to sniffles and then to tears. Max the Siamese woke up immediately. Elephant was already at full bawl. Max looked at his brother. Rex hopped off his bed, limped to Elephant's side, and hugged his pudgy shoulders.

"There, there, baby . . . Don't cry. It'll be all right."

"I want pee-pee," Elephant sobbed. "He doesn't let me."

"He's going to right now," promised Siamese, his yellow eyes shooting daggers at Sportsman. "He's going to let you like he's never let anybody anything ever."

Humpback, who until then was lying quietly on the top bunk, shot up.

"Enough!" he howled and chucked his shoe at the pan on top of the door.

The pan crashed to the floor amid deafening clatter and torrents of water. Elephant startled and went silent. Crybaby whimpered and pulled up his feet. The floor was turning into a lake.

THE BACKYARD

INTERLUDE

Humpback played his flute, and the backyard listened. He was playing very softly, for himself only. The wind whirled the leaves in circles. Then they were caught in the puddles and stopped. Their dance ended. They ended. Now they would turn to mush and dirt. Just like people.

Softer. Softer still. The slender fingers flitting across the holes, the wind throwing the leaves right in the face, the coins in the back pocket cutting into the skin, the bare ankles freezing, covered in goose bumps. Comfort is a piece of sibilant wood. Calming, lulling, if you allow it to be.

A leaf fetched against his foot and was stuck. Then another one. If you sat without moving for hours, Nature would include you in its cycle just like another tree. Leaves would cling to your roots, birds would alight on your branches and crap down your shirt, rain would wash down your furrows, and wind would bury you in sand. He imagined himself such a treeman and laughed. He laughed with only half of his face. His red sweater, patched on the elbows, let in the wind through the threadbare wool, and it prickled. He didn't have a shirt under it. This was a punishment he set for himself. For all transgressions, both real and imagined, he always punished himself. And almost never commuted his own sentences. He was unforgiving toward his skin, his arms and legs, his fears and fantasies. The itchy sweater was penance for his fears in the night. Those that made him wrap his head in the blanket, making sure that there was no gap left for He Who Comes In The Dark to creep in. Those that forbade him from drinking water before bed, to save himself from the torment of needing to go to the bathroom. The fears that no one knew about, because their owner occupied the top bunk and no one from below could see what was going on up there.

Still, he was ashamed of them. He fought them every night, lost every time, and punished himself for the loss. This had been his way for as long as he remembered. It was the game he always played with himself, gaining the next level of maturity through mortifications imposed on his body. All of his victories smelled of defeat. By winning he only conquered a part of himself, while remaining unchanged at the core.

He fought his shyness with vulgar jokes, his aversion to fights by being the first to jump in, his dread of death with thoughts about it. But all of that, repressed and suppressed, still lived inside and breathed the same air he did. He was both shy and rude, quiet and loud; he bottled up his virtues and exposed his vices, pulled the blanket over his head, praying "O God, don't let me die," and attacked those much stronger than himself.

He had his poems, written in code on the wallpaper next to his pillow, and he scraped off those he got tired of. He had his flute, a kind gift, and he hid it in the space between the wall and his mattress. He had his crow, and he stole morsels of food for her from the kitchen. He had his skeins of wool, and he knitted beautiful sweaters.

He was born hunchbacked and six-fingered, ugly, apelike. At ten he had been moody, his lips always bruised, his awkward paws destroying everything they touched. At seventeen he became more delicate, taciturn and quiet. His face was the face of an adult, his eyebrows met above the bridge of his nose, his wild unkempt hair the color of raven feathers spread out like a gorse bush. He ate indifferently and dressed slovenly, wore black under his fingernails and rarely changed his socks. He was ashamed of his hump and the pimples on his nose. He was ashamed that he didn't need to shave yet, and smoked a pipe to look older. His secret vice was soppy romance novels, and the heroes of his poems died slow, horrible deaths. He kept books by Dickens under his pillow.

He loved the House. He'd never had any other home and had never known his parents. Here he grew up as one of many, and he was used to tuning the world out when he needed to be alone. His best flute playing happened when no one was listening. Then everything came out right, every song sounded as if the wind itself whistled into the instrument. He thought sometimes that he wanted someone else to hear it, but he also knew that if someone were listening it wouldn't have come out this well. In the House it was customary to call those with humps "angels," in reference to the folded wings on their backs. This was one of the very few tender names that the House allowed itself to give to its children.

Humpback played, keeping time on the wet leaves with his splayed feet. He inhaled the peace and the kindness, and placed himself in the circle of clarity that never would allow the pale hands of those who *confuse the soul* to worm their way through. Other people sometimes drifted past, behind the fence, but they did not disturb him. In his mind, the Outsides did not exist. There was only him, the wind, his songs, and those he loved. All of that was inside the House, and outside of it was nothing and no one, only the empty and hostile city that lived its own life.

The wind was burying the yard in leaves. Two poplars, the oak, and four nameless bushes. The bushes grew under the windows, clinging to the walls; poplars occupied the two outer corners of the fence, and some of their roots left the domain of the House. With its massive arms the oak pushed at the shed that it neighbored and overshadowed its corner of the yard completely. It had sprung up here long before the House came to be, and it remembered the time when all of this was orchards and storks made their nests in the trees. How far did its own roots extend?

The empty ball court with old crates for seats. The empty kennel, its roof leaking, the rusty water bowls in front of it full of rain. The bench under the oak, plastered with beer labels. Trash cans. White steam issuing out of the kitchen. Multicolored music out of the windows on the second floor.

Mangy cats stole along the boundaries of the yard. Crows marched across the bare lawns, pushing wet leaves. An aquiline-faced boy in a red sweater sat on an overturned crate and played his flute, locked in a circle of empty loneliness. The House breathed on him through its windows.

SMOKER

OF BATS, DRAGONS, AND
BASILISK EGGSHELLS

The dorm was rocking. Humpback and I were sitting on the bed. Noble, Tabaqui, and Blind were on the floor passing around bottles and jars, sniffing, sampling, and pouring the mysterious contents of some of them into others. Tubby, in pink pajamas, watched them from behind the bars of his portable playpen.

I was watching through the bars of the headboard.

Humpback was whittling something from a blackened knobby root with his pocket knife. He had on his outside coat, decorated with Nanette's droppings, and his shaggy hair was full of shavings.

"The pine needles are past their prime, is all I'm saying," Tabaqui was droning halfway inside a jar of something murky and brownish. "The bouquet is completely off."

"Take the other one, then," Noble said. He took the jar himself, sniffed, and put it aside. "This is last year's vintage. And quit jolting it, you are disturbing the sediment."

Blind licked the drops he'd shaken onto his hand from another bottle, scowled, and said, "What's oil doing here? Is this salad dressing or something?"

"Hey!" Tabaqui yelped. "Where did you get that from? That's a scorpion drowned in sunflower oil! It's medicine! I always store it separately!"

Noble brought the bottle closer and peered at it.

"Could be. Yep, there it is, floating there. You dummy, why did you have to do it in an opaque bottle? You can hardly see the bugger."

"I used what was available at close proximity," Tabaqui said sulkily. "Your choices are somewhat limited when you are holding a live scorpion in your hand, you know. And I distinctly remember putting a warning label on it. Must have dropped off at some point."

"What use would your label be to Blind? What if *he* drops off right here? We'd be leaderless on the eve of a military coup."

At this, Noble broke into a smile. It was tender and wistful.

It immediately brought to mind Tabaqui's saying: "Noble only smiles once a year, and that when someone breaks a leg."

Or when someone takes a swig from the bottle with a scorpion in it, I added silently.

"Blind, tell me, do you know any spells against poisons?" Tabaqui inquired anxiously. "Or how about a guarding amulet?"

Blind was already busy with the next bottle. He threw the cork from it into Tubby's playpen and coaxed a drop onto his finger. He definitely didn't look like someone in deathly peril.

"On second thought, what's a mere scorpion to him?" Tabaqui said, mostly to himself. "He's eaten much worse stuff than that. Just the other day, and other days besides the other day."

Tubby, happy as a lark, was playing with the cork. He tossed it into the air with his two-fingered pincers and then tried to catch it. The cork kept falling through his grasp, but that didn't faze him. Then he stuffed it into his mouth and started gumming it like a pacifier.

I watched them for a bit more and then turned over on my back. Humpback's whittling was spraying the shavings in all directions.

"Sorry," he'd say every time some of it fell on me.

"It's all right," I'd answer.

Humpback's eyes were like moist prunes, and his eyelashes were so long they looked glued on.

"By the way," he said, interrupting our monotonous exchanges of pleasantries, "Shuffle says that Pompey is practicing knife throwing, imagine that. He's rumored to hit the mark from ten paces three times out of five now."

"Who were you talking to just now?" Tabaqui said from down on the floor.

"Everybody," Humpback said.

I turned over on my stomach again and pushed apart the bags hanging on the headboard.

"Then stop doing it. Basically, everybody already had enough of that talk from Lary."

Tabaqui extracted a half-decomposed chili pepper from the jar he was holding, shook off the liquid, and chomped on it.

"Now this one is pretty good," he said and closed his eyes. "There's only one thing that's currently perturbing me. By the time Pompey achieves perfection in his quest for accurate knife throws, Lary will have eaten all of our brains out with a spoon. He's already on edge. Attacking people left and right. Well, he won't be attacking anyone anytime soon now, but still. He's clearly not himself. I think we all need to do something about it."

"Why isn't he going to do it anytime soon?" I said.

Noble sent another one of his radiant smiles my way.

"Yesterday we convinced Lary that he had killed you."

My next question got stuck in my throat.

"He was bawling his head off somewhere in the bowels of the House," Noble continued, "bidding good-bye to his faithful Bandar-Logs. It'll be some time before he lives that down."

"And you're just reveling in the agony of your fellow human being!" Tabaqui said indignantly. "Happy that he almost hanged himself! Gleefully recounting this whole disgusting matter!"

"I'm sure Sphinx would've taken him out of the noose before anything bad happened," Noble said airily. "He's very considerate like that . . . sometimes. And besides, I get this feeling that you already forgot it was your idea all along."

I was looking at Noble and thinking that at the time Sphinx was wringing me out in the bathroom, he already knew what his packmates had done to Lary. And that what they had done was by far the best protection for me that could be imagined. But he never said anything. He was testing if I was capable of snitching, and then testing if I was ready to be considered a snitch in the mind of Lary, whom I did not particularly respect. And maybe a bunch of other things as well, I couldn't even imagine what. So that's why I felt like I was navigating through some sort of test. Because I actually was. I knew I wasn't going to forgive him this for a long while. And I also knew that I'd never tell anyone about it.

Tabaqui continued to expound excitedly on Lary's mental state, and it all boiled down to his conviction that Lary would be best helped by a nice cup of herbal tea. Noble countered that Lary would be best helped by Pompey's untimely death. Listening to this made me realize that I'd been hearing rumors of some kind of coup for a while now, and that the nick of Pompey, Leader of the Sixth, was often mentioned in relation to it. When I had still been a Pheasant, this kind of talk never really concerned me, but now I was suddenly worried that there was some piece of common knowledge I didn't have any idea about.

"So it's Pompey who is behind this coup?" I said. "What does he want with it?"

Tabaqui, Noble, and Blind all raised their heads and stared at me. Or rather, Tabaqui and Noble did. Blind just raised his head. All three holding jars and spoons, all three in colorful bandanas to keep their hair out of the way, they hilariously resembled three witches busy with their potions. Tubby in his playpen could pass for a homunculus. Even the bottled scorpion fit. I giggled at the thought.

"What does he want with it?" The smallest weird sister, the one with the most hair, shrouded herself in cigarette smoke and went into a trance. "What-does-he—"

"One sentence!" the second one snapped. "And that's an order."

"What?" Jackal said indignantly, ruining the image. "Blind, have a heart, or Smoker shall forever remain unenlightened!"

This threat did not appear to have any effect on Blind.

"I see," Tabaqui drawled menacingly. "So this is how you want to play. All right, so be it."

He cleared out some space around him as if preparing for takeoff, sat up, and cleared his throat.

"Hear a tale then, O Smoker, and know that it is the true tale of Pompey, whom you might know a little about and who lately has been behaving in a not entirely satisfactory manner by taking things upon himself that he hadn't before, even though 'before' is an imprecise notion in this context, seeing as there was a 'before' for some of us here where he did not figure at all, and so it is completely beyond our kenning what exactly his behavior was in the place where he found himself prior to the moment when he found himself with us, making it at best questionable that at that time he did behave more adequately, since this man has obviously traveled far from the spirit of true Tao by becoming thoroughly steeped in the effluvium of the Outsides and is therefore capable of earnestly imagining that he could be an adequate substitute for Blind in his demanding position, which delusion might, however, be more mundanely attributed to his being fed up with the constant overpopulation of the particular precinct entrusted in his care and thus yearning for your everyday peace and quiet, in which case the preferred course of action to alleviate this condition would have been to transport himself bodily within the confines of the Cage for a period of no less than three and no more than five days, undoubtedly resulting in deeper self-awareness and spiritual cleansing as well as development of a more public-minded level of conscience, or, not to put too fine a point on it, a more introspective state of being, but no, he needs something entirely more bombastic and earth shattering, he desires to conquer and to vanquish and to tickle his multitudinous ingrained insecurities, where the manifest insecurity of his person is easily apparent to anyone in sight of his cravats and sideburns, his manner of locomotion and body language, but especially the faces of the bats that he keeps adorning himself with, for those are the faces of creatures doomed to endless suffering, afflicted with all the infirmities, known and unknown, of their chiropterous kind at the same time, a regular Ozzy Osbourne he, except that, instead of mercifully biting off their heads, he condemns them to fester around his neck for months, take poor unfortunate Poppy, having shuffled off this mortal coil not quite last Wednesday, and lo! today Suzy is already in its place, considering that this is the best we can expect from someone completely ignorant of the science that is biology,

who could not even be bothered to notice that Suzy is male, despite it flashing balls
the size of walnuts, though it still isn't going to make any significant contribution in
the grand scheme of things since it, too, is not long for this world, this Suzy guy is, as
Pompey buried quite half a dozen of its brothers already, making its demise a question
only of time, besides it likely is a matter of indifference to a bat what name is attached
to it as it breathes its last, while if I were representing the Society for Prevention of
Cruelty to Animals I'd be very interested to know the name of the scoundrel buying
those wretches wholesale just to look cool, even though it's highly debatable how much
coolness can possibly be squeezed out of the bedraggled body of a bat, it's not like it's
a coral snake, now that really would be something to write home about, whereas he
who is not at home with the thought of his own death is quite unlikely to wrap said
snake around his neck since that would require significant expenditure of time and
effort to win its trust when instead one can so easily pave his way in this world with
feeble bones of innocent leather-winged victims without even bothering to notice their
gender, and it is quite likely that only the complete and utter impunity Pompey enjoys
with respect to this specific question is what facilitates his mistaken belief that he is
supposedly capable of trampling underfoot the bones of a considerably less innocuous
creature without breaking stride, by which creature I of course mean Blind, but you
must have already gathered that, my esteemed packmates, so this last clarification can
be considered extraneous."

Tabaqui paused and then nodded proudly at Blind.

"I trust that was within the rules. Even though limiting me in this fashion was
really rotten of you."

The room was totally quiet. Even the boombox had gone silent. Even Nanette
stopped stirring. It was as though, all this time, Jackal had been chanting a monumental spell putting the whole world to sleep. Noble was cradling an open jar and swaying
from side to side with his eyes closed. Blind had slumped against Tubby's playpen.
Humpback stared at the twisted root in his hands, evidently having no idea anymore
about what he was doing with it. Their faces seemed drowsy and somehow unwell,
bordering on sickly. Tubby was the only one immune to the spell. He was peacefully
pulling on Blind's hair and droning softly.

Once it became crystal clear that everyone else was completely bewitched,
Humpback startled and translated, blinking sleepily.

"What Tabaqui is saying is that Pompey hankers after Blind's job. I'm not sure
this really came through, what with all those bats and other crap."

"Objection!" Tabaqui said hotly. "I was acquitting myself quite eloquently, and,
what's more important, very vividly. To try and reduce this oration to a digest is
criminal."

"True," Humpback said. "Except that Smoker might be a bit stunned, since it's his first time, and so not really in a position to give it its due."

Noble opened his eyes and peeked in astonishment into the jar he was hugging through all of this.

"Would it be possible," he said, "to limit this monster next time to a certain number of words instead of sentences?"

"Of course not!" Blind said. He straightened up and snatched his hair out of Tubby's grasp. "Just think of the many different ways one single word can be repeated."

We all thought of it and groaned. Tabaqui inclined his head like a great actor acknowledging the applause of his audience.

At dinner I couldn't eat properly. I was shaken up by the information about Pompey. The well-being of his bats was the last thing on my mind. I didn't like the word *coup*, not one bit. I felt myself in the middle of events about which I had only a very hazy notion, or rather no notion at all, and I liked that even less.

How does the House change Leaders? Do they fight each other? Or is it pack against pack? And if so, why is the Fourth so unruffled in the face of the coming massacre? Because there was no other way that a fight between them and the Sixth could be described.

I guess that's the end of the peaceful life, I thought. As if my life in the Fourth was ever peaceful.

The green peas were drying out on the plate, and the meat loaf was already caked with congealed fat. I was hungry, but I still couldn't eat. The ceiling speakers were drenching us in marching music, so anyone in the canteen wanting to have a conversation had to shout in order to be heard.

The black-and-white Pheasant table. The quiet horror of the glances examining neighbors' plates. Half of the Pheasants were on individual meal plans, each one different, so everyone's plate contents were always a concern. There were calories to be counted.

Rats at the next table. The explosion of color and the tide of insanity.

Then Birds, in their nightmarish bibs over black.

The Sixth was all about camaraderie. Looking at them, it would seem that the group consisted exclusively of jovial practical jokers. I wouldn't want to find myself on the receiving end of their jokes, and their bursts of loud merriment looked suspect, but so what. They were trying their best.

The Third, Fourth, and Sixth had it tough. Rats and Pheasants were the Naughty and the Nice. Both of them overdid it to such an extent that everyone else had to squeeze in between somewhere. Birds were a bit better at it, Hounds a bit worse, and

the Fourth, in addition to having no designation, was just too sparsely populated to
. . . to fully participate in the game.

Once I managed to *say the word*, I suddenly was free to realize that this "game"
would have to include much more than just appearance. It was the right word, and,
having caught it, I understood that I had been looking for it for a long time. For the
word that would contain the key to everything happening in the House. All it took
was the recognition of the fact that the Game encompassed *everything* around me.

It was too improbable that every single one of the pathetic, whining conformists
would assemble in one group, while all the unhinged anarchists would go to the other.
Which meant that someone somewhere must have designed this at some point. Why?
Now that was a different question.

My own perspicacity was making me sweat. I wasn't even hungry anymore.

So one day, my imagination churned, they became so frightfully bored that they
compiled the script of the Game and vowed to never deviate from it under any circumstances. For everyone his role and everyone in his place. And that was the way it
had gone since that time. Make-believe and following the script. Willingly for some,
less so for others, but everywhere and always. And especially in the canteen, where the
audience was always the biggest. No wonder some of them, Pheasants for example,
eventually could allow the Game to overrule even basic human nature.

Within this structure everything started making sense, easily and beautifully. The
scales had fallen from my eyes as I looked around.

Rats. Almost all of them underage, sixteen or less. Their acid-colored mullets
masked teenagers in the throes of age-appropriate angst. Probably this was why they
looked so natural playing at deranged instability.

Birds. Birds made me pause a little. All right. Black is just a color. Unpleasant
faces, but I probably could make my own face look like that if needed. Vulture . . .
the House monster. I looked at him through my newly opened eyes and tried to strip
away the chaff. Mourning . . . rings . . . black polish on long manicured nails . . . long
hair and eye shadow. Throw all of that out, forget even the fact that he made his bed
in a coffin, erase every trace of his nasty habits—what would you have left? A gaunt,
hook-nosed fellow. An unpleasant person, to be sure, but not a monster by any stretch.

This is where I switched off temporarily, because the unpleasant person suddenly
turned around and stared at me. Must have felt himself being exposed. He looked at
me with those sleepy yellow eyes of his and I lost the ability to function, skewered by
that stare.

Assured that I had been neutralized and was ready to be served, Vulture smiled,
showcasing the unnaturally long crooked teeth. It felt like someone forcefully dragging
a blade over glass.

It took me a couple of minutes to get my composure back, and even then something kept nagging at me. Like when you watch an old black-and-white movie and this creep in a ton of makeup is constantly polishing his fingernails and looking around unblinkingly, and it suddenly freaks you out and the next moment makes you ashamed for falling for his cheap tricks.

All right. That meant only that he was a very good actor. He inhabited the character. If anyone was supposed to be a Game master, it was a House Leader. It must have been they who actually invented it.

To test my theory, I decided to expose Red.

Rat Leader proved to be not particularly amenable to exposure. If you took away the green shades occupying the whole upper half of his face and the bloodred buzz cut, supposedly his natural color, what were you left with? Nothing at all. A tailor's dummy made up as a Rat would have done just as well.

That fairly took away my thunder. To cheer myself up again, I turned to Pompey.

He sort of looked a bit like Sphinx. I guess it was his height. And the bald head. Except Sphinx's was real. And Pompey left a small lick on top. Jet black and greased to a shine. He was also fatter. That is, fleshier.

I stripped away the leather biker jacket, like the ones so beloved by Logs, and shook off the face powder. Then picked the poor bat off the collar, bearing in mind that its name was Suzy and that its days were numbered. What was left looked . . . ordinary. A handsome guy, but nothing special.

I couldn't understand before why a guy like Pompey would pretend he was a walking corpse. Now I knew it was all in accordance with the rules of the Game. Leaders needed to be pale and ominous. Pompey was naturally swarthy, so he must have gone through a lot of face powder to maintain the standard. The image of Pompey with the puff in his hand, putting the last touches of deathly paleness on his face, made me swoon and giggle.

The script accounted for everything. Every detail. Which way the part in Pheasants' hair went. How black was the underwear of a true Bird. What books were allowed for Hounds. Maybe Rats would have liked to skip the hair coloring once in a while, but they forced themselves, for those were the rules of the Game. It was even quite likely that Birds secretly loathed anything that grew, pots or no pots.

The final insight was a very simple one. I was leading up to it through all the preceding ones, deliberately, slowly, leaving it for last, so that in the end I could place it on top flamboyantly and be done with the whole thing.

The overthrow of Blind by Pompey—or rather, the widely advertised intention thereof—must have been a part of the Game as well. To always run the same tired script wasn't much fun. From time to time the play needed some variety. The war declared by Pompey provided just such variety. Hound Leader scares the Logs, practices throwing knives, generally behaves "in a not entirely satisfactory manner," to quote Jackal. The audience shivers, Log spies run between different camps with the latest dispatches. People have something to discuss. Everyone's engaged and no one's afraid. Except Lary, but Lary is a simpleton taking everything at face value.

I looked around the canteen again. It was all so obvious! And so stupid!

I wanted to laugh out loud and scream that I was onto all of them now. All of their bats, throwing knives, coups, face powders, and scorpions in oil.

It must have somehow manifested itself on my face, because Tabaqui suddenly threw down his fork and demanded to know why the hell was I looking so smug and stupid.

"This," I said and stuck out my tongue at him. Just the tip. I immediately remembered how Jackal could not stand being mocked, but it was already too late.

He went livid faster than if someone had dumped boiling water on him. Coughed the half-chewed piece of food out on his plate and asked Noble to hold him as fast as he could.

"Did you see that? Did you see that feathered bastard disrespect my advanced age? Everyone see that? I'm going to see the color of his guts!"

He was saying all of this between coughing fits, but it sounded deadly serious.

Noble took the butter knife off Tabaqui and remarked that my guts being spread out on the floor of the canteen would put everybody off their food.

"He thinks that he's received enlightenment!" Tabaqui continued through bouts of coughing, even turning slightly blue. "That he understands it now! Is there life after death, is there life on Mars, and is the Earth round! Look at him, sitting here all bloated!"

"He's been kind of puffy ever since your speech," Humpback said. "I guess he's just not used to it all."

"I'm not bloated!" I protested. "I'm not bloated, I'm not puffy, and I'd appreciate it if you all left me alone!"

"Hear, hear," Black said from the other side of the table. "Tabaqui, why are you at his throat all of a sudden? Can't a guy just think whatever it is he thinks in peace?"

"Peace!" Tabaqui shrieked. "Is that what you call peace now? When one of your packmates fills up with self-importance, turns into a complete bastard, and on top of that squints at you contentedly? And I'm supposed to just shut up about this? To live alongside this disgusting mug? Not likely! If he thinks he can walk around with that kind of face, he should get himself a veil. I personally am not going to let it slide!"

"Look, he's just pissed off now," Sphinx said. "See for yourself. And calm down, will you."

But it took quite a while for Jackal to calm down. He would chew his food looking away and then suddenly turn around, throw me a wicked stare, and turn back. It was not at all funny, even though it seemed so to Noble.

I tried to look stone-faced while wheeling out of the canteen. I wasn't mad at Tabaqui. Not even a bit angry. If anything, I was admiring his sharpness. Who would be happy if someone were to debunk their favorite game? Tabaqui's reaction confirmed that I really was on to something. I just had to learn to keep it to myself.

Black patted me on the shoulder as he passed.

"Don't let it get to you," he said. "They're all nuts, some more than others."

"They're not nuts," I blurted out. "They're players."

Black gave me a surprised look.

I couldn't understand what was more surprising to him: my words, which he didn't understand, or my insightfulness.

They lived in filthy cages, and they ate raw eggs by sucking them out through cracked shells. Their ears were sharp and rough to the touch and their claws were like curved swords. No disease could ever befall them, except colds and scabies, from which they died . . .

. . . it shined its purple eye on me and I understood that it was her, the Great Hairy, the one who lives under the beds in the places where the dust collects, the one who turns the floorboards over in search of mold. I asked her to tell me my future, but she never did that. "There is nothing more horrible than knowing what awaits us tomorrow," she said and gave me one of her fangs in consolation . . .

And within that castle dwelt a knight renowned throughout the land for his prowess. They called him Dragonslayer, for he had killed the last dragon, and that was no mean feat since it was very hard to find. Those who would speak ill of him maintained, however, that it wasn't a dragon at all, just a large lizard from the Southern Realm . . .

It looks like a small black cylinder. It cannot be seen by sunlight, and it definitely cannot be seen in the dark. One can only bump into it by accident. Every night it hums softly as it steals time . . .

I was lying in the dark and listening. It was hot. My head was swimming from the cocktail, in which I could vaguely discern vodka, lemon juice, and something like pine-scented shampoo. The boombox, buried under the layers of blankets, was playing organ music. Everywhere around me were someone's arms, legs, pillows, and bottles. It was the first time that I'd experienced the room with all the lights off. The stories kept coming. Some were interrupted just when they got going, others started instead, and then the earlier ones returned when I'd already lost the sequence of events, and the overlaying snippets wove themselves into fanciful patterns that were very hard to keep track of. I tried, though.

. . . it is the hour when the bighorns venture out on the glistening paths leading down to the water, and they bellow. Trees bend from their calls. And then the hour comes when all the fools are placed in boats and sent up the moon river. It is said that the Moon takes them. The water near the shore becomes sweet and remains sweet until sunrise. Those who catch this hour and manage to drink the water turn into fools themselves . . .

I laughed and spilled some wine on my shirt.

"Why would anyone want to drink it," I whispered, "if it's so dangerous?"

"There is none happier than a true fool," the invisible storyteller said.

The voice sounded like Sphinx. But I didn't think I was distinguishing the voices correctly. I'd drunk too much, I guessed. The glass kept refilling itself, and an empty bottle was sticking in my ribs on the right side. I couldn't be bothered to push it away.

There aren't too many basilisks left in the Black Forest. They have mostly gone to seed, and their gaze is rarely lethal. But if you trek farther in, where the moss covering the tree trunks glows purple, the ones you meet there are the real ones, since they've never seen light. That's why no one goes there, and of those who do, few return, and of those who return, none had seen any basilisks. So how do we know that they still exist there?

Someone jostled me.

"Hey, your turn. Tell us something."

I rubbed my face. My fingers were sticky. I licked them. The drowsy apathy was carrying me away, up the moon river. To where the bighorns were waiting.

"I can't," I said honestly. "I don't know anything that's like these stories. I'd just spoil everything."

"Give me your glass, then."

I thrust the glass in the direction of the voice.

"I'll have the pine, please. But not too much. I'm already tipsy."

I specified the pine because I saw Tabaqui splash some of the contents from the jar with the chili peppers into the other three bottles. I wasn't sure I'd be able to survive a sampling of the resulting brew.

"There isn't much left anyway. Don't drop off, though. No sleeping on Fairy Tale Night. That would be bad manners."

"Do these nights happen often?"

"Four times a year. There's one every season. And also the Monologue Night, the Dream Night, and the Longest Night. Those are once per year. You've missed the first two."

The glass returned.

"The Night of the Big Crash, when Humpback falls out of his aerie," the voice continued to mumble indistinctly. "The Night of the Yellow Water, when Lary remembers his childhood . . . We should check in on him, by the way. He skipped two rounds already."

Someone at the foot of the bed started checking in on Lary. Judging by the sighs and moans reaching me from over there, he was fast asleep.

"Hey you, sleepyhead. Wake up, you owe us a penalty story."

Lary yawned broadly, like a tiger. There was a pause.

"There was this pretty girl who once got run over by a train . . . ," a husky and desperate voice finally said.

"Right, shut up. Go back to sleep."

Lary snorted contentedly, crashed back wherever it was they had just excavated him from, and began snoring immediately. I laughed. My shirt was clinging wetly where I'd spilled the liquor. The boombox stared at me with its red eye.

. . . when Hairy needs to hear something she makes a hole in the wall, and when she needs to see she sends her rats to see for her. She is born of the foundation, and she is alive while the house is still standing. The older the house, the bigger and wiser its Hairy. For those she likes, she makes her domain benevolent and gentle, and for the others—the other way around. In the ancient times, people used to call her spiritus familiaris and made offerings to her. They hoped she would protect them from dark influence and the evil eye . . .

I wondered whose story that was. I couldn't make out the voice. I even suspected that they'd switched off the lights specifically to confuse me. And that they were now telling these tales in resonant, disguised voices for the very same reason.

. . . because ever since the time that the knight nailed the two-headed skull up in the Grand Hall, he was beset by the dragon's curse. The eldest sons in his line were born two-headed. Some said differently. That it wasn't the knight who came out victorious in that

long-forgotten battle, but the dragon, and that it was the lizard who lived in the castle now in the guise of a human, and that for this very reason he never allowed anything bad to be spoken about his two-headed progeny, but instead loved them more than all others . . .

The cry of the midwife toad is terrible and can be heard from far away. If you didn't know beforehand, it would be impossible to believe that it is just a toad crying. It buries its eggs in wet leaves and shovels earth on top of them. You can find them wherever it is the dampest, by the roots of the oldest trees. When the little basilisk is about to hatch, the shell starts to smolder. You should never pour water on it or otherwise try to extinguish the fire, as it's a very bad omen. It must be allowed to extinguish itself. The black slivers that remain can bring luck if sewn into leather or suede and worn constantly . . .

"I wouldn't mind getting some of that shell," I said, trying to chase away sleep. "Anybody here got any? Are there any basilisk hunters around?"

Everyone laughed.

"Or a two-headed dragon skull for you, maybe?" Tabaqui said indignantly. "That little nipper doesn't miss a beat!"

"No. No skull, I don't want to fall prey to a curse," I said.

"But a bit of free luck would not be amiss?" the mysterious basilisk expert said.

"It's luck, how could it be?" I said.

"Have it, then. But remember: you carry a part of the Forest with you now. May your desires be pure."

Someone's hand brushed my hair. I lifted my head and a pouch on a string slid down my neck.

All around me people rumbled indignantly, disapproving of my sudden fortune.

"Outrageous!" Tabaqui shouted.

Something bumped against the back of my head. It was small but expertly tossed. A quarter of an apple, as it turned out.

"I've been living here for ages, constantly at everyone's pleasure, entertaining day and night. I've become all frayed and withered, and not a single wretched creature in this place has ever offered me to try on a piece of basilisk eggshell! This is the gratitude for all my pains, for years and years of misery," Tabaqui ranted.

"I don't think you've ever asked," the former owner of the amulet said gently.

The voice made me shiver slightly, and that's how I knew it was Blind. Even though the voice was not entirely his.

"Horse pucky!" Tabaqui exploded. "Are you saying respect must be begged and wheedled now? Justice! Where's justice, I ask you?"

He was either really very deeply upset, or he was playing it up brilliantly. Either way, I felt uneasy.

"Would you like to have it for a while?" I said and reached for the string.

"No way!" he squeaked. "An amulet belonging to someone else? You're off your rocker, dearest! Better a cursed dragon tailbone!"

"Speaking of dragons," Sphinx interjected. "We got distracted. So what about those, the two-headed ones?"

"Nothing." A lighter clicked and I saw it was Noble lighting up. "I am the last son in the whole stupid lineage. One-headed, as you can see. We're freaking extinct, and I'm certainly not complaining."

The ending of this story caught me a little off guard. I laughed.

"Cool. So was this a curse or the dragon himself?" I said.

The burning cigarette end zigzagged in the air.

"I've no idea. I only know the tale, and that we have a two-headed lizard on our coat of arms, with a supremely idiotic expression on both of its mugs," Noble said.

"You've got a coat of arms?" I said.

"It's on every handkerchief and every sock," Noble admitted with disgust. "I keep trying to lose them everywhere and they keep coming back. Would you like a sock or ten? I'll throw in a free lighter as well. And let's talk about something else, all right? Like what happens to those poor idiots floating in the river?"

"Who knows?" Sphinx said. "They float. Maybe they wash ashore somewhere. Or maybe the Moon really takes them. It's not about them, it's about the water in the river."

"Moon River!" Tabaqui exclaimed. "I knew it! I knew this was about the dear old concoction!"

I recalled the beginning of that story: *Those who manage to drink the water turn into fools.* I was just about to ask how come Noble didn't turn into one when I felt his hand squeezing my elbow as a mute warning. An impossible trick, to move so quickly over a bed full of people. I was curious if he managed to shut up Jackal as well. Or did Tabaqui decide on his own to shut up? I definitely wasn't going to ask that.

"How about we open the windows?" someone suggested. "It's getting stuffy."

The other end of the bed developed some movement, there were yawns and cigarettes being lit.

"And some more water. We ran out."

"Let Smoker go get some. He's not speaking anyway."

"He won't make it."

"I'll go," someone suggested, jumping off the bed. "Give me the bottles."

I heard bottles clinking. I grappled for the one sticking in my side, passed it over, and felt that I could breathe freely again. Turned out it had been making me really miserable all this time.

"Humpback, sing the one about the purple ghost. That's a beautiful song."

"I'm not in the mood. I'll sing the one about being caught in the act," Humpback said.

Someone jostled me and made me spill the wine again.

> *Please don't hurt me, I'm a little old rat,*
> *just a little old rat, I swear!*
> *Only this piece of old yellow cheese,*
> *and that's the full extent of my sins,*
> *I swear to you, yes, I swear!*

"Wicked," someone whispered and giggled softly.

> *Only a burrow, two runs in it,*
> *my bedroom is at the very end.*
> *There are four of us hiding inside,*
> *I'm the oldest, Death will come for me soon.*
> *Please, please, don't hurt me tonight,*
> *let me return, return to my hole!*

Doleful sighs in the dark.

I fingered the pouch on the string. It was soft, worn, and sewn shut. There was something sharp inside, and it crackled where I was probing. Maybe it really was a piece of shell. Or a corn chip. My own movements felt sluggish, and my thoughts chased each other around in my head. I tried to assemble them into something halfway coherent, but I only ended up with some fuzzy snippets. *Rip the pouch open . . . to see . . . Check Noble's socks. Ask him why he didn't want anyone to know about Moon River.* At the same time I was conscious of the fact that tomorrow I wouldn't remember much of what I was thinking tonight. Or much of anything really.

Lary woke up and began telling a story about the abominable snowman. I recognized his voice easily, even when drunk. His snowman was really made of snow. He was quickly shushed. Apparently Lary had been telling this same story for years now, and everyone except me already knew it by heart. Lary said that they were just afraid. That it was the scariest tale in the world and that not many people were able to listen to it.

Then the water arrived. The glass disappeared somewhere, so I was waiting for the bottle making the rounds to get to me, but someone upended it on the way, spilling water on the bed. Everyone started yelling and jumping about. I got hit with a book, then another book, and a pillow. I scrambled out from under them and immediately dove right back, blinded by the bright light.

Once I came to and could open my eyes, I emerged again and right away found the glass. It was lolling in the folds of the blanket, quietly bleeding the last drops of pine. Blind's hand was on the wall switch. He was the only one not screwing his eyes desperately as he gleefully waited for the groans to die down. In the other hand he held three dripping bottles, his impossibly long fingers interwoven around their necks, so I figured that he was the one who'd offered to go get the water. The chain of command sure manifested itself in mysterious ways in the Fourth.

Half of the pack had already migrated down. Humpback and Alexander opened the windows and tossed mattresses on the floor. I tried to climb off the bed as well, something I couldn't reliably manage without help even when sober. Black caught me just in time, turned me the right way up, and deposited me on the mattress. I thanked him effusively, if not quite coherently. The boombox went back on, the lights went back out. Alexander threw a blanket over Noble and me, then another one over those who were lying next to us. Blind distributed the bottles.

I lay there wrapped up in my corner of the blanket. I was content. I became a part of something big, something of many arms and legs, something warm and chatty. I was probably its tail or paw, or maybe even a bone. Any movement made my head spin, but still I couldn't remember the last time when I'd felt so comfortable. If, that morning, someone had told me that I was going to be spending the night like this, mellow and happy, drinking and listening to stories, would I have believed it? Probably not. Stories. Fairy tales. In the dark, complete with harmless dragons, basilisks, and stupid, stupid snowmen . . .

I almost cried from all the empathy for my packmates that was now flooding me, but managed to stop myself. Those would have been the wrong tears, drunken and maudlin.

"I'm beautiful," said one of the ugly ones and started crying.

"And I'm ugly," said the other and started laughing . . .

And the night went on.

THE HOUSE

The House belonged to the seniors. The House was their home—counselors existed to maintain order in it, teachers to make sure seniors weren't bored. Seniors could make fires in the dorms and grow magic mushrooms in bathtubs, there was no one to tell them off.

They would say things like "a spoke of my wheels," or "the lurch is stale in the bones," or "vigorously present body parts," or "liturgically challenged." They were shaggy and motley. They threw sharp elbows and icy stares.

They could marry and adopt each other at will. Their malicious energy made the windowpanes rattle, but the cats luxuriated in it, acquiring an arcing glow. No one could enter their world. They invented it themselves. The world, the war, and their places in it.

No one remembered how their war had started. But they were now divided into Moor people and Skull people, into red and black, like chess pieces. On the eve of their rumbles, the House froze and waited with bated breath. The juniors would be locked in their dorms, and that's why for them the rumbles were always a burning, itching secret behind the two turns of the key. Something beautiful, something into which, someday, they would grow themselves. They waited for the battles to end, desperately scraping at the locks and pressing their ears to the doors. The ending was always the same. The seniors would forget to unlock them, and the squirts would remain prisoners of their dorms until morning, when the counselors returned. Once liberated, they would rush to the battlefield, sniffing around for the traces—of what, they didn't know, for there never were any. They would learn the details later, from the overheard snippets of conversations. Then the Great Game entered into their little games in the backyard, teased and twisted until they grew tired of it.

Once he reaches the doors of the Fifteenth, Grasshopper tiptoes like an enemy infiltrator. There are voices coming out of the room. Suddenly they stop, and all he can hear is soft rasping. Grasshopper peeks into the half-opened door.

Purple Moor sits with his back to the door, not two steps away. Grasshopper is mesmerized by the sight of his neck. If someone were to be covered with myriad little tattoos, and then they all mingled and ran together, it would look like this neck. The ears seem tacked on above this strange neck. Moor is wheezing softly, and the prickly words bubble out of him with each jerk of his head. The small pink rat ears move out of sync, as if of their own volition. Grasshopper looks at Moor, at the back of his wheelchair, which sports an umbrella holder and also some kind of hook and many other strange protuberances and implements he's never seen on other wheelchairs. He also tries to listen to the wheezing more closely but still cannot make it out. A bespectacled wheeler in pajamas talks back, respectfully holding a hand to his mouth. Then he notices Grasshopper and his eyes open wide; his lips form the word "Out!"

Moor's curly-haired head starts turning. Grasshopper shrinks away from the door and flies down the hall like the wind. He is the only one among the walking juniors who is barred from Moor's rooms. Numbers 15, 14, 13. Others can enter, but not he. In the Moor's room one can serve—carrying this and that, boiling water, shining shoes, or washing dishes. Or slicing bologna for sandwiches that Purple One consumes in enormous quantities, one after another. This is the price of socializing with the seniors. For those who fail at their duties, Moor keeps a belt somewhere in his wheelchair. This belt features prominently in the juniors' nightmares. Moor's belt, Moor himself, and his voice—the rasping wheeze of Livid Monster. The boys curse Purple One when returning from his rooms and parade the welts his belt left on their hands.

Grasshopper secretly envies them. Their wounds, their stories, and their complaints—everything that unites them in their hatred of Moor. It's their adventure, their experience. He's not a part of it.

Grasshopper slows down. Now he's crossing into Skull's domain. These three rooms equalize Grasshopper with the rest of the boys—they are just as barred from here as he is. They also sneak through on their tiptoes. They've never been there, but they know everything about how the rooms look inside. They know that one doesn't have any beds at all, just the mattresses that are stacked in two enormous piles every morning. Then the wheelers while away the hours playing checkers on top of those mountains. The floors are sticky in there, and the windowsills are crowded with rows and rows of empty bottles. Everyone sits on thin red straw mats. Skull lives in this room. The narrow-eyed predator, the owner of the soul-deadening nick, warrior, Leader, and living legend. The idol of each and every junior, the hero of all their games, the unattainable ideal.

There's also the Eleventh, with a real bamboo hut in the middle. With the star attraction—Lame's hookah. With Babe the old cockatoo, who can swear in three different languages. The boys know the exact time to go past the open door to catch a glimpse of hunchbacked Lame blowing bubbles in his transparent water crock.

And then the third room, the one with the messages on the door. Where Ancient lives with his box of amulets and the two fish in the tank. Ancient, who can't stand bright light. This room is more mysterious than the other two because its door is always closed. Grasshopper sees Ancient's room in his mind as he goes past; it's easy for him because he's been in there and seen it for himself. He presses his chin against the amulet under the shirt, regretting that he can never tell anyone what happened to him behind this door. Ancient's gift brings him closer to the seniors. Power that is equal to Skull's; he carries it in secret, hidden from the world. Every day it becomes harder and harder to keep believing in it. He walks on, and the mystery walks with him, and also his pride and his doubt.

There are also two more packs of walking juniors in the House. They have their own dorms, and Grasshopper tries to avoid those.

The Singings pack is in a state of permanent cold war with the Stuffagers. Actual fights are rare, but both packs watch their sides of the hallway closely to warn the enemies away.

The inhabitants of the Cursed room are not bothered with that. Their room is considered the worst since it is the only one on this floor with the windows looking out. Outcasts live there. Those who were banished from the other packs. There are four of them. Sometimes Grasshopper thinks that this is what Sportsman is driving at. To force the Cursed status on him. So he never goes near that room. The mightiest amulet in the world would be powerless to turn him into a second Skull were he to become one of them.

For Grasshopper, the House resembles a gigantic beehive. Each dorm is a cell, and each cell a separate world. There are also empty cells—classrooms and playrooms, the canteen and locker rooms, but they are not shining at night with the honey-amber light from their windows, so they are not real, in a sense.

Sometimes he stays outside in the yard late into the evening, on purpose, to count the living cells in the coming darkness and to think about them. This always leaves a melancholy taste in his soul, because only four such cells exist for him behind the blazing windows in the entire enormous hive of a building. Four little worlds that are accessible to him: Elk's room, Ancient's room, and the two rooms of the Stuffage. This thought makes him a bit depressed. He knows all too well that

Stuffage is not his home, never will be his home. He doesn't want to escape from the darkness in it or to unwind after classes, and there's no one waiting for him there if he's late. Stuffage is a place in itself. For many it is home. They cordon off their beds, mark them with signs of their presence the way dogs mark their territory with urine. They pin up pictures over the headboards, make shelves out of old crates, and throw their things on them. For them the beds are private fortresses, bearing the imprints of their owners. His bed is bare and anonymous, and he never feels completely safe, whether lying down or sitting up in it.

Each window means a room, with people living inside. For them that room is home. For every one of them except me. My room is not my home, because there are too many strangers in it. People who do not like me. Who do not care whether I come back there or not. But the House is so big. Surely there must be a place in it for someone who does not like to fight? For two someones. This thought cheered him up. He felt like he'd stumbled upon something important. Found a way out. All he needed was a room of his own, a room without Sportsman, Whiner and Crybaby, and Siamese, and the rest of them. Naturally, there still would be more people living in it besides Blind and himself. A lot more, actually. Because all the living quarters in the House were accounted for. Every little nook capable of providing a bit of privacy was taken over by the seniors. Which meant that he needed a dorm. And a dorm meant at least ten people. If only he could find them . . . Even four would do! Then they could occupy the room where Rabbit, Bubble, and Crook slept. They only spent the nights there. Switch places with them and have it for themselves. That would be really cool!

Grasshopper sighs. He knows those are just idle dreams. Even if he and Blind did move into an empty dorm, it would still remain a part of Stuffage. And if anyone, say Humpback, decided to join them, Sportsman never would permit that. The place where three of his Pack sleep would be as much a part of Stuffage as the sleepers—a part of the Pack. Come to think of it, he might not allow even the two of them to leave. *Isn't there anything we can do, anything at all?*

Thirty-four days after his first visit, Grasshopper once again stands before the door of the Tenth. He has on a green sweater over his shirt, boots instead of sneakers, and a zipped corduroy jacket instead of a blazer. His lips are moving as he reads the messages again. This helps him calm down. He moves closer to the door and raps on it softly with the tip of his boot. Then, without waiting for an answer, just like Blind did back then, he brings his heel down on the handle, opens the door, and enters. The smoky gloom falls on him like a stuffy tent.

The mysterious shiny world of the seniors smells. The room looks exactly the same as it did a month ago. Time stopped here, got tangled in the invisible net, caught in the glint on the bottoms of the bottles under the bed, precipitated in the bedpans, settled on the wings of the insects pinned to the walls. The butterflies, so pretty in the sunlight, are uniformly black in the eternal dusk of the room, resembling nothing so much as winged cockroaches. The boy's breath is shallow; he is trying to tame his fear. The fish tank still glows green, the smoke still curls in the air. The striped mattress is still in the same place.

Ancient, wrapped in a blanket, turns his bony face around. He is wearing dark shades that make his skin seem even whiter than it is.

"What's this?" he asks. "What are you doing here?"

"I came to ask about the great power. May I?"

Ancient frowns, then remembers and smiles.

"Have a seat. Ask. But make it short."

Grasshopper approaches Ancient's mattress and lowers himself to the floor in front of it. Since their previous meeting, he has become a month older, a full month at this age of rapid growth. His face is sad and somber; his nose still bears the traces of freckles, a reminder of the summer gone by.

Ancient smokes, dropping ash in the folds of his blanket. The mattress is covered in wine stains. The ashtrays are full of orange peel. The plate is occupied by the remains of a sandwich going stale. All of this has a calming effect on Grasshopper. Those things seem to bring a measure of domesticity. He clears his throat.

"This . . . Great Power," he says timidly. "I can't feel it anymore. For some reason. Could it be that the amulet's broken? I've never opened it, I swear. I could feel it when I put it on for the first time. But not now. So I came."

The black holes of the sunglasses glimmer teasingly in the dark.

"And you thought you were going to move mountains? Then you're just a silly little boy."

The boy bites his lip, unable to look up.

"I wasn't thinking about any mountains. And I'm not silly. It's just that I had something then, so I thought that was the Great Power. And now there's nothing."

Tears make his eyes sting. He holds his breath to gain control over them. Ancient, intrigued in spite of himself, takes off his glasses.

"Tell me what you were feeling. I can't know that until you tell me. Let's talk."

"It was . . . like arms. Not like they grew out all of a sudden. More the other way around. Like I could choose to have them or not have them. As if arms are not something everyone needs." Grasshopper is shaking his head and rocking back and forth. "I can't explain. It's like I was whole. I thought that's how the Great Power was."

"You were whole? When you left here, you were whole?"

"Yes."

Grasshopper finally lifts his gaze and looks hopefully into the albino's wine-colored eyes.

"When did it go away? When you returned to your dorm?"

"No. It was there through the night, and the next morning, and for a while after that. And then it went away. I thought it would come back, but it didn't."

Ancient's colorless eyebrows shoot up.

"And even when you tried to do something that you couldn't do by yourself, you still felt whole? Is that what you're saying?"

Grasshopper nods. His cheeks are burning.

"I was a bird," he whispers. "A bird that could fly. It may walk upon the Earth when that's what it wants, but if it decides . . . as soon as it decides . . . Then it just flies."

Ancient leans over to him, across the mat, the plates, and the ashtrays. His face no longer seems purely white.

"You felt that you could do whatever you want whenever you decide to want it?"

"Yes."

"You are a marvel, my boy."

"It's not me! It's the amulet!"

"Ah, yes, of course," Ancient agrees. "I seem to have forgotten. Well, it looks like it came out even stronger than I thought. I wouldn't mind making one like that for myself. Pity that's impossible."

"Why?" Grasshopper's voice is full of sympathy.

"Things like that are only given to you once." Ancient stubs the cigarette in the ashtray. "So you're saying it stopped working?"

Grasshopper shifts uneasily and licks his parched lips.

"That's why I came. I mean, I thought I'd wait at first. In case it returned. I waited and waited, and then I decided to come. Ancient, can you help me? Only you can fix it. Put it back."

Ancient realizes too late that the trap has sprung. He makes a face and looks at his watch.

"I'd love to, but I'm afraid we don't have much time left. They are going to return soon. And we can't discuss things like that when others are around. So, some other time. And the power might still come back by then."

"Tonight it's a double," Grasshopper reminds him. The suspicion that Ancient is trying to get rid of him drains all color from his voice. "The movie is a double feature," he repeats softly.

"Really? I didn't know that."

Grasshopper gets up.

"You can't help me," he says and shrugs his shoulders, looking down intently. "I would have thought it was all fake, except I still remember the way it was in the beginning. And besides, the water pan fell down," he adds desperately. "They were mopping the floor when we returned. It doesn't just happen like that, when it all comes together, does it? By accident? It doesn't, right?"

"No. You're right, nothing happens by accident. Sit down."

Grasshopper sits back down eagerly, legs folded. Ancient's annoyed face stirs up hope inside him. The seniors are powerful and subtle. There will come a day when he's going to be like that, too.

"Are they still bullying you? I seem to remember Blind telling me about it."

"It's less now," Grasshopper answers readily. "They got bored, I guess. Just . . . pick on me sometimes, that's all."

"All right." Ancient ponders something behind the closed snow-white eyelashes. "Tell me again how you felt that Great Power of yours. There must be a way to revive it. We may still find it. I need to hear one more time."

Grasshopper shrugs his shoulders again to throw back the sleeves of his jacket and tries to explain everything one more time from the beginning. Ancient looks almost asleep, but he's not sleeping. The lamp, turned to the wall, casts a golden halo on it. The fish bump against the glass of the tank with their puffy lips.

"I see," Ancient says after Grasshopper stops talking. "I understand now. Well, this happens sometimes. I thought I was giving you power, but instead it was something else. Something much better. Only now you lost it. That happens too."

Grasshopper's lips tremble. Ancient pretends not to see that. The smoke writhes transparently between his fingers.

"And the reason is," he continues softly, "that you are still too little for that amulet. I warned you, I never make them for children. But you can turn it back on. Even if you aren't able to do it right away, I'm almost sure you will when you're older. It's for an adult, see."

Grasshopper isn't even trying to conceal his disappointment.

"And now? What about now? I can't wait that long."

Having caught Ancient's rising irritation, Grasshopper rushes to explain.

"It's not because I want it right now. I swear! But they all say that I'm not good for anything, and even those who don't say it must think the same. They're all stronger than I am because they all have arms. All of them," he says with quiet horror. "And if I am going to remain like this until I grow up, there would be noth-ing I could do about it then. They are all going to remember that I was useless. Always. How am I supposed to become the next Skull then?"

Ancient clears his throat and waves the smoke away.

"Good question. Don't you think you just might become someone else instead? Two Skulls would be a bit much for one House."

"All right, not Skull," Grasshopper agrees. "Someone else. But only if that someone else is like Skull."

Ancient averts his gaze, unable to look at the empty sleeves and the burning eyes.

"Yes," he says. "Of course."

His face is angry now, scaring Grasshopper, even though the anger is not directed at him.

"Right," Ancient says. "Tell me, who's the most powerful man in the House?"

"Skull," Grasshopper says without hesitation.

"And who's the smartest?"

"Well . . . they say . . . you?"

"Listen, then, to what the smartest man in this big gray box is telling you. There is one way to give the amulet its power back. Only one. It's very hard. Harder than anything. You'll have to do everything exactly as I say. Not once, not for a couple of days, but for many, many days. And if you fail to do it completely and fully, even once, even if it's the teeniest, tiniest thing . . ."

Grasshopper shakes his head vigorously.

"If you miss something, or forget, or just get lazy"—Ancient pauses ominously—"the amulet will lose all of its power forever. Might as well throw it in the trash."

Grasshopper freezes.

"So think about it," Ancient concludes. "You still have time."

"Yes," Grasshopper whispers. "Yes. I'll do everything. I'm not going to miss or forget."

"You didn't even ask what it is that you're promising to do."

"I forgot," Grasshopper admits. "What is it I'm promising to do?"

"Things," Ancient says mysteriously. "Some of them may even seem dull or boring. For example"—his extinguished cigarette zigzags in the air—"I might order you to think magic words. Every morning as you wake up and every night before you fall asleep. Or say them to yourself very softly. They may sound simple, but you'll have to repeat them like you mean them. Every time. Or here's something I might say." Ancient smiles at his thoughts. "I'd say, 'Today you're not allowed to utter a single word.' And then you must be silent."

"What about classes? I can't be completely silent in class."

"There are no classes on weekends."

"What if the counselors . . ."

"You see?" Ancient throws up his hands. "You're already arguing with me. Looking for an out. It doesn't work like that. Either you agree or you don't."

Grasshopper blinks.

"Go hide in the attic, if you have to. But whatever you do that day, you do it in silence. And that's one of the easy ones. They'll get harder as we go along. For example, several days of not feeling sorry for yourself. Or not getting angry. That one is very hard. Not even Skull can do that."

The mention of Skull cheers up disheartened Grasshopper.

"Are all the tasks going to be like that? Like . . ." He searches for the right word. "Brainy?"

"The spirit is more important than the body," Ancient proclaims. "But if you are referring to the physical side, don't worry. We'll do that too. You're not going to have it easy."

"Will I have to fight?"

"Not for a while. It's not essential, really. But for starters, you're going to kiss both of your heels."

Grasshopper smiles.

"How so?"

"Simple." Ancient spreads out the blanket, shakes out the crumbs, and wraps it around himself again. "I'm going to say: 'On this and this day you are to appear here before me and kiss your heels.' One, and then the other. While standing, of course. Anyone can do it sitting down. And you're either going to do it, or forfeit the whole task."

"When are you going to say that?"

"Not today. And not tomorrow. First things first."

In Grasshopper's misty gaze Ancient reads the future, and it definitely includes attempts at kissing the heels. Very soon. Ancient hides his smile in a glass of lemonade. He takes a very long sip, and when he puts away the glass he's somber again.

"All right, that's enough," he says. "I shouldn't even have told you all of that ahead of time. It's late. Go, think it over carefully. I'd drop the whole thing if I were you."

Grasshopper rises up reluctantly.

"I've decided. I'm not going to change my mind. I will be silent, and I will be whatever else. Can you give me a task now?"

Ancient looks at his watch.

"That's it for today," he says. "The tasks will have to wait until tomorrow. I need to remember all the magic words. And a lot of other things too. Now go and think. Good night."

"Good night."

Grasshopper walks backward to the door, nodding all the while. Once he's in the hallway he just stands there in uncertainty, as if not knowing where he's supposed to go. The bright lights are hard on his eyes after the darkness of the room. Finally he turns and shuffles away along the corridor. His boots scuff listlessly at the floor. He is walking full of the innermost secrets and strange visions. Of magic words, of pitiless and angerless weeks, of big Skull and little Skull, of Bruce Lee kissing his own heels, of Blind asking "Why aren't you saying anything?" Of voices around him: "He's become so strange lately." It lies heavy on Grasshopper, but also suddenly fills him with pride.

"Not even Skull can do that," he mutters. "For him that would be too hard."

Humpback is on his haunches by the doghouse, petting the resident dog and rubbing it behind the ears. Grasshopper comes over. Humpback gets up and follows him to the fence. To the place where the bushes hide the secret tunnel to the Outsides.

Humpback's shirt is covered in stains and splotches. He's wearing sunglasses that used to belong to one of the seniors; one side is cracked. They keep sliding down his nose, exposing the conjoined half-moons of his eyebrows. The yard is reflected in the twin round mirrors. His cap is covered in pins and badges. He takes off the shades and the cap deliberately, like a swimmer about to go into the water. On the other side of the fence, in the outside world, the five scruffy stray dogs all react to this gesture in unison: they whine and brush the ground impatiently with their tails.

"Down!" Humpback commands. "Sit!"

The passage into the Outsides was constructed by the seniors. When autumn arrives, the bushes around it grow thinner, and then it can be seen from a distance. That's why dried leaves are piled around it. But the dogs still know where it is, and when Humpback approaches the right spot, they become even more agitated.

"Shall we?" Humpback says and reaches into the pocket of Grasshopper's coat. They exchange knowing smiles.

Humpback produces a grease-stained package, hides it under his shirt, crouches down, and crawls into the bushes. The camouflage leaves stream on top of him like a rustling waterfall. The hole in the fence is now evident, and the whimpering dogs jostle each other to sniff at the black-haired, shaggy head that has suddenly appeared on their side.

"Sit!" Humpback shouts, trying to make them back down.

Surprisingly they do sit, in a docile circle, with only their tails still thumping the ground. Each receives its share, and then there are just chomping noises. It doesn't take long. When it's all gone, Humpback lets them sniff him, at his hands and his pockets, to assure them that he's not hiding anything. He goes back the same way and emerges covered in clods of wet earth. They shovel the leaves back into the bushes. The dogs snap at each other and run back and forth along the fence.

"Wild animals," Humpback observes thoughtfully, watching them. "No one needs them. All by themselves . . ."

"Newbie!" the boys shout to each other as they run.

The word is passed down the chain, even the walls seem to vibrate as they absorb it. Wherever a member of the Pack was peacefully excavating his nostrils, or tossing a ball, or trying to coax a cat to come closer so he could tie a bottle to its tail, this enticing vibration in the walls and in his own legs prompts him to abandon all other pursuits and run, overtake the ones running in front, and pick up the airborne word: "Newbie!" And then, putting on the brakes in front of the door of the Sixth, elbow aside those who came first—to look, to inhale that scent that new arrivals always bring in. Only the children of the House can feel it. The fleeting scent of the mother's warmth, of hot chocolate in the morning, of packed lunches, a dog, maybe even a bicycle. Scent of one's own home. The farther it drifts back in time for the denizens of Stuffage, the sharper they sense it on someone else.

And so they run, they rush and hurry, only to freeze once arrived and sniff at the air and see just a scrawny little boy on crutches, smiling plaintively, showing his braces, a boy with a ragged haircut, with one of the shoes so strange that it obviously cannot contain a regular foot. Grasshopper runs with the rest of them, and gawks with the rest of them too. His eyes are open wide, he shoves and jostles those in front of him. He's not after any scents, as he hasn't learned to distinguish them yet. For him the newbie means simply a boy who looks strange and smells of the Outsides. What he also means is the end of the war, end of humiliation, a ticket into the Pack and the peaceful life. But when he hears that word tossed around in excited whispers, he still cringes, as if they were talking about him.

The boy is surrounded.

"Hey you, newbie!" they laugh.

One of the Siamese pulls up the boy's pant leg, and the Pack examines the foot with the air of experts. The newbie sways uncertainly on his crutches.

"They'll cut it off. Like all of it," says one of the Siamese.

"Naturally," affirms the assembled choir.

"Mama's boy," Hoover adds dreamily. "Gonna be without a leg." And he forcefully inhales the sweet scent of home.

Grasshopper realizes that he's waiting for the familiar insults: "Elk's Pet" and "Blind's Tail." They are not uttered, but it seems like they will be in a moment. They really are on the tips of the tongues. The boys have got so used to shouting it out in a certain sequence that they are confused and angry at the sudden drying out of their reservoir of curses.

Grasshopper steps back. He is uneasy. The joy he was feeling is quickly overshadowed by despair. He is stepping closer and closer toward the door, until he's out of the circle, out of the room, until he can see only their backs, and still he can't erase the image in his mind, the image of the boy drooping on his crutches, the boy who has taken his place and assumed his horrible designation. Grasshopper is now standing behind everybody else. Farther behind than necessary, to show his noninvolvement. When the ritual runs its course and the boys start to drift off, he doesn't move. He waits until the last one of them goes away, then waits a bit more and enters the dorm.

THE FOREST

Blind was walking waist-deep in the coarse weeds. His sneakers squelched. He'd managed to take on water somewhere. His heels clung to the wet rubber, and he was thinking of taking off the shoes and continuing barefoot. He decided against it: the grass could cut, there were thorns in it, and also disgusting slugs that, once squashed, were almost impossible to wash off. There were other things too, something resembling soggy cotton balls, and something else, like clumps of tangled hair, and all of that inhabited the noxious grass, ate it, crawled in it, intoxicated by its vapors, gave birth, and died, turning into muck. It was all grass, if you stopped to think about it, all flesh was as grass and nothing more.

Blind took a dainty snail's shell off a tendril that slashed at his hand. The snails clung to the tops of the weeds and knocked against each other, sounding like hollow walnuts. He slipped the shell in his pocket. He knew the pocket was going to be empty when he returned, but he still took something with him every time, out of habit.

He threw back his head. The moon washed out his face. The Forest was very close now. Blind quickened his step, even though he knew he shouldn't; the Forest did not like the impatient and could draw back from them. It had happened before: he'd search for it and not be able to find, feel it nearby and not be able to enter. The Forest was moody and fickle. Many roads led to it, but all of them were long and winding. You could go through the swamp or through the noxious meadow. Once he'd ended up in it by crossing an abandoned dump strewn with busted tires, rusting iron, and broken glass; there he gashed his hand on a piece of sharp metal and lost his favorite rope bracelet. That time the Forest grabbed him of its own accord, picked him up in its tree-trunk arms and pulled him inside, into the stuffy thickets of its damp heart.

The Forest was beautiful. It was shaggy and mysterious, and concealed deep burrows and the strange denizens of those burrows. It never knew the sun and never let the wind through, it was inhabited by the dogheads and the whistlers, giant blackcap mushrooms and bloodsucking flowers grew in it. Somewhere, Blind was never quite sure where, exactly, there was the lake and the river feeding it, maybe even more than one. The road to the Forest began in the hallway, at the doors of the dorms behind which boys snored and whispered, on the moaning rickety floorboards, right behind the indignantly squeaking rats scurrying to avoid him in the dark.

Blind was ready to enter it now. The noxious meadow ended. He lingered, inhaling the scent of the wet leaves, and then heard the footsteps. The Forest vanished in an instant and took the smells with it. The footsteps drew closer, it was obvious now that the walker limped. He also reeked of nail polish and mint gum. Blind smiled and stepped forward.

"Hey! Who's there?" Vulture whispered, shrinking away.

A match flared.

"Oh. It's you . . ."

"You have frightened my Forest, Gimpyleg," Blind said lightly, but the voice betrayed his disappointment.

"My sincere apologies!" Vulture sounded genuinely upset. "But there is someone coming through right behind. Heavyweight, too. Why don't we clear the way?"

"All right."

They stepped closer to the wall. Vulture leaned on it gingerly, trying not to get the stains on himself. Blind pressed against it from head to toe. Somewhere in the vicinity of the Crossroads, a door slammed. Moonlight pierced the corridor. Then the sound of footsteps and breathing. Something heavy was treading the path. It was pushing through, moaning and huffing, the debris from the tops of the trees cascading over its back. The steam curling from its nostrils brushed their faces, making them press even harder into the wall. The beast stopped, inhaled nervously, trembled, and thundered off, noisily breaking the trunks along the way and leaving a blackened trail of trampled earth in its wake. Blind turned to Vulture.

"That was your Elephant."

"Come off it, Blind! Elephant is a wimp, he would never go out by himself in the night. Even in the middle of the day he is scared of being alone."

"Still, it was him. Go see for yourself if you want."

"I don't. If you say it was him, then it was. Which is very strange. And not a good sign. Would you like to go and have a smoke now?"

Vulture pulled open the door to one of the disused classrooms. They entered, closed the door behind them, and sat down on the floor. They lit up and made themselves comfortable. Then lay down, propped on their elbows. The smells of the meadow returned. Time rushed past. Gray House lurked within its own mute walls.

"Do you remember, Blind . . . You were talking about this wheel once. The huge ancient wheel, with so much stuff clinging to it that it's not entirely clear it is a wheel anymore, and it turns. Very slowly, but still it turns. One could get run over, while the other is carried up high. Remember? You said then that it was possible to predict its motion by the squeaking noise, long before it actually completes the turn. Listen to the squeaking and tell."

"I remember. It was just silly talk."

"That's as it may be. But do you hear the squeaking now?"

"No. It is not turning in my direction, if it's turning at all."

Vulture coughed. Or laughed.

"Just as I thought. An odd fellow. I wonder what it was that he wanted."

"Past tense already?"

"So it would appear. He is not one of the old ones, and that's all there's to it. Take us, for example. We know things, even if we don't exactly know what it is we know. He doesn't."

"I think the words are getting the better of you."

"As does everything lately. It's a weird old thing, the world. And you are saying that it was Elephant rambling past just then, like a rhino with a screw loose. What am I supposed to make of it? You know I'm scared of things like that. Harmless little Elephant goes out at night sniffing, for some reason . . . Now what do I do? I'm upset, you see. I guess I'd better check on him."

"Of course. Go."

The door squeaked. Blind traced Vulture's progress, turning his head as if he really could see, then closed his eyes and sank into a cozy slumber. And the Forest returned. It overtook him, breathing into his ears, tucking him into its moss and dried leaves, hiding him and rocking him to sleep with the soft lullabies of the whistlers. It liked Blind. It smiled at him. Blind knew that. He could sense a smile from a distance. The burning ones, the sticky and sharp-toothed ones, the soft and cuddly ones. Their fleeting nature tormented him, that and his inability to subject them to the probing of his fingers and ears. A smile couldn't be caught, grasped, examined in minute detail, it couldn't be replicated. Smiles fled, they could only be guessed at. Once, when he was still little, he heard Elk asking him to smile. He could not understand what was required of him then.

"A smile, my boy, a smile," Elk said. "The best of the human features. Until you learn to smile you're not quite human yet."

"Show me," Blind requested.

Elk bent down to him and let Blind's fingers probe his face. Blind encountered the wet teeth and jerked his hand.

"It's scary," he said. "Can I please not do that?"

Elk sighed resignedly.

A lot of time had passed since then, and Blind had learned to smile, but he knew that a smile did not make him more appealing, like it did others. He stumbled upon the wide-mouthed faces on the tactile pictures in his books, found them on toys, but none of those were something that made itself visible in the voice. Only listening to the smiling voices did he finally understand. A smile meant a light switching on inside. Not for everyone, but for many it did. He knew now what Alice must have felt when the Cheshire Cat's toothy, sarcastic smile was floating in the air in front of her. That was how the Forest smiled. From above, in a boundless mocking grin.

Blind rose and staggered forward, stumbling against tree roots. His foot dropped into someone's burrow. A whistler startled and went silent. Blind bent forward, felt in the grass and grasped it—a tiny one, covered in peach fuzz and smelling of a young cub. He cradled it against his cheek. The whistler was breathing softly, its heart ticking in his fingers. A worried whistle issued from about ten paces ahead. The baby in his hand squeaked in response. Blind laughed and placed it on the ground. The grass rustled. The baby rushed to its mother, squeaking along the way, and soon their joined whistling faded in the distance. Before continuing on, Blind sniffed at his hand to better remember the baby's scent. An adult whistler smelled different.

He couldn't feel his legs. They became alien and bent in all the wrong directions, as if made of rubber. That irked him. He soon grew tired of snatching them out of holes and avoiding mud and puddles and decided to sit down. His legs folded the wrong way again. It also seemed that there were more than two of them now. He was probably turning into something, but the transformation wasn't complete yet. He heard the laughter of the dogheads. They were still far off, running, giggling, bumping against each other. Blind shot up and tottered away on all six of his legs, long and articulated. The stray leaves clung to them, but they made for an easy gait. He hid in the nearest hole and waited in silence. The dogheads thundered past. The disgusting guffaws faded. Blind peeked out cautiously. Something hooted in the canopy and dropped a cloud of rotted wood on him. He shook himself off and counted the legs again. This time there were two. The night was stifling. Blind pulled off his sweater and threw it away. Then took off the waterlogged sneakers, tied their laces together, and dropped them into the hole.

He touched the gnarly trunks as he went by, his ears pricked. Slender, silent, invisible against the trees, he was a part of the Forest, its offshoot, a changeling. The Forest was walking alongside him, swaying its treetops far above, dropping its dew on the warped floorboards.

Blind stopped at the clearing. The gigantic moon drenched him in silver. He crouched, feeling the light bathing him, feeling his fur stand on end, electrified by this light. He pinned back his ears, closed his eyes, and howled.

A lingering, mournful sound enveloped the Forest. It was full of sorrow, but also of Blind's joy, of the closeness of the moon, of the night's own life. It didn't last long, and then Blind bolted into the thickets to sniff at the mossy trunks and dance on the wet leaves and roll around on the ground. He was boisterous, scaring off the small creatures, covering his fur in debris, leaving wolflike prints in the puddles. He ran after a stupid mouse and chased it into someone else's burrow. He peeked into a tree hollow and got hissed at. He excavated an underground lair and ate its owner, a fat, juicy one, spat out the fur, and moved on. The moon was hidden by the trees now, but he felt it as vividly as he'd feel someone standing behind the door or hiding in the bushes—it was that close, and the trees could not hinder it. He leapt over the brook without getting his paws wet, ran back and forth along the shore, found a puddle and gulped it all in, tadpoles included.

A frog, miraculously spared, cursed him piercingly in its language and scampered off to find another hiding place. He stretched on the wet sand, his sharp-eared head on top of the folded paws, listening to the Forest noises and to the grumbling in his stomach, then leapt up and bounded farther along the path, since he didn't like to spend too much time near the water.

He soon was within earshot of the dogheads' howls again, but decided not to hide this time. Instead he howled back in defiance, but they did not accept his challenge and were soon gone, quarreling among themselves. He followed their trail for a while. He would have caught them had he wanted to, but it was a game, not a real hunt, and he liked running games more than chasing games. He suddenly switched direction, as if he'd thought of something he had to go and see about, and from then on ran purposefully, with his nose to the ground, paws moving fast. His tail, up in the air and full of thorns, broadcast his concentration to the world.

Then the Forest ended. Vanished just as instantly as it had appeared. Blind wasn't upset, and he didn't think of going to search for it again. He stopped. Exactly on the edge dividing the darkness and the light rectangle on the floorboards, the yellow glow cast by the opened door. Behind the door, shaggy shadows darted over the tiles and talked in muffled voices. On Saturdays and Sundays the teachers' bathroom was poker territory. The only player in his pack was Noble.

Blind was motionless, and the flame of the candles played in his wide-open eyes. He stood there for a long time. Then he lit a cigarette and moved on. He crossed the strip of light, not hiding anymore, went past the moonlit clearing of the Crossroads, the open door to the bathroom, the door to the staff room, the canteen. The stairs smelled of cigarette butts; he stepped on one of them, still warm, and slowed down.

Down the stairs. Another long, empty corridor, and at the very end of it—more stairs and the door to the basement. He swayed, and his feet slid on the steps. He steadied himself against the wall. Picked the lock with a piece of wire and entered.

The basement was dusty and stuffy. Blind sat on the concrete floor facing the door, buried his chin in his knees, and froze. His armpits flowed down into his jeans. The cigarette clung to his lips. A ringing in his ears. Three little bells and one cricket. He rolled over to the wall, rose up to his knees, and ran his fingers along the scratchy brick surface. Feeling for the emptiness behind one of them. At first he had needed to count steps from the corner to find the right one, but now he knew instantly. Blind carefully removed the brick. In the opening there was a bundle wrapped in newspapers. He shook the dust off his fingers and inserted both of his hands into the hiding place. The old paper rustled. He extracted the parcel, put it on the floor, and unwrapped it.

There were two knives inside. Blind liked to touch them. Sometimes he would cry when doing it. At one time the parcel had also contained a monkey skull on a chain, but he had given it to Sphinx, so now there were only the knives.

One was a gift. It had been given to him so long ago that he didn't remember exactly when it happened, and remembered only that it had always been a secret—first so that no one would take it from him, and then just to keep it away from prying eyes. The knife was beautiful. The blade thin as a thorn and sharp on both sides. No one had told Blind it was beautiful, he just knew it. He'd never questioned the seniors of his childhood, and so one of them giving a child a toy like this did not appear strange to him at all.

The other knife was the one they'd used to kill Elk. It was neither beautiful nor particularly handy. A regular kitchen knife marred with rust. He always shuddered when he touched it, but at the same time his pain was dulled by the strange feeling of the impossibility of what had actually happened. This pitiful piece of iron in his hand couldn't have killed Elk. A mouse never would gnaw down a mountain, a mosquito bite never would harm a lion, a sliver of steel never would destroy his god. So he kept the knife and visited it regularly, touching it to refill himself with unbelief again and again. To imagine that Elk wasn't dead, that he'd vanished, disappeared, cast off the House that had betrayed him.

It was time to go back. Blind stuffed his knife in the pocket, wrapped the other one in the paper again, and lowered it into the hiding place. The brick slotted back into position. *My sweater,* Blind remembered. *I need to pick it up.* He went out, clicked the padlock shut, and mounted the stairs. The stairway to the second floor he took at a run. He was almost out of time. The night was fading away. The Forest was quickly devouring it. The hallway, the doors, the silence. The first sounds of morning were on the cusp of bursting in, and then he would be invisible no more. It was an unpleasant thought, and it made Blind hurry up.

SMOKER

VISITING THE CAGE

I felt like a corpse the entire day after Fairy Tale Night, and only started showing signs of life late in the afternoon. And it came in stages. First I mustered enough strength to wheel down to the bathroom and meet a sinister red-eyed monster there, who then turned out to be myself. I had to do something with him, so I decided washing him would be a good start.

Alexander helped me undress. I wouldn't have managed. My hands shook as if I had been drinking for thirty years straight. I refused to believe that one single bender was capable of reducing me to such a sorry state. After parting with my pajamas—they were so saturated with pine scent and alcohol that I easily could have used them to scare away mosquitoes—I went to sit in the shower and then returned to the dorm.

It was around six. I still wasn't able to divine precise time without the aid of a watch. I clambered onto the bed somehow, took a pad from under the pillow, and started drawing whatever. The backpacks and bags on the bed rail, all in a row. Tabaqui's head, peeking out of the blanket cocoon he'd wrapped himself in. Noble, yawning.

The backpacks came out the best. Tabaqui was almost completely hidden, and Noble turned away as soon as he noticed that I was trying to draw him. So I cross-hatched the backpacks, filling them with volume and increasing their hanginess, put the shadows underneath, and had started to fill in the patterns when Tabaqui crawled over and all but lay on top of the pad, clogging the line of sight from me to just about everything else.

"Why have you stopped drawing?" he asked with surprise when I put the pad back.

"Your head is in the way," I said honestly. "Also I don't like people pushing my arm."

Tabaqui decided to take offense. He rolled over and turned his back to me. I knew by now that he could not remain offended for long, and I ignored it. But I didn't want to draw anymore. I wanted to eat.

"Anything edible left?" I asked.

Noble nodded at the nightstand.

"Sandwiches. There must still be a couple in there. Help yourself."

The throw draped over the bed was never quite pulled taut. It always bulged and rippled in impassable folds. To crawl over them was excruciating. I tried. Tabaqui said that I looked like an unfaithful wife whom a sultan ordered rolled into a carpet before drowning.

Noble helped me untangle myself—an outstretched hand—presented the packet of sandwiches—a heave to the nightstand—and returned to his corner—another heave. About two paces for someone with working legs. And he managed not to upset anything, not to bump into anyone, and naturally didn't get snarled along the way. Since only yesterday night Noble had done the same thing in total darkness, on the bed crammed with bodies, this shouldn't have been a surprise. But this time he never deigned to part with his magazine, which, somehow, he continued reading, *which meant that one of his arms was otherwise engaged!* I was astonished. It wasn't simply that I felt inferior next to him. I was ready to burst into tears.

It wasn't enough for the man to be offensively beautiful and to pull off these impossible feats, no, he had to do it without even noticing! Honestly, had he been preening about, showing off his superiority, he would have been easier to tolerate.

Noble was gnawing at his finger and flipping through the magazine, his face permanently screwed into a disgusted grimace that indicated whatever he was reading was complete trash. He was floating someplace he did not particularly want to be, but could not force himself to descend back down to the godforsaken real world. Even if it was only to look where he was crawling and ascertain whether he was taking what he wanted from the nightstand.

"Noble," I said, "sometimes I get this impression that you're just faking it."

He glanced at me distractedly.

"Meaning?"

"Meaning that you're not really a wheeler at all."

He shrugged and went back to his magazine. "Everyone's entitled to their impressions." He didn't say it out loud, but sometimes it wasn't necessary to actually say something for it to be understood.

"Could it be that you really are heir to the dragons?" I said. "That you're actually flying all this time, and we just can't see it?"

"Want an explanation?" someone interjected suddenly.

I looked around.

It was Black. He was lying on his bed with a notepad under his chin, chewing on a pencil. Looking like a large sheep dog with a thin bone in its teeth.

In the time I'd been living in the Fourth, I had already gotten used to two of its inhabitants always being silent. Alexander and Black. Theirs were different silences, though. Alexander was silent like a mute, while Black was silent with a message. *I really should keep my mouth shut,* or something along those lines. So used was I to his silence that I drew a complete blank when Black suddenly spoke. I even dropped my sandwich. Which naturally landed butter-down. And egg-down as well.

"What?"

"I said I could explain," Black repeated. "If you'd like."

I said that I would. And tried to recall what I'd been asking about.

Black sat up and pulled off his glasses.

No one ever sat on Black's bed except him. Nor lay down on, fell onto, put his feet on top of, or threw dirty socks over. Nobody put anything on it at all. That bed, always crisp, perfectly tucked and turned, seemed thoroughly out of place here. As did Black himself. As if at any moment he could sail away on it headed for some distant shores. To where his species lived in its natural habitat.

"It's simple, really. See this bed?"

Black pointed at Humpback's bunk over his head. The upper section that would have stayed behind even if the lower part did set sail.

I said that of course I did.

"What do you think would happen if you were to be hung off of its side? So that you only held on to it with your hands, like on a high bar?"

"I'd fall down," I said.

"And before you fell down?"

I couldn't quite catch what kind of answer he was expecting. I earnestly traced the sequence of events in my head.

"I'd hang there. And then fall down. Hang for a while and crash."

"What if you were to be hung like that daily?"

It dawned on me a little.

"Are you saying I'd hang for a bit longer every day?"

"Good job! Smart boy."

Black bit on the pencil again and went back to his notebook.

"But I'd only need to fall down once, and then there wouldn't be anyone to hang anymore. I'm not a cat, after all."

"That's exactly what Noble thought. Once upon a time."

Noble threw away the magazine and stared at Black. It was a withering stare.

"How about enough?" he said.

I realized with a shudder that the picture Black drew for me was, like trashy movies liked to point out in the credits, based on actual events.

"But that's impossible," I said. "That's torture!"

"And that's what Noble used to think too. He's still touchy about the subject, as you can see."

"I thought I asked you to shut the hell up."

Noble's look would have been quite enough for me to shut up immediately if I'd been in Black's place. But I wasn't him. He was him.

"Chill, will you," he said to Noble. "Don't ruin your complexion."

What happened next almost made me believe half the tales told the night before.

Noble swept to the edge of the bed. From there he probably got to the floor, but I wasn't sure. Black managed to sit up. And even to take off the glasses. But when he stood up he already had Noble hanging on his shoulders. Then he was trying to peel off Noble while Noble was trying to throttle his opponent. It was a grisly sight.

The snarling figure made up of two figures stumbled awkwardly around on the floor, bumped into furniture, upended the nightstand, and crashed on the bed, burying a screaming Jackal.

Then they rolled over to my side. I pressed farther into the bars of the headboard, petrified. Two faces, contorted . . . breathing heavily . . . saliva . . . so close. Too close. Tabaqui went on wailing. *One more roll,* I thought with resignation, *and it's good-bye Smoker.* They'd break every bone in my body.

They didn't roll. Black managed to shake off Noble and spring up on the bed. His boots shuffled on the covers under my nose, then he jumped off and I finally could breathe easier.

It was unclear who emerged victorious. Noble, curled up in a ball by the bars, looked lousy. Black, wiping blood off his face and neck with the bottom of his shirt, wasn't much better. Judging by that last throw, he'd won. But judging by the speed of his retreat from the bed, he wasn't quite sure that he had.

Not-quite-crushed Tabaqui fared best of all. He was sitting on two pillows and cursing so elaborately that it immediately put my mind at ease regarding him.

"You should be exterminated, you and your ilk," Black said when Tabaqui paused for a moment. "Like rabid dogs."

"Bastard!" Noble answered. "Pigface!"

Black spat out a broken tooth into his hand. Studied it for a while, dropped it, and made for the door.

A multitude of pill bottles had tumbled out of the overturned nightstand. Black slipped on one of them just as he was going out and almost fell. This slightly cheered up Noble. Very slightly.

When Sphinx, Alexander, and Blind came back, it was their turn to roll around on the pill bottles. Threading his way between them, Humpback deposited Tubby in his pen and said that we obviously hadn't been bored.

"Bored?" Tabaqui exclaimed. "You guys completely missed the best thing ever! It was epic, if I say so myself! The battle of Hector and Achilles! I'll be damned!"

Sphinx examined the trashed bed strewn with broken glass, then looked at Noble and said that he could definitely observe the battlefield and the body of Hector left on it, but couldn't quite determine the whereabouts of Achilles.

"And that's how it's going to be for a while," Tabaqui explained. "He's somewhere out there. Quenching gushers of blood."

"Got it," Sphinx sighed. "We'll keep that in mind." He offloaded Nanette to the windowsill. "Good thing we hadn't left the bird with you."

The next hour I spent crawling under the beds, collecting the bottles and vials. Tabaqui pretended to help me. His fervor regarding the fight was wearing really thin. In my opinion, Noble and Black resembled animals more than heroes of antiquity. The whole deal was disgusting.

"Let me tell you, dearest, the heroes of antiquity were not much better," Jackal said. "Worse, in fact," he added thoughtfully, as if refreshing Homer in his mind.

I decided to crawl away before he started to quote his favorite passages from the *Iliad*. Because I had a sneaking suspicion about which ones would turn out to be among the favorites.

After we tidied up the room, Blind palpated Noble and declared that he had a cracked rib.

The Sepulcher was out of the question. Noble allowed himself to be swaddled in elastic bandages and sat hugging a pillow, pissed off as he could be. He informed us that the bandage was restricting his airflow, while the rib prevented him from lying down, and that he was now doomed to sleepless nights of oxygen deprivation.

Tabaqui assured him that he would never abandon a friend in need. And he immediately didn't. He sang to Noble. He played the harmonica for him. He bucked him up with disgusting concoctions complete with floating chilies, of which he himself liberally partook as well, so that Noble wouldn't feel singled out. There wasn't a living soul capable of getting any sleep under Tabaqui's tender ministrations.

When Black returned, he was running a fever. Tabaqui sounded the alarm. He said that this was a clear sign of infection taking hold in Black's bloodstream, and that Black was soon to tread in the valley of death.

Black was serenaded and plied with drink as well.

At three in the morning they started singing in harmony.

Accompanied by their horrible singing, I dozed off. When I woke up I saw Humpback, naked, standing on the bed armed with a broom. He was holding it as if it were a bayonet aimed at an invisible foe. He looked like a complete nutcase. If I were to find myself alone in the room with him, this would have scared me witless. But Jackal was right next to me, while Alexander and Lary, swearing softly, milled in the space between the beds, moving the nightstand for some reason. Their appearance wasn't a big improvement on Humpback's. They were both in their briefs and in rubber boots. Lary's boots alone were a sight, what with the pointed toes curled upward.

The wide-open windows let in the blackness of the night, and the door into the hallway was also thrown open and even prevented from closing by a stack of books. A breeze was wafting through the room.

"There it is!" Lary whispered. "We got it now. Humpback, ready with the broom!"

Humpback stopped fidgeting, stood at attention, and said, also in a very firm whisper, that this might cause it harm.

"Sissy," Lary groaned.

They jerked the nightstand away. Lary dove into the opening between it and the wall with surprising agility, and seemed to hurt himself quite badly. Humpback dropped the broom. Alexander jumped up on the bed.

This convinced me beyond any doubt that all of them had gone temporarily insane. Tabaqui lifted the broom off me and handed it back to Humpback. He then said sweetly, "We're hunting a rat. I hope you were not too inconvenienced?"

I wasn't, but I did not particularly want to observe the extermination, either. I'd loathed stuff like that since I was a baby, be it rats or spiders. People around me seemed to get a kick out of this attitude for some reason.

"Freaking wimps," Lary said from behind the nightstand. "Totally useless."

Humpback and Alexander blinked. Humpback indistinctly repeated something to the effect of being afraid to hurt it.

I started putting on clothes.

"Where are you headed?" Tabaqui asked incredulously.

"I thought I'd go for a spin."

"A spin where? It's dark in the hallways."

I'd completely forgotten that, but rallied and said I'd take a flashlight.

"You can't. There's been an increase in activity by maniacs and people with split personalities. Your flashlight would draw their attention."

I looked around.

"Where's Noble?"

"Now *he* is in fact out there." Tabaqui nodded. "But he's among his own kind, where you have no place."

I decided not to press him on that "own kind" remark.

"What about Sphinx?"

"He's with Tubby, grazing in the bathroom. To save the kid the aggravation."

Humpback and Lary conferred and started tossing empty bottles under the bed. Black, shiny with sweat and looking unhealthy, inquired from his bunk whether he might be allowed to die in peace.

"They barge in from the yard," Tabaqui chirped. "As soon as it turns to winter, they just swarm the House. While the cats, they come later. They like to roam while the roaming's good. So you see, in the meantime there's this disconnect."

The poor rat, having had enough of the bottle barrage, darted to the center of the room and crouched in front of the open door. It definitely wasn't thinking straight, because it didn't even try to escape.

Lary tossed the floor-cleaning rag on top of it. Humpback stormed the resulting bump with a hoarse wail, grabbed it, and pitched it out into the corridor. Then he kicked the door closed. The books that were keeping it open went flying.

"Cool!" Lary screamed and hugged Humpback.

"There," Tabaqui said, satisfied. "See, that didn't take long at all."

I was just grateful that picking up the empty bottles off the floor wasn't going to be my responsibility. And also that the rat survived.

"Do you think it suffered much when I threw it like that?" Humpback asked.

"Come on, it was fine. It was inside a rag," Lary said, obviously unconcerned for the rat's well-being.

Tabaqui assured Humpback that the rat was completely content, both in flight and upon landing. Black again asked if he could now get his final rest.

That's when Blind came in, holding the rag that formerly held the rat.

"Are you guys mental?" he asked.

"You mean it hit you?" Tabaqui said, trembling with anticipation.

"It hit me."

"And were you surprised?"

"We both were."

Blind threw the rag away and flopped on the bed. He was barefoot and frazzled, his sweater was tied around the neck, debris was clinging to his wet legs, soot covered his fingers, and he smelled funny. Of damp, and what seemed like fresh grass. There was also a thin ring of dirt around his mouth. I thought that the place he'd come from wasn't a normal place. That it maybe had something to do with the basilisk eggshells. I also tried to figure out which type in the Jackal's classification he fit into—maniacs or those with split personalities. I wasn't too sure at the moment.

Then Sphinx returned, with Tubby clinging to his back. He sat next to Blind and stared at him. Then he spoke.

"Wipe your mug. Were you eating dirt again?"

"It wasn't dirt," Blind said blissfully, using his sleeve.

More of a maniac, I decided.

Tubby slid off Sphinx, rolled to my side, and started tugging at my pajama buttons, trying to tear them off. Alexander was busy making tea.

"It's going to be light soon," Humpback said. "How about we get some sleep?"

That wasn't to be. Half an hour later Noble came back. The dawn-welcoming elf clad in elastic bandages. Also in someone's beret, with some trinket around his neck and even more drunk than several hours prior. He unloaded crumpled wads of cash out of his pockets and picked a quarrel with me over my foot accidentally slipping under his pillow. He said many hurtful things about my legs, made a show of changing the pillowcase, and scrambled off again.

Once he wheeled out, I suddenly realized what his new adornment was. It was Black's tooth on a silver chain.

And the next night I spent in quarantine. In this small room all covered in foam rubber. And in cheery chintz, yellow with blue flowers, over it. There was a commode, half recessed in the wall, masquerading as a trash bin with a hinged top. Also upholstered in foam rubber and chintz. And finally, a frosted white lamp on the ceiling. Nothing else. A perfect place for sleeping and contemplation. I wish I could have sought refuge there during my first year in the House. Like once a week. But I didn't know it was this good. The House dwellers had long appropriated this resort for their needs, and there were only two ways to get in. Either as a punishment for some transgression, or by cajoling permission from the Sepulcher. I didn't know about the second option. And of course I had no idea that a visit to the Cage could be regifted, which was exactly what Tabaqui had done.

Physicals were a weekly occurrence for about half of all House denizens and a monthly one for everyone else. When I was still with the Pheasants, we also had the so-called A-list, comprising those who went in every day. Six Pheasants qualified for it, and the rest all dreamed of joining them. A-list meant a less strict daily routine, the right to a nap in the afternoon, and a separate meal schedule complete with low-calorie salads and vitamin drinks. Every physical was a solemn event, so it was important to enter all your health concerns on a special notepad. I had used mine, dutifully divided into days and hours, for doodles, so they had taken it off me.

Today was the first time I'd been for a physical with the Fourth. While we were waiting for our turn, Lary created an installation from used gum, crowned by a fresh cigarette butt in the middle, on the wall of the hospital wing. Tabaqui spent the time drawing horrific black and white stripes and polygons on his face.

"It's our duty to entertain the Spiders," he explained. "Their lives are pointless, they have lousy jobs, so inventive KISS-style makeup is sure to raise their spirits."

The KISS-style makeup did not raise anyone's spirits. It did arouse suspicions, though. Tabaqui was thoroughly scrubbed in the treatment room to make sure he wasn't trying to conceal some skin ailment. Finally, all pink, squeaky clean, and literally wet behind the ears, he wheeled out of the treatment room waving a white scrap of paper resembling a store receipt.

"How about this?" he boasted, parading the scrap in front of us. "That's respect, that is! Here, in the Sepulcher, I'm a VIP!"

"Whatever do you want with it?" Noble asked. "It hasn't even been a week since the last time."

"It's a present for Smoker," Jackal explained. "I happen to enjoy giving out presents every once in a while."

"Are you sure he's going to like it?" Noble said doubtfully.

"Just let him try not to!"

I listened to them without any clue as to what they were talking about. One thing was clear: I was supposed to be overjoyed about something that Tabaqui was planning to give me. So as he wheeled to me and shoved his scrap in my hands, I endeavored to look happy. I must have succeeded. At least Tabaqui was pleased.

"Smoker is ecstatic," he said to Noble. "And you thought he wouldn't be able to appreciate it. You're just a poor judge of character, that's all."

And he took off toward the exit in his Mustang. I folded the gift and followed. At the landing, the one they called "Antesepulchral," I put on the brakes and tried to decipher the scribbles on the paper. All the rest had wheeled or walked ahead. The writing, which I failed to understand, looked like a sloppily made out prescription. I was ready to give up and go back to the Sepulcher to ask Spiders what it said. Could it be some sort of confirmation of my former Pheasant privileges, put down on paper for some reason? Then Black mounted nearby. He didn't even ask if I was happy or not. I must have looked like I still wasn't able to make heads or tails of my present.

He just took the paper and said, "It's a quarantine referral."

He's joking was my first thought. My second was that Tabaqui had played a dirty trick on me.

"Just as I thought. You're clueless," Black sighed. "Listen, I understand it's none of my business and all, but are you always grabbing whatever people shove at you?"

"No, I'm not usually," I said. "But Tabaqui said it was a present."

"Tabaqui's presents especially must be X-rayed before you even think of touching them," Black explained. "Right, just be more careful next time."

He returned the scrap and turned toward the stairs.

"Hey!" I called out, panicked. "Black, wait!"

"What?"

He stopped, slightly annoyed, as if this idle chat was keeping him from something important.

"Why would Tabaqui do this to me? Is it something I've done?"

Black stared ahead sullenly, chewing his gum, and cogitated.

"Why would he? Well, he happens to think that it's great to end up in the Cage. Pleasant."

"What's so pleasant about it?" I said angrily.

If Pheasants were to be believed, the quarantine was a kind of solitary cell for the most dangerous miscreants. And, on certain subjects, I did tend to believe them.

"What's pleasant?" Black's habit of slowly repeating the question he'd just been asked could drive anyone with less patience completely crazy. "Well, it's so quiet, you see. There isn't anyone else in there and it's very quiet. Soundproofed. It really is kind of nice. I, for one, like it there."

"Look," I said quickly. "Since you like it . . . how about I give this to you and you can go to that quarantine place instead of me?"

Black shook his head.

"Won't work. It specifies a wheeler. You can swap with Noble, though. Or with Tabaqui himself."

He left, and I stayed back, very puzzled. On the way to the dorm I deliberated my course of action: injure Jackal terribly or go sit in quarantine? All signs pointed to the second choice. Suffer for a bit and then just forget the whole thing. I somehow was certain that Tabaqui never forgot and never forgave. I had no idea where this certainty came from, but by the time I reached the doors of the Fourth I was convinced that I had no business refusing this present. If Tabaqui was sure he was doing me a favor, who was I to disagree?

And sure of it he was. Beaming and businesslike, he was darning the sleeve of a denim jacket—the special Cage jacket, as he explained, for those being sent "over there." I was to put it on without delay, because otherwise I might miss the opportunity to do that, and also just in case.

It turned out to be so heavy as to make me think it was lined with lead. Tabaqui let me hold it but snatched it right back, spread it out on the bed, and began the performance entitled "Secrets of the Enlightened." Alexander, Lary, and Humpback all crowded around, observing with interest. I felt like a child who was being packed off to a costume party by his entire family.

The jacket was in fact two jackets. The lining was so thick that it could be a separate garment on its own. It fastened to the shell with concealed zippers and buttons and could be taken out completely. Jackal explained the sequence twice. The shell contained the principal hidden pockets. Two tins with cigarettes, one in each shoulder pad. Boxes of pills in the elbows. "This is headache, this is insomnia, this is diarrhea," Jackal rattled off rapidly, "and here are the instructions. All color-coded." Two lighters and two ashtrays in the bottom, one of each on the left and on the right. "Because there are some people, you know, who like to stub out the cigarettes directly on the floor, which is a bit of a fire hazard in that place."

"In fact, you should cut down on smoking there," Humpback jumped in. "Or you'll suffocate. No ventilation at all."

"There is that hole in the ceiling," Noble countered. "Besides, it's not like he's going to smoke a pipe."

"Pipe smoke is much less toxic," Humpback said, taking the bait. "Yes, there's more of it, but at least it doesn't stink."

"Depends on who you ask."

"Quiet!" Tabaqui snapped. "This is vitally important information, and I would thank you to not interrupt with your petty squabbles."

The lining went back in, concealing the stashes.

"Now . . . ," Tabaqui said, raising his finger. "The second layer. All nice and legal. Observe closely, and whatever you think is extraneous we can remove. Although, to be honest, there is nothing extraneous here."

The legal layer consisted of a Walkman with ten cassettes, a chocolate bar, a note-pad of Jackal's poetry, a packet of nuts, a pocket chess set, spare batteries, a deck of cards, a harmonica, and four horribly dog-eared paperbacks. It was little wonder that I found it hard to breathe once I donned the jacket. And even though it was Tabaqui who offered to get rid of anything extraneous, he was extremely critical when I said I'd like to leave behind the harmonica and the cards.

"I can't play the harmonica," I tried to explain.

"Exactly! This is the time to learn."

"And I don't do solitaire."

"I'll give you a guide!"

Sphinx jumped off the windowsill and joined us. Humpback extracted two stale rolls from the left pocket of the jacket. Tabaqui observed them sadly.

"They haven't been there for that long. They're still quite digestible."

"Tabaqui, enough," Noble said. "Who is going to the Cage, you or Smoker?"

"He is!" Tabaqui exclaimed. "Except he is a complete novice, and should listen to the wisdom of his more experienced packmates!"

From the breast pocket I excavated a stack of word puzzles, another notebook, and a pen.

"That would be mine," Noble said and put out his arm. "You can leave it, it's fine."

I gratefully handed the wad to him and turned my attention to the books.

"*The Poetry of Scandinavia*," I read on the cover.

"If you're not into it, I'll take that," Humpback said eagerly.

It dawned on me that each of them contributed to the jacket when it was their turn to sit in quarantine. That's how it became so heavy. Everything that they considered useful was in there.

Now it was Lary's turn to astonish me. He was swaying indifferently back and forth on the heels of his monstrous boots while the jacket was being gutted, and then suddenly offered, "I have never been there, not once. I have this, you know . . . claustrophobia. I can't even go in the elevators."

I was so stunned I didn't know what to say. It was the first time Lary had talked to me. I mean, not really, but the first time he addressed me as a human. As an equal.

"Oh," I managed. "I see."

"I'm afraid of *it*," he continued in a whisper, drawing closer. "People tell things. But you're cool. You're on top of it."

"Hey!" Tabaqui said. "Stop this defeatist nonsense on the eve of the departure. This is going to be rest and recuperation. Lary, leave him alone, take your morbid look somewhere else!"

Lary shuffled away obediently. Tabaqui continued his lecture. He said that there actually were two quarantine rooms. The blue one and the yellow one. And that the blue one was not for the faint of heart, but did wonders for the soul, while the yellow one was just pure bliss all around.

"The blue one makes you depressed, and the yellow stinks of urine, because the flush always gets stuck," Sphinx said. "And they are both only blissful if you dream of being alone. Was that ever your dream, Smoker?"

"I think it is now," I huffed, weighed down by the miracle jacket. I couldn't even bend my arms, because of the stashes in the elbows. "Are they . . . coming for me soon?"

They did come fairly soon.

They were already wheeling me out like a motionless dummy when there came another surprise, this time from Alexander. He ran to me and handed me a flashlight.

"They say that the lights are completely out at night. Here, take this, in case you need to find something in the dark."

I couldn't bend my arms, but my fingers were in perfect working order, so I grabbed the flashlight. And I had a second to look into Alexander's eyes. They were the color of strong tea. And they were speckled.

I also had time to say "See you" to the rest of them. To Jackal, who was waving to me sentimentally. To Lary, milling at the door. To Noble, who nodded from the bed. To Sphinx, sitting on the headboard. To Humpback. To everyone.

Cases, as they were called, were stationed on the first floor, two per shift. They lugged heavy stuff, if there was any to be lugged, transported the wheelers if it was suspected that the wheeler in question might object to his transportation, swept the yard, fixed this and that, and from time to time traversed the hallways with grim determination, carrying empty stretchers, for some reason. Also guarded the front door, instead of the actual guard, who was guarding the door to the third floor. But mostly they drank. Cases figured prominently in most of the local jokes, even those told by Pheasants.

The one accompanying me was too decrepit even for jokes. An old drunk with trembling hands and an unsteady gait. I was very concerned with the way he breathed. I couldn't shake off the mental picture in which he keeled over before delivering me to where I needed to go, and then I would be stuck right there in this impossible jacket until they figured out the circumstances of his demise.

We crossed the third-floor hallway. In the tiny anteroom between two identical doors, he told me to turn out my pockets.

"Sorry," I said earnestly. "I can't bend my arms. You'll have to do it yourself."

Case decided I was trying to trick him.

"I wasn't born yesterday, my boy," he said reproachfully. "I'm too old to play these games with you. Come on, let's go."

And so I escaped being searched. As soon as the lock clicked shut behind me, I left the confines of the jacket and stretched out on the foam floor, relishing my new freedom. I was just lying there looking up into the ceiling.

It was not until about half an hour later that I suddenly understood: I was completely alone. And it was going to be this way for a while. Tabaqui really did give me a present. I just didn't know enough to appreciate it at the time.

I was about to doze off but then remembered what Alexander said about the lights and willed myself to action. I needed to prepare. I wasn't sure I could handle the extraction of the stashes from the jacket in the dark, even with the aid of a flashlight. I sat up, pulled the jacket toward me, and began disassembling it. Everything I took out I sorted into piles. I wasn't even halfway through this when I needed a smoke, so I had to just shake the remaining stuff out and take care of the lining. There must have been a hundred different places I had to unfasten. I finally got to the cigarettes, folded the jacket into a cushion, put it under my back, and lit up.

The Poetry of Scandinavia, Dashiell Hammett's *The Glass Key*, *The Annotated Book of Ecclesiastes*, *Moby-Dick*. All four extremely worn, with pages falling out. Shaking *The Glass Key* also produced Jackal's notes on it and a withered slice of salami. *Moby-Dick* had a library stamp informing me that Black had checked out the book two years ago. The plastic cover bulged with paper scraps and also contained two photographs. I took out the photographs.

One was of Wolf. He was the guy who died at the beginning of last summer. I'd only been in the House for a month then, so I didn't remember much about him. Skinny, frazzled, a frowning stare. An unlit cigarette in one hand, the other on the strings of a guitar. Rather grave face, as if he knew what was going to happen soon, although I guess we all have photos that could be used for the "he knew" purposes if needed—just because a person refused to smile. And this particular photograph was designed to be funny. A baby bird was sitting on Wolf's head, and this must have seemed amusing to the person behind the camera. You couldn't see the bird all too well, though. The corner of a striped blanket hanging from the upper bunk was in the way. I figured that Wolf must have been sitting on the common bed and that Lary, as usual, had not made his, and that it was summer. After a more careful examination I recognized the bird as Nanette. Still a chick. I shivered.

They found Nanette sometime in early June, which meant that the guy in the photo had only a little time ahead of him before dying under mysterious circumstances. But that wasn't really important for me. Not that he died, or the way he died. It was the way he looked. He was home. He had a home and he was in it. I was never going to be like that in the Fourth. Not until I'd lived there for many years.

Wolf had been a part of the Fourth, but no one ever mentioned him while I was there. There wasn't anything in the room that was said to have been his. I'd forgotten all about him, to be honest. Pheasants were really fussy about their deceased, and I had gotten used to such treatment. Two photographs in black frames hanging in the classroom. Two cups behind the glass doors of the cabinet in the dorm, never to be taken out. Two towel hooks in the bathroom, eternally empty. The dead of the First lived in its rooms alongside the living. They were quoted, recalled fondly, their parents continued to receive the collective holiday greeting cards. I'd never seen either of them, but I knew all about their likes and dislikes. Whereas Wolf had never existed, never was in the Fourth. This photograph was the first and so far the only trace of him that I had seen.

I took out another cigarette. Started flipping the pages of *The Glass Key* to shake off the mood, and fell into it without even noticing. Caught myself finishing the fourth cigarette and decided that I smoked too much. Took stock of my reserves. I still had sixteen left. I thought that if someone were to come in right now, to bring in lunch, for example, he'd immediately know that I'd been smoking. And would take away everything. So I left three cigarettes out, preemptive sacrifices to a possible search, shoved the rest back into the jacket, and more or less covered the stashes with the lining. Then I tidied up a bit, spread out the jacket again under myself, and took out the second photo.

A bunch of kids on the steps of the back porch. Standing, sitting, hanging off the railing. It must have been a hot day. Faces in splotches of sun and shade.

I managed to recognize most of the faces. First of them—Black, of course. The heavy gaze, the blond bangs, the square jaw. All there. He looked a bit less imposing and a bit more round faced, and, if anything, even more morose than now.

Then I found Humpback, Elephant from the Third, and Rabbit from the Sixth. Rabbit hadn't changed at all. Humpback was disguised by motorcycle goggles and was hugging a crossbow. Elephant towered above everyone, a smiling mountain, like a scaled Kewpie doll, with a rubber giraffe peeking out of the pocket of his overalls.

This was turning out to be an exciting activity.

The next one was Blind. He was barefoot, crouching in the corner of the shot so that half of his head was out of the frame. The top button of his shirt came down almost to his navel, and his hair hung lower than the end of his nose. If he were to stand up, the hem of the checkered shirt would have fallen below his knees. I thought it strange that the counselors allowed him to go around the House dressed like that.

I looked for Sphinx but couldn't locate him.

There was Beauty, a tender angel; he was playing dead, draped over the railing. And Solomon, from the Second. Not yet the fat Rat he became, but already quite a plump young of the species.

Then I saw Lary and laughed out loud, choking on smoke. Awkward, big-eared, spindly Lary. He was standing with one leg proudly set apart, displaying the knee scraped myriad times, and no one, not even the sunniest romantic, would dare drone about "happy childhood" looking at this picture, because it was clearly impossible to have both a happy childhood and a nose like his. An owner of a matching nose, and bugged-out eyes to boot, was standing next to Lary. Obviously Horse from the Third. Of all the people in the photograph, Lary's visage took the cake. I even felt something resembling tenderness toward him. Cruel was the life of little Bandar-Logs. And that made them grow up hostile. And suffering from claustrophobia. And stuttering. Because no one loved them. Because they weren't smart, they weren't handsome, they weren't even cute. Lary and Horse were the last ones I could recognize. And Sphinx was still nowhere to be seen.

The two identical fair-haired guys in identical striped vests kept tormenting me. And a boy in front, with a perfectly spherical head, also was somehow familiar. I kept turning the picture this way and that, trying to match the faces to various inhabitants of the House, but wasn't able to place five of them. Finally I grew tired of this and just looked at the picture.

It was a wild, ragtag gang. Dirty, shaggy. They all probably had worms. You couldn't make them behave no matter how you tried, but at least no one was making a face. They wanted to look presentable, even though they could probably guess it wasn't working.

Protective amulets and all that other crap worn around the neck was all the rage, even back then. I counted sixteen pouches, plus talons, teeth, and bones, in bunches and separately; bolts, nuts, nails, rabbit feet, and a wide assortment of tails. Lary and Horse preferred their protection shiny and clanking. Elephant was bedecked in little bells, while the blond twins wore keys. My gaze registered those keys and it finally dawned on me.

I closed my eyes for a second and looked again.

Of course! The cold, round, staring eyes, the hooked noses . . . Little Vultures! So alike that I wouldn't even venture to guess which of them was the real one.

I wondered where the second one went. Immediately came a thought that even one was plenty, but I chased it away, ashamed, as I remembered the perpetual mourning of the Third.

It could be that Birds were not in mourning for Vulture's lost twin. That they just liked black. Honestly, I didn't really want to know. But in any case, Vulture had no twin brother in the House anymore, and thinking that it was good that he didn't was a foul thing to do.

I put the photograph back and took out the first one again. Looked at it. Then lay back and stared at the ceiling.

The dead inhabited every room in the House. Hidden in every closet was its own decomposing unmentionable skeleton. When the ghosts ran out of space, they moved out into the hallways. Then came the protective sigils on the doors and amulets around the necks, to ward off the uninvited guests, while at the same time the resident spirits were welcomed and flattered, consulted and listened to, serenaded with songs and stories. And they talked back. With scribbles in soap and toothpaste on the bathroom mirrors. With purple-hued drawings on the walls. Also with night whispers, right in the ears of the chosen, while they were taking a shower or bravely catching some sleep on the Crossroads sofa.

The unholy mess of Pheasant stories, superstitions, House proverbs, and silly sayings chased itself around in my head, becoming more and more weird as it went. When I finally tamped it down, I realized with surprise that I seemed to know the House a bit better. A tiny little bit. At least, I understood some things I was never able to before. The passion of the House dwellers for tall tales of all kinds did not spring out of nothing. It was their way of coping, molding their grief into superstitions. Which in turn morphed into traditions, and traditions were really easy to accept. Especially when you're a child. Had I come here seven years ago, I too might have considered talking to ghosts an everyday affair. I'd sit right there on Black's old photos, with a crude bow, or a sling in my pocket, proudly displaying an amulet against poltergeists that I'd fortuitously acquired in exchange for some rare stamps. I'd avoid some specific places at some specific times and still go there on a dare. It might have led to a stutter, who knows, but at least my life never would have been boring, unlike the one I actually had, the one that hadn't been spent here. I was a little bitter that this untamed childhood had passed me by. Yes, it didn't have any open spaces in it, no rivers or forests or abandoned cemeteries, but neither did my real one. I would have learned all of the House's rules and regulations, and how to tell ridiculous stories, to play guitar, to decipher the scribbles on the walls, to read fortunes in chicken bones, to remember all the former nicks of all the old-timers. And maybe, just maybe, to love this crumbling building, which I now would never be able to. The longer I thought about this the sadder I felt. I took out the last sacrificial cigarette, lit it, and sat there tracing the tendrils of smoke floating up toward the lamp and dissolving in its light.

THE HOUSE

Sepulcher is a House within the House. It's a place where the world works differently. It's much younger; when it was created the House was already starting to crumble. It is the subject of the scariest stories of all. It is hated and reviled. Sepulcher has its own rules, and it enforces them without mercy. It is dangerous and unpredictable; it sows discord between friends and pacifies enemies. It unrolls a separate path for each visitor: when you travel it to the end, you'll be either found or lost. For some it's their last journey, for others—only the beginning. Time itself slows down there.

Grasshopper looked out the window at the snowdrifts and the black silhouettes on blue. The morning at the hospital wing began with rounds, before dawn. The cars navigating the icebound roads, honking impatiently, the stomping of feet in the hallway, the lit-up windows of the houses—all pointed toward morning. But if the sky were to be believed, it was still night. Classes had been canceled because of the snowfall, and the inhabitants of the House had been celebrating the unexpected vacation for two days straight. The windows of the hospital wing looked out to the yard. Each morning and each night, Grasshopper climbed up on the windowsill and looked at the boys throwing snowballs and building white forts out of the drifts. He could tell them apart by their hats and parkas. The voices did not penetrate the double-paned glass.

It had been two weeks already since he'd been referred here for prosthetic fitting. At first Grasshopper had thought that it would be over in a few hours. He'd be given arms—not real ones, of course, but at least somewhat useful—and then he'd be on his way. Only when he ended up in the hospital wing did he realize how little he knew of these things.

He liked it here at first. The unhurried life, the cleanliness, the silence. The Stuffage boys weren't picking on him and the nurses were friendly. Sepulcher seemed light, airy, and peaceful, the nicest place on Earth. Elk brought him books and helped with his homework, just like during his earliest days in the House. Grasshopper couldn't understand why this place was considered bad news. Where did the morbid name "Sepulcher" come from? The word itself used to scare him before he'd come here.

It was fine. Then he started feeling lonely. Especially when the snow came. He missed Blind. And something else too. Grasshopper, now bored, forgot about the books and moved to the windowsill. The nurses would shoo him off, but he climbed right back. He dutifully performed everything he was told to do with the prosthetics, even though he knew that he was unlikely to ever need those skills. They warned him to take care of the prosthetics, and that was when he knew he wasn't going to wear them. They'd just get broken in the very first fight, either accidentally or on purpose. To spend all this time in the Sepulcher was meaningless. So he was spending it looking out of the window.

"Just like a forest creature on a leash," the nurse said as she came in. "You'll soon be back with your friends, don't you worry. And it'll be so much more fun playing with them too."

He was waiting for her to tell him off for sitting on the windowsill again, but she seemed to have tired of that.

"Do you miss them?" she asked with concern.

"No," he said without turning around.

It was light already, and the nurse turned off the lamp. He could hear the jangle of the cutlery and the groans of nightstands being moved. The yard was empty, as were the streets outside and the ruins of the snow fortresses. The nurse left, the door clicked shut behind her, and all was silent again. Then someone came in and stopped behind him.

"I wonder how cats go around in the snow when the snow is higher than cats?"

The voice was unfamiliar to him, but Grasshopper didn't turn around.

"They jump," he said, still looking out to the yard.

"You mean dive in headfirst and jump out again every time? Or are they building tunnels?" The voice smiled. "Like moles?"

Grasshopper turned. There was an unfamiliar boy standing next to him, looking past him out the window. His lips were quaking with laughter, but his eyes remained somber. The most striking thing about him was the clothes. He had on the white top from the hospital pajamas and fraying blue jeans underneath. The sneakers on his feet were black with dirt. Laces undone. His hair was smeared with something white where it fell over his forehead. He didn't look like a patient. He didn't look like anyone Grasshopper had known. The sick were supposed to lie in their clean beds, while the healthy and the able were not supposed to sneak around the Sepulcher entering other people's rooms. But that wasn't the strangest bit. Where in the spic-and-span Sepulcher could one find that much dirt to soil his feet?

"The snow moles," the boy said dreamily. "They burrow in the winter and come summer they turn into cats. And in the spring, just after the transformation, they emerge from the ground screaming. The March shrews. With their piercing shrieks."

Grasshopper jumped off the windowsill.

"Who are you?"

"I am a prisoner of the Sepulcher. I wrenched the iron ring to which I've been shackled out of the wall and directed my steps here."

"Why here?"

"Because I'm a vampire," the visitor said sincerely. "I came to partake of fresh blood. You wouldn't deny a sick man, would you, my child?"

"What if I would?"

The boy sighed.

"Then I'll just die. Before your very eyes. In horrible agony."

This piqued Grasshopper's interest even more.

"All right. Partake, then. But not too much. Not so that I'd die. If you can do that, of course."

"Very noble of you, my child," the boy said. "But I am sated today, therefore I reject your offering. The bodies of nurses, bitten and drained, are even now marking the way from my dungeon to this door."

Grasshopper imagined this vividly. A nurse, and another one, and another . . . All lying there, bitten, pale, their eyes rolled back.

"Hilarious," he said.

"Like you won't believe," the visitor agreed. "Listen, could you hide me here? They're after me. Wooden stakes and all that."

"Sure," Grasshopper said eagerly, looking around the room. "Except there isn't anywhere you could hide. You're too big to fit inside the nightstand. And if you go under the bed, they'd see you."

The guest smirked.

"Leave that to me, O kindhearted youth. The old bloodsucker knows his business. Would you mind if your bed were to become a little bit higher?"

Grasshopper shook his head vigorously. The boy walked to the bed and started turning some kind of lever there. The bed did rise. The guest peeked under it, apparently satisfied.

"There are these elastic bands," he explained. "Very handy. Unless they're too tight, of course."

He approached Grasshopper and looked at him intently.

"I like you, young man," he said earnestly. "And now let us say our good-byes."

"You're going," Grasshopper drawled dejectedly.

The boy winked. His eyes were brown, but of such a vivid hue that they seemed almost orange.

"Only as far as under the bed."

He waved, got on all fours, and crawled under the mattress. Then he scrambled around there, swearing softly, and disappeared.

Grasshopper ran to the bed and listened intently. It was very quiet. You could only distinguish the guest's soft breathing if you bent down all the way to the floor. Grasshopper returned to the windowsill. He was deeply intrigued, but he knew that the nurses must find him in his regular position should they check his room. He rested his chin on his knee and peered into the window, watching and not seeing the yard and the boys now teeming there. He was afraid that anyone coming in would see his flushed cheeks and hear his thumping heart.

They came for him at the assigned time and took him to the playroom, where the prosthetics and the tasks to be performed with them were waiting. When he came back, the nurse was already in with lunch, so he couldn't check if the vampire was still under the bed. And after lunch came Elk.

"How's my student doing?" he asked, opening the door. He had a stack of books in his hands. The white lab coat made him look even taller.

"Chirping nonstop, like a budgie," Nurse Agatha complained, wiping Grasshopper's mouth. "Didn't eat a thing," she added as she lifted the tray, inviting Elk to observe the smeared mashed potatoes and the wrecked meat loaf.

Grasshopper had indeed been talking without taking a breath. He dreaded pauses and silence. That's when the nurse would hear something else and look under the bed. He doubted the visitor was still there but couldn't risk it if he were.

"Curious," Elk said, looking Grasshopper in the eye. "He's not usually the chatty type. He is an indifferent eater, though."

"Well, he sure is chatty today," the nurse said, putting the tray on the nightstand and covering it with a napkin. "It's your turn now. I'm getting a headache with this boy and his stories. Never in my life have I heard so much nonsense at once."

"I'll do my best," Elk said, sitting on the bed and putting the books on the chair.

"He really is a little angel," the nurse cooed. "I almost thought we were boring him here. But he seems to have shaken it off today. Talking and talking, like he couldn't stop."

"I wonder what's gotten into him," Elk said with a smile.

Grasshopper looked at him and shrugged.

Elk suddenly grew serious.

"Any news of the runaway?" he asked the nurse.

The nurse frowned and started whispering.

"None. I wouldn't put it past him to be outside the House by now. The doctor is going crazy. He asked you to make sure and drop in."

Grasshopper pricked his ears while casually studying the spines of the books Elk had brought.

"Certainly," Elk assured the nurse. "It is a serious problem."

"Yes," the nurse said, getting up. "What could be more serious? You try and feed him. Maybe he won't talk you to death."

She walked out, leaving the lunch tray behind.

Elk turned to Grasshopper.

"Listen, kid, have you by any chance met a boy here today, in blue jeans and with the gray bangs? About your height?"

"No, I haven't. Why?"

"Nothing," Elk said and smiled at the ceiling. "Just that if you do, could you tell him that he's getting a lot of people in a lot of trouble? Including me."

Grasshopper nodded.

"I'll be sure to tell him that. If I see him," Grasshopper said. "What did he do?"

Elk lifted the napkin for some reason and studied the contents of the tray.

"Many things. Enough for ten people. Are you going to eat this?"

"No," Grasshopper said. "Well, maybe later. Not now."

"All right," Elk said and stood up. "Come on, let's get you dressed. We'll go for a walk. You need some fresh air once in a while."

Grasshopper reluctantly slid off the bed. Elk dug in his pocket, produced a slip of paper, smoothed it out, and placed it on the pillow.

"A letter for you," he said. "Read it and let's go."

Grasshopper looked at the crumpled scrap with a single word: *Miss*. He knew Blind well enough to guess that he meant "I miss you." Blind was missing him!

"Thanks," he said to Elk. "How is he? Are they picking on him?"

"I don't know," said Elk. He seemed very tired. "I know so little about you, really."

They walked up and down the hospital wing's deck, protected from the wind by the convex overhang. Elk was relating the news of the Stuffage, Grasshopper just half listening. After the walk, Elk took him for the second session with the prosthetics. Then he watched a television show in the hall, which was allowed every other day. Then dinner with Nurse Maria, plumper and younger than Nurse Agatha. This time Grasshopper ate in silence, completely sure that the visitor was long gone. No one, not even a vampire, would be patient enough to hang under the bed for this long.

"I'll come at nine to turn the lights off," the nurse warned. "Don't sit on the windowsill. It's dark out, anyway."

As soon as the door closed behind her, Grasshopper jumped down and peeked under the bed. The vampire was lying on the floor, looking straight back at him.

"Oh," Grasshopper said. "You're not hanging anymore? She could have seen you, easily!"

The boy slowly crawled from under the bed, like a tortoise, and sat up wincing with pain.

"You try hanging on those straps for four hours straight," he snapped. "Naturally, I took breaks, when nobody was in here. But I think," he said with concern, "Elk is onto me. He came back and checked the tray. And I ate almost all the meat loaf."

Grasshopper laughed. It was very funny, imagining a vampire secretly devouring his meat loaf. And Elk, checking on the meat loaf. Sniffing at the plate. Why wouldn't he look under the bed, though? He probably didn't realize someone could hide there.

"Sure, laugh," the vampire said. "Make merry. Of course, you can't imagine how it is when you hold on to the elastic straps feeling the deathly breath of a wooden stake aimed at your heart. All for one measly dried-out piece of meat loaf. What's so funny now?"

"Stakes can't breathe," Grasshopper whispered, now weak from laughter.

The vampire said sternly, "It was a figure of speech, my boy. I turned three hundred last Tuesday, so I'm allowed to mix my metaphors once in a while, don't you think?"

"You are," Grasshopper admitted. "And I like the way you mix them."

"Well, we'll see how you like this night. I intend to assume my true withered appearance and listen to your pleas for mercy as my teeth prepare to stab into your flesh!"

The vampire broke off and sighed heavily. "Listen, can I lie on your bed for a bit? I'm stiff as a board. Is it OK that I'm dirty like this?"

He slipped off his sneakers and stretched out on the bed. His feet were even dirtier than his shoes. Grasshopper sat next to him. The vampire winced.

"My back really hurts," he said sadly.

"That could be because you're so old," Grasshopper suggested.

"You think so?"

The vampire was looking very pale, and this scared Grasshopper.

"Should I call the nurse?" he asked timidly.

"You mean for dessert?"

"I mean for help." Grasshopper laughed.

The vampire smiled.

"No. I am in the mood to while away the night talking to you and generally enjoying myself, not receiving the ministrations of a nurse. Let's not waste any more time. Tell me, how is it going out there, in the House? I miss the life outside the Sepulcher."

"No," Grasshopper said, climbing on the bed. "You first. And then I'll tell you anything you want. I thought about you all day. I can't stand the mystery anymore."

"What was it you thought? I bet it was about how cute that vampire was."

"I thought about . . . ," mumbled Grasshopper. "What did you do that Elk was speaking of? Why are you a runaway? Why are you hiding?"

The vampire frowned.

"I didn't do anything. Just ran away. But it's no use. It's the fourth time I've done it. I even tried setting fire to the place. They just don't care. I mean, I did get to them. They started locking me up. So this time I ran away because of that. So that they wouldn't think they outsmarted me. They won't have a minute's peace until I'm out of here."

"How did you manage to get out?" Grasshopper said breathlessly. The guest was quickly acquiring the halo of a heroic martyr in his eyes.

"A friend helped," the vampire said reluctantly. "A true soul. Don't even think about asking for the nick, I won't tell you anyway. So I thought this room was empty, and I came in. When I saw you sitting over there I liked you right away. I knew you wouldn't go calling them. Even though you looked like you believed all that stuff I was saying."

"I didn't," Grasshopper admitted. "But it would've been really cool to have a vampire hiding under my bed."

"See, just as I said. You're weird." The guest propped himself on one elbow and looked at Grasshopper closer. "I like weird ones. What do they call you?"

"Grasshopper."

"I'm Wolf. Your nick, you know . . . doesn't fit somehow. I would've given you a better one. When did they bring you in?"

"This summer. There wasn't anyone here. Only Elk. He took me in. But there has been another newbie already after me," Grasshopper added hastily.

"I bet Sportsman hates you," Wolf ventured.

Grasshopper frowned.

"Yeah," he said curtly. "He does."

"And everyone else is picking on you to try and suck up to him."

"Used to," Grasshopper said. "How do you know about me?"

"I don't. I know nothing about you, but I do know about them. Which people get along with them and which don't. Also I overheard you talking to Elk when he gave you the letter from your friend. Who they may be picking on while you're not there. Who is he, by the way?"

Wolf perked up. He clearly enjoyed talking about life outside the Sepulcher.

"Blind," Grasshopper said. He knew Wolf would be impressed, and Wolf was impressed.

"You're kidding."

Grasshopper kept proud silence.

"My hat's off to you," Wolf said respectfully. "I never would have thought of Blind as friend material."

Grasshopper was hurt.

"He is too, just like anyone else!"

"Or of him being picked on," Wolf continued, ignoring the outburst.

Grasshopper turned away. Wolf patted him on the shoulder.

"Don't get mad, OK? I can be nasty sometimes. Especially when my back's acting up. Tell me everything from the very beginning. When they brought you in. And from there on. And then I'll tell you lots about everyone."

Grasshopper did. His story was interrupted by the nurse who came in to wash his face and tuck him in. After she left, Wolf got out from under the bed and climbed under the covers next to Grasshopper.

"Please go on," he said.

Grasshopper spoke for a long time. Then they lay in silence for a while. Grasshopper knew that Wolf wasn't asleep.

"I wish I could get away from here," Wolf said miserably. "It's been six months already. You have no idea . . ."

Grasshopper imagined that Wolf started crying.

"You will. I'm sure you will," Grasshopper said. "Don't worry. It just can't be that someone needs to get out of something and can't."

"You're really nice." Wolf hugged Grasshopper and pressed his cheek against him. The cheek was wet. "If I manage to get out, I promise to fight for you to the death. You'll see. Will you remember me if I don't get out?"

"I swear!" Grasshopper said. "I'll always remember you."

In the morning, Nurse Agatha discovered Wolf sleeping in Grasshopper's bed. Her scream woke up both of them. Wolf head-butted the nurse in the stomach and stormed out into the hallway. Grasshopper ran after him and watched, dumb-founded, as Wolf, navigating between the bawling nurses, knocked over the trays with food and medications. His path was marked with broken glass, cotton balls, and scrambled eggs.

They caught him in the side corridor, where Wolf unfortunately bumped into two men at once and was carried off into a private room, to the accompaniment of angry shouts from the nurses. He was soon followed there by stone-faced Spider Jan. The second doctor and the janitor, the ones who caught Wolf, were busy pouring iodine on the bite marks and pulling up trouser legs to inspect the contusions where he'd kicked them. Half of the nurses gathered around and began rehashing the incident, while the rest started picking up the wreckage.

Grasshopper, stunned and wild eyed from the sudden awakening, was standing mutely by his door.

"I thought you were a good boy," Nurse Agatha said, walking past him. "And you turned out to be a liar. They are taking all this trouble with you, fitting you with prosthetics, and this is how you repay them for their efforts?"

"You can shove your prosthetics!" Grasshopper said furiously. "And your efforts!"

He turned on his heel without another glance at the nurse, who was rooted to the spot, and went inside.

In the room, now empty, he looked at the unmade bed and at the blanket on the floor. Then he hooked the chair with his foot and hurled it against the wall. The sound of the crash, the cup slipping off the nightstand and breaking to pieces, the sight of the overturned chair—all of that calmed him a bit. Nurse Agatha was clucking concernedly in the hallway.

"There," Grasshopper said at the ceiling. "Now they're just going to chain me up next to Wolf. And he won't be alone anymore."

But no one chained him up anywhere—not next to Wolf and not by himself. Doctor Jan gave him a scolding in his office. Elk apologized for him and promised to get him out of the hospital wing. Nurse Agatha said that he really was a good boy who just happened to fall under bad influence.

The principal patted him on the head and said, "No harm done. The child was understandably upset."

"Let Wolf go," Grasshopper said.

The only one who heard that was Elk.

That evening he was visited by a girl in light-blue pajamas, with flaming hair, like a red poppy. He'd never seen anyone with hair so bright. He never imagined that such a color could exist. Well, maybe on some clowns. The girl came in and approached Grasshopper's window, proudly clutching a bunch of strange fuzzy flowers. Her head was illuminating the white room like a very small, very concentrated fire.

"Hi," she said.

Grasshopper said hi too and climbed down from the windowsill.

The girl placed the flowers on the nightstand and said, "I am Ginger."

She had big ears, the skin around her nose was a bit reddish, and her eyes, unexpectedly, were almost black, framed by red lashes. It took some time for Grasshopper to register all that. It was not easy to look away from her hair. Grasshopper was surprised that she thought he needed to be told something so obvious.

"I can see that," he said. "Hard not to."

"No," said the girl, shaking her head. "This is me introducing myself. Ginger. Get it?"

He did.

"Grasshopper," he answered.

The girl nodded and looked around the empty room.

"It's boring here," she said. "Clean and boring."

Grasshopper didn't say anything.

"Want to come with me? That's an invitation," she said.

"Is that permitted?"

Grasshopper seriously doubted that he would be allowed as far as his room's door, after everything that happened.

"It's not. But no one will say a word. You'll see. Coming?"

They went out into the shining white corridor of the Sepulcher, which muffled their steps. The frosted-glass doors were opening and closing. Seniors in pajamas lounged in chairs, flipping through colorful magazines. Nurses flew from one room to another like snowballs. Grasshopper was following Ginger, expecting that at any moment someone would shout at him, but no one did. Nobody asked them anything. They walked and, alongside them, their reflections appeared and disappeared in the mirror sides of the cabinets lining the wall, one after the other. Blue pajamas and white ones. And the fire of her hair flaming up and extinguishing itself as they passed.

It's as if we have vanished, Grasshopper thought, astounded. *We're walking, but we're not. No one sees us or hears us. This red-haired girl has put a spell on the entire Sepulcher.*

Snow still fell outside the windows. They turned down another corridor, where the floor was shiny, and went to the very last door.

"Here we are."

Ginger pushed the door.

The room was really tiny. Three beds, strewn with clothes. Fully developed piles of magazines, notebooks, paper, brushes, and jars of paint. Drawings adorned the walls, and a green budgie jumped up and down excitedly in its wire cage. The room resembled Stuffage and even smelled like Stuffage. Grasshopper stepped on some orange peel and stopped, a little embarrassed. Ginger jumped onto one of the beds at a run, shook away her slippers, swept off the trash, and introduced her mate.

"This is Death."

A handsome boy with a mop-top haircut smiled and nodded at him.

"Hi," he said.

Grasshopper startled when he heard the nick.

"So you must be . . ."

Death nodded again, still smiling.

"Have a seat, will you," Ginger called, pushing another pile off the bed. "You can stare at him later, we have time."

Grasshopper sat down next to her. He knew about Ginger's friend. Death was the boy who never left the Sepulcher. The counselors, when talking among themselves, always said that he wasn't "long for this world." Death was a bed case. He never walked. He never even used a wheelchair. He'd lived in the Sepulcher since time immemorial, and Grasshopper always imagined this permanent resident to be greenish-pale, almost like a corpse. There was no other way to imagine someone who hadn't been long for this world for so many years now. But Death turned out to be a small, tender boy, with eyes occupying a good half of his face, and long dark-red hair that looked varnished. Grasshopper was staring at him while Ginger was picking cards off the blanket.

"Wanna play?" she asked.

She and Grasshopper climbed onto Death's bed.

For the next hour they became fortune-tellers. They prophesied to each other happy futures and all wishes coming true. Then the cards went flying to the floor and Ginger pulled up her pajama top and showed Grasshopper the tattoo she had on her stomach. The tattoo was made with a ballpoint pen and already a bit smeared, but one could still recognize something vaguely eagle-like, with a human head.

"What's that?" Grasshopper asked.

"I don't know," Ginger said. "Death thinks it's a harpy. I was shooting for a gryphon, actually. What do you think?"

"Could have been worse," Grasshopper said politely.

Ginger sighed and wiped the fuzzy parts off with her finger.

"It had been," she admitted. "The previous couple of times. Honestly? A great artist I'm not."

They sat in silence for a while. Death was fiddling with an orange. Grasshopper was searching for a topic to discuss.

"Is it true there are ghosts here, in Sepulcher?" he asked.

Ginger rolled her eyes.

"You mean White? He's never a ghost. He's just a halfwit. Which is not to say that there aren't. Except they don't walk into people's rooms mumbling nonsense, the way they tell it in your Stuffage."

"What do they do, then?" Grasshopper said.

Ginger directed a demanding look toward Death.

"What do they do, Death?"

"Nothing much," he said shyly. "They just walk the corridors sometimes. You'd be lucky to notice them, really. They're very quiet. And very beautiful. And White is the opposite of that. He ran in once when it was dark, stumbled, made this awful racket, and then started howling like a dog. I almost died I was so scared."

"White was one of the seniors," Ginger explained. "He would stick two lit cigarettes in his nose, wrap himself in a sheet, and sneak around scaring kids. They caught him and sent him away somewhere. He was really nuts."

Grasshopper imagined a really nuts, sinister senior in a sheet and looked at Death with a newfound respect.

"I'd surely die if I saw something like that," he said. "Or at least wet my pants."

"I did wet them." Death smiled. "Doesn't mean I was going to just admit that."

Death was growing on Grasshopper by the minute.

"What about those, the real ones?" Grasshopper asked. "Have you seen them?"

"They're not scary at all. I saw them and I wasn't afraid. They don't hurt anybody. They had enough trouble themselves in their time."

Grasshopper realized that Death wasn't making this up, and felt butterflies waking up in his stomach. Death was either crazy himself, or really had seen ghosts.

"He's not making it up," Ginger confirmed. "He's a Strider, by the way."

"He's a who now?" said Grasshopper, confused.

"Stri-der," Ginger repeated slowly, looking disappointed. "You mean you don't know who they are?"

Grasshopper was overwhelmed with a desire to lie that he did. But then he remembered that he had actually heard the word used. Once, Splint the counselor had grabbed him in the hallway. They were walking together, the three of them—Splint, Elk, and Black Ralph—arguing about something. Grasshopper said hello and wanted to go past them, but Splint seized hold of his shirt collar.

"Hold still, child!" he shouted. "Tell me, quickly, do Jumpers and Striders exist in nature?"

"Who are they?" Grasshopper asked politely.

The counselor's face was now very close to his own. The eyes behind the thick glasses were darting back and forth. He seemed scared of something.

"You really don't know?"

Grasshopper shook his head.

Splint let him go.

"There," he exclaimed. "Out of the mouths of babes! He has no clue!"

"That is not a valid argument," R One said sourly, and the three of them went on walking and arguing.

Grasshopper had forgotten all about this incident. Counselors sometimes acted no less mysteriously than seniors. So much so that sometimes it was hard to understand what they were talking about.

"Are they the same as Jumpers?" he asked Ginger carefully, risking ridicule.

"Of course not!" she said indignantly. "So you do know?"

"Only the words," Grasshopper admitted.

Ginger looked at Death. He nodded.

"Jumpers and Striders," she said in a schoolmarm voice. "Those who visit the Underside of the House. Except that Jumpers are kind of thrown there, while Striders can get there by themselves. And also go back whenever they want. Jumpers can't, they have to wait until they're thrown back. Clear now?"

"Yeah."

It wasn't clear to Grasshopper at all, but he decided he'd rather die than admit it. "What about you? Are you a Strider or a Jumper?"

Ginger's face darkened.

"I'm neither. Yet. But I will be. One day, you'll see."

She started flipping through a magazine she picked up from the pillow, as if she was suddenly bored by the conversation.

Death just smiled.

"How did you like Wolf?" he asked. "He's something else, isn't he?"

"You know about Wolf?" Grasshopper said in astonishment.

Ginger put down the magazine.

"We know everything about everybody. Even about those who aren't here. And those who are, we know more about them than anyone else. You did great to hide him. I filched those flowers for you from one senior girl. She didn't need them anyway, she has like hundreds more of them. And they would at least make you less lonely, and your room won't look so empty. Except we forgot to put them in water. They'll go all wilted before you get back."

"I thought you invited me just because."

"There's no such thing as an invitation just because." Ginger smiled. She was silent for a while before saying, "And not only because of that either. Also because you're a bit ginger too, like Death and me. We gingers need to stick together. We're a gang, get it? We are different, not like everyone else. They always try to blame us for everything, and nobody likes us. Well, most of them don't—there are exceptions, of course. That's because we're descended from Neanderthals. I mean, we're their children, and those who are not ginger are descended from Cro-Magnons. It's all there in this one magazine, scientific. I can show it to you if you want, I stole it from the library."

Grasshopper wasn't sure about the "gang" business. Or that it was the right word. But he was ready to be descended from anything if it meant so much to Ginger. Her mind and her words were jumping around too fast, the topics changed too abruptly for Grasshopper to catch up, but he did notice that Ginger was admitting to theft a bit too often and that she wasn't too bothered about it. He tuned out for a moment and stopped listening to her, which turned out to be a mistake since she started talking about Wolf.

"I let him out. And I'll do it again if need be. I hate it when people are being locked up, especially kids, that's just cruel, that is . . ."

"So the true soul he was talking about was you?" Grasshopper said, relieved.

"Of course. By the way, if you get locked up someday, you can count on me. I help lots of people in lots of ways. Pass some notes, or even bring in visitors at night. Stuff like that."

"How come the nurses haven't killed you yet?" Grasshopper said.

Ginger dismissed this with a wave of her hand.

"They are not allowed to touch me. They're afraid."

Death giggled and looked at the girl admiringly. "When they punish her, I get really sick. Right away. And I can't get sick, or I'll die. I can't even risk getting upset. Like at all," he said.

"Can't do nothing about me," Ginger said. "Death is their favoritest patient, they're always fussing around him like crazy. And I'm his best friend. So they don't bother me."

Grasshopper finally understood why this room was such a mess, why Ginger was free to invite anyone she pleased, and why nobody had come in yet to check on what they were doing. The nurses' proscriptions and rules had no power here. *Being not long for this world certainly has its advantages*, Grasshopper thought.

He spent the rest of the evening in this room. They dined on oranges. They played every board game they could dig out from under Death's bed, and when it was time to return to their rooms they staged a pillow fight and upended the budgie's cage. The feathers from the busted pillow floated in the air and settled down on the floor next to the chips, cards, and Monopoly money.

Grasshopper felt good. He liked both Death and Ginger, even though Ginger was on the bossy side and Death was too timid to ever go against her demands. As soon as Grasshopper reached his own room, dark and empty, he went straight to bed. This was the second happy night in a row that he'd spent inside the Sepulcher. Only one thing preyed on his mind. Wolf was still locked up somewhere, all alone.

The nurse was pointedly aloof the next morning.

"Jumping around all night, like a savage. In someone else's room, too," she ranted, pushing spoon after spoon of oatmeal into Grasshopper's mouth. "Dinner, bedtime—all by the wayside. And the way you left that room! A regular pigsty. What a disgrace!"

Grasshopper swallowed dutifully and thought that no one was feeding Ginger in this fashion, and that Death was surely eating by himself too. Although to him they might be doing something else, something even more disgusting. The nurse kept grumbling and frowning and then suddenly froze, spoon in hand.

"Who, pray tell, showed you to the bathroom? Or didn't you go at all? Held it in?"

"I did go," Grasshopper said, surprised. "Ginger helped."

The spoon dropped. Nurse Agatha upraised her hands and let out a very strange muffled yelp. Grasshopper was watching her with interest.

"You! A big boy! A girl helping you to . . . do it! Shame on you! The horror!"

Elk entered just in time to hear all about horror and shame.

"What happened?" he asked.

This infuriated the nurse even more.

"These children have not an ounce of modesty in them!"

Grasshopper stared sullenly at the oatmeal smeared on the covers.

"Why are you yelling like that? You help me all the time."

Something went *plop* in the nurse's throat.

"I am a woman!" she said. "And a nurse!"

"That's even worse," Grasshopper said.

Nurse Agatha stood up.

"All right, that's enough! I am going to tell the doctor. It's well past time we put an end to this nonsense. And you! A counselor! You should be ashamed for your charges!"

The door slammed, but Grasshopper was able to catch the beginning of a diatribe concerning good-for-nothing counselors like Elk. The end of it got lost in the distance. Elk used a napkin to scrape off the oatmeal and gave Grasshopper a sad look.

"Kid, I think you have terminally disappointed Nurse Agatha. You're too forward."

Grasshopper sighed.

"We turned off the lights so I wouldn't feel weird. And she didn't look at all. What's so bad about it?"

"All right," Elk said, rubbing his forehead. "The bit about the lights we're going to keep to ourselves. Deal?"

"Deal. I won't tell if you won't," Grasshopper said and then frowned. "Am I . . . perverted?"

"No," Elk said irritably. "You're normal. Are you going to eat this?"

Grasshopper made a face.

"I see," Elk sighed. "I'm not making you."

"Do they give Wolf the same thing?"

"They give everyone the same thing. Unless they're on a special meal plan."

"Can I go see him?"

"That's a question for the head of the department, not me."

"They're going to tell him I'm perverted. And that I have no shame. They're going to tell everyone, to make them think I'm disgusting."

Elk was picking up and replacing the cutlery on the tray.

"Elk, listen," Grasshopper said, trying to catch his eye. "Is Wolf not long for this world too?"

Elk's face went red in splotches, and his eyes flashed angrily.

"That's ridiculous! Who told you that?"

"Why wouldn't they let him go, then?"

"He's undergoing treatment."

"This place is very bad for him," Grasshopper said. "He can't stay here any longer."

Elk was staring out the window. He looked worn out. His face was lined heavily, especially around the mouth. For the first time ever, Grasshopper wondered how old Elk was. He thought that Elk was probably much older than Grasshopper's mom. And that the gray hairs on his head outnumbered the not-gray ones. And that his face looked even older when he was upset. Grasshopper had never thought about these things before.

"I talked to the department head. Wolf will be discharged soon. They're not keeping him here for their own amusement, you know. You should be old enough to understand this."

"I do understand," Grasshopper said. "So can I see him?"

Elk gave him a strange look.

"You can," he said. "On one condition."

Grasshopper squeaked excitedly, but Elk raised his hand.

"Wait. I said on one condition. You'll be transferred to his room, and you'll stay together until you're both discharged, but only if you can make him do everything the doctors say. No running, no pillow fights, no games except those they allow. Are you up to it?"

Grasshopper frowned.

"Maybe," he said evasively.

"Forget it, then. Not good enough."

Grasshopper thought about this. Would he be able to make Wolf do something Wolf didn't want to do? Or not do something? It was hard to imagine. Wolf didn't listen to anybody, so why would he want to listen to Grasshopper? But then, he'd cried that night, cried because he wanted more than anything to get out of there. He just didn't believe he could anymore.

"I agree," Grasshopper said and shifted under the covers. "But you have to give me your word, Elk. Swear that they're going to let him out."

"I swear," Elk said.

"Let's go, then!" Grasshopper sprang up and started jumping excitedly on the bed. "Quick, before he dies there all alone!"

"Wait," Elk said and grabbed Grasshopper's ankle. Grasshopper crashed back down on the pillow. "We'll have to wait for the doctor and the nurse."

"Listen, Elk, are they ever going to discharge Death? And Ginger, she's this girl here, is she long for this world? What about this senior, White, did you know him?"

Grasshopper was getting a sizable escort. Doctor Jan was carrying his things, the nurse had the linens, and Elk took the books. The doctor and Elk talked on the way, but Nurse Agatha was keeping silent, and her pursed lips were informing Grasshopper that she no longer expected much of him, wherever he might be transferred. Grasshopper was trying to slow himself down.

"Well, then," the doctor said as he stopped and bent down. He was tall, taller even than Elk. "Changed your mind yet?"

Grasshopper shook his head.

"All right."

The bars on the windows were the first thing he noticed. They were white, and they protruded into the room, checkered boxes encasing the windows that blocked the view. Multicolored Winnie-the-Poohs and Mickeys frolicked on the walls. Wolf was lying on the floor, facing the wall, his pajamas pulled around his head. He did not turn around when he heard the door or their voices, and Grasshopper didn't want to call to him. The nurse made the bed, shaking her head and muttering under her breath. Doctor and Elk went to the window. Grasshopper's stuff went on the nightstand, his books on the floor. The nurse busied herself with the bed for far longer than necessary. Wolf hadn't stirred. Doctor Jan and Elk were talking in whispers about something unrelated.

On his way out, Jan pulled Grasshopper's ear affectionately and said, "Courage."

It was as if they were leaving him alone in a cage with a real wolf.

Finally they all left. The lock clicked shut and all was silent.

Grasshopper looked at Wolf. He felt uneasy.

I don't know him. I really don't know him at all. He may well not be glad to see me. Maybe I should have stayed in my own room and gone with Ginger to visit Death every night.

He looked at the jumping Mickeys again. Some morbid joker had provided them with sharp fangs.

Grasshopper sat down next to Wolf and said softly, "Hey. Hey, vampire . . ."

SPHINX

VISITING THE SEPULCHER

I am looking into the eyes of my own reflection. Intently, without blinking, until my eyes start tearing up. Sometimes I am able to achieve the sense of complete detachment, sometimes not. It's either a decent way of calming your nerves or a waste of time, depending on your inner state when approaching the mirror and the lessons you carry away from it.

The mirror is a mocker. Purveyor of nasty practical jokes unfathomable to us, since our time runs faster. Much faster than is required to fully appreciate its sense of humor. But I do remember. I, who used to look into the eyes of a bullied squirt, whispering, "I want to be like Skull," now meet the gaze of someone who looks much more like a skull than the eponymous character. To compound the joke, I am now the sole possessor of the trinket that was responsible for his nick. I can appreciate the humor born behind the looking glass because I know what I know, but I doubt many would wish to pay for that knowledge by spending countless hours talking to mirrors.

I know an achingly beautiful man who runs from mirrors like they were a plague.

I know a girl who has an entire set of mirrors around her neck. She looks into them more often than she looks around, so the world for her exists in little upside-down fragments.

I know a blind person who sometimes freezes watchfully in front of his reflection.

And I remember a hamster attacking its own reflection with the fury of a berserker.

So don't tell me there isn't magic hidden in mirrors. It is there, even when you're dead tired and not good for anything.

I stop detaching and catch the eyes of my reflection.

"Jeez," I say. "What a monstrosity . . . At least put some clothes on, my friend."

The monstrosity, naked, covered in scratches, eyes crazed with insomnia, looks back reproachfully. He's got a Band-Aid over his right eyebrow, his left ear sticks out, flashing red, and dried-up blood covers his busted lip.

Chastised by the mute reproach, I turn away.

"All right. Sorry. You're perfect. Just a bit out of sorts is all."

I wiggle the bath towel from the hook onto my back and smooth it out over my shoulders with my teeth. Now draped in the fluffy white toga, I can emerge from the bathroom.

"There are people who live their lives as if running some kind of experiment," Sightless One said about the recent events. Beats me why this desire to experiment takes over so many at once. With no breaks in between. Noble, then Black, and finally me. There's a certain logic to it. Is this the way flu epidemics start? This virus of aggression and apprehension flies from one person to another, multiplying unstoppably. A dark period in the life of the pack, and one hard to snap out of.

I freeze, close my eyes, and try to identify it, this abomination that managed to sneak in from who knows where. To know its smell, corner it, return it back to where it belongs. But I feel nothing, apart from the two sleepless nights pressing down on my eyelids. Well, that and the smell of someone's socks, apparently buried in the pile of boots and sneakers. The shoe cemetery needs to be dealt with at some point, before we start getting mice addicted to the toxic vapors.

I open the door. The room is empty and quiet, which makes it seem smaller than it is, even though it should be the other way around. But this is not how it works here. Considering that Humpback always brings trees with him wherever he goes; that Alexander is shadowed by an invisible choir belting out the "Lacrimosa"; that Noble is always in his ivy-walled castle and only puts down the drawbridge when he feels like it, while Jackal is capable of spawning another half-dozen of himself at any moment; and that it's a blessing that at least Lary is not dragging the corridors inside when he walks in the door, and Tubby only does his magic when cooped up in his pen . . . Considering all that, it's not surprising that our room, overflowing with all those different worlds, would seem smaller now than when we're all in it.

I sit on the bed. I'm hungry, but I need sleep even more. I rest my forehead against the bars and switch off for a while. Until there's a quiet rapping on the door and the swish of rubber tires.

It's Smoker.

He's glowing, renewed after visiting the Cage. He's a nice guy, he doesn't bring anything here except himself. And his nightmarish questions.

I give him a one-eyed birdlike look. The other eye can't see from behind the hanging strip of Band-Aid.

"Hi!" he exclaims, but darkens immediately. "What happened here?"

I feel pangs of guilt. Those who are returned from the Cages should be met jubilantly. This is how it goes, ever since the times when nobody went there of their own accord. And I'm a tired scarecrow right now, incapable of performing the requisite rituals.

"Had a disagreement with Black. How are you doing? Everything all right?"

Plump, rose-cheeked Smoker, with those shiny bangs all the way down to his eyebrows. He passed the test of the Cage. Of course he's all right, I can see it clearly, but I have to ask to make sure. Cages are not good places. Not the worst in the House, but still pretty bad. I'm glad Smoker didn't have a reason to find that out. Even though being glad about it is not a good idea.

"Everything's great," he confirms. "It's like I've been reborn! All thanks to Jackal."

"I'm happy you feel that way."

He wheels next to the bed and looks at me probingly.

"Why did you fight with Black?"

Meaning: how on Earth have you and Black managed to have a fight. Even though my expertise in that area is an undiscovered country for him, he finds it easier to imagine me fighting as compared to stolid, emotionless Black, which is the way he sees him. Also, he's deathly afraid of hearing something along the lines of "You know, kid, we just had a certain difference of opinion" as the beginning and end of conversation. He's afraid because that's exactly the kind of explanation he usually gets, and it makes him depressed. It interferes with his need to feel grown up. He has all the reasons to be afraid right now. The temptation to get rid of him with a pair of meaningless sentences is overwhelming. The explanations will only invite more questions, and then eventually I will run out of answers. But Smoker is impossible to get rid of. He opens his palm and all of himself is right there on it, and he just hands that to you. You can't throw away this naked soul, pretending like you don't understand what it is you've been offered and why. That's where his power comes from, out of this devastating openness. I've never met anyone like that before. I sigh and silently bid good-bye to the idea of getting some rest before the pack is back.

"You see . . . Noble decided to try Moon River. The effect of this stuff on the human consciousness is unpredictable to the extreme. Some just feel sick. Others start behaving strangely. There are those who experience absolute bliss. Which doesn't look nice on the outside. I knew a guy who after a dose of River started talking in iambic pentameter. And then there was one who completely forgot how to talk . . ."

Smoker's attention is so rapt that I'm barely in time to stop myself from expounding on all side effects of River I've had the opportunity to learn about.

"You get the idea. Drinking it makes you a human guinea pig."

He nods. "I understand. It's a drug. So what happened to Noble?"

I shoot a quick look to the wrinkled covers in the corner of the bed. The place where the dragon was sitting. Frozen. Lifeless.

"He went stiff. Turned to stone. Wouldn't respond to anything. That's not a particularly bad reaction, by the way. The important thing in those circumstances is to stand back and not interfere. Except someone needs to be nearby. Just in case."

Smoker sighs with relief. He wasn't here to look into the wide-open eyes of the live statue for five hours straight. Or to hear Lary's whining and Jackal's prophesies. There is nothing scary for him in what I'm saying.

I am trying to stick the damned Band-Aid back in its place by rubbing it against the bars of the headboard, but no such luck. Breakfast will be over soon. Time to wrap up the story.

"Black volunteered to stay with Noble over lunch. When we returned, Noble wasn't here. This moron hauled him over to the Sepulcher. I've no idea if he lugged him all the way there himself or asked Spiders for help. But it doesn't matter, really. That's about it."

Just as I expected, this is clearly far from "it" for Smoker. He looks so shocked that I begin to suspect that something must have filtered through from my side, something bad. I felt like I was talking without bringing any emotions into this, and anyway I am already far removed from the way I was yesterday, but some feelings are very hard to hold inside, they find a way out. My dislike of Black is one of those. As is his dislike of me, naturally. Smoker doesn't need to be burdened with this, but I might be too late, at least on my own account. He's already caught some of it.

"I think"—Smoker's eyes flee, hiding behind the lashes—"maybe he thought that would be for the best? Maybe he was afraid for Noble and decided that he'd better make sure. In the hospital wing they know how to take care of people after . . . after things like that."

"Of course. They know a lot of things there. And Black wanted what was best. And what's best, in his opinion, is that we get rid of Noble. He's much too unstable."

"That's a strange way of putting it, Sphinx . . . It's not like they'd eat him alive there."

That's the most unbearable feature of all newbies. They constantly need obvious things explained to them. I feel like an idiot doing that. Especially when I'm wrapped in a wet towel. But I am also firmly against avoiding it, since sooner or later we always run into problems stemming from things left unsaid. From one of us being misunderstood.

"The medical records kept in the Sepulcher," I forge on bravely, "have these stickers on them. Yellow ones, blue ones, and red ones. They are also put in the personal files. I'm not going to talk about yellow and blue right now, but one red stripe means that you are antisocial and unbalanced. Two, you have suicidal tendencies and require a psychologist. Three, you have a psychiatric disorder and require inpatient treatment, which the House is not capable of providing."

Smoker frowns, trying to remember if he saw any stripes in his personal file. I want to laugh, although heaven knows there's nothing funny about this.

"One," I say. "You've been thrown out of your group, that's a sure way to get it. But everyone has one, so don't worry. Here only Tubby managed to avoid it."

"And Noble has . . ."

"Three. And I'm afraid that, barring a miracle, someone is going to finally notice them this time."

"Does it mean he has schizophrenia, then?"

I take a huge breath, but then the strengthening roar and clatter of an avalanche rolling down the hallway reaches my ears and all the nasty words stay where they were. Smoker also hears the sound of the imminent arrival of the well fed.

"Oops. I guess I better go someplace," he says. "While there isn't anyone there."

He manages to sneak out just as the avalanche reaches our door. Jackal, riding his Mustang, is the first to burst in. Yogurt mustache, a pack of sandwiches under his arm.

"Why, hello, Sphinx! Doing a one-man strip show? Could have waited for your friends!"

Humpback shoves him aside, places a packet of juice on the nightstand, and goes on to take Nanette out for feeding.

"Yummy sandwiches, look!" Tabaqui tempts me. "I can even put some sauce on top."

Alexander, a bunch of clothes in his hands, pushes his way through.

"This is cheese and this is cream cheese," Tabaqui persists. "All lovingly made by these very hands!"

"Smoker's back. Why don't you ask him if he's hungry?"

With a triumphant yell, Tabaqui backs out of the door and, by the sound of it, proceeds to break down the door to the bathroom.

"Smoker! Light of my life! Are you in there? Talk to me!"

Alexander finishes buttoning my shirt.

"Are you going to go see Noble?" he asks.

Sure. That's about the last thing I need right now. Go to Noble and explain to him the circumstances leading to his current whereabouts.

"Leave me alone," I snap. "Can't you see I'm not in a condition to drag myself over there?"

He just holds the jeans for me. He doesn't argue, he doesn't question me, and this makes me that much more miserable.

Jackal, the sunny go-getter with the yogurt mustache, the exuberant noisemaker, is back. Along with Smoker, who's chewing on a sandwich from that packet, and Humpback, who slaps Smoker's back excitedly, preventing him from enjoying his food with a barrage of questions about his time in quarantine.

"How's the Cage? Is the blasted thing still standing?"

Smoker nods. "Of course it is. Still there. What could possibly happen to it?"

I observe the lightning-fast disappearance of the sandwiches and swallow hard.

"You're so thin," Lary observes with concern. "Was it hard for you over there?"

Smoker nods again, then mumbles through the layers of the sandwich, "Hate those yellow flowers!"

Which precipitates another explosion of reminiscences from Humpback and Jackal about the hours they spent in quarantine.

"So the last time I was there, I . . ."

"One night is nothing, I was in for four in a row once . . ."

"Yellow is child's play! Now blue, on the other hand . . ."

While they are all comparing notes, I suddenly discover Blind's hand on my shoulder.

"I think," the Great-and-Powerful pronounces thoughtfully, "that it might be a good idea for you to walk down to the Sepulcher. Have a talk with Janus. You two are friends, after all."

Another one. The destination is the same, the quest just got harder, and Blind, unlike Alexander, I cannot just brush off. I mean, I could, but that would be unwise.

"Is that an order?"

Sightless One is surprised.

"Of course not. Just a suggestion."

He lets go of my shoulder and walks off, not giving me even a moment to grumble. Time to run to the Sepulcher. And I mean run right now, before Tabaqui joins the well-meaning advisers, before Humpback tells me all he thinks about it, and before Lary volunteers to accompany me there. We've been living side by side for far too long. Our sides have merged, and we all share common habits now. Soon we won't even need to open our mouths anymore to express an opinion, everyone will already know everything.

The classes drift by silently, not involving me in any way. Rain is drumming on the windowpanes. The gray ribbons of the raindrops snake down the glass. So sleepy. I catch myself dozing off with my eyes open, and I even see something like a dream.

A dimly lit passage through subterranean corridors. There's a window ahead of me. A dull, flyspecked rectangle of whitewashed glass. Wolf is sitting on the sill. With his back to me. He has on his old patterned sweater with holes in the elbows.

"Wolf!" I call to him.

He turns around and looks at me. The familiar white scar over the lip. His lips don't move, but I hear his voice.

"This mouse hanged itself under the pillow in my hole," he whispers.

I'm shaken awake by Skank's yelp and see her round, piggy eyes right in front of my face. She looks frantic.

"Where is the mouse?" she demands in a shaky voice, directing the end of the pointer at my nose. "Where is it?"

Then I'm thrown out and therefore free to do as I please. Or, rather, as I do not please. I have to go to the Sepulcher. I swing by the dorm in hopes of finding the remains of Smoker's feast, but there is nothing but crumbs left, so I slink away, defeated. The corridor rolls by, refusing to tell me anything new. Well, maybe it does, but I float through it like in a vacuum, deaf and blind to its pronouncements. I am pleasantly surprised that this turned out to be possible after all. This goes on until I reach the Sepulcher. Here I shake off the fog. Beyond this threshold is a domain that does not suffer being trod upon in this state of almost terminal exhaustion. The Sepulcher demands an appearance of vim and vigor. Even if you're already a corpse.

The hallway is immaculately clean and blindingly white. And soaked in this horrible mediciney smell. I am intercepted by two female Spiders rolling out on the glistening floor.

"What's this? On whose authority? Get out!"

And my unrecognizably plaintive voice pleads, "Just for a moment. A teacher sent me. It's very important."

"To the head of the department!"

A plump index finger directing me farther down the corridor.

My tail is sweeping the floor, my lips are stretched in an obsequious grin. I take off again.

The Spider queens stare suspiciously. A person like me is only to their liking when he's bound, suspended from the ceiling, and stuck all over with wires and tubes. To better suck out his blood. An armless creature running free is a disgrace, verging on a crime. In my mind I give them the finger. My rakes are not capable of that feat, of course. The rest of the way I take at a trot.

Janus's office. Jan is the nicest, most conscientious Spider there is. I love him dearly, but our relationship has soured a bit lately, so I'm worried. I rap the rake against the frosted-glass door and push it open a bit.

"May I?"

"Oh, it's you." He swivels around in his chair. A long-faced, big-eared graying ginger with an amazing smile that he rarely lets out. That's why he's called Janus. He's two different people depending on whether he's smiling. "Come in, don't stand there."

I enter. His office is not as white as the rest of the Sepulcher. You could almost imagine you were somewhere else. Leopard's drawings in thin wooden frames on the walls. Janus's office is the only place in the House where you can still see them in a civilized environment. Yes, whatever remains on the walls is closer, more accessible, and all around more fun, but a wall is a wall, it's hard to preserve things on it in exactly the state they were meant to be when created. Especially if they do go ahead with that renovation, painting over everything everywhere—then the drawings will be lost forever. Only these will be left. These, and the ones I have stashed away. Here, all we have are the spiderwebs and the trees. The largest sheet shows a gloomy white spider, its face unmistakably that of Janus. It's hanging forlornly from a thread in the middle of a tattered web. There aren't many people who'd hang a portrait like that in their office. But Janus did. He hung it, and the others, even though they all reek of the hatred Leopard had for the Sepulcher. I approach the glass-covered white desk.

"Can I see Noble?"

Janus doesn't answer. I can see he's set against it. But he's never going to say "Get out" straight off. That's not his way.

"Who was it you had a scrap with? Come here, let's have a look at you." Jan pulls out a desk drawer and starts rummaging in it. "I said come here. Do you enjoy this?"

"Enjoy what?"

"Fighting. Hitting someone in the face with your feet."

He finally fishes out something and dumps it on the table. A white-and-cyan package of surgical tape.

"That grimy thing over your eye, it needs to be changed."

Jan gets up, puts me in the swiveling chair, and peels off the strip of Band-Aid on my forehead. I see that it really is on the grimy side. It's not the end of the world, of course, but I need to be nice to Janus, so I sit quietly and allow him to do whatever he thinks has to be done.

"Now you see," he mutters, picking over my wounds, "he needs to be by himself for a while. People do need that sometimes. You understand that, don't you?"

I do. And he's right. But let him explain this to Alexander. To Blind. To all of them.

"I understand."

"Good. Go back to your group and tell the guys not to send anybody else. Later, maybe. But not now. Principal's orders."

I shudder. "Why? He usually doesn't interfere with your business."

Janus is purposefully looking at the landscape beyond his window.

"He doesn't, and then again he does. In extreme cases."

I feel sick. That's a death sentence. I look at Janus and see him suddenly pull away from me, himself, his desk, and then the whole room, growing smaller, more and more indistinct. The walls glide past, carrying him farther and farther from me, while the pictures seem to grow and crowd me, the webs on them hanging from the ceiling to the floor in nightmarish distorted polygons. I close my eyes, but this only compounds the horror, because I start hearing voices. The barely perceptible whispers of those who got tangled in the web and perished here. Leopard. Shadow. This is a terrifying place. The worst in the whole House. It stinks of death, regardless of how well scrubbed and polished they keep it.

Someone is shaking me so hard my teeth are clattering. I see Janus's face right in front of me. The web is gone.

"What's going on?" he asks. "Are you all right?"

"Don't do this," I say.

He lets me go and straightens up.

"You can't do this."

Janus shakes his head.

"It's not my decision anymore. I am really sorry. What's happening to you?"

What's happening to me? The Sepulcher is happening to me, which is peanuts compared to what lies in store for Noble.

"My apologies. This place gets to me very badly."

He pours water into a glass and gives it to me. I drink it out of his hands, completely forgetting about the rakes.

"This place?" he asks. "This particular place?"

"You know exactly what I'm talking about."

"Yes, I think so. It's those weird superstitions of yours. Are you completely sure you're not sick?"

I don't answer. There is no one here who can be completely sure about it. If anybody, a Spider should know this. Janus looks down and bites his lip. He is terminally curious. I don't have to wait long for the questions to start. He takes cigarettes out of the drawer and I realize that there might be more questions than I thought. Jan sits down on the edge of the desk.

"Where does this angst come from?" he asks. "Why? I see it too often to just dismiss it out of hand. When people start breaking out in a cold sweat in this very office . . ." He looks around, as if making sure that this is indeed still his office. "I'd like to know the reasons for it. I could understand if this were only happening to you. I'd just refer you to a specialist and that would be the end of the problem." He puffs on his cigarette, observing me closely. "You can answer or not, it's your choice."

"I'll answer. But I don't think my answer, such as it is, will satisfy you. This is a bad place. For every one of us. There are good places and bad places here. This one is bad. How it became this way is a long story."

Janus patiently waits for me to continue.

"And since you're not going to let me see Noble anyway . . ."

His forehead breaks out into a concertina of ripples.

"Are you trying to bargain?" he asks incredulously. "With me?"

"Yes, I am. Just so you know, I wrote a scholarly article once exactly on the topic that interests you, so I'm quite competent to discuss it. A long article complete with references to the classics and an inventive title, 'Sepulcher: Outside or Inside Us.' This, as you might have guessed, is me talking up my side. I understand it is common when bargaining."

Janus looks at me with such sincere amazement that I almost laugh out loud.

"You've lost me," he says. "What article? Where?"

"Just an article. In a magazine with a circulation of ten copies."

He exhales, relieved.

"Oh. I get it. It's your own magazine. What's it about?"

"Everything. It comes out twice a year, so we're never short of topics. The authors hide behind unrecognizable pen names, and everyone writes about whatever is of interest to him. I wrote about the Sepulcher, and the next issue featured a very lively discussion in the letters to the editor. Those might be even more useful to you than the article itself."

Janus nods. "We're haggling over two issues. A yearly subscription. It's a pig in a poke. Two pigs."

"In exchange for one visit to one dragon. I think that's fair."

"Nothing doing," Janus says, clearly disappointed. "That would mean me abandoning my principles. Indulging my own petty curiosity. I'd be ashamed of myself afterward."

"Your call."

I sigh with relief, even though he did refuse. It's good that he did. I didn't really want him reading my creation. It revealed too much. Almost as much as Leopard's drawings. I steal a glance at them and look away. It wouldn't do to go down for the count again. I transfer my attention to Janus, do my best to keep my eyes on him. He looks around in an exaggerated manner, trying to see something that he wouldn't be able to, no matter what. Then stubs out the cigarette in the ashtray.

"You look terrible," he says. "Go get some sleep, grab something to eat, calm down, and then come back."

He sounds irritated. My nightmares are getting on his nerves. They must be visible to the naked eye by now.

"Go," Janus repeats. "We're all tired. There are no classes tomorrow. I might let you see him then."

"It doesn't work that way," I say patiently. "I'd be happy to do exactly that, except I can't. Until I see Noble I can neither sleep nor eat nor look my people in the eye. I can't just go back empty-handed and crash into my bed. I will have failed to do that which I was sent to do. How can you not see that?"

"You mean I have to cater to your whims now?"

"It's not a whim. You know it isn't."

"He needs to rest. To be away from your people. You would only exacerbate his condition if you showed up in this panicked state."

"He'll have plenty of rest where you're sending him. And it will exacerbate everything much more than I ever could. Do you know how we speak of those who leave the House? The same way we speak of the dead. You're not letting me talk to someone who is going to be dead soon."

Janus climbs down from the desk. Rubs his face. A gaunt, hunched figure, looking more now like Leopard's drawing of him than I've ever seen.

"You know what?" he says. "If you spend one more minute in my office I'm going to start dreading to stay here alone. Imagining heaven knows what until I become convinced that this is indeed an evil place. I have no idea how you manage to force this on me, but I'm having a hard time fighting it."

"I'm not forcing anything," I say. "It's the way I feel."

"Let's go." He opens the door and holds it for me. "I am fond of my office and of my sanity. So the sooner you get out of here, the better for both of us."

I get up.

"Are you going to let me see him?"

"That's where we're headed. Do you think I should ask him first if he'd like to see you?"

We're walking down the Sepulchral corridor. He's striding ahead—a slender white tower. I can barely move my feet fast enough to keep up with him. I am all wrung out like a sponge, someone could use me to wipe the floor. Sure, I've gotten what I wanted, but I have nothing left for the main event, the whole point of this enterprise. We turn a corner. Janus slows down by a long opaque cabinet, takes out a white lab coat, and throws it over to me.

"Wait here. I'll just be a moment."

I wait, staring at an installation of cacti in pink flowerpots hanging off a wire frame, somehow resembling a spiderweb. Another one. This blind offshoot of the main corridor, clad in the whitest linoleum, glistens under the lights, proudly presenting the essential quality of the Sepulcher—its total sterility. I could eat my dinner off it, if I wanted to. But I just lower myself down on it and lean against the wall. And try to calm my frayed nerves with a simple mantra. *You are not a patient here. You're just coming through. Running through. You can leave whenever you want. Remember it and hold on.*

In that long-ago article on the Sepulcher, I picked apart the very word "patient." Dissected it, broke it down into elementary particles. And deduced that a patient is no longer a human being. That those are two mutually exclusive notions. When a person turns into a patient he relinquishes his identity. The individuality sloughs off, and the only thing that's left is an animal shell over a compound of fear, hope, pain, and sleep. There is no trace of humanity in there. The human floats somewhere outside of the boundaries of the patient, waiting patiently for the possibility of a resurrection. And there is nothing worse for a spirit than to be reduced to a mere body. That's why it is Sepulcher. A place where the spirit goes to be buried. The dread permeating these walls cannot be extinguished. When I was little I couldn't understand how this name came to be. We inherited it from the seniors, along with the horror this place instilled in them. We needed time to grow into it. A lot of time and many bitter losses. It's as if we were filling a void, a space carved out by those who came before us that somehow turned out to fit us perfectly when we filled it completely. When we understood the meaning of all the names given long before our time and went through almost all the motions that had been already played out. Even our innocent little *Blume* was a great-great-grandchild of an earlier incarnation; our very own baby and at the same time a reappearance of an old ghost. I'm willing to bet that if someone were to discover the archives of its predecessors, he'd find plenty of screams of rage against the Sepulcher, identical to mine.

Janus steps out and nods at the door.

"You can come in. I'll be back to check on you in a quarter of an hour. We'll see how your presence reflects on him. If I find that he's becoming upset, that will be the last time you are allowed anywhere near here."

"Thank you," I say, and enter.

The whiteness of the tiled walls is blinding. The room is tiny. Semiprivate—that is, for two. There are no windows. Noble is sitting up, blanket up to his knees, in an ugly gray gown with string ties hanging down from the collar. On the nightstand by the bed—a tray with a bowl of oatmeal and a glass of milk. The silly gown becomes him. As does everything I've ever seen him wear. Tabaqui has this theory that Goldenhead would remain beautiful even if he were to be dunked in shit. And the more benign tar and feathers would make him absolutely stunning. Someone who's not used to the visage of the Dark Elf is usually overwhelmed in his presence, buried under a mountain of insecurities. But someone who is used to it, and is also very hungry, should be able to redirect his attention to, say, a bowl of oatmeal. Which is exactly what I do.

How beautiful it is! Small pink flowers run along the border of the bowl; a golden puddle of melted butter occupies its center. The oatmeal is already starting to acquire a tender crust, but obviously is still warm. Not too hot, not too cold, just right. I am mesmerized by it, consumed by the desire to attack it, to chomp and smack my lips and lick the bowl clean, slurp in the milk, and then fall asleep right there. It's funny, the more vividly I imagine all this, the hungrier I get. My legs are about to give under me. I am this close to fainting. Noble stares at me in surprise.

"Hi," I say tersely, not able to peel myself away from the sight of the bowl. "How are things?"

Yeah. I'm clearly babbling. What things? That was a stupid question. But I had to say something, hadn't I?

Noble grimaces.

"What things? What are you talking about?"

I am silent. A sullen, hopeless silence. The oatmeal is getting cold. Noble frowns. "Are you hungry, by any chance?"

How polite and thoughtful of him.

"Purely by chance—very much so!"

"In that case . . ."

But I'm already not listening. I fall upon the oatmeal like a hawk and exterminate it. Apparently I make use of a spoon, because when the meal is finished I notice it stuck in the grip of my right rake. The wrong way around, so it's a mystery how I managed to eat the whole thing with the thin end. But that's not important. I miraculously avoid being suffocated, I still tremble with the now-satisfied craving, and I can gratefully lower myself down on the edge of the bed.

"Noble. Thank you. I know it may sound corny, but you have just saved my life."

Noble's chin quivers.

"I noticed. I'm sorry, but it was rather obvious."

I too begin to appreciate the humor of the situation. The putative savior and bringer of consolation showed up bruised, stared at oatmeal with crazy eyes, and then devoured it as soon as he got half an invitation. Inhaled a sick man's lunch.

"Oh. I guess that wasn't very nice," I admit.

Noble bursts out laughing. I join him. We laugh until tears come, loudly and hysterically. A pair of mental cases. I'm afraid the oatmeal might ask to get out. But the merriment switches off just as abruptly as it started. Noble darkens.

An uncomfortable silence. Exactly what I was dreading all along. There is a wall growing between us. And an iron door with a crest on it—over three stripes bright red, a two-headed overgrown lizard rampant.

"Who was that bastard?" Noble begins, and his tone is painting the fourth stripe: *Prone to violence, represents danger to himself and others, requires strict isolation.*

"It was Black," I interrupt hurriedly before a fifth or, heaven forbid, sixth stripe becomes visible. "And don't look at me like that. It's my fault too. I should have smelled a rat when he suddenly was so eager to be left with you. If it's any consolation, I have just about sent him to his grave."

"And he, you," Noble scoffs.

"He'd wish."

Silence again. It would've been better if he'd swear and curse. He's exceedingly good with the meaningful silences. Long ones, too. So we just sit there, and the silence envelops us in a suffocating cloud. It's laced with something strange, though. Noble is more confused than angry. It might be the result of the treatment he's getting, but then again it might not.

"What's going to happen to me?" he asks, just as I lose the last shreds of hope for our conversation.

"I don't know. It depends."

That's not entirely honest, but I can't just lay it all out. That there's practically no hope. Noble is still shocked, as if I did tell it like it was.

"Shit," he says. "Of all the stupid, stupid things."

My own uselessness is devouring me. Soon there will be only bones left. A familiar feeling, one I've had too often ever since Wolf died. Then it turned out that I could get used to living with it. Now I'll have to drag myself through all of that again. Endlessly repeating to myself that it could have been worse. That at least Noble is alive.

"Listen," he says, "have you ever used River?"

"No. Didn't even try. Not River, not White Rainbow, and not Seven Steps."

Noble looks at me oddly. He is dying to tell me something and at the same time is afraid of doing it.

"Would you believe it if I told you that I ended up in some godforsaken place and spent at least four months there?"

He asks me and looks away. His fingers are teasing the edge of the blanket, his lips are contorted in a grin, as if I have already started clucking in protest, made a sign of the cross with the rakes and fainted.

Would I? I examine him closer—and only now see that which I should have seen right away, were it not for the oatmeal. He looks older. Gone are the last traces of baby fat, the formerly soft cheeks have been chiseled out. His entire face looks sharper. Looking at him, it's not at all certain that he's not twenty yet. This indeterminability of age, the principal feature of a Jumper, is staring at me so blatantly that it's all I can do not to swear out loud. You had to be someone like Black not to notice it.

My emotions are apparently on open display. His grin becomes even more self-deprecating.

"Yeah, just what I thought. Now you too think I've gone loopy."

"No, I think that I have. That I'm completely off my game. Damn, not to recognize a Jumper from two paces! What an idiot!"

He blinks in confusion.

"Sphinx? What's going on?"

I get a hold of myself. What the hell did I come here for? To demolish someone's dinner? To parade my exhaustion around, not notice anything, and then, after being shoved face-first into it, to fly off the handle? He trusted his innermost secret to me, and this is how I repay him?

I close my eyes. These are things you're not supposed to talk about. But I've already ruined just about everything, and this is the price I have to pay.

"The landscape looked kind of abandoned," I begin hurriedly, with my eyes still closed, "a cracked blacktop, fields on both sides, houses here and there. Most of them boarded up. Nothing really memorable . . . except maybe the diner. More or less on the side of the road. I think it's the first inhabited place for about every other Jumper. There are some who bump straight into the gas station, but not many."

My head starts spinning. Very slightly, but it's still a warning sign.

"I'm sorry. I'm not supposed to talk about this. I don't know what happened to you afterward and where you ended up, but the beginning of the road to the Underside of the House is the same for everyone. Almost everyone. Am I close?"

I unscrew my eyes and see Noble's eyes occupying half of his face. A sleepwalker who's suddenly been woken up. Now would be the perfect time for Jan to come back and see this insane look. I turn around to check if the door has just opened.

"Noble. Enough. Get yourself together. I never said anything. Leave the blanket alone, count to a hundred. I don't know, have some milk. Jan is coming soon. If you keep staring like that they're going to pump you full of drugs and pack you off in a straitjacket."

Noble nods spasmodically. I can see he's desperately trying to follow my advice. Maybe even the "count to a hundred" thing. His face assumes this faraway look. He gets as far as eighty-six, by my estimates.

"But you said you've never had anything like that!" Noble blurts out. "How could you know?"

"See, Noble. The House is a weird place," I say. "Here people have identical hallucinations. Or at least they start identically. And it's not necessary to swallow or chew anything to get them. You know, I think that if any of the concoctions that the so-called experts are conjuring up here were to be brought into the Outsides and given to someone there, nothing would happen. Maybe a stomachache, but that's all. Hard to be sure, of course, but that's what I think. I could be wrong."

"So I'm not crazy?" Noble recaps, in a calmer manner. "Or if I am, I'm not alone."

"That last part looks more like it."

This is where Janus finally comes in. Noble is carefully playing at nonchalance. I straighten up, concern and compassion incarnate. A grandma who finally got to pamper her favorite.

"How are you doing here?" Jan queries. "Fighting yet?"

We raise a unanimous protest. Jan notices the tray with the empty bowl and nods approvingly.

"You can stay just a while longer," he tells me. "Half an hour at most."

Jan disappears.

Now I could stick around with Noble until tomorrow morning if I wanted to. No Spider queens are going to show up to throw me out.

"I need a cigarette," Noble whines as soon as the door slams shut behind Janus.

I send the rake rummaging through my pocket. It gets predictably stuck in there, scratching around like a trapped insect. Useless thing. Noble pulls me toward him, frees up the unfortunate appendage, and takes out the pack. Then in the other pocket we find a lighter. I climb off the bed and sit down on the floor, with my back against the nightstand. We puff in unison. Noble's drags are greedy; mine, despondent.

"Go on."

The sight of my shaking bald pate must be especially depressing when viewed from above.

"Sorry. Can't. You don't talk about these things."

"Yeah, figures. The House Laws, may they be forgotten. Right?"

"The Laws don't enter into it. That's just how it goes. Take me, for example. I'm not superstitious, but it's quite possible that, should I choose to share my experiences with you right now, my next visit to the Underside might not end well. I wasn't planning on dropping by over there anytime soon, but you never know. No one knows much about things like that. And where you don't know about something, you don't talk about it."

We smoke in silence. The floor under me is all covered in gouges left by the wheels of the bed. The walls are tiled to about three feet from the floor, blindingly white, reflecting the light from the lamps. I acutely feel that the circumstances are inappropriate, the setting is inappropriate, and the topic is inappropriate. But there is going to be more, no doubt. Noble is too unsettled right now to put on the brakes just because I asked him to. I have no doubt that, sooner or later, this way or that, this is going to rebound on me. The small of my back is freezing, the nightstand drawer handle is digging into my spine, but I'm exhausted beyond apathy and simply unable to move.

"How do you know about the others, then?" Noble asks. "Somebody must have been talking at some point."

Now this is called "stalking the prey." Even though we seemed to be talking about something else, but then what else is there? I lift up my head. From here I can only see his elbow and whispery tendrils of smoke. He shakes the ash off into the oatmeal bowl. Barbaric, that is. But better than having it all over the linens. I am jealous of him. Nobody ever explained anything to me back then. No matter how I phrased my questions. No matter from what side I tried to sneak in or how artfully I disguised the interest. In my case none of that made any difference whatsoever.

"Noble, listen," I say soothingly. "Why don't you try answering that question yourself. You're not Smoker, after all. Think."

This is Blind's approach. Boy, would he be amazed if he heard me using it. He himself switched on the meaningful silences in situations like this one. I was supposed to hear the hallowed "Think for yourself" hidden in those silences, do my own thinking and then, provided I arrived at some insight, keep it to myself. Very convenient. If it somehow fell on the Pale One to teach someone how to swim, he'd just toss the subject overboard and wait for the results. I am the only graduate of this drastic method of learning. Sometimes I feel proud of my own resilience.

While I am deep in the recollections of the good old days of my apprenticeship, Noble suddenly brightens up.

"Fairy Tale Night?"

"Precisely!"

Blind's education system had no use for positive reinforcement, but then, I'm not him.

"Do you know what it was called before?" I add. "Night of Permitted Talking. But that would be too obvious, you see."

"The poems . . . The songs . . . ," Noble mumbles. "Somebody might let something slip when drunk. Tabaqui's drunken songs do sound very weird sometimes . . ."

I turn toward him and rest my chin on the edge of his bed. This is both comfortable and risky. If I lose control, I am going to fall asleep. Noble would never forgive me if I did.

"Right," I say drowsily. "And? You're making great progress. You're exactly right about being drunk. And about the songs. Also you might want to visit the poets' assemblies some Thursday evening in the old laundry room. Sit through an hour and a half of inane wailing and figure out some interesting details in the process. Though not an experience I'd like to repeat."

Noble cogitates for a while longer.

"I'm coming up empty," he admits. "No more insights. Unless there are people who are even less superstitious and can talk about it openly."

I can see that he is indeed empty. His face looks tired. I decide to take pity on him.

"The walls. Do you always read everything that's on them? Of course not, no one does. Except those who know what to look for and where. Now you, for example, are a card player. So you know where the latest scores are displayed, right? While nonplayers would never find them in a million years."

Noble slaps his forehead.

"Of course! I was an idiot! All those hundreds of times . . ."

Done. For the next couple of days we are going to observe our packmate glued to the walls. We'll have to pry him off at mealtimes. This is when it hits me again that he most likely won't have that couple of days, and the thought paralyzes me. No walls, no poets' assemblies. I completely forgot about this while trying to affect serenity, and went over the top. The loss is already gnawing at my insides. It won't do to show this to Noble, who is still right here.

"Do you understand what this means? That it happened to you? It's the House taking you in. Letting you inside. Now, wherever you might be, you're a part of it. And let me tell you, it doesn't like its parts to be scattered. It pulls them back. So all is not lost."

Noble makes a face and flattens the cigarette against the long-suffering bowl.

"Do you really believe what you just said? Or are you trying to make me feel better?"

"I'm trying to make myself feel better, why? But as Ancient used to say, when words have been spoken they always have a meaning, even if you didn't mean it when you spoke them."

He laughs and rummages in the pack for a fresh cigarette.

"I have no idea who this Ancient character is, but if he really did say all that then I guess I can feel a bit better. 'Ancient' sounds important. Almost like 'Aristotle.' You can sleep here if you like. Looking at you, I'm not entirely sure you're going to make it to the dorm."

Sleep in the Sepulcher? Oh well, why not. I can see Noble doesn't want to be alone here. I get up and go sit on the other bed. There are two of them here, just for the occasion. It even has linens on it, all tucked in and ready.

"You're right. I'm not much of a conversationalist right now. And I also doubt I'd make it all the way back."

I stretch out on the cot, on top of the slate-colored blanket. This is indescribable bliss.

"Thank you," I whisper with my eyes already closed. "This is the second time today you are saving my life."

He laughs again.

"Hey, Sphinx."

I am not quite sure if he called to me right away or if I was already asleep for some time.

"Sphinx, listen, would I be able to go to the Underside from somewhere else? Like from the Outsides?"

I climb out of the sleep, clutching at it at the same time, like at a warm blanket being pulled off.

"What? Don't know." My own voice sounds alien to me, muffled by the non-existent blanket. "I don't think anyone's tried. There wasn't anyone to try. Also, you know what . . . Those lands, they're not as harmless as you might think. There are some pretty scary places too. It's just that I figure you weren't stuck there for more than two months."

I continue to mumble. It is important, the thing he's asking about, I should try to explain . . . The sleep overtakes me, throws sticky cotton wool in my face, and it's hard to speak. I crash into it. Into a heavy, suffocating dream, where a man with steel front teeth and a face covered in small scars calls me "little bastard," thrashes me for the smallest of missteps, and threatens to feed me to his Doberman pinschers. He has five of them. Five scraggy, razor-faced, completely insane creatures in transport cages. My duties include feeding them and mucking out after them, and I hate them almost as much as I hate our common master. They hate me right back. I am thirteen, powerless and alone, and certain that no one is ever going to save me. *It's because of him that I learned to reach for beer when I was thirsty. There was never any water in his damn truck.*

I awaken suddenly, screaming as if slapped, and jump up all covered in sweat. The hoary nightmare is still ringing in my ears with the throaty "ho-ho-ho" that makes me cringe in almost physical pain.

It's dark, except for the nightlight above Noble's bed. Goldenhead is hard at work over my cigarettes. He is still sitting up very straight, deep in thought. The tobacco smell has defeated the scent of the Sepulcher. No amount of airing is going to get rid of it now.

"Rise and shine," Noble acknowledges me perfunctorily.

I lean back over the cot, still bearing the imprint of my body, over the damp spot where my head was, and wipe my forehead against the scratchy blanket. Then I go over to Noble's side. There is an aching in my bones as if someone jumped all over me while I was sleeping. Come to think of it, that's not far from the truth. Noble hands me a short stub of a cigarette.

"Sorry. No more left. I was bored. Here, they brought dinner."

And they never said anything, either about the smoke or about my prostrate figure. Beauty is a horrible weapon. It even has an effect on Spider queens. Not much else does.

Noble inserts the cigarette end into my clamp, avoiding looking me in the eye.

"You were screaming. And talking. Scary stuff."

I take a drag, scratching the itchy spot on my forehead under the tape with the rake-prong.

"It's the Sepulcher. It gets to me. Almost always does. I shouldn't have fallen asleep here."

"Who was that man? Does he exist?"

The tiles reflect our voices in a barely perceptible echo.

"Could be. On the Underside. Unless someone snuffed him. Let's not talk about it."

"Let's." Noble pushes the hair from his face and finally looks at me full on. Like this is the first time he sees me. "It's late. I guess you must be going. Provided they did not lock the front door."

I really must be going, but I am loath to leave him here, in the place where Steel-Toothed just came for a visit, albeit in a dream. Noble is scared, which means he's more susceptible to demons of all kinds, should they like to drop in. On the other hand, I need to replenish the stocks of food, cigarettes, and other useful items, and also tell people I was going to be spending the night in the Sepulcher.

"Right. I'll go check the door. If it's locked, I'll come straight back. If it isn't, I'll go see the guys. And bring some chow."

Noble nods.

"OK. It's really bright out there, be careful."

I make a wave with my rake and open the door into the shining snow-bound corridor.

The Sepulcher at night is a haunted castle. I hate its bluish lights. They turn faces into death masks. I reach the end of the side corridor and turn the corner. Now my sliding reflection is caught between the glass doors of the cabinets on both sides. I walk briskly. There's nowhere for me to hide, but I am somehow sure that it won't be necessary. And that's how it turns out. The night nurse's area is illuminated like a giant aquarium, and in its center floats the gorgon's cold face. If she were to open her eyes I'd have to turn into stone, rely on the inability of certain predators to notice stationary objects. But the Spider queen is asleep. Her eyes are closed, only the round-rimmed glasses glint menacingly.

Not only is the front door not locked, it's even open a crack. It catches me by surprise, but once I'm out on the landing I see the orange points of light glowing rhythmically and stop worrying. They're here. And they've been here for a long time already. Their bags are full of food. They brought bottles of water, blankets, the coffeemaker, and probably even utensils. Someone rises to meet me. They are all accustomed to the dark by now, so I am the only one here who can't see anything, but judging by the sureness of his movement, this someone must be Blind.

"Janus says it doesn't look good?"

Could be either a question or a statement. You can never tell with Pale One.

"More or less."

"Let's go." He addresses those left sitting against the wall. "Get up. Sphinx will show the way."

Which I do. Our grotesque cavalcade floats past the aquarium with the illuminated gorgon, past the glass cabinets and opaque doors. We are nothing but long, transient shadows. The most extravagant of them is the one consisting of two, Tabaqui atop Lary's shoulders. It's the tallest and the most disheveled. Neither Black nor Smoker is here, but Alexander is lugging sleeping Tubby, whose reflection in the cabinet doors resembles nothing so much as a massive backpack. I let them go ahead and bring up the rear, looking at them with love and admiration. This is my pack. It can read minds and grab meanings out of thin air. It is both awkward and awesome. Thrifty and quarrelsome. I allow myself to dissolve in the tenderness toward them—Black isn't here, so there's no one to knock the sentimentality off me. But Lord Almighty, how few we are. I catch myself falling behind instead of blazing the trail and quicken my steps. Out of the corner of my eye I catch the last reflections in the last cabinet—Alexander under his softly snuffling burden, Sphinx right behind him, and then one more silhouette, flashing the white sneakers as it steps in sync with us until I turn around and it vanishes. I feel much better. And then, solely for that last invisible one, I start composing a poem out loud. It comes out incredibly silly, just the way Wolf liked them.

> Green locusts falling from the sky today,
> The gray suburban hills are full of voices.
> It takes two sacks to walk from fields back home,
> Just two, filled to the brim with chirping noises . . .

THE HOUSE

Stuffage welcomed them with jeers and giggles.

"Blind's Tail is back!" Muffin shouted.

Whiner and Crybaby played a drumroll on the bottoms of leaky pails.

"Blind's Tail! Blind's Tail!" they sang mockingly.

Their voices did not express hostility. It was more surprise. As if the month Grasshopper spent in the hospital wing had erased him from their lives.

Wolf was greedily lapping up the scene.

"And . . . And Grayhead is with him," Muffin added hesitantly.

Almost the entire group was wearing sweatshirts with loud, garish messages. Grasshopper figured that those had become fashionable while he was away. The sweatshirts were declaring:

I'm on Fire!

Life Is One Big Disappointment

Keep Off!

The colorful slogans made the faces above them seem more grown up.

Sportsman was lounging on his bunk, legs dangling, and flipping through a magazine. He didn't even glance in the direction of Grasshopper and Wolf. *Not a Slave to Circumstances*, Grasshopper observed the slogan on Sportsman's sweatshirt. Wolf put down their bags.

"Hi, Blond!" he said to Sportsman.

Whiner and Crybaby immediately ceased the racket. Sportsman paid them a brief look over the magazine.

"Muffin, tell those two that I've been Sportsman for ages now."

"He's been Sportsman for ages, he's not Blond," Muffin repeated dutifully.

Wolf made an incredulous face.

"He's not? And somehow his hair isn't any darker."

Muffin turned around in search of a clue, but was ignored by Sportsman, who was engrossed in the magazine.

"Sport's hair is none of your business," Muffin said significantly. "Or yours!" he snapped at Grasshopper, even though Grasshopper hadn't mentioned hair at all. With him, Muffin felt himself on firmer ground.

Plump and rosy cheeked, he was pacing back and forth, preventing them from coming in. They waited at the door for him to get tired of it.

"So." Muffin stopped and adjusted his pants. "You, mama's darling. Your bed belongs to the newbie now. To Magician. So you're going to sleep in that room. And be grateful that at least we're not sending you to the wheelers."

Grasshopper had already noticed someone else's stuff on his bed but didn't say anything.

"We don't need sissies like you here," Muffin said. "Or like him!" Muffin's finger pointed at Wolf now. "Especially his kind we don't need at all."

"Was that Sportsman's idea?" Wolf asked.

Sportsman didn't deign to respond. He just stretched out on his bed, yawned, and flipped another page.

"Tail's got arms now," he said, still not looking up from the magazine. "I wonder . . ."

Grasshopper looked at his prosthetics and blushed. Wolf's eyes narrowed.

Muffin bustled about, completely oblivious.

"Now beat it. This is the Pack's room. Not for the sissies crawling around the Sepulcher."

Wolf shoved him away.

"All right, I'm a sissy," he said with disgust. "And you're all tough guys here. Especially you and Champion. Or whatever he calls himself today. Blond. So. Since you've thrown us out of here, we're going to live in that room now, and we're going to have our own sissy rules, so the tough guys like you better keep out. Got that?"

Grasshopper couldn't wait to leave. He furtively stepped on Wolf's foot.

"Wolf. That's enough. Let's go."

Wolf picked up the bags.

"We're going," he said. "To our room. And whoever doesn't feel like a tough guy can come with us. There's plenty of space."

Whiner and Crybaby banged on their drums, a bit uncertainly.

"Hey!" Bubble protested, wheeling up to them on his skates. "What do you mean, your room? I sleep there too!"

"Not anymore," Wolf declared. "You're a tough guy, aren't you?"

Bubble looked himself over.

"I don't know. I'm not sure."

"Enough of this," Sportsman said, putting away the magazine and raising himself off the bed. "You heard. Beat it, before it gets beat for you. Bubble is going to sleep wherever he wants, and you just shut up!"

The pack was silent. The newbie, the one on crutches who could do magic tricks, was looking at Grasshopper sadly. *He'd like to come with us,* Grasshopper realized. *But he's got my bed now, they'll never let him go.*

They went out into the hallway. Someone belatedly whistled behind their backs.

Grasshopper laughed.

"That's exactly what I wished for."

"I know," Wolf said.

They entered the room next door. Wolf turned on the lights. The room was bare and ugly. Steel cots in two rows, with rolled-up mattresses on them. Only three had linens. Blind was sitting by the wall and raised his head as they entered. He hadn't grown at all—or he just didn't look like he had. His hair had gotten longer. The fashion for sweatshirts with messages apparently hadn't reached him. He was wearing a checkered flannel shirt, an adult one. Elk's shirt, much too long for him.

"Hey, Blind!" Grasshopper said happily. "It's me. And Wolf. They threw us out. And here you are!"

"Hey," Wolf said, putting down the bags.

"Hello." Blind rustled.

"A sad sight," Wolf said, looking around the room. "But we'll soon transform this into Gardens of Paradise."

Grasshopper perked up.

"Can I do the transforming too?"

He couldn't wait to try his new prosthetics.

"I said 'we.'" Wolf nodded. "We, living here. Blind, is that OK with you?"

Blind was listening intently, with his head slightly to the side.

"Yes. Do all the transforming you want."

Wolf went up to the tucked-in beds.

"Which one is Bubble's bed?"

"Second from the window."

Wolf grabbed everything from that bed and hauled it to the door. Then he returned for the linens.

"Are we going to evict Crook as well?" Grasshopper asked hopefully.

Wolf stopped.

"Don't know. I guess he can decide for himself."

Wolf deposited Bubble's things in the hallway and came back.

Behind the wall, Stuffage was alive with voices and stomping feet. Wolf ran up to the windowsill and plopped onto it, paying no attention to the dust.

Grasshopper sat down beside him. Wolf was devouring the scene down in the yard. He had a proprietary look on his face. Grasshopper was used to seeing Blind look that way, but never Wolf. *How are they going to get along?* he thought apprehensively and looked back at Blind.

Blind was still sitting at the wall and listening. He wasn't listening to the noises of Stuffage. He was listening to Wolf. Guardedly and inconspicuously.

Were it not for Wolf, he'd talk to me. Tell me what's been happening while I was away. Show that he's glad I came back. Like really show, not the way he did now—everything on the inside and nothing visible.

Grasshopper felt sad.

"Blind," he said. "Do you know what it says on Whiner's and Crybaby's sweatshirts? *Leave the Loner Alone.* Both of them."

Blind smiled.

Wolf snorted from the windowsill, "One loner and one loner make two loners. And ten more loners would make for an entire ocean of loneliness."

"They called us sissies," Grasshopper explained. "And said that there was no place for us there."

"I heard," Blind replied.

Grasshopper went to sit next to him. Elk's shirt covered Blind down to his knees. The rolled sleeves looked like tubes around his wrists. The corners of his lips were covered in something white. He must have been eating plaster off the walls again. Grasshopper moved closer to Blind and inhaled the familiar scent of plaster and unwashed hair. He'd missed him, but he didn't know how to express his happiness and how to make Blind feel it too. He could only sit next to him in silence. Blind remained still, but now he was listening to Grasshopper. Without turning his head he inhaled forcefully through his nose and then licked off the white residue.

I must have my own scent too, Grasshopper realized. Everything did. People, houses, rooms. Stuffage certainly had it. This room did not smell of anything yet. But that would soon change.

Grasshopper stretched his legs and closed his eyes. *This is my home,* he thought. *Right here. Where Wolf and Blind are going to wait for me and worry if I'm away for too long. This is what they call Gardens of Paradise.*

The next morning, Wolf started working on the room. He dashed off to Elk and to seniors, then went down to the yard, returning each time with heaps of this and that and laying it out along the walls. Grasshopper never went out. He and Blind were guarding the room. Wolf procured paints, both liquid and spray, an old easel, a stepladder, and some fraying brushes. He also arranged empty paint cans and stacked old, yellowing newspapers on the floor. Grasshopper was getting tired of the commotion and of Wolf running around holding all these items, but then Wolf declared everything ready for the work to begin.

Grasshopper helped him spread out the newspapers. Wolf mounted the stepladder and started painting the wall white. The old portable radio was belting out slow blues, coughing and making unfunny jokes between the songs. Grasshopper walked over the newspapers, anticipating the multiple colors of the Gardens of Paradise and singing along softly whenever the tune turned out to be familiar. Blind was scrubbing the windowsill, grayish water flying everywhere.

The lunch bell came unexpectedly for all of them. Wolf stayed back while Grasshopper and Blind went to the canteen. Sportsman's eyes were shooting daggers, Muffin made faces, blue-eyed Magician looked at them plaintively and forlornly. This was the first time Grasshopper was using his prosthetics in full view of others, and the embarrassment was making him eat very slowly.

"Sportsman is looking at us weird," he whispered to Blind.

"He'd do better to look after his own."

"Why?"

"Wolf has more cunning than he," Blind replied cryptically.

He squeezed a piece of meat loaf between two slices of bread and shoved the resulting sandwich in Grasshopper's pocket. Another sandwich just like that one weighed down the other pocket. On the way back they bestowed two greasy stains on Grasshopper's jacket.

In addition to Wolf sitting on the stepladder, they also found Humpback and Beauty in the room. Humpback's hamster was running around in the tub installed on one of the beds. Its glass bowl, spotlessly clean, was drying out on the windowsill. Beauty, his tongue hanging out from the effort, was diligently, if inexpertly, rubbing a wet rag on the lampshade. Humpback, hunched over, was drawing an unidentified animal on the wall. Its legs rose up like columns. When Grasshopper and Blind entered, he nervously straightened up and hid the pencil. All that was near the floor. Higher up, the white wall exploded in green and blue triangles, red spirals, and orange splashes. *Blind can't see this,* Grasshopper thought with disappointment.

"What do you think?" Wolf asked from up on the stepladder.

"Yes!" Grasshopper said. "This is exactly it!"

"And these"—Wolf pointed with the brush at Beauty and Humpback—"are fresh Poxy Sissies. Now we are five. And the hamster."

That's why Sportsman was so mad, Grasshopper thought.

"Can I finish this now?" Humpback asked no one in particular.

He turned back to his monster and started putting stripes on it. His head was covered in orange drips too, making him seem a continuation of the wall.

"We brought food," Grasshopper said. "Runny meat loaf."

They all skipped dinner. By evening they'd painted the entire wall. The upper part bristled with the flying spirals and triangles, while the bottom was taken over by bizarre animals. Humpback's striped creation was there, as was a slender-legged wolf with teeth like a buzz saw—Wolf's contribution. Also a smiling hamster. Beauty painted a red blob, then smeared it and started crying. They all pitched in and teased it into an owl.

Grasshopper couldn't hold a brush. Wolf wrapped a rag around one of the fingers on his prosthetic hand and dipped it into the can, and a giant porcupine with slightly crooked quills joined the parade of animals. Blind drew a giraffe. It was empty inside and resembled a tower crane, so Humpback colored it in. When they stopped, paint was everywhere. On the newspapers, the clothes, their hands, faces, hair, even the hamster—everything. Elk came by to ask why they didn't show up for dinner and froze as he opened the door.

"Oh," he said. "This is something else."

"Beautiful, isn't it," Beauty whispered. "We did everything ourselves."

"I can see that," Elk said. "But you are spending the night in my room."

"No," Grasshopper said, agitated. "We can't! If we leave here, Sportsman and all the rest of them are going to come and ruin this. We can open the windows, to air it out. There's hardly any smell at all! Please?"

Elk gingerly stepped inside and immediately got stuck to the newspapers.

"A rebellion?" he asked Wolf.

Wolf nodded. "They threw us out themselves."

Elk studied their stained faces, the floor and the cans of paint, then the wall.

"I think I see a vacant space right there," he said.

A green dinosaur shaped like a kangaroo came to live in the vacant space, and Elk's suit acquired beautiful emerald spots.

"Yes, well," Elk declared, getting up from his knees. "It is indeed contagious. And now we go and wash up." He shoved the brush into the paint can. "Are the other walls destined for the same fate?"

"We'll think of something," Wolf promised.

"No doubt," Elk said. "Go open the windows."

They opened the windows and threw away the newspapers. Elk took Grasshopper and Beauty to the bathroom. He washed them by turns. As soon as the scrubber left Grasshopper to attack Beauty, Grasshopper would fall asleep. Surrounded by the white tiles, under the thundering hot waterfall, swaying and grabbing the bars of the drain with his toes to stop himself from falling down.

Beauty's squeals, muffled by the noise of the shower, faded into the distance, then Elk's hands came back and jostled him, the soapy brush reappearing, and Grasshopper woke up again. Then he was being carried, swaddled in a towel, and he still kept his eyes shut even though he wasn't asleep anymore, because he didn't feel like walking. He only peeked out of his fluffy cocoon once deposited in the room.

Humpback, Blind, and Wolf were sitting side by side on a bed. The wall stretched before them in its drying splendor, and Grasshopper again became sad that Blind could not see it. Elk covered him with the blanket, and Grasshopper snuggled in the warm burrow. The voices rolled over him, bubbling indistinctly, but he couldn't make out the words. He was sinking into sleep but managed to call out.

"Blind . . ."

Someone smelling of paint appeared silently by his side.

"You know what," Grasshopper whispered. "The dinosaur . . . It's raised off the wall a bit. You could see it when it dries up . . . If you touch it . . ."

The paint-smelling apparition answered something, but Grasshopper did not hear it. He was asleep.

The next morning, Wolf changed the lightbulbs for brighter ones. They made shades for two of them out of colored craft paper, and Wolf covered them with Chinese characters. The third one occupied the shade Beauty had been washing. After Beauty left, Humpback washed it all over again, but Beauty didn't know that and so every time he walked under it his face was illuminated by a smile, itself like a lightbulb under the dark bangs.

They guarded the room in shifts all day. The wall was almost completely dry now. The Stuffage Pack was suspiciously quiet. From time to time one of them would sneak out and shuffle outside the door, trying to peek through the lock. Or they would knock and run away before someone could open. Wolf and Grasshopper were on guard during lunchtime. Wolf sat on the windowsill looking out into the yard. Grasshopper lay on his bed. The hamster scratched in its bowl. The room on the other side of the wall was silent. Then someone knocked. Wolf had been jumping up and down all morning, opening the door only to find emptiness behind it and hear the sound of running feet, so he didn't even move.

"You'd think they'd give it a rest during lunch, at least," he said.

The knocking resumed. Grasshopper got up.

"May I?" a squeaky voice said, and a big-eared head insinuated itself into the crack.

Grasshopper closed his eyes. Then he opened them again.

"This can't be a wheeler?" he said.

"It is," the visitor said. "Amazing, huh?"

And he rolled into the room.

Stinker the wheeler was known far and wide. Grasshopper had heard a lot about him, even though he'd never met him in person. Those who had, all confirmed that Stinker was the nastiest wheeler in the House. The walking juniors considered all wheelers whiny and nasty, but even the other wheelers had branded Stinker as such. That's probably because he was. The mere sight of him made seasoned counselors wistfully count the years remaining until retirement. His roommates harbored secret desires to throttle him in his sleep. Stinker was nine, but he'd already managed to pack a lot of achievements into his life. His fame, or rather infamy, preceded him.

"I came to have a look," Stinker said. "Are you going to throw me out?"

"Look," Wolf said, "if you're really interested."

Stinker stared at the wall. Grasshopper and Wolf stared at him. Stinker was small and ugly looking, with incongruously big ears and round eyes. His pink shirt sported greasy stains. Grasshopper had never seen such dirty hands. Still, it was nice of the wheeler to have come all the way here to look at their wall.

"Like it?" Grasshopper asked.

Stinker turned away from the wall.

"Dunno. Maybe I do. And maybe I don't. Are you a separate pack now? With your own separate room?"

He knows already, Grasshopper thought with surprise.

"We're not a pack," Wolf said. "We are Poxy Sissies. We spread disease. If someone asks, you tell them that."

"Oooh!" Stinker's large eyes lit up with excitement. He now resembled an owl out to hunt. "That's a good one. I'll remember that." He looked around. "You are only using five beds. Sort of too few of you for this whole room."

"So? Quite enough for disease-spreading."

"That's true." Stinker picked bashfully at his dirty hand. "Here's what I thought . . . Could you maybe use one more Poxy Sissy? I'd volunteer. I can spread disease too. I'm really good at that."

Grasshopper looked at Wolf. Wolf looked at Grasshopper.

He's going to agree, Grasshopper thought, horrified. *He might not know what Stinker is. They held him in the Sepulcher for too long.*

But it looked like Wolf did know.

"We don't need anyone else," he said.

Apparently this was the answer Stinker expected. But he continued to stare at Grasshopper. His round owlish eyes were too big. They seemed boundless if you looked into them for a while. They glowed with a strange inner light, drawing you in, like a sky bristling with stars. Grasshopper looked for a bit longer than was safe.

"You can come," his unwieldy lips said by themselves. "If you want to."

Stinker blinked, and the glow of the faraway stars was extinguished. He wiped the nose with the back of his dirty hand. Then sniffled and exposed the picket fence of his sharpish teeth.

"I'll just go grab my things. Won't be a minute."

He turned around and rolled out. Surprisingly quickly. The door slammed behind him. His victory song filled the hallway. Grasshopper took a step backward, staggered, and sat on his bed.

"What have I just done?" he said.

"Oh, nothing much," Wolf said, still looking at the door. "Only invited the most famous dirtbag in the House to live with us."

Grasshopper was ready to cry.

"Wolf. I swear, I didn't want to. I don't know what happened. He was looking and looking, and I said . . ."

"It's all right. Don't worry." Wolf sat down next to him. "When he comes back we'll just tell him we changed our minds. By a majority of votes. I never agreed to anything, after all."

Grasshopper buried his face in the pillow. He felt awful. This most horrible, nasty person, the nastiest ever, and he'd invited him here, into his home, his very own room. It was like he wanted to spoil everything.

The noise of many returning feet rolled down the corridor, gradually subsiding as their owners filed into the rooms. The Stuffage Pack thundered by, roaring, banging on their door as they ran. Then Humpback entered, with a big packet of food. Blind came next, carrying two bottles of milk. Beauty timidly brought up the rear, and his hands were empty.

"We got hot dogs," Humpback started brightly, then stumbled. "What happened? Why are you sitting all miserable like that?"

"Stinker the wheeler's just been here," Wolf explained. "And Grasshopper said he could move in with us. It just happened. He didn't want to."

"Stinker?!" Humpback and Blind exclaimed in unison.

Grasshopper stood looking down at the floor.

"We could say it was a joke," Humpback suggested. "Say that Grasshopper was joking. You were joking, weren't you?"

Grasshopper was doing his best to fight back tears.

"We'll think of something," Wolf said uncertainly. "Maybe he was joking himself. Maybe he wouldn't come anyway. This has never happened, for a wheeler to join the walkers. We'd just say we said it by accident. Whatever. Just to make him go away."

Beauty was looking forlornly up at the ceiling. At his lightbulb. Or, rather, at his lampshade.

They sat in silence for a while. The food was going stale on the floor. Grasshopper, with his eyes closed, was picturing Stinker. How he was packing his things. Opening all of his secret places in front of everybody. Telling the other wheelers that he was moving to the colorful room. And they were laughing at him, not believing him. "Who needs you there?" they would say. "The walkers were joking." And Stinker would continue to pack.

Grasshopper imagined this so vividly it almost knocked the breath out of him. He opened his eyes.

"No," he said. "I can't do this. I told him he could come. He knows it's not a joke. He'll run here with all of his stuff . . ."

Grasshopper went silent. There was something in his throat that wasn't letting him continue. He buried his face in his knees, and the knees immediately became wet.

"Hey. Stop this," Wolf said. "We are going to talk to him ourselves. What's come over you?"

Humpback sniffled loudly into his clenched fist. Grasshopper lifted up his face, tears streaming down, and looked at Wolf.

"You are going to talk to him and throw him out. And I'm going to sit silently and pretend it has nothing to do with me? He believed me. Me, not you. And now it turns out my word means nothing. What does that make me?"

Wolf looked away.

"Let's do it the way he wants," Blind said. "Let him keep his word. Just don't let him cry. By the way, this Stinker guy, is he heavy like a tank?"

Grasshopper didn't have enough time to be surprised by Blind's words. They all heard the strange grinding noise and jumped up together. The door flew open. There was a trunk looming behind it.

"Help!" came the voice from the other side. "I can't push it in alone!"

Wolf and Humpback hauled in the trunk. They had to turn it lengthwise. It was followed by Stinker, hugging a bloated backpack and clad in a parka. A striped knit hat with a pom-pom on top crowned his head.

"Here! I brought you all this," he proclaimed. "Look . . ."

Then Stinker saw Grasshopper's tearstained face and went red. Very slowly, from the tips of his enormous ears down.

"Oh," he said and pulled off the multicolored hat. "Oh. I see."

"You see what?" Wolf said gruffly. "Squeeze in and close the door. Or the entire Stuffage is going to be here any minute."

Humpback went around the trunk and knocked on it.

"What do you have here? A matching furniture set?"

Beauty peeked inside.

"Oh wow. There's like a bulldozer in there," he said.

"That's not a bulldozer! It's a juice maker," Stinker said, visibly hurt. "I made it myself. A very useful appliance to have around."

Grasshopper wiped his runny nose on his knee and smiled.

"What about this?" Humpback fished out a scary-looking steel contraption.

"A bear trap," Stinker said proudly. "My own design as well."

"Also a useful appliance to have around," Blind said acidly.

Wolf and Humpback were diving inside the trunk, producing more and more stuff. Beauty was afraid to touch any of it, lest he break something. Blind examined everything with his fingers before setting it down on the floor. Stinker was providing a running commentary.

"Kettle. Photographic trays. Tool set. Stuffed horned viper. Portable coatrack. Guitar . . ."

"Wait," Wolf interrupted. "You can play guitar?"

Stinker scratched himself and looked at the ceiling.

"Not really, no."

"Why do you have it, then?"

"It was a parting gift. From former roommates."

"Ah. You mean you took all you could. Was there anything left at all?"

Stinker sighed.

"Nightstands. And beds, too."

He stared at the floor with a guilty look on his face. Grasshopper and Humpback laughed.

"I see," Wolf said. "So in the morning they're going to come for the trunk."

"No, they won't," Stinker said firmly. "They wouldn't dare. I warned them that I'd move right back if they tried."

Humpback slipped on the bear trap and landed in the salad bowl. Grasshopper doubled over on the bed.

"Hey! Hey," Wolf said. "I'm not allowed to laugh like that!"

Then all was hysterics and moans. Even Blind was laughing. Stinker squeaked loudest of all.

"Move right back! Blackmailer! Former roommate!"

"You haven't seen all of it!" Stinker yelled. "There's still a lot left!"

They yelped, shaking the beds with their laughter.

Suddenly Wolf straightened up and said, "Shhh! Hear that?"

They stopped and listened to silence. The silence of Stuffage listening intently to them laughing.

Stinker couldn't play guitar, but he could play the harmonica. He knew nineteen songs, happy as well as sad, and he played them all. And the trunk did contain a lot more fun stuff. For example, a jumbled mass of wires in which Humpback managed to entangle himself.

"Security system," Stinker explained. "With alarm."

"Great," Wolf said. "Certainly useful to have around. For us I'd say even indispensable. Let's connect it."

The door was soon crisscrossed by wires so thickly it was scary to look at. Then it turned out that the alarm didn't work.

"No problem," Stinker said. "Probably a break in the current somewhere. I'll have a look later."

Grasshopper took Stinker's failures personally. But the security system was so far the only major setback. The trap definitely worked. They found out when Blind stepped in it. The juice maker worked too. They installed the coatrack in the corner, where it accepted the weight of two jackets and one backpack. Stinker was knocking himself out making a good impression. He didn't miss any opportunity to show that he was capable of doing everything by himself, and to prove it, he would flop out of the wheelchair and crawl briskly around the room. He demonstrated his skills at climbing on the bed and back into the wheelchair, and even attempted to scale the windowsill, but crashed down halfway. He rubbed the mark on his chin, and his eyes looking at Grasshopper seemed to say: *Can you see how hard I'm trying?*

Wolf went to his bed with the guitar and tried to play it, without much success. Beauty sat mesmerized before the juice maker, regarding his own reflection in its shiny sides. Blind was listening to Stuffage, sitting by the wall with his injured leg held aloft.

When Stinker finally wheeled off to the bathroom, assuring everybody and everything that he needed absolutely no help with "things like that," Humpback said to Wolf, "This Stinker is not a bad guy at all. Why is everyone picking on him? They all say there's no one nastier in the whole House. And he's really nice."

"Yeah," Wolf said, "he's fine. A cute little baby who's a bit into blackmail. Caught Blind in a trap, fell down from the window, and by a complete coincidence gobbled four of our hot dogs."

"He was hungry," Grasshopper interjected. "He didn't go to lunch."

"I didn't either," Wolf sighed. "On the other hand, if no one comes here to claim this guitar by tomorrow, I'll personally feed him two more lunches."

Grasshopper exhaled. *It's lucky that Stinker thought of grabbing that guitar,* he thought. *And it will be lucky if they don't come for it.*

"I wish I had an orange," said Beauty plaintively. "Or a lemon. Something squeezable."

He gingerly touched the switch on the juicer and jerked his hand back. He was very afraid of breaking it. Everything he touched broke, for some reason.

"Sportsman is having a fight with Siamese," Blind said. "They stole his magazine with the naked ladies."

"That's sad," Wolf said. "The moral fiber of that boy leaves much to be desired. You are a regular listening device, Blind. Do they know about Stinker yet?"

Blind shook his hair.

"No. But they did hear the harmonica."

Stinker came back. He parked by the door and started fiddling with the wires, whistling a tune softly.

"Where can I get an orange?" Beauty asked. "Anybody?"

"Where can I get a guitar tutorial?" Wolf said. "You guys think Elk might have one?"

The piercing wail of the alarm shook them all badly. Beauty pressed his hands against his ears. The alarm raged on for two minutes, then silence returned.

"It's working," Stinker said happily, staring with his shameless round eyes.

Leaving for breakfast the next morning, they left the security system armed and also installed the disguised trap by the door.

"Maybe we'll find someone in it when we get back," Humpback said.

The presence of Stinker at their table caused a furor in the canteen. Sportsman pointedly got up and went to sit farther away. His pack followed. The long junior table now had a neutral zone in the middle. Even seniors noticed it.

"Look, the squirts are splitting up," Boar, one of the seniors, said.

"The little shits are growing," Lame replied dismissively. "Into big shits. Just like us."

The juniors overheard this exchange, straightened proudly, and blushed. *The seniors just compared us to themselves!*

The wheelers were regarding Stinker sulkily. But he happily absorbed the attention, all the while creating a pigsty around his plate.

On the way back to the room, Grasshopper stopped before the message board. *Separated at Birth.* Showing this evening. Both parts. So there wouldn't be anybody in the Tenth except Ancient. Grasshopper ran to catch up with the rest of them.

Stinker asked permission to draw something on the wall. Wolf dug out the cans of paint and showed him an empty corner. Stinker labored long and hard.

He first drew everything in pencil, then used paint—there was nary a peep from his corner all the way till lunch, save for doleful sighs and scratching, representing the throes of inspiration.

Wolf managed to procure the guitar tutorial. He was studying it very closely, but to Grasshopper it looked like he couldn't quite concentrate on what was before him. Beauty had wheedled an orange from someone and was now sitting in front of the juicer, not daring to switch it on. Grasshopper and Humpback had mounted a typewriter on the nightstand—another gift of the trunk, which no one except Grasshopper took any interest in. Grasshopper realized immediately that this was something he really needed. Hitting a lettered key with the finger of his prosthetic was much easier than trying to draw that same letter so that someone else could guess which one it was. Pens always slipped out of the artificial fingers, and the letters came out all angular and broken. When Grasshopper saw the typewriter, he perked up and asked for it to be placed on his nightstand.

While Humpback was busy feeding paper into it and typing whatever came into his mind, Grasshopper was imagining how he'd write a letter to Death and Ginger and drop it in the hospital mailbox—there was an actual box on the door to the hospital wing.

Stuffage sounded even rowdier than usual.

"Are they planning to attack us?" Humpback said.

"Or already attacking each other," Grasshopper suggested.

Humpback rattled out the word *attack*.

"Or maybe this is the sound of Sportsman's empire crumbling," Wolf said. "And we are soon going to be hit by its splinters."

Somebody scratched softly at the door.

"See what I mean?" Wolf said. "The splinters are flying."

Beauty quickly hid the orange behind his back.

"Could be someone coming for the trunk," Blind said.

But it was, in fact, Magician. Sad little Magician in a striped shirt, with a crutch under one arm and a sack of clothes under the other.

"Hello," he said. "Can I come in?"

He looked like someone who'd narrowly escaped some catastrophe.

"Did something really blow up there?" Humpback asked, alarmed.

"They let you go?" Grasshopper said incredulously. "I thought they never would."

"Two newbies arrived at once," Magician explained bashfully. "So I grabbed my stuff and got out. They have other things to worry about now, and I always wanted to move in with you. Can I please stay here?"

He briefly looked at the wall.

"Did you bring anything useful?" Stinker inquired.

"He can do magic tricks," Grasshopper said quickly. "With cards and with a handkerchief. And with everything."

"You're in. Choose a bed," Wolf said. "Who are the newbies?"

Magician marched to an empty bed, thumping his crutch, and put his things on it.

"One is normal," he said. "And the other is scary. He's got this spot. Like someone poured chocolate on him. Almost his entire face." Magician pressed a hand to his own face. "Oh, wow, a guitar!" he exclaimed and put the hand down, mesmerized by the instrument on Wolf's pillow. "Where did you get it?"

"Can you play?" Wolf said quickly.

Magician nodded. He couldn't pry his eyes off it.

"We're in luck," Wolf said. "I was going crazy with this tutorial. Come on, play something."

Magician thumped over to his bed. Wolf shifted to make space for him.

While Magician was getting comfortable with the guitar, he also cleared his throat significantly, as if he was about to sing.

"'A Taste of Honey,'" he announced.

Grasshopper recalled that he always announced his magic tricks in the same artificial kind of voice.

Magician started playing, and indeed also singing, even though no one had asked him to. He must have decided to showcase all of his talents at once. He had a high-pitched, piercing voice, and he pulled off both playing and singing with confidence. It was obvious that he was really good at both, and that this voice was not an impediment for him. Everyone clustered around, except Stinker, who was still busy with his drawing.

Magician was wailing in his tragic falsetto, swaying back and forth over the guitar, singing along with the licks, *pa-dam, pa-dam*, shaking his bangs, and staring distractedly at the wall. By the end of the song his voice was hoarse, and he had tears in his eyes. The next song he played without singing or announcing its title. The third one he dubbed "Tango of Death," and in it he bungled the melody once. Magician's songs made Grasshopper sad, and not only him but the others too, apparently.

"I can also play the violin," Magician said after dispatching "Tango of Death." He added, "And trumpet. And also accordion, a little bit."

"When did you manage all this?" Wolf said, surprised.

Magician twanged a string a couple of times.

"I just did. Just like that."

Suddenly his sharp face lost the veneer of self-satisfaction and twisted in a grimace. He turned away.

He must be remembering something from the Outsides, Grasshopper thought. *Something good that happened to him there.*

"Do the trick with the handkerchief," Grasshopper said. "You know, your best one."

Magician started digging through his pockets.

"It doesn't work every time," he warned. "I really should be practicing more."

Stinker wheeled away from the wall and regarded Magician with interest. Behind his back, in the corner that had been assigned to him, something creepy was now visible, with a flattened nose and bugged-out eyes, and covered in spots. Everyone turned to the something and forgot all about the magic tricks. Even Magician quit his search for the handkerchief.

"What is that thing?" Wolf asked, horrified. "What were you trying to make?"

"It's a goblin," Stinker explained smugly. "Life-sized. Isn't he pretty?"

"Yep," Humpback said. "So pretty we'd better cover him up."

Stinker took this as a compliment.

"No, really?" he said. "Is it heart-stopping?"

"Certainly is," Humpback confirmed. "Especially if someone wanders into that corner at night with a flashlight. That'll stop it for sure."

Stinker giggled.

"Can you show me how to make juice?" Beauty said and handed him the orange.

Stinker grabbed it and peeled it in a flash. Divided it into sections and stuffed them in his mouth. He then explained to a stunned Beauty, "Not enough for juicing. Much better to just eat it." He generously handed Beauty the last sloppy, half-squashed section and said, "Here. Have this. It's good for you. Vitamin C and all."

SMOKER

ON MUTUAL UNDERSTANDING
BETWEEN BLACK SHEEP

Silence. And the smells of dust and mold. That's what the Crossroads is at night. I was sitting beside the barrel where something raggedy and moribund was trying to grow, touching this skeleton of a plant and reading the messages. They covered the barrel from top to bottom. Boar, Poplar, Nail . . . All unfamiliar nicks. The darkened letters looked like old carvings, partially obliterated. But some things were still legible.

Crossroads was illuminated by two wall fixtures. One with a purple shade, in the corner with the TV set. The other, with a cracked blue glass cover, over the low, battered armchair by the opposite wall. The central space between them, containing the sofa, the withered plants, and myself, was shrouded in darkness. I almost had to read with my fingers, the way Blind did. Or sometimes with the help of a lighter. A rather pointless pursuit, but still better than nothing.

THE COELACANTHS ARE EXTINCT, BUT NOT REALLY, a message declared cryptically. Next to it, one Saurus intimated: FOLLOWING THE PATH OF THE COYOTE. Exactly where, he did not elaborate. To extinction, probably. Below it was a poem dedicated to a girl. AND TO YOUR LEGS, AND TO YOUR ARMS, AND RUMPTY-TUMPTY-TUMPTY-TUM . . . The poem was incredibly clunky, and obviously had in mind some specific girl. Otherwise the author wouldn't have mentioned her "piebald curls." I wasn't sure what "piebald" meant exactly, but applied to hair it definitely wasn't a color worthy of poetic praise.

We didn't have much contact with the girls. None, as a matter of fact. Even though their wing was connected to ours by a common stairway. As far as I knew, no one ever used it to go up to them. They occupied the third floor; the second was taken up by the sick bay, and I had no idea what was there on the first. Probably that mysterious swimming pool with its eternal renovations. The only time we ran into them was on Saturdays, during movie nights. They sat separately and never joined in any of our conversations. In the yard they always kept to their own porch. I didn't know where all those strict rules came from, but obviously not from the principal's office. Or they would have been broken. Which they weren't.

The other section of the poem related the story of some records being given to someone. And of a book THAT YOU HAVE SO GRACEFULLY DROPPED ON MY HEAD, WITH NARY A SHRUG OF YOUR SHOULDERS . . . The only place where one could drop a book on someone's head would be in the library, standing on a stepladder. And girls never went to the common library.

The more I thought about this, the more intrigued I became. I remembered an episode that I'd witnessed in the yard once, in my very first month of being here.

Beauty, from the Third, and a wheeler girl, whose nick I didn't know, were playing with a ball. This must have been the weirdest game I'd ever seen. The petite, dark-haired girl, with a little face as white as a china cup, threw a tennis ball down from the porch. Then, by miracle (with the role of the slightly clumsy miracle performed by Beauty), the ball would find itself back on the porch. Actually, Beauty missed more often than not. Then the girl had to wheel down and search for her toy in the bushes. In over half an hour, Beauty managed to throw it accurately, so it landed at her feet, only four times, and I'm not sure those weren't just accidents. But each time she would smile. It certainly seemed that she was smiling at her own happy thoughts, because neither she nor Beauty ever looked at each other. Only at the ball. Watched it appear in front of them, time after time, as if from some other dimension. The girl was much better at it. Beauty kept losing his concentration and trying to trace the ball outside of his territory, but the girl . . . I could have shot a gorgeous short film starring her: *The Girl and the Ball: Playing with Shadows*. I was mesmerized by this spectacle. I didn't realize that I was watching two lovers, and that this game was the closest they could allow themselves to be to each other. Back then I just figured that they didn't know each other too well and were a bit embarrassed about it.

I was thinking about that time when Black appeared. Sleepy, surly, in a pajama top and untied sneakers. He'd put them on like slippers, flattening the backs. He approached, limping visibly, and inquired if I knew what time it was.

I didn't. Like every other inhabitant of the Fourth I no longer had a watch. I mean, actually I did. Buried deep in the bottom of my bag.

"Quarter to midnight," Black said. "The hallway lights are going to be out soon, and I doubt you thought to bring a flashlight along. You are going to get personally acquainted with every wall on your way back."

"I was reading this poem," I said, pointing at the barrel. "Very unusual. It's about this girl. Can't figure out who wrote it. Can you believe it, it says that she was dropping on him—that is, on the guy writing all this—some books, and also giving him records. Who could that possibly be? Do you know?"

Black glanced briefly at the barrel.

"It's old stuff, from six years ago," he said indifferently. "They graduated. Can't you see, it's all blackened and stuff."

"Oh! I see! Boar, Poplar, Saurus—they're all from the previous class." I was a little disappointed in the mystery being resolved in such a mundane fashion. "So that's why I couldn't find a single familiar nick."

"I think you managed to dig up just about the only place where their scribblings are still visible. Beats me how you found it," Black grumbled, lowering himself onto the sofa. His face contorted as he did it, and he gingerly straightened his leg once seated.

"It was so quiet in the dorm. It felt . . . different. Alien, somehow. You were asleep, and anything I touched made an awful racket for some reason," I said, trying to explain why I'd scrambled out of there.

"Yeah." Black shrugged. "You think I don't understand? I woke up and it's, like, all dark and silent. Like I was in a coffin. I could hear my own heart beating. All I could do not to scream."

I had a really tough time imagining Black screaming because he was scared. So I laughed.

"Really," Black said. "You don't believe me?"

He took a pack of Lucky Strikes out of his pocket and lit up. I was completely floored. I was sure he didn't smoke.

"I don't, usually," Black said. "Only when the day is particularly shitty. Like today."

He smoked in silence and with great concentration. Like everything he did: eating, drinking, reading . . . Every action he performed possessed this thoroughness, as if announcing to the world: "Now this is how it's supposed to be done." Probably that was why no one ever interrupted him while he was doing something. When he found himself in need of an ashtray, Black rummaged under the sofa with the same absorbed look on his face and hauled out a flat copper saucer in the shape of a maple leaf. The old-timers would do magic tricks like that sometimes, producing unexpected objects out of the most unlikely places.

"Listen," he said, installing the leaf on the sofa's arm, "I wanted to ask you something. How come you stayed? Why didn't you go with them?"

I paused. It was not an easy thing to explain. In all honesty, I didn't want to leave Black alone. After his conversation with Sphinx in the morning, when I saw the way they looked at him, or rather, avoided looking at him . . . It all had this horribly familiar feel. Familiar and unpleasant.

"I'm not sure," I said. "I guess I'm still too much of a Pheasant. I can't even imagine how this could work—turning up at the hospital wing, at night, without permission, carrying supplies. For me that would be the same as, I don't know, busting into

Shark's office and stealing his fire extinguisher. I thought I would be out of place there. And it's not because I'm scared. I just don't see the point."

Black nodded.

"I get it. It's the same with me. I wouldn't have gone even if this whole thing with Noble hadn't happened. In times like this someone has to stay back and secure the base."

It seemed that, despite the approaching lights out, Black wasn't in any hurry to leave. He was, if anything, open for a discussion. Or maybe it was just that his leg hurt and he was simply resting it. I decided to go for it and clear up some things that had been bothering me ever since that talk with Sphinx.

"I'm sorry if this is not a comfortable topic," I said, "but why is it that Sphinx dislikes you so much?"

Black choked on the smoke.

"Sorry!" I repeated hurriedly. "It's just that the impression I got—"

"It's not an impression," he interrupted. "And that's a mild way of putting it. It's not just that he doesn't like me. He hates me. But generally that wouldn't be any of your business, agreed?"

"Sorry," I mumbled again. "Of course it isn't."

Black disgustedly crushed the cigarette stub against the ashtray.

"When Sphinx first got to the House, I did kick him around. It's been nine years already, but he never forgot. Good memory, for that kind of thing. He's so cool and tough now, but back then he was a spoiled mama's darling. Crying into his pillow every night, tailing Blind's every step. You know, everybody's little pet. All of them fussing around him, wiping the snot off his nose."

I remembered the photo out of the *Moby-Dick*. Where I couldn't find Sphinx. Maybe he hadn't arrived at the House yet. Or maybe he was somewhere else, crying into his pillow, as Black put it.

"So," Black said, shoving the ashtray back under the sofa. He bumped into something there, pulled out a pink rubber bunny, and stared at it in apparent surprise. "What was I talking about? Oh, right. It's a long story. Everything was fine until he came in. And then it all went screwy. First he wanted a separate room. Then he wanted separate friends. And whatever he wanted, he always got. Half of my pack defected into that damn room of his. All drawn in by his pretty smile."

Black was fiddling with the rubber bunny, regarding it thoughtfully, as if he was in fact seeing something else there in front of him.

"And ever since that time we kind of can't stand each other. Silly, I know. I bet you're thinking right now, 'This is nonsense, those grown-up guys still nursing their childish grudges.' Well, these grudges keep getting reinforced. A lot of other things get added in. And they keep adding. Like this one, with Noble. Sphinx makes it look like

I doomed him to something horrible. When in fact all I did was save him. But would anybody say it like it is? Of course not, how could they? There is only one truth, and Sphinx is the one telling it. He's the smartest here, and we're all like nothing before him."

"He certainly has charm," I offered carefully.

"You should have seen him when he was nine," Black chortled. "The shining light of the House. One smile and swoons all around. It's not the same now. He's been cranky lately. But he's still got it, no question. So I'm surprised you haven't dashed off after him to the Sepulcher, trailing smoke. Usually that's more or less the effect he has on people."

It wasn't a pleasant experience, listening to what Black was saying, but in some sense I'd brought it on myself. And maybe, just maybe, there was a grain of truth in all of this.

"Are they going to take Noble away now?" I asked, in a clumsy attempt to change the subject.

Black was wiping dust off the bunny and didn't even look in my direction.

"Probably. I wouldn't be so hung up about this. But for the guys in here, there's nothing worse in the whole world. For them, there's no life in the Outsides. As for me, I'm counting down the days until graduation. I guess I'm a black sheep in that regard."

Being a seasoned and much-persecuted black sheep in my own right, I nodded understandingly. Now I knew what made Black different from the others.

"I understand," I said. "That's how it was with me too, the last half year."

"And that's why I find you easy to talk to," Black said.

I nodded again. We were silent for a while. This mute understanding was growing between us, and we were afraid words might spook it. It's not that I considered Black to be right about everything. But I had to admit that talking to him was indeed much easier than talking to Sphinx or Humpback.

"Noble is not well," Black said suddenly, apparently trying to get everything that was bothering him out in the open. "Tried to kill himself a couple years ago. Once, twice . . . Sphinx got to him. With his drills, like a sergeant. Amazing how he's crawling around now, right? Well, you should have seen the way Sphinx was driving him. Followed him one step behind, and as soon as Noble stopped he'd step on his legs. So Noble was in turns crawling and yelping. Crying and still crawling. A sickening sight. And Sphinx kept following and stepping on him."

I had to close my eyes when I imagined what he was talking about.

"Black, stop it," I said. "This is too much."

"Sure," Black said. "It's better not to know. To continue thinking that Sphinx is this sweet guy. Very helpful, if you want to blend in."

I let that pass. I was still trying to come to terms with the image of sadistic Sphinx trampling someone's legs with a beatific smile on his face. I had a hard time even imagining this. But at the same time I realized that Black wasn't lying, and this contradiction was driving me crazy.

"Black, I'm sorry," I said finally. "I didn't want to interrupt. I guess I am better off knowing things like that, at least to . . . to better understand what's what. But I need some time to adjust. To absorb the information."

"I'm fine with that," Black replied. "I didn't tell you all this so that you start avoiding Sphinx from now on. That's not the point. The point is that Noble is nuts. He's sick. Always has been. Even before Sphinx added to it. He needs treatment. So when Sphinx goes all righteous on me, telling me that I, wouldn't you know, behaved despicably, I want to just laugh it off. But when six other people, who, by the way, all witnessed everything I've told you about, when those six all agree with him, that's no longer funny. Make sense?"

"Yeah."

Black took out another cigarette.

"Just wanted, you know, for at least one person in this damned zoo to understand. Just one."

He lit up. I saw that his knuckles were scraped, and his hands trembled so much that he couldn't quite connect the end of the cigarette with the lighter's flame.

I was sitting there, stunned, torn between anger and pity. I understood him. I understood him all too well. But I didn't want to. Because it meant becoming a black sheep again. Only this time there'd be two of us. And I so wished to become a full-fledged member of the pack. To be with them, to be one of them.

"I understand you. I do. I'm sorry if it doesn't look that way from the outside."

"No, I'm sorry. I guess I shouldn't have dumped all of this on you."

But he was obviously glad I'd said that. And I realized that this was it. There was no going back. I chose Black.

I was trying to convince myself that maybe this wasn't quite the end of the world when Black finished his cigarette, tossed the butt over the back of the sofa, and got up, favoring his aching leg.

"Let's roll," he said. "Now we're definitely not going to make it before it's dark."

He stuffed the pink bunny into his pocket.

We didn't make it even as far as the Second when the lights went out. They blinked twice, and then it was dark. I'd been forewarned and prepared, but still I startled. Black was right: if I were to find myself alone in this inky blackness, I'd just be stuck wherever I was when it came. But Black did have a flashlight. Now I was holding it, and he was pushing the wheelchair.

I was still digesting our conversation and must have been doing a lousy job of lighting our way, because at some point Black stopped and told me to point the flashlight straight ahead. I apologized and raised it higher.

The murals on the walls looked different. They loomed out of the darkness in fragments, most of them unfamiliar, even those that I passed several times each day. And when faced with the White Bull I simply gasped in astonishment. Black understood and stopped, giving me the opportunity to fully illuminate the drawing.

The Bull was swaying forlornly on its slender stick legs, watching us with its human eyes and thinking about something sad. It was the most amazing bull in the whole world. It was drawn in an affectedly primitive, childish manner, and its expressiveness went straight for the heart.

"Look at it," I whispered.

Black stepped forward and scraped the wall where it had started peeling, costing the bull half a horn.

"It's coming off. Vulture tried putting clear varnish on top, that's why it looks dull now."

The image of Vulture as a custodian of wall art was such an incongruous one that I could only mutter something indistinct. The House was a strange place indeed, and every day brought me new evidence of this.

"Who painted this?"

Black looked at me funny.

"Leopard, who else? Oh yeah, I keep forgetting you haven't been here that long. You can't mistake his drawings for anyone else's." He thought for a while, then added, "Leopard was Leader of the Second. Some three years ago. Red's third after him."

He seemed to force that last bit out of himself, but I got the impression that the details would have been forthcoming if I started asking questions. It was strange but refreshing knowledge: that my every question would be answered concisely and exhaustively. With no equivocating, clowning around, references to Pheasants, or long discourses about the Ways of the House. I immediately decided not to abuse this, and to begin by not digging further into the topic of Leopard's disappearance. Especially since Black's tone of voice very strongly hinted at the answer.

"There are others," Black continued as we went along. "Other drawings. They're almost all around the Third now. There were even more near the Second, but those were all painted over. Still, *Bull* is the best. I took a couple of shots using a flash, but they didn't work out that well. I should try again. There's been this talk about repainting the walls for some time now. Then it'd be gone forever."

At the door, Black fumbled in his pockets and produced a key. This was the first time I saw our dorm locked, and it sharply drove home the fact that Black and I were indeed alone. Black was fiddling with the balky lock and I was illuminating the door. All along the door's edge the wall was covered with the repetition of the letter *R*. The pattern almost dissolved into a meaningless ornament, but it was still composed of that letter. I remembered that I'd seen it on the walls quite often.

"What does the letter *R* mean?" I asked.

"That's our counselor," Black said. "Ralph. He had both us and the Third."

I'd never heard of a counselor named Ralph, so I assumed that he was no longer alive either. Like Leopard the wall painter. The House was filling up with corpses at an alarming rate in response to my every question. Even if it concerned something that might initially appear entirely innocent.

"Is he dead?" I said, expecting confirmation.

"No."

Black pushed me in the door and clicked the wall switch, but the light in the anteroom did not come on. He swore, went a bit farther, and switched on the light inside the dorm. Coming back, he tripped over something and swore again.

"Filthy thing!" he was saying when I wheeled in, shielding my eyes from the bright light. "Slipped in, the dirty bitch!"

"What?"

"A rat, that's what! Another one!" Black was peering under the common bed, in a demonstrably hopeless attempt to discern something there. "What do you think I tripped over just now?"

"Could be anything . . ."

"There are no anythings when your Leader's blind." Black straightened up, moaned, and rubbed his leg. "When was the last time you saw something thrown on the floor here? I can tell you that the last thing Blind ever tripped over was Lary's boots. Ever since that time the boots spend each night with Lary, on his bunk."

I giggled. Black shot me a disapproving look.

"You're one weird guy," he said. "This isn't funny at all."

He helped me climb on the bed and put the kettle on. I cleared up the strata left by Tabaqui—he seemed to regard the trip to the Sepulcher as kind of a night out, and the garments he had tried on and discarded were left covering the bed in an untidy mound. I then made myself more comfortable and asked Black where did Ralph the counselor go and why were his initials such a popular motif among the wall artists. In all honesty, I didn't care much about all this, and was asking only to rinse out the unpleasant sediment that was brought up by the conversation concerning Sphinx. I was afraid Black might return back to that. But Black wasn't in the mood to discuss counselors.

"He left," he said tersely. "About six months ago. Packed his stuff one day and hightailed it out of here. I have no idea why they still write and paint his nick. Could be someone misses him."

Black's face showed quite clearly that if anyone did miss this mysterious R, it definitely wasn't him.

"I see," I mumbled thoughtfully.

Black sat down across from me and arranged the cups, the teapot, and a pack of cookies on the tray. I crawled closer. He passed me the cup and turned on the player. Good thing, too. Without music our tea party would have been too gloomy. Even with music it was pretty sad.

I had a strange dream that night. I saw myself in the second-floor hallway. It looked the same as it always did, except it was divided down the middle by this thick plate of glass, all the way from the floor to the ceiling. There were people on the other side. Indistinct figures floated there, like fish in a bowl, bumping into the glass and pressing their faces against it. I saw a pale guy wearing sunglasses, with hair as white as snow, a girl with very long braids, and an ugly, dark-faced creature flying around in a wheelchair. There were a lot of them, and all of them wanted to get in. Some had translucent wings. Their side also had light fixtures on the walls, but theirs looked somehow different: they glowed green, almost emerald, like giant fireflies. I was observing all this from the door to our dorm.

Then Noble pushed my wheelchair aside, walked out of the room, and threw a crystal ball at the wall. The ball hit the wall and bounced off, making a long crack in it, reaching all the way down. Noble walked into it, like between the folds of a transparent curtain, and the glass sealed itself behind him, becoming whole again. He waved to us and walked down the green firefly corridor. On his own legs. He wasn't floating or swimming, he just walked, and the strange winged shadows darted around him and returned back to the glass, to look at us and to try and say something to us, something that we couldn't hear.

There were whispers and commotion behind my back. Then Tabaqui and Blind hauled out this huge cauldron of boiling, bubbling liquid and splashed it at the glass. It made an ugly stain. The hissing, poisonous stain started spreading, growing in all directions, and shaped itself into a smeared letter *R*. The glass under it crackled, and all the creatures that were flying around on the other side crowded near it and started banging on the glass, while everyone on our side moved away from it, dragging me and my wheelchair with them, the crackling and hissing was becoming louder and louder . . .

I opened my eyes and immediately saw the reason for my waking up. The open window was flapping in the wind, and the glass in it rattled noisily. Black, who apparently woke up at the same time as I did, climbed up, slammed it shut, and secured the handle. The wind was so strong that the glass still vibrated, only more softly. Black went back to bed, and I related my dream to him quickly before I forgot. When I finished, I realized that there had been no rush to tell it—it was still before my eyes as vividly as the moment I awoke. Black said that my dream was bullshit. He said it in a very annoyed voice, and I regretted keeping him up.

The next time it was Sphinx who woke us. I guess it was about half past five.

He kicked open the door and yelled, "Behold, a pale rider on a pale horse! Comes the cloud of locusts, and the dead are rattling their bones! Just look at this!" He ran to the window. "The fog is gray like the backs of gray mice! Hordes of mice are advancing! There is going to be no ground left soon, only the fog, clad in gray garments. It started stealing upon you in the night. Look now, before there is nothing to look at!"

Is he drunk? I thought, burying my head in the pillow. Sphinx abandoned his fog quest, mounted the headboard, weaving his legs between the bars, and stared at me. With his crazy eyes in dark circles. I chirpily inquired how Noble was doing.

"He's doing like Saint Francis's favorite chipmunk," Sphinx said and giggled.

"Sphinx. We are trying to sleep here," Black murmured.

"Sure, while the fog is creeping ever closer!"

"It can do all the creeping it wants."

"That what you think? All right. Don't say I didn't warn you."

Tabaqui unloaded himself on the bed, crawled over me, and commenced the construction of his nighttime nest. Humpback, with Nanette in tow, climbed up to his place. Alexander started the coffeemaker. Lary deposited Tubby in his pen, knocking over another bottle and bumping into the nightstand in the process.

"Oh god," Black moaned, putting the pillow over his head.

"Do not invoke His name in vain, you despicable person."

Sphinx stared at me for a while longer, shaking his head, then slid down on the bed and switched off, like a busted light. Tabaqui took special care to climb out of the nest and pull the blanket over him, then sniffed at him thoroughly and, apparently satisfied, crawled back into his pillows.

When the morning rituals began, two hours later, we weren't able to rouse Sphinx. He never acknowledged the gentle patting or calling him by name, and when someone tried to shake him he snarled that this someone was going to have his head bitten off, so Humpback decided to leave him alone.

The morning turned out lousy. It was gray and wet all the way through, like a slippery cap of some mushroom in the forest. On days like this all the door handles resist harder than usual, all food scratches the mouth, the early birds are disgustingly perky and are not letting anyone lounge in bed, while the night owls are miserable and snap at every other word. Sphinx, usually the first among the disgusting early birds, was out of commission for the time being, and so his role in terrorizing the inhabitants was taken up by Humpback, who jetted around like crazy, imitated a rooster, rang a handbell, tooted on his flute, poked the sleepers with chair legs, and dumped clothes on them.

Lary, moaning and groaning, dangled his feet in tattered socks from his bunk. Tabaqui was already chomping on something that was dripping all over the blanket.

Blind, in his acid-green shirt, was smoking in the open window. I dug deeper and deeper under the blanket, fully aware that I wouldn't be allowed to continue sleeping.

The boombox wailed "Oh! Darling" by The Beatles. Tabaqui was singing along in a falsetto voice, right in my ear. He even lifted the blanket to make sure he aimed correctly. It was useless. I crawled out.

While turning the wheelchair around by the window, I looked out. The wires of the fence weren't there. The houses and streets all had disappeared. It was completely quiet. Even Nanette's kin had scrambled somewhere. Blind turned his sharp face toward me. The mist in his gray eyes very much resembled the one outside the window.

"Backs of mice?" he said.

"Rather big blobs of cotton wool," I said. "Or maybe clouds."

At this he nodded and turned away.

At breakfast we were given boiled water to drink. It was supposed to ward off colds. Another one of the administration's pet ideas. There was no music after we came back, and no card playing. Everyone was catching up on more sleep. Now even the yard itself disappeared, and the gray clouds (or was it really backs of mice?) came up to the windows.

They brought Noble in after lunch.

"He's coming," Lary announced, bursting in with the clatter of a wild mustang. "And those . . . Shark and the others . . ."

The others turned out to be two livid-faced Cases and, surprisingly, Homer.

They wheeled Noble in, installed him on the bed, and clustered around. Noble was sleepy and grumpy, dressed in the hospital gown—one of those things that rob faces and bodies of individuality, making everyone look the same. Alexander took his clothes out of the closet. Noble was changing into them while the principal's retinue stood there and gawked.

"You are his comrades, you could have helped," Homer said.

"I can handle this," Noble said curtly, sliding into his jeans.

"Such a nervous boy," Homer said, aghast. "Nervous and abrupt."

"If only that was the worst of it," Shark replied, his eyes darting around the room, looking for traces of criminal behavior.

By some miracle we didn't even have a single ashtray out, so all his efforts were wasted.

"You have thirty minutes to pack," he said. "And none of your tricks. Leave nothing behind, you're not coming back here."

"Go fuck yourself," Noble said.

Homer's eyes rolled back in his head, and he seemingly stopped breathing. Tabaqui giggled. Shark swung around so fiercely that I shrunk back.

"One more peep out of any of you and you'll regret the day you were born," he hissed.

There were no more peeps out of anyone. Homer left, still unable to come to terms with the shock he'd just suffered, while Shark remained to observe Humpback and Alexander pack Noble's stuff. It all fit in two bags. One of the Cases took them away. Noble climbed in his wheelchair and looked at us. He hadn't uttered a single word during all of this, apart from what he'd said to Shark. And had he restrained himself, Shark might have given us the opportunity to say our good-byes in private. The other Case grabbed the handles of Noble's wheelchair, and, for some reason, Alexander placed Humpback's jacket on Noble's knees. It was a heavy leather jacket, originally black but currently black and white, because it was first worn out until it became white and then blackened back with dirt and soot. This monster, bedecked in badges and touched up with paint here and there, was dubbed "dinosaur skin." Tabaqui claimed that it was bulletproof. But Noble seemed delighted.

"Thanks," he said, looking at Humpback.

This was where the levee broke. The Case had to jump out of the way.

When Noble was wheeled out, he resembled a scarecrow. He had on Alexander's sweater, a veteran of many a general cleanup; Tabaqui's craziest vest; Lary's belt with the monkey-head buckle; Sphinx's fingerless glove on his left hand; and Blind's seashell on a string around his neck. Also there was Nanette's feather behind his ear and Tubby's bib in his pocket. I had nothing I could give him except cigarettes, so I gave him a pack, but then remembered about the amulet, the one allegedly containing basilisk eggshell, and handed it over to him as well.

No one went out to see Noble off.

THE HOUSE

The heat descended on the House, and with it came volleyball fever and vacations. The inhabitants of the House discarded it like a tired shell and hatched out into the sun—anyone who could walk or ride, yell and watch, and especially those who could run and hit the ball. The House was utilized for breakfast, lunch, dinner, and sleep, but the locus of the civic activity moved to the yard, where the opening of the volleyball season was proudly celebrated.

The court was bisected by the net and framed by the chairs and benches. Those had all been bristling with warning signs since early morning, and by the time breakfast was over there was nowhere to sit or escape from the sun. The elite spectator spots were shielded by a canopy. Everyone else had to make do with parasols.

The walking boys would rush to claim the crate seats right after breakfast. The Stuffage gang, the Singings from the Nesting, the unfortunates of the Cursed room. Sometimes fights broke out for the best spots. The junior wheelers came out later, together with seniors, secure in the knowledge that the counselors would take care of their seating arrangements. The walking weren't thus privileged, so they had to wage war for every crate. On the other hand, once the game began they were promptly shooed away, sent to bring water, lemonade, and cigarettes, only to find their places taken up when they returned. They then had to settle down directly on the dirt, but even there they had no respite from demands, since some-one soon was parched from shouting too much, another needed sunglasses to cover blinded eyes, and everybody was continually thirsty. For the walking juniors, the games consisted mostly of running errands. Surprisingly, they seemed to enjoy this. They enjoyed everything that had to do with the seniors' entertainment. The sun, the ball flying up to the heavens, the sunglasses on every face, and the general air of screaming insanity.

Poxy Sissies were the last to make their appearance in the yard. They therefore had to contend with the worst seats, in the very back, but that did not bother them in the slightest. They were hardly interested either in the game itself or in those seniors who flitted around the court accompanied by the fittest among the counselors. They had their own delights. Blind practiced discerning the fortunes of the teams based on the shouts from the crowd. Beauty gnawed on his fingers and dreamed of catching the ball if it happened to fly in their direction. Magician absorbed the applause and the catcalls, imagining himself on stage. Grasshopper studied the seniors.

The Moorists and the Skullers divided the yard in half. The watershed was represented by the counselors' seats in the middle under the canopy of honor. That was where Elk sat as well. "I'm too old for things like that," Elk told Grasshopper when asked why wasn't he playing too, like Splint and Black Ralph.

Moor's place was sacrosanct. The large multicolored umbrella dominated the landscape. Moor descended to the yard trailed by five attendants. The bodyguard, also wheelchair pusher. The girl with a flyswatter. The girl with the warm blanket. The girl with two thermal jugs. The bologna slicer. Moor settled under the umbrella. The girls positioned themselves on the chairs around it. Nail, the pusher-bodyguard, remained behind the wheelchair. The bologna slicer (a floating assignment) put down a mat by Moor's feet. This resembled nothing so much as a tribal elder's preparations for departure from his native village. Grasshopper always thought how much more fun it would be if someone were to sit next to them and bang a drum. And the girls could rattle something. Then the picture would have been complete.

Skull's people occupied the opposite end. There were no masters or servants there. Skull himself sat on a simple bench. Not in a hundred years would you suspect that he ruled this place, except everyone knew that he did.

When Grasshopper looked at him, Skull seemed to radiate an invisible halo. It was not apparent to the eye, but it separated him from the background, made him brighter. Like they do with light in old movies. And the fact that he was just sitting there, lost in the sea of mere mortals, only strengthened the effect. The sun beat down on him, but he became only more bronzed and handsome with each passing day. His skin did begin to peel, but only later, and you couldn't tell from a distance anyway.

Next to Skull, but under an umbrella, sat Lame. He was wearing his green blazer, and Babe the cockatoo was sitting on his shoulder. He wasn't paying much attention to the game, probably finding it not entertaining enough. Babe was watching for both of them, though, becoming very agitated and pulling feathers out of its own breast. On the third day there was a bald spot the size of a coin, and after a week it grew to the size of a hand. Grasshopper waited to see how this would end. Was the bird going completely naked, or was it planning to leave something? Babe stopped when it plucked its belly clean.

Ancient never went out into the yard. He couldn't stand direct sunlight. Witch was a frequent guest, though. Witch, Grasshopper's godmother, whose one glance could curse a person to the very end of his days. Witch always put on a wide-brimmed black hat so that out of her entire face only her mouth remained visible. And still people shunned her. Witch's occult powers made them nervous.

Grasshopper observed the seniors until the heat and the noise made him sleepy. Then he closed his eyes and sailed off, along with his crate and with Blind sitting next to him, into the blue sea. The yard became a beach, the spectators turned into quarrelsome seagulls, and then the ghost of the Other House took shape among the sand dunes and imaginary palm trees, took shape and became closer and closer every day.

Two weeks of the volleyball fever turned the denizens of the House into sun-burned savages. Even counselors took to wandering the hallways in T-shirts with lighthearted slogans. The principal, swept along by the general spirit of freedom, barricaded himself in his office and cut his phone cord. There was a feeling in the air of the upcoming exodus, which Grasshopper felt as all-enveloping edginess.

Then the day came when a modest sheet of paper appeared on the board, proclaiming the date of the departure, in exactly one week, and also warning about "one piece of luggage per person." The volleyball was immediately tossed aside. The announcement concerning the bag limit was made every year, and was therefore traditionally taken as a personal affront and an infringement of basic rights. Naturally, every infringement required pushback. And push back they did. The seniors acquired bags the size of trunks. The juniors had to improvise, sewing additional pockets and elastic bands to their old ones. The pockets held on tentatively, looked ugly, and didn't really add any capacity. Which is why both Stuffagers and Poxies spent their entire days packing and unpacking, in search of the precise formula for the contents of a bag before it finally burst at the seams.

This was a deeply engaging and tense activity. The boots were having their stiff fronts forcibly softened. The clothes got pieces hacked off with scissors. Everything that could not possibly be carried along was hidden and then relocated endlessly between secret places. The bags were sat on, in order to more thoroughly flatten everything that was already in them, because there were always more things that simply had to go inside. Elephant wanted to take his potted begonia. Beauty needed the juice maker; Wolf, the guitar; Humpback, the hamster; and all the useful appliances Stinker was declaring necessary just "for the road" wouldn't have fit in ten suitcases. Grasshopper wandered among the heaps of clothing strewn on the floor and commiserated with everybody in turns. He tried helping, but soon came to the conclusion that his own methods of packing did not suit anybody but himself. His handful of shirts, shorts, and socks added up to a meager pile that took barely half of his own bag, and he turned the rest over to Stinker and Humpback, who'd run out of space in theirs.

Blind did not pack. Once again, he wasn't going anywhere because Elk was staying at the House. The boys' laments dashed against his cold smirk.

Uneasy with his own idleness and bored by the commotion in the room, Grasshopper fled into the hallways, but the virus of insanity already had taken hold there too. New roller skates and recreational wheelchairs tested, rubber boats and mattresses inflated, and even tents pitched—a mystery, considering the certainty of having a roof over their heads where they were going.

The wall calendar slowly filled with fat crosses over the days that remained. Stuffagers walked around in diving masks and rubber fins.

Grasshopper would seek refuge in Elk's room, but Elk also had a wall calendar, and the counselors also had to prepare and pack, and the one-bag limit applied to them as well, and the hassle of their preparations spilled out into the corridors.

Grasshopper went down to the yard. Here he could sit in peace, with his back to the House, listening to the ocean in his head—the shuffling of the waves and the rustle of the faraway citrus trees. The piled-up abandoned crates and benches, the last remnants of the volleyball epic, looked depressing, and he tried not to notice them.

One day before departure, the House finally was at peace. The bags, each marked with the initials of the owner, were packed and stashed under the beds. Humpback completed the construction of a travel nest for the hamster. Wolf's begging for permission to take the guitar bore fruit. Stinker hid everything he couldn't take in inaccessible places. Elephant was persuaded to temporarily part with the begonia. All that remained was the wait.

In the night, Wolf's back started acting up. By morning it was much worse. Poxies received a visit from the Spiders. The specter of the Sepulcher was quickly taking shape for Wolf, and the dread of it overcame the longing for the ocean. He spent the entire day in bed, just as he was told.

Elk came by with encouragements and gifts, the nurses with tests and vague threats. Wolf transferred the permission for the guitar to Magician, along with the guitar itself. He also promised Beauty to take care of the juice maker, and assured Elephant that he'd personally water the begonia daily. The black marker crossed out one more day on the calendar.

That night no one slept. The screams and singing of the seniors splashed out of the open windows. On the other side of the wall Stuffagers roared, practicing their traveling song. Sissies sat around the imaginary campfire and told horror stories of drownings and stinging jellyfish. It was supposed to cheer up Wolf, and he dutifully pretended that it did.

Grasshopper again went down to the yard, now free from the crates and chairs, sat one more time with his back to the House, and listened for the waves and the citrus trees. For the groaning of the Other House. Only now, for some reason, those sounds were not getting any closer to him, but instead faded into the distance. He waited until they disappeared completely into the unfathomable void, then jumped up and ran back into the House. The darkness felt suddenly threatening.

Early the next morning, in the wee hours that usually found the yard empty, with only the first window blinds being raised here and there, Grasshopper was standing next to the porch with everyone else, waiting for the buses. He shivered in the morning chill, tried to keep his eyes open, and avoided sitting down in order not to fall asleep. The wheelers pulled the coats tighter around themselves and coughed meaningfully. The walkers smoked and glanced impatiently at their watches. The bags formed a neat pile against the wall. The junior girls were allowed to sit there, and two of them were already using the opportunity to catch up on some sleep, resting their curly heads on the bloated canvas balloons. The counselors fussed around the junior wheelers, distributing motion-sickness pills and also hygienic bags for when the pills weren't enough. It was very quiet. Almost the entire complement of the House was outside in the yard, and the silence hung unnaturally and unpleasantly.

It's probably because no one slept last night, Grasshopper thought. *And also because this day is finally here.*

The seniors had watches, but the juniors didn't, and they continuously inquired about the time. The seniors barked back lazily. Stinker, bundled up in his wheelchair, glowered at anyone who came close to his bag. Humpback yawned and tried to discern familiar dogs in the Outsides. The dogs were usually excavating the trash cans at this hour, but they hadn't appeared yet.

Sportsman went around the yard with his packed fishing rods slung over his shoulder. Whiner and Crybaby, racked by incessant yawns, followed his every step. Grasshopper sighed and fought off sleep.

The combined yell of a hundred throats startled him. Those who were sitting on the stairs shot up and started waving their arms. The first bus crawled in through the open gates. It was white and blue and resembled a big candy bar. Humpback and Grasshopper shouted "Yay!" with the others and charged.

They were immediately pushed back to the porch.

"That's for the wheelers," Humpback whispered. "The first one is always theirs."

"Why were you running, then?" Grasshopper said indignantly.

"No idea," Humpback answered happily. "It just sort of happened."

The principal climbed on the first step of the bus.

"Women and children first!" he shouted and fluffed his beard significantly. "Please make way for the ladies and the juniors in wheelchairs!"

Stinker giggled. The wheeler girls and juniors began loading. They were rolled up the ramp, unloaded inside, and then their bags were brought in and the wheelchairs folded up and stowed in the luggage compartment.

This took so much time that Grasshopper got bored watching. Humpback went to say good-bye to Stinker, whose turn finally came. Siamese furtively picked up the cigarette butts tossed away by the seniors. Then the second bus arrived, and the third right behind it, and it was pandemonium. The juniors with their bags darted between the seniors' legs and tried to squeeze into every available opening. Moor's people and Skull's people chose one bus each. The fourth bus, which stopped halfway inside the gates, ended up mixed, and nobody wanted to ride in that one. Counselors reasoned and harangued. The principal shuttled between the two buses, imploring the seniors to stop this silliness. Grasshopper climbed into the Moorists' bus, took pains to stake out a place, and went back down, only to go into the mixed one. Then he switched to the Skullers' bus and left his bag there. He insinuated himself into the throng of Stuffagers, brushed by Singings and Curseds, loudly called out to Poxy Sissies, changed seats. Finally satisfied that no one would be able to tell with any certainty which of the buses he boarded, he went around the one standing closest to the trees and squatted down beside it.

He was trembling, expecting that any moment now someone would call his name. Someone who was paying attention to his meanderings. But the bustle of the loading continued and no one went around the buses looking for this one Poxy Sissy. Grasshopper, still in a crouch, scrambled under the nearest tree. It turned out to be a bad hiding spot. He did not linger there and went straight behind the doghouse. Now this was the safest place in the whole yard. The dog, otherwise busy barking at the departing students, jumped back to sniff at him, but soon got distracted again by the buses. Grasshopper exhaled. He sat on the ground, free from the dog's probing attention. He couldn't help himself and sneaked a look out.

The pile of bags was no more. No juniors could be seen either. The counselors all milled by the steps of the mixed bus. Grasshopper pulled his head back and never peeked again, afraid that someone would spot him out of the bus window. He heard the door close behind the counselors, then a bus revving up and trundling out, followed by the other three, then the gates slamming shut, the sound of the engines fading and finally gone. The dog barked through all of it.

When silence returned, Grasshopper remained in his hideout for a while more, taking stock. He'd pulled it off. There was no way to undo what he'd done. The last bus had left, carrying Poxy Sissies, and with them went away the ocean and the myriad great games that they'd been inventing all spring. It was not easy to let go of all that, but he couldn't allow himself to even dream of staying back until the very last moment. He just knew that when that moment came, he was going to try.

A doggy nose buried itself in his hair, paws pushing against his shoulders. He shoved the dog, jumped up, and ran out from behind the shed. The yard, free of the clutter and commotion that had reigned all morning, was now even more thoroughly empty. The spots where the buses stood could still be drawn up precisely, as the cigarette butts, matches, candy wrappers, and other litter marked the boundaries of the three enormous rectangles. Grasshopper threaded his way through, avoiding stepping inside them for some reason, and entered the House. This is where he met the silence.

The rich, sultry, velvety silence he'd forgotten all about since the last summer. It enveloped and dominated. The few minutes that had passed were enough for the silence to flood the entire House, from the roof down to the cellars. The House felt bigger.

Grasshopper ran ahead, suddenly afraid that he might be completely alone. He knew it not to be so, but could not overcome the silly, childish dread of stillness and emptiness. The hallway still smelled of seniors, of their anxiety and impatience.

This scent would soon be gone, the cleaners were going to sweep it out with the trash and cover it with floor polish, the rooms becoming bare and featureless, like when he first saw them. He sped up and burst into the Poxy room at a run. It was empty. Wolf's bed was made up. Grasshopper sat on it, shook out the sand from his sneakers, and told himself there was no reason to panic. Wolf wasn't in the room, but that didn't mean he wasn't somewhere else. And Blind, he must have been somewhere too. Grasshopper remembered the last summer and realized that he was looking in the wrong place. He needed to find Elk. Elk had spent the previous summer in the principal's office.

Grasshopper ran back out into the hallway and dashed toward the principal's office. He kicked the door—and there they were. Wolf, Elk, and Blind. They were sitting on the windowsill, and didn't seem surprised to see him. It was as if they knew he'd come. Wolf smiled, and Elk nodded very slightly, in approval of his choice. They shifted and made space for him. Grasshopper squeezed in and finally felt completely happy. And also that the summer was going to be a gorgeous one.

And it was, it was. It had mornings in pink and gold, and the soft rains, and the scents wafting into the room between the curtains. And the bird.

They saw it that one time on the back of the bench under the oak tree. It was beautiful, bright as a painted toy, all striped and with an orange crown and a curved beak. The whole summer was like that bird.

Elk drove them out to the country in his Bug. Bug was a car seemingly assembled from parts of ten different cars, all of them picked up at the junkyard. It leaked from the top and the bottom, it got winded on long drives, and sharp turns sometimes made it shed its mysterious components. It liked to choose for itself where it would go next, and they had to concede, otherwise the engine would just quit, and Bug would be stuck in the most inopportune places and remain silent and inert until granted full independence again.

But wherever Bug decided to park itself, it was fine with them. They would lie under the warm sun, explore the roadside puddles, eat sandwiches. They never returned to the House empty-handed. In the bed of a dried-up creek, Blind unearthed an ancient candlestick, green with age. Grasshopper found a pack of cards on a trash heap, but they had naked ladies on them so Elk tossed them right back out. Wolf took to hauling in scary-looking insects; no one knew where he got them. Elk found an old looking glass in a leather case.

In the evening they set up tea on the deck and told scary stories. And one time they didn't make it back for dinner. Bug threw a fit and they had to spend the night inside it, with only the remains of sandwiches and one bottle of water between them. That night all the stories were about victims of shipwrecks and getting lost in a desert. The water had to be rationed. Blind said he heard hyenas laughing in the distance, and Wolf maintained he saw a mirage of three palm trees and a stone well.

After another excursion, they became five. A plump white puppy of an emphatically mutt lineage became their best discovery, so that's what they named it. She turned out to be a girl. Discovery was hopelessly plebeian and hopelessly bad mannered. The boys' pants were soon covered in white hairs and greasy stains. The legs of the principal's desk acquired a shabby, distinctly chewed look. Elk whittled chewing sticks for Discovery. They were strewn everywhere, and the dog gnawed on them rapturously, but the desk legs, boys' ankles, and Elk's boots never escaped her attention either.

A couple of times they took sleeping bags up on the roof and spent the night there. Elk told them about the stars and their names. They packed flashlights, thermoses, and blankets, and once even took Discovery, because otherwise she missed them and howled pitifully in the empty office. They tied her to the chimney up there, but she liked this even less than being alone downstairs.

And there was the flying of the kite. It was yellow and purple, and it had narrow, slit-like eyes. It hung over the yard, smiling mysteriously and fluttering its tail. They took turns yanking its cord and observing how the wind changed the expression on its face. And one time their dinner featured food prepared according to customs of the Australian aborigines. They tried to obtain fire by rubbing sticks together, but eventually gave up and used the lighter. The food was expectedly horrible, but the aborigines did not mind and were completely satisfied. That was when the strange bird came. It also brought the rain that lasted for three days, and the air smelled of autumn. Bug went back into the garage and they had to wash Discovery's paws every time she came in from the yard.

When the Grayhouse folk finally returned, excited, tanned, and overflowing with stories and experiences, their arrival was met with resignation. Because it meant that this summer was over, and because all of them, except the grown-up, knew that there would never be another one like it.

The seniors and the juniors, the cooks, and the counselors filled out the House quickly and expertly, as if there was never a time when they weren't there. The principal's office ceased being the most interesting place in the whole House and became just the principal's office, a place of daily pilgrimage for teachers and counselors, of plans and phone calls. Became that which it was supposed to be. Discovery was exiled down to the yard. The narrow-eyed kite flew a couple more times, then ended up forgotten in the attic. The tale of the wondrous bird and the three-day rain failed to interest anyone. The walls of the Poxy room were now taken up with strings of seashells and tree nuts.

SMOKER

POMPEY'S LAST STAND

In the Grayhouse Forest for two days straight
Water leaks from the skies.
Shake off the moss, wake up your mate
And dance, and look in his eyes!

But you don't see the eyes and you don't have a face,
Wet is your fur and tight your embrace.
Then you will find that there is no truth
Stashed in the hollow's black mouth.

Let your hand inside, take it out and read,
Tiny black beasts on the whitest paper.
Then run away, because you need
To shout the words that they whisper.

To shout the truth that's not there at all,
That's up to you to create,
In the prickly grass leaving the scrawl
Of your heavy six-taloned gait.

Sing as you run and shout as you dance,
You're a freak, so let out a scream—
Let the whole world know you've been born by chance
Of the tree and the forest stream.

Chorus:

Quick! Quick! Go bite a tick!
Drape the ears over the cloak!
We'll dance all night and we'll sing our delight!
We, the proud Gray Forest folk!
"The Rain Song"

The silence that had devoured the world once the pack moved to the Sepulcher continued even after they'd returned. The noisy morning dissolved in it without a trace. After classes, Sphinx and Blind both climbed on the windowsill and smoked there without a single word, each using his own ashtray. Humpback took Tubby out for a walk. Alexander hid himself on Humpback's bunk. Tabaqui sat there like a prairie dog, all hushed and mournful, his sorrow on full display. The boombox hissed idly. The nastiest silence there is, the silence of many people being silent together. We stewed in it until lunch, and in the canteen I realized I couldn't stand it anymore. It weighed on me like something that was alive, something suffocating. Then I noticed that ours was not the only quiet table. The entire canteen was silent. Even the music, usually thunderously loud, seemed hushed. I could hear cooks talking and jangling the cutlery in the kitchen behind the wall. This is where I got really scared. Trembling-hands scared.

The lunch-end bell clanked once and went dumb, as if by magic. Usually it was followed by an immediate explosion of clatter, with the Second rushing to the door tripping over themselves, clearly showing that the air in the canteen had suddenly become impossible to breathe. They didn't go anywhere this time. A couple of wheelchairs peeled off the Pheasants' table, circled the exit, and returned.

"I detect a whiff of mayhem," Jackal observed. "Can you feel it?"

It was hard not to. As soon as we rose to go, we were intercepted by the delegation arriving from the table of the Sixth, three Hounds in all, and Laurus solemnly presented Sphinx with some kind of note.

"'Pompey requests the Leaders of all packs to assemble in the Coffeepot for an important discussion,'" Sphinx read out.

He shrugged and passed the note to Blind.

As soon as those words were said, everyone started talking at once. The silence was shattered. Logs began their rounds between the tables. Pheasants clustered together to better guard against a perceived assault.

"This is an outrage!" Vulture shouted above the fevered din of voices. "People are in mourning here!"

Pompey raised his hands in a mollifying gesture.

"I commiserate," he said. "But business is business."

Vulture scowled dismissively, and Birds reflected his grimace in a dozen bad mirrors.

We were wheeling out in a throng of chattering, hopping Rats. Then there was a traffic jam at the doors, composed mostly of those who wanted to keep alongside us, trying to read our faces. The Great Game abruptly shifted into active mode.

The sky was whitish outside the windows. The fog seemed to wrap the House in a big blob of cotton wool. And it also became very chilly. Like the temperature dropped several degrees in an instant. Or maybe it was just me getting the chills from all this.

Near the Coffeepot the throng thinned out a bit. The Pheasants dropped away, and the rest coalesced into groups. The Leaders marched into the Coffeepot one after the other. Once they were gone, the volume of the conversation went down significantly. Everyone waited.

The Rats were emitting muted snippets of music.

"I told you," Lary mumbled, chewing his unlit cigarette into shreds. "I warned you. And now this . . ."

"So, what now? A rumble?" I asked, trying to sound casual. The way it came out almost made me gag.

"No, a candlelit dinner, *mon poilu*," Tabaqui snapped.

Humpback said that there was no sense in all of us sticking around. He himself didn't move an inch.

"You're right," Sphinx said. "Anything important we'll find out from Blind."

He also stayed put.

Alexander gave Tubby a bread roll. Humpback lit a cigarette.

Even knowing perfectly well that all of this was just a game, I still felt nervous. Everyone was in character a little too well.

Finally the door of the Coffeepot opened. Pompey emerged first. He turned toward Hounds and stuck up his thumb. Hounds roared approvingly. Blind and Vulture came out together and shuffled away, immersed in a hushed conversation. Red never appeared at all. It was as if the others had eaten him whole in the course of the meeting.

"Oh god," Lary moaned when he noticed Pompey walking in our direction.

The packs, having already started to disperse, quickly resumed their places in the dress circle.

Pompey came closer. Tall, swarthy, with his chic Mohawk. But no bat, I noticed. Maybe it had already croaked.

"Can we talk?" he asked Sphinx.

"You already had a talk with Blind, what else do you want?"

Pompey took out a cigarette. He stood there among us like he was in his own room. Not anxious at all. Even a little showy. For some reason, we were the anxious ones.

"I've recently learned of this old Law," Pompey explained between puffs. "It made me very sad. This, you know, prehistoric crap . . . And it's exactly the reason I've dragged this out for so long. I just refused to believe it. I know all the guys were saying it was not in force anymore. But still . . ."

Hounds drifted closer, not wanting to miss even a single word.

"It is my opinion," Pompey continued, looking distractedly over our heads, "that it was invented by cowardly Leaders. So that made me apprehensive, as you can imagine."

The invisible ice could be chipped off Sphinx with a pick.

"But you're not apprehensive anymore?" he asked.

"I overcame that," Pompey announced proudly.

"Congratulations."

"But I would still like to make sure. Is your pack following it?"

"No," Sphinx said. "Anything else?"

"You are behaving a bit rudely," Pompey said, frowning. "In the big scheme of things I'm looking out for your own interest."

Tabaqui, behind Pompey's back, very realistically imitated throwing up.

"There's no need," Sphinx said. "We are all free."

"Well, that's nice," Pompey sighed with relief.

"It's not nice."

"You mean you're in favor of that shit?"

Sphinx shook his head. His look, directed at Pompey, was more calculating than anything else. Like he was weighing something in his mind, trying to come to a decision.

"No," he said finally and turned away. "It's useless."

Pompey assumed a businesslike air. He even threw away the cigarette.

"All right, out with it. What's this about?"

"Nothing. Where's your bat?"

This question took Pompey completely aback. At first he was surprised. Then offended.

"Is that supposed to be funny?"

"Not at all."

Pompey's face darkened.

"We'll continue this conversation tomorrow. Bats and all. Maybe your head will clear up a bit by then."

"Maybe," Sphinx agreed. And laughed. Really laughed, not faking it.

I sighed, relieved. Finally someone blew it. Went out of character, spoiled the game for himself and others. I was really glad that he did, even though I couldn't explain why. So people invented a game for themselves, what was so bad about that? I was sure that this was the end of it, that Sphinx's laughter would now spread to others and everyone would abandon the script.

None of that happened.

Pompey feigned taking umbrage, said "Right. See you," and stomped off to join with Hounds. The Sixth surrounded him, shielding him from us.

Soon after, Rats, each in his own little cloud of music, slowly drifted away. There was nothing more that seemed to be happening in front of the Coffeepot. Tabaqui circled around on his Mustang, hanging over the side with his face almost to the floor, apparently looking for something. Alexander was pulling threads out of his sweater.

"What are we waiting for here?" Humpback asked. "Or is this where the new place of encampment is?"

"This is where the saliva of the Great Hound is," Tabaqui piped happily, peering into something invisible on the floorboards. "I knew it! He spit right over here somewhere. He was really pissed, so it's genuine hate spit. Someone stepped in it slightly, I'll admit that, but still, putting the voodoo on him now would not be a problem at all."

"Don't even think about touching that!" Sphinx barked.

Tabaqui's giggles became even more ecstatic.

Humpback wheeled Tubby, covered in bread crumbs, past us, and I followed them. I desperately needed some coffee. I also needed to ask Black a couple of questions.

When we reached the dorm, Blind was nowhere to be seen. Black was sitting on his bed. Tabaqui took all kinds of sacks and boxes out of the storage, dumped them in a huge pile, and proceeded to dive into it, emerging from time to time wearing something new and inquiring whether or not it suited him. Tubby bumped his head against the edge of his pen and started wailing. Alexander hauled him onto the common bed too.

By the time the commotion died down a little, Black had already managed to make himself scarce, so I couldn't ask him anything. I crawled over to Sphinx, lying there all mysterious and inaccessible with his feet up on the bed frame, and inquired what was in that prehistoric Law that Pompey was talking about.

Until I asked the question, everyone was seemingly busy with their own pursuits, but now they all quit what they were doing, came closer, and stared at the two of us.

"I just adore Smoker," Tabaqui mumbled, pulling another sack full of indescribable stuff closer to the bed. "Listen to the crisp way he frames his questions!"

Humpback looked at Sphinx with what seemed like pity and passed me the coffee. Alexander was hanging off the bed frame, still holding the sugar bowl. These

people were real experts in turning anything into a circus show. Must have been years
of practice. I already regretted not having wheeled out after Black as soon as he left.

Sphinx did not even deign to sit up. He lay looking up at the ceiling, his prosthetics folded up on his belly. He did explain, though. That the Law to which Pompey
took such exception was called "the Law of Choice." That it was so old that no one in
the House remembered who invented it and when. And that it required any moron
who followed it—that was exactly how Sphinx phrased it, "any moron"—to die for his
Leader. If, for example, a coup was in the making, under this Law the Leader must be
defended even at the cost of one's life. Sphinx talked like he was quoting directly from
some moldy textbook. In such lofty tones that at first I didn't catch the full meaning
of what was being said. Once I did, I almost spilled my coffee. Humpback, who was
sitting next to me, gingerly propped up my cup. Tabaqui was in hysterics, giggling
and snorting like crazy.

"What's choice got to do with it?"

"It had to do with it that the Law could be ignored. In theory."

"Sounds very much like prehistoric crap," I said, agreeing with Pompey.

Tabaqui supplied that the ancestors were simple and austere people and therefore
possessed nasty laws in great abundance. "Dark ages, Smoker, dark ages, believe you
me." And he started giggling again.

I inquired whose ancestors he meant by that.

"Ours, of course," Jackal replied. "Right here."

"It could be that they thought this Law would protect Leaders from most coup
attempts," Sphinx suggested. "Apparently it even worked for a while. They assumed
that the better the Leader, the more people would make their choice in his favor, and,
correspondingly, the less chance the usurpers would have. Even though it's obvious
what it would inevitably degenerate into, if only you think about it for one minute."

Lary's head emerged from the space between the beds and positioned itself with
its chin on the edge of the mattress.

"That was the seniors' undoing," it announced. "Blasted Moor had forty hooked
on Choice. So obviously, not many survived."

I asked who Blasted Moor was.

"You're not old enough to know things like that," Lary responded grimly and hid
his head again.

I did not mention that, in that case, it would have been a good idea not to bring
him up at all. I decided to continue being polite and to take part in their stupid games
the best I could. So I asked Sphinx what he meant when he told Pompey that it was
"useless."

"It was useless to try and talk him out of the fight," Sphinx explained. "He
wouldn't have understood."

"Don't tell me you were going to!" Tabaqui exploded. "You're out of your mind! How would that look? Just think about it!"

Sphinx sat up.

"I don't care how it looks," he said. "I should have tried. He's still a human being."

"He's an idiot! A complete dolt!" Tabaqui screamed.

"That's not a reason to kill him!"

"That is too a reason!"

They were shouting with their faces right against each other. Their noses almost touched. It was as if they were alone. As if there was nobody else around.

"It is very much a reason," Tabaqui repeated, a bit softer.

Sphinx looked into his eyes for a while more and then turned away.

I took a deep breath. The Great Game reached unprecedented intensity. They almost managed to convince me that it all was for real, that they weren't playing. That it was a matter of life and death. The faces of everyone present must have reflected the same appreciation of their talents.

"So?" I said. "That means no one can save Pompey now?"

They looked at me like I was seriously ill. With compassion and concern. This marked the end of my attempts to contribute to the Game. I realized that I'd done quite enough contributing for one day. I was sick of playing a simpleton in need of edification.

So I said thank you. I said that they had now helped me to understand everything and that I was content. Their eyes popped out of their heads, like I'd completely lost my mind.

I drank my coffee and never asked anyone anything.

We were walking and wheeling in total darkness. Slowly, like tortoises. The flashlights weren't much help. The two pale dots under the wheels and a mass of people bumping into each other both ahead of and behind me. Three packs stumbling together in the dark, and it was a good thing Hounds had already gone downstairs. When we passed the doors of the dorms they cracked open, and we could hear the whispering of those left behind—both those like our own Tubby and the others, a little more aware of the world around them. The poor souls tried to make themselves inconspicuous, but it was still unnerving as hell.

Then we saw someone ahead of us, on top of the stairs, shining an industrial-strength beam down the steps. I was sweating and in desperate need of a cigarette. The Crossroads television resembled a hunched figure. Our progress seemed to be echoing through the entire building, and I was waiting for the invasion, at any moment, of counselors and Cases, running to find out what was going on.

The steps smelled of bleach and mouse droppings. The person in charge of lighting the way was doing a really thorough job. He formed groups of six, went down ahead of them himself, illuminating every step and then returning for the next batch.

The first-floor corridor was much more expansive than ours—four wheelchairs could ride abreast here and still leave enough room for a pair of walkers. We were moving much faster. We passed the locked doors to the entrance hall, the movie room, the video-game arcade, the rows of photographs, the rows of fire extinguishers, the laundry window . . . The gym was open, and all the lights were on inside. We could put the flashlights away.

It was already packed, but more and more were arriving. It was also surprisingly quiet. The conversations didn't rise above a whisper. Hounds occupied the mats, managing in the time they were here to surround themselves with tea in thermal flasks, pass around the paper cups, and in general assume the air of gracious hosts entertaining troublesome guests.

Sphinx, Black, and Humpback made straight for them. Blind remained standing by the door. I followed Tabaqui around like a shadow, but he apparently decided to renew acquaintances with everyone in the room, so we kept circling and circling the gym, saying hello and engaging in pointless banter with every random person. I finally grew tired of this and fell behind.

Pompey was sitting on a separate mat a little way off from the other Hounds and smoking, dropping ash on the floor. Around his neck he had a colorful kerchief tightly twisted into a slim rope. His leather pants were on the verge of splitting open under the assault of his muscular thighs. He did not participate in the talks with Sphinx, which told me that the details of the Great Battle were being hashed out without input from its participants. Then I realized that I had no idea what the plan was—whether Pompey was supposed to prevail or be defeated. I just knew it had to be agreed upon in advance.

Sphinx returned, with Humpback and Black. Sphinx then went to the door and engaged in a whispered dialogue with Blind. The wheelers of the Sixth remained where they were. The walkers got up but also didn't go anywhere. Then the walkers of the Second and Third assembled in the center of the floor. They held hands and formed a large circle. Then the wheelers were introduced into it, and then finally Black, Humpback, Lary, and the remaining Hounds. Every one of ours and of Birds was positioned so that he had members of other packs on both sides. Once the guys from the Sixth joined in, the circle grew to the size of a boxing ring. It looked silly, but was done very efficiently, as if the House held weekly drills in creating circles like this. I was marveling at the unusual spectacle, but then someone called me. Turned out I had to go and take my place as well.

"Wake up, will you," Tabaqui hissed when I wheeled by him.

"Alexander hasn't gone in either," I said by way of an excuse.

Tabaqui gave me a withering look, pursed his lips, and turned away. I was stationed between Angel from the Third and Monkey from the Second. The former was intently studying something on the ceiling and yawning. The latter fidgeted, made faces, and smacked his lips. Angel's hand barely touched mine, while Monkey now gripped my hand, now shook it, now almost pushed it away. I got the impression that neither one of them perceived me as a human being at that point. I was just a fragment of the chain. Nothing more.

Once the movement ceased, Pompey rose from the mat, stretched, and entered the circle, bobbing under a pair of clasped hands.

"Does it always happen like this? Like a kids' game?" I whispered to Monkey.

He looked at me distractedly, made another face, and said that he had no idea what I was talking about.

Sphinx led Blind toward the circle. Blind then also went inside.

"Why this merry-go-round?" I asked Monkey again.

"What do you mean why? So that everyone can see properly, you fool! And so that nobody's hands . . ."

Monkey didn't finish. A collective cry made us startle and crane our necks. The chain broke. Pompey lay prostrate on the floor, kicking his legs and making strange bubbling noises. Sort of like a cooing dove.

Is that all? I thought, stunned.

What I saw next made me sick. Pompey was clutching at his throat, and between his red fingers there was a knife handle. I closed my eyes, and then heard everyone exhale in unison. That could only mean one thing. But I still waited, not able to make myself look again. When I did, Pompey wasn't moving anymore. Just lying there, a sad bulk in a widening pool of blood. Not a single person among those sitting and standing around could have any doubts that he was dead.

The circle was still standing, even though no one was holding hands anymore. It was very quiet. We all looked at Pompey in silence.

I realized then that I was going to remember this for the rest of my life. The corpse on the glistening green paint, the track lights reflecting in the dark glass of the windows, and the silence. The silence of the place where too many people were silent.

Blind crouched down near Pompey, felt for the knife, and pulled it out. The wet noise almost made me throw up. I waited for the rising contents of my stomach to settle down a little, then turned the wheelchair around and dashed toward the doors. The only thought in my head was to leave this place as soon as I could.

I was speeding blindly down the corridor and definitely would have crashed into something at the very next turn if Tabaqui hadn't caught up with me.

"Hey! Where are you going? Stop right there!"

He grabbed my wheelchair and forced me to stop.

"Smoker. Calm down. You've got to calm down," he kept repeating.

I told him I was absolutely calm. He produced a flashlight from his backpack and we proceeded along. Very slowly.

Tabaqui was trembling and mumbling, "Not with me, barred from me, find yourself another skin, walk up the river, join with the moon, but never with me, not now and not soon . . ."

I laughed.

"Please stop with the crazy," he said, "or we'll have to slap your cheeks and pour water on you. And I don't think anyone wants to do that at the moment."

"What is it you want to do at the moment?" I said. "Lots of demands on your time?"

He didn't answer.

"That's not a reason to kill him!" Sphinx shouted in Jackal's face.

"That is too a reason!" Jackal shot back.

"You're not old enough for things like that," Lary said.

"So?" I said. "That means no one can save Pompey now?"

And they all stared at me. The way people look at complete idiots.

Which was exactly what I was.

"Oh god!" I said. And laughed. And couldn't stop myself. Tabaqui stopped and waited out my bout of mirth.

"And that rat," I said. "Remember the rat? I thought you were going to kill it. Whack it with the broom. But you weren't planning to, were you?"

I saw the reflections of the flashlight in both of Jackal's big round eyes. Two yellow dots.

"You were never going to hurt it. The rat? No way. Right? But it was only Lary who was really afraid of Pompey. And you all knew that Blind was going to simply kill him . . ."

Tabaqui was still looking at me without saying a word.

"You all knew," I said. "When you were joking about his bats. When you were telling stories. When you were singing songs. Sphinx was sure of it when he was talking to him today . . . Now I understand . . ."

"So?" Tabaqui said. "Let's say we did know. So what?"

He wasn't disgusted, and he wasn't sorry. Not a single bit. It was obvious even here in the darkness. And if not for Sphinx . . . if not for his "That's not a reason to kill him," I'd have had to assume they were all like this. "That is too a reason," Jackal had answered. Yes. They kill in this House. And there I was with my "no one can save Pompey now." Sarcastic. Mocking. Even they were surprised. Of course they were. I'd outcynicked them all.

I laughed again. I laughed and laughed, and then I literally choked on the laughter as it turned into a spasm. I vomited. Right on my legs. I didn't have time to lean over or turn to the side.

Tabaqui gasped but didn't say anything.

Alexander, with another flashlight, caught up with us at the bottom of the steps. He looked me over, grabbed the handles of the wheelchair, and ran. Jackal was speeding alongside. I screwed up my eyes very tightly and tried not to think of anything. Least of all, of the Great Game. This silly, amusing game, born out of boredom.

Once we reached the bathroom, Alexander unloaded me on the floor and undressed me down to my briefs. I was sitting on the wet floor, trembling. He took away my clothes and returned to wash the wheelchair, and still I was sitting there, naked. Then he and Humpback shoved me into the shower stall, turned on the water, and closed the door. I stretched out in the little tiled alcove, under the jets of water cascading down my back, and listened to their voices, muted by the frosted glass, mingling with the sound of the shower. Listened to them talk while they were washing my wheelchair.

"Grabbed all the knives and razors and hauled them away," Humpback said. "Even the nail files. Gone. He has his own hiding places."

Alexander mumbled something indistinct.

"Used a pillowcase to wrap them. Mine, for some reason. I wonder why."

Squeaking of the wheelchair. Silence.

"We can give Smoker my pants. At least they won't be falling down. But I'm all out of clean shirts."

I closed my eyes and put my face inside the water stream. This way I couldn't hear anything else. Much better. If only they'd left me alone, I might have spent the night there, numbing myself in the shower, and then maybe feeling a little better in the morning. But they pulled me out. Pushed aside the door and dragged me onto the towel spread out on the floor.

As I was drying myself, in came Lary, took my place in the stall, and started splashing around like a manic seal without even bothering to close the door.

Sphinx entered and froze in the middle of the bathroom with a perplexed look on his face, as if he forgot what it was he needed here.

I emerged from under the towel. There was a stack of clothes on the stool next to me. I saw a gray-checkered shirt on top.

"I'm not wearing that," I said. "Take it away."

Humpback looked at me quizzically. As if there was something incongruous about me not wanting to put on that shirt. Blind's shirt, I'd seen him wear it, not once and not twice. As if it wasn't obvious that I had no desire to wear anything that was his after what had just happened.

Lary started singing, there in the shower, loudly and out of tune. Singing and slapping his protruding ribs.

"Damned exhibitionist," Sphinx grumbled. And yelled, so suddenly that I startled, "Close the damn door!"

"All right," Humpback said and took the clothes away from under my nose. "We'll figure out something tomorrow. There's nothing left to do today but sleep, anyway."

He draped the towel over me, helped me into the wheelchair, and rolled it out. The wheelchair was still wet after the washing. I slid around on the seat and grabbed the handles tightly to prevent myself from falling out.

"You are a really fastidious person," Sphinx said.

I looked back.

His stare was ice cold.

"I'm not fastidious," I said. "I'm normal. And you?"

His eyes narrowed.

"And I'm not."

No one had ever looked at me that way before. With such boundless loathing. Then he closed his eyes. Like he didn't want to see me at all.

"God," he said. "You're not worth half of his fingernail. You . . ."

Humpback quickly turned the wheelchair, rolled me out into the corridor, and slammed the door. There was commotion and hissing on the other side of it, as if both Alexander and Lary had grabbed hold of Sphinx to prevent him from going after me. Humpback galloping all the way to the dorm only confirmed that suspicion. He dumped me on the bed and immediately ran back.

I lay down right away. Still wrapped in the towel. Pulled the covers over my head, screwed my eyes closed, and tried my best not to burst into tears. I held on until all the sounds around me ceased. Until they stopped walking around, talking, shifting stuff, and settling down. Only then did I allow myself to cry. I hoped against hope that no one could hear me. Something ended that night, and it was more painful than an entire life spent among Pheasants.

The next day was the day of interrogations and searches. Surly figures in uniform roamed the hallways. They entered classrooms, asked questions about Pompey, and searched for the knife. They didn't spend too much time in our dorm. Rifled through the desk drawers and nightstands, tapped on the walls, and left.

Lary periodically carried out reconnaissance missions and returned with the latest news that nobody cared about. If one were to go out into the hallway he'd be able to see Hounds being brought one by one into the staff room to compare testimonies.

That was exactly what Lary was doing, loitering in the hallway. He just liked to call it "reconnaissance."

Around seven in the evening, all of the outsiders left. Shark assembled the teachers and the counselors in his office for an emergency meeting. At ten, two hours later than usual, they rang for dinner, and we all went to the canteen. The classroom doors were already adorned with black ribbons. Shark was waiting for us. His speech was long and heartfelt, and could be summed up in a single point: anyone who knew anything about the circumstances of Pompey's death was cordially invited to drop by the principal's office for a nice private talk.

We went to bed early that night. There were spells scribbled in all four corners of the room to ward off the vengeful ghosts. Tabaqui hung a collection of protective amulets above his head. Humpback jumped up every half hour, directed the beam of his flashlight at the door, exhaled with relief, and crashed back on the bunk.

BOOK TWO

EIGHT DAYS IN THE LIFE OF JACKAL

THE HOUSE MALE STUDENTS

FOURTH	THIRD	SECOND
	BIRDS	RATS
—	—	—
BLIND	(VULTURE)	RED
SPHINX	LIZARD	SOLOMON
TABAQUI	(ANGEL)	SQUIB
HUMPBACK	DODO	DON
(NOBLE)	HORSE	VIKING
BLACK	(BUTTERFLY)	(CORPSE)
LARY	DEAREST	(ZEBRA)
ALEXANDER	GUPPY	HYBRID
SMOKER	BUBBLE	MONKEY
(TUBBY)	(BEAUTY)	MICROBE
	(ELEPHANT)	TERMITE
	(FICUS)	SUMAC
	(SHRUB)	PORCUPINE
		CARRION
		RINGER
		TINY
		WHITEBELLY
		GREENERY
		(DAWDLER)

AS OF BOOK TWO

SIXTH HOUNDS	**FIRST** PHEASANTS	LEGEND
—	—	—
	GIN	(PARENTHESES): JUMPERS
CROOK	PROFESSOR	**BOLD:** STRIDERS
(OWL)	BITER	
GNOME	GHOUL	
(SHUFFLE)	STRAW	
LAURUS	STICKS	
WOOLLY	BRICKS	
RABBIT	(CRYBABY)	
ZIT	GYPS	
TRITON	HAMSTER	
SLEEPY	KIT	
GENEPOOL	BOOGER	
DEALWITHIT	CUPCAKE	
SPLUTTER	SNIFFLE	
HEADLIGHT	(PIDDLER)	
HASTEWASTE		
EARS		
NUTTER		
RICKSHAW		
BAGMAN		
CRAB		
(FLIPPER)		

RALPH

A SIDEWAYS GLANCE AT GRAFFITI

He went up the stairs and entered the hallway, certain that he was not going to see anyone there. The canteen buzzed with voices, coming through to him muted, like a bee swarm humming in an old hollow tree. *When it is inside the hollow, and you're outside, and you haven't yet realized what that hum is, there, in the tree, and what are those strange spots darting around you, and once you do realize you're already at a full run . . .* He walked slowly, the duffel bag weighting down his shoulder. Open doors revealed the empty classrooms, laying fallow before the last period. The doors here could sometimes open so suddenly as to deliver a good smack on the forehead, so he'd long ago acquired the habit of walking on the other side, the one that used to have windows, keeping his distance from the doors. He remembered it and almost laughed at that thought.

Thirteen years. Enough time to blaze a trail, had the floorboards underfoot been something else, had they been earth and grass. A wide and permanent trail. His own. Like a deer might make. Or an . . .

This place used to have windows. There was much more light in the hallway. No one would have even considered boarding them up if not for the writings. The windowpanes were completely covered with them. *They* would cover the entire surface with scribbles and ugly drawings, and as soon as the windows were washed or replaced, the whole thing repeated itself. The windows never had a full day when they looked presentable. And it only happened in this hallway. The first floor never had windows looking out on the street, and the third housed too many counselors. He remembered it well, how one time, after the windowpanes were once again replaced (hoping against hope that this time *they* would finally see reason, except that had never happened), *they* simply slathered black paint all over the new, squeaky-clean glass. He remembered his feeling that morning, when he first saw the disgusting black-framed rectangles. It was the feeling of dread, the horror of the dawning recognition—he understood what those windows represented to them, literally demanding this barbaric treatment. At the next general meeting he voted for the windows to be eliminated.

It was not childish pranks. Oh, it looked that way at first, but even then there were signs—they never did anything like that in dorms and classes. Seeing the blacked-out glass, he realized to what degree his charges were afraid of those windows and how much they hated them. *Windows into the Outsides.*

He was now walking on the side that formerly had windows. This made the hallway a little too dark, but he doubted anyone in the House remembered that it had not always been so.

The windows debacle taught him a lot. He was young then, and he wanted to share his apprehension with somebody. Somebody who was older and more experienced. He wouldn't think of doing that now, but back then it had seemed like a good idea. So he did it, once, for the first and the last time ever. After that he never talked about things he felt.

They shielded themselves from the side that was looking out to the street. The other one, the yard side, did not bother them, even though it seemed to open up to the Outsides just the same. But the yard and the houses visible from there and the vacant lot and everything around it they had already accepted, included in their world. There was no need to surround the yard with a concrete fence, the other houses worked fine in that capacity. There was nothing like that on the street side. *They are trying to erase everything.* Those were his words. He remembered saying them, even though it had happened long ago. *Everything except themselves and their own domain. They refuse to acknowledge the existence of anything that is not the House. This is dangerous.* Elk laughed and said that he was imagining things.

They know perfectly well what the Outsides is and how it looks. They go to camps every summer. They enjoy watching movies.

He knew then that he'd never be able to explain. The danger was not in ignorance. It was in the word itself. The word "Outsides" that they had stripped of its former meaning and pressed into their service. They had decided that House was House, and Outsides was a thing apart, instead of being something that contained the House in it. But no one had understood. No one had felt anything even when looking at the blackened windows. It was only he who became scared when they had sprung the trap, taking away his ability to look at that which they refused to see. Elk was smart, but even he had never understood them. *The poor kids, they were hard done by . . .* Elk had believed that. And the graduation of the window tormentors hadn't taught him anything either, even though in the days before their exit the House had been saturated with sticky horror, making Ralph gasp in its noxious fumes. He had already wanted to run even then, but he kept hoping that as soon as those seniors were gone everything would change, the others would be different. It even worked for a while. A very short while, as the next batch was still too little to fight reality seriously. Then it turned out that they were just as good at it as their predecessors, maybe even better, and all he had left was to watch them and wait. He insisted that they were given too much freedom, but anytime he mentioned this he got the "unfortunate children" reply, and those words made him wince, just as they themselves winced when they heard something like that. So he watched and waited.

Waited until they grew up, molding themselves and their territory. Until they reached the age of leaving. Their predecessors had tried to throttle the passage of time in their own way: twelve suicide attempts, five of them successful. These had simply dragged everything around them into the maelstrom of their exit. That vortex had claimed Elk as well, even as he still thought of them as harmless children. It was possible he had understood something, but by then it was already too late.

Ralph often wondered what had been going through Elk's mind in those last moments, if he had time to think about anything at all. They had just brushed him aside like a grain of sand, a piece of debris that for some reason clung to them as they ran. They didn't mean it, they loved him, to the extent they were capable of love. It's just that they didn't care. When their personal Apocalypse had struck, one counselor was of no consequence. No one could have stopped them, not two, or three.

Had he survived that night, he would have understood what I figured out long before then. The world into which they are thrown once they turn eighteen does not exist for them. So if they have to leave, it is imperative that they destroy it for everyone else too.

That graduation left behind a blood-soaked void so horrible that it frightened everyone. Even those who had no direct connection to the House. The management had been replaced, and once it had been, all the teachers and counselors left. All except Ralph. He stayed. And getting to know the new principal, a man very far removed from humanistic ideals, proved the deciding factor. Those who had not run away after the June events rushed for the exits after the first talk with the principal. Ralph was convinced that this time everything was going to be different. That he would be able to do everything in his power to stop them when the time came. He had that opportunity now, knowing that there was no one who would interfere with him by playing the "poor little kids" card.

He watched them from the very beginning, and he began to see the ways in which they were changing even before the transformation started happening. He took the Third and the Fourth, the strangest and the most dangerous, even though it was silly back then to think of them this way. He waited for a long time, not knowing what he was waiting for, until finally he noticed it: something was out of place in their rooms. The rooms were somehow different from others. And as the rooms changed, so too did their inhabitants. The change was subtle, untraceable for any but the most sensitive observer; it had to be felt on the skin, inhaled with the air, and there had been times when weeks passed before he was able to really once again enter the place they were creating for themselves, creating by imperceptibly transforming the one that actually existed. With time he became better and better at it, and then, to his horror, he noticed that this domain, this invisible world, was not immune to incursions from other, completely random people. There could be only one explanation: this world came to exist on its own, or was on the threshold of existence. That's when he ran. But even as he was running, he knew that he would be back, to see this through, to watch the credits, to find out *how it ended this time.* He had accepted that there was nothing he could do to stop whatever was going to happen, he just needed to know what happened. Because even while he was learning from those who came before, *they* were learning too, and much faster. They wouldn't need to paint over the windows. He was sure that they only had to convince themselves that the windows weren't there. And then, likely as not, the windows would cease to exist.

The Crossroads piano was glinting, unsheathed. He stepped on a piece of tape, a red snake curled underfoot. He was treading the middle of the hallway now. *Still his own trail . . .* The three letters *R* jumped out at him from the wall. Bold as a signature, as a badge of his presence.

He froze. His name wasn't Ralph at all. This nickname, name-nick, he'd hated from the moment he got it. Precisely because it was a name. He'd much prefer to be called Shaggy, or Pansy, whatever, if only it sounded like a nick instead of a name that could be mistaken for his own. So naturally, because of this, of his loathing of "Ralph," it had stuck to him for this long, outliving all of his previous designations. Those who had christened him had left, and then those who had been squirts when it happened had left as well, and now the ones who hadn't even been there back then were grown up, and still he remained Ralph. Or just a letter, a capital letter with a number. The letter was even worse. But it was the only way they wrote him up on the walls, and even talking among themselves it came up more and more often, the loathsome nick being made uglier by the even more loathsome abbreviation.

He stopped in front of the door that didn't have a number on it, with the glass transom on top. Here one more *R*, done in soap on the glass, greeted him. He slammed the door behind him and thus rid himself of his own nick until the next time he needed to go out into the hallway. This was both his office and his bedroom. He was the only counselor who spent nights on the second floor. Shark firmly believed that it constituted a colossal sacrifice on his part, and Ralph did nothing to suggest to him otherwise. It was enough to mention in passing, "I am at my post at all hours," and he received everything he wanted, right away.

Ralph made a point of maintaining the heroic image of selfless service, even though the fear of the second floor he saw in other counselors and in Shark himself almost made him laugh. You had to have an extremely hazy understanding of *them*, or rather none at all, to imagine that they would go busting into a room and sticking a knife into a counselor just because. Because they were generally wicked, or because they had nothing better to do. He guessed at the existence of the Law. No one told him anything about it, of course, but by observing certain patterns in their behavior he deduced not only that the Law existed, but even some of its tenets. One, for example, made teachers and counselors untouchable, and it protected him unswervingly. The exceptions to it could come raining down only in that fateful time, the two weeks before graduation.

So it was useless to think about that, much less fear it, and he wasn't going to move to a different room now only because something could possibly happen in six months' time. He'd already committed the biggest folly of all by returning. Compared to that, worrying about his personal safety would be ridiculous. And whatever else, he wasn't about to spend his last months in the House in interminable conversations with Sheriff, or inebriated Raptor, who were both known to barge into any room on the third floor as if it were their own. Two bottles of beer were, in their opinion, reason enough to come for a visit, so once armed with those they didn't even bother to knock. The counselors traditionally drank. They weren't drunks, like Cases, they just drank. The difference was subtle and, admittedly, rather hard to notice at times, but they would all certainly take offense should someone have pointed that out to them. Cases were much harder to rattle. But there were some things even they resented. For starters, they didn't like being called Cases.

There weren't many people in the House who knew that Ralph was the one who'd given Cases their name. He didn't mean either their overall shapes or their mental state, as the common interpretations ran, but exactly cases, of bottles. Pinning a name on someone in the House was easy. All you had to do was walk out into the hallway at night, choose an appropriate place on the wall, scribble something on it, either illuminating your way with a flashlight or by touch, making sure that your entry did not stand out too much. It was going to be read anyway. The walls for them were the newspapers, the weekly magazines, the road signs, the advertising supplements, the communications office, and the museum of fine arts. All he had to do was put his word in and wait for it to have an effect. What happened next wasn't up to him. The name could have been forgotten and painted over, or accepted and taken up. Ralph never felt himself younger and more alive than when he went prowling in the night armed with a can of spray paint. That was all you needed, a flashlight and spray paint. Once he moved to the second floor, the task became even easier, but then he was almost caught, twice in a row, and had to stop adding his two cents to the House names, fearing that sooner or later he would be discovered and unmasked. He did not want to undermine their trust in the walls, since he himself received much that was useful from the same source. It required only diligence in reading and deciphering their scribbles. The wall was his entrance into their world, a ticket without which the admission would have been completely impossible. He learned to grasp new messages at a glance, distinguishing them from the tapestry of the old ones, once he knew the lay of the land. He never stopped to look closer—that could arouse suspicion. One unfocused glance, and he carried a riddle with him until the time when he could decipher it at night in his room, at his leisure over a cup of tea, the way others spent their time on a crossword puzzle.

Sometimes he succeeded, other times he didn't, but he never despaired, because he knew that the next day would bring another crop of messages worthy of thinking over. One thing bugged him, though, the abundance of swearwords, since they also demanded careful reading in case they concealed something important. Once the House inhabitants started hitting puberty, he even had days when he regretted his habit of reading everything they put out on the walls. Later the swearing abated, except around the Second, where it was still easy to drown in it.

He wasn't looking at the walls as he was walking down the corridor now. The intervening half a year changed the landscape to the point of unfamiliarity. He didn't want to overload his brain on the very first day of his return, trying to peel away everything they'd added in six months—where the crop of a single night was sometimes more than enough. But he still could not shield himself from the proliferation of the *R*. The letters jumped out at him, outlined and separated from the common muddle that was snaking over itself in places where the concentration of words and drawings was highest.

There might well have been intent behind this. But then, who was the target of it, he or they themselves? What was it supposed to be—a remembrance or a greeting? Something they were afraid they'd forget, or something they wanted to forget but couldn't? He was gone, but at the same time he was still here. Never before had Ralph encountered the nicks of the dead written on the walls. They were never spoken of again, their things either distributed between the living or destroyed. Closing the gap, that's what it was called. One night of mournful vigil and then every sign of the person's existence was erased, especially from the walls. The same thing happened to those who left the domain of the House. They were convinced of the inevitable annihilation awaiting them in the Outsides. The departed were treated the same as the dead, while he'd managed to both move out and still remain embedded in the walls, by their own hands. They must have known he was going to be back. But how could they? How could they be so sure of something that he himself had doubted until the last moment?

Ralph dropped the duffel on the floor and sat on the sofa. Of course they knew. *And now I know that they knew. Even though I haven't really studied the walls yet. They deliberately wrote it so that it caught the eye, so that once I was back I'd see immediately that they were waiting for me.*

I might even start acknowledging that they pulled me in, wrapped me in the spell of the letters. Start imagining them dancing around those writings, mumbling incantations and drawing magic sigils. Thinking that the only reason I returned was because they willed me to. I've only been here for a couple of minutes and the insanity is already setting in. Or maybe that's what it takes, that anyone here needs to be at least a little mad? That this place does not tolerate those who aren't?

He knew he was right, at least somewhat. One couldn't just walk out of here and then walk back in again. The House might not accept him. This had happened to others, he himself saw it not once and not twice, so he knew what he was talking about. *Something* might not accept him. It could not be put in words, it could not be subjected to logical analysis, this *Something* that was the House itself, or maybe its spirit, its essence. He wasn't looking for the right word, or for any word at all. It was just that, coming back, he knew that the final decision was not up to him. Not to him, not to *them*, and to Shark least of all. The House would either let him in or it wouldn't. So maybe it was the House they tried to placate, marking its walls with his initials. To accustom it to the idea of him returning.

"All right," Ralph said resignedly. "You can consider yourselves thanked." *I wonder what it is they need from me. Or is it just that tradition now demands the sacrifice of a counselor before graduation?*

He got up and tried to chase the silly thoughts out of his head. *If all they needed was a counselor, they've got plenty already, I'm just one more . . . And by the way, no one needs a crazy counselor, not them and not me.* He went to the window, tugged at the latch, and opened one of the panes. The cold gust burst into the room, banishing the staleness of the unlived-in space.

The crumpled clouds were hanging level with the top of the window, filling midday with the shadows of an evening-like dusk. He wiped the dust off the windowsill, sat down, and lit a cigarette, relaxing. Then threw away the end and listened. The hallway was alive with voices.

The House songs and whispers . . .

He heard feet thundering past his door, then the wheelchairs squeaking. Ralph moved to the sofa and switched on the radio. Music. He increased the volume.

Someone stopped in front of the door. Two of them. Then more. He heard the muffled conversation but couldn't make out the words. The meeting ended. The heavily shod boots of the Log messengers disappeared with the reports, and Ralph switched off the radio. He went to the door, one of those delivering a smack to the face when opened. But they were in time to jump away.

"Oooh . . . Oooh . . ."

At the opposite wall, two awkward, big-eared Logs were bowing to him respectfully. "You are back! You are listening to the radio . . ."

"Yes," he said. "As you can see."

They proceeded to simultaneously bow and shift imperceptibly to the right. *Quick, run, tell, be the first to inform everyone!* The biggest story of the day was standing right there, in the flesh, but the rules of etiquette prevented them from storming off, racing each other and yelling at the top of their lungs, announcing the news to the entire House. They suffered in silence, flaming ears, bitten lips, and all, while their eyes continued the feverish examination of Ralph. Whoever noticed something extraordinary would be king for the day. Those who already left were the first to know and were now going to be the first to tell, but those who stayed were the first to see, and they were trying to squeeze out every last drop of this feeble advantage now that the option of surprise was taken from them. The eyewitness accounts were supposed to be elaborate and deeply moving, and Ralph felt himself being mined for the moving and elaborate details, the greedy tentacles of their probing eyes burrowing under his skin.

"Dismissed," he said.

Bandar-Logs didn't move an inch, only upped the degree of passion in their stares. He decided to take mercy on them.

"I am going to the Third."

Logs gasped and galloped away, treading on each other's feet, all glistening black-leather vests and clanking rivets.

Ralph walked slowly, giving the couriers time to fulfill their purpose. Walked and looked at the walls.

The domain of the Second. Headless female forms, impossibly ample hips, spherical buttocks, bountiful breasts . . . The spaces between those were given to public criticism of the artists' abilities, verses discussing the same basic concepts, and, of course, swearing.

By his own tail, Solomon Rat

LOOK OUT! YOU KNOW WHAT I MEAN!

Swim canceled due non-stndrd clthng

Did it again. Will do again.

Rats were standing in the open doorway of their classroom, giggling, bowing and scraping in unison, as if their strings were being pulled simultaneously by one invisible inebriated hand.

"Good afternoon . . ."

Fresh from a dive in the dumpster. Scalded gray fur, glassily vibrating whiskers, the stench of garbage and naked tails covered in slime.

"Welcome back. How are you?"

Ralph walked past.

Foreheads, cheeks, and chins covered in drawings. Dark shades of any and all shapes and sizes. Rats detested bright light and shielded their eyes from it.

"Welcome back," the wall sneered at him next. The greeting was accompanied by a veritable picket fence, eight exclamation points in a row. *When did they have time?* He left the Second behind. The scenery changed to red triangles, bulls, and antelopes. The writings here were few and compact. Leopard's drawings were protected from encroachments. Ralph did not look too closely. A green arrow, pointing straight ahead:

THE PATH OF THE DRUID. FEEL THE GROUND IN FRONT WITH A POLE. S.CE EVERY FRIDAY AT FULL MOON.

What does "S.ce" mean? Could it really be "sacrifice"?

The doorframe of the Third remained unoccupied. Ralph entered and immediately heard the crunch of seeds underfoot. Seeds and dead leaves. Pods bursting noisily as he stepped on them, spreading whitish dust. Birds in the shadow of verdant vegetation, smiling. Fleshy leaves and thick trunks of various plants masking the window frames. And the smell of freshly dug earth.

Enormous, red-cheeked Elephant nodding his head, surrounded by potted violets. Purplish end of the spectrum. Beauty over the withering geranium, Butterfly under the lemon tree. Vulture perched on the stepladder, floating over the classroom all the way up to the ceiling. Two small pots with cacti kept him company there. Lizard's desk, home only to a plate of sprouted wheat, looked austere.

Birds smiled. *Chirping in the thickets . . .* There was no fear, no hostility. It could almost seem that they were glad to see him again.

Ralph sat down at the teacher's desk. A thick, whitish sprout plopped in front of him, like a grub that's lost its grip somewhere above.

Vulture dismounted from the stepladder, hobbled to the desk, muttered "My apologies," grabbed the sprout, swallowed it, and added, "Told you time and time again: if it's rotten, prune it back!"

He passed his handkerchief over the desk.

"Thank you," Ralph said.

Vulture smiled beatifically.

A cup of coffee appeared from nowhere in front of Ralph. As he was regarding it in surprise, duckweed sprang up on the surface.

"As you can see," Vulture said, "one is hard pressed to keep track of everything at once. It pains me greatly, it really does."

Ralph tried to get his mind back together.

"While I was away . . ."

"We all missed you," Birds announced happily.

Vulture beamed with pride.

"And this Pheasant flew over to the Fourth," Elephant said, picking his nose. "Who knows why. Not us, but them. Who knows . . ."

"The affairs of the Fourth are not our concern," Lizard snapped. "Keep your mouth closed!"

Angel struck a pose.

"The House is not quite the House without you, esteemed Ralph. So I keep telling them, constantly! Just ask them, go ahead, ask . . ."

"Happy to hear it," Ralph said. "Anything else?"

"A song!" Angel crowed, delighted. "Dedicated to you! Finished rehearsing it only yesterday! Permission to perform?"

Finished rehearsing . . . yesterday? A song?

"Denied," Ralph said. "Songs will have to wait."

Birds sighed in disappointment. Angel, infuriated, sank his teeth into his own arm.

"Excuse me?"

There was a small man at the door, bald, wearing a blue suit. He was studying Ralph, squinting myopically.

Ralph rose up.

"I don't believe I've had the pleasure," the small man said, stepping inside.

"I am a counselor," Ralph explained. "Back from vacation. Just came to visit with the boys. I won't interfere with your lesson."

"Not at all," the teacher fussed, "please, talk all you want. I'll come later."

"We have already talked. I don't want to disrupt. I'm sorry."

Ralph went around the bald man and into the hallway.

The teacher squeezed out after him.

"You are *their* counselor, aren't you?" The pudgy hand grabbed the sleeve of Ralph's jacket. "Would you agree"—the teacher's eyes opened wide and his voice went down to a whisper—"would you agree that they are rather . . . unusual? This smell . . . and this . . . prevalence of plant life. Would you agree? The sheer amount of it . . . And the smell . . ."

"I certainly would," Ralph said politely, unclasping the teacher's fingers. "But it's time for your lesson."

"Yes," the teacher said, looking despondently at the door. "It is. But I am certainly experiencing a palpable discomfort. Please don't misunderstand me. This is vexing."

The cloying scent of a bog wafted through the crack in the door.

"You'll get used to it," Ralph promised. "Give it time."

The teacher slumped and disappeared inside. Vulture immediately filtered through the door in the other direction.

"Lay it on," Ralph said. "Everything that's happened. And make it brief."

Vulture leaned against the wall.

"Nothing has happened in *my* pack," he reported. "And prying into other people's business—that would be against my upbringing."

"No one's asked you to do any prying."

Vulture smiled, exposing red gums.

"The biggest news is that Pompey is no longer with us. Untimely succumbed to a stab wound. Might be considered a suicide, but then again it might not. I would call it that."

"Would others?"

"The others could regard it differently."

Ralph thought it over.

"So it was not, in fact, a suicide?"

Vulture shook his head pensively. "It is a question of semantics. When a person spends a considerable amount of time and effort digging a hole in the ground, carefully installs sharpened stakes on the bottom, and then finally jumps in with a cheerful shout, I call that a suicide. But people are free to express a different opinion."

"All right," Ralph sighed. "Anything else?"

"The rest is trifling. I am having a hard time imagining what could be worthy of your attention. Maybe the one about the Pheasant transferring from the First to the Fourth. Sphinx's godson. He is yours now. Also Noble was taken away to the Outsides. The Fourth is in mourning . . ."

Vulture stumbled and fell silent, wincing as if his own words disgusted him for a moment.

"Is that all?"

"Well," Vulture sighed. "If we are to include the happenings of an earlier time, Wolf died. Back over the summer, soon after you left."

"What happened?"

"Now this, no one really knows."

A gangling, blondish apparition with bugged-out eyes suddenly came into view.

"I'm sorry," it muttered, squeezing in the door past them.

"You're late!" Vulture screamed testily. "You son of a Log, will I ever see the end of this?"

Horse moaned, shaking his hair, and disappeared inside. Vulture spat a chewed-up lemon leaf after him.

"Bastard," he said. "Useless weed!"

His face suddenly contorted; he clutched his knee and hissed in pain.

Ralph watched him intently.

"Anything else?"

Vulture was looking up at him impassively, with unseeing eyes. He descended into the pain and locked himself in it. This conversation was over.

"All right, you may go. You don't seem to be feeling too well."

There was no one who could tell for sure if Vulture was faking it or if he really was in such bad shape. He lowered himself to the floor, hugged his leg, and bent over it as if it were a sick child, swaying gently back and forth and singing to it softly through clenched teeth. Ralph waited, not sure if he should offer help. Then shrugged and continued down the hallway.

It was empty. Teachers' voices droned monotonously from behind the classroom doors. A faucet was running somewhere.

Birds . . . He probably should have listened to that song. The song that they allegedly just finished rehearsing. Now he'd never know if it really existed or if it was entirely Angel's spontaneous invention. On the other hand, it was possible that under the inspired direction from Vulture's ringed fingers they would have closed their eyes and opened their mouths, and the voiceless singing would go on and on, whipping them into a frenzy . . . And he'd have no idea how to react.

Ralph stopped and studied the wall and a trail of smeared black footprints. They went up vertically, from the bottom to the ceiling, then across it and down the opposite wall. Someone had expended a lot of time and energy to make it look like Spiderman had dropped in for a visit. That, or someone figured out how to walk upside down.

Pheasant in the Fourth. Sphinx's godson. That by itself didn't tell Ralph anything. He knew very little about Pheasants. Wolf. And Pompey. Mentioning Wolf made Vulture's leg hurt. Pompey . . . Jumped into a hole of his own making . . . Made a mistake? Maybe went against the Law? A riddle wrapped in a mystery. But Ralph knew he was not in a position to demand more. Vulture never snitched. Everything he said, Ralph would have found out anyway. From talking to Shark, if no one else. But when told by Vulture, the information took on a greater importance. Unlike Shark, Vulture knew what he was talking about and always gave Ralph a chance to decipher his pronouncements.

It became a secret game for the two of them, a game in which Vulture played on his side, his only partner in the whole House. This was the measure of Great Bird's gratitude for the night he had spent in Ralph's room—that night two years ago, following Vulture's attempt to gnaw through the walls of the hospital wing and devour its inhabitants. He should have earned himself a one-way ticket to the madhouse, but had ended up instead in Ralph's room. Ralph kept a souvenir of that night, a bloodstained towel. He had scraped Vulture's mouth with it, trying to stifle his howls. Ralph had been too busy to think about anything except keeping his hands out of harm's way, but when, through the opened windows, he had heard the Third respond, he realized what it was—a funeral lament. The towel, and the upholstery on the sofa ruined by Great Bird's teeth. Once he started crying, Ralph let go of him, and for the rest of the night Vulture sobbed with his hooked nose buried in the pillow. Ralph watched and waited. In silence, not making any attempts to soothe him.

At dawn Vulture got up, all swollen and somehow blackened, hobbled to the shower, and stood there until the morning bell rang. And then he left. Ralph spent the morning in the hospital wing with Birds, liquidating the aftermath of Vulture's performance. The Leader of the Third was nowhere to be found for three straight days. On the fourth day he appeared in the canteen in the blackest mourning and had been wearing it ever since. He might not have had many praiseworthy qualities, but he never forgot his debts and those to whom they were owed. This was how the game started, the game of "If you're so smart, figure out what I meant by that." Ralph also knew that, were he to stumble, there was always going to be a clue left somewhere. It might not be obvious, more in the manner of the wall puzzles, but a clue nonetheless. And besides, Vulture was always concise and to the point, and never talked in poor verse, the way walls sometimes did.

He called Pompey's death a suicide. Pompey had dug a hole for himself and jumped into it, getting a stab wound. Doesn't really sound like a suicide. Too circumspect. Allegorical. Not exactly wall verse, but close.

Noble is a whole other deal. Him and his mother. Who would never voluntarily take her much-too-mature son back home. So, not home, somewhere else. Where? Who knows?

And the most unpleasant one is, of course, Wolf. After mentioning his name Vulture didn't let slip even a vague hint. And that was exactly the moment when his leg started hurting. Coincidence? From what little Ralph knew about Vulture, nothing was ever a coincidence with him. Bird was certainly capable of enduring sudden pain without batting an eye. And Wolf had been one of those who'd changed reality around them. One of the strongest in that regard. A potential challenger. Could this be the answer?

The dull lights cast a yellowish pall on the hallway. Sheriff was hobbling toward him—the Second's sugar daddy and horror show. In a word—Rat, only older and bigger.

"Wow." Sheriff winked from under the bill of his cap and dissolved in a big smile. "Why, hello, pardner! What the hey are you looking for in this stinkin' swamp?"

Ralph momentarily faked surprise and joy upon meeting an esteemed colleague and effected a high-five.

"Guess I couldn't stand being away from you."

Sheriff burst out in a fit of laughter and disappeared behind the door of the Second, still giggling. *The tail, thick as a rope, slithered in after him, and Rats stepped aside to make way for it* . . . Rats giggled too, rubbing their hands.

When Ralph returned to the door of his room he found a note stuck to it with a pushpin: *This is insulting. You could have dropped by.* It wasn't signed, but there was no mistaking Shark's hand. Ralph teased the pushpin out, stuffed the note in his pocket, and went to see the principal.

Shark was waiting for him in the nonbusiness part of his office, sunk in a low armchair upholstered in cheery chintz with yellow-blue flowers. Knees above his chest, nose in the TV. He shot Ralph a sideways glance with his mottled eyes and gestured at the chair next to his.

"So you're back."

Ralph sat down and immediately sank in up to his chest as well. Shark's countenance provided irrefutable evidence of the approaching end of the working day.

"I'm leaving soon," Shark confirmed, as he sucked in the clear liquid sloshing in his glass without the help of the straw and stared at Ralph. "I don't see any reason to be waiting here for the classes to end. No reason at all. Do you see any reason? Because I don't. Nobody does. But that's the deal, apparently. I'm supposed to sit here until I'm blue in the face, even though no one cares if I do or not. No one comes, no one knocks, no one asks anything. Ever. But here I sit. Performing what's left of the principal's duties. Chained here like a dog, from eight till four, and don't even think of taking off the tie, because who knows what might happen! I have to be ready for whatever it is. If this looks like I have it easy, trust me, I don't. It is far from easy. Welcome back, dear fellow. These past years have been kind to you. Still spry."

"Six months is years now?" Ralph said, surprised.

"It is." Shark nodded. "In combat situations each month counts as a year. So, all in all, you've been AWOL for six years, which means that you should've been terminated long ago. This is not to reprimand you in any way, mind. I'm just keeping score."

"Thanks."

Ralph looked at the screen.

Shark didn't appreciate being ignored. He reached for the remote. The screen blinked off and Ralph turned the chair to face the principal. Shark's finger was waving at the bridge of his nose.

"What was the duration of your leave supposed to be? Two months. Two. Not six. You realize, of course, that you're through here. And have been for a while. But"—the finger made a circular motion—"I forgive you. Do you know why? Because I like you. And I understand why you decided to scram. Why is it that I understand? Because that's the kind of person I am. Caring and understanding."

Ralph relaxed and stretched his legs. Listening to Shark's crazy talk was a part of every counselor's job description, and had long become a matter of routine. He was thinking about Wolf. And Pompey. And the hole. What exactly was the "hole" that Pompey, according to Vulture, had dug for himself? What did Great Bird mean by that? Still, thinking about Pompey was easier than thinking about Wolf. He didn't want to think about Wolf at all.

"But who's going to understand me? Nobody, that's who. I stand alone, abandoned by everyone. Now one of my subordinates returns after a six-month absence and he doesn't even consider stopping by to say hello. I have to write notes to him! And only then does he come. What's the best word to describe this? I'll tell you. That word is 'shit.' Everything that surrounds me is shit."

"I'm sorry," Ralph said. "I would've come even without the note."

"When?" Shark's mottled eyes lit up angrily. "Tomorrow? Or maybe the day after? I demand respect. Or you can all go to hell. I'm the boss here! Am I right?"

The principal fell silent, sighing heavily into his glass.

Ralph stole a look at his watch. There were less than twenty minutes left until the end of the last class, and he wanted to drop by the Sixth before Hounds scattered throughout the House. That meant arriving there directly after the teacher left.

"You," Shark said, placing the glass on the floor and slumping dejectedly in his chair. "You're the only counselor worthy of the name in this entire hellhole. And you just up and left, ran away to the coast. Abandoning us here to be carved up."

"No one's carving up anyone."

"That's what you say." Shark's scratchy voice was pouring soft sand into his ears. "And you're the only one to say that." He sniffed at the palm of his hand and frowned.

Ralph waited patiently. The principal wasn't drunk. He was in the state that the less politically correct counselors dubbed his "period." There was no sense in trying to debate him now.

"I am very sick," Shark volunteered suddenly, staring directly into Ralph's eyes. "They don't believe me, but it's just a question of time."

Ralph affected concern. "What's wrong?"

"It's cancer," Shark said darkly. "That's what I suspect."

"You've got to go and have it checked. Might be serious."

"No use. I prefer to remain in the dark. So that when I'm killed, at least that will save me from a more drawn-out and miserable death. Which is a comfort. A rather cold one."

"There are different ways of being killed."

Shark flinched. "No kidding. Are there also different ways of saying nasty things to a terminally ill man, instead of, oh, I don't know, maybe trying to cheer him up?"

He sat there for a while, looking like he was ready to breathe his last right that moment, then looked at his watch and stirred nervously.

"Oh . . . There's a game on today. Damn! Forgot all about it!" He jumped up and looked around the office. "Right. Switched off everything. Now only the lights. And the door."

He searched his pockets.

"Want to go grab a bite?"

"No. The trip took it out of me. I think I'll turn in early."

Ralph took the keys proffered to him and turned off the lights. Shark was looking at him proudly.

"It's good to have you back. We'll fill you in tomorrow morning. Don't think your vacation is not going to really cost you in the end."

"I have no doubt it will."

Ralph locked the door and returned the key ring to the principal. He jangled it, hunting for the key to his bedroom.

"Why did Noble's mother take him away?"

"You know already," Shark said with admiration. "As usual. One foot in the door and already knows everything. I've always said you weren't quite normal. In the best possible sense, of course."

"So why did she?"

Shark finally located the key and painstakingly separated it from the others.

"Lost confidence in us. We weren't watching the guy closely enough. That's how she put it. And something about the climate here being unhealthy. A stunning woman. Hard to argue with her. I didn't even try."

"Did she take him home?"

"I don't know. None of my business. I never asked."

"She could have switched schools . . . If this one wasn't good enough for her."

Near the canteen they were greeted by a piercing bell. Ralph couldn't help wincing. Shark looked at him disdainfully, like a crusty captain might look at a former sailor long out of practice.

"You've gone weak," he observed. "Weak and lazy. And here's me holding you up as an example to the youth."

Still grumbling, he mounted the stairs. Ralph stood there on the landing for a while, watching him go, and then returned to the hallway.

The Sixth was never quiet. Even when all of them were silent, a trained ear could still catch a kind of buzzing, the hum of a spinning engine hidden in the walls. *That invisible swarm.*

The voices died down as he entered. Hounds spit on the cigarettes, extinguishing them, cascaded down from the windowsills, rolled back toward the chairs, and attempted to switch on the silence. This enabled him to hear the droning: the susurration of their thoughts that never quieted down, since there were always too many of them in this place. The song of the Sixth. They wore bright colors—not quite at the Rat level, but close—assaulting the eye with the splashes of scarlet shirts and emerald-green sweaters. But the walls of the classroom exuded a dull grayish sheen, trapping them in an impenetrable airtight rectangle, so that the windows started to seem like crude drawings stuck on the gray substance.

As soon as he closed the door behind him, he felt how stifling this vacuum was, robbing him of breath and movement. The ceiling hung too low over his head, while the walls moved slowly inward, flowing into the floor and pressing on him with a rubbery colorlessness. *They can engulf you completely, trap you like an insect, and then when the next visitor comes you'll already just be a part of the decoration, a mural indistinguishable from the rest of them, a stuffed specimen of the Sixth.*

"I want to speak with the new Leader," he said. Waited until the bout of coughing from those who choked on the smoke subsided and added, "Or with whoever considers himself to be one."

They shifted and looked down. All of them in leather dog collars—store bought and handmade, with studs and rivets or decorated with beads. He knew the answer even before anyone spoke. There was no Leader. The Leader of the Sixth was the only one of them not obligated to wear this token of belonging to the pack. Only he could walk around with his neck open. Of course, a collar could have been serving as a kind of disguise, hiding a Leader who didn't wish to be exposed to outsiders. But not a single Hound even glanced at another, no one became a momentary center of attention. There was no one among them who had taken the place of the late Pompey.

They cringed and studied their hands, as if ashamed of something. *What of? That they can't find anyone to rise above the others? Their headlessness? Their loss?*

"There is no Leader," someone in the back offered. "Haven't elected him yet."

"When did Pompey die?" Ralph asked.

"A month ago," long-faced, bespectacled Laurus said. "A little less than a month."

"And no elections yet?"

Hounds crouched, exposing the backs of their heads, trying to hide something disgraceful, something that pained them. The quiet hum in the walls grew in intensity. The walls advanced on Ralph, shielding the Sixth, but before the slippery curtain closed in on him . . .

The lamps behind the wire mesh spilling yellow light. The glistening green lake of oily paint, then a scream . . . A dark silhouette writhing on the floor, spraying blood . . .

Then the walls took over, blotting out the flying shards of the vision, discoloring and erasing them. Ralph had seen enough to understand that whatever happened to Pompey, they were all there, the entire pack, and the memory of what they saw, the bitter taste of it still in their mouths, was poisoning their existence. He was now carrying their pain and their fear—of whom, he could not yet see. They were too closed, too resistant to his attempt to understand more fully.

Every pack was built like a ladder. On every step a living soul. If the top step broke, the next one became the top. A headless pyramid immediately grew a new head. This happened everywhere and always, excluding Pheasants, of course. Every pack had not only a first, but also a second. Even Birds, with Vulture being an enormous distance, seventeen unoccupied rungs at least, above everyone else—even Birds had Lizard, ready to take the place of the Leader should anything happen to him. The only way for this order to be broken was to have someone from way below usurp the power. But then he became the Leader himself. The fact that neither of these things had happened with Hounds pointed to a third possibility. And whatever it was, it had nothing in common with the first two. Ralph hadn't the slightest idea what it could be. *I wonder what the gym has to do with all this?*

"Curious," he said.

He only realized how long he'd been standing there thinking about all of this when he saw the darkness outside the windows and felt that the pack had been exhausted by his presence. The more nervous gnawed at their fingers and made faces. The wheelers fidgeted quietly, bringing their sallow faces together. The engine in the walls buzzed in fits and starts. Everything around him was completely gray. The Sixth was stuck in its protective fence, they all now looked as if they were drowning—or had long ago drowned—in a fish tank that hadn't been cleaned in the last million years.

Ralph went out without saying a word. The Sixth's relieved exhalation was cut off from him by the door slamming back. It was immediately pushed open again, and the pale visage of Bandar-Log Zit appeared in the crack as he traced Ralph's steps.

Between the Sixth's classroom and their bedrooms Ralph moved slowly, reading the walls. Sloughing away the fresh writings like the skin off an onion, revealing old ones, smeared and by now barely visible. Dogs' heads with collars. The appeal to the "members of the umpire committee" to assemble in the yard on Saturday night. He squinted. *There it is.* A cat with a human head, crossed out with red paint. A black triangle with a hole through it. An eye inside a spiral, covered in jagged notches. All of them new. Not less than a month old. He looked again to make sure he saw what he saw. The meaning of these symbols was no harder for him to read than his own nick. The cat was Sphinx. The triangle, Black. The spiral with the eye, Blind. All three signs had been used for target practice. That was no coincidence.

Blind was crouching in front of Ralph's office, tracing invisible circles on the floorboards with his finger. His long black hair fell over his eyes. The knees peeked out of the ripped jeans. He raised his head when he heard the steps. An emaciated figure with colorless eyes, faceless and devoid of a discernible age, like a drifter who had long forgotten the date of his birth. At the same time as he was standing up, he was also getting younger and younger with lightning speed, and when Ralph reached him he was met by a mere boy.

Anyone would have written this off as a trick of light in a dimly lit corridor, a mirage that disappeared when seen up close. Anyone but Ralph.

"Hi," Ralph said, unlocking the door.

"Hello."

Ralph let him in and followed.

Blind froze once inside. Ralph had to fight the urge to take him by the hand and lead him to the chair or the sofa. *He's blind, helpless in unfamiliar surroundings, and look at that oversized sweater, the sleeves going down to the tips of his fingers, and those holes at the knees.* He closed his eyes, trying to evict the insidious image out of his head. *This is the master of the House in front of you, you dummy!*

Ralph went to the window and said over his shoulder, "Have a seat."

And immediately turned around, not sure of what he'd see: a futile search, ineffectual grasping for solid objects in the surrounding emptiness—or a sure swiftness of motion. Ralph wouldn't have been surprised if Blind were to stay frozen in place, either. Or asked him for help, stumbling over the words. But Blind just did as he was told—sat down where he was standing, cross-legged by the door, and secreted his hands under his armpits.

"I can't see you this way," Ralph said, rummaging in the stuff piled on the sofa in search of his cigarettes. "Only the top of your head. How much hair falls on your plate every time you have lunch?"

"I never thought to count," Blind said. "Is it important?"

"It is slovenly."

Ralph found the pack, lit a cigarette, and sat on the sofa.

He smoked in silence, allowing Blind to get comfortable. Or uncomfortable. Blind wasn't moving. It was obvious that he could sit here like this forever. *If this is the game you want to play . . .* The only thing betraying Ralph was the cigarette; otherwise he had turned into stone as comprehensively as Blind. The ash growing at the end of the cigarette prevented him from disappearing completely. Blind didn't have any ash to worry about. The bog-green sweater, exposing glimpses of body through its chunky braiding, had turned into parched lizard skin, the cyanotic eyelids folded over the eyes. Blind was no longer there. Ralph imagined that he was entertaining an ancient reptile, or a fancifully turned tree knot, or even a shadow of the knot. Whatever it was could remain motionless for a very long time. Ralph never had enough patience to find out exactly how long.

"Tell me what happened to Wolf. And how it happened."

Blind immediately flowed back into the boyish persona and eagerly leaned forward.

"He did not wake up. No one knows why."

Ralph looked at his cigarette, or what was left of it—a column of ash miraculously clinging to the filter.

"Is that all you can say? Try again, please. In more detail this time."

Blind shook his head.

"We were sleeping," he said. "In the morning everyone woke up, and he didn't. He behaved normally the night before, didn't complain of anything."

Ralph tried to imagine this.

Strictly speaking, Blind wasn't lying, but the incongruousness in his words was akin to a lie. Ralph was well aware of the connection they had to each other. It cemented them into packs, it drove the Third to the doors of the hospital wing the night Shadow died. *Why were they compelled to come there on that day and at that hour, all of them, even the blockheaded Logs? Was it like a bell tolling, a bell that only they could hear?* He'd seen them more than once, the hunched figures by the walls of the Sepulcher. They weren't smoking or talking, they were just there, sitting quietly. It wasn't exactly a wake, rather a way of participating in what was unfolding in a place where they couldn't be. Was it possible that they, who could sense death through thick walls, might not sense it in their own room? That they wouldn't wake up when one of them was dying?

"He was dying five feet from you and you felt nothing? Nothing was bothering you?"

"It wasn't even five feet," Blind countered. "We wouldn't have been sleeping if we'd felt anything."

"I see," Ralph said, getting up. "Why do you think I wanted you to come? Anyone from your group could have told me exactly the same thing. If you're going to insist on continuing this charade, there's the door right behind you."

Blind crouched lower.

"What should I have said so that it's not a charade? What would you like to hear?"

"I would like to hear what you, the Leader, have to say about a member of your pack not waking up one morning. If I am not mistaken, it is your responsibility to make sure they do wake up. Yours and no one else's."

"Strong words," Blind whispered. "I cannot be responsible for everything that might happen to them."

"How about knowing why it happened? Or are you not responsible for that either?"

Blind did not answer. As soon as Ralph made a motion toward him, Blind's posture changed, dissolved in a deceptive softness. *A familiar trick. Poor little House kids. This is precisely how some of them react to a perceived threat. And this is exactly when one has to be extra vigilant.* Blind relaxed, but his eyes, those clear pools stapled to fair skin, froze. Turned into ice. A chilly, snakelike stare. Blind didn't know how to hide it.

"If you want to look harmless, get yourself some shades," Ralph said, surprised at himself.

"The pack becomes nervous if I wear them," Blind said, his voice tinged with regret. "Sphinx especially. I can't ignore him."

"What does he think about Wolf's death?"

"He tries not to think about it."

"As far as I know he was rather attached to him, wasn't he?"

Blind laughed unpleasantly.

"What a strange turn of phrase . . . Attached. Yes, he was. With a steel cable. A very thick one."

"What happened to this cable that night?"

"I don't know. And I am not planning to ask him."

"Are you a heavy sleeper? Would you wake up if someone moaned next to you?"

A shadow of rage flitted across Blind's face and was gone.

"I would wake up if a mouse scurried next to me. Wolf did not moan. There was no sound from him at all. He had no time to even realize . . ."

"Ah, so that's how it is!" Ralph straightened up. "Now we're getting somewhere. How would you know what he did have time for and what he didn't? To hear you say it, you were fast asleep along with the rest of the pack."

"I just know. He was also asleep. Or his face wouldn't have been so peaceful. His fear would have awakened us all. It must have been the most peaceful death in the entire history of the House."

"If it were Sphinx instead of Wolf, and if I were to tell you of his death using the exact same words you've just used to tell me about Wolf's, would you be satisfied with my story?"

Blind hesitated before answering.

"I don't know. You're asking too much of me."

"Are you glad he died?"

He shouldn't have said that. Ralph realized it as soon as the words had been spoken. Too late. For a quick couple of seconds Ralph really expected Blind to spit pure poison at him.

"Don't you think there are things about me that do not concern you? What I feel when someone from my pack dies is my business. Don't you think?"

Blind closed his eyes, listening to something that only he could hear, and then changed his tone of voice completely.

"I am sorry. I did not mean to offend. If you needed to ask me that, then I owe you an answer." And then obligingly—Ralph caught that external force, something almost palpable making Blind strip naked in front of him—added, "I was not glad. But there is no one else I'd rather exchange for him. Not one. If this is what interests you. If it's what you meant when you were talking about me being glad. I am also innocent of his death, if you meant to ask *that*. And if you meant my dislike of him—yes, that was true. I did not like him. Just as he, me. There were times when I imagined that I would have been glad if he . . ."

"Enough," Ralph said. "I apologize. That was tactless of me."

Blind hugged his shoulders. Ralph could not shake off the feeling that he was witnessing Blind being skinned alive. Or having his carapace cracked open. And that Blind was doing it to himself.

"All right," Ralph said. "Your honesty is even worse than your silence. And if I asked you about Pompey, you'd say that you have no right to be talking about the affairs of the Sixth. Is that correct?"

Blind nodded.

"And you also haven't the foggiest idea how he died?"

"I do. But I am not allowed to say."

Ralph sighed.

"Right. So why do you suppose I ask Leaders to come here when I need information? Well, I can tell you, it's not because I enjoy listening to them brush me off with empty talk. Dismissed. You may leave."

Blind got up. "You forgot to ask about one more person."

"I didn't forget anything. It's just that I am no longer enjoying this conversation. I'm not in the mood to continue it. Go away."

Blind did not go anywhere. His face clouded with apprehension, as if he knew he had to undertake a daunting task with no hope of being able to accomplish it.

There, Ralph thought with relief. *He's going to ask for something, and I'll learn what can make Blind turn himself inside out.*

"What do you want to ask me for?" he said.

"Noble. For you to find out something about him. It's been a month since they've taken him, and we haven't heard anything. Where he is, or how he is."

Ralph did not answer, trying to hide the astonishment. The nicks on the walls, painted over; the things, distributed; the funeral laments, performed—all this he had seen and heard and known about. Those who left the House were a part of this knowledge, one of the facets he was absolutely sure of. And yet what Blind had just asked for, even the mere mention of someone who was supposed to have ceased existing, to never have existed the moment he was taken from the House, blew that sureness completely out of the water.

Blind waited patiently. Ralph's cigarette suddenly burned his fingers.

"You're dismissed," he repeated. "Go."

"What about Noble?"

"I said you may go."

Blind's face froze. He opened the door and disappeared. Ralph did not hear anything; Blind moved soundlessly.

Ralph remained standing, looking up at the glass panel on top of the door. The letter *R*, inverted back to front, oozed into the room, a warning and a caution, reminding him that he was but a part of the House.

Maybe that's the real reason for my return. To find out what happened to one of them now that he's gone where they can't reach him. And to bring them the answer . . . They've been waiting for me.

TABAQUI

"His form is ungainly—his intellect small—"
(So the Bellman would often remark)
"But his courage is perfect! And that, after all,
Is the thing that one needs with a Snark."

—Lewis Carroll, *The Hunting of the Snark*

I don't like stories. I like moments. I like night better than day, moon better than sun, and here-and-now better than any sometime-later. I also like birds, mushrooms, the blues, peacock feathers, black cats, blue-eyed people, heraldry, astrology, criminal stories with lots of blood, and ancient epic poems where human heads can hold conversations with former friends and generally have a great time for years after they've been cut off. I like good food and good drink, sitting in a hot bath and lounging in a snowbank, wearing everything I own at once, and having everything I need close at hand. I like speed and that special ache in the pit of the stomach when you accelerate to the point of no return. I like to frighten and to be frightened, to amuse and to confound. I like writing on the walls so that no one can guess who did it, and drawing so that no one can guess what it is. I like doing my writing using a ladder or not using it, with a spray can or squeezing the paint from a tube. I like painting with a brush, with a sponge, and with my fingers. I like drawing the outline first and then filling it in completely, so that there's no empty space left. I like letters as big as myself, but I like very small ones as well. I like directing those who read them here and there by means of arrows, to other places where I also wrote something, but I also like to leave false trails and false signs. I like to tell fortunes with runes, bones, beans, lentils, and I Ching. Hot climates I like in the books and movies; in real life, rain and wind. Generally rain is what I like most of all. Spring rain, summer rain, autumn rain. Any rain, anytime. I like rereading things I've read a hundred times over. I like the sound of the harmonica, provided I'm the one playing it. I like lots of pockets, and clothes so worn that they become a kind of second skin instead of something that can be taken off. I like guardian amulets, but specific ones, so that each is responsible for something separate, not the all-inclusive kind. I like drying nettles and garlic and then adding them to anything and everything. I like covering my fingers with rubber cement and then peeling it off in front of everybody. I like sunglasses. Masks, umbrellas, old carved furniture, copper basins, checkered tablecloths, walnut shells, walnuts themselves, wicker chairs, yellowed postcards, gramophones, beads, the faces on triceratopses, yellow dandelions that are orange in the middle, melting snowmen whose carrot noses have fallen off, secret passages, fire-evacuation-route placards; I like fretting when in line at the doctor's office, and screaming all of a sudden so that everyone around feels bad, and putting my arm or leg on someone when asleep, and scratching mosquito bites, and predicting the weather, keeping small objects behind my ears, receiving letters, playing solitaire, smoking someone else's cigarettes, and rummaging in old papers and photographs. I like finding something lost so long ago that I've forgotten why I needed it in the first place. I like being really loved and being everyone's last hope, I like my own hands—they are beautiful, I like driving somewhere in the dark using a flashlight, and turning something into something completely different, gluing and attaching things to each other and then being amazed that it actually worked. I like preparing things both edible and not, mixing drinks, tastes, and scents, curing friends of the hiccups by scaring them. There's an awful lot of stuff I like.

What I don't like are clocks and watches.

All kinds.

For reasons too tedious to enumerate. So I won't.

Today the House saw the return of Ralph. The man of mystery. A fossil of sorts, the only living witness among the counselors of times gone by. It's not that we particularly missed him, but with him it's somehow a bit more lively around here. Those who had joined the House in the last three years are picturesquely apprehensive of him, contributing to a unique aura whenever he's prowling the hallways. An aura of awe. I'll say it straight. This man is our Darth Vader. Clad in black, horrible, and inscrutable. The only thing missing is the wheezy helmet. And as soon as he returned, things got interesting.

The one to bring in the news was Lary, naturally. At the last period. We didn't have time to discuss it, since the class had just begun, so we had to stew until the bell. But then it started coming hard and fast. Every five minutes someone else visited us with a special report on the current whereabouts of R One. I suggested pinning a map of the House on the wall and sticking flags in it marking his movements, but no one offered help in making the map. And trying to draw it alone is no easy task. I should know. Pity, though. Ralph would have felt himself flattered by such evidence of attention to his person. It was my considered opinion that, upon return, he sank into a depression and would have benefited from cheering up.

The return in question had been a foregone conclusion, but it's been foregone for such a long time now that everyone got kind of used to the way things were, and so when Ralph did indeed return we were a bit shaken up. For us it meant that we now had someone who could put out the feelers to find out what had happened to Noble. Which meant that he'd returned in the very nick of time.

"Aha," Sphinx said, regarding this matter. The "aha" was said in That Sort of Voice, and I immediately and bitterly regretted not saying it myself.

Sometime later it becomes clear that one simple "aha" by itself wouldn't cut it. We need to somehow make the "aha" known to Ralph.

Humpback suggests we send a delegation with a petition. Sphinx disagrees, because it would—get this—look like intimidation. I suggest we send me. Everyone disagrees, for some reason. Sphinx says that if anyone goes, it should be Blind. With this everyone agrees, except Blind. Blind suggests we write a letter and send Tubby to deliver it, the reason being that Tubby has this sincerity about him. I like the idea. I have my doubts concerning Blind. Concerning his abilities as a supplicant. He's not the right person to add a good quaver to the voice at the right moment, or to exhibit persistence and even a certain blockheadedness. Whereas I certainly am. And I am flabbergasted that the pack is seemingly unable to appreciate that. Tubby would be the next-best choice, our wingless messenger pigeon, innocence incarnate coupled with an exhaustive lack of any understanding of events around him. But they don't want him either. And what a subtle move that would have been! Ralph would be drowning in tears in his dusty office.

The majority of votes go to Blind.

In the meantime Lary returns, bearing the latest news. R One had a stopover in the Sixth. He's still there, and the Sixth is suspiciously quiet. Could he have gobbled up all Hounds in one gulp?

I decide to investigate.

The hallway is bustling. Logs flit hither and thither, bug-eyed, conducting whispered conferences. The door of the Sixth is already jammed solid with investigators listening in. Stuck to it with their ears and starting to turn blue in futile attempts at not breathing. There's clearly no way to infiltrate them. I drive back, slightly disappointed. On the way I get almost knocked off my Mustang by Lary and Horse, galloping away from the Sixth. Having pushed me and Mustang out of their way, they prance off, neighing happily and not even noticing that they've bumped into something. Much less what that something happened to be.

I am back just in time for Blind's departure. Sour faced, he grudgingly trundles away in the direction of Ralph's office. Humpback, Sphinx, and Alexander go out of their way to cheer him up and give him useful advice, but for anyone willing to look closely it's obvious that the Leader is far from enthusiastic. If not for Sphinx's chirpy "aha," still lodged in my memory, I really could have become dispirited when faced with this spectacle.

Some part of my doubts must have rubbed off on Humpback.

Looking at Blind's receding back, he muses, "Are you sure we shouldn't have sent Nanette instead?"

"To have her crap all over Ralph's office?" Sphinx says.

I offer that it's very much uncertain what the effect of Blind's visit will be on Ralph's office.

"Blind has a well-developed sense of duty," Sphinx says by way of response.

This sentence sounds so officious that no one has any desire to argue with it.

And then we wait. I gnaw at my fingers, feeling more and more downcast by the minute. Since Noble's extraction, the common bed has become disgustingly spacious and desolate. Smoker does nothing to ameliorate the situation. Nor would three or even four Smokers. Noble's emotions are irreplaceable. They had kept the environment beautifully charged.

Don't you dare crawl over his covers, or breathe on his pillow, or fart by his ear! And what a pleasure it was to do exactly that, anticipating that his patience was just about ready to blow—and then watch the books, pillows, and general fur go flying. And to observe frightened Smoker. There's nothing to be frightened of anymore. We don't have another Noble in our midst.

I take out the harmonica and launch into three Waiting Songs in a row. I loathe waiting, so Waiting Songs are about the gloomiest that I have. I never could stand more than three of them together myself. And people around me usually run for cover after the first one. This time no one says a word.

When it becomes completely unbearable, I put the harmonica away and open a book of Indian fairy tales. I read them often. It's a very calming experience. I like the laws of Karma most of all. "Whosoever injures a donkey in this life, shall become one in the next." And don't even start about the cows. A very neat system. The only problem is, the deeper you get into it, the more you wonder who it was that you injured the last time around.

The fairy tales distract for a while, and then I start fretting again. What's Noble to Ralph? Nothing. Especially now. Would R One agree to bother looking for him only because we'd like him to? And if he would, would he then let us know if Noble is not doing well wherever he is now? I keep asking myself these questions, more often out loud than not, so by the time Blind finally comes back, everyone is already prepared for the worst. No small feat on my part.

"No dice," Blind says, leaning against the headboard. "I got no reaction from him at all."

And that's it. We are left with the soothing option of observing Blind, who spreads his elbows and stares into the sightless void, and Smoker, who keeps creeping farther and farther from him—imperceptibly, as he imagines. Blind's reticence sometimes verges on pathological. We all wait with bated breath, and he's just hanging there draped over the headboard, as if that was the full extent of the information he has to impart.

We all look at Sphinx. Sphinx gets the message.

"What did you talk about?" he asks.

"That's right. Pliers," I whisper to him. "And hooks."

Blind shakes his bangs over his eyes and separates himself from the world.

"Wolf," comes the indistinct reply from behind the curtain.

"And what else?"

"Only Wolf."

This, I'll have you know, is a man who is capable of recalling any conversation word-for-word, and acting it out doing voices. Regardless of how long ago it happened.

"What about Noble?"

"I mentioned Noble at the very end, when he told me to go away."

"And?"

"And I got squat." Blind hunches still further. Now we have a perfect opportunity to study the back of his head. "It's like he didn't hear me."

"That's a good sign," Sphinx enthuses.

I exchange looks with Humpback. Lary's eyes converge on the bridge of his nose, which for him signifies an increase in brain activity. Even Alexander looks puzzled.

Sphinx sighs.

"It's never the case with Ralph that he didn't hear when someone said something," he explains. "Therefore, he mustn't have liked what Blind was saying. And why would that be? There was nothing out of the ordinary in what he asked for. But to actually find out how Noble is doing, it's necessary to get to him first. That is, travel somewhere and then argue with someone to get permission for a visit. I don't think any counselor would undertake a thing like this happily. But on the other hand, if he knew that he wouldn't be doing any of that, he would've just said so. Ralph is perfectly capable of saying no. So it's a good sign that he didn't."

We exchange looks again, smug ones this time.

Lary scratches his chin and says, "There's only one thing I don't understand . . ."

But what that thing is remains shrouded in mystery. We dutifully wait for about three minutes, but Lary only scratches himself and sighs, so we finally lose interest and return to the daily grind.

For some completely unknown reason, or for no reason at all, Black chooses this particular day to get drunk. When he appears in the room he's already made good on this decision, that is, he's totally plastered, so any objections are completely useless. Different people behave differently when drunk. Black becomes unpleasant. It's not that he's a picture of friendliness even when sober, but when he drinks he gets aggressive. So he shuffles around the room in circles, like a Terminator that's blown a fuse, and tries to pick a fight. He tries and he tries, never quite losing hope, right until the dinner bell. He even continues his pointless efforts at the table, so clumsily it pains me to look at him. His disgusting behavior finds any sympathy only from Smoker. Why—beats me.

SMOKER

ON APHIDS AND UNTAMED
BULL TERRIERS

Daily Survival for a Wheeler: A Manual

Chapter 1

It is recommended that any mention of the Outsides be completely avoided as a conversation topic, with the exception of situations in which it is being mentioned:

> *a. absent any connection to the speaker;*
> *b. absent any connection to his interlocutor;*
> *c. absent any connection to their mutual acquaintances.*

Including the Outsides in sentences constructed in present or future tense is discouraged. Past tense is permissible, but not advisable either. Mentioning the Outsides in future tense with respect to the interlocutor constitutes a grave insult to the latter. Two people speaking to each other in those terms are engaging in a kind of perversion, acceptable only between very close packmates.

—JACKAL'S ADVICE COLUMN, *Blume*, vol. 7

"Because you live cooped up here. In an enclosed space. Don't you see? Completely engrossed in yourselves and in this place, like . . . like chicks still in the shell. I think that's the source of all your perversions."

"Perversions?" Sphinx coughs, and smoke streams from his nostrils and between the teeth. "How's that?"

Smoker hesitates.

"You know . . . that stuff . . ."

"Elaborate," Sphinx suggests. "That's a strong word, *perversion*. I'd like to understand what you mean by it."

Smoker glumly picks at a bead on his sweater. This sweater, in gray and green wool, was knitted for him by Humpback. Around the collar and the sleeves he attached glass balls with black pupils, the kind people use to ward off evil eye.

"You know," Smoker says, looking up at Sphinx. "You know perfectly well."

"Let's say I do. Let's say I just need you to spell it out."

Smoker looks away.

"I meant your games. The Nights, the fairy tales, the fights, the wars . . . I'm sorry, I just can't see that as something real. So I call it games. Even . . . even when they end badly."

"Is this about Pompey again?" Sphinx scowls.

"Him too. But not only him," Smoker adds quickly. "It could have been someone else. Well, all right, it is about him. Doesn't it strike you as over the top—to cut someone down only because he wanted to be the coolest guy here? Here, in this tiny, moldy figment of a world . . . Sphinx, could you please not look at me that way? You know I'm right! No Leadership can possibly be worth this."

They are alone in the canteen emptied of people. Chairs pushed away from the tables piled with dirty dishes, tablecloths spattered with sauce and sprinkled with bread crumbs. The door out into the hallway is cracked open.

Sphinx leans back in his chair.

"Smoker. Try to understand," he says, avoiding looking directly into the flushed face of his vis-à-vis. "What for you means nothing can be everything for someone else. Why is that so hard to believe?"

"Because it's wrong! You're too smart to live like this, with your eyes always closed. To believe that the world begins and ends with this particular building."

An elderly woman appears in the doors to the kitchen and stares at them, lips pursed. Sphinx stops rocking his chair, brings it closer to the table, and carefully places the cigarette end he was holding between his teeth on the edge of the plate.

"This is a question of freedom," he says. "Which can be discussed until forever, breaking only for sleep, tea, and movable feasts. Would you like to do that? Tell me, if you please, who is more free: an elephant stomping across the savanna or an aphid sitting on the leaf of whatever plant they sit on?"

Smoker is mesmerized by the cigarette expiring sadly on the plate.

"That's a silly example. Neither possesses consciousness. I'm talking about people."

"An elephant doesn't? Really?" Sphinx is surprised. "All right. Let's leave the animal world alone, if you wish. You can put out my cigarette, by the way, if it's annoying to you. Take a prisoner and a king . . ."

Smoker winces. "Please! Spare me. You're not going to try and convince me that the inmate is the one who's more free? Empty words. Do you really want to identify with a prisoner? Or an aphid?"

"I am simply trying to explain . . ." Sphinx looks past Smoker at the kitchen door. The washing lady just came out, resolutely pushing a wheeled cart in front of her. "But I see that I'm talking in a vacuum. You're not listening. Everyone chooses his own House. It is we who make it interesting or dull, and only then does it start working trying to change us. You can choose to agree with me or disagree. It really is your choice."

"I can choose nothing," Smoker fumes. "It was all chosen for me. Even before I took the first step inside. They chose the group, and that automatically made me a Pheasant. No one had asked my opinion. And if I were to go to the Second, I'd have no choice but to conform to the Rats' ways. To the idiotic image that they chose for themselves without me and long before me. Is that your idea of freedom?"

"But you didn't make a good Pheasant, did you?"

"I sure tried!"

"Not hard enough, or you would've been one by now. You decided not to. Made your choice."

"While we're at it, it's as much your fault that I didn't as it's mine," Smoker says hotly. "You ruined my reputation!"

Sphinx laughs. "Is that regret I hear?"

"Well, no . . ." Smoker accidentally dunks his sleeve into the plate still holding the remains of dinner and pushes it away gingerly. "I don't regret that. But after all that happened, you should be the last to lecture me about freedom of choice," he concludes feebly, rubbing the napkin over the sleeve.

Sphinx watches him with interest. "Look. You're not in the First now, and not in the Second. What's eating you? What kind of role do you think you're being forced to play?"

"Of someone exactly like all the rest of you."

"You don't mean we're all exactly alike?"

Smoker throws away the crumpled napkin.

"You don't even see it. You don't realize how similar you are. You're so alike it's scary!"

Sphinx looks at him in mock surprise.

"We are? You don't say. Silly me, thinking that there's very little in common between me and Black. So little that it's making communication between us almost impossible. And I also notice that for some reason you decided to adopt his views regarding everything that's around us. So it's becoming more and more difficult for me to communicate with you as well."

Smoker smiles.

"I see. A dressing-down for consorting with the black sheep."

"Who's black sheep?" Sphinx says, amazed. "You can't mean Black, surely?"

"Exactly. The only one not sharing your own view. An undesirable."

Sphinx laughs merrily. "Black? Very funny. There's only one question where he deviates from the majority, and that's the question of his own stature."

"I can always talk to him about the Outsides," Smoker counters. "To him, but to no one else."

"True," Sphinx says. "Of course he needs his own shtick. And if it happens to get on everyone's nerves, so much the better. But don't get suckered in. He's been here since age six. The Outsides for him is just as much of a fiction as it is for Blind. He's only ever read about it in books. Or seen it in the movies."

"But at least he's not afraid of it."

"Is that what he told you?" Sphinx gets up. "All right. Let's stop it here. If you could, for a moment, get unstuck from feeling tragically misunderstood, you might have some time left to understand others. If you could limit your exposure to Black it would do you a world of good. If this stern woman weren't approaching our table right now with such grim determination I could have enlightened you some more. If this door did not lead out into the corridor it would lead somewhere else . . ."

He goes to the door, pushes it with his shoulder, and goes out without looking back.

Smoker, distraught, wheels after him.

Black said: "Try talking to him seriously. You'll see him start hemming and hawing. You just haven't had a chance to observe it. I have."

Smoker scans the corridor for signs of Sphinx, but he's already lost in the sea of people walking and wheeling the other way.

Was he hemming? Hawing? The sleepless night stings his eyelids, the countless cigarettes scratch at his throat.

Sphinx walks quickly. At the entrance to the hallway he stops and lets his eyes find the familiar whitish spot on the floorboards.

You should have seen it, Smoker. Seen what they had wrought when their time came. If you'd have seen that, then for the rest of your life you would've kept your mouth shut *about the Outsides, about open and closed doors, about chicks in their shells. If only you could have seen.*

"Young man!" the bitter woman in an apron calls after Smoker. "I would thank you not to smoke in the canteen ever again. And give me your name. I shall have to report you to the principal."

Smoker turns around.

The hag is holding a tiny cigarette butt between her finger and thumb. Left there by Sphinx. Smoker regards it closely. *Did she wait on purpose until I was out here, to have an opportunity to yell at me in front of the entire House?* The headache comes on suddenly, gripping his head in a vise.

"Your name!" the narrow, slit-like mouth demands again.

"Raskolnikov!" Smoker shouts back.

The woman nods, satisfied, and disappears behind the door to the canteen. Smoker continues on his way, wondering whether she would have dared to threaten Sphinx in this fashion. And why nothing had been said about this in all the time the two of them were sitting inside.

When he passes the Coffeepot, where Logs sway amid the clouds of smoke, he sees Lary waving at him from his perch at the bar and wheels in.

"What's with staying back in the canteen? Secret talks?"

Horse picks his ear with a sharply filed fingernail.

"Lary, tell me, who's more free, an elephant stomping across the savanna or an aphid sitting on the leaf of whatever plant?"

Lary scratches his chest under the numerous crosses, nuts, and bolts hanging on it.

"How should I know, Smoker? I guess that would be the eagle who's flitting about over all of that. Why?"

"Eagles don't flit," Bubble from the Third jumps in. "They soar. They plow the sky. They own it and have it in all possible respects."

"Idiot," Lary spits back. "Never talk about things you don't understand. It's the ships that plow the oceans. And plows plow the earth."

Black-vested Logs sigh in unison.

Smoker continues along the hallway. He sees a poster, bordered in black: *In loving memory of Ard. Ghoul, our dearly departed brother. Memorial service for the deceased. Classroom 1. Poems, songs, dedications. Everyone who knew and loved him is invited to join the First on the 28th of this month at 18:00 hours.*

Smoker recalls the sallow face with protruding horselike teeth, and the interminable harangues on the dangers of smoking and the attending illnesses tied to this nasty habit. Who knew and loved him . . . What about those who knew and hated him?

The piggy little visage of Pheasant Sticks peeks from behind the poster.

"Are you coming?" it says. "You especially are invited."

Sticks is holding the poster up by means of two wooden handles. It's made of heavy-gauge cardboard, too heavy for him, but he's so proud of the task entrusted to him he's positively glowing.

"As someone who knew him. Even though you're in that other group now. You should come."

Smoker can't restrain himself in time.

"Isn't that supposed to be 'drive,' not 'come'?"

Sticks's face contorts in a grimace.

"You're a mean one. Good thing they threw you out."

He yelps and lets go of the poster. Then leans over, grabs one of its ends, and quickly wheels off. The flapping end rattles against the floorboards.

Smoker regards his fist thoughtfully. The knuckles are skinned in one place. He licks the raw pink spot.

What is it to which the person in question is trying to draw attention? It would seem that it is just his footwear . . . advertising his handicap, putting it in everyone's face. Therefore he is accentuating our common unfortunate condition . . .

Smoker starts laughing. Very softly.

Tiny spots everywhere, aphids spread over the leaves, the leaves are covered with multitudes of aphids, the leaves, the trees, the forests.

He laughs. He drives along.

You should come. How should you come? Go on wheels, but never mention it.

A MESSAGE, the wall cautions. Smoker stops to read it.

BOYS, DON'T BELIEVE THE TALK ABOUT THERE BEING NO TREES OR PINECONES IN HEAVEN. DON'T BELIEVE IT'S ONLY CLOUDS UP THERE. BELIEVE WHAT I TELL YOU. FOR I AM AN ANCIENT BIRD, AND MY BABY TEETH FELL OUT SO LONG AGO I CAN NO LONGER REMEMBER THEIR TASTE.

ALWAYS WITH YOU IN MY THOUGHTS. YOUR DADDY VULTURE.

Trees. Pinecones. An old bird with teeth. Looks more like a pterodactyl.

By the time he wheels into the dorm, Smoker is hooting hysterically.

"That's no leaf!" he shouts at Sphinx. "And no savanna either! Aphids, elephants, and toothy pterodactyls! What kind of savanna would hold all of that together, huh?"

Sphinx stares. Smoker is extracted from the wheelchair and deposited on the bed. His laughter gradually becomes more subdued. Then he just lies there looking at the ceiling. A wet rag plops on top of his forehead. It smells of spilled coffee. *I think they wiped the table with this thing before putting it on me.*

"Smoker, what's wrong?"

He's silent. Sniffing at the rag.

"That's just the autumn blues. It'll pass."

"Or it won't."

"The siren call of home," Jackal sighs. "He misses his birthingplace. Wait, that can't be the right word."

"He's just realized that he's the dregs of society," Humpback proclaims thoughtfully. "It was a flash of lightning illuminating his entire existence. Zap! And down he goes."

"Are you doing this on purpose?" Smoker says. "So that I'd have to throw up?"

The rag slithers down to his nose.

Blind noodles on the guitar, his hair touching the strings.

"Boys, don't believe the talk," Tabaqui and Sphinx sing in unison.

"There being no trees or pinecones," Humpback's voice carries upward to the ceiling, clear and precise.

"In Heave-e-e-e-n!"

Smoker closes his eyes.

The bed groans under the bulk of Black, who just lowered himself on it. His face is of a more livid hue than usual, and his breath is heavy. He's drunk. This makes Smoker nervous.

"Was I right or was I right?" Black says.

Smoker sits up.

"Don't know," he says. "Can't say."

"Right about what?" Jackal inquires. "Who was right and about what?"

Black turns to face Sphinx.

"I bet you talked for a long time, but then it turned out he never said anything. He's good at that. Flapping his gums for hours, and then you can't remember a single word for the life of you."

Smoker lies down again. He's hoping that if he manages to lie absolutely still, his head will stop aching. Humpback comes closer and shakes an enormous striped knit stocking at him.

"Hey, Smoker. This is where the Christmas presents are going. What would you like? Make up your mind in advance, in case we need to order something from Flyers."

"A working pair of legs," Black responds for Smoker. "That's what he really needs. Is it going to fit in your festive sack?"

Humpback blinks glumly.

"No," he says. "It won't."

And walks away.

Smoker feels embarrassed. Everyone is looking at him. At him and Black. Not exactly with disapproval, but with a kind of weary resignation, as if they have worn out their welcome. Both of them. And even though what Black just did was the exact same thing Smoker himself had done to Sticks, he's still uneasy. He wants to distance himself from it somehow.

"Black. Please don't," he says.

"I don't give a crap about all those rules and manners," Black says, his tone of voice indicating clearly that he's over the edge. "All those taboos. Don't say this, don't mention that. I'm going to talk about whatever I want to talk about, got that? This is the last year for all these ostriches with their stupid heads in the sand. They only have six more months to keep it down there, but look at them, Smoker. Just look at the way they lose their collective shit anytime anyone tries to say anything about it!"

The deathly stillness that follows these words scares Smoker, but also fills him with an unexpected gloating.

Humpback, crumpling the handkerchief, his face slowly reddening.

Tabaqui, in his cloak of many colors, frozen solid, with the bite of food he was chewing visible under the skin of the cheek.

Blind, fingers on the strings almost as thin as the strings themselves. His face remains hidden.

Sphinx on the headboard, like a perched bird, eyes closed.

"One's all about chicks and shells, the other—ostriches," Sphinx mumbles. "One set of metaphors for both."

"Why don't you please shut up," Black says, breathing heavily. "Like you didn't piss yourself. You're the same as them!"

"Sure. Not the same as you, thank God." Sphinx sighs. "All right, if you're done trying to mess with our heads . . ."

"Oh no-o-o," Black smirks drunkenly. "I haven't even begun. That was . . . by way of introduction. Letting Smoker have a nice, clear look at you. At the way you . . ." Black is shaking with mute laughter, unable to speak. "At the way you all alerted. Dogs, every one of you. Crazy, huh?"

He wipes the tears off his cheeks.

"Black, what were you drinking?" Humpback asks, panicked. "Talk to me. How are you feeling?"

Tabaqui makes frantic swallowing motions, trying to dislodge the piece of a bread roll stuck in his throat.

"Great!" Black shoots up and displays a wide, toothy smile. "I am feeling great!"

Smoker moves away a little. Black grabs his shoulder and whispers loudly in his ear, drenching him in alcoholic reek, "Did you see that? No, I mean it. Did you see them?"

"Yes. Yes, I saw them," Smoker says, wincing. Black has him in a steel grip. "Black, I saw everything. Calm down, please."

"You saw them, right?" Black shakes him. "Remember it well, and just wait till graduation day comes. We're going to have so much fun!"

It's not fun for Smoker right now. He yelps when Black tightens his grip even more, and tries to pry his fingers apart, hissing in pain.

"Black, let go! Please!"

Black releases him, and Smoker falls back on the bed with a sigh of relief.

"But tell you what, graduation is nothing. What I would really, really like to look at is them in the Outsides. Just a glimpse, you know! A minute or two! Because I can't imagine them there, I really can't, you know. I am trying and trying, and I simply can't." Black screws his eyes tightly shut. "Maybe I could help one of them cross the road or something," he mumbles.

Blind recognizes himself in Black's fantasies and smiles.

"Or hold back my dog if it decided to jump on them."

Tabaqui finally defeats the roll and issues an indignant squeal.

"Your dog? What do you mean, your dog? Where did that come from? It's not enough for you to roam the Outsides stalking your former packmates with the intent of dragging them from curb to curb, you have a *dog* now? Is it trained to hunt us? So that all you need to do is just sic it? Make it sniff the socks you swiped from us and then say, 'Get 'em, my precious.' Is that it? That disgusting . . . Disgusting . . ."

"Bull terrier," Sphinx prompts in a whisper.

"Right! Bull terrier! That man-eating horror! That ghastly, revolting beast! What kind of sick shit is that?"

"Tabaqui, pipe down." Blind laughs. "He said he's going to hold it. I'm facing a real possibility of being dragged across the street whether I like it or not, and I am not complaining. Even though I might have left all of my worldly possessions on the other side. Both the begging bowl *and* the piece of cardboard with 'Blind, destitute, please help' on it."

"Hold?" Tabaqui screams, his eyes ablaze. "Hold? Ha! You can't stop those bulls when they get an idea in those idiotic stumpy heads of theirs. They're all completely loony. And this one is going to be specially trained! Don't you get it?"

"But Black, he's not some kind of wimp, see," Sphinx says, shaking his head. "Besides, it's going to be his doggie, his pride and joy, his sweetie girl. Hunt together, eat together . . ."

"Shut up, you morons!" Black screams. "Assclowns!"

"I can just see it. The morning stroll. Him in a gray checkered overcoat, and the bachelor's delight by his side in a gray sweater. He is holding Blind's old sock in his hand . . . In a plastic bag, to better retain the scent . . . They're out on their daily quest."

"Shut up! You are all scared shitless, that's what!"

"Of course we are," Sphinx confirms, frowning. "We're petrified, believe me. One look at your dog . . ."

"That god-awful abomination," Tabaqui jumps in.

"Especially when you can't really see it," Blind adds.

"That bandy-legged gait."

"That pirate squint."

"That studded collar. Oh my, oh my!"

"And the gray sweater."

"Leave my dog alone!"

Black's scream is drowned by the squall of laughter. Sphinx slides down the bed frame and crashes on the floor.

"Cretins! Nitwits!"

Black shakes the common bed, then overturns it, growling, and storms out, tripping over his own legs.

"Crazy bastards," comes his voice from the anteroom, his retreat punctuated with crashing and clanking.

"The mop. The water bucket," Alexander whispers, carefully fishing Smoker from under the mattress.

Sphinx flings the blankets aside with his feet.

"If he's busted the boombox, he'd better not be coming back. I'm going to kill him personally."

"Did you see the way he went at us for that crummy dog?" Tabaqui exclaims happily, crawling among the shards of broken glass. "He could've crushed us all! Now that's power. That's what I call a proud owner!"

Smoker feels his head, realizing that, to his total surprise, it doesn't hurt anymore. He couldn't help laughing with the others, and now he's racked with guilt. As if by that he betrayed Black. Black, lonely and furious, expertly provoked and goaded. Could he maybe not have seen that Smoker was laughing?

Humpback and Alexander turn the bed back up and start picking up stuff off the floor.

"Actually . . . ," Humpback says thoughtfully. "Actually, bull terriers are remarkable animals. Very brave and very loyal."

"Who says they aren't?" Blind asks.

Humpback shrugs.

"I don't know. I got this impression that you are not too fond of them."

Tabaqui clucks contentedly.

The boombox suddenly screams at full tilt, and Blind quickly hushes it down.

"It's alive. Black is in luck today."

Sphinx wiggles his shoulders to make the jacket settle properly. One of his cheeks is covered in wet tea leaves, and the collar of his shirt turned brownish.

Smoker discovers a goose egg on his head. That must be the reason for the missing headache.

"By the way, what makes you think that the dog Black is going to have out there will be a bull terrier?" he asks Sphinx.

THE HOUSE

The House had several places where Grasshopper liked to hide. One of them was the yard after dark. He liked his thoughtful places. That's what they were for, those special spots where he could hide, disappear from the world and think. And in a strange way the places themselves influenced the thinking.

The yard distanced him from the House. When he was down there, the House allowed him to look at itself from a different angle, through different eyes. Sometimes it looked like a hive. Sometimes it turned into a toy. A painted cardboard box with a removable roof. Everything in it was real—the figurines, the furniture, all the way down to the tiniest things—and at the same time he could take off the cover and see who and what had moved where. It was a game.

He played it, and other games too, with their own thoughtful places. Behind the large sofa in the waiting room, smelling of dust, where the accumulated fluff, like pieces of a gray rag, floated away when he breathed on them or simply moved a bit. That's where the heart of the House was located. Steps echoed through it, voices of those passing by reflected in it, but the estrangement and the invasive thoughts of others could not reach here, he was left alone with his own mind and his own games. He was in the belly of a giant, and he listened to the rumbling around him, felt the beating of the enormous heart and shook with the coughs. Part belly of the giant, part darkened movie theater, and also part Blind, a very small part, because it prompted Grasshopper to strain his hearing for the soundless stirrings, to guess the meanings of conversations by a few stray snippets, and the identities of people by their steps, all in the hazy slumber of thinking. The thoughts that came to him here were viscous, translucent, invisible; the strangest thoughts he ever had. To snap out of this game he needed to lie down on the floor. To feel the coolness of the boards and the slippery leather of the sofa's upholstery. To reclaim his body and the world around him from the nothingness he dissolved them in.

He stretched his legs, probing the strange feeling of their length, their strength, the springs coiled inside. The power was everywhere, but the strongest part of it was lodged in himself, making him wonder how he managed not to fly apart—this much power could not possibly have fit in the slim body wedged between the wall and the back of the sofa. It yearned to whirl in a wild tornado, spiraling out of control, sweeping the lightbulbs off the ceiling, tying the floor rugs in knots. Grasshopper, tucked away in the giant's stomach, became the giant himself. Then it faded, melted away, as did all of his games sooner or later. But when he scrambled out from behind the sofa he still remained light as a feather, felt small and insubstantial. He was a giant in the body of a mouse, and his giant power shrank to the size of a walnut and sneaked into the flimsy suede bump on a string around his neck.

The power was akin to an enormous genie reduced to a vortex to slip into a minuscule bottle. This game was his favorite. Its scent was that of the amulet, of Ancient and his room. All his secret games originated from Ancient's room, grew out of his tasks that nourished Grasshopper's amulet just as Ancient's hand fed the triangular fish in the green tank. He played the game of the thoughtful places, the game of lookies, the game of catchies, and all of them he carried out of Ancient's room, all of them were transparent and inconspicuous like the powdered food of the triangular fish.

Lookies required him only to look. Look and see more than those who were immersed in themselves and their worries. Turned out they didn't see much at all if they didn't look closely. If they didn't need to. To play lookies, you had to watch not only someone you were talking to but also everything that was happening around you, as much as you could without turning your head or shifting the eyes from side to side. Who stood or sat where, and what they did. What was in its usual place and what moved or disappeared. The game was boring if he regarded it as a task, and exciting if he just played it. It made his eyes hurt and filled his dreams with jittery flashes. But he did start to notice things he hadn't before. As he entered the room he now saw drops and splashes, indentations in the pillows, objects moved from where they were before—the traces of events that had happened in his absence. He knew that if he played it long enough he'd learn to uncover who left those traces, the way Blind knew them by their scent or breath. Blind had been playing hearies and rememberies since birth—the two invisible games, out of four, that were open to him.

Grasshopper waited. One day out of seven belonged to Ancient. On movie nights he performed his magic using words and cigarette smoke in the darkened room—the weary, cantankerous senior in a threadbare dressing gown, the red-eyed shaman privy to the mysteries of the invisible games. Grasshopper read the words on the door as if they were incantations: *No knocking. No admittance.* Then he knocked and admitted himself into the stuffy room, where both the Purple Ratter and the Dog That Bites lurked in the dark, and the shadows whispered *Spring is the time of horrible changes*, where the table lamp was wreathed in tendrils of smoke, and the Gray Shaman told him, "Well, here you are." And dropped amulets against evil eye in wine puddles. Amulets stared at him through the red liquid, the fish stared through the glass of their tank. Grasshopper's back broke out in goose bumps, and it was the scariest and the most beautiful time in the whole world.

When several hours later he was in his bed half-asleep, he imagined that there was something sharp living inside him, something that became sharper still with each visit to Ancient, who was slowly honing it on a magical whetstone.

Grasshopper and Humpback were observing the dogs. Humpback was also shaking snow and dirt out of his coat. Dogs sniffed at the earth under their feet. The most impatient of them had already bolted, run away to other places that also might somehow provide something edible.

"It's not enough," Humpback said. "Not even close to enough for them."

"But it does give them a bit of strength," Grasshopper noted, "so they can go and search for more food."

They walked away from the fence. Hoods hanging low, shoes squelching in the mud, they shuffled across the slush of the yard. The white markings on the asphalt peeked through where the snow had already melted. In summer those indicated the volleyball court. Humpback came up to one of the cars that some teacher had neglected to put inside the garage and prodded the iced-over fender with his finger.

"Cheap trash," he said. "This car, I mean."

Grasshopper liked old cars, so he didn't say anything. He squatted to look for the icicles on the underside of it, but there weren't any. They shuffled on, toward the porch.

"You know what? I feel much better now that we fed them," Humpback said. "All the time that I think about them I feel . . . uneasy. But then when I feed them it goes away."

"I see these black cats sometimes," Grasshopper offered distractedly. "Sneaking under the bed. Or under the door. They're really tiny. Strange, huh?"

"That's from your fuzzy looking. Everyone keeps telling you to stop the fuzzy looking. But you keep doing it. I'm surprised it's only cats and not, I don't know, elephants running around. Like Beauty's shadow, you know."

"That way I can see much more," Grasshopper said, trying to defend the look-ies, more out of habit than to really convince Humpback.

Some tasks he couldn't really keep secret. Poxy Sissies caught on to lookies almost immediately. And they hated it. It was very hard to hold a coherent conversation while playing lookies. Grasshopper still couldn't, no matter how hard he tried.

"Yeah, right," Humpback snorted. "More indeed. More of the black cats that don't exist."

"What's the shadow that Beauty sees running around?" Grasshopper asked in a clumsy attempt to change the subject.

"His own. But it's kind of alive. Don't go asking him, though. He's scared of it."

They came to the porch and tapped their shoes on the steps to shake off the dirt. A senior girl was sitting on the railing, smoking and looking out into the yard. Witch. She didn't have a coat on, only a suede vest over a turtleneck. Grasshopper said hello. Humpback did as well, but secretly crossed his fingers inside his coat pocket, just in case.

Witch nodded. Water was dripping off the roof and ricocheting right onto her pants, but she paid it no attention. Or maybe she just liked sitting in this particular place.

"Hey, Grasshopper," she called. "Come here."

Humpback, who was holding the door for him, turned around. Grasshopper dutifully approached Witch. She threw away the cigarette.

"You can go," she told Humpback. "He won't be long."

Humpback shuffled his feet by the door, looking at Grasshopper sullenly from under his hood. Grasshopper nodded to him.

"Go. Look, you're soaked."

Humpback sighed. He pulled the door wider and entered it backward, not taking his eyes off Grasshopper, as if pleading with him to reconsider before it was too late. Grasshopper waited until he was gone and then turned to Witch. He wasn't scared. Witch was the most beautiful girl in the whole House, and his godmother to boot. Not scared, but definitely uneasy under her fixed stare.

"Have a seat. We'll talk," Witch said.

He sat next to her on the wet railing, and her fingers pulled the hood off his head. Witch's hair reached to her waist, like a shiny black tent. She never did anything to it, allowing it to flow freely. She had a very white face, and her eyes were so dark that the pupils flowed imperceptibly into the irises. Genuine witch eyes.

"Remember me?" she said.

"You were the one who named me Grasshopper. You're my godmother."

"Yes. It's time we got acquainted more closely."

She sure chose a strange place and time for it. Grasshopper was getting wet sitting on the railing. And it was slippery. And Witch wasn't dressed properly. As if she'd rushed to get closer acquainted with him so fast she didn't have time to grab a coat. He dangled one leg and touched the floor with his toe to steady himself.

"Are you brave?" Witch asked.

"No."

"That's too bad," she said. "I wish you were."

"Me too," Grasshopper admitted. "Why do you ask?"

Witch's black eyes flashed mysteriously.

"Getting to know you. You like dogs?"

"I like Humpback. And he likes dogs. Likes to feed them. And I like to see him do it. But I do like them too."

Witch pulled one leg up, put the foot on the railing, and lowered her chin to her knee.

"You could help me," she said. "If you'd like, of course. If you don't want to, I'm not going to be angry."

A drop found its way down Grasshopper's neck. He shivered.

"Doing what?" he said.

This must have had something to do with dogs and being brave. Or maybe he just imagined that because she'd mentioned those things.

"I need someone to carry my letters to a certain person." Her hair fell down over her face. "Do you understand?"

He did. Witch was of Moor's people. Letters were for one of Skull's people. That much was obvious. It was also bad. And dangerous. For her, and whomever the letters were for, and whoever would deliver them. It would have to be a secret from everybody. So that's why she asked about him being brave. And that's why the yard, the twilight, no coat, no hat. She must have spotted him out the window and rushed straight down.

"I understand," Grasshopper said. "He's one of Skull's people."

"Yes," Witch said. "You got it."

She reached into the pocket and took out cigarettes and a lighter. Her hands were turning red from the cold. He noticed loose threads hanging off the patch-work suede vest.

"Scared?" she asked.

Grasshopper didn't answer.

"Yeah, I am too," she said. Then lit the cigarette. Dropped the lighter, but didn't pick it up. Hid her hands under her armpits and hunched over. Silvery water beads glistened in her hair. Witch swayed back and forth on the railing and watched him.

"You don't have to," she said. "I am not going to put a curse on you. If you believe that nonsense. Simple yes or no, that's all."

"Yes," Grasshopper said.

Witch nodded, as if she never expected a different answer.

"Thank you."

Grasshopper was swinging his leg, soaked all the way to his underwear. And he didn't care about being wet anymore. The yard was sinking into the deepening blue. He heard dogs howling somewhere. They might have been the same dogs Humpback and he had just fed.

"Who is he?" Grasshopper asked.

Witch slid off the railing and picked up the lighter.

"Who do you think?"

Usually Grasshopper liked guessing games, but right now he was too cold, and Skull's people were too many to recall each of them one by one and try to imagine if she could have fallen in love with them or not.

"I don't know," he said resignedly. "You'll have to tell me."

Witch leaned closer and whispered in his ear. Grasshopper's eyes opened wide. She laughed softly.

"Why didn't you just say so? Like first thing! Why?"

"Shhh. Quiet," she said, still laughing. "There's no need to shout. It's not really important."

"How could you not say it?"

"To make sure you didn't agree only because of that. I wanted you to think it over properly."

"It will make me so happy," Grasshopper whispered.

Witch laughed again, and again hid her face behind hair.

"Of course," she said. "Of course it will . . . Still. Don't you want to think about it?"

"Where's the letter?"

She warmed her hands with her breath and took an envelope out of a vest pocket.

"Take this to your friend," she said. "He'll give you another one, bring it back to me. Tonight. First floor, by the laundry room. After dinner. I'll be waiting. Or maybe you'll have to wait a little. But be careful."

"What friend?" Grasshopper said, surprised, but then understood. "Blind?"

"Yes. Try to do it so that no one sees you."

"And you didn't say anything about Blind either. Why?"

Witch put her hand in his pocket, stuffed the letter all the way down, and then buttoned the flap.

"You were testing my courage," Grasshopper said. "Testing *me*. But I would have agreed anyway."

Witch brushed his face with her fingers.

"I know."

"Because you're Witch?"

"I'm no witch. I just know. I know many things."

She pulled the hood over his head.

"Let's go. It's getting cold."

Grasshopper was not feeling cold at all. Quite the opposite.

"Tell me," he whispered when they were climbing the stairs. "Tell me, what is it you know about me?"

"I know how you're going to be when you're older," she said.

Black tent of hair and long legs. Sharp clatter of steel-shod boots on the steps.

"Really?"

"Sure. It's obvious."

She stopped.

"Run along, my godson. It would be best if we weren't seen together."

"Yeah!"

He took the rest of the stairs at a run and only turned back when he reached the landing.

Witch raised her hand in a farewell gesture. He nodded and took off again. He ran without stopping the rest of the way. The soaked jeans clung to his legs.

What does she know about me? What am I going to become when I'm older?

Blind wasn't in the room. Magician, his bad leg propped on a pillow, absentmindedly tortured the guitar. Humpback's bunk was topped by a triangular white tent. This tent, made from bedsheets strung over wooden slats, came crashing down every morning, and every night Humpback resurrected it. He liked his privacy.

Grasshopper looked at the tent. Someone was moving inside it now. The walls bulged and flapped. But the entrance was tightly closed, so that no one could peek in. Grasshopper sighed with relief. Humpback was in and busy with his own concerns, not keeping watch by the door armed with probing questions, as he'd feared.

Stinker was also busy, stringing pieces of apple, planning to hang them up for drying. Humpback's coat, wet and plastered with dirt, lay on the floor.

Wolf dangled his feet off the windowsill.

"What we need in the yard is a field kitchen," he said. "For all the stray dogs. Then you and Humpback could don those white toques and the dogs would form a line. Each holding a bowl in its front paws."

"Wolf, can you see how I'm going to be when I grow up?" Grasshopper said.

"Some things, I guess," Wolf said, surprised. "Why?"

"No reason. I just thought you might know."

"You're probably going to be tall. And thin."

"And covered in spots," Stinker squeaked. "All the seniors have zits. Face like a strawberry patch. You're going to be sort of spotty reddish blond. Oh, and sideburns. The unkempt kind."

"Thanks," Grasshopper said darkly. "What about yourself?"

"Who, me?" Stinker waved the unfinished string of apples in the air and closed his eyes dreamily. "Yes, yes, I can clearly see myself! Six years from now. A fine specimen of a man. No one is immune from the overwhelming charms of my piercing gaze. Women go weak-kneed and drop at my feet. In droves. All I need to do is lean over and pick them up, the poor darlings."

"When you do that, try not to trip over your ears," Wolf warned. "Or they'd think a mosquito fell on them."

Stinker turned away, scandalized. Humpback's tent wobbled and produced a shaggy head.

"Wolf, this book is disgusting. This one run through with a sword, that one run through with a sword. I've had enough. I'm going to have nightmares about them now."

"Then stop reading. It's your choice, no one's making you."

Humpback pulled in his head and angrily fastened the flap. The tent shook again. Wolf and Grasshopper watched it with concern until it stopped listing to one side.

"They're going to take me to the Sepulcher for a day or two," Wolf said. "Tomorrow morning. But only for a short while."

"Why?" Grasshopper asked. "I thought you were cured."

Wolf lay on the floor with his hands behind his head.

"They want to stuff me in this corset. So that I go around with the Sepulchral shell on my back. Like a tortoise. Old and wise."

He tried to make it sound like a joke, but there was something in his voice that Grasshopper hadn't heard for a long time.

"Are you scared?" he asked.

"I'm scared of nothing," Wolf said.

His eyes became very angry. Grasshopper winced.

"Please don't, Wolf . . . Your thoughts now smell different than your words. It's so obvious."

Wolf propped himself up on his elbows.

"Say again? Thoughts have a smell now? And you can hear it? I'd understand if Blind was saying this stuff. But the only one who talks like that is you. How come?"

Wolf was mocking him, but the sharp thorns in his eyes had faded away, and Grasshopper relaxed.

"Just a shitty turn of phrase," Stinker mumbled.

"Shitty yourself," Humpback countered from within the depths of the tent, defending his friend. "It's beautiful. Grasshopper talks poetically."

Grasshopper laughed. Humpback peeked out again.

"What do we do if they don't let you out? Could that happen?"

"In that case I'll send over a note with precise instructions," Wolf said.

Stinker perked up.

"We'll follow them to the letter," he promised. "The House shall be quaking all the way down to the foundation, or my name is not Stinker. We'll chain ourselves to the gates of the Sepulcher. Douse each other in kerosene and play catch with matchbooks. Top-notch treatment guaranteed."

"I believe you," Wolf said earnestly. "You're just the type to pull it off."

It was dark and lonely down at the laundry room. Grasshopper sat on the floor by the locked door, waited for Witch, and tried to think about nice things. And not about hearing someone's ragged breath nearby. Or how that someone seemed to be creeping closer. Or how that hole in the wall glinted suspiciously. Like there was an eye behind it.

The hallway here smelled of bleach. The feeble lamp hardly illuminated it, and the library stacks a little farther on were shrouded in complete darkness. Grasshopper tried not to look in that direction, to avoid seeing the inky shadows of the revolving racks where seniors dumped old issues of magazines. He didn't like those shadows a single bit. And the more they stayed motionless, the less he liked them.

The groaning of the elevator distracted him. Grasshopper listened intently. The doors clanked, and someone's steps swished over the linoleum floor. He got up.

Witch stepped out into the pool of light.

"Sorry I'm late," she said. "Must be scary waiting here all by yourself."

The shadows of the cabinets and the eye in the wall went right out of Grasshopper's head.

"What's scary about it? There isn't anyone here," he said. "I have the letter in my pocket. And I gave that other one to Blind. Just as we agreed."

Her hand slipped into his pocket and took out the envelope. Grasshopper expected her to hide it, but instead she ripped it open and began to read. Grasshopper kept his eyes down. The letter apparently turned out to be very long.

"Thank you," Witch said as she finished reading. "I hope you weren't too cold back in the yard. It was darn freezing out there."

"I wasn't."

He watched as she produced a small lighter and put the flame to the corner of the envelope. The fire sprang up in her hands. She turned it this way and that with the fingers, dropped the last remaining scrap, and stomped on it.

"So that's that," she said, rubbing the ashes with her heel.

That was when Grasshopper got really scared. He knew that the letter was a dangerous thing to be carrying, but only now that Witch had burned it did he realize that he'd been walking around with that danger in his pocket and had even managed to forget about it sometimes.

"It's all right," Witch said, guessing at his horror. "Don't think about it. We'll try writing each other less frequently. But you and Blind shouldn't be talking about it. Even when you're alone."

"Blind wouldn't be talking about it even if we were alone in the middle of a desert," Grasshopper said. "Blind never talks about things that don't concern him. Or those that do, actually."

"That's good. Come out into the yard from time to time. After dinner. Alone. If you see me there, don't try to talk to me, just walk by so I can put the letter in your pocket. Deal?"

Grasshopper nodded.

"Is it hard . . . being Skull's girl?" he asked, blushing at his own indiscretion.

"I don't know," Witch said. "Compared to what? Probably not any harder than being Moor's girl, I guess."

Grasshopper chewed on his shirt collar a bit.

"You said you knew what I'll be like when I grow up. Could you tell me? It's kind of important."

"It's hard to explain," Witch sighed. "It's more like a feeling than a picture. But I can promise you that girls are going to like you."

"They're going to drop down at my feet," Grasshopper said wretchedly. "Defeated and helpless. I'd only have to pick them up without stepping on my ears. My zits and patchy sideburns will drive them crazy."

Witch gave him a puzzled look.

"I've no idea who it is you just described. It definitely has nothing to do with you. Go back. I'll hang out here for a while."

"Good night," Grasshopper said.

She thinks I'm stupid now, he thought dejectedly. *All because of Stinker.*

Grasshopper was fighting the typewriter. He only had the first few lines of the letter: *Hi, Wolf. How are you? We are good. Waiting for you. One day is already over, and the second is half-over. So tomorrow we are waiting for your note with . . .* The word *instructions* was giving him trouble. Grasshopper had already found and discarded two different ways of spelling it. Humpback hovered over his shoulder, sighing loudly but not daring to offer help.

"I think it has two *i*'s," he blurted finally.

"You mean *iinstructions*?" Grasshopper said acidly.

Humpback went red.

"No. I didn't mean that. Not both of them in the beginning."

"Keep it to yourself, then."

"Send my regards," Stinker squeaked from the bed.

"I haven't gotten to the regards yet. And stop interrupting! Or I'll never finish."

Grasshopper conquered "instructions" and paused to think about what was next, absentmindedly gnawing at the finger of his prosthetic hand.

"You're going to break it," Humpback warned in a whisper.

Grasshopper put away the finger.

There was a knock at the door.

"Enter," Stinker yelled in a high-pitched voice.

The door squeaked and admitted bashful Siamese, the pride and horror of Stuffage. Both of them at once, pressed against each other.

Grasshopper directed a panicky look behind their backs, waiting for Sportsman to come barging in on their heels, and the rest of Stuffage with him. But the twins were alone. They took a few more steps and froze, still inseparable, glued together. Same clothes, same face—indistinguishable like two coins.

"What do you want?" Grasshopper asked.

Blind stopped caressing the book with the indented pages and raised his head.

"We need to talk," Siamese said.

"Very suspicious," Stinker noted. "I don't think I like the sound of that at all."

Siamese apprehensively shuffled their feet. Tall, lanky, thin lipped, and . . . *kind of hinged,* Grasshopper thought unkindly. Aquiline noses peeking from behind flaxen bangs, round gold-colored eyes, cold and unblinking, almost a seagull's stare.

"Did Sportsman send you, or are you by yourselves?" Blind asked.

"By ourselves," Siamese said in unison. "We came because . . . we wanted to ask . . . could we also . . . move to your room?"

They seemed to press their sides against each other even tighter. Sighed loudly several times and fell silent.

"Where did that come from?" Humpback said.

Siamese didn't answer. Outside of their domain they looked subdued and not as ghastly as they usually did, but nowhere near pleasant either. The elbows of their white hoodies were of a blackish tint, and each had a badge on a chain around his neck. One with the letter *R*, and the other with the letter *M*. The badges always turned themselves blank-side up, making them pretty useless for distinguishing which of Siamese was which.

"So you're not letting us?" the left Siamese asked glumly.

Grasshopper didn't have time to answer. The door slammed open and excited Magician, looking past Siamese, waddled into the room.

"Wolf's coming!" he shouted. "Honest! They let him go!"

"Hooray!" Stinker said.

Everyone transferred their attention to the door. Grasshopper thought with relief that now he didn't have to finish typing the letter. Humpback huffed jubilantly right behind him. Stinker grabbed the binoculars, for some reason. Siamese stealthily shuffled to the side, whispering among themselves and throwing sullen glances at Grasshopper.

"I am the knight in armor of purest plaster!" Wolf declared, appearing at the door. "And I seek a squire, loyal to the end and properly fit to kneel and bind my shoelaces, for I, clad thus in armor, am akin to a tortoise fettered by its carapace."

He approached Grasshopper and poked him with an umbrella handle.

"Come, be my squire, noble youth. A bag of gold rewards each year of your service. And should I perish, this splendid armor passes on to you, and you can fetch good coin for it."

Wolf lifted his sweater and tapped on the plaster.

"You won't regret it. Your life shall be filled with wonders beyond measure."

Grasshopper nodded.

"I gladly accept. But we have Siamese here . . ."

Wolf squinted at the twins.

"My trusty helmet obscures my vision," he said. "But tell me, noble youth, isn't this just evil spirits tempting me by choosing to assume two visages so like each other and reveal them to my gaze?"

Siamese exchanged glances.

"Spirits, of course." Stinker giggled. "Who else? And now they want to live with us. If we agree."

Wolf thumped the umbrella on the floor. It opened.

"Sorcery," Wolf muttered, closed the umbrella, and turned to Stinker. "Your words are indeed puzzling to me, young friend. This cave where we have assembled does not belong to us. By God's infinite grace any vagabond is allowed to enter, dry his cloak by the fire, and regale us with tales of his adventures. Thus he repays us for our hospitality. If these two are not an infernal apparition, even though the similitude of their faces burdens my senses heavily, by all means do invite them closer to the fire and assure them of our goodwill."

Siamese gaped at Wolf, dumbfounded, their seagull eyes unblinking.

Wolf tapped the floor with the umbrella again.

"Are you of low birth? For what reason do you conceal your names from us, as if ashamed? Could it be that you have covered them with dishonor? Could it be that you are in fact Cain's issue, cursed to forever roam the world?"

"Nnnooo . . . ," one of the Siamese moaned. "We're . . . We're not that at all!"

"Knights is what we are," the other offered brightly. "Caught in a storm."

Wolf lifted an eyebrow and fixed the brothers with a suspicious stare.

"Warm yourselves, then," he said finally, "and relate your story to us."

He sat down on the floor. Magician, Humpback, and Grasshopper quietly took their places around him. Siamese exchanged glances and sat down too, cross-legged and identically hunched.

"Are you in trouble, knights," Humpback whispered. "Wolf can keep up this charade until lights out."

Magician, without even waiting for further instructions, placed the guitar down at his feet, propped it up with a chair, and strummed it a couple of times.

"Ah," Wolf said. "The splendid minstrel and his harp. You are here as well."

Magician nodded smartly, picking at the strings.

"And there is the captive monster, once the devourer of innocent maidens, but now repentant."

Stinker contrived to look deeply repentant. He did it mainly by hanging halfway off the bed and sounding a mournful wail.

"It rues its misdeeds greatly," Wolf translated. "Daily it recounts the unfortunate girls in its prayers, imploring mercy from their enraged shadows."

"Oh . . . Oh . . . ," Stinker moaned. "Theresa, Anna, Maria, Sophia . . ."

"Let us not dwell on that," Wolf interrupted. "We have visitors."

Now everyone was quiet. Magician continued strumming the guitar. The hamster stomped over Humpback's sweater, sneezing from time to time. Siamese felt the collective attention on their persons and shifted uneasily.

"You said you didn't need tough guys," the left Siamese said to Wolf. "And we're not. We don't like them either. And they don't like us. We're by ourselves. If no one picks on us, then we don't pick on anyone. And they call us thieves any chance they get. And they do pick on us. And now those newbies."

He sighed.

"But you're not going to take us in, I know."

And he threw a sideways glance at Grasshopper.

Because we used to beat you up, Grasshopper completed the sentence in his head.

"Could you take Elephant, at least? He's scared of that newbie, Spot. He spooks all the time and starts bawling. Take him in, huh? He's very quiet when he's not scared. He just plays all day by himself."

"Would he go without you?" Grasshopper asked. "He likes you."

"We'll talk to him," Siamese promised. "He's a very reasonable kid."

This was Max. Grasshopper managed to distinguish the letter *M* on his badge.

"Just show him this wall." Rex giggled. "You won't be able to pry him off it."

"Until after dinner," said Blind, who had been sitting silently in the corner all this time. "Then he's going to remember about you and start bawling. And then it's either take him back or take you in. Or jump around him all night with handkerchiefs at the ready."

Siamese blushed and pressed even closer together.

"Bring Elephant," Wolf said, "and you both come too. Just quit confusing us. And using Elephant to guilt us."

Rex stood up and helped up his brother.

"Thank you," he said with a smirk, "O Plaster Knight."

It was a crooked smirk. The only kind Siamese were capable of. Rex wanted to say something else, but his brother tugged at his sleeve.

They're completely different, Grasshopper thought, surprised. *You only have to look closer.*

The twins departed. Humpback looked over the beds and whistled.

"Now we are ten Sissies. Full complement. But they'll never be able to climb the top bunks. Them, or Elephant either."

"I'll move upstairs," Wolf said reluctantly. "And Blind will also have to. There's no other way."

Stinker swayed on the pillows.

"They are burglars," he said. "And thieves. They've got a crapload of lockpicks and other things that are useful to have around. They can rob us clean and sneak back to Stuffage. We'd be left with nothing."

"Let them try," Wolf said. "We'll set your goblin loose on them. Hey! Speaking of which, cover it up quick before Elephant comes. Or the entire House is going to come running here when he starts wailing."

Humpback and Magician pushed the nightstand against the goblin and then placed a salad bowl on top. The radio went on top of the bowl.

"There's only this ear peeking out," Magician said. "But you can't see whose ear it is, so he won't be afraid of it."

"This is the way art is suppressed nowadays." Stinker sighed. "I only poured my entire heart into that goblin."

"That much is obvious," Humpback said. "Your black soul is right there for everyone to see."

"It sure is noisy in there," Blind said. "In the Stuffage, I mean. I'd even say raucous."

"Could it be they're not letting them go?" Grasshopper said hopefully.

"Something like that," Blind said, creeping closer to the wall and pressing his ear against it.

Magician turned down the radio. Now all of them could hear the noise behind the wall.

"Tell us, Chief Keen Ear, what's the news?" Wolf said.

"Keen Ear yourself," Blind shot back. "Sounds like they're getting beat up. But I can't tell for sure. Can't hear much besides Elephant raging."

"So that wasn't a ruse," Wolf said contentedly. "Them coming here, I mean."

Wolf looked at Grasshopper. Grasshopper frowned miserably.

"They're kind of ours now," he said. "They're Poxy Sissies too."

Wolf nodded. "Exactly what I was thinking."

"We have to go fight for them," Grasshopper sighed. "If they're ours."

Running to the rescue of Siamese was the last thing he wanted to do.

"You mental?" Stinker said indignantly. "There're only five of you. They're going to dispose of you and then mount an assault on the room. And take all the useful things. It might even happen that I could suffer as well."

Grasshopper slipped his foot into his shoe and extended the leg toward Wolf.

"Could you tie this up, please?"

Humpback was already holding the second shoe.

"Come on, hurry up, let's go," he said. "They're two against them all."

Magician armed himself with a spare guitar string. Blind peeled his ear off the wall.

"They're already out into the hallway," he said in a featureless voice. "No need to rush."

Humpback slapped the other shoe on Grasshopper's foot and ran for the door. Grasshopper, tripping over the laces, dashed after him. They raced each other out of the room.

Siamese were indeed there. Them and the entire Stuffage. One Siamese was visible. He held off the attackers with a duffel bag. Next to him on the floor, where the other one appeared to have been tripped, something spiderlike was whirling about, waving its multiple arms and legs. Humpback let out a battle cry that sounded like a car alarm going off, and jumped right into the thick of battle. Grasshopper swung his leg at someone's backside sticking out of the spider and continued to punch whoever came up to the surface. Blind sneaked by, but Grasshopper was too busy to trace his further movements. The seething mass was already whelping enemies—Muffin rose up, groaning, and Crybaby readied his fists. Looking at them, Grasshopper suddenly realized, to his horror, that he'd forgotten to take off his prosthetics. This was the most important thing, more important than the shoes, more important than anything in the world!

"Don't you dare!" he screamed at the top of his lungs into the closest face and swung at it with his foot. The face disappeared, but another one took its place, which Grasshopper also hit, yelling, "Don't you dare!"

I broke his nose! I wonder whose nose?

The battle raged around him. Grasshopper tried to get to Wolf, who was fighting nearby, but someone's hand grabbed his ankle. He stomped on it with the free foot; the untied shoe flew off and immediately was lost in the melee.

All Grasshopper could think about was that they mustn't break the prosthetics. Someone shoved him in the back, he fell over on top of Crybaby, and then someone fell on top of him. Someone heavy. Crybaby squealed. Grasshopper writhed, knocking his knees against him. Someone was sitting astride Grasshopper's back and pummeling him. It hurt, but judging by his whimpering, Crybaby was hurting even more.

"Look out!" somebody screamed.

He saw spinning wheels. Stinker's wheelchair came to a stop right by his nose.

"Look out," Stinker squeaked again and brandished an umbrella.

Muffin loosened his grip and Grasshopper, now freed, was able to roll aside.

"Take that, fiend!" Stinker exclaimed and speared Muffin with the umbrella.

Grasshopper kicked Muffin in the belly. Muffin, defeated, crawled off, but there appeared Whiner, swinging a hockey stick at Grasshopper. Grasshopper managed to kick him, but the unshod foot could not do much damage. The stick struck Grasshopper in the ear. The ear flashed. The second blow landed on the prosthetic.

"You broke it," Grasshopper whimpered and rushed Whiner, forgetting all about the stick. For some reason Whiner threw the weapon away and bolted. Grasshopper ran after him. Somebody tripped Whiner, he tumbled, rolled over onto his back, and squealed, terrified. Grasshopper was bearing on him inexorably, like a comet, leaving trampled hands and feet in his wake, the enemies scattering around.

Then someone grabbed him and lifted him off his feet. Grasshopper started kicking, attempting to free himself.

"OK, cool it down," a grown-up voice said.

Suspended above the field of battle, Grasshopper saw Magician using his crutch to beat back Rabbit and Crook, Stinker's overturned wheelchair, Stinker himself wildly flailing the umbrella in all directions, Sportsman rolling on the floor tangled with someone—and seniors. Lots of them. Swearing and laughing, they were pulling the boys apart.

The back of Grasshopper's head pressed against something sharp. He froze, struck by a sudden realization, and turned around. A small skull on a chain scraped against his cheek. Grasshopper couldn't make himself look farther up.

I kicked Skull!

His head spun. He felt faint and sick to his stomach.

Skull turned him around and lowered him to the floor.

"Well? Better now?"

Grasshopper swayed on the spot. A tattooed arm shot out and steadied him.

"I didn't know," Grasshopper whispered. "I didn't know."

"You didn't know what?"

Skull's gray eyes were sprinkled with tiny dots.

He's got speckled eyes. Dappled. How curious.

The seniors shoved the boys into the dorms. The door of the Stuffage bristled with grimacing faces. The faces spat and shouted abuse.

"Shoo!" the seniors yelled back.

Sportsman and Blind were the last to be pried from each other. Magician and Humpback, holding the tattered remains of their shirts, disappeared into the Poxy dorm. Siamese crawled on the floor, picking up the spilled contents of their bags. Elephant followed them one step behind, drowning in tears.

"Outrageous!" Splint, the counselor, was screaming. "All of you! To the principal! Right now!"

Elk was stuffing Stinker into his wheelchair. Stinker was putting up a fight. Grasshopper had some time by now to collect his thoughts. He turned back around, planning to apologize to Skull, but found that he wasn't there anymore. He was already leaving with the other seniors. Grasshopper caught a glance from one of them, and then heard: "That armless squirt, he was fighting like a tiger!"

The seniors laughed. Skull stopped and looked back at Grasshopper. Very somberly. He was the only one not laughing.

"To your dorm, on the double," Splint hissed in Grasshopper's ear, and he ran, limping on the shoeless foot. He was burning with shame. The seniors didn't know that he only fought like a tiger because of prosthetics. They would have laughed even more if they knew. Except maybe for Skull.

"Principal's office in half an hour!" Splint shouted behind him.

The sinks in the bathroom were mobbed by the casualties. There was water all over the floor. The sock on Grasshopper's unshod foot got soaked through.

"The plaster armor is like the most useful thing to have around. The enemy forces disable themselves, you don't even have to do anything. Just get yourself open and wait for someone to take a swing at you."

Wolf emerged from under the faucet and looked at Grasshopper.

"Oh. There you are."

"There he is!" Stinker screamed. "The Vanquisher of Stuff! The Avenging Foot! The Heel of Death! Yay!"

"The crutch is useful too," Magician bragged. "You should have seen the way I caught Crook with it."

Humpback splashed loudly, bathing his busted lip. One of the Siamese, a little worse for the wear, probed a loose tooth.

"They accused us of stealing," he said, extracting the finger from his mouth. "And we like never even saw those pins of theirs."

"I'm not sadistic," Stinker said in a singsong voice. "No, I am not. But I can be quite severe when roused. Part of my character. My own part."

He wheeled over to Grasshopper.

"There's a streak of severity in you as well when roused, old man," he said. "But still, you can't hold a candle to me in that regard. All shrink in fear before me."

Stinker was completely unscathed, so he didn't really have any business in the bathroom. He just wheeled around on the wet tiles, splashed water from the low sink on everyone, and sang an elaborate ode dedicated to his own heroic exploits. The boys, covered in scrapes and bruises, proudly pressed wet towels to their wounds and studied themselves in the mirror. Grasshopper took a look as well. His ear was livid, and blood caked under his nose. He liked what he saw.

"Hark, knights," Wolf said. "Tonight at the round table we shall recount the glorious battle. Praise our valor and mourn our losses. Sing war songs and bring together our chalices in honor of the fallen."

"Stinker seems to have started already," Humpback said.

"I didn't start anything! And quit admiring yourselves, it's my turn now."

Stinker wheeled at them from behind and pushed them away from the mirror.

In the dorm, the other Siamese was comforting Elephant, Elk was stuffing cotton wool in Blind's nostrils, and Beauty was pacing the room, gnawing at his fingernails.

"Get yourselves cleaned up," Elk said. "Then we'll go visit the principal."

"Us?" Magician said indignantly. "What about them?"

"Them too, don't worry. Where's your shoe?" said Elk, glancing at Grasshopper's feet.

"I've got it," said Stinker and fished it out of the wheelchair, followed separately by the dripping shoelace. "I kept it as a remembrance. A souvenir."

"Couldn't whatever problems you had be solved peacefully?"

The knights kept silent.

"Right," Elk said, looking at his watch. "Be at the principal's office in ten minutes. We'll talk."

He walked out.

"Hey, what's that?" Humpback said and touched Grasshopper's shoulder.

Elephant, sitting on the blanket, was surrounded by pins forming a colorful mosaic.

"Here! Look at this one. Pretty, huh?" Siamese implored, bringing the pins one by one closer to Elephant's wet face. "Just look at it . . ."

Siamese's contribution to the wall consisted of a stork and a crocodile. The stork was standing on one leg and therefore occupied very little space, while the crocodile was apparently flying, splayed above the wolf and the owl. Elephant worked for a long time, and when he finished painting there was a flower in the corner, looking very much like an inkblot.

Stuffagers threw the pot with the broken plant out into the hallway. The only thing belonging to Siamese that they didn't manage to bring over. Siamese found it on their way back from the canteen, picked it up and tried to revive it, but it withered anyway, so they had to bury it in the yard in an old shoebox.

Everyone was quietly preparing for the next fight. Stinker mended the umbrella. Siamese grew out their nails. Magician whittled himself a cane. Every night they had a war council. The time spent in the canteen was taken up by threatening stares and scary faces. Then they grew tired of all that.

Wolf joined the music club and started disappearing with the guitar after lunch, and then tormenting Sissies with monotonous chords for hours on end. Magician dug up the book titled *The Illusion of Reality* in the library, fashioned a top hat out of cardboard, and tried to make the hamster disappear under it. Hamster refused. It just startled and crapped more than usual. Beauty pressed juices. Stinker composed long, heartfelt letters to charitable organizations and private citizens. The letters featured *the unfortunate paralyzed boy, the poor orphan preparing for dangerous surgery,* and *the sightless baby who loves music more than anything in the world.* Every letter was accompanied by heartrending drawings. Stinker's hope was to acquire a plethora of things that might be useful to have around.

Siamese Max wrote letters too. To himself. He did them in pencil on sheets of toilet paper and sorted them in envelopes with strange legends: *When You Want to Cry, When You Want a Bicycle, When You Think You're Ugly, When You Envy the Leg.* The leg in question was most likely his brother's second one. The one Rex had, and Max could have had. Stinker showed his letters to everybody. Max never showed his to anyone. He only ever read them to himself, and rarely, at that, only when his mood corresponded to the legend on one of the envelopes.

Grasshopper came out into the yard every night. When Witch showed up, he went in search of Blind, a letter deep in his pocket. Sometimes it was Blind who passed a letter to him—then Grasshopper went down to the ground floor and waited by the laundry-room doors. He got so used to it that he kept forgetting about the danger, only remembering when he saw Witch burn the letters in front of him.

Blind took to disappearing at night. Humpback tried every possible way of constructing the tent, but it still crashed. Then came the rains. Elk said of them that they smelled of spring. The yard became a muddy mess. Humpback's dogs stopped coming. They were thinking about having offspring and were therefore too busy. Siamese Max got knighted.

TABAQUI

In one moment I've seen what has hitherto been
Enveloped in absolute mystery

—Lewis Carroll, *The Hunting of the Snark*

Just your regular day. The wind rattling the glass, everyone yawning silently. The wind is relentless, so Alexander opens the windows and lets it in. Then it tortures the frames until they moan and chases the curtains so that they become frighteningly like things that are alive and struggling to break free and fly away somewhere. Pity they can't. Would have been a sight to watch.

Third period is highlighted by a visit from Ralph. He comes with his own chair. Puts it in the corner and sits on it like he's stuck until the bell rings.

He hasn't changed at all. A stint in the Outsides can sometimes really do a number on a person, but there's no trace of it on him. It's like he went away only yesterday, and today he's already back. The familiar jacket over the familiar sweater. The gloved left hand, the one missing the two fingers, and those eyes. The eyes of an inquisitor. Makes you shiver. When the lesson ends he stands up and stares at us. He's leaped over. It's so obvious. I marvel at his lack of discretion. Really, someone should tutor him, though I'm having a hard time imagining who that might be. Yes, he's not exactly young, but he's not stupid either, and quite capable of understanding things. In the Outsides it's considered impolite to visit someone else's house naked. In the House it's impolite to enter by leaping over. This is like climbing into a window and sitting at the dinner table without so much as greeting the hosts. Or going through someone's bedroom and pulling out the dresser drawers. Or . . . I don't know what else to compare it to. And Ralph, when it comes down to it, is not really to blame. Just a wild creature. Untamed.

Now he's asking Smoker how he's doing in the new environment. Smoker says he's fine. No complaints. Has everything, requires nothing. He also contrives to look as if this is not so. Ralph nods and departs. Noble isn't mentioned at all.

After lunch I'm the last one to get back, because I lingered, shooting the breeze with Shuffle. Upon arrival I'm met by the packmates milling at the door. Not entering it, though.

"Something the matter?" I ask.

"The door," Lary says, poking it with his fingernail, the one that's longer and even uglier than the rest.

"So?" I say. "It certainly is, everyone knows that."

"Locked," he says.

There goes the nail again, pointing out to me that it's the door that's locked, in case I, heaven forbid, would think that it's actually the wall.

"Who the heck would need to lock himself in?" I ask.

"That's what we've been thinking. Who the heck," Lary says and looks back at Sphinx.

Sphinx is all pensive. Spring cleaning of the soul, no doubt.

"I would expect some knocking going on right about now. Maybe even a bit of shouting. And then whoever answers would be the one who's locked in there," I suggest.

"True. But what for?" Humpback says. "Why would they want to do it?"

We exchange glances. Me, Sphinx, Humpback, Lary, Smoker, and Alexander, with Tubbs in tow.

"It's probably Blind?" Humpback offers tentatively. "He wasn't there at lunch."

"He must be thinking about something important," Lary says, brightening. "And here we are knocking. Might be very awkward."

Sphinx and I exchange glances again. Failing to remember any previous occasion when Blind would lock himself in the dorm to think. I drive around the circle once and return.

"Or maybe Black. Killing himself. What? Quite possible, after what happened yesterday. You know . . . Us saying nasty things about his precious dog . . . and stuff. He's a proud man. Couldn't live it down," I say.

"Shame on you," Humpback says. "We're on edge as it is."

I do two more rounds. Alexander squats down by the wall, apparently tired of standing. Humpback is scratching at the number 4 on the door. Rubs off the lower half.

"Damn!" Sphinx blurts out. "Are we going to stand here all day like statues in front of our own door? I feel stupid."

"They're all watching," Lary says bashfully. "Maybe we can move?"

I look around and see that indeed they are. Watching and even crowding in places. A nasty predicament. I get a rolling start, planning to smash into the door and jostle whoever is on the other side, but Vulture chooses this particular moment to approach, so I have to make it look like I've decided to practice driving.

"Issues?" Vulture inquires. "Anything wrong with the door?"

He is leaning foppishly on a cane and swinging a key chain on his pinkie. Naturally, there is more than just keys on it.

Sphinx hesitates.

"I'm not sure we should."

"Should, definitely should," I say. "Who knows what could happen. We need to investigate. Still, my money is on Black hanging there. He hasn't quite been himself these last few days. Brooding."

"Heavens!"

That was Vulture.

Humpback shakes a fist at me.

The picks jangle, the long wire snakes inside the lock, the hallway audience moves closer, tongues hanging to the side from curiosity, and in the distance I spy Red, cruising in our direction at top speed with a vicious grimace on his face, but we burst inside—with me being pushed in front of everyone else—and manage to slam the door before the noses of those trying to stick them in our business. Vulture gets a pass, since he helped and is therefore entitled to the information.

I quickly cross the anteroom.

"What's that?" Sphinx asks behind my back.

Someone seems to have had the gall to squeeze in. Shameless is what it is. The intruder is Red. He spits a couple of words into Sphinx's ear. Sphinx nods and hisses at us.

"Hold on!"

I have no intention of holding on to anything, Red or no Red. I push the door and enter the dorm. It's empty like a family vault. No one's hanging, no one's on the floor with his veins split open, no corpses at all, in fact.

"Look at that," I say. "No one's here."

Lary breathes spasmodically in my ear.

Humpback asks, "So who's locked it, then?"

And here we see legs dangling off Lary's bunk. Two of them. Lary gasps and grabs hold of my hair. Legs dangle. Long ones, clad in black stockings. One has a white pump on, the other just the stocking, with a hole in it so that the pink toes are sticking out. There's something very familiar about those legs. They descend, lower and lower, and then Long Gaby appears at the other end of them, crashes to the floor, and winks at us quite insolently. The shadow around her eyes is all smudged and runny.

Lary lets go of my hair and claws at his heart. Humpback screws his eyes shut and shakes his head. I don't get it. What's the big deal? So she's a bit on the scary side, but not excessively so. And live Gaby is certainly better than dead Black. Just my opinion.

Gaby is a local celebrity. She's celebrated for her height and lack of brains, but mostly for her surplus of sex drive. Different approaches to deal with it were proposed and tried, to absolutely no avail. The management then decided to refer to it obliquely as "noncompliant behavior." That "noncompliance" was fought doggedly until everyone got tired both of it and of Gaby herself, and Long was allowed to live as she wished, to her and everyone else's joy and benefit.

"Hey," she imparts in the husky voice of a habitual drunkard, and leans over to her stilts, cinching and tucking something down there. The short sweater reveals a pink bodysuit underneath, and her hair is decorated with candied lemon peel, Lary's delight. Lary moans softly.

"What have you been doing here?" Humpback inquires.

Gaby just grins with the purple-lipsticked maw, not taking the attention off the stockings. The answer to Humpback's question comes from Lary's bunk, in the form of Blind appearing over the edge. He's noticeably purple in places. The places she pressed against. He leans down limply and lets fall the second white shoe. It lands with a thud.

"Merci," Gaby rasps, fitting it over her oversized appendage.

She struts to the door, majestic and content, heels clicking, and is intercepted there by Red. He looks exceedingly pimpish, his newfound occupation written all over him. They ride off into the sunset, she towering over him by a full head, he throwing back furtive glances. The door slams shut, and then it's very quiet, apart from my exuberance. I have to drive around for a while to calm down. Vulture is still standing there, with a look like he was just force-fed a whole lemon.

"My bed. My bed," Lary mutters. "They defiled it."

"What?" Sphinx says and sits where he stood. To think this over, I guess.

Blind slips down. I wheel over and study him thoroughly. Because I need to know.

"So?" I say. "How was she? To the touch, I mean. Not too bony?"

"I'll be going now," Vulture says mournfully. "It appears you have no further need of my services at this time."

No one stops him, and he departs.

"Thanks for your help!" Sphinx shouts at his retreating back. "Sorry!"

"How was it?" I ask Blind again. "Do you feel a new man now?"

"Leave me alone," he says. "Right now I don't feel anything."

"My bed!"

Lary still can't quite handle this. Runs around. Then climbs up to his bunk, and from there comes a mournful wail.

"Thank you. That you didn't choose mine," Humpback says. "Really big thanks, Blind."

"Not at all," Blind says and sits down next to Sphinx. "Sorry about the door. I didn't have time to go find another place."

"No harm done," Sphinx says, casting his gaze upward, where Lary continues the lamentations. "What exactly did you do to his bed? He sounds frantic."

"Nothing much." Blind suddenly perks up. "You know what, it really is fun. Would you like a go? I can call her back. We'll throw everyone else out. Except Lary, he can stay . . ."

Lary tumbles down and stares at Blind, horrified.

"No, thanks," Sphinx says. "Not with her, no. I'd have nightmares. Until the day I die."

"Is she that ugly?" Blind asks dejectedly.

"She is a creature from the pit of hell!" Lary shrieks, arms upraised. Then he turns back to Blind. "Linens exchange, right now. Or I never sleep up there again."

"As you wish," the Leader agrees readily.

Lary studies him with suspicion. Blind's linens deserve a separate song that I never seem to get around to composing. Lary is a pig, no argument, and often goes unwashed, but at least he doesn't stumble around the House barefoot. Or cough up hairballs on the pillow.

"I'll think about it," Lary proclaims.

"Enough," Sphinx says, getting up from the floor. "Your linens forgot what color they were supposed to be. Long ago."

"And now you could sniff at them," I pipe in. "Turn your sleepless nights into erotic revelations."

Lary spits in my direction, clutches at his head, and sits down on the floor.

"Tomorrow there will be a new Law," Blind says matter-of-factly. "So I'm trying to figure out how we're going to announce it. Wall? Or Logs?"

Stunned silence. For quite a while. Finally Humpback clears his throat.

"Ri-ight," he says. "Red, he's not stupid. He knows which side his bread is buttered on."

"Of course he's not stupid," I say. "Never was. He's a Leader, whatever else he is."

More silence.

I climb on the bed and sit there, digesting the news. Too much news for one day. Long Gaby, new Law . . . New Law means girls. Here, there, and everywhere—them visiting us, us visiting them. The way it had been before, the way it hasn't been for a long time. It's an unusual thought, and I can't quite construct the image no matter how hard I try. I'm out of habit. Or, rather, it's gone completely, but come tomorrow it'll have to be revived, the habit as well as the communication skills, because tomorrow they are going to be here: the girls. That means skirts, perfume, braids, hair spray, ponytails, and long eyelashes with ends curled slightly, and smoky eyes, and tender names for the wheelchairs, and narrow fingernails, like Noble used to have, and they are born of our ribs but their voices are much, much softer . . . Do they like tea? And if they do, what with? And where do we get the "with," and who's going to invite them over, not me, that's for sure, but someone would have to . . .

"Breathe!" Sphinx yells at me. "Breathe, silly! You're turning blue!"

I catch myself in time and resume breathing. A marked improvement.

"Thanks," I say. "I seem to have paid too much attention to certain thoughts, and they sort of filled me up and spilled out."

"Sing them, then," he says. "You're constitutionally not cut out for silence."

True, that. I think better when I talk. And singing works better still. Part of my alien internal design.

Black comes back. Drops the dumbbells in the corner, stares at Blind's purple spots in wonderment, and goes off to the showers. There's no one to tell him about Gaby and the new Law, because Lary trotted off to inform Logs and I am not yet ready. I have to sort out everything. After that—oh, how they're all going to wish I'd shut up, but until then I'm as silent as a grave.

Blind is still slumped on the floor, chin between his knees. Humpback trains Nanette to attack intruders. Alexander strips the linens off Lary's bed and shakes out the blanket and duvet. Nothing much going on, in short. I decide to go down to the yard, where my thoughts will have more space to roam. I might even get sad there for a bit, regarding various sad circumstances. I haven't been getting sad properly for a long time about anything, apart from Noble, that is, and haven't gone to the yard alone either. I grab my coat and ride. Alexander stops torturing the duvet and goes to see me off.

I'm alone in the yard. I like being out alone, everyone knows that. There's no rain, but the weather is cold and kind of raw. The big puddle, where the water is clear in the middle and murky at the edges, is reflecting my head. It's black and unkempt. I resemble a porcupine. I stare at it. Then it gets boring. I throw a small stone into the puddle. Then another one.

The clouds are running out of room in the sky and start jostling one another. I pick up another stone. This one is an unusual color. Seems to be white. At least, that's how it looks in the dark, but there's no way to tell for sure. I pocket it, to have a closer look later. Rustle of rain; the first drops slide down my nose. I throw back my head, opening my mouth. Heavenly tears cover my face but my mouth doesn't feel anything. The rain's still too thin.

Alexander's outline in the window. He looks down and waves. Wants to know if I need to go up yet. I wave back and sway from side to side.

That's my answer. The rain doesn't bother me. I'd even like it to become stronger.

Alexander disappears. He'll come and pick me up before dinner, plenty of time for me to change clothes then. For now I'm content.

I think back to that one time I was sitting here. It was raining then as well, and harder too. The steps were shiny black, and water was running down the wheelchair ramp in rivulets. I was thinking about something. Or maybe dozing off. Can't tell for certain. Rain, sun, wind; they all impart strength. So I sat and waited for it to soak into me to the last drop, to the point of translucency. Once sated, I decided to go back. I didn't go up right away, but took a ride along the first floor instead.

And right there, in the hallway, there they were. Standing side by side. This fat fire-breathing woman, a regular human volcano. Red coat, black hat. Crocodile leather bag. Lips like an open wound. Cheeks like slices of bologna. Teardrop earrings. There was a puddle at her feet, from all the water that had dripped down, she was shuffling in it and stewing silently. And the man next to her. Pale and pasty like a mealworm. A snout for a nose, lips pursed. Tortoiseshell glasses. Pity the tortoise! Pity the crocodile! I wouldn't want to be in their place.

Also they had a snit of a girl, about fourteen. Gangly, blondish, red albino eyes. Also in a red coat. And a boy of about ten. Spitting image of his father. Clearly the pet of the family. Piggy eyes, snout nose, lips coming to a point—all there. Coat—red-and-gray check. Obviously. The entire brood was flashing way too much red.

And a little apart from them, leaning against the wall, stood Scarlet Dragon. The only really red one in the whole gang. Red is a tricky color. Deceitful. You can wear it and put it on your face all you want, and only become even grayer. It is the color of conjurers, clowns, and killers. I like it, but not always and not everywhere.

I am Tabaqui, dispenser of nicks at first sight. Godfather for scores upon scores. In every incarnation the master of tales, the royal fool, and the keeper of Time. And I can always tell a dragon from a person. Dragons are not evil. Just different. If I saw him alone first, not surrounded by his family, I might not have spotted him right away. But this was easy.

He was thin and covered in freckles. Old battered jacket, patched-up homemade sweater, jeans fraying at the knees. His eyes contained a whole different world in them. An entire abandoned planet. Long, slender fingers gnawed raw.

I looked at the hands of the others. Short, stubby sausages. Rings biting into the flesh. Big hands, small hands, all of them the same. He was of another blood. Different hands, different eyes, different body. He also was the only one wearing old clothes, so old that they were now as familiar with him as he was with them, enveloping and caressing him.

I smiled. I can't remember the last time I liked someone that much from just one look. He tried to return the smile. Imperceptibly, with just a corner of his mouth.

Then Shark came out. The woman let out a stream of excited babble and stepped forward to meet him, trailing mud. The man tagged along, holding the youngest by the hand. Those family pets do have a knack for getting lost. And getting into trouble. You might say they're born with this talent. The girl, scratching at a zit on her cheek, was looking sideways at Scarlet One. I wondered how he was feeling. He stood there somber and silent.

Shark put all of his teeth on display and invited them to the office. They all filed inside. Except for him. Once the door slammed after them I wheeled over to it, took out the plug, which is only allowed in the most dire of circumstances, and proceeded to watch them. I'm always curious about parents. Especially of that kind.

The woman was bawling. Making crunching noises into her handkerchief, smearing lipstick with it, licking the snot off her lips, and grabbing at her face. Robustly and affirmatively. The man perspired demurely. The coat he had on was really heavy. The children pinched each other. Shark nodded thoughtfully.

"Our house has gone to hell! To hell, you hear?" the woman proclaimed, interspersing this information with incessant sobs.

Shark nodded. Yes, he heard. The House he spent his time in wasn't much better, in fact, so could they maybe get to the point?

"He is killing us," the woman explained. "Slowly. Day after day. He is tormenting and humiliating us. He's a murderer! A sadistic killer!"

"You wouldn't know, looking at him," Shark said politely.

This statement made the woman in the red coat explode.

"Of course!" she shrieked. "Of course! Why do you think we brought him here? No one believes us! No one!"

Shark had seen some really strange people in his life, but this was a bit too much even for him.

"We do not accept youths with criminal tendencies," he said sternly. "This is not a penal facility."

"He's not criminal," the man interjected. "That's not what we meant."

"You see," the woman said, realizing she'd gone overboard. She switched from crying to an intimate whisper. "He always knows everything. About everybody. It's horrible. He is one of them . . ." She winced, searching for the right word.

"Savants?" Shark prompted, intrigued.

"If only! Worse, much worse! All kinds of things happen when he's around. Things appearing out of nowhere. Technology breaking. Televisions . . . one, then another. And the cat's gone mad! The poor creature couldn't take it anymore."

She went on, but Shark lost interest. He didn't like crazies. His face clearly showed that he'd tuned out somewhere around the bit about the cat.

"Are you sure?" he asked perfunctorily when the woman paused. Just to be polite.

"Yes! Anyone in my place would be sure."

And she trotted out a litany of ironclad proofs, prominently featuring her own little kids. Those underage piranhas. Apparently "they would not let pass a single word that wasn't true."

"Tell this nice gentleman if Mommy's telling the truth."

The truth detectors, busy shoving and pinching each other behind her back, took a short break from their activities and eagerly nodded a couple of times.

"And those baldies are tagging after him," the boy added. "They're like completely nuts. They pee in our building by the elevator. They'll keep coming until we get him out of there. Or until they throw us all out."

Shark goggled, but didn't pursue it further. Apparently, though, the love of truth had its limits, because this contribution earned the boy a whack upside the head from his mommy, and he shut up.

"We are decent people, you know," she said proudly. "We'd never invent something like this. We've never had any deviations on my side of the family, thank you very much."

The man cringed guiltily. On his side of the family they clearly did.

"We showed him to the best specialists," the woman said, dabbing the corner of her eye. "But he pretended to be normal. Made fools of us. One time they even said that it's us who needed to be checked. The indignity of it! The humiliation!"

Crunch, sniffle, snort.

Shark scratched his head.

"I don't see how we could be of help. Our specialization is children with diminished physical capacity. You might be better served by . . ."

"He's epileptic since age ten," the woman interrupted. "A horrible sight. Just horrible. Would that work for you?"

"Well, not exactly, that's a different area altogether . . ."

This is where I stopped listening. It was clear enough. The administration was going to pump them for money and then accept the newbie. The house is full of healthy people with scary stuff in their medical histories. And others who are written up for something completely different from what they have. Boring. The Scarlet One was still by the wall. Now I knew what made him special. So I wheeled over to him.

"Ask to be put in the Fourth. We don't have a television. Never had. And cats only come in winter. Even if you make a couple of them crazy, no one is going to make a big deal out of it. Got it?"

His stare was unblinking. I never got an answer. So I decided I'd done what I could, nodded at him, and went back. When I looked at him over my shoulder he wasn't looking at me. He was thinking. I made it up to the second floor in record time, sprinted to the door of the dorm, coaxed Sphinx out into the hallway, and told him everything. Then we both went down and I showed him the Scarlet One.

Sphinx frowned.

"Mommy's clearly hysterical and imagining things. You're too gullible, believing every story you hear."

"Mommy is bonkers, that's a fact. But she hasn't got enough imagination to make up something like that."

We went closer. Soon the pasty family spilled out of the office. We couldn't hear them from where we were standing, but we'd seen and heard all of this a million times already. It never varied except in the details. Small details. The tank woman floated up to him, patted his head, flapped the red lips for a bit, and walked on. The man shoved something in his pocket. Money, what else? The girl looked directly at us, while the pet piglet was chewing gum and blowing bubbles. They burst and covered his snout in translucent film. He used his nails to scrape it off and shove the gum back in his mouth. Finally they all left and we returned to the dorm.

They brought him an hour later. Shark did, personally. We had to listen to everything Shark had to say concerning the cramped conditions in other dorms, and then about the camaraderie that was supposed to unite those less fortunate. Once he'd blabbed his fill he sailed away.

Scarlet One was looking down at his feet all that time. And we were looking at him. The corduroy jacket was too big for him, and the sweater under it was too small. He stood a little splayfooted, and apart from the freckles, we couldn't make out much about his looks. His eyes were of indeterminate color, speckled, as if reflecting the freckled face. Fingernails gnawed off. He was incredibly calm. No one who's just been brought in could be this calm. Everyone liked that in him. I didn't have to look around, I just knew that they did. I was happy for him.

"Epilepsy," Noble grumbled. "Just the thing we were waiting for. Someone having convulsion fits right here in full view."

"You're exaggerating," Wolf said. "Besides, what about your own first day here? Equal to at least three fits at once, if I remember correctly."

"Such a quiet kid," Humpback said. "Nice, even. I vote we take him."

While they were discussing him in this fashion, Scarlet One just stood there looking down. His face was completely impassive, like Blind's when he's listening to music. I wasn't taking part in the discussion. I alone knew what he was. He was a dragon, a scarlet dragon, a fairy-tale visitor from a different world. Because sad people with knowing eyes and mysterious abilities do not appear in piranha families for no reason, or by accident. I was worried about Sphinx, though. His usual perspicacity seemed to have evaporated.

Sphinx stepped forward.

"You are going to stay here only if we agree to it," he said. "You'll get a nick and become one of us. But only if we agree."

I exhaled. Sphinx was not in the habit of explaining these things to newbies. Of explaining, period. He must have felt something too. Just didn't want to admit it.

Scarlet One looked at him.

"Then can you please agree," he said. "So I can stay."

He said "you" to Sphinx personally, as if he knew which one of us made the decisions about who stayed and who went.

"I'm so tired," he added. "Really, really tired."

He didn't mean us, he was talking about something from his past.

"All right," Sphinx said. "We accept you. But you have to swear that you're not going to blow up electronics, attract thunderstorms, or turn into animals."

The pack giggled at the joke that was not a joke at all.

"I don't know how to do any of that," the newbie said earnestly. "But I understand you. If that's what is required, then I swear."

The pack was hysterical. I was the only one not laughing.

And that's how Alexander came to live among us.

A newbie is always an event. They're just so different. It's exciting just to look at them. Watch them and observe how they change, little by little, how the House pulls them in, making them part of itself. I know many detest newbies because they're a handful at first, but I happen to like them. I like observing them, pestering them with questions, pulling jokes on them. I like the strange scents they carry in. Many things, not all of them capable of being put in words. One thing's certain—where there's a newbie, there's always excitement.

That's the way it was with Noble, and with everyone who came before him. Everyone I ever saw, really. But not Alexander. It's as if he didn't come in from out there but materialized, more of this place than any of us. With the shadows cast by the bars on the windows already etched into his face, with the voice as soft as the rustle of the rain. Possessing memories of each of us. He seemed to have been born here long ago, absorbing all of the colors and smells of the House. He kept his word. He's never done anything that someone else would not be doing. He was quiet, pointedly so.

He did have fits from time to time, breaking and ruining everything in his wake, but that happened rarely. There was just one thing he did allow himself—chasing away our bad dreams. I saw how he did it: he would jump up all of a sudden, walk over to someone who was asleep, whisper indistinctly in his ear, and go back. We were no longer awakened by screams—either our own or someone else's. Our nights became more peaceful. Except for those that came after Wolf . . .

I catch that thought by the tail and try to turn it back.

DO NOT THINK ABOUT THAT!

Except those nights. When even Alexander could do nothing. When . . .

ENOUGH! NOT ALLOWED!

With a desperate effort I manage to put the brakes on it. Then I realize I've been crying for a while. Good thing the rain's picked up. Coming down for real now. I throw back my head, intent on getting soaked. Then I start shaking. The cold managed to creep under my coat and vests while I was occupied. Teeth start chattering. Time to go.

I wheel over to the porch and wait. The darkness falls suddenly and swiftly. Shadows are floating past the curtains on the windows. The music seems to be louder than usual, or maybe I'm just imagining it because of the rain and the darkness and me here all alone, forgotten and abandoned. I feel sorry for myself. Then I feel very sorry. Then extremely sorry.

"Tabaqui! What's wrong?" Alexander thunders down the steps, holding a jacket like a tent above his head. "I thought you wanted to stay."

"I did, and then I didn't anymore. And the ramp is too slippery, as you can see. So I had to call for some help."

He drags me into the elevator. I shiver and rattle my teeth, rather theatrically. He leans over, looks me in the face.

"What was it you saw, Tabaqui? I can feel it."

"Lots of things. You're not old enough to know."

"Sorry. I won't leave you by yourself for that long next time."

On the way to the dorm I explain to Alexander that liking a drizzle is an altogether different thing from liking a downpour. The latter happens to play havoc with vehicles not designed for prolonged exposure to the elements, and a wheelchair should be kept dry regardless of one's love for rain.

"Mustang has been in service for a long time now, and is deserving of attention and respect. Even if its churlish rider, also owner, is not."

"Tabaqui, stop it," Alexander pleads. "I'm going to have a hard time sleeping tonight as it is."

While he's drying and dressing me I take the stone out of my pocket. This time I manage to take a closer look at it, even though it's not easy with the towel scrubbing my head. It is oblong and light blue in color. Both the color and the shape seem familiar, resembling—what? I keep fiddling with it, turning it this way and that, trying to figure it out.

Alexander wraps me in a dressing gown and deposits me on the bed under the blankets. I burrow even deeper and keep thinking. The stone is warm in my hand. We go to sleep together, and the dream I have is about it and about that which it resembles.

I wake up to soft guitar chords. It's dark except for the red Chinese lantern hanging low above the bed. It gives off barely enough light. I stare at it for a long time, until I start swaying in unison with it.

Somewhere very close—Sphinx's voice. He's singing, something about "the hole in a black truck tire against brown grass." Muffled noise on the other side of the wall, like there's a party going on. I pull off the covers and sit up. Could it be that I missed dinner? That's something that doesn't happen very often.

> *Sunlight mixed with dust*
> *rises behind a truck*
> *on the dirt road*

There's something awfully familiar about Sphinx's song. Vulture's head is nodding over the guitar's strings. And what looks like Shuffle's feet are hanging off the headboard. His right one especially is very distinctive.

"Are you awake?" Humpback whispers. "You're not ill, by any chance? You've missed dinner."

"If I am, then chance had nothing to do with it. What's that noise?"

"Celebrating the new Law. Or have you forgotten? So we're also kind of celebrating. The old gang's here."

I remember. Everything, including my dream. The stone in my hand is wet. Now I know exactly what it looks like. And it's a very strange coincidence.

> *Not a word! Not a word!*
> *Flies do all my talking for me—*
> *and the wind says something else*

Right now the important thing is my dream. I need to fulfill it. That's what I think.

The pale pinkish glow of the lantern. The plates of shard-like sandwiches. Glasses clinking, black wine sloshing inside. The old gang: Vulture, Shuffle, Elephant, Beauty.

My hand reaches for the harmonica, but flees by itself. Not now. Need to remember . . . I grab the nearest sandwich and eat it.

walking back into the retreat house

Humpback breathes tenderly into the flute. Sways, bumps into me. Someone is chomping loudly behind my back. Irritating.

after Two-Week Retreat

The guitar passes on to Shuffle. A succession of somber chords. The sandwich suddenly comes to an end, and then another one. Now it's Vulture droning hoarsely:

> *A thin red-faced pimpled boy*
> *stands alone minutes*
> *looking into the ice cream bin*

When he comes to the "Cabin in the Rockies" we're interrupted by an explosion of noise from the dorms up and down the hallway. I crawl in the direction of Vulture's voice.

"Listen. Could you maybe lend me your stepladder? It's very important. And I'd like to avoid answering the question 'Why,' if you don't mind."

He's pink, like everything around him that's illuminated by the lantern. Leans over, reeking of wine.

"No problem at all. Of course. It's yours, for however long you need it."

He has a short whispered conversation with someone invisible and turns back to me.

"You drive over with Beauty. He'll tell the boys, they'll bring it out."

"Thanks. I'll call for him when I'm ready."

I crawl over the sandwiches, legs, and bottles—and here I am on the floor, and the stone is in my pocket, and I'm dying to find out if I can accomplish what I decided to do before lights out. Everyone's making merry. I hate leaving them now, but time's a-wasting.

I put on the warmest clothes I can find. The tools I need are in the anteroom, in the boxes under the coat hangers. The bulb here is dim, but after the flashlight it's almost blinding. At first all I manage to dredge out are rags and old ossified shoes—useless crud. Shuffle's guitar perversions in the room grow even more elaborate. I fret and worry, until finally there comes out the thing I was looking for: the brush with the can of white paint and some more rags stuck to it. I take them and some other small things that might prove useful, call Beauty, and wheel into the corridor with him.

He comes inside the Third while I wait by the door. The Nest is quiet, unlike the other dorms—all clatter and wailing. The common room is full of jumping, mulleted shadows. Our Lary must also be there somewhere.

I have my warmest vest on, but I still shiver. The can, covered in dry paint drippings, I hold in my hands, and the rest—the scraper, the knife, brushes—I try to stuff in my pocket, where they collide with the remains of something edible. I shake out those. The rats who happen to run this way tonight are in for a treat.

The door of the Third opens and lets out Guppy.

"Hey," he says. "Where do I put the stepladder?"

I show him. They bring the ladder. Guppy huffs and puffs and clanks its metallic parts, while Beauty mostly bumps into its legs. He's not much help, in short. Bubble, in pajamas and yawning, drags himself out as well.

"Damn Logs all bolted. Celebrating some crap or other," he whines. "Now we're supposed to lug this. It's heavy, and here we are with our health condition."

"Daddy's orders are Daddy's orders," Dearest says. He also has on pajamas, but is holding a suspicious-looking bottle under his arm.

"How about a swig in honor of the new Law?" he offers as he wheels closer. "Everyone's so happy, wouldn't do for us not to join in."

So while they install the stepladder, we drink some homebrew junk, made by him personally.

"Now give me a hand up," I say.

Two more stumble out to look at them lifting me up. Bubble worries that I'm going to fall. Angel worries that I'm going to throw up right on Vulture's stepladder. At the top I can see much more clearly how dirty and spider-infested the ceiling is. The wall is dark and dirty as well. I take care of insulation—spreading Guppy's blanket under me. The top step is tiny, I have to keep the paint can balanced on my knees. To go tumbling from here, hitting all the steps on the way down, is a scary thought.

I sigh quietly, wave to the Bird throng below, and start drawing. Just as I expected, they soon grow tired of craning their necks trying to decipher my scribbles and freezing their tails off in the process, and slowly drift away. My head is spinning from the vile hooch Dearest calls tequila. What I'm drawing is the outline of a dragon standing on its hind legs. It is coming out strange: a bit like a horse and a bit like a dog. I would have done better in a more convenient spot, but this'll have to do. I give it teeth and sharp talons on the front paws. Talons are important. Once it becomes obvious that it's a dragon I'm looking at, I crack open the can and fill it in.

Gunk, hair, and assorted debris that drowned in the can long ago—my poor dragon is now covered in all of this. When the white brush follows its jagged spine, my hand starts shaking. Time and I, we're not exactly on the best terms, but it appears I may pull it off, even though it's too early to tell for sure. I can't sit here and wait until the dragon dries completely. With the pocket knife I start gouging out a hole for the eye.

This is hellishly difficult. The hole is almost ready, and then the can suddenly jumps off my knees and disappears below. Awful racket. It rolls around down there for a while, then finally gets stuck, and I'm still busy with the eye. The hole is already quite deep. I probe it with my finger. Now for the lilies. I scratch them into the wet surface of my dragon with the tip of the knife, the crude fleurs-de-lis, all over. Once I'm done, the dragon is no longer just any dragon, it's Noble, because lily equals Noble if you want to draw him quickly and recognizably. I sign my work.

By the time the lights go out I'm almost finished. I rummage in my pocket for the magical stone the color of Noble's eyes. The dragon, the ceiling, me—we all disappear in the darkness. I'm not scared. I take out the flashlight, point it at the eye socket, and insert the stone. It's holding. It fits, or maybe just sticks to the wet paint.

I fulfill my dream. Here it is—the ghost dragon, covered in lilies and with Noble's eye. It's running with the talons pointing at our room. That means return. Maybe something else as well, I have no idea. My job was just to put it here. I switch off the flashlight and sit there in the dark. I'm all sticky; probably covered with paint.

I don't know how much time passes before there's stomping, flashlighting, and cooing from below.

"Coo-ee yourselves," I say. "I'm up here. Could you maybe have waited until morning? My rotting carcass would have been so glad to see you."

"Pipe down," Sphinx says. "It's no one else's fault if you decided to spend the night on this idiotic contraption."

"He-ey!" comes in Vulture's drunken voice. "I would thank you for not dumping on my princely perch!"

They point flashlights at me and giggle. Then someone trips over the can and steps in the paint. Now I'm the one giggling.

"Damn!" Humpback yells. "There's shit all over the floor! He was making a trap for innocent passersby. Using bird crap!"

They finally take me off the ladder and carry me away. The actual carrying falls to Alexander, and everybody else just stumbles along, waving flashlights and singing.

If there's one thing I hate, it's being the only sober member of a drunk crowd. But by now it's useless for me to try and catch up with them. Not even with the help of Dearest's tequila.

They carry me inside and file in. Humpback is bringing up the rear, whistling into a flute. The dorm is so trashed it's scary. The nightlights leave a trail on the ceiling. Alexander puts me on the bed, and the rest keep circling the room in a conga line. Must be looking for dungeons and caverns.

Nanette is sleeping splayed out on the sandwich plate. I take her off, grab the last remaining sandwich, and eat it. The rest of the plates are empty. My favorite place is occupied by Elephant, fast asleep, clutching some kind of red ball. On closer inspection it proves to be our Chinese lantern.

Red and Blind are waltzing, but mostly walking into furniture. Humpback is trying to tootle on the flute in time with them. Blind is counting off loudly: "A-one-two-three . . . One-two-three . . . One . . ." Each standalone "one" makes them freeze in place. Humpback then bumps into them and freezes too.

"To the girls," Vulture proclaims, sniffing at his glass thoughtfully.

Who knows what he can be sniffing there. Anything liquid within reach has already been gobbled up. I set to gnawing on the remains of the sandwich. In this crotchety state I disgust even myself.

Sphinx plops down next to me, winks, and imparts, "A dragon be a mythical beast . . . While a white dragon, doubly so, because in addition to all of its other qualities it is also an albino, that is, an anomaly even among its own kind."

"You noticed," I marvel at him. "Managed to see! In total darkness!"

"I notice everything. Besides, it's not like you climbed all the way up there just to give the ceiling a fresh coat of paint."

Then we sit and watch the others gradually switch off. Someone's singing from the direction of the window. Loudly and out of tune.

"Whose is this?" I ask, lifting an unfamiliar prosthetic by the strap. "I didn't know we had anyone else of that sort here."

"It's a joke," Sphinx says darkly. "A funny, merry joke. Humor among thieves, you might say."

I decide not to pursue this and instead busy myself with going to sleep. Feeling worn out, grimy, and elderly, but also like someone who has responsibly carried out his duty. Also cold. As soon as I manage to get warm and cozy and finally drift off, I'm immediately woken up by Black. He's rattling the coffeepot against the bars of the bed and reading Kipling aloud. Some of those not yet asleep try to get him to pipe down, while the rest are having some kind of scholarly argument. I don't want to sort through the details, and I fall back asleep.

The second time it's a hyena's laugh that wakes me up. It trails off into sobs. Everyone except the hyena is fast asleep, and even the lights are out.

The third time I startle at dawn, who knows why. The party's over. The gray morning slithers in through the windowpanes. Insensate bodies stacked haphazardly, snoring. All is still and quiet, except for the barely audible ticking. That's the bitch that woke me up. I seek it by ear, by smell, I home in on it. It's a watch, lurking in the folds of the blanket. I lean over the edge of the bed, grasp for an empty bottle, place the watch on the floor, and smash it, using the bottom of the bottle as a hammer. It takes but a moment, and the ticking stops.

Black, asleep on the floor, raises his head and stares at me dazedly. Then falls back down. I drop someone's sweater on him and crawl back into my paint-smelling burrow.

THE CONFESSION OF THE SCARLET DRAGON

"You sin, you pay."

This had been pounded into me by Gramps, my crazy grandfather. I hope he burns in hell right now, because if such a place really exists he and those like him must end up in it. I cursed him with all the curses known to me, and they wore him down eventually. Very slowly, because he knew how to fight these things; besides, we were of one blood, he and I, so I received a portion of my own curses on the rebound. Let him burn, like a gas burner burns, heating up everything around him, as he never gave me even a smidgen of warmth.

The white plaque on the wall, letters of some unknown alphabet, four dozen shaved heads; whispered prayers and incantations. ". . . use the lemon juice, god-damn it, rub them until your arms fall off, because whoever saw an angel covered in freckles from head to toe? There ain't no such thing! You must of done it just to spite me!" So—never a single ray of light, always the dusk of the curtained rooms. Maybe they really did appear in the most visible places to spite him, covering the skin that never saw the sun, the skin rubbed raw with lemon juice. White toga smelling of lemons, a withered wreath of chamomiles with white centers. And the constant "Give us a miracle, reveal it to us!" Miracles that weren't, and painted nails, and colored lenses that made the eyes water. But "Fuck it, it ain't no angel if he's not blue eyed!" He swore like a sailor as soon as he was out of earshot of his beloved brethren, his "sons and daughters." The sanctimonious piety went straight into the trash when the last of them disappeared behind the door, and the monstrous dwarf sat down to his three-course fish dinner. Wreath hanging askew, thin fish bones extracted from the depths of the munching orifice. He had no use for napkins. Never. "They are an extravagance, unbecoming of the godly, you hear me, O winged one?" Also unbecoming of him was cutlery. And unbecoming of me—a table, a chair, and even "Angels don't eat, ha-ha, they are satiated by Holy Spirit!" Angels. Are curses becoming of them? Of course not. They discharge in your own body, pure sizzling electricity filling out every last hair instead of arcing to the one they were directed at. And then one day, a simple enchanted fish bone that's done its job. That was the first real miracle I wrought: to pass from MY FATHER'S HOUSE, in capital letters, to a house. It could even be called my mother's, if only I ever had the slightest inclination to call it that. Exchanging house for house and Angel for Moron, because "He can't even read, the retard!" And "What have we done to deserve this?" They didn't need any miracles at all. Miracles scared them. Except those they saw on the Tube. It was their god, even though they didn't bow before it or whisper prayers to it, just stared at it through the clear lenses of their glasses, but the effect was still the same both here and there, the only difference being that there I at least had been useful for something.

The papers wrote about the old swindler who'd managed to enchant scores of people. The Tube proclaimed it, so it must have been true. It was not true: he was just a dirty old man who lost his mind. But the Tube never lies, it is beyond suspicion, so they took me to the god's house, to rinse the traces of Gramps's sins out of me with holy water. They washed me and christened me, but still the letters kept coming, and the crazies with shaved heads kept stalking me and falling headfirst onto the pavement, grabbing me not by the hem of the toga, as before, but by the bottom of my sweater or coat pockets, tearing them clean off, and "Oh god, I am so tired of this! The coat was brand new! It cost us a fortune! We should not let him out of the house. Disgrace for the entire family!" So—curtains drawn again, lights always on, the Tube humming constantly, the shaved heads stumbling around outside the house, sniffing the walls, scratching at them, seeking the angel that became a kind of addiction for them. Therefore, what they were seeking had to be removed. Didn't matter where to, otherwise it was simply dangerous; after all, "they urinate down by the elevator, the neighbors are furious, and that incessant knocking in the night, and the phone calls, intolerable, simply intolerable!" And so, my mother's house exchanged for the House. This exchange followed a prayer. The only genuine one out of thousands. The only one where I asked something for myself. I wasn't even sure what exactly it was I asked. But it was answered, or it just might have been a coincidence, even though I happen to know that there are no coincidences, and I entered Gray House. The place that existed for me and those like me. Those not needed or, if they are, needed for all the wrong reasons.

Once I saw it, I immediately understood that this was it, the thing I'd been asking for. The writing was on the wall. Literally. It read: WELCOME, ALL YOU ABORTED, YOU PREEMIES AND POSTIES! ALL YOU DROPPED, THROWN OUT, FLIGHTLESS! WELCOME, CHILDREN OF THE WEEDS! I knew how to read, even though those in the mother's house claimed otherwise. I entered, believing that I was given according to my prayer. Entered as Alexander, shedding both the Angel and the Moron, both of them forever, because "If you want to stay with us, there are going to be no miracles. None, you hear? Not bad ones, not good ones, and not even indifferent ones." I said yes and, under the all-seeing gaze of those green eyes, became Alexander, as far from The Great as could be, the eternal shadow, the ever-ready pair of hands. I tried. I really tried, even though saying yes was much easier than always remembering that I had. The gray walls of the House talked to me through the graffiti: "Tired of being a slave yet, freckle-face?" No, I wasn't, not at all, it was not slavery; besides, what do you know about being a slave? You just know the word, and you have this picture of a black man picking cotton. Uncle Tom, Uncle Sam, whatever. Have you ever seen those with shaved heads being led by the invisible rings in their noses? Have you ever heard about an angel in chains? Are you familiar with lemon-scented mornings, with chanting at dawn? Or the miracle of the exploding Prophet of the Holy Tube? Or the cat that decided to taste freedom, the least miracle in God's quiver of miracles; I did not enchant it, however much everyone was sure that I did, it was simply a miracle, given to it not by me but through me . . .

Every house has its rules that must not be broken. Every house has its three-headed dog keeping order. Gramps; Mother; Sphinx. They all hemmed me in with proscriptions, installed barriers keeping me from myself, but only one of those worked, the one put up by Sphinx. Because that's what I wanted. Sphinx is not to blame here. He hadn't brought me into this world or sold me to insane relatives, and he never robbed me of my childhood or starved me half to death. All he did was give me this one rule, and he never demanded anything else. And . . . After all, it was I who wished for peace and quiet, for the new life as one of many, it was I who uttered the prayer that transported me to the House. That's why it was not slavery. Of my other houses I talked only to Sphinx. He was the only one who knew everything. He was the invisible thread tying me to the previous lives, and at the same time teaching me to live this new one. He was not afraid of me at all—I would know, I have long learned to distinguish the fear hidden in the thin shells of human faces. Why him? I have no idea. It just happened. He did remind me of the shaved heads at first. But all he had in common with them was the bare skull. I'd never ever seen that doglike expression in his eyes. "Find your own skin, Alexander, find your own mask, talk about something, do something, never stop, you must be there every moment, people must feel you. Got it? Or you'll disappear." Talk about what? Do what? Where to go seeking masks I've never worn, for words I've never known? He yelled at me, then calmed down. "All right, whatever. Forget it. If you can't think about anything, don't. After all, that's also a kind of mask. But when your body is present in this room, you have to be as well. Be present and busy, always, unless you want to be stared at or drawn into discussions." And . . . Day and night, cigarette butts swept into the hand, a wet rag over the clumps of dust, a sponge over the coffee stains, a spoon into the waiting mouth, and always the eyes, more piercing than Gramps's. Don't look into them, never look into them. Forbidden. Taboo. And "Al, air out the room," "Get me the pants," "Help me into that stupid shirt," "Bring over the wheelchair." Splinters in the fingers, always wet, aching, bleached white by the detergent. Scrapes. Fingernails, weeping. And "Look at this guy, he's switched off again. Hey, Alexander, what's that you're thinking about?" "The Conqueror's head has left the building. Give him the mop, that'll bring him back." "He's a card, that Alexander character. All he ever wants is housework." The House walls, the House Laws, its memories, its fights, its games, its tales—that's all well and good, calm and soothing, if it were not for the fear that's always nearby, that only can be pushed away for a short while, very short, because sooner or later it returns, bristling with even more sharp spikes than before. It's the fear of the inevitable end to all this, the public flaying of the new, freshly grown skin. The fear of long-legged Sphinx carrying the secret of the real me. He who has power over someone surely would wield it?

"Are you afraid of me, Alexander?"

The green eyes leave smoking holes in me. I cringe. I shout back, "Yes! Yes! I am afraid! So? Wouldn't you be, in my place?"

"If I could be both you and myself at the same time, no, I wouldn't. And you don't have to either. Trust me, I want nothing from you."

It was the truth, but I could not allow myself to believe it. He was taming me, quietly, step by step, and I didn't realize it. He made me read and then discuss books with him. Listen to music and talk about it. Make up ridiculous stories and tell them to him. First to him only, then to others. He squeezed the fear out of me and made me trust him. I was happy, and not afraid of his eyes anymore. Not afraid of anything anymore, even though the oath was not lifted from me, I had to remember that. But I was too warm and cozy, it melted me, the warmth that he was giving me, gifting me, making up for everyone who'd withheld it from me before. The warmth I was receiving from all of them, receiving and giving back. I forgot. I never should have done that. My hands acted by themselves, quietly stealing their pain. I carried it, burning hot, and washed it off under the tap. It floated away down the drains, my legs were shaking, I was tired and empty; it was so beautiful, and it was not a miracle at all, honest, so I never broke my promise. That's what

I thought then. A new world assembled itself around me, resplendent in golden sunrises and furious sunsets, I jumped up from the bed before everyone else and ran out barefoot into the hallway, to seize the most beautiful hour, to knead the dust with my feet, to feel my body, my running legs. I turned on a lukewarm shower and sang—both ancient hymns and the songs I'd learned recently, scaring the cockroaches, splashing in puddles. That was what I was. Alexander covered in freckles, Alexander pale and thin, Alexander unknown to anyone, Alexander who gnaws at his fingernails, Alexander who needs to eat more, Alexander with his buck teeth, Alexander who's going to be sixteen soon, who has the entire world and eight friends, who is happy.

I wasn't doing anything for them. Almost nothing. Even though miracles were as necessary for them as air and water, and there I was, silent, simply living among them, and all I wished was to really become one of them.

I secretly gave them bits and pieces of miracles—so small that you could pass them around, stuff them in a pocket and then pretend there was nothing there, nothing at all. I was good at it. Until one of them discovered my secret. It was inevitable. They all had a keen sense of smell, the Tube and the venom of the multitudes on the outside never dulled it. And I was careless. Little Jackal knew that Alexander was not like anyone else. Blind suspected something. And Wolf . . . It's funny and sad at the same time: he was the one I feared the least of all, and the one to whom I gave more of the forbidden miracles. The burning substance that clung to my hands when I passed them over his spine tried to poison me in the time it took to carry it to the sink. My palms swelled with his pain, and I was grateful for it. Gratitude and love, those were their lessons for me, and I came to expect those from them. Foolish. Sphinx knew what he was doing when he warned me that day: "There are to be no miracles. None, you hear?"

If two are placed within the stuffy, soft-walled limits of the Cage, they are at the same time close and alone. Too many hours to spend this way, in closeness and isolation. And . . . "I'm not stupid, Alexander, I can feel it. Wolves can always feel things like that." And "Don't you trust me, goddamn it? Aren't we friends?" I should have heard that, should have remembered the toothless grin and the gray mane of that other one who so loved to pepper his speech with "damn it." I should have locked myself with a million locks there and then, as soon as I was given that warning, but I'd forgotten my previous lives. The warmth of this life melted my resolve, and I talked to him the same way I talked to Sphinx, offering myself to him, but he wasn't Sphinx, not even close, I realized it right there, in the stifling confines of the Cage, when he bared his crooked fangs and smiled: "You're mine now!" I realized that the trap had sprung, that it was already too late. I was chained again; not an angel this time but rather a demon, because that was what

he needed, and I always morphed into whatever was needed, with only one exception. "Hey, quit whining! It's not like I want a lot from you!" I cried and hugged
his knees, I crawled at his feet like the least of the shaved heads, I screamed with
the pain of the reincarnation. "What are you bawling about? I'm not hurting you,
I'm not doing anything to you, leave my feet alone, you miserable weirdo!" I fled
into the corner, but he pulled me out again, he shook me and slapped my cheeks
with cold, detached curiosity. Of course I knew what he wanted. Wolf's innermost
wish was no secret from anyone. "I don't want him dead, understand? I'm not
a murderer. Let him just walk away. Leave the House, go into the Outsides and
never return. Got that?" The walls like pillows in flowery chintz, white lights, his
sweaty face and angry hands . . . And "Stop the hysterics! What's so scary about
what I'm asking?" What he was asking was hideous, but I couldn't find the words
to explain why. It's better to kill someone than to make him a slave to your desires.
Wolf didn't know that.

Are curses becoming a demon? Of course. But I didn't do anything. I resolved
to remain Alexander until the last possible moment, until I couldn't anymore.
Knowing that tomorrow the end would come, Gray House would learn the truth,
and then I'd be torn apart by the seekers of miracles. Alexander would be no more.
Someone else would take his place, and there would be a different House, without
Sphinx, without Tabaqui, where I would be completely alone, like a gutted insect
slapped between two pieces of glass to be studied through the thick lenses of a
microscope. "I'll tell everyone about you, miracle worker, every Pheasant will know,
every stray dog. They're going to tear you to pieces, understand?" I crawled away
and lay on the floor. My head was swimming, needles pricked in my hands, I was
burning up. My answer, my refusal, I buried deep inside my soul, along with the
coming fall out of a window—or maybe off the roof, the roof was even better—and
the broken rusty chain that could never again be used to bind me, forever and ever
amen . . . Then the deliverance came, I freed myself of myself and roared away,
through walls and ceilings, through clouds and rain, into the burning blackness
of space.

For two days after that he left me alone, did not remind me. But I was tired
of the fear. It all happened by itself. My curse pierced him in the night, and he did
not wake up. I ran away from my sin, I locked myself in the bathroom, I prayed and
cried. I went looking for the way up into the attic. I didn't find it, neither the attic
nor the way to get there. Then I went down to the yard and climbed up the fire
escape. I stood at the edge of the roof when the sun came up, bathing the world
in gold and turquoise, and the swifts jetted overhead with joyous noise, and still I
stood there, unable to make myself jump. It turned out to be harder, much harder
than I thought. I was all swollen with tears, I swayed and pleaded with the wind to

help me, but it was too feeble for that. Then I heard a horrified scream—I imagined it was Sphinx—and my legs pushed me on their own accord. I took a step, slipped, scrambled for purchase on the rounded edge of the steel plate, fell, and grabbed it with my hands. And immediately realized that I was not going to let go. No matter what. Not if I had to hang like that for a long time, not if I got tired, not even by accident. I hung there and cried. Then I pulled myself up and lay flat on the roof, legs still dangling. The palms of my hands were on fire, there was blood on them, and also something was trickling down my leg and pooling in my shoe. I knew that I was forever a coward, and I hated myself. The sun was beating down on me. The edge of the roof dug under my ribs. One of the girls saw me out of the window of their wing, I heard her shouting and pulled farther up, so I was fully on the roof. But I could not get up and climb down. This was how the two long-limbed Spiders found me. They grabbed me and took me with them.

Later I tried doing it again, in a different way, but it didn't work the second time either . . . Blind came to visit me in the Sepulcher. He had on this one-size-fits-all white gown; it would have fit two more of him easily. He climbed on the bed, sat there cross-legged, and listened to my silence.

"Why?" he asked.

"There is a great sin on me," I said. "I cannot be redeemed."

After Wolf I knew better than to trust them. I waited. What would this one say? The one hiding inside himself. Not nice at all, the way Wolf had seemed. Quite the opposite. It could have been anything. He could turn into Sphinx. I remembered the oath I gave him and then broke: "If you want to stay with us . . ." If he did that, I'd have to go away. Or he could turn into Wolf and make a razor blade out of me. I never told him who it was that I was supposed to forever tether to a post beyond the House gates. He could have decided he owed me something, and I didn't want that.

"Come back," he said. "No one is going to find out."

"Why?" I said. "And how do I pay for it?"

"Stupid," Blind said. And left.

So I went back. Life goes on, and my sin is still on me. While I live, it will be thus. I have no way to atone. Ghosts constantly stream through these walls, but only one of them bares his fangs at me. He is everywhere. On the windowsill when I pull away the curtain, waiting for me in the shower, even at the bottom of the bath when I am about to climb in, looking at me with burning eyes from underwater. I am almost used to it now, and don't go to pieces anymore every time we meet. I go to bed later than before and rise earlier, to make sure my nights are dreamless—because in the dreams he can do whatever he wants with me. I'm tired of him, and he of me, but we cannot get rid of each other. The pills help, but only for a while.

Every morning I go down to the yard to feed the stray dogs running around in the predawn hours on the other side of the fence, in the Outsides. They know I'm going to show up and wait for me there. All it takes is the secreted half of my dinner, and they are ready to talk to me about their vagabond life, and listen to me talk about mine. They live in a pack, and so do I. We have a lot to discuss. I never ask them if they know what sin is. But I suspect they do. Sometimes, very rarely, I work miracles for them: healing gashes on their paws, growing fur over burns, or conjuring a phantom of the Great White Bitch that resembles a polar bear a bit. They like to chase it along the fence. Then we go our separate ways. They leave to tend to their quarrelsome business, and I return to the House. Occasionally I meet Blind in the hallway, as he's returning from his nightly wanderings. More often on my way down to the yard, but sometimes also on the way back. I often think that if I were to come out at night he would be everywhere, in myriad different disguises, just like my ghost. But I never go out at night. I'm afraid of the dark.

I'm afraid of the dark and of my own dreams. I'm afraid of being alone and of walking into empty rooms. But most of all I'm afraid I might end up in the Cage again, this time by myself. If that were to happen most likely I'd stay there forever. Or snap and bust out of it in some nonhuman way, and that's even worse. I don't know if I'm going to burn in hell or not. Probably yes. If it exists. I can only hope that it doesn't.

TABAQUI

DAY THE THIRD

They roused him with muffins—they roused him with ice—*
They roused him with mustard and cress—
They roused him with jam and judicious advice—
They set him conundrums to guess.

—Lewis Carroll, *The Hunting of the Snark*

By the time I pry open my eyes, the morning has already morphed into the day. Guests are gone, as are all traces of them ever having been here. Alexander sweeps out the broken glass and cigarette butts. Lary is sitting all forlorn, his head wrapped in a towel. Someone seems to have put thistles in my eyes and filled my throat with especially scratchy saliva.

"Hey," I say in a frail voice. "What's the time?"

Alexander drops the broom and stares at me in horror.

"Must be dying," Lary says to him, ruefully shaking his betoweled noggin.

Al gasps and runs out, forgetting to close the door behind him. I shouldn't have scared him like that. A simple recitation of the list of all the places where it hurts would have sufficed. I already regret what I said. Though it's flattering, to be capable of arousing an emotional response of this magnitude.

"And you had to choose the first day of the new Law for it," Lary continues selfishly.

"No one chooses the day of their death," I say.

The pack has an entire arsenal of treatments for every ailment, mostly contradictory. First Humpback dutifully pokes me in various places as prescribed by ancient Chinese wisdom. Then, following Sphinx's method, I am stuffed into a bath hot enough to cook me alive. I do not protest, because Sphinx's method knows only two variations: scalding hot or freezing cold. They fish me out, pull a sweater over my naked body, slather my back with something that feels like fire, wrap a scarf around my neck, and put socks on my feet, preceded by a thorough alcohol rub.

At this point in the course of treatment I no longer can distinguish whose method is which and try to rip off all of that stuff, but they hold me rather fast while Blind produces a jar of honey from his secret stash, a very small one, and proudly parades it before me. As if I'm still capable of being moved by such things. Then they feed it to me, and force me to wash it down with milk. I have to suffer it until I begin melting under the layers they've wrapped me in, sweating milk and coughing out cream.

Pity me, who is in favor of only one method of healing the sick: tender loving care.

Sphinx entertains me by reading from *The Mahabharata*. Humpback plays the flute. Lary mashes lemons with sugar in a bowl, while Blind keeps watch, preventing me from slipping away. I grow so tired of these ministrations that I manage to fall asleep inside the fiery, honey-infused cocoon, and all the sarcastic repartee regarding tormentors and torturers, ready to escape from me and enlighten the pack, remains unsaid and tickles me all through the night, insinuating itself into my sweaty dreams.

TABAQUI

"For, although common Snarks do no manner of harm,
Yet, I feel it my duty to say,
Some are Boojums—" The Bellman broke off in alarm,
For the Baker had fainted away.

—Lewis Carroll, *The Hunting of the Snark*

By next morning my sore throat is gone. I myself am almost gone as well. All that's left are bones and some kind of syrupy substance. At the physical everyone remarks on my perky countenance and milky scent. Mentions of milk make me want to throw up, but this detail happily passes unnoticed by Spiders. Considering the atrocious torture I've been subjected to, I came out of it remarkably well.

The days of the physicals are always on the jittery side, because you never know what the pesky Arthropods might uncover in your internals. And when they confirm that there's nothing wrong with you personally, it's time to start worrying about everyone else, and the rest of the day is taken up by recuperation of the nervous system. So those days are mostly quiet, given to apprehension and then exhaustion.

Already filtered through eight different tests and a swarm of Spiders, but still a center of attention as the weakest link in the pack's chain, I lounge on the pile of blankets with Humpback's gift, a packet of walnuts in the shells. I crack and eat them, chasing them with raisins, and a thought occurs—it's not that bad, being a convalescent. On the other hand, I'm not allowed out into the hallway, and therefore not able to look at the girls and smell for myself the new Law in action. Sphinx keeps saying that there's nothing interesting going on out there, but I don't believe him. How can he know what is or isn't going on in other places when he's right here in the dorm? Also, I'd like to check up on my dragon. I haven't had a chance to look at it properly yet. But both breakfast and lunch are served to me in bed, and even Sphinx, charged with guarding me, takes the meals without leaving his post. So I'm left with nuts and raisins. And they are about to run out.

"If you keep grumbling, I'll invite Long Gaby," Sphinx says threateningly. "Then you'll have your new Law right here in all its inimitable glory."

"I'll have a coffee, please," I say to Alexander, and to Sphinx I reply, "You're bluffing. You're not man enough."

"You're this close to getting it," he warns.

But all of that becomes irrelevant, because Long comes by herself. Without waiting for any invitation from any of us. Slams the door and saunters in with that giraffe-like gait. Plops down on Alexander's bed, crosses her legs.

"Well, hello, dudes," she rasps.

The skirt is almost nonexistent, and we are treated to a view of the elastic on top of the black stockings and a band of white skin above it. Great legs, no argument there. Something to feast the eyes on, especially as compared to the face. Black lifts up his glasses. His eyes open so wide they're almost square. He stares at the legs and then at Sphinx.

"What the hell's that?" he says.

"*That* is me, dearest," Gaby wheezes. "Who did you think it was?"

Black blackens. He's still unaware of the whole business with the locked door, and now he's imagining things that are doubtless intriguing but unfortunately do not have anything to do with reality. He thumps the book down and rounds on Sphinx.

"Was this your idea?"

"Black, come on," Sphinx sighs. "Of course not. You seem to have a very strange impression of me."

"Whose, then? You were mentioning her just now!"

"Now that was a joke. Besides, what's your problem? The new Law is in effect, everyone is free to invite whomever they want."

"That's right," Gaby pipes in, lighting up. "Chill, man. Who knows, maybe someday it's going to be your lucky day too."

"Who?" Black screams, ripping off his glasses. "Who invited you?"

"Blind." Gaby winks. "Like the boss of your boss, unless I am mistaken."

Black sits back down. At first he seems paralyzed. Then he pulls the book back and buries himself in it. Looking right through it. Gaby puffs. I resume teasing the nuts out of the shells. Looks like a very promising development.

Sphinx's polite comments regarding the weather and the teachers result only in Long snorting merrily and recrossing her legs, which are impossible not to look at. So I don't fight the urge and gawk freely. Sphinx does as well. Humpback and Alexander seem to prefer studying the ceiling. Finally Gaby becomes bored just sitting there, gets up, and starts pacing about the room.

"What's this you have here? And this? Ni-ice . . ." Boobs on the table, butt sticking out in our direction, oohing over the record stacks. "Oh, wow. Cool stuff. I think I heard this one. And the one on the B-side here is, like, the shit! I didn't know you guys were into this."

Humpback goes pale and cranes his neck. I become uneasy too, especially when she proceeds to shake the records out of the sleeves and turn them around, leaving dozens of paw prints on both sides.

"Look at all that dust," Long says. "Do you wipe them, like, ever? Shame."

She extracts a handkerchief and spits on it.

"Halt!" Sphinx screams, shooting up. "Freeze, bitch!"

Humpback, who jumped at the same time, falls back on the bed and wipes the sweat off his face.

"Would you like some nuts?" I inquire.

Long dutifully stands frozen exactly where Sphinx's yelp caught her, and probably cogitates whether she should take offense or not.

"Bad for the teeth," she grumbles, taking a step away from the table. "You guys are, like, jumpy. Yelling and stuff. What if I'm gonna stutter now?"

"It's the day of the physical, you see," I explain. "Everyone's on edge. You might even say it's traditional."

Long leans against the headboard and tilts toward me. "Yeah, they tried poking me too. So? I don't give a shit. Like I never been poked before, right? Now this one time when I got raped . . ."

I choke on the nut and cough it out on the blanket. Gaby kindly whacks me on the back with a fist. In search of a more convenient angle, she basically drapes herself over the headboard, and my perspective into the neck of her blouse becomes infinitely more fascinating. This has a terrible effect on my coughing. I almost suffocate.

"You poor thing," Long sighs. "It's no fun being sick, right? It's OK. It happens. Now this one time when I got sick . . ."

"Enough," Black says and gets up. "I'm just going for a walk. There's got to be a limit!"

He walks out, slamming the door so hard everyone startles.

"What was that about?" Gaby says.

"Nothing, never mind," Sphinx says hoarsely. "Busy, I guess."

"Yeah, right. Went to sit in the john with a book, I'll bet," Long snorts. "Those four-eyes are all the same. What's with the voice? Are you, like, sick too?"

"Something with the vocal cords."

"No way," Long marvels. "That was some shout, you know what I mean?"

"Exactly," Sphinx agrees. "Not bad at all."

Gaby peels herself off the headboard. The bed groans gratefully.

I blink my eyes back into focus. She shuffles to the door.

"I'm off, then. The world awaits. My regards to Blind. And to your bookworm too. You get well."

"I'll make sure we tell them," I say. "You're welcome anytime, don't be a stranger."

"Stranger, that's not me," she says. "But I guess you figured that already, am I right?"

A farewell grin framed by purple lip gloss, and she disappears. The heavily perfumed air is stifling. I thoughtfully swallow the last nut and sweep the shells together.

"What was that you just said? Welcome anytime?" Humpback says. "I'm going to remember that, Tabaqui."

"That's called being polite," I explain. "It's what you say when guests are leaving. Especially when it's a lady."

"I see," Humpback says.

He goes to check on the records. On their overall condition and especially on the absence of traces of saliva polishing. I drink my coffee and flip the cards of my solitaire. This new Law looks like fun. Whatever else, it certainly brings variety.

When Black returns, Smoker starts pestering us with questions. Who was Mother Ann? It's all Sphinx's fault. He let it slip to Black that he, Sphinx that is, is not Mother Ann to be chasing Blind's girlfriends out of the dorm. Honestly, that was a fib. He was never going to do the chasing himself. But Long is unlikely to come back here anytime soon if I know anything about Sphinx, and I do, believe me. Black does as well, but he's too thick to see things that are right under his nose. Which is why we all waste so much nervous energy.

"So who was she?" Smoker asks.

Asks me, imagine that. It's not an easy question. I can see Sphinx grinning. Easy for him. He's not the one being questioned, so he's not the one who has to answer.

"Well, you see," I begin reluctantly, "she was this woman who lived here ages ago . . ."

A lousy way to start. But what else do I have? Should I have started with us inventing distractions for ourselves? With songs? Maybe Wolf's jokes, like that snowman that we put Lary's T-shirt on, even though we had to disassemble and rebuild it to do that? Fairy Tale Nights? It's impossible to recall everything that has been tried at one time or another just to prevent ourselves from dying of boredom.

"About a million years back she ruled this place," I said.

She did. As a principal.

Sepia photographs, fraying at the edges: a plump woman in a nun's habit, hands folded over her stomach. Cheeks most likely red, palms calloused. When it got cold she'd wear fingerless mittens. Those hands had to do a lot. Tin buckets full of icy water. Shovelfuls of coal. Each dorm—or *dortoir*, as they were called—had either a fireplace or a stove, smoky and sooty, and every day fuel for them had to be brought up from the sheds in the yard to provide heat for everyone.

Kids in heavy hobnailed boots. Meager coats with large round buttons. Winters meant constantly chapped cheeks. "Almshouse for Deprived Children." The House bore this unctuous Dickensian sobriquet with pride. That's what it said on the plaque attached to the squat cast-iron gates. Every Saturday they polished it with sand, as they did everything that was supposed to shine. It was a huge plaque, for in addition to that name it also had to fit the names of the twenty-eight trustees. Each one of them had a postcard prepared and sent out every holiday, in clumsy kids' handwriting, plus a letter from M. A. herself. *With the renewed expression of true gratitude . . . Praying daily that you remain in God's good graces.* Maybe they really did give those daily prayers, who knows? Each trustee meant a small measure of joy for the inhabitants of the House, and joy was in short supply back then.

We were down in the basement, Sphinx and I, diving into the strata of crusted papers held together with wire. Some had almost disintegrated, others survived intact, but all of them, every little scrap, reeked of damp—as if they had absorbed miles and miles of swamps. It was a pleasure to dig. There was only one other person who shared this passion for clawing the House's past out of its most secret nooks, and that was Sphinx. For the rest of them even the most precious finds from the basement were disgusting junk. But Sphinx . . .

"Oh, wow," he whispered, holding a bundle of yellowed invoices. "Jackpot."

We pored over them, trembling with anticipation, just to add another tiny detail to the picture that was invisible to everyone except us two.

Cloth, gray.

And the children of the House of old dressed up in gray uniforms.

Wool, skeins.

And Sisters Mary and Ursula, each on her own stool, started clicking the knitting needles, one sister per *dortoir*, one stool per sister, and woolen socks, hanging lower and lower, snaked out of the hands roughened by incessant washing and cooking.

Step by step, scrap by scrap, we reconstructed the House. *That* House. We knew how the rooms looked, knew what its occupants did, and not even M. A.'s passion for stretching the stores of apples long into the winter could hide from us. Why would she insist on that? We didn't know. But we burrowed into the contents of that basement like two insane moles. From 1870 to the last graduating class. Throughout our research we lugged to the dorm reams of what Wolf termed "hopeless garbage," with Lary serving as the muscle. The previous graduating class was the only part of it all that interested the pack. I compiled two scrapbooks out of the most fascinating documents, and then we cooled a bit on the whole excavation enterprise.

So now it falls on me to tell Smoker about Mother Ann. I almost have to laugh, because it's impossible to explain without explaining what the House was back then. I continue to deliberate whether I should try, while my mouth keeps running on auto-pilot. At some point even I myself become curious: What's that I've been babbling about all this time?

"To get on her good side you had to be very God-fearing, and know a lot of ancient texts by heart, mostly the ones that are impossible to remember, and when she was dying in her bed she made the sisters bring all the linens in the House to her room and counted and recounted them. But then she was already not right in the head. And when she died and her assistant became the principal, they said they saw the ghost of Mother Ann going from dorm to dorm, checking, counting, and rechecking, in other words, not resting in peace at all."

Smoker blinks and frowns. It takes him some time, because he's busy, but I notice it anyway.

"What? You don't believe me? Sphinx, tell him!"

"It's true," Sphinx says. "It was exactly the way Tabaqui's telling it."

"How can you know that?"

"We know everything. Anything and everything that is the House!"

I deliberately don't mention the basement, but my bragging suddenly rings true. I sense this truth and marvel at it. There. That's what we were looking for. For *everything that is the House*. There comes a time in the life of everyone to start asking who their great-grandfather was and to listen to the family lore, so Sphinx and I descended into the basement and told the musty tales to ourselves. I shiver. We became too much a part of this place—and it, of us. It's almost as though we had created it. There was nothing in the basement where it mentioned the ghost restlessly roaming the rooms looking for linens to count.

That night I finally manage to escape into the hallway. Under the pretext of going to dinner, but most likely because Sphinx got bored guarding me. No girls in sight, and my dragon looks really tiny from below, barely visible. The eye glistens, but to distinguish the details you'd have to be a giant. On the other hand, the stains from the overturned paint can are quite readily visible. One might even say eminently visible. I drive over them on purpose, to declare my involvement.

Dinner is disgusting mashed potatoes, all lumpy. A person such as I, who gorged himself on nuts and raisins all day, can only look at it with contempt. The girls are right there when I wheel back. Two of them at once. They sit on the Crossroads sofa, picking at the exposed foam rubber and flinging the pieces out the window. There's a gaggle of Hounds assembled around them. Nothing really interesting. Besides, they're blocking the way so I can't move closer and hear what they're discussing, or otherwise take part in the proceedings. I only can note that they are Succubus and Bedouinne, and that the evisceration of the sofa is being performed rather gracefully. That's the extent of my research for tonight. Long doesn't make another appearance either, even though I spend the rest of the evening waiting, desperately hoping that she does.

THE SOOT OF
THE STREETS

SHARDS

The Wheeler's Entertainment Manual

1. *Racing club. Heartily recommended for any wheeler seeking excitement. Wheelchair races over hard terrain. Scheduled competition dates. Seasonally awarded cup, "The Silver Whee."*

2. *Cooking club. Weekends, Biology room. If you can cook something, anything, you're welcome to join. If you can't but would like to learn, you're especially welcome. Note: ingredients usually not provided.*

3. *Poetry society. If you can string together a couple of lines, you're in. If you can't manage even that, do not despair. Your ability to listen will be enough. Preferably with appreciation. Note: if you can't do appreciation, find yourself another place. Poets are touchy!*

4. *Enthusiastic bodybuilders. Advantage—the only prerequisite to join is athletic trunks. Disadvantage—you guessed it: they're enthusiastic!*

5. *Card players. This one is members-only, with very strict entry requirements. If you're not in yet, forget it.*

Also:

—*Astrologers, Cof., every Wednesday;*
—*Swap, Tuesdays, first floor;*
—*Billiards, game room, anytime;*
—*Guitarists, laundry, every Monday, Wednesday, and Friday;*
—*Novelists, Cof., every Saturday and Sunday;*
—*Contacters, every month on Friday the 13th, Crossroads at night.*

WHILE JUMPERS AND STRIDERS DO NOT REALLY EXIST!
Have a nice time.

—JACKAL'S ADVICE COLUMN, *Blume,* vol. 22

"Stop it," Smoker says. "No one can know those things."

"We know everything," Tabaqui enthuses. "Anything and everything that is the House!"

Sphinx smiles at Jackal and nods. Jackal smiles at Sphinx and nods. They're both grinning, making Smoker want to throw up. He again feels that everyone here has conspired to torture him.

"Don't ask, then," Sphinx offers. "Keep quiet and be happy."

"Would you like it better if I were a mute?"

Sphinx jumps up.

"Let's go. We'll have a stroll. Smell the soot of the streets. You look a bit pale."

Smoker reluctantly climbs off the bed.

"What do you mean, soot of the streets? Is that another joke?"

"Why is it that you never listen when people tell you things?" Sphinx asks on the way. "Even when they're answering your questions?"

Smoker is trying to keep up.

"Listen? To who? Tabaqui?"

The hallway allows them to squeeze through the gauntlet of compassionate chuckles. The walls shout at them: **KILL YOUR INNER CUCKOO! ENTER THE NEXT LOOP!**

"Tabaqui would be a good start. He answers questions better than any of us. Tries to, at least."

Smoker slows down.

"Are you serious?"

"Absolutely."

Smoker reddens if his eyes accidentally fall on girls. Sphinx strides widely and purposefully toward some unseen goal, and Smoker recalls the mysterious soot of the streets, about which he never got an explanation.

"Are we really going outside?"

"What do you think?"

"Damn! Stop brushing me off with those what-do-you-thinks! I don't! I don't think! Would it kill you to actually say something when you open your mouth, for a change?"

Smoker cringes, scared by his sudden outburst and also by Sphinx's face, which is suddenly level with his own.

"Smoker," Sphinx says. "Do you like crawling on the floor?"

Smoker shakes his head in desperation.

"Somehow that's what I thought too," Sphinx says, straightening up and bumping the wheelchair away with his knee. "In which case, please behave yourself and don't raise your voice at me. I can understand that it's fascinating stuff: probing the limits of Sphinx's patience. I am often fascinated with this myself. But not today. I'm not in the mood. So let's get one thing straight . . ."

He resumes the stride without finishing the sentence, and what the thing is that should get straight remains a mystery.

Smoker wheels after him, even though he's not sure he should. It seems that Sphinx is already regretting the company. On the other hand, he hasn't told Smoker to stay back either. Upon reflection, Smoker decides that he should go forward, as if nothing has happened. He loses sight of Sphinx near the stairway, but when he drives down the ramp to the first-floor landing he discovers him standing there, waiting.

"No offense, Smoker. When I ask you what you think, it always has only one purpose: I would really like to make you think. Let's go back to the beginning. Was I serious when I told you that it's better to listen to Tabaqui than not to listen to him?"

"Come on. That was not really a question."

Sphinx peers into the trash can full of cigarette butts.

"Do you like this smell, Smoker? The one emanating from this vessel? I doubt it. Even taking your nick into consideration that would be a . . . perversion."

"Why do you ask, then?"

Sphinx kicks the can and sniffs at the air.

"How about the soot of the streets? Answer me this one, and I'll answer yours. Did you think I was taking you into the Outsides? That I regularly take strolls there at night, when I'm in a bad mood, and that this time I decided to take you with me? Dressed like this?"

Smoker takes out a pack of cigarettes.

"I was just wondering what it was that you called the soot of the streets. Was that so wrong?"

"But you didn't ask it that way. You asked if we were going outside."

"Why are you picking at my words? You understood perfectly well what I meant." Sphinx kicks the can again.

"Smoker. This is really bad. When your questions are more stupid than you are. And when they are much more stupid, it's even worse. Like the contents of this trash can. You don't like its smell. And I don't like the smell of dead words. You wouldn't try to turn this over and shake out the butts and the spit on my head? But you're willing to bury me in rotted empty words without a second thought. Without a first thought, in fact."

Smoker, pale and frightened, teases a cigarette in his fingers. "All right, I'm getting on your nerves. You could just say so. I won't be asking any more questions, then."

"Ask about things you don't know."

"Right. Mother Ann, for example. And get answers that I can't understand. Very enlightening."

"Tabaqui tried to tell you. It's not his fault that you were determined not to believe a single word."

"Because it was perfect nonsense. Why is it that *his* trash is fine with you, Sphinx? How come *his* words don't feel dead to you? He's constantly running his mouth. If every word he said were a cigarette butt, the House would be buried under them. It would be one huge mountain of butts."

Sphinx sighs.

"Only for someone who doesn't know how to listen. Learn to listen, Smoker, and you'll see how much easier your life becomes. Jackal can teach you a thing or two about that. Pay attention to what he says. To the way he frames his questions. He takes only what he needs. And as for running his mouth . . . Yes, he does that. And yes, he likes to embellish the truth. But in that avalanche of words there is always the answer, somewhere in the middle. Which means it's not empty words anymore. Yes, listening to Tabaqui takes a knack. But it's definitely not impossible. Others seem to manage."

Smoker looks at Sphinx indignantly.

"Sphinx, don't make Tabaqui this great guru figure. Please! Just admit that he's of a privileged class. That he can get away with things others can't."

Sphinx nods.

"He is of a privileged class. And he can get away with things others can't. Happy now? I didn't think so. What is it you actually want?"

Smoker doesn't answer. Sphinx leaves the landing and starts down the first-floor corridor. Smoker follows him a few feet behind. He's so hurt he can't speak. He drives along and thinks about how hard the black sheep have it. How no one likes them.

"Maybe I'm spoiled," Sphinx says, not turning his head. "By Alexander. His wordless understanding. Or even Noble, who was too proud to ask questions. Maybe I'm biased, or simply irritated. But I also see you behaving very strangely, Smoker. Like there's something I am supposed to ask forgiveness for. From you."

Smoker catches up with him.

"Is it true you used to beat Noble, forcing him to crawl?"

Sphinx stops.

"It is *a* truth. Black's truth."

"But did it happen?"

"It did."

The first-floor corridor—lantern-like lights, linoleum crisscrossed by wheelchair tracks. Someone is torturing the piano in the lecture hall. Hounds yip in the changing room. Sphinx takes a quick look inside all the doors they're passing. He's looking for Blind, and he keeps thinking: *Is it possible that Smoker doesn't see how like a street this place is? Doesn't smell the soot in the air, doesn't feel the snow falling invisibly?*

They meet Blind at the very end of the corridor. He is knocking the stuffing out of a vending machine, hoping to get back the coin it swallowed.

"Thirsty?" Sphinx asks.

"Not anymore."

One last punch, and the machine spits out a paper cup. Blind picks it up.

"Nine," he says. "Nor a drop to drink, in any of them."

"Blind, this machine has been dispensing nothing but empty cups for the past hundred years."

Next to them Bubble, from the Third, is roaring down the highway, slamming into the oncoming cars and shaking the game console.

"You wouldn't happen to have met Red in these parts?"

"What happened to your voice?" Blind inquires. "You sound hoarse."

"Safeguarding the pack's property from long-legged sluts," Sphinx says darkly.

"Oh? Gaby has been?"

Sphinx is overcome with a burning desire to kick Blind. Shatter his ankle, make the dear Leader lame for a while. A long while.

"She has," he manages, restraining himself. "And I sincerely hope that she won't again. That you are going to take care of that."

Blind listens intently, head to one side, then steps behind the machine, taking his legs out of Sphinx's reach.

"My bad," he says. "I shall be more careful next time. Who's that with you? Smoker?"

"Yeah. I took him out for a walk."

"He's uneasy, isn't he," Blind says indifferently. "Didn't I tell you? Black damaged him."

Smoker, mute with indignation, looks up at them both. Two shameless, self-absorbed bastards discussing him as if he weren't here. Bubble's screen switches off, the machine squeaks the first few measures of the *Marche Funèbre* at him. He listens to it bare-headed.

In the lecture hall, pimply Laurus pushes the stool away from the piano and dabs his forehead with a handkerchief.

"Now do something less boring," the audience demands.

Laurus smiles haughtily at no one in particular. These people know nothing about real jazz, and there's no use in trying to explain. The wheelers in collars burst out in applause. They applaud the smile, not the music.

Smoker, abandoned, drives around the first floor. Smelling the soot of the streets. He pointedly wheeled away from Sphinx and Blind, and is now regretting having done that. He should have stayed and listened to what else they had to say about him. Once the first angry flash subsided, Smoker began to suspect that what he had heard was meant for his benefit. And that once he left they switched to something unrelated. And that Sphinx received another confirmation that he, Smoker, doesn't know how to listen.

"To hell with you," he says. "I don't have to listen to your stupid remarks."

"Whose?" someone asks probingly.

Smoker raises his eyes and meets the Cheshire Cat smile beaming at him, as performed by Red.

"Nobody's," he mutters distractedly.

He still can't get used to members of other packs engaging him in conversation. Their readiness to actually exchange words confuses him, as if he were still a Pheasant.

Angry at himself for that, he says swiftly, "Sphinx and Blind. They were talking about me right in my face, like I wasn't there. It really pissed me off."

"Woooow," Red drawls, his smile becoming even wider. "Lofty stuff. Not for the likes of little old me."

Smoker winces. He's being made fun of again. But the innate respect for a Leader, albeit a total buffoon such as Red, prevents him from turning around on the spot and leaving.

Red proceeds to proffer a pack of cigarettes like it's no big deal, then flops down on the floor and lights up himself. His hair is the color of caked blood, and his lips are just as bright, so it looks like he's wearing lipstick. Chin scraped while shaving, a bundle of dried chicken bones around his neck. In a word—weird, as all Rats are, but even more so up close.

"Red," Smoker says, surprising himself. "What do you know about Mother Ann?"

Red throws back his head. The shades flash with the reflections of the hallway lights.

"Not much," he says and drops the ash from the cigarette right on his pants, white with the flower ornament—staggeringly dirty pants. "History is not my forte. Looks like she was the principal here at the end of the last century. Religious as all get out. Saints talking to her personally, that kind of thing. Joan of Arc gone to seed. I guess being a nun would do that to you. The hospital wing got added to the House on her watch. Before that they only had this one puny room with a nurse and two beds. Also you had to trek over to the town for every little thing. Back then the House was in the boondocks."

"How did you get to know all that?"

Smoker is astonished at Red's knowledge. Also at the fact that he can apparently talk in a normal, human way. From what he'd observed, Rats communicated mostly in grunts.

"I have no idea," Red says with a shrug. "Everyone kind of knows it. See, it's this way. When you want to find something here, you go dig in the old papers. There are stacks and stacks of them in the basement. If you're looking for something specific, it could be tough. The newer stuff is closer to the entrance, and the really old ones are in the cabinets by the walls."

Smoker winces again, this time at the thought that Red—yes, Red!—could dig through musty papers in search of the House's history. Jeez! If someone were to have asked Smoker half an hour ago, he would have confidently said that Red was illiterate.

"That's where Tabaqui got it from."

Smoker isn't asking, more stating a fact. But Red hears a question.

"Tabaqui!" he laughs. "Tabaqui got it more than everyone else put together. He was the one doing the digging. Digging, sorting, and making us read that crap. You should ask him, he'll tell you in vivid detail."

Smoker puffs so hard it makes him cough. Waving the smoke out of his face, he says hoarsely, "Oh, he did. Just didn't think to mention the documents."

"Yeah, likes to play coy," Red agrees, yawning. "That's the way he ticks."

Sphinx appears before them.

"I was looking for you," he says to Red.

Red sits up straighter.

"Looks like you found me."

"You fixed up Blind with Gaby. All right, I suppose that if I don't like it, that's my problem. But I'm not going to tolerate regular raids on our room. I'm warning you, if she ever tries to show up again . . ."

Red jumps up, diligently hamming up being scared. Smoker can't stop himself from laughing.

"You're going to regret it," Sphinx concludes. "Am I clear?"

"Better than clear. But what if Blind . . ."

"I've already talked to Blind."

Red takes a clownish bow.

"I'll do my very best. Count on me anytime. Zeal and eagerness, that's my motto, amigo!"

"Cut it out," Sphinx says.

"Cutting it out right now!"

Smoker snorts again. Sphinx and Red seem not to notice him. Sphinx studies Red's features thoughtfully, as if trying to recall something. Red scratches himself.

"Anything else I can do for you today?" he says.

"If it's not too much trouble, could you take off the glasses?" Sphinx asks.

"Ah, catching me at my word. That's not very nice. But what the hell. Don't get used to it, though."

He turns his back to the corridor, looks around furtively, and sweeps off the glasses.

And disappears. At least, that's what Smoker sees. That Red is no longer there. Dark eyes framed by copper eyelashes stare dolefully at Sphinx, and the delicate face of their owner belongs to some stranger who cannot possibly be Red. The shaved eyebrows, the scratched chin, the sickening smirk—gone. Those eyes, the eyes of an angel, erased them, transforming the face beyond recognition. The apparition lasts all of two seconds. When Red puts the glasses back on the angel vanishes. What's left is the familiar perverted neurotic.

"Oops," he says, licking his lips. "The fun is over."

"Thanks," Sphinx says, without even a trace of irony. "I missed you, Death. Really missed you."

"Keep missing," Red snarls. "There's no Death anymore. So let's leave the strip show for some other time."

"Red, I'm sorry." Smoker interrupts the conversation. "I understand it's none of my business, but these glasses really make you look ugly."

"Why do you think I'm wearing them? To look cute, maybe? Also, why do you think everyone in the Rat Den sleeps with his head in a sleeping bag? Same reason. So that I don't have to duct-tape this fucking optical device to my face at night. Let me tell you, my exalted position does not really jibe with looking like a manga character."

"I figured that out recently," Smoker says. "That Leaders in the House are supposed to look like walking corpses. I wonder why."

"Smart boy," Red says. "You figured right. And one more thing: even for an honest-to-goodness former corpse it's not an easy job to look like one. I'm not a piece of blue cheese, you know."

"How do you know what they look like?"

"I happen to have a certain insight."

Red giggles, bows to Smoker, rattling the chicken bones around his neck, and departs. Disgusting red-lipped fool, despicable Rat Leader. With insights into reanimated corpses.

"You know, Sphinx," Smoker says, looking at Red's receding back, "I used to play this game with myself: I imagined changing people's clothes. Leaders, mostly. Undressed them in my head, shaved, changed hairstyles, things like that. It was very entertaining. Except I never could get anywhere with Red. I thought that was because of the glasses. Because they obscure most of his face. But now I see that I couldn't because it is simply not him under those glasses."

Sphinx looks at Smoker with sudden interest.

"Strange games you have, Smoker. Uncommon."

He doesn't ask any more questions, doesn't say anything at all. He just leaves because someone called to him, but Smoker is so encouraged by this show of apparent interest that, on the way back to the dorm, his mood becomes almost sunny. Could it be that things are not as bad as he feared? That even Sphinx is capable of normal human interaction? His conversation with Red was almost friendly, after all. While rattling up in the elevator, he hears the giggling of a couple on the stairs and the wet sound of their lips separating. On the landing above them, someone's playing the guitar.

Girls. The new Law.

In the Fourth's bathroom, Lary, perched on the edge of the toilet seat, takes out an empty compact, opens it, and starts squeezing out the pimples using the little mirror, wincing and hissing in pain. Still hissing, he dabs on some aftershave, closes the bottle, and secretes it behind the commode.

Vulture is curled up on the still-made bed in the Third's dorm. His pant leg is rolled up and the exposed knee is wrapped in a wet towel. It isn't helping.

"More music," he growls, not opening the eyes, and Birds trip over one another to turn up the boombox volume. Elephant looks at his Leader, then toddles over to the window. There, on the windowsill, in a festive red pot, stands Louis the cactus. Vulture's favorite. Its flower hangs down forlornly, a sad shard of the desert.

"Well?" Elephant whispers to the cactus accusingly. "Can't you see? He's hurting. Help him."

Snowflakes, barely visible, stream past the window. First snow of the year. Elephant lifts his head to admire them and forgets about Vulture.

In the First's classroom, Pheasant Gin, with a black ribbon around his arm, calls to order the "Memorial service for the dearly departed brother Ard. Ghoul." Pheasants rustle paper sheets with suitable poems selected for the occasion and sigh, waiting for their turn to speak.

In the library Black is thumbing through the encyclopedia, the entries starting with *F*. Between the pages he spots a folded scrap of paper. He unfolds it. *Freedom can only be found inside you,* someone is telling him in slanted handwriting.

Smoker is studying a catalogue of Bosch's paintings. When he looks up he sees Tabaqui staring at him.

"Why the long face?" Jackal asks.

"Why not?"

"Listen to him," Sphinx said.

Smoker listens.

"Why?" Jackal asks again.

He takes only what he needs.

"Sometimes it's like I don't know you guys at all."

Tabaqui generously throws open both of his vests.

"Well, here I am! For all to see. What's not to know?"

Under the vests he has on a grubby T-shirt. With red giraffes prancing on blue background.

Dinner is over. Counselors, up on their third floor, shut the House out behind double locks and try to convince themselves it doesn't exist. Kitchen workers start their cars and roll out of the yard. The first snow, wet and sparse, becomes momentarily visible in the headlights.

At the bottom of the stairs going up to the girls' quarters, Lary, wearing the prettiest of the shirts left behind by Noble, is saying good-bye to Needle, a tall blonde girl.

"There's nothing to be scared of," he keeps saying. "They're nice guys, you'll see. They are going to like you. I promise."

Needle is shaking her head. Her bangs fall over her right eye.

"No way! I'm not going there. Don't even think about it!"

Lanky Gaby stuffs the photograph of Marilyn back under the mattress and sits on top, pulling her black-stockinged legs closer under her to keep from the cold. There are three more identical pairs of stockings draped over the heater, drying. Gaby takes them one by one and puts her hand inside, trying to find two with the least number of holes, so that she can scratch together a decent-looking pair.

In the First, Pheasants, waving black ribbons, break out in a collective song, doing their best to "bravely fight back the tears at this trying hour." Their singing is exhausting for Smoker in the Fourth, even though he does not hear it. Cards float down on the blanket—Tabaqui is playing solitaire. Sphinx is toying with the cat: he flips it over with the nose of his shoe and then deftly avoids the sharp claws. Black is lying on Humpback's bed, face to the wall. He can't be seen from below, but everyone knows he's there. He's not asleep. He is reading Humpback's poems written on the wall in crayon. He feels ashamed for doing it, like someone not averting his eyes from a private letter left open in front of them.

The lights go out. The last Log stragglers left in the corridors rush to their respective dorms. An Asian-looking girl in a wheelchair, Doll, switches on a small green flashlight on a chain and raises it above her head. Beauty walks next to her, miraculously keeping his balance even in the dark. Doll is beautiful. Petite, with a remarkably smooth, cloudless face. Logs that are running by, lips at the ready for the next piece of gossip, giggle and slam into walls, unable to look away from her.

Black has moved to his own bunk. He's trying to remember the poem that he especially liked, the one about the old man who pulled the dog out of the river. Up above him, Humpback is industriously rubbing the wall with his saliva-moistened handkerchief, erasing that very poem. Smoker sighs and tosses about in his sleep. The nightlight throws pink highlights on the bumps and folds of the rumpled blanket.

Between the bumps and folds of the rumpled blanket a white building starts to grow. It inches upward, becoming a twenty-two-story tower. The little dots of the windows light up. Smoker flies up to the fourteenth floor and peers into the window. Father, Mother, and Brother, all rigid and unmoving, creepily resembling mannequins, sit on the sofa in the living room and look back at him.

He flies inside, awkwardly flapping his arms and wagging the lower part of his body.

"There you are, sonny . . . Finally. Come sit with us."

Now he's in his bed, the curtains are drawn. It's dark in the room. The floor starts to vibrate.

"What was that?"

Like a marching column, they enter in rows. Identical black-and-white magpie clothes, identical haircuts. Pheasants.

"Come on . . . Get up," comes the squeaky voice of the late (he died! I remember now!) Ard. Ghoul, and the long limp noodle of his finger aims directly at the middle of Smoker's forehead. That place immediately erupts in pain, as if he got hit there. "Up!"

They must know I can't!

Smoker doesn't move. The whiny voices around him keep repeating, "UP! GET UP! RISE AND SHINE!" until he begins to cry.

"You didn't come to my memorial service," Ghoul hisses, screwing the tip of his finger into Smoker's aching head.

"At this trying hour!" Pheasants sing in unison. "The hour of farewells!"

Is this my memorial service now? But I'm alive!

There's a pot with a geranium on the nightstand. Smoker peers into the foliage and notices a tiny green spot on one of the leaves.

"Come here," Sphinx's voice whispers. "Come on, don't be afraid."

The leaf grows until it blocks out the room. Each vein in it is the size of a tree, the soft fuzz covering it is a wild meadow. Sphinx, in a green cloak with translucent wings, is swinging his legs at the edge of the emerald savanna.

"See? That was easy. No reason to be scared."

"Is this where we are going to live now? Forever?"

The leaf trembles, echoing with distant thunder.

"What was that?"

"That? Oh, that's elephants running," Sphinx says, waving the long antennae growing right above his eyes. "Running . . . running . . ."

"That's right, sonny," Father says, putting his hand on Smoker's knee. They are back on the living-room sofa, Mother and Brother are next to him. "You see, sometimes they just run through here, minding their own business."

Smoker stares at the enormous print of an elephant's foot on the brownish carpet.

The trapdoor to the House's attic lifts up, creaking. Blind squeezes into the opening, then places the hatch back without getting off his knees. The hatch has a large iron ring on top, and nothing on the bottom—it's Blind's personal entrance. He shakes the dust out of his clothes and creeps along the attic, treading softly on the floorboards. There are five steps from the trapdoor to the chair, but somehow only four and a half the other way. He knows that the old chair with the busted seat is waiting for him in the exact same place he left it. No one else ever comes here. Just him and Arachne. She hangs in the corner—tiny, almost invisible. Pretending to be dead. Blind lowers himself onto the edge of the busted seat and takes the flute from under his sweater.

"Listen, Arachne," he says into space. "This is for you only."

It's quiet. The attic is the quietest place in the world. Then the sound streaming from under Blind's fingers, plangent and trembling, fills it up. Blind does not know yet what he wants. It has to be a kind of web. Arachne's webbed trap—enormous and all-encompassing for her, imperceptible for everyone else. Something that is at the same time the snare, the House, and the entire world. Blind plays. He has the whole night ahead of him. He follows familiar tunes. Humpback makes them beautiful, but Blind leaves them dry and frayed at the edges. He can only make beautiful things that are fully his own. Chasing that feeling, he does not notice the steps of the night going past, it walks through the attic and through him, dragging his songs away. Arachne grows bigger and bigger. She fills the corner and spills out from it; the silver web envelops the attic. Blind and Arachne, now enormous, are in the center of it.

Arachne trembles, and her trap trembles with her, the translucent spider harp strung from the ceiling to the floor. Blind senses its vibration, hears its chiming, Arachne's innumerable eyes burrow into his face and hands, burning them, and he smiles. He knows that he's doing it right. Not completely yet, but very close.

The two of them play together. Then they are three, the wind joining in with the song of the flues. Then four, welcoming a cat's gray shadow.

Blind cuts the song short. Arachne shrinks back into the dusty corner, no bigger than a fingernail again. The cat flees into the crack in the floor. Only the wind, completely unhinged, continues wailing, rattling the flues, knocking on the skylight, tugging at the window frames . . . The glass erupts and tumbles inside, coating the floorboards in snowy dust.

Blind, barefoot, calmly walks over the shards to the window. He thrusts his arm through the middle of the ring of glass knives, takes a handful of snow from the roof—it's soft and fluffy under the hardened crust—and drinks it.

"I am drinking the clouds and the frozen rain. The soot of the streets and the sparrow's footsteps. What are you having, Arachne?"

Arachne is silent. The wind flees, recedes, inconsolable. The cat, overflowing with the song, flies down through the building, a furry arrow. Its double, one floor below it, crosses the hallway, tumbles down the steps, halts, and starts to clean the paws and the chest. The cat aims lower and lower, reaches the landing saturated with the scent of other cats—and is reunited with its double. Three rounds of the cat dance follow, the all-knowing noses touch, the stories get told: one about the adventures of the trash can in the night, the other about the spider concerto. Then it is the running, paw to paw and rib cage to rib cage, past the dark screen of the switched-off television, past the sleeping bodies, until finally they take a turn into an opened door, into stuffy darkness where their master is sitting, cradling another cat in her lap. Their vaults onto the master's sharp shoulders are mirror images of each other. The coats mingle and flow into a single furry blanket.

THE HOUSE

The wind rattled the glass. The roof dripped water. Blind heard the faint tinkling and then Beauty's sigh as he snuggled in the puddle he'd just made without waking up. Stinker's nose whistled softly. Blind stalked past the beds, clutching the sneakers wrapped in the blanket to his chest. Siamese, side by side in their bed, lay in the exact same pose, down to the clenched fists. Wolf, on the top bunk, hugged the guitar. When he tossed and turned in his sleep, the strings thrummed. The room was full of phantoms. Blind heard them all. Each one was like a clear song to him.

Sleeping Beauty was dwarfed by the snowcapped mountain of the enormous juice maker. It worked continuously, spewing forth multicolored cascades smelling of fruit. The torrents whirled around Beauty's bed, ushering it into the orange ocean, and the meager puddle of urine was lost in that kingdom of juice, utterly insignificant.

Over Magician's bed a masked man rustled his star-studded cape, the master of top hats and swimsuit-clad women sawn in half. The squalls of applause from the unseen audience made the other ghosts startle.

Elephant slept silently, like a small hill under the stars. There was a whispering susurration from the top bunks: Humpback's parents dropped in for a visit, faceless figures in bright clothes. Blind never listened to their conversations. Up there were only them and Wolf's nightmares: dark labyrinthine corridors, sucking him further and further into their emptiness, and the heavy steps thundering behind. Wolf whined, and the guitar, anchored to the headboard, answered softly, soothing him.

Blind passed the phantom of the juice maker and stopped. From the direction of Grasshopper's bed came the velvet drawl of that senior girl: "Listen to me. When you grow up you're going to be like Skull. I know, for I am Witch."

Blind took a step forward, stumbled over someone's shoe, and the dream phantoms vanished, spooked by the noise. He pushed the door and found himself in the anteroom. The floor was cold against his heels. He put on the sneakers and went out into the hallway.

He walked lightly in his rumpled clothes, trailing the edge of the blanket after him like a cape blotting out his footprints. Stopping in one particular place, he plucked a piece of wet, crumbly plaster off the wall and ate it. Then another one, unable to resist. His dirty face was now spotted white. He walked past senior dorms and classrooms, went up the stairs and through the counselors' hallway, dry and clean; walls here didn't have cracks, were not a source of plaster. A television droned behind one of the doors, and Blind lingered, listening to it. At last he came to Elk's door. Pushed down the handle gently, assuming a savage crouch, ready to bolt at the slightest sound. The door opened, and he entered, feeling the way ahead with his hand to prevent himself from banging into the bathroom door, but it was securely closed. He quietly crossed to the bedroom door and leaned against it, taking in the silence and the barely audible breathing of the one sleeping inside. Blind listened, at first standing up, then squatting down. He was listening to the soft song that was whispering to him: "He is fine, he is sleeping, his sleep is dreamless." Then he spread the blanket and lay down by the door, a watcher, a protector of that sleep. No one knew about this, and no one was supposed to know. He was oblivious to the sliver of light under the door, of course, but his sleep was mindful, and when there was a cough and a groan of bedsprings on the other side of the door he shot up like a dog hearing someone's footsteps. The sound of a match being lit, the rustle of pages. Blind listened.

He read for quite a while. Read and smoked. Then the springs groaned again, released of the weight, and slippers shuffled to the door. Blind flew away under the coatrack. The coat and the rain jacket pressed together, hiding him and the crumpled blanket. Elk went to the bathroom without noticing anything. Back the same way, the click of the light switch. The door slammed shut. Blind emerged from his hiding place, returned to his former spot, put the blanket down, and lay back. He placed his head on top of an open palm and fell asleep. His dreams were clear that night.

The first thing Siamese Rex did when he went down to the yard was to check the traps. There were three, and two of them he'd constructed himself. But this time the one that worked was the third one, even though he'd placed the least hope on it. The concrete hole. It was unclear who had built it and what for, but it sure made for a nice trap. Rex baited it by throwing fish entrails down and then camouflaged it with pieces of lumber. He couldn't check on it every day because of the rains, but he did visit it from time to time. The smell of the entrails grew stronger each day. Finally he heard a rustle and low growling when he passed by.

He crept to the edge of the hole, got on all fours, and peeked under the plank. The stench of rotted fish hit him full in the face. A ginger cat, ragged, dirty, and wet, arched its back and hissed at him. Rex whistled excitedly and toddled away. When he returned, his pockets were full of stones. The cat must have figured what was in store for it and attempted to jump out. Rex shot it down with a piece of brick. Then he proceeded to toss the rest of his haul. The planks interfered with his aim, and most of the stones missed the target. Rex was afraid that the cat would either bolt or start screaming. The cat was indeed yelping now, drawing attention to itself. Rex was slow to notice Lame, and once he did it was useless to pretend that he'd just happened near the hole by accident.

Lame, the hunchback with golden curls, an unpleasant stare, and a twisted leg, was one of Skull's people.

"Having fun?" he said, stopping next to Rex and looking down into the hole.

The cat was frantic, throwing itself against the smooth concrete walls. It might have gotten out if not for the injured paw. Three legs were not enough for the jump.

"Get the animal out," Lame said, lighting up.

Siamese started to back away. Lame grabbed him by the scruff of the neck.

"I can't. It's too deep. If I take the planks away it'll get out by itself."

Lame didn't say anything. Rex began to take off the lumber. Once the last plank was gone, he looked back at Lame.

"Get it out," Lame repeated indifferently. "Before I throw you in."

Rex leaned forward and made a plaintive purring sound, but the cat did not respond. It was hiding somewhere. Siamese sighed and slithered into the hole. He was afraid to jump. Because of the leg.

Lame stood right at the edge. Rex shot him a glance, saw the evil slit of the lipless mouth, closed his eyes, and crashed down to the bottom of the hole.

The cat went completely berserk. It took to the walls, mewling and scrabbling for purchase. Rex felt the leg, making sure it was intact, and then tried to grab the protesting cat.

"It scratched me!"

"Get it out," the implacable voice said again.

The cat drew zigzags in the air around Rex. He tried to catch it by the tail. It doubled over with a muffled yelp, claws out, then jumped on Rex's head and out of the hole, leaving ginger hairs in his hands. Its scream trailed off in the direction of the garage and then ascended to the sky.

Rex crouched, waiting. His scratched face and hands smarted. At first he saw only the sky above him, but then Lame appeared, surrounded by his golden halo of hair, in a striped blazer the color of mustard. He was holding a piece of brick. Siamese stared at it in horror.

"Let's play," Lame said. "You're going to be the cat, and I'm going to be you. It's a great game. Ready?"

He flung the brick down. Rex gasped and shielded his head.

"Isn't that fun?" Lame said. "But if I were you I'd try to duck instead. Or you might get hit, you know."

He tossed two more stones and then yanked Siamese out by the collar. Reeking of fish, limp as a rag, Siamese sagged in his hands, eyes closed. But as soon as Lame lowered him to the ground, Rex perked up and dashed toward the House sideways, like a crab. Lame gave him one last look and sat down on the plank, smoking and dropping the ash down into the hole.

The boys of the Poxy room were playing catch with the boxing glove. The radio screamed. Magician covered the hamster with his top hat, then pulled the hat back and sighed sadly. The hamster, still not used to the top hat, was gorging itself on potato peel to calm its nerves. Siamese Max, wearing a polka-dot shirt, was sitting on the windowsill, pressing his nose and lips against the glass and looking fretfully down at the yard. He was worried. So worried that he was ready to throw up.

"Blind went away somewhere in the night again," Stinker said, hugging the glove he'd just caught. "Where, I wonder?"

"If you're so curious, go follow him sometime and see for yourself," Wolf suggested.

The glove smacked him in the jaw, and he swatted it away.

"I was going to," Stinker said. "Except he'd hear me. So there wouldn't be any sense in my doing it."

"Leave the poor rodent alone," Humpback said to Magician. "Can't you see, it's eating like crazy because of you?"

"That means it's working," Magician enthused. "It must be eating to put on some extra weight, because it's afraid of disappearing!"

Siamese Rex came in, covered in dirt and scratches, steeped in the stink of rotted fish. He stumbled to the bed and lay on it, face to the wall, without even glancing at his brother.

I knew it, Max thought miserably. *Something happened to him down there. Something bad.*

Sissies tactfully avoided asking questions. Hamster, free of the attention, sneaked under the bed. Wolf started drawing a tattoo on his cheek.

Siamese lay very quietly. The only part of him that was moving was his hand, scratching words into the wall with a razor: DEATH TO LAME. Max came closer and looked over his shoulder.

The House was awake. The teachers and counselors might have been sleeping, the dogs and the television, but not the House. From its bowels, from right under its roots, music emerged, seeping through the walls and ceilings, making the House tremble slightly. The nexus was in the basement.

The dark figures of Poxy Sissies crawled along the dark hallways. Magician's crutch thumped softly. Elephant huffed, burdened by the weight of Stinker on his shoulders. The cavalcade of white nightgowns proceeded down the stairs. They opened the front door and went out into the yard, blackened by the moonless night. Still in lockstep they stole closer to the basement windows and sat down on the ground next to them. Then lay flat. The basement had been turned into a bar, and the seniors were going wild down there. The windows flashed orange and green, the glass vibrated to the jumps of the dancers. It was a crazy kaleidoscope with human silhouettes whirling inside. The boys looked in breathlessly.

There was only one thing more awesome than the seniors' fights, and that was their entertainment. Beer benders, otherworldly dances of the glued together, wheelchair waltzes, and the wild, screeching music. Who knew how and where they got it from. Sissies peered intently into the low windows, desperate to prove to themselves and each other that they could see something there, even though nothing could be discerned apart from the changing lights. But they were free to get both deaf and blind, and to die of envy. They lay with their noses patiently stuck to the cold grating, blinked in unison with the flashes, and after some time started to truly believe that they did see something.

Grasshopper, wedged between Siamese and Magician, inhaled the colors: now orange, now green, white, blue . . . and the wailing music. Every time the song rose to a high-pitched squeal he expected that, right at that moment, accompanied by the din and clatter of this beautiful orgy, a senior girl would burst out of the basement window astride a broom and soar into the black sky, trailing sparks and unbridled laughter. It would be Witch, of course.

"I GOT TO RAMBLE, OH, YEAH, BABY, BABY!" the song shrieked.

She would leave a jagged hole in the glass, and then everyone else would fly out of that hole. They would glide down to the ground and then spike right up—one, then another, and another, streaming along the ragged clouds, turning into laughing demons as they went. And the only thing left of them in this world would be their amulets on torn strings. That's what the song was about. The seniors swayed, jerked, flamed in different colors, but remained rooted to the floor. They could not fly away, the basement was holding them, tethering them to itself. There was no one to break the glass for them.

"OOH, BABY, BABY!" The song was ringing in Grasshopper's ears. The colors flashed. Orange! Green! White! Blue!

His breath was ragged in the throat, his mouth open, he was coiled like a spring.

"IT'S CALLIN' ME!" Green! White!

Grasshopper gasped, turned over on his back, and kicked out with his feet as hard as he could, right at the glass. It rained shards, and then Grasshopper was lifted bodily from both sides and hauled away, but not before freeing his legs, stuck in the grating. After just a few steps he managed to spring up and run with the others, even ahead of the others, because the song continued to scream at him: "OOH! OOH! OOH!" Except now it urged them to flee. They flew up the stairs, with him still in front, and thundered down the hallway, tripping and chortling loudly. The three lame among them imagined that they were racing the wind, the two hauling the third thought that they were really fast, and even the largest one, huffing miserably behind, was sure he was running. And all of them heard the clatter of the hot pursuit on their heels. They burst into the dorm, crashed on the beds, and burrowed inside, the way lizards disappear in the sand. The suppressed laughter was trying to get out of them. Then there wasn't a stir anywhere, except for the shoes being taken off under the covers. The first shoe hit the floor, then another and another, and every time they froze and listened. But everything was quiet. No one chased after them, no one came in to check if they were really sleeping. Taming their breaths, they pretended to be asleep until they got tired of it, then slowly, one by one, climbed down from the beds and crawled to the middle of the room, the place where the invisible fire was always lit in their cave, surrounding it in a barefoot semicircle.

"What did you do that for?" Magician asked.

"They dropped me," Stinker squeaked. "Twice! One time was on the stairs. I could have fallen to my death."

Elephant just shuddered, sucking his thumb.

"I wanted to let them out," Grasshopper explained. "So they could fly."

The hands of the Poxy Sissies, dirty from the asphalt and the rusty grates, reached out to feel him.

"Hey. Are you all right?"

"It all comes from the fuzzy looking," Humpback said. "I knew it."

"Someone had to let them out," Grasshopper said. "Set them free. That's what the song was about."

He fell silent, straining to hear the song again across the two floors dividing them. But it felt different now, like someone just listening to music in the distance. No one was calling him to action.

"I'd give anything," one of the Siamese moaned, "to be grown up now. And to be there. Like them. Why do we have to grow so slowly?"

"I saw him. Skull," Magician bragged.

"No you didn't," Wolf said. "You're just making it up."

Beauty was hugging the juice maker.

"It was . . . It was like juice," he said dreamily. "Like it was all covered in juice. Orange. And then strawberry. And then I don't know what kind."

"As soon as my letters get there, we'll have all of that too," Stinker said. "Dancing at night. Big deal. They just guzzle beer and scream. Some entertainment. We'll do loads better."

"You can still hear them," Wolf said. "Down there. Maybe they didn't even notice that busted glass. Or maybe they don't care when they're having fun like that."

"Let's have fun too," Humpback suggested.

"We haven't got girls," Grasshopper said. "Or the basement. Or the record player with the stereo system. But once we get all that, we're not going to just shuffle in place. We'll fly away."

"Right." Stinker nodded. "You're going to kick out the glass for us, and we'll just soar into the sky. In white nightgowns. Like ghosts! You gave your word, so remember that."

"No one is going to make me wear a nightgown, ever," Humpback grumbled. "Not when I'm grown up. Just let them try . . ."

Grasshopper edged along the wall, constantly stepping in the piles of sawdust. Pearlescent smoke permeated the café; clouds of it drifted from table to table. Music oozed from the speakers. The seniors were in conversation mode, elbows spread on the table mats, heads close together, smoke curling out of nostrils. He stole by them silently and found a corner between the switched-off television and the fake palm tree. There he crouched down and froze, letting his gaze wander among the tables.

Those actually were classroom desks with tablecloths on top. The ashtrays took over for the pencil holders. The seniors had thought up this café themselves, and designed all the furniture. The counter they made out of crates covered in fabric.

Behind the counter, Gibbon, a long-limbed senior, tended to the sizzling, spitting coffeepots, juggled sugar bowls, cups, and spoons, poured, mixed, whipped, and arranged his creations on the waiting trays.

The audience on the slender-legged stools placed all along the counter observed him rapturously. They leaned on it, wiggled corduroy-clad bottoms on the mushroom seats, teased the half-moon coffee stains with their fingers, raided the sugar bowls. Those were the delights available to the walkers. Wheelers had to make do with the tables.

A cardboard monkey on a string hung from the palm branch over Grasshopper's head. He looked at it. Then looked back at the seniors. The speakers on the walls hissed idly. There, in the distance, among the clouds of smoke behind the counter, Gibbon wiped his hands on the bar towel and changed the record. Grasshopper buried his chin in his knees and closed his eyes. This was not the song. But he believed. Believed that if he sat here quietly, not going anywhere, they'd put the song back on.

The windows darkened gradually. Most of the tables were already occupied. The seniors' voices droned in the background, dissolving into one rustling stream. This song danced, clanking the tin cans and squeaking from time to time. It was like a conga line of cheerful people, wiggling their hips, stomping in the sand, and shaking tambourines.

Grasshopper took in the smells of coffee and smoke. Could it be that coffee was the potion that made you a grown-up? That if you drank it you became an adult? That's what Grasshopper thought. Life had its own laws, they were innate, not invented, and one of them was about coffee and those who drank it. First they let you have coffee. Then, as a result, they stop insisting that you go to bed at a certain hour. No one actually lets you smoke, but there's not letting and then there's not letting. Which is why there aren't any seniors who don't smoke, and only one junior who does. Seniors who smoke and drink coffee become very excitable, and next thing you know they're allowed to turn a lecture hall into a bar and not sleep at night. And to skip breakfast. And it all started with coffee.

Grasshopper, still with chin between knees, closed his eyes drowsily. The cardboard monkey swung on its cord. Someone tossed a beer can in the air and caught it again. A web of cracks ran down the windowpane. Rain. The rumble of thunder crowded out the music. Those at the tables laughed and looked at the windows. Gibbon wiped down the counter.

Grasshopper waited patiently.

The dancing people were still drumming and singing, relentlessly vivacious, alien—to the rain, the dusk, the faces at the tables. Only the smell of coffee was in tune with them, and the fake palm. *Why is it that no one hears how out of place it is here? Them and their sunny songs?* Finally, with the last shake of the hips and the last rattle of the tambourines, the dancers departed, to Grasshopper's relief, leaving behind only an empty rustle, like the crackling of a dying fire. That soft sound was soon drowned out, as the rain took over.

Gibbon changed the record again. A guitar lick, overlaid on the rain. Grasshopper perked up and raised his head. The voice he recognized immediately, as soon as it came in. It was a different song, but the voice was the same voice that had screamed at him from the basement. Grasshopper sat up straight. The voice whispered and moaned over the tables and the heads of the seniors. The setting sun pushed aside the streaming water and the low clouds, and the room turned to purple and gold. It didn't matter that this wasn't *the* song. Grasshopper was sure that he knew this one too, had always known it. Knew it like he knew himself, like something that always had been, that he and everyone else needed in order to simply go on existing. This was the café, not the basement, but the voice kept on calling. Inviting to come with it, out into the wall of the rain. Where? No one could know. And there was no need to break the glass this time. Just step out through it, parting it like water, then through the rain, and up from there. The tables dissolved in the music, leaving only the checkered puzzle of the tablecloths. Time stopped. Rain beat out the drum solo on the faces and hands. Then the purple faded, the gold melted. Only Grasshopper's hair still flamed in the dark corner.

That song came to an end, but the voice on the record had others. More magic for those who knew how to listen. Grasshopper listened until Gibbon changed the record, and it had a different voice, one that couldn't make him recognize it. The heads of the seniors resumed their swaying, the fingers busied themselves with glasses and ashtrays. A cat with a glossy back slinked under the tables, mewling pitifully, and got a cigarette and a mint thrown down for its troubles. Grasshopper sighed. This new song didn't even have coffee people in it. It didn't have anything. Only a shrill woman.

Two girls wearing bright-red lipstick wheeled away from their table. One of them picked up the cat and cradled it. Someone turned the light on, and there was a short burst of switches clicking. Lights under green umbrella shades were coming on everywhere. The woman was singing about being dumped. Two songs in a row now.

Grasshopper got up, separating himself from the wall and the warm nook behind the television. The palm tree swayed. The monkey turned its empty, unpainted side to him. He threaded his way between the tables, a white streak in the cloud of smoke. An underwater kingdom of green shades and green faces. He went to the counter and asked a question.

The seniors leaned down from the mushroom stools and said, "What was that?" Gibbon, in his white apron, regarded him from above like he was something not worthy of attention.

Grasshopper repeated the question. The faces of the seniors scowled sarcastically. Gibbon took out a marker, scribbled something on a napkin, and placed it on the edge of the counter.

"Read this," he said.

Grasshopper looked at the words.

"Led Zeppelin," he said timidly. "Where is it led?"

The seniors sneered.

"Everywhere! It's made of lead, dummy!"

Grasshopper blushed.

"Why?"

"To better smash the windows with," Gibbon said indifferently, and they broke out laughing again.

The laughter chased Grasshopper out, burning with shame, but not before he stashed the wad of the napkin in the grip of the prosthetic.

How did they know? Who told them?

Across the walls of the Poxy room, animals were flying. Goblin lurked in wait, ready to ambush an unwary stranger. Grasshopper sat down in front of the nightstand with the typewriter and relaxed his grip. The napkin wasn't there. The not-quite-hand could not make a proper fist. Grasshopper shut his eyes tightly, then opened them and rattled out the words that he remembered even without the aid of the napkin. Then pulled out the sheet of paper and stuffed it in his pocket. He was upset. By the zeppelin. Because he didn't understand what a zeppelin could possibly have to do with it. They were bulky and unwieldy, and they'd been extinct for a long time. And also because the seniors knew about the glass. About him breaking it.

"The most hurtful thing," he said, "is that it was one of you who told them."

"What?" Humpback said, leaning down from his bunk.

"Nothing," Grasshopper said. "Whoever did it heard me."

Beauty was wearing a paper crown with rounded edges. His smile was missing a tooth. Stinker, in a crown exactly like Beauty's, also grinned, but with inquisitive anticipation. His smile was abundantly toothy. One of the Siamese was cutting pictures out of a magazine. He raised his icy stare at Grasshopper and turned back to clicking the scissors.

"Who said what to who?" Stinker blurted out. "And who was supposed to hear?"

Humpback leaned over again.

"About the glass," Grasshopper said. "That it was me who broke it. The seniors know."

"It wasn't me," Stinker protested. "I'm blameless. Never, not to a single soul!"

Siamese yawned. Humpback shifted angrily under the covers.

Elephant was fiddling bashfully with the pocket of his overalls.

"I told them. That Grasshopper . . . wanted to let them out. Very much. Was very upset. So I told them."

"Who?" Stinker said, shifting the crown askew and picking at his ear. "Who did you tell?"

"Them," Elephant said waving his hand vaguely. "That tall one. He asked. And also the other one, he was standing there too. Was that wrong? They weren't angry."

Elephant's guileless blue gaze sought out Siamese, and his thumb moved in the direction of his mouth.

"Was that wrong?"

Siamese sighed.

"How hard did you get it?" he asked.

"I didn't," Grasshopper said, approaching Stinker and nodding at a pocket. "Take this out, please. I wrote something, for your letters. For you to mention."

Stinker tugged at the pocket, snatched out the sheet, and peered into the words, then brought them right under his nose and sniffed greedily.

"Wow," he said. "I'd say . . . You think that would be useful to have around?"

Humpback climbed down, took the paper from Stinker, and read it too.

"Zeppelin? What's that mean?"

"I could, of course, write that a poor paralyzed baby is desperately into the lighter-than-air craft," Stinker drawled dreamily. "No problem at all. But how can we be sure they'll understand it correctly?"

"That's the name of the song," Grasshopper said. "Or the band. I'm not sure. That's if Gibbon wasn't trying to pull a joke on me."

"We'll find out," Stinker said, putting away the paper. "And then it's going on the list."

Elephant trampled heavily to Grasshopper's side, right over the magazine cuttings.

"I want a crown too," he whined, pointing at Beauty. "With pointy bits, like this one."

Stinker handed over his crown.

Elephant quickly put his hands behind his back.

"No! Like this one. Beautiful!"

Humpback took the crown off Beauty's head and slapped it over Elephant's. He had to push it down a bit to make sure it didn't fall off. Elephant went back, beaming and holding very straight.

"No bawling this time," Humpback said happily. "We're in luck."

Elephant sat on the bed and felt around his head gingerly.

TABAQUI

"'Tis the voice of the Jubjub!" he suddenly cried.
(This man, that they used to call "Dunce.")

—Lewis Carroll, *The Hunting of the Snark*

Tuesdays are Swap days. I haven't been down to the first since Pompey. That floor somehow ceased to attract me. You can call it cowardly, I guess, but it's more to do with waiting it out. There are bad places and there are temporarily bad places. That temporary badness can be waited out. That's what I ponder all morning. How I miss the Swap days and how enough time has passed since Pompey for the first floor to stop being a bad place.

So after classes I take stock of my belongings. Of everything stuffed into the bags and boxes. Can't find anything worthwhile. That's what comes from not swapping for so long. When you're away from that business for a while you lose the nose for it. I am scraping the bottom, turning over the deepest piles, and come across the long-forgotten flashlight with the naked lady. That is, the handle has this form, so you're supposedly holding her at the waist. Ghastly thing. Very slightly dented. I'll take it. But this abomination immediately makes me feel ashamed, so I pick out three strings of bead necklaces. Walnut shells, date pits, and coffee beans. It's a bit painful to part with those, but I can always make more. I have the technology. All of this fits into one bundle, a very small one.

I dive into the record stacks, the back rows. Yngwie Malmsteen. Exactly the kind of thing that's just begging to be swapped. Lary's going to go bananas, but I'm certainly a better judge of what is or isn't useful to have around. Besides, it is quite likely that I won't find anything to swap it for, and then I'll just put it back. In fact, I'm almost certain that this is how it'll be. I put the record into a plastic bag, so it's less conspicuous. Time to drive.

The din hits me on the landing, and all I can see when I look down are figures rushing to and fro. More people than usual. Many more, come to think of it. I can't quite grasp why, but once I'm down there I notice that half of the swappers are girls, and then I'm surprised at my own surprise. It's not as if they wouldn't have anything worth swapping. I keep forgetting about the new Law. This makes me slightly uneasy. I'm really introverted by nature, and I don't like being ambushed. Yes, the Law, that's all nice and good, but not when you haven't been expecting it to jump out at you. Which I wasn't. But I've already wheeled down here in front of everyone, it wouldn't do to just turn back.

I drive slowly past them—sitting and standing, hawking this and that. I try to look the way I always look. Like they have always been loitering here, nothing special about it. It's not too hard to look unruffled in the throng of primped-up Rats and Hounds. You're almost invisible in it. Takes an effort to muscle through, even.

Owl's already in his favorite corner with cigarettes, Monkey's camped out with the stickers behind the drinks machine, but most everyone else is lost in the sea of girls. Nobody has their wares out. You're supposed to ask, and I hate that. Looks like I came all the way down here for nothing. Who needs my gaudy flashlight and homemade necklaces? People are here for the opportunities to hook up, and all that changey business is just a pretext. Still, I make it to the other end, so that I can return with my head held high.

"Whaddya have?" Gnome asks.

His spots make him look like a fly agaric. He's looking over my head and doesn't give a crap about what I have. He's asking just because. Next to him, sullen Gaby is holding a huge poster of Marilyn and yawning like a crocodile.

I drive by quickly. There's a short line in the records corner, four Hounds and two bespectacled girls. Before them an empty space, and before that a single girl, all alone. Suddenly I'm stuck near her. Had to stop to catch the record that chose this moment to try to slide off Mustang and slither out of the sleeve at the same time. And then . . .

I see it. It's on her knees, the vest of many colors. Decorated with glass beads. Shiny and flashy. A small sun. It's impossible, of course, that a thing like this could have been brought just to be swapped, but I'm still mesmerized. It has this effect on me. She looks up. Green eyes, a shade darker than Sphinx's. And hair so long she seems to have tucked the ends under her, like it's a mat.

"Hey," she says. "Like it?"

Like it? What kind of question is that? I need to go back and find something valuable. The boombox could get me killed, but there are always Noble's shirts. And my lucky amulets.

"I don't have anything in exchange," I say. "Only useless trinkets. I have to go now."

She stands up. What's her nick? Mermaid, isn't it? She's tiny. Didn't she used to be a wheeler, though? Or maybe I'm mistaking her for someone else.

"Try it. It's a small size. Might be too tight."

Malmsteen slips down again.

"No, no need," I say, trying to yank the guy back. "I was just coming through."

My ears start burning for some reason. Burning and getting in the way.

"But you liked it. Try it on," she says, pushing the vest at me. "Come on. I need to know how it looks on someone."

I take off the two I'm wearing and put on this one. Do the buttons. It's totally mine. In all possible respects.

"Cool," Mermaid says, circling the wheelchair. "Perfect fit. Almost like I made it with you in mind."

I start to undo it.

"Oh no." She shakes her head. "It's yours. A gift."

"No way." I pull off the vest and hand it to her. "That's not how it's done."

Well, all right. I had this unsavory habit once. Coming down to the first on a Swap Tuesday with nothing, choosing something I fancied, and then asking the owner, "Mind just giving this away?" And they did. What choice did they have? Then they started running away at the sight of me, or hiding their stuff. That's when I quit wheedling gifts. Got tired of it myself. But I never would have taken something like this for free. I still have my pride, after all. So I keep shaking this marvelous vest at her, begging her to take it back.

"I brought it so I could give it away," she keeps explaining. "But only to someone who would get it. You get it, so it's yours now. Take it, don't make me angry."

Hair the color of milky coffee, falling below the knees. Green shirt, pairs well with her eyes. She'd be perfect for my bead necklaces. So I untie the bundle. And the first thing to fall out is the tawdry flashlight. Horribly embarrassing. But she's only seeing the necklaces. It's obvious, just by the way she looks at them, that she knows her stuff.

"Beautiful," she says. "Did you make them yourself?"

"Take them," I say. "All of this isn't worth one single pocket on your vest."

"This one."

She picks up the date pits and puts them around her neck. There aren't many girls in the world who would look good in that. She's one.

"These, too. Don't make me angry," I say, shoving the rest at her.

I've got to rush, because I spy with my little eye that Lary is trying to force his way through the mass of swappers, and he looks loaded for bear.

"Bye! Thanks for the present!"

Driving away swiftly. Lary is almost there, except he happens to step on someone's cigarette stash and is consequently waylaid for an important discussion. So I have a momentary reprieve that I intend to use fully.

"Hey! Who's up for giving me a lift to the Fourth? Cash on delivery!"

Three solicitous Rats jump in to volunteer. Microbe and Sumac I reject. Not enough brawn. So Viking gets the job. He hoists me on his shoulders, and we're off to the races. I am positively dashing in my new vest, and he makes a handsome mount.

"Hold it, bastard!" Lary squeals somewhere behind us. "Stop!"

Naturally, we don't stop. It's a chase, the thing I like more than anything in the world. Viking's legs are pumping, white boots flashing. Jostling me rather hard.

"Yoo-hoo," I shout. "Step on it!"

Viking flies up the steps. The yellow bangs keep falling over his eyes, so I tuck it away. Wouldn't do for him to stumble. Then I dig his earbuds from under his collar and stuff them in my ears. The cords are barely long enough, so it's not very comfortable, but now we have music along for the run.

Indeed! One never knows how many delights one simple Swap Tuesday can bring.

We run. The music is plenty bumpy. Viking is plenty fast. I maintain a tight grip on my bundle. Then I spot a familiar shiny dome in the sea of hallway heads.

I tear out the earbuds and shout down to Viking, "Whoa! Right here is fine."

He puts on the brakes and unloads me on the floor. Right under Sphinx's feet.

"What's with the horsemanship?" Sphinx inquires.

"That's not horsemanship, that's a matter of life and death," I explain, paying Viking.

"Where did you get this gorgeous vest? I don't think I've seen it before."

Lary arrives, spoiling the story of the vest.

"You swapped it!" he screams. "My Yngwie! Sphinx, let me at him! I'm going to kill him!"

Sphinx, naturally, does not let him. Lary is spraying snot and spit, looking like he's about to go apoplectic at any moment.

"Keep yourself together," I say to him. "There are Logs all around us. What are they going to think? I've never swapped your precious Yngwie. As Sphinx's legs are my witness."

"Where is it then, you bloodsucking merchant?"

"Back in the wheelchair, I guess. Downstairs. Where I left it, having had to depart urgently."

Lary smacks himself in the face, turns around, and runs back.

"Wouldn't be surprised if Rats get to it first," I tell Sphinx. "You know how they are. No respect for other people's property."

"Look who's talking about respect for property, Tabaqui," Sphinx says, crouching down. I climb on his shoulders. "If his record gets swiped, you're giving him one of yours. Got that?"

I don't say anything. What can I say? Sphinx knows perfectly well that Lary has no use for any of my records. Just as I, for his. From up here I get a good view of the upper portions of the wall murals, so I busy myself studying them, even though Sphinx is striding too fast for a really close look. Once we reach the dorm I bend down to his ear.

"You know what? I think I'm going to give him a flashlight instead. It's very nice. Even a bit risqué, in a sense. Deal?"

The time between lunch and dinner drags on the longest, so by dinnertime I'm usually almost bonkers from all the waiting. But that's only if the day was dull; if it was not and there is something I can tell others about, that's different. I do have something today, and so I tell, to everyone in turn, until I myself grow tired of the repetitive details. Lary is the only one who refuses to listen. He comes back hauling his Yngwie, slots it in place, shakes a fist at me, and goes away. One might even think he's totally uninterested in finding out where I got the new vest.

I take it off to get a closer look. Then put it back on. Then take it off again. It gets better and better every time I do it. Even Nanette thinks so. She struts around and tries to peck off the beads. I have to use a magazine to shoo her off. It's a whole week until next Tuesday, if you count today, but I decide to stock up on the swappies, especially in view of a sack of freshly cracked walnut shells.

Putting on headphones to better filter out the distractions and sundry pack business, I start stringing the shells on a piece of fishing line, picking the smallest and the cutest ones. The radio is tuned to some garbage for the toddlers.

It's shameful what they feed the Outsides kids. Hair stands on end, honest. I mean, "The Snow Queen" by itself isn't half bad, but they chose to give the narration to this deep female voice doing sexy whispers and moans, which gives the story a rather unexpected flavor.

"The boat drifted with the stream," she sighs hoarsely in my ears, "little Gerda sat quite still without shoes, for they were swimming behind the boat, but she could not reach them, because the boat went much faster than they did. 'Perhaps the river will carry me to little Kay,' said she; and then she grew less sad." The voice stumbles, overwhelmed with emotion.

Another shell. And another.

Black comes to rummage in the nightstand, then in the desk drawer. Finally finds a razor and goes away. He's already got a beard to worry about. I've got nothing in that department.

"'I have often longed for such a dear little girl,'" a vampire voice hisses. "'Now you shall see how well we agree together.'"

Someone's hair is being combed, with a suspicious crunching sound.

"'O-o-oh, I'm so sleepy, what is happening,'" Gerda squeaks. She's forty if she is a day. Fascinating stuff. The necklace is almost ready, and my fingers are in agony. You might think making holes in walnut shells is easy, but it's not. I hang the first string on the nail. Looks like it'll be a good one. The shells are all almost identical.

"'Caw! Caw! Good day! Good day!'"

Judging by the voice, Raven is off the wagon. His spouse seems to be the first character in the entire thing who is actually young. She caws in a tender soprano. I pick out the second piece of fishing line.

Humpback runs in. He has this peculiar face, so it's obvious that something big has just happened. I drop the shells and look at his lips. I used to be able to read lips when I was younger, but that was so long ago, and besides he keeps turning away, so I can't quite make it out. I guess I'd better take off the earphones, except I'm scared. Because I think I saw him say "Noble." Which is impossible.

"'Yes, yes; for certain that was Kay,'" enunciates the on-the-wrong-side-of-forty Gerda in my head. "'Oh, won't you take me to the palace?'"

Out of the corner of my eye I notice that Sphinx is also a bit frazzled. He stumbles backward to the bed and sits down, staring at Humpback. Blind comes in. He looks strange too. And then—Noble's wheelchair, pushed by Ralph, with Noble in it.

"'They are only dreams . . . Dreams of noble gentlemen . . .'"

To hell with the headphones.

Silence. It's so quiet that I can hear the thrum of the House in the walls, and even the noises of the Outsides. Real silence, the kind we don't often have. Ralph is looking at us, and we're looking at Noble. Then comes the loudest dinner bell I've ever heard in my life. Ralph turns to leave and bumps into freshly shaven Black.

"Sorry," Black says to him, and then "Oh!" as he notices Noble.

"Not at all," Ralph says and walks out.

We keep staring at Noble. It really is him. Alive, in the flesh, not in a song or a dream. You can touch him, smell him, pull his hair. I need to find out how long he's going to be here and all kinds of important stuff, but I'm stupefied and can't snap out of it. Noble is hunched down in his chair. Pitiful looking, exactly the way I pictured him when playing the harmonica. Closely cropped hair. Not a buzz cut, but it would have been better if it were, because the person who gave him this was clearly bipolar. Hair sticking out in untidy clumps, and between them the skin is visible under the stubble, like he's got ringworm. Whoever thought of cutting Noble's hair, especially in this fashion, can't be considered normal, that much is obvious. Noble has on Humpback's leather jacket and my old vest. His eyes seem bigger than before, face looks smaller, fingers tease the badges stuck all over the jacket, and he never raises his head. He looks like hell, and the worst of it is that everyone just stares silently.

I begin swaying fretfully. The bad situation is getting worse and worse, until Blind sneaks out to the wheelchair and offers cigarettes to Noble.

"Here, have a smoke. You're unusually quiet."

Noble grabs the pack the way a drowning man grasps at the life preserver. And my stupefaction is suddenly gone. So is everyone else's. I turn on the afterburners, but I'm still the last one to reach him. Noble is being swarmed, jostled, sniffed, and shouted at. I join in the festivities at top volume. In the middle of the celebrations he breaks down and starts crying.

"OK, that's enough," Sphinx cuts in immediately. "Dinner, everyone. Leave him alone."

I am not about to leave Noble alone, no way. I climb on his lap, to have better access to his ears, because right now it's important to tell him stuff, like how I missed him. I don't care if he listens or not. When he drops the cigarette, six more are thrust at him from all directions.

"Look at your hair," Humpback says, ruffling the ugly 'do. "Horrible. Who would do something like that?"

"How's my vest been treating you?" I ask. "Because if you like it, I'm not going to ask for it back. Especially now that I have this brand-new one."

"Are you . . . staying?" Sphinx says carefully.

Noble nods.

"Yay!" Humpback shouts, tossing Nanette in the air.

Blind feels Noble's head and whistles sadly.

"And we have this new Law, imagine that," I begin, but Sphinx cuts the story short.

"Dinner! On the double!" he shouts testily.

They pry me off Noble and carry me away, even though I struggle valiantly. In the hallway I catch up with Humpback, who's apparently talking to himself.

"I knew he was a solid character."

That would be Ralph, obviously. A bit farther away are Sphinx and Blind, and Sphinx is saying, "Smells of the nuthouse."

That would be Noble.

I put on some speed and bump into their heels. I don't give a hoot what Noble smells like as long as he's back, and all this talk is perfect nonsense. The only thing to do now is sing and rattle things. So I sing. I sing, I run rampant, I throw cutlery. I make a huge sandwich for Noble and douse it in syrup. It, the plate, the tablecloth, and myself. I fish meatballs out of the soup, also for Noble. Two end up on the floor for each one I salvage and I stuff them into a second sandwich. Soon I'm swimming in the syrup-and-soup lake. Sphinx gives me a furious eye but doesn't say anything. It's Lary who speaks.

"If anyone asks, I'm not from the same pack. 'Cause that's just embarrassing."

Then we drive back. I rush ahead, but then fall behind because I remember about Ralph and start searching for him. I guess I wouldn't have asked him anything even if I saw him, but until I do I can't be sure. For example, where did he bring Noble from? It's very intriguing, and you can't just go and ask Noble, because you can't. Not done, not allowed, not polite—in a word, forbidden. Unless Noble tells me on his own, which he won't, that much I gathered. That's why I keep looking for Ralph, but he's nowhere to be found, so I go and catch up with the others, who got distracted receiving high-fives from those who already heard the news.

I gladly would have joined in, except the damn sandwiches keep oozing and staining everything, so I am confined to waving my hand as I drive by. It appears that I spot a couple of girls among the well-wishers, but I have no time to investigate further because I'm in such a hurry.

TABAQUI

DAY THE SIXTH

Let us take them in order. The first is the taste,
Which is meagre and hollow, but crisp:
Like a coat that is rather too tight in the waist,
With a flavour of Will-o'-the-wisp.

—Lewis Carroll, *The Hunting of the Snark*

Watching Noble the next morning, I notice a lot of strange things. He gets a coffee stain on his sweater and doesn't rush to change out of it. Drops his pillow on the floor and doesn't even notice, and when he does, neglects to change the pillowcase. Gives Lary two of his nicest shirts. When I, purely by accident, put on a pair of his socks, he doesn't make a scene and seems genuinely surprised by my sincere apologies. Tiny trifles, sure, but it's those trifles that composed the significant part of the Noble I knew, and it's strange to see him not doing things he used to do, and the other way around— doing things he never would have done. He seems to have left a lot of other stuff in the Outsides along with his hair, and I have no idea what that is so I'm undecided if I should be happy or sad about it.

"See, people, here's the deal," Lary imparts on the way from the canteen after breakfast. He's got on Noble's blue shirt with white egrets on the front, and he looks gorgeous in it. "I say to him, 'Sorry, Noble, I've been using some of your stuff while you were away. You know how it is, taking a girl out, can't do that in the rags I had.' So I say that to him and I wait for the fireworks. And he's like, 'Sure, take them, they're yours now. And take these too.' Dumps it all out in front of me, and goes, 'Take whatever you want, come on.' So I took some. And then he gave me his lighter. 'Have it,' he says. You know, the one with the dragon. And all I did was say to him, 'That's a really nice lighter you have, Noble.' I didn't mean anything like that, honest, and he's like—bang, stuffs it in my pocket. 'You have it, if you like it,' he says."

"Next thing you're going to beg the underpants off him," Humpback grumbles. "Have you no shame? Leave the guy alone."

"I didn't mean nothing. Just said how nice it was."

Humpback and I shake our heads. Lary reddens and goes quiet. When we reach the classroom he steps in front of us, barring the way.

"All right. Screw the lighter. So I did figure he'd give it to me if I mentioned it. But you tell me this. Would I have, like, even considered that he might do that? I mean, before? No way. So you tell me, what's wrong with him and why is he behaving like he's not himself? I mean, he looks like our Noble and stuff. But he behaves kind of alien. Doesn't that bother you? You know what I'm saying?"

"Go to hell," Humpback says, shoving him in the chest. "Get out of the way. I don't have time to stand here listening to your garbage. How's that lighter doing, burning your butt yet?"

Lary carefully studies the egret in the center of his shirt, the biggest one, afraid that Humpback might have stained it. Then fingers the fabric.

"What's with the shoving?" he says. "I call them as I see them, if you don't want to listen—fine, don't. Still no reason to go shoving. You think I'm not happy they brought him back? I too am happy! But there is this concern, you see, and I'm just saying. Because all those stories about changelings, they're not for nothing, you know. Food for thought is all I'm saying."

Humpback moves for his collar, but Lary wiggles away and runs into the classroom. Humpback and I exchange glances.

"Pitiful excuse for a human," he says. "I should have smacked him one."

I fiddle with my earring, turning it around and around.

"Probably. He's always asking for it. But there is something in what he's babbling. I noticed too. Noble did change. A lot."

Humpback frowns, surprised.

"Of course he did. Grown up, that's all. And also he missed us. Lary is a nitwit, he doesn't get it, but I would have expected more from you. Where're your eyes? And ears and everything else?"

He pushes me inside and retreats to his seat. I sidle up to the desk and take out my notes. The ear is burning because I tugged at the earring, but the cheeks do because of Humpback's words. I stare at Noble. He's right here, at the next desk, and I can stare to my heart's content. He's already hard at work over my notebook, correcting something in my scribbles. I hadn't asked him to, but he did that before, too, without being asked. Refined aquiline face, unnaturally beautiful, bent over the grubby pages. Even the bald spots and the entire disgusting haircut are powerless to ruin the impression. The hair is not yellow like before, but more on the milk-chocolate side, the way it used to show near the roots. And a barely suggested shadow of a beard. A ghost of a beard. Because of it, or maybe because Humpback's words are starting to have an effect, I can see that Noble has indeed grown up. Is that all it is? Only this and nothing else? I spend the whole class thinking about it.

The snow is a curtain outside the window. It falls and it falls, easing up only by dinnertime. The entire yard is now only bumps and folds under the white sugary blanket. Very beautiful. Even the Outsides is not quite itself, and it's completely quiet, as if the House had been transported to a wintry forest. Pity it's dark, or it all would have glistened and sparkled.

After dinner everyone rushes out. I drive down too. I like snow, even though wheelchairs have a habit of getting completely stuck in it, which is unpleasant, but on the bright side there are many delights that are only available when it's been snowing.

I pick out a convenient spot and dump myself out into the snowbank. Then I assemble a store of snowballs, and then everyone passing by gets a snowball to the head. My aim is perfect, as usual; as long as I have things to throw, they always land where I want them. Noble soon joins me. The two of us give a good thrashing to the walkers of the Sixth and to Lary and his gang. Logs are uniformly clad in striped pompom hats, so aiming at them is ridiculously easy.

By the time the girls come out, everyone is fairly warmed up and wound up. The first barrage greets them right on the porch. They don't even have time to step down. But there's enough snow on the porch too, and it offers better opportunities for hiding, so they recover pretty soon and answer with an avalanche of their own. Noble and I are in a completely open spot and cannot run away, so most of it arrives our way. I am flattened against the snowbank and temporarily incapacitated, and by the time I manage to crawl out, the battlefield is strewn with half-exploded ordnance and Noble is wounded in the mouth. He barks out curses mixed with snow.

"What was that word you used to describe them?" I inquire. "'Tender'? Or was it 'charming'?"

Before Noble has a chance to answer, a girl in a blue parka gets him right on the bridge of the nose. He yelps and proceeds to prepare the snowball of vengeance, the size of a melon. While he's thus busy I provide cover for him, picking off the hats that poke above the railing, but the blue parka girl manages to plonk him twice more. Finally Noble rises up and tosses his deadly missile at her feet. An explosion of snow and screams. The blue parka goes down like a bowling pin. I was doubtful that this thing would fly at all, so I'm amazed and humbled, and say so to Noble. He looks at me askance.

"You don't think I hurt her too much, do you?"

"I think she only fell to flatter you," I say. "It's unlikely she got hit that badly."

Noble doesn't believe me and crawls to see for himself. "Crawls" is the wrong word here. It's a slow word. Noble moves very fast. Well, right now he's hampered by all the snow. By the time he reaches the porch, the girl's already up and shaking the snow out of her hair. He asks her something from below. She laughs, shakes her head, and plops down into the snowbank next to him—so that he doesn't feel himself awkward next to her standing. That's how they continue the conversation—wet and plastered with snow. Like a comedic duo that just climbed out of a gigantic cream pie. But I don't have time to observe them—someone is shelling me from behind the railing. I have to respond, even though the adversary is hidden and all my snowballs dash futilely against the porch. I wait for the someone to peek out, but she's smart and keeps down. Which interferes with her aim, so her snowballs miss too. You might say we're missing each other.

Then I accidentally look up and see Sphinx's outline in the window of our dorm. It doesn't matter that it's just an outline, and it doesn't matter that his mouth, invisible to me, is almost certainly smiling. I still know what he's thinking when he looks over our snow battles. Half of my life was spent on windowsills staring down and dying from envy. So one look at his distant shadow is enough for me to lose the desire to frolic.

I toss the lovingly prepared snowball aside and crawl toward Mustang. After an eternity of being pelted from all sides I finally reach it, only to discover that Mustang is wet and slippery. Some clown had the bright idea of using it to shield himself. I try to climb in but keep slipping. Takes me three tries. Then I realize that the snow around me is so trampled that there's no way to drive through. Mustang lists to one side, stalled irretrievably. A gloomy sight. Horse and Bubble, kindhearted Logs of the Third, offer help. They roll me up the porch ramp, and we are immediately mobbed by the girls begging me to play with them just a bit more. That's unexpected and flattering, and I perspire anxiously all the way up to the second floor and to the doors of the dorm, recalling how they dubbed me "William Tell" and asked me to stay. And that's considering that the yard was fairly swarming with guys. Every walker of the House plus the wildest of the wheelers.

The hallway is empty. Only Blind's out, shuffling to and fro and kicking wet sawdust with his feet. When I wheel into the dorm, Sphinx is still by the window, inquiring testily of Alexander who Noble is cavorting with, buried up to his neck in snow, and who's that girl running circles around Black, eyeing him salaciously.

"How is it possible, Sphinx," Alexander says, "to see the salaciousness in the eyes from up here?"

Now warm and dry in my dressing gown, I sit over the chessboard. Sphinx is right across from me. Knitting his brow, demonstrating to the world how the little gray cells are working overtime, but in fact engrossed in the sounds filtering from the yard.

"Put the kettle on," he tells Alexander. "They're going to barge in soon and start whining and demanding tea. You'll be running off your feet."

Alexander plops the kettle on the hotplate and joins us on the bed. I have this ambush brewing, hidden in the corner of the board, and on no occasion should Sphinx notice it, so I sing the distracting Confusion Song and pointedly stare at the other corner, where a decoy attack is being prepared. Blind is sitting with his feet on the table, yawning and rummaging in the tool chest, already half-gutted. The screams in the yard grow less and less loud, then migrate to the hallways. Squeals, thundering feet: someone's galloping down the corridor while being destroyed with snowballs.

I feign great interest and turn toward the door, but when I glance back at the board, the inventive attack is in ruins and Sphinx is pushing my queen off with the rake-prong.

Queen in the ashtray means the game's all but over.

"The snow's coming here," Alexander says.

The door screeches and here they are, white as a gaggle of snowmen: Black, Humpback, Noble, and Lary, and two girls with them, the blue parka and the purple one. They're all in hysterics. Lary, giggling moronically, smashes a large snowball in the center of the board.

The pieces scatter. Sphinx, scowling, uses his knee to wipe his face. The scowl is quite a friendly one, but Lary thinks better of dumping the second snowball on us and with the same idiotic grin breaks it over his own head.

Black and Humpback help the girls with their heavy clothes. Coats are tossed on the windowsill, hats are taken off, and scarves unwound. The blue parka turns out to be fiery red. It's Ginger, of course—sharp face and inky eyes. And the purple one is Fly, swarthy and toothy, covered in moles. Now that I've identified them I'm free to jump up and down on the pillows and screech invitingly.

They immediately plop down on the floor. Sphinx sidles up, or down, to them, while Black and Humpback proceed to bustle, putting out the plates, cups, and ashtrays. They all leave wet squelching footsteps that Alexander keeps surreptitiously running the rag over.

I slither down to the floor too. We sit in a semicircle. Most of me is under the bed, only my head is peeking out. Tea's served. A compelling installation of wet socks on a string stretches over our heads all across the room, spreading fragrant dampness. Drying boots stick out of the heater. Ginger and Fly are both wrapped in blankets, with smoke curling upward from under the makeshift hoods.

Lary is engrossed in excavating his nostril, imagining that he's doing it discreetly. Noble and Humpback also put on blankets. Alexander roams the room offering tea, and the boombox is burbling unobtrusively. In short, a nice evening of pleasant domesticity. Not quite the way we would have done it by ourselves, though, or even with the Old Sissy Guard, because girls are girls and their presence is somewhat limiting. It's one thing to imagine yourself sparkling with wit, but the wit itself does not readily present itself. Only stale, belabored jokes, not worthy of being thought of, much less enunciated. Better to keep silent. So I'm silent for a spell. Breathing in and listening to others.

They're rehashing the snow battle. Can't seem to get enough of it. Ginger's bare feet peek from under the blanket. The feet are milky white and scratched, the curled-up toes move when she speaks. Fly makes faces, sways, and giggles. Then she chokes on the smoke and sweeps the corner of the blanket off her head, so we now see her sharp teeth and the metal rings in her ears, five in each. Eyebrows dusted with glitter. She looks like a thieving ragamuffin. Maybe because she constantly pouts, or maybe because she keeps flaring her nostrils. Takes no great leap of imagination to picture her doing something like stealing horses. Also, she talks too fast. Even for me.

Ginger is silent. Either smoking or gnawing at her nails. Looking at the two of them, an outside observer would say: now here's a shy and quiet girl, and here's a gregarious and talkative one. All nice and clear, choose whichever one suits you better. But those of us who knew them from a tender age know that it's not so simple. Because Fly was the one who never said a single word for five straight years, from age six to age eleven. She was neither deaf nor mute, but she'd flee under the bed anytime anyone tried to approach her. Whereas Ginger had been at one time dubbed Satan by the counselors. Not even I have distinguished myself with a nick like that. So she's about as humble and mild mannered as I am. And she's grown quieter and quieter each year.

I pull at the edge of her blanket.

"Hey, Gingie, do girls still get sent to the Cages?"

She leans closer to me.

"Of course. But to the ones in our hallway, not those on the counselors' floor. Godmother never allows Cases near us. They're always drunk and tend to let their hands wander too much. So she does the honors herself. Locks us in and lets us out. She's the only one with the keys."

"Wow," I say. "That sounds just like her."

Counselor Godmother is the House's Iron Lady. Looking at her you start imagining that she must be jangling and clanking as she walks, like the Tin Man. But the only sound you actually hear is those heels clicking.

Lary inquires about Blondie, the new counselor. Girls' counselors are a favorite topic with Logs, and they absolutely adore Blondie. Ever since they first laid their eyes on her.

"Still feeling out the place," Fly says. "She's kinda cute, but on the nervous side. I don't think she's going to take an entire shift. Running errands for others is just about her speed. And that hair, it's real, imagine that. A natural strawberry blonde. Gorgeous shade."

Lary swallows and lets out a wistful sigh. As far as I'm concerned, blondes like that are better off being buried alive. Well, this one might be cute, I wouldn't know. I've only seen her twice, and both times I could only look at the watch she had. Huge thing, the size of a large onion. Ticking like a bomb. Disgusting. So her hair was the last thing on my mind.

"Our Tubby is totally in love with her," Sphinx says. "I was walking him down on the first. And she'd just left Shark's office, straight at us. Tubby tossed himself out of his wheelchair and made a beeline for her. At a ridiculous speed. No one could've expected that."

"And?" Fly says, opening her eyes wide.

"Nothing," Sphinx scowls. "Gummed her a bit, that's all. But you should have heard the screams."

We are silent for a while, out of respect for Tubby's broken heart. Ginger has emerged from under her veil. Humpback's red shirt and her own fiery hair—the impression here is of a flaming torch. You just can't go and set black eyes into a face like that. It's scary. The skin does not exactly crawl, but definitely feels scratchy.

Fly keeps turning her head this way and that, looking for something.

"Where's your crow? I heard you had a crow living here. I'd love to take a look!"

Humpback goes to take out Nanette. The poor bird, already tucked in for the night.

"How's Mermaid doing?" I ask. "You know, the small one with the longest hair," I clarify, because I'm still not sure about the nick.

"Ask her," Fly says, pointing at Ginger. "They're from the same room. The Dreadful Dorm."

Ginger's eyebrows jerk up. She's not looking at Fly; her chin is buried in her knees, finger sweeping the lips distractedly.

"I mean, distinctive," Fly backpedals. "The most unusual, I mean . . ."

Humpback returns with sleepy Nanette in an irritated torpor and parades her before the girls. Fly carefully pets the gunmetal feathers. The bird startles and pulls the translucent film over her eyes. Were she in a bit more conscious state, the enemy's fingers already would have been pecked to a bloody mess.

"Isn't she a darling . . . Beau-utiful . . . ," Fly coos obliviously. "So cute."

The cute darling looks daggers and is already starting to wheeze threateningly, so Humpback whisks her away back to the perch.

"Such a sweetie," Fly persists. "I could've just eaten her up!"

"Before you do, make sure you have a spare set of eyes handy," Black says. "It's not a darling at all, really."

"Nah," Fly pouts, not taking her eyes off departing Nanette. "She's a sweet girl, she can't be a meanie."

"So, how's Mermaid?" I ask again. "I had a little talk with her yesterday."

Ginger looks at my vest and smiles.

"Mermaid's doing fine," she says. "She's one of those people . . . Well, maybe they only look like that, I don't know. But anyway, they're rare, those people who never have any problems. Or at least behave as if they don't have any."

We all look at Alexander. He blushes and gets tangled in the coffeemaker's electric cord. We turn away, giving him time to untangle.

I have a strange aftertaste in my mouth after this exchange. As if I, too, know how she is, the girl who creates the most wonderful vests in the world and then gives them away to the first stranger she meets. This conversation calls for a smoke. Ginger and I light up in unison, except her cigarette, unlike mine, gets six lighters thrust at it from all directions, and the most insistent of them belongs to Noble, and I suddenly realize that he's been kind of strangely bright red of color, and the looks he's been giving Ginger are also strange. Probing and fiery. Predatory, one might even say. It is so obvious that I grow uncomfortable, and throw a sideways glance at Sphinx: Has he noticed yet?

Well, if he has, he's not letting it show. He's twirling the ashtray with the rake, all sleepy like. He and Wolf always looked like that when something piqued their interest. Deceptively relaxed.

"I tried my best to protect the ear." Lary wades in with a non sequitur. "And still it got walloped. A nasty one, too. Hope it's not going to get infected like the last time."

He feels his ear and then examines the fingers. As if, when he touched it, the infection could have fallen out.

"You don't look like your ears would be giving you trouble," Fly notes kindly.

Lary considers this. Should he take it as a compliment?

We discuss the latest Gallery. The actual paintings there could be counted on one hand, but Lizard from the Third exhibited himself, painted. That was a sight to behold. Looking at Lizard is a scary proposition even under normal circumstances. But body-painted . . . Talking about the Gallery shakes Smoker out of his funk and he tells us about a couple of exhibitions he happened to attend back in the Outsides. Then we discuss the Fortune-Telling Salon. I worked there for a week as Madame Zazu, fortune-teller and palmist extraordinaire, and can impart some inside info. Fly and Lary proceed to gossip about the girls' counselors—that is, Fly gossips while Lary nods excitedly. Ginger and I get into an argument about Richard Bach, also in a gossipy way. We both agree that he isn't too bad as a writer, but as far as women in his life are concerned, he behaved like a complete bastard. Take, for example, his search for the One, where the aspiring girls more or less had to pass a private pilot's exam at some point.

"And smokers were cut right out," Ginger fumes. "Because, get this, he doesn't smoke! As if she couldn't just quit if it came to that."

I still want to talk more about Mermaid, but can't work up the courage.

Blind wants to know when Rat is expected back from her foray into the Outsides. Rat is the House's principal Flyer, and he placed a large and expensive order with her. Ginger doesn't know when Rat will return. No one knows. Not even Rat herself. Black tries to find out where Rat sleeps when she's in the Outsides and generally how she manages to stay there for extended periods of time, but neither Ginger nor Fly can tell him anything about that because they, too, have no idea.

Ginger looks up to the ceiling.

"You used to have this wall with all those animals living on it," she says out of the blue. "And you kept the door locked. And put snares behind it. Traps. Or so they said. I dreamed of that wall so often that at some point it became very important to see it for real. So I sneaked into your dorm through the window."

"There are bars, and nothing to step on," Noble whispers, not taking his burning eyes off her.

Ginger glances at him and chuckles.

"There were no bars back then, and there's this crumbly ledge along the wall. I followed it about halfway and got scared. I was stuck there for an eternity, unable to move. Until the seniors spotted me. It was horrible."

"They picked you off," I venture. "Fetched a stepladder and talked you down."

"No. They stood below and watched. With interest. So I had to get going."

"Yeah." Humpback shudders. "They were good at that. Watching with interest, I mean. Don't ask . . ."

"Quiet!" I crawl closer, anticipating something very important to be revealed any second now. "Go on," I urge Ginger. "So, what happened? You climbed in and . . ."

"And there I was in your room," Ginger says, half smiling, fiddling with the cigarette in her fingers. "At first I was just glad that I made it. That I was standing on a solid, dependable surface. Then I studied the wall. It turned out to be completely different from what I had imagined, but it was still so amazing. Like it was boundless, stretching out into infinity on both sides." Ginger spreads her arms wide, demonstrating the vast expanse. "It's hard to explain. I didn't have much time, I knew you were going to be back soon, and I still had to make myself climb out of that window, travel along that horrible ledge, and slide down the drainpipe . . . I found this thick marker in the nightstand and drew a bird on the wall. It came out so ugly, so . . . insignificant.

Spoiled the entire wall. It got me so depressed that I almost didn't notice how I crawled out. Cried myself to sleep that night."

"And two days later you returned to paint it in," Sphinx says. "To make it white. You signed it *Jonathan*. And then Jonathan started leaving us presents."

"Oh god," Humpback moans. "So Jonathan was you all along? And there we were, fiddling about with the traps and everything."

"Now *this*, my friends," I explain to my fingernails, "is what's commonly known as a shock to the system. When you suddenly find out what's behind an unsolved mystery. In the twilight of your years. The fastest way to a psychological trauma, I'll have you know. You see, Black, we kept finding these . . ."

"I get it," Black interrupts me. "You don't need to spell it out."

But he doesn't. Neither he, nor Noble and Alexander, nor Lary. The only ones who would get it are Vulture, Shuffle, Beauty, and Elephant. If we told them. But no one else.

Soft rustling. Humpback searches his pockets. Blind rummages in some hidden recesses as well. I unhook the earring. Our hands meet over the blanket. Humpback's palm cradles a small brass bell. Blind has a coin on a string. I'm holding the earring.

"*To the foul-smelling pirate from Jo, the one flying across oceans,*" I recite. "Except the note is long gone, of course."

Ginger bites her lip.

"You've kept it! After all this time!"

"Those are gifts from Jonathan." Sphinx laughs. "Treasure. If I'm not mistaken, Noble also inherited one. The seashell."

Noble grasps at the shell, gripping it tightly. Looks almost obsessive doing it.

"Oh, and by the way," I add. "Blind always ended up with the most gifts, for some reason. Some greedy people, such as myself, used to take offense."

Ginger reddens. In her eyes I read a reproach, a plea to stop burrowing into the memories and a lot of other things that make my tongue freeze and my head receive belated insights concerning the real reasons certain people made an appearance in this room tonight.

"Interesting," Black remarks, sipping his tepid tea and not looking at anyone in particular. "So Jonathan played favorites?"

Ginger blushes even deeper, but straightens up defiantly and shoots back, "He did. Still does. So?"

If I were Ginger I wouldn't be saying things like that, not under the heavy gaze of Noble's burning eyes. In fact, with him looking like that, which is inhumanly beautiful, I'd have probably lost the ability to speak altogether. But girls are mysterious creatures. If she thinks she likes Blind better, there's nothing anybody can do about it.

After all, it's not for nothing Jonathan risked her life climbing the ledges and sneaking into other people's windows.

"I know this one solitaire," Fly says, breaking up the awkward silence. "Dream a Little Dream, it's called. Almost never comes out, but if it does it means that your innermost desire will come true. Cool, huh?"

"Wicked," I say. "Do it right now. I am full of innermost desires."

Alexander passes the deck and pushes the cups out to the edge of the blanket. Fly begins dealing, stumbling through the rules. Ginger shivers and wraps the blanket tighter around herself, pulling in her bare feet.

"If you're cold, you can take my socks," I say. "You can return them whenever. Next time you come here."

She agrees and Alexander goes to the wardrobe to fetch the socks.

"How about my sweater?" Noble says plaintively. "It's really warm."

"There," Fly says, crestfallen, holding the last remaining card. "This always happens. Didn't I say it never comes out right? I think it's designed that way, to keep you from getting bored."

She turns to Noble.

"Can I have your sweater instead? I feel kinda cold too. Freezing, actually."

Noble nods impassively.

"Sure."

"What's your innermost desire?" I ask Fly. "The one that never comes out right?"

She waves the card at me.

"Get away! You can't say it, or it'll never come true."

Humpback and Lary yawn furtively. Ginger pulls on my socks.

"Nice place you have, guys," Fly says. "But it's getting late. Anyone got the time?"

"Shhh!" everyone hisses, and Fly, startled, puts her hand over her mouth.

"What?" she mumbles into her palm. "What did I say?"

"That which you just mentioned should not be mentioned in front of Tabaqui," Humpback says, shaking his head. "It really shouldn't."

"What was it I mentioned?" Fly whispers. "I don't remember."

Humpback and Lary tap their wrists, miming nonexistent watches. Lary does it with a look of utter disgust on his face, probably channeling me. Now poor Fly's completely confused.

"What is it? Some kind of disease?" she asks.

This entire conversation, and especially the gestures accompanying it, do start to make me sick. Slightly. I do not appreciate my psychological peculiarities being put on display, and crawl farther under the bed. Then I put my hands over my ears. Now let them say whatever they want. By the way, a mere mention of a watch is never enough for me to fly off the handle, they're well aware of that. When I crawl back out they are already discussing something else, and getting ready to leave.

The girls have discarded the blankets. Fly's own speckled sweater is peeking out from under Noble's gray one. She tugs on both, admiring her reflection in the wardrobe's polished door, and cheerfully displays her teeth. Lary, putting on boots, heaps praise on her belt buckle that I completely failed to notice. Alexander rolls up the blanket formerly known as tablecloth. Sphinx and Blind are also going out, while Noble, who wheeled off into a corner to give everyone some space, watches Ginger from over there like a predator stalking its prey with a penetrating, unblinking stare.

I emerge fully, loath to miss even the smallest detail. But there isn't anything to miss anymore: the guests are leaving, the evening morphed into the night, and the radio DJs are cheerfully greeting the insomniacs—in short, the predawn stupefaction is right around the corner. The saddest of all moods. Few are those who could gabble through the night with unrelenting intensity, like me, for example. Ginger is still wearing my socks and doesn't seem to want to take them off before heading out, which means there's a possibility of her coming back. On the other hand, she could always send them over with someone else.

"Bye," she and Fly say to me, Noble, and Alexander.

Everyone else is planning to walk them home. With flashlights.

"Bye, Jonathan," I reply. "Come again."

She nods uncertainly and steals a sideways glance at Blind. Blind, of course, is not aware of that, but, honestly, he might have guessed. The others dutifully hold off inviting her back for a few seconds, giving him first dibs. When they do, they invite Fly as well. Lary, giggling, tells her to bring Gaby along. Idiot, that one.

Finally they file out. The whole crowd, leaving behind me, Alexander, Smoker, and also Noble. Ginger's departure takes the sparkliness and fieriness out of him, leaving him dull and sullen.

I climb on the bed and start tidying it up. Spread out the plastic bag, shake the ashtrays out over it, add the half-eaten pieces of this and that, peel the gum blobs off the railing. Make a pile out of the textbooks and notes. Once the mess is localized and pushed to the edge, I create a burrow near the headboard and dive in. It's warm and cozy here. Alexander's broom swishes softly. Noble is completely quiet. I condense a cloud of drowsy fog around myself, a small one, to make it even cozier, and start remembering.

Jonathan. The ghost haunting our room. Probably the only case in the entire history of the House when a room had its own ghost. We were extremely proud. Countless times we had discussed the gifts he was leaving us, trying to decipher who he was. Countless times we had invented more and more elaborate snares and traps, only to come up empty again and again. Which served as irrefutable proof of his nonhuman nature. At first we had suspected our neighbors from next door. Then, the seniors. But neither could possibly know about our traps and snares, while Jonathan somehow evaded them all. Having despaired of catching him, we set to uncovering his identity through his handwriting. We diligently collected samples for comparison by stealing homework left in the staff room to be graded. We accumulated a sizable pile and were just about to destroy the evidence when a janitor stumbled upon it and told the administration on us.

I shuffle through the memories of that time. Funny how no one had even considered to snatch a girl's notebook. Because, quite obviously, Jonathan was male. One thing we couldn't grasp, though: Why hadn't he chosen a more inventive nick? Why a simple name? Once the hopes of catching him had evaporated, we started leaving notes for him.

Why Jonathan?

In lieu of an answer, we received a skinny book about a seagull. We had collectively read it aloud, as was our custom back then. Because of Blind, because of Beauty, who could barely put letters together, and because of Elephant, who didn't even come as far as the letters. So it was an obvious solution. Naturally, Wolf was best at reading, so he'd get the longest chapters. For some reason everyone agreed that I was the worst. We learned about Jonathan Livingston Seagull, but that hadn't really helped us in figuring out the identity of our mysterious visitor. The book hadn't been checked out of the library, so it didn't have a card we could examine for clues, and pointedly dropping the word *seagull* around did not lead us to its supposed owner. Among seniors almost everyone had read the book; among juniors we were the only ones.

Are you a seagull? was our question to Jonathan in the next letter. Jonathan maintained his silence, leaving us instead a suspicious brownish feather. We kept the feather and showed it to anyone who had even a passing familiarity with ornithology. The scholars concluded that the feather did not belong to a seagull, but whose it was they couldn't say.

I remember all of this and many other things besides, fall asleep, wake up again, remember some more, and suddenly it strikes me that I have missed a chance to unravel one of the mysteries that had so tormented us when we were kids. How did she know in advance about all of our traps? The fact that Jonathan turned out to be Ginger doesn't explain anything at all. The more I think about it the more it bugs me that I didn't think to ask. Now I have to wait until the next time she comes. And what if she never comes again? This thought strips the sleepiness clean off. I toss and turn, I sigh, I call myself stupid. Well, all right, so I did a stupid thing. But what about the others, the supposedly smart ones, huh? No one thought to ask about what's most important! Unless . . . Unless they did. Of course! I shake myself up, peek out of the burrow, and look around.

Asleep. All of them, snuffling shamelessly. Smoker on the other end, Sphinx to the left of me, while Noble is nowhere to be seen. There's a lonely silhouette on the windowsill, though, gazing at the stars. Very romantic. Must be him.

I kick Sphinx in the ribs.

"Hey! Hey, wake up! I need to ask something, quick."

"Tabaqui! You bastard!" Sphinx shakes his bald head sleepily. "Never in my life have I met anyone half as nasty as you. What is it now?"

"Have you by any chance thought to ask how she managed to evade all our traps? You know, the most important and fascinating thing?"

"I have," Sphinx grumbles and lowers his head back on the pillow. "But I'm not telling. Not until you mend your dirty ways."

"Sphinx, please! Pretty please! Or I won't be able to sleep . . . Tell me . . ." I keep jostling him gently in sync with my entreaties. "Sphinx, tell me . . ."

He sits up again.

"Damn it, Tabaqui! I would have told you everything when we came back, except you were asleep, and I respected that, by the way. And this is the gratitude I get . . ."

"I wasn't asleep!"

I indignantly crawl out.

"See that? I'm fully dressed. Wouldn't I be in pajamas if I were really asleep?"

"I see. So what I was supposed to do is dig up your nest and check if you're dressed or wearing pajamas?"

"Yes, you were! Especially considering that I wasn't asleep at all. I was thinking."

Blind sits up on his mattress on the floor.

"Just tell him, Sphinx. He's going to chew us all up by morning if you don't."

"She got it from Elephant," Sphinx says reluctantly. "That's all there is to it. And in return she allowed him to touch her hair."

I remember now. Every time Elephant saw Ginger he would try to reach for her hair, huffing, "Want! Want!" Something of an unusually vivid color in a place where other people don't have anything interesting—that's all he saw. And more than anything in the world Elephant liked to touch unusual things: soap bubbles, cats' tails, burning matches.

I sigh, disappointed. What a mundane explanation for the most intractable enigma of our childhood. It would have been better not to know.

"So that's it," I say. "Simple and boring."

"And for that you had to wake me up," Sphinx says vengefully.

"Yes. The suspense would've killed me. And now we can all sleep in peace."

Blind lights up, and Sphinx sidles up to him to mooch a couple of puffs. My burrow is in shambles. I have to construct a fresh one. I quietly hum a new song, stacking the pillows. Mysteries revealed, Jonathan unmasked! Now that I've had time to think, that's a great thing, and the rest is small details, not worth getting upset about.

> *Truth is the greatest friend. Now we can sleep in peace.*
> *Certainty came in the night. There was a knock at the door.*
> *The snowball crashed on the board! Then she entered the room!*
> *Bearing the torch of Knowledge. Here's how the story goes . . .*

"Do you like her?" Sphinx asks Blind, a shadow from where I'm sitting.

I cut the song short, afraid of missing the answer.

"No," Blind says after a pause. "Not really. She had this disgusting habit when she was little. She'd knock me over and run away laughing. It really ticked me off. Elk told me never to hit girls, or I'd have given her a thrashing."

"Yeah, that's right," Sphinx says thoughtfully. "She always tried to shove you. I couldn't really understand it. She wasn't usually that way."

I position myself by the entrance to the freshly constructed burrow, hugging Sphinx's pillow.

"Yep," I say. "In civilized societies little boys pull the hair of the little girls they like. And put dead mice in their pockets. To say nothing about tripping them. Which is how they express their love. We borrowed this kind of behavior from our prehistoric ancestors. Those were simpler times. You see a girl, you ogle at her, you whack her on the head with a woolly-mammoth bone—and that's your wedding, right there. Later generations were more interested in peeking under the long skirts of their girl companions, where they, being smart to those ways, wore lacy underpants. Besides, the sight of a crying girl all spattered with mud is so touching. They unleash a maelstrom of feelings in the heart of the suitor, those pretty tears."

"I doubt Blind looked particularly pretty when tripped up," Sphinx mutters. "To say nothing about tears and lacy underpants. You're over-philosophizing it, Jackal."

"I thought I specifically mentioned the civilized societies? Of course, here it's the other way around."

"Let's get some sleep," Blind says. "Or next thing we know, Black was crazy about me and that's why he was pummeling me all day long. To marvel at how beautiful I was when in tears."

"Why not?" Sphinx sneers. "A fascinating concept. Except it would mean that with me it was simply love at first sight. Black clearly liked my tears much more than yours. And I had such a lot of them to share with him."

"Guys, will you stop with the gossiping?" Humpback's voice drones from the upper bunk. "He's sleeping right here, you know, and you're babbling this god-awful nonsense about him."

"Play us something soft, Shaggy," Sphinx asks, looking up. "A nighttime serenade. Jackal chased away our dreams, and all that's left is gossip. Distract us."

"Yeah, go on. That way no one sleeps," Blind says.

Humpback stirs, then swings his legs down and begins playing. I jump into the burrow, intending to fall asleep to his flute, so I need to hurry before he stops. But I don't pull my head in yet because Sphinx and Blind are still up, which means they might still discuss something interesting. Except they don't. So there we are. They're silent, I'm silent. Humpback plays, warding off the gossip.

THE HOUSE

Grasshopper felt something as soon as he stepped inside the Tenth. A change not apparent to the eye. Ancient was hunched over the chess board cogitating, chin on knuckles.

Grasshopper crouched down on the floor.

Ancient never greeted him. He behaved as if Grasshopper didn't leave and come back, as if their meetings were not separated by hours and days. Grasshopper had gotten used to that and had even come to like it.

He looked at the amulet box. Empty. Ajar, it lay on the mattress next to the board. *There. That's what's changed. Why?*

Ancient traced Grasshopper's gaze and let the long fingers rummage inside the box. Then brought them closer to his eyes and shook off the dust.

"No more left. I've given it all away."

Grasshopper craned his neck and peeked in.

"Really, all of it?" he asked hesitantly.

"Yes."

Ancient clicked the top shut and put the empty box away.

"So there will be no more amulets?"

Dejectedly, Grasshopper waited for an explanation. A lock of hair fell over his eyes, but he was afraid to move to push it away.

"I'm leaving. Going home."

Here, in Ancient's room, these words sounded strange. Like he wasn't the one who actually said them. How could he have a home? Ancient was where he was. He had been born here, he grew up here, and he became ancient here. That was obvious to anyone looking at him and talking to him.

Grasshopper shuffled his shoe over the dark wine-stain spots.

"Why?"

Ancient moved one of the pieces and flicked another off with the fingernail.

"I am nineteen," he said. "It's well past time."

These words also shifted something. Just like his mention of a home. He couldn't be any age. He was outside of age, outside of time itself—until he broke the spell by saying the number. And it still didn't explain anything.

"Everyone else is staying until summer. Why aren't you?"

"It smells bad here," Ancient said. "It smells worse and worse. You know what I'm talking about. You should be able to sense it. It's already pretty bad, but it's going to get much worse at the end. I know. I've seen it before. I remember the last graduation, the one before ours. That's why I want to leave earlier."

"So you're running away? From your own people?"

"I am," Ancient agreed. "Legging it, you might say. Without the legs."

"You mean you're scared?" Grasshopper said doubtfully.

Ancient scratched his chin with the base of the queen.

"Yes," he said. "I am scared. There will come a time, much later, when you'll understand. Then you too are going to be scared. Graduation is a bad time. It's a step into the void. Not many can simply take it. It is the year of fear, of the crazies and the suicides, of insanity and nervous breakdowns. All of that disgusting stuff that spews out of those who are afraid. There's nothing worse than that. Better to leave before it starts. Which is what I'm doing. Because I happen to have that opportunity."

"So you're making the brave choice," Grasshopper said.

Now it was Ancient's turn to be surprised.

"I wouldn't say that. More the opposite."

Grasshopper wanted to ask about himself and his amulet, but didn't. Ancient was preparing for the step into the void, for the brave choice that looked like the cowardly one. This was the moment to be silent and not interfere. So Grasshopper was silent.

"I am taking those two gluttons with me," Ancient said, pointing in the direction of the fish tank. "Along with their room. They're not going to even notice. They won't know that they've been moved to the Outsides. Sometimes I wish I could trade places with them."

Grasshopper looked at the fish.

He's afraid . . .

He pitied Ancient, and he pitied himself. *What's going to become of this room?* The Den of the Purple Ratter. Without Ancient in it, it would lose its identity. No longer the Den, just dorm number ten.

"No, I haven't forgotten about you." Ancient placed the queen on the black square. "It's strange how often I've been thinking of you. Why is that, do you think?"

"Because of the amulet?"

"What's the amulet got to do with it? You don't need it. You don't need the tasks either. You're wide open. You just absorb it all."

"I do need it." Grasshopper swayed on his heels. "Very much. Ever since I got it, it's all been . . . right."

"I'm glad for it." Ancient shook a cigarette out of the pack. "That it came out better than all the others. And also for you."

Grasshopper suddenly grew agitated.

"What happened with the last graduation? What was it you saw back then that you don't want to see again?"

Ancient fiddled with the cigarette, not lighting it.

"What's the point in talking about it? You'll see it all come summer. With your own eyes."

"I need to know now. Tell me."

Ancient glanced at him from under the half-closed lids.

"The last time was like a sinking ship," he said. "This time is going to be worse. But don't be afraid. Watch and remember. Then you can avoid the mistakes made by others. We are all given two graduations for a reason. One is to watch, so that you can know. The other is your own."

"Why is it going to be worse?"

Ancient sighed.

"The House had one leader back then. Now there are two. It's the House divided. That's always bad. And in the year of graduation that's the worst thing. No more questions now. It might be that I'm simply wrong, talking nonsense. It's going to be either this way or that way or, more likely, something completely different will happen, something that neither I nor you nor anyone else can even imagine. Predictions are useless here."

"All right," Grasshopper said, nodding.

The look Ancient was giving him felt strange. A faraway look.

He's saying his good-byes, Grasshopper realized. *It's still a long way till summer, but he's saying good-bye now. There will be no more conversations like this one.*

Ancient sighed and turned to the board.

"Come closer. I am going to teach you this game."

His fingers rushed from square to square, setting the pieces.

"Your army shall be White. Mine is Black. These are pawns. They only move forward one square. Except their first move can be two squares at once."

Ancient looked at Grasshopper again.

"Don't think about bad things now," he said. "Empty your head of everything I've just said. Now look here . . ."

He climbed out of the attic through the window and looked around. Most of all it resembled a desert. This gray, bare, parched desert, with aerials in place of cacti. Flat, except for the solitary hill of the other attic, looking tiny from up here. And the sky, all around him. Grasshopper clung to the window, afraid to venture away. Wolf winked at him and climbed out to the roof. The iron plates rattled.

He sat down, dangling his feet, and called to Grasshopper, "Come on. Put your foot on the box here."

Grasshopper climbed up and cautiously lowered himself next to him. Once he got his breathing under control he could take in the view. They were at the very top of the House. Even higher than the roof. You could even see the Outsides from here, brightly striped, washed clean by the rains, ready for the summer. The dump surrounded by the fence, the round tops of the trees, the jagged remains of the crumbled walls—where, to their parents' utter horror, the Outsides children liked to play. He could see the bright splotches of their raincoats among the ruins even now. A boy on a bicycle rolled down the street. Grasshopper looked in the opposite direction. The street was wider on that side, and in the distance he could glimpse the same bus stop from where he'd walked with his mother on the day he first entered the House.

"If they find out I dragged you here, they're going to kill me," Wolf said. "But this is a really good place. Do you like it here?"

"I don't know," Grasshopper said honestly. "I have to think about it."

He looked down again.

"I guess it's a good thinking place. Except I'm not sure if the thinking here is of good or bad things."

"Tell me what you're thinking about, then," Wolf said. "I'll tell you if it's good or bad."

Grasshopper watched a bus as it disappeared from view. Then he looked back at Wolf.

"Promise you're not going to laugh. In the place where we used to live, I mean, Mom, Grandma, and I, there was this park near our house. On one side, and on the other side this huge store, and a little farther down, the playground. The store sold mirrors. And other things too. Our house was right in the middle of all this. On the same street as the park and the mirror store. You know what I mean?"

Wolf shook his head.

"No, not really."

"When I remember our house, I also remember all of that. The way it stood on the street, and what was around it. You see?"

"I guess so," Wolf said, rubbing his ear. "There is nothing like that here."

"Yeah, nothing. Worse than nothing. It's like all of this has been painted on," Grasshopper said, nodding at the streets. "A picture."

"And if you go out," Wolf said thoughtfully, looking down, "you'd punch a hole in it. Tear the paper and leave a hole. What's behind it?"

"I don't know," Grasshopper said. "That's exactly what I was thinking about."

"Nobody knows," Wolf said. "The only way to find out is to do it. I don't want to think about this."

"Then it's not a good thinking place. When you don't want to think about something, but it still thinks about itself. And how does it feel to you?"

"With me it's different," Wolf said, pulling his legs up and placing his elbows on his knees. "I like the roof. It's the House and at the same time it isn't. Like an island in the middle of the ocean. Or like a ship. Or the edge of the world. Like you could crash straight down into outer space from here—falling, falling, never reaching the bottom. I used to play here by myself. Imagining all that: the ocean, the sky . . ."

"And now?"

"And now I don't anymore. Haven't been here forever."

The rectangle of the roof glistened with glass shards. They gleamed and sparkled like diamonds. In the other corner they saw yellowed newspapers, empty bottles, and chair seats, all color leached out of them.

"Who's left all that here?" Grasshopper asked.

"Don't know. Seniors, I guess. I'm not the only one who knows about this place. People come here all the time. I like it more when it's windy and raining. It's completely different from how it is now. A ship in a storm. I can run around in the rain and I know for sure that no one would gawk at me from the windows. The important thing is to be careful not to slide to the sloping part."

Grasshopper imagined Wolf running around on the wet slippery roof and shuddered.

Wolf laughed.

"You just never tried. Look."

He stood up, swayed, righted himself, threw back his head, and shouted into the vast blueness of the sky, "Aaa! Ooo! Yoo-hoo!"

The sky swallowed his scream. Grasshopper watched, his eyes wide in astonishment.

"Come on. Don't be scared."

Wolf helped him get up, and then they were shouting together. Grasshopper's uncertain cry was gobbled up by the sky in a flash. He shouted louder, then louder still. Suddenly it came to him: How beautiful it was to be shouting at the sky. How there was nothing in the world more beautiful than that.

He screwed his eyes tightly shut and screamed until he was hoarse. He and Wolf flopped down on the warm metal and looked at each other with insane eyes. The wind breathed into their flushed faces. The black scissors of the swallows scythed overhead. It was so quiet that they felt a ringing in their ears.

It's as if I'm empty, Grasshopper thought. *Everything that was inside me flew away. This empty me is the only thing that's left. And it feels good.*

Wolf grabbed his sweater.

"Hey! Careful, or you'll fall down. You look like you're drunk."

"I feel fine," Grasshopper mumbled. "I feel good."

The wind mussed their hair. The aerial wires crisscrossed the sky. The sparrows, no more than fluffy balls when seen from here, used them as swings. Wolf's nose was on the verge of breaking out in freckles.

It's the scent of summer, Grasshopper realized suddenly.

The summer was coming for real.

The dorm was busy poring over the box of photographs.

"Look!" Humpback shouted as they entered. "Look at what Max-'n'-Rexes hauled in."

They moved in closer. The photographs were of the seniors. They hadn't been made in the House. Siamese pointed at one of the photos.

"Remember this gate? How it jumped off the hinges because Sausage was swinging on it?"

"And here's my head!" The other Siamese pointed at an indistinct blob in the corner. "You can see our window, right there!"

They crowded around, greedily searching for snippets of something familiar in the world populated by the seniors. And finding them. Behind the backs, over the shoulders, here and there, in bits and pieces. And then trying to connect those bits, weave them into a cloth.

Grasshopper went to sit on the bed. He didn't like such discussions. He'd skipped the first summer trip, and the time when he did go, they got sent to a fancy spa where the staff was so intent on providing a quality experience that there was no possibility of any unregimented fun. It was very nice, but you can't enjoy the swimming pools and the gyms and even real horseback riding when there's a whole army of insistent helpers always tagging along. Everyone, or at least everyone whom Grasshopper heard rehashing it over and over again, agreed that in the entire history of the House they never had a summer break as lousy as that one. Actually, if not for them, Grasshopper might even have imagined that he'd had a great time. But the House people were, if anything, traditionalists. There were only two places that were acceptable to them outside the boundaries of the House: a disused ski area somewhere in the mountains, and the old resort on the shore. Nothing else even came close. The distinction "House" was extended to those places as well, they were its annexes, its feelers stretched an unfathomable distance. Grasshopper knew both of these Houses as if he himself had visited them many times. He even had a preference for the one by the sea. The oldest one. Creaking and wheezing, with its sagging beds and warped wardrobes, its water-stained walls and ceilings, its flapping floorboards, with one shower stall for each four dorms and constant queues to use the toilets.

"The ceiling dripped in our room!"

"Elephant sat on a chair and broke it, remember?"

"Sport banged on the wall to shut up the guys in the next room and punched a hole clean through."

"Remember the centipedes in the bathroom?"

"Centipedes? How about silverfish and water beetles?"

The boys tossed the phrases like footballs, reveling in the flaws of the Other House, and Grasshopper was listening to them jealously. The Other House, the little brother of This House. There might even be some secret connection between them. Maybe they exchanged things. Rats, or ghosts, or something else interesting. You could see the ocean from the windows of the Other House. And at night you could hear it. There the counselors immediately fell in love with the tanned girls on the beach and forgot about their responsibilities, and when it rained the building leaked, so they all locked themselves in, like a tortoise retreating into its shell, cursed the weather, and played cards through the night—juniors, seniors, counselors, all. They played and listened to the jingle of the drops hitting the pans placed under the holes in the roof.

"Did you steal them from the seniors?" Grasshopper asked.

Siamese blinked at him.

"So? They've got loads of them, and we didn't have any. At least now there's this."

"I didn't mean that. I just asked. Where's Stinker?"

"Got called to the principal," Magician said. "Didn't you notice how quiet it was?"

Stinker wheeled in, flashing the badges that covered him from the neck all the way down to his knees.

"Hear that?" he squeaked, gasping. "There are fourteen packages in the principal's office, and loads of letters! But to hell with the letters. The important thing here is the packages. All of them mine!"

"Would those be the responses to your letters?" Humpback ventured.

"None other!" Stinker made a circle around the room, spokes glistening. "I ask you, have you ever heard anything this outrageous? They're not letting me have them. Asking who sent them and why. How's that their business? They were sent to me, which means they're mine. So it follows they must hand them over."

"So you turned around and left, just like that?" Wolf said.

"As if! I made a scene. Now I need some time to recuperate, and then I'll go back and make another one. Except I need a poster. Mind drawing it for me?"

Grasshopper laughed.

"Nothing funny about it," Stinker said indignantly. "This pile of useful stuff is rotting away in the principal's office. Not funny at all! Come on, quick . . . Get to the drawing! And writing!"

He wheeled over to the nightstand and rustled some papers.

"Don't we have a large poster board? I don't get it. It's like the most useful thing to have around."

"We could use a bedsheet," Magician piped in with enthusiasm. "We can cut it in half . . . We'll need a couple of sticks for the handles."

"One handle is enough," Stinker said sharply. "I'm going to need my other hand to blow the trumpet."

They sat on the floor in front of the remains of the sheet and nibbled on the brushes thoughtfully.

"Something along the lines of *Don't Tread on Me*," Stinker insisted. "Or *Hands Off* . . . something or other."

"Or maybe *Packages for the Owner*?" Humpback suggested.

"We could do that too," Stinker agreed reluctantly. "Even though it sounds trite."

Beauty fondled the paint cans. Elephant drew a sun on the floor. Wolf got to writing *Packages* in blue paint.

"Careful. Keep it on the line," Stinker fretted. "Make the letters bigger."

"We could just pick the lock," Siamese Rex said, "and carry everything away. At night. Then we wouldn't need to write anything."

"No way! Stealing something that's rightfully mine? No, they must hand it over themselves," Stinker said, smoothing out the sheet. "They're bound to regret their decision. They're going to beg me: 'Come, oh, come and take them!'"

"Fourteen packages," Magician sighed reverently.

"See what I mean? Totally worth the effort."

Once the slogan *Packages for the Owner* was ready, Magician demanded they make another copy, for him. Wolf said that two identical banners was boring, and in the time it took the "Packages" one to dry they wrote *Down with Dictatorship* on the other half of the sheet, and also *Hands Off Student Property* on a poster board. Then they glued handles to the sheets.

"Faster! Faster!" Magician urged.

"Can we come too?" one of the Siamese asked.

"Later," Stinker said sternly. "You're the second line. For when we get exhausted. Then it will be your turn to shout 'Shame!' and rattle something."

Beauty suddenly grew agitated, stuttering excitedly, "Four apples! Four! That's a lot!"

"Beauty will provide juice," Wolf translated. "And Siamese will bring it over. To revive your stamina. The juice of four apples."

Beauty beamed. Stinker patted his arm.

"Thank you. Your valuable contribution to the just cause shall not be forgotten. I'll give you a lemon to make the contribution even more valuable."

Magician, Stinker, and Humpback took the slogans and left. Siamese went looking for something they could rattle. Beauty bustled around the juice maker. Elephant brought him one more apple. Wolf lay on the floor and closed his eyes.

Grasshopper sat on his bed. He was dying to find out what Stinker was going to do, but was self-conscious about it. It was going to be something noisy and shameful, and the entire House was going to come gawk at it. Siamese dug out the salad bowl, the bear trap, and the ladle, and then set to picking up the scraps of paper off the floor and closing the paint cans, gingerly stepping around Wolf.

"Fourteen packages," they whispered to each other, licking their lips.

Beauty reverently operated the juice maker. Elephant held the pan under the spout, watching it fill up with the transparent yellowish juice.

Then they too headed off. Elephant carried the bottle of juice. Beauty carried nothing. Siamese carried the things they were going to rattle. Beauty fretted. He could only manage to make it through the door on the third try, and for that Siamese had to wedge him between themselves and march him out like a prisoner between two guards.

Wolf lay on the floor. Blind lay on his bed.

Blind can hear everything anyway, Grasshopper thought. *He doesn't need to go. He's both here and there at the same time.*

Grasshopper slid down from the bed and sat on the floor.

"Ancient's leaving," he said. "Forever. He's not going to be in the House anymore. He's afraid of something. Something that's going to happen in the summer before the seniors have to leave."

Wolf opened his eyes.

"How do you know? You mean you talked to him?"

Grasshopper nodded.

"He remembers the last graduation. He says there's nothing worse than the last year."

"That's true," Wolf said, propping himself up. "I'm only curious why he would talk to you about things like that. Or did you . . . overhear what he was saying?"

"No. He told me himself. Only me, no one else."

Wolf lay back down.

"Curiouser and curiouser," he muttered.

Blind stirred on his bed. When he rose, he had a dusty plastic bag in his hands. He traipsed over to Grasshopper, dropped the bag in his lap, and went back. Grasshopper stared at Blind's present in surprise.

Wolf turned over, grabbed the bag, and peeked inside.

"I think this is what you wanted," he said and shook out some cassette tapes on the floor. Old and battered, some without the inserts, flashing the scratched labels.

"That's your Zeppelins," Blind grumbled. "The ones making you go crazy in the head. He told me that these are it exactly. The one who gave them to me."

"Thanks," Grasshopper whispered. "Thanks, Blind. Where did you get them?"

"It was a gift," Blind replied curtly. "From someone who couldn't say no."

It was obvious that this wasn't Elk he was talking about.

"Doesn't matter. Just enjoy."

"One more blackmailer," Wolf remarked thoughtfully. "Rather a lot of you guys for one dorm."

It was Skull who gave it to him, Grasshopper thought. *Blind is carrying his letters. So Skull is the one who couldn't say no.*

Blind lay there with his hands hidden under his armpits. His black hair shined, obscuring his face.

"Who was it that couldn't refuse you, I wonder," Wolf said probingly.

Blind didn't answer.

Wolf turned to Grasshopper.

"He never answers. Almost never. Then he says something and goes silent again. Just once I'd like to hear the rest of the story, find out if it actually happened."

Grasshopper shook his head.

"What is it you'd like to hear?"

"A complete sentence. So I could understand what he was saying. I don't mean now in particular. I mean usually."

Grasshopper looked at Blind.

"I can always understand what he's saying. Even when he's not saying anything at all."

Wolf's orange eyes glanced in the direction of Blind.

"You, maybe. But I don't."

"Well, I don't understand anything when you're silent," Grasshopper admitted. "And sometimes even when you're speaking."

"How about enough?" Blind said. "Another round of this, and you'd both stop understanding anything."

"What do you hear?" Grasshopper asked.

"Stuffagers are all there, and a lot of seniors. It's Siamese's turn now. They're howling and banging."

Grasshopper gingerly picked up the tapes and put them back in the bag. There were five, and only two had cases.

"But how am I supposed to listen to them?" he said sadly. "We don't have anything for that."

"There are fourteen packages being rescued as we speak," Wolf reminded him. "If I know anything about Stinker, at least one of them is going to contain something that would play your Zeppelins."

Grasshopper was suddenly restless.

"Should I maybe go and shout too?"

"There's enough shouting as it is," Blind said. "I'm surprised the principal is still holding."

"We'll go in half an hour," Wolf said. "Fresh reinforcements. It would be more useful that way."

Grasshopper peeked into the bag to count the tapes again. There were still five of them. No more, no less.

"Was there anything else Ancient told you?" Wolf said smoothly.

Grasshopper looked at him in surprise.

"That he was leaving. That it smells bad here. And it's going to get worse. I mean, not in those exact words. About the seniors, in short."

"Our dear morons," Wolf said. "I see."

Grasshopper frowned.

"Why are you calling them that?"

"Because it's the truth."

"Is Skull a moron too?" Grasshopper said indignantly.

"He more than others."

"Then give me the rest of the sentence. Like you demanded from Blind. So that even I understand. Why are they morons? And then about Skull. Separately."

"No problem," Wolf said, looking at Blind. "There's one House. It needs to have one master. One leader for all."

That's what Ancient said, Grasshopper thought. *Or something like that.*

"But that's why the two of them fight. They want to be the one you're talking about," he said.

"They've been fighting for a long time. Too long. Might as well quit. It's ridiculous," Wolf said, shaking his head. "If in all that time they didn't manage to prove they could rise above everyone else's wants and not-wants, then neither of them is worth anything."

"Skull could rise!"

Wolf smiled. He was still looking at Blind. Blind wasn't stirring. He could be listening to Wolf, or to Stinker, far away.

"Strange thoughts you have," Grasshopper said.

"They're not strange. They're obvious," Wolf said. "Child's play. You need to build up on them. Like floors in a building—one, two, three, ten . . . Then they might start looking wise and deep. But until that time, seniors are seniors. And all we can do is bask in their smoke and die from envy listening to their records. Like this one guy I know."

"I wasn't dying from envy," Grasshopper protested.

"I was," Wolf admitted.

"Still," Grasshopper said stubbornly, "Skull is not a moron. And Ancient isn't. You're just jealous."

"Can't you hear it?" Blind said suddenly.

This time they did—the faraway voices and shouts. Grasshopper took another peek in the bag with the tapes and then looked at Wolf.

"All right, let's go," Wolf said, getting up. "Go and support Stinker's possessive urges. Something tells me he's going to get rechristened after today's show."

"Into Crocodile?" Grasshopper said.

"Nah. Won't work. Crocodiles gobble up something and then lie there sleeping, like statues. He's much too noisy for that. And I don't think he ever sleeps. Or has enough to eat."

Grasshopper stuffed the tapes into the nightstand so they'd be safe from Siamese.

Blind didn't get up.

"Good luck," he said lazily.

"Do you think we'll have to shout?" Grasshopper said.

"We'll see. We'll play it by ear. Maybe we won't have to."

Wolf let him go out first.

The hallway was almost empty, but there was a throng of people at the other end, by the doors of the staff room. The garish shirts and jackets on the seniors' backs shielded the proceedings from them better than any fence. They couldn't see Stinker and the cohorts, but they could hear them fine. The clanking of metal on metal and the screams "Down with tyranny!" echoed through the building.

The closer Wolf and Grasshopper got, the louder it became. The seniors weren't standing in one place. Some of them moved away, laughing, and their spots were immediately taken by others who had just arrived. When Ulysses the wheeler peeled off with a disgusted grimace on his face, Wolf and Grasshopper quickly squeezed in. Now they could finally see.

The posters swayed uncertainly in the feeble hands of Poxy Sissies. Magician, jaw firmly set and eyes bulging, held his above everybody else's. Stinker, gone livid with the effort and bedecked in badges, brandished *Packages for the Owner*. The half sheet was draped around the handle limply, the writing wasn't legible, so he simply waved it like a flag. Poker-faced Siamese furiously rattled the salad bowl and the bear trap. Elephant looked on, elated.

"Down with tyranny! Down with counselors' despotism! Down . . ." Stinker droned.

"Down with it!" the choir picked up on the exhale.

Elephant whined softly in agreement. Beauty hid himself among the wheelers, keeping his head low so as not to stand out.

Stuffagers, all present, formed a semicircle and swayed to the beat.

The seniors just laughed. Grasshopper thought that there was significantly more shouting than would be expected, and then realized that, to his surprise, Stuffagers were screaming as well.

"Down with teachers!" Crybaby squealed. Whiner incongruously proclaimed, "World peace!" Crook, waving his crutch, demanded, "Living space for the cripples!"

But Stinker's voice sailed clear above the din. His screams joined with the crashing of the salad bowl and the tooting of the tin trumpet to create one hellish, unbearable cacophony.

Seniors, still laughing, inserted fingers in their ears.

"Could it be that the principal has already jumped out the window?" Wolf shouted to Grasshopper.

Principal hadn't jumped anywhere. Safe and sound, albeit distinctly greenish in color, he opened the doors of the staff room and waved his hands, trying to shout over the commotion. Short, with a pugnacious gray beard, he resembled a retired pirate, except he didn't smoke a pipe, wasn't covered in tattoos, and generally was closer in appearance to a gnome—if not for the shaggy head of an old sailor.

"Attention, squirts!" Boar the senior shouted, raising two fingers in the air.

The seniors guffawed. Stinker, red faced and majestic, waved his little paw, commanding the others to pause. Siamese ceased their racket. Principal's voice finally broke through the general hubbub.

"At once . . . Outrageous . . . Ankle biters . . ."

"Quiet!" Stinker ordered.

The principal produced a handkerchief and wiped his face.

"If I may be allowed to speak," he said and had to wait out an explosion of laughter. "I hoped to prevail upon this young gentleman to consider sharing his bounty with others. But I'm afraid that the way this is going I won't live to see the day. We'll continue the investigation into where these packages came from and why. In the meantime he can take them away. The sooner the better!"

Siamese whistled. Humpback applauded. Splint the counselor appeared behind the crestfallen principal's back, pushing a cart. Black Ralph, hands in pockets, marched alongside him, while Elk was bringing up the rear carrying a box full of letters. The cart was piled with packages. A mound of boxes in bright wrappers.

"What's that?" the seniors inquired.

"Packages for the owner," Stinker said and nodded to Humpback and Magician. "Prepare to accept the goods."

The cart was transferred from Splint to Humpback. Magician, in one practiced theatrical sweep, covered it with the *Hands Off* sheet, hiding the contents from the prying eyes. Sissies trooped in the direction of the Poxy room, pushing the cart in front of them. The Stuffage boys made way, flabbergasted. As the procession filed past the rows of seniors, they looked at Stinker approvingly and sneaked peeks under the cover.

"That's one wicked squirt," Lame said with a tinge of respect in his voice. "He's going to crawl far."

Stinker nodded left and right, graciously bestowing his toothy smile on the assembled admirers.

"Wait," he said suddenly, stopping the escort. "Just one moment."

He wheeled over to the cart, rummaged under the sheet, extracted the smallest package, in bubble wrap with stars plastered all over it, and tossed it to Whiner.

"There. This is yours, guys. Thanks for the support."

The seniors applauded. Whiner ogled the package in disbelief.

"Drop that thing right now," Sportsman hissed, shouldering his way through. "Wheelers' handouts! Drop it, I said!"

"No, I won't," Whiner said, clutching the package tightly. "Why should I? Get your own things and drop them if you want."

Sportsman slapped Whiner across the face. Wheelers rumbled indignantly.

As he was catching up with Sissies and the cart, Grasshopper looked over his shoulder. The principal was still standing at the entrance to the staff room. The counselors on both sides of him patted him on the shoulders soothingly. Principal's vacant stare was fixed directly in front of him.

Could he really have gone crazy? Grasshopper thought. *I mean, it's possible . . .*

"I want that cart back!" Splint the counselor shouted after them, his glasses glinting. "Miscreants!"

A COMPLETELY DIFFERENT CORRIDOR

Every time she returned to their place, she wondered at the difference between the two corridors and never could understand what the secret was. It wasn't that theirs was narrower and shorter. It wasn't the windows (that one didn't have them), and not the area rugs either . . . But tonight she finally got it: their corridor wasn't a corridor.

The old principal . . . The former principal (that white beard; she couldn't recall the face anymore) favored girls, and it was reflected in the disparity between the corridors. The white beard had been long gone, but the favorable treatment persisted. Only four per dorm; yes, they were tiny, more cells than rooms, but still only four, and you could always close the door. And those area rugs, balding and fraying, and the cords on the curtains, and the television sets. White beard put them up in every dorm, but he'd been long gone, and the televisions broke down gradually until there were only two left. One of those two was glowing now by the wall, and in front of it, on mattresses and blankets dragged out of the dorms, an enraptured *(whatever could they be expecting to learn?)* selection of females from various rooms positioned themselves. Stumbling in the dark between their arms and legs, stepping on the pillows and mounds of apple peels, she finally figured out the difference. Their corridor was not a place separate from the dorms, it was their continuation, one common dorm, a place where after dark anyone could crash down and sleep.

The ghostly glow flitted across the faces. She extricated herself from the tangle of prone bodies, opened the door (in daylight you could distinguish a smeared silhouette of a cat on it), and entered the room. Greenish dusk, four mattresses on the floor, and the glinting eyes of the one dubbed Catwoman. She switched on the light and tossed the backpack on the floor.

"I'm back. Sure is quiet here."

"Everyone's out," a soft voice answered. "Didn't you see them *there*?"

A slight stress on *there*, just enough for a sensitive ear.

"No, they've all filtered back to the rooms," she said reluctantly. "Haven't seen anyone. Why are the lights out? Your eyes hurt?"

"*Mine* don't."

Stressed again. Barely noticeable. Eliciting the question: Whose do? And if asked, the answer to it would be forthcoming. Catwoman had only two ways of influencing those around her: her voice and her eyes. She used both of them to the fullest. And that wasn't counting the cats. *Those eyes, on top of the pile of clothes and the three fur coats, are best avoided.* She turned out the contents of her pockets onto the mattress. The gifts from "there," from "them" and "those." Pitiful stuff they might be, but they were still destined for eternal repose in the drawers, wrapped in cloth or shiny gray paper, because gifts were never thrown out or given away.

The bottomless holes of the night in the windows. Catwoman shrugged the jacket onto the mattress, shedding the three identical smoky-gray cats with it and exposing sharp, bony shoulders. The long razor face, the swaying needles of the colorless hair. The cats tried to climb back, she chased them off, then whistled to one of them, sending it on an errand. The cat trotted to the window and pulled on the cord, flooding the black holes of the window with white. It then returned to the mattress, shaking its paw in disgust.

"If only they would make coffee," repeated those who were never tired of the show.

"If only they would," Ginger whispered.

She couldn't tell the cats apart, no one could except for their owner. She crouched down next to the gifts and turned them over distractedly.

"So whose eyes do hurt?"

Catwoman draped herself in the jacket and the cats again.

"Rat's," she said. "She returned."

Ginger craned her neck warily.

"Where from this time?"

"How would I know? Bottom of the river, she says. Where sand people live among the seaweed. I would've thought one Mermaid was enough."

"True."

Ginger picked up a hair. Mermaid's, unendingly long. Trying to lift it off, she stretched her arm all the way up, but the end still remained on the floor, lustrous and invisible, coiling and snaking under the mattress. The cats observed her eagerly from their perch. Their eyes and their master's. Ginger rose.

"I'll go look for her. I'd like to hear about the river."

A switch for the corridor lights at every door. Another privilege. As the light flooded in, the indignant cries flared up and subsided into irritated murmuring. She scanned the scene and found what she was looking for. There, by the wall, hunched behind the backs of the TV watchers. The lone figure in the leather jacket. The lights went back off. Ginger threaded her way between the bodies and the transient wafts of perfume, bent down, and shook Rat by the shoulder.

"Hey, Rat! Hey! Get up!"

"Why would you wake her? Don't do that," came the plaintive voices. "Let her sleep. Let her dream."

Ginger jostled harder.

The eyes flamed in the dark, burning her.

"Why are you disturbing my dreams? Tearing at my clothes? Why?"

Thin as a rail (to recognize a girl in her took a special effort), eyes like two black puddles, hair dyed black and plastered down with spray, a much-too-short black leather jacket, pale lips. Rat, not one of, but Rat the Flyer, the traveler into the Outsides, the owner of (guess under which of her nails) the half-moon razor, picked herself up off the floor and took a muddled look at the screen.

"Oh god," she said. "Fount of knowledge."

The bodies in front of the TV shifted uneasily. The floorboards squeaked.

"Let's go."

Ginger pulled Rat's sleeve. Rat followed docilely, crushing the stray body parts underfoot. But not a shout, not even a peep out of anyone, because you never knew: one, whether she's in her right mind, and two, under which of her nails.

"We thought you'd be missing your toes. And your nose. That they'd freeze and fall off."

"You mean like the tail back then?"

Rat crashed down on the mattress under the gym ladder, each bar with a gaggle of bells on a string. They sang in unison, just the way they were going to sing now every night when she stirred in her sleep.

The cats pawed, hearing the familiar song that became unfamiliar.

"You were away for a whole month, and it's been snowing."

"Has it?" Rat said, rummaging in her pockets. "I've brought you a present from out there. Wait . . . it's here somewhere. There."

Ginger crouched next to the open palm, in which sat a ring.

"Take it. The stone is amethyst. You can get it out and put it somewhere else."

"Who did you take this off?"

"A corpse." Rat giggled. "Take it. For luck."

She turned to listen to the screams of the TV. Catwoman was sitting with her eyes closed. Four-line snippets of lyrics mingled with paint flows on the walls.

Mermaid (where does her hair end?) came in playing the guitar, holding it like a ukulele, and stared at them expectantly. A gentle soul, conversing only in whispers (and definitely nothing under the nails).

"Gingie. Tell me," she said. "How was it there tonight?"

Ginger wasn't in the mood for talking about "them" and "there," but she knew there was no avoiding it. All three were waiting for the story. Waiting quietly and patiently, not even acknowledging her feeble "Same as yesterday." Even she who'd just returned, not knowing anything and not understanding what "there" meant, even she waited too. Ginger sat down, hugging her knees.

"Why don't you go and see for yourself. Quit bugging me."

They were just staring, motionless. Outside the door, the TV shrieked excitedly. Ten eyes, if you counted the cats.

"It's completely different *there*," she began with a sigh.

The gifts lay on the mattress, looking pathetic to anyone who would like to laugh at them.

WALKING WITH THE BIRD

Step, step . . . There goes Bird, the one feeding on carrion. He comes and he goes, and *clomp-clomp* goes his poor crippled paw. Way, give way! There's never ever a day that we're not here at this hour. But it's useless to expect the populace to expect us. They still impede, they still interfere, running by, jostling and bumping. Not me, of course, but the shadow of my brother, which is almost as annoying. I'm strolling, divining the times to come. It's only going to get worse. The new Law will take care of that. It will take care of many other things besides the aforementioned, but that's not my concern, now is it? Or is it? Concern, that's what we Leaders are made of. We're supposed to nip the unnippable in the bud, or at least fret dutifully concerning the inability to thus nip. There's exactly zero sense in that. And a lot of headache into the bargain.

Animals and birds hobble here and there, the inhabitants of the zoo and their keepers. Some greet me, some maintain silence. Snow sparkling on the ledge of the Crossroads window. I'm overwhelmed by the desire to Jump, to roam in the fields of the Underside of the House. But I can't. For "by succumbing to your desires you lose the self and turn into their slave." This maxim is all that remains in my mind of the old Jumpers' Code, destroyed during the Troubles. Sightless One can probably quote it chapter and verse, but for me that one snippet is plenty.

I walk up the pain in my knee and return to the Nesting. My dear jungle. The pillars thereof of ivy, the bottom thereof of ferns. Bitter green flesh all the way around. What's that smell? Someone's indiscretion. Nothing to do with me. Everyone here lives on carrion, not just me. I hop on the roost to give myself a boost. That's the only way to see anything in here, from up high. The inhabitants mostly cling to the ground, and there're nooks galore. And we're the ones called Birds, go figure. Whatever, it wasn't us who dubbed us that. I take the red ribbon out of the plastic bag and tie it to the top rung. That's a sign. Of the upcoming verbal incontinence of old Daddy Vulture. The awful racket dies down, the populace crawls closer and waits. All kinds of deformities, both external and internal, all of them staring at my beak. That's the way they've been born, so what can you do? I drop a carton of cigarettes down, as a token of benevolence. It is caught jubilantly. I can toss them goodies all day long, and it'll never be enough.

"Listen, children," I begin.

They do. They're good at it. All of them. Scary, that.

"Here's the deal," I say unto them, "concerning the girls. I seem to notice that you never invite anyone. That's not good. Making friends and inviting them—that's good. Look at Beauty, he's got a girlfriend, but he doesn't invite her. That's the latest fashion here in the House, wouldn't do for us to fall behind. Saunter forth. Give the Nest a bit of spit and polish, tidy up, throw away the rubbish. Clean and sparkling, and the only smell should be of Elephant's violets."

They get it. Nodding. Elephant more eagerly than others. He heard his pretty flowers mentioned, so he's happy, poor soul. Butterfly flips his paw over Angel's shoulder. Angel wrinkles his nose. Hilarious. What do those two need with girls?

Dearest giggles.

"I just lo-o-ove girls," he proclaims in falsetto. "Such darlings! Could it be they would bring us something? Them being so kind and all."

Sure, why not. They very well might. Lipstick, for example. I wouldn't bet on kindness, though.

"Don't even think about wheedling gifts from them," I say.

Dearest rolls his eyes dolefully and preens his feathers.

"Wheedling? Eww-w! I'm not that way!"

"What the hell?" Lizard says. "Girls mean trouble. They go here, they go there, and then there's gossip all over the House. Some darlings! They can take their gifts and shove 'em."

"Don't do anything worth gossiping about, then," I say.

Beauty glows. Tries to dim the light show with the eyelashes, but it still shines through. One handsome guy. The only one here. He's not going to invite Doll, of course. He's got enough sense for that.

Lizard slaps him on the back and brays, "Our Ro-o-meo!"

Beauty goes livid, hisses and spits. The image is ruined for the next half hour.

"Shut up!" I shout from my aerie.

They do.

Every possible variety of senility, all in one Nest. You could come in with the medical reference and check off the symptoms one by one. I've got crazies to suit any taste.

Horse's snoring. I toss a matchbook at him. He perks up and tries to look like he was alert all that time. Who's he kidding?

"Hooray for Vulture!" Bubble suggests out of the blue.

I have to wait out the assortment of odd-sized hoorays.

"Was that clear to everyone?" I inquire.

They nod. They scratch. With grating and huffing noises. As I look over them, a thought occurs: a girl's got to have no brains at all to accept the invitation. Horse's glum mug. Bubble's multicolored one. Butterfly's, rotting from both top and bottom. Lizard's, bumpy. Beauty alone is a sight for sore eyes, him and Elephant. And they are all uniformly green. That's from bad lighting. I look at the lightbulb. Something's buzzing around it. Something that has not yet croaked in this cold. I take a swipe at it and miss.

Lizard doubles down coughing. Choked on smoke. Eight flippers pound him on the back. A Boschian masterpiece. In the dark.

"Lord, thy will be done," I say to the bulb.

Uproarious fun. It's a chronic condition with the pack. Whenever I am serious they imagine that I'm joking. I untie the red ribbon, fold it, and stuff it back into the bag. The buzzer goes off. They startle. It's time for Angel's drops.

"Still. Why do we need this?" Lizard drones. "Girls! We were doing fine without them. We should keep it that way. Now what? With half a year left . . . Blind took a roll with Long, and hey, there's the new Law? Now we can't even walk the hallways in peace."

Angel opens his mouth and waits. For his portion of dew.

"Blind is off limits. Hallways are not. Girls are for chatting up, and inviting whenever feasible. That is all. Understood?"

Angel is waiting. Elephant bashfully giggles and covers his mouth. Beauty nods. Bubble grins.

"That's nice. Go with my blessings, children."

I slide down from the roost and hobble away. Away from the Nest. Away from everyone. Elephant catches up with me and presents me with Louis in the pot. To buck me up and for general cheer.

So we are three walking now. Me, Louis in the crook of my elbow, and the stooping figure in Levi's and black sweater. He treads limping on his left foot just as I am listing to the right. The soundless ghost of Shadow, brother of mine. This place belongs to him as much as it does to me. In fact, he's even more of the House than I am, since he could never leave it. I can see him whenever and wherever I wish, he's always around, but always occupied with some kind of posthumous business, always on the run. He never even looks in my direction. Could be that he's upset with me. We only ever talk in my dreams, and in the morning I have to struggle to remember them. Max is the reason people seldom come closer to me than three paces when I'm not walking. Many of them feel his presence.

There's Black. Walking slowly toward me.

He nods at me, I nod at him. We don't like each other very much, but *noblesse oblige*. What it demands is that we greet each other and chat whenever we meet. What about? I don't know. The weather? Each other's health? Shadow makes a sour face. We move on. I start whistling softly. The daylight hours belong to the girls now. They're also out strolling. Along with their hangers-on and gawkers-at. Flea-ridden Hounds in collars. Birds, bare-necked and in pajamas. Logs, ever fashionable, swarming. What do you call a Log's girlfriend? Logess or Logmaid? Logette, maybe? They rustle and whisper, they laugh, throwing sharp stares from under the fringes. Their presence turns the corridors into something that I don't know how to describe. The floorboards keep whimpering as balding Vulture treads them.

Plump Splutter sees Vulture, yanks off his beret, and assumes the Hound pose of respect. Head down, tail sweeping the floor. I go around him, Shadow plows through, and it's not entirely clear what causes Splutter to shudder, his respect for me or the unpleasant feeling one gets when Shadow walks through him. I would have liked to bring clarity to this question, but my feet carry me on. I have lots of questions that will forever remain unanswered. We knew not what we were doing when we christened Shadow as Shadow. Wasn't that inviting the fate that did befall him: to wander eternally, to cleave and be one flesh, to be always silent? Most of the other ghosts I know are quite chatty. He's the only one to keep total silence.

The Crossroads sofa features beastly Gaby. Legs open wide, the skirt barely there at all. The connoisseurs of private parts huddle around, peeking in eagerly. Gaby's having fun, swatting at them with her purse and squeaking coyly, but doing nothing to limit the view. When they see Great Bird it's all silence and jerky jumps away. I part that silence and take it with me, the silence, the flushed cheeks, and the sickening feeling of being somehow involved. A stern grandfather happening on a granddaughter in a compromising position. Disgusting. And funny at the same time.

A familiar tune assembles thread by thread out of thin air and pulls me in. I slow down. The Coffeepot's entrance. Guitar gently weeping. Rats swaying their motley heads blissfully, pressing into the tiled walls. All the slender-legged stools are packed, but mine's free as always, projecting emptiness two seats deep. Only Shuffle, the troubadour of our youth, is pressing right against it, his nose buried in the strings.

I come in and sit down. Shadow takes the seat to the left of me. Louis goes on the right. An empty cup. I look in and it fills up. I nod, I drink, I take out the key ring and count the keys. Eighteen, just as expected. The same result time after time after time. Someone with gills and one nostril floats closer. Wheezing. Puts out a claw. A silver earring. Nice, but there's no place to put it. It would ruin the general concept. The gills droop sadly. More wheezing. A tiny key, about the size of my pinky nail, is tendered. Silver as well. I try it on. Now this I have to get.

"How much?"

The claw extends four fingers. That's as many as it has. I draw the wallet out from the secret pocket. I pay up. I have this soft spot for keys. Especially when they're useless. Doggy breath behind my back. That would be Shuffle.

"I hope the music isn't bothering you?"

"Not at all, old man. Quite the opposite. Pity you're not singing. How about it?"

He smiles, a mute question in his eyes. "You, of all people, should know I don't have the voice for it."

I know. He only sings when he's drunk now. Not having the voice doesn't stop him when he's not sober. He launches into "Immigrant Song." By itself, without the singing, it's harshing me, but I can handle it. By the time he gets to the end, the Coffeepot is packed. Rats' skulls mostly, making my eyes see spots, but then Rodents are huge fans of the Big Song, wouldn't do to throw them out of the dear old feeding trough. I put on dark shades instead. All there's to it. One hundred percent improvement. The skulls acquire a gray uniformity, the nerves settle down. We can listen in peace again.

At the first strains of the Lady and her "Stepladder to the Skies," Sphinx wanders in. Three perches empty in short order. He mounts one of them and goggles with his black beetles set deep into the virginally clean skull. An amazing specimen. I pull off my shades because he needs to be appreciated in color, and we continue listening. Sphinx begins to pipe in softly. Rats sway. Shuffle's guitar picks up steam and breaks into arpeggios. Sphinx picks up steam and breaks into scream-whispers. I pick up steam too and start keeping time with my foot.

Someone jumps up and closes the door, just in time to prevent the invasion of more riffraff. This charming evening is going to end in a scuffle, because that's the way it is with Rats, but we're not there yet. We're good. Especially me. Shuffle scratches his nose, Sphinx grins. Music is a perfect way of erasing thoughts, bad and otherwise. The best and the oldest.

We're chilling for about half an hour, and then a depressed junior Rat suddenly bursts into tears and digs out a razor. They can't help themselves. That's about the only redeeming quality in a Rat, his constant readiness to off himself, anytime, anyplace. Himself or those around him. That old fart Don Juan Matus would be happy. But not many others would. I, for one, detest these things.

The Ratling is sawing at his wrist, drowning in snot. Shuffle, entranced by the performance, stares and bungles the melody. End of the fun. Rats file out reluctantly, hauling off the youngling to be patched up. Nice-looking scarlet puddles on the floor. Sphinx sighs. I put on my Number 5 shades, in the cheery orange-yellow range. They're a big help when talking to the Poxy brethren.

Sphinx notices the freshly acquired nail-sized key and approves. It's the little things that matter. We drink our coffee and shoot the breeze. First about Breughel. Then about Leopard. Neutral, inoffensive talk. Also a kind of escape. We're swimming in cigarette smoke, coffee stains are barely visible through the white clouds, and here are the Birdies peeking in timidly, looking for their Leader. I snap at them without turning around, and they're not there anymore, and never were.

"Obedience to the point of reflex," Sphinx says. "What are they so afraid of, Yelloweyes?"

"My hulking bulk."

I choke, cough, and it turns out that Birds didn't vanish completely. Two appear out of nowhere to pat me on the back. Shadow's ghost laughs on the stool next to me, also coughing. No one's patting him.

The conversation drifts peacefully toward Santana. I'm ready to melt and dissolve in the nearest coffee puddle. It's so pleasant that it gives me the creeps. For an inhabitant of the Nest, a conversation with someone who knows how to talk is a rare pleasure indeed. We're yammering away. Shuffle is cleaning his travel bag. He keeps his finger picks in it, and it is, frankly, filthy. Scratching at it won't help, it's time for a washing machine. And Shuffle himself would benefit from being thrown in after it. I smile at my cup and fiddle with the ring on my finger.

Moonflower and *Amigos*, oh yeah . . .

The smell of the nearby toilet filters into the Coffeepot and spoils the mood. That's sad. A learned discourse is a necessity. Especially for this one Bird I know. Poor thing . . . I pity him dearly sometimes.

Bald One finishes the coffee, or whatever passes for it in the Coffeepot, bids us good-bye, and leaves, taking care to step around the mess left by the young Rat cutter.

"So how about it? Are you coming tonight?" I ask Shuffle.

Doghead pales and fiddles with the crutch.

"Eh . . . I mean, I'd love to, but . . . Your place . . . You know, it's kind of . . ."

"Disgusting," I say. "Sure. If we're so revolting to you, you don't have to come."

I climb down from the perch and take off. I am positive that he's coming.

I hobble lively. The House is in the throes of spring madness. It's contagious. You can come down with it in every nook and at every corner. I'm running from it as fast as I can, but they still manage to slither into the memory, the stupidly content faces with the winking slits of the eyes, the beautiful dazed faces smiling at each other. The soft jangle of chains on the girls' slender necks, in lieu of the collars. The wheelers whispering to each other, locking fingers and wheels, reading palms, divining their wingless fates. This is not a good time to be abroad alone. The House belongs to them. All of it, the cracks and the leaking pipes, the walls and the writings on them, acquiring another, mystical meaning . . .

Sad. I'm hobbling, lame as that unfortunate devil. The leg starts to heat up. We're in store for a night of torture, with my own bones doing the honors. It's rare indeed to have such a strong stimulant at one's disposal. Let's be grateful for what we've got.

I take off the glasses and wait. I know that in another moment the White Rabbit is going to sneak by at the end of the corridor, galloping at full speed, late for his Carrollian shindig. And there he goes. Flashing for a fraction of a second. You just have to know where to look, or you'd never catch him. I rest for a bit longer and then crawl forward again . . . *Step, step . . . There goes Great Bird, the one feeding on carrion . . .*

TABAQUI

DAY THE SEVENTH

You boil it in sawdust: you salt it in glue:
You condense it with locusts and tape

—Lewis Carroll, *The Hunting of the Snark*

Winter is the time of the great cat migration. They don't come one by one; no, they arrive all at once, each taking their posts by the familiar doors, waiting for permission to enter. When Noble and I wheel out of the dorm in the morning, the first thing we see is a rat's corpse. The one offering the bribe is sitting unassumingly beside it. An extremely skinny, extremely mangy ashen-striped tigress in white socks. Mother to countless offspring and a bane of rodents everywhere.

"Hey, Mona Lisa!"

Noble reaches down excitedly to pet her. Mona vaults onto his knees and rubs her scrawny side against his sweater.

"Whoa, that's a big one," Lary remarks from somewhere behind. "King sized."

Meaning, of course, the late rat. We let Mona in the room and proceed to the canteen. The basic arrangement is repeated in front of the Third. Two more rat carcasses and cats waiting over them. There's only nine of us at breakfast. Whenever it is snowing, Tubby goes into hibernation. He doesn't do breakfast or lunch, snacking on whatever morsels we bring back, and only if we manage to shake him awake. Winter's here.

Ginger comes in after classes, returning my socks and Noble's sweater, and then she, Noble, Humpback, and I go down to the yard. It's empty and snowy. The House dwellers do not like to frolic in full view of the Outsides, so the snow battle, if it's to be at all, is postponed until darkness. We make a crumbly snowman and take it back inside. It drips sadly in the middle of the room, becoming a puddle with clumps of snow in it. Humpback declares that such is life.

Then we sit down to dry off and have tea. Ginger teases Humpback's hair into a mass of braids, but only on one side. She gets bored, and also there's interference from Nanette, jealous and showing it. Humpback puts the bird on top of his head, and she immediately calms down and stops screeching. I say that even one-sided braids look nice, and Noble says that he misses his hair like crazy, because the way it is now it can't be plaited at all. I play the Snow Song—it's not as good as the Rain Song and is also much shorter, but on the other hand it fits this winter day better.

At lunchtime Dylan arrives, fashionably late for the great migration. Sphinx's favorite, son of Mona, coal black and the loudest singer we know. Except you have to wait until spring to hear his songs.

"And where's your tribute rat?" I ask him.

He just turns around and walks away, the shiny back swaying as he goes. A supremely self-absorbed animal.

The floor is covered with sausage ends and saucers of milk. The windows, with the crystal patterns left by the frost.

It's evening now, and it's snowing again.

The crow and the cats are testing each other's alertness. Humpback, one side of his head still in braids, is trying to soothe them with the flute. Lary powders his zits, cinches the belt, turning a bit blue as a result, and runs out in search of adventure. Noble wheels out immediately after. No one has come out for the snow battle, for some reason. I sit on the sill and wait, but it's empty down there. Empty and dreary. I study the frost patterns on the windowpanes and discover myself in them, endlessly repeated, all kinds of me—on Mustang and without it, shaggy and well-groomed, there's even one clad in the new vest. I scratch out a tiny window for that crystal me, to make his life easier and more pleasant. Sphinx frowns as he observes me do it.

"It's kind of a superstition," I say. "You see, there's another me here."

"Oh. Yeah," he says, "you can find all kinds of stuff in there. Tell me this, though. When you were painting that dragon on the ceiling . . . you wouldn't happen to have drawn it a heart? Shot through by an arrow? You know, accidentally."

"No," I say. "That would have been too corny. All I did was give it an eye. In accordance with the instructions received in a dream."

Lary comes back. He's still on the purplish side. Circles around the room a couple of times, sighing like a hungry ghost.

"I'll bring her," he says suddenly. "To say hello. You're going to like her. She's a really cool girl, you'll see."

We wait. Lary waits. Watching Humpback all the while, for some reason.

"Sure, why not," Humpback says. "What are you looking at me for? It's not like I make the rules around these parts."

"You see, we love each other," Lary explains. "You see? I mean, for real. Could you, like, have a friendly conversation with her when she comes? You being my friend and all."

Humpback stares in horror.

"What about? What do I need to talk to her about?"

"Well, there's knitting, for one," Lary says eagerly. "You should see the sweaters she makes! Crazy! Almost as good as yours. Honest."

Humpback wilts. Everyone knows he likes to keep that skill private. Everyone, including Lary. But apparently real love interferes with the basic functioning of memory.

"Friendship demands sacrifices," I say soothingly when Lary runs out again.

Smoker asks who Lary's girlfriend is. We shrug in unison. No one knows. All we know for sure is that there isn't another Gaby in the House. There are plenty of other horrible creatures besides her, though, and Logs' standards are notoriously loose, so we all fret a bit, Humpback more than others.

We don't have to wait long. Lary comes back accompanied by this flaxen-haired stick of a girl, unsteady pencil-thin legs perched on top of high heels. She takes position behind Lary's back and marvels at us from there. He reddens in apparent delight. Another second and he's going to melt like a blob of tomato paste.

"Allow me to introduce Needle. She knits gorgeous sweaters. Like really gorgeous. I've seen the last two myself. They're in huge demand. Cool, huh? Humpback?"

Humpback shoots me a desperate look. Then clears his throat and asks what gauge of knitting needles she, that is, Needle, prefers. You couldn't hear him at two paces.

Needle smiles pitifully. It's time to ride to Humpback's rescue. And Lary's, even though he's a nitwit. I take charge. When I speak, everyone hears what I say.

"Patterns? What kind? Cables, twists? Herringbone? Oh, eyelets, how lovely!"

It takes me half an hour to establish that the girl's favorite color is beige, that she was born in November and is therefore a Scorpio, that she likes tea but not coffee—at which point Lary pours two cups of tea into her—that she gets sunburned easily, can cook oatmeal but not much else, and also puts on a bit of mascara but no other makeup, thank you. Finally Lary takes her away, satisfied, and I can breathe easier.

"Thanks, Tabaqui," Humpback says. "I'm in your debt. Whatever you need. I mean, whatever I can get."

"Don't mention it," I say airily. "Even though chatting her up was no mean feat, that's for sure."

Noble returns. Also red faced and crazy eyed, almost like Lary. Green sweater decorated with white lizards running across the front, wet hair combed back to conceal the bald spots. I go to work on cracking nuts. Sphinx is swinging back and forth atop the nightstand, clanking its innards. Noble, looking very strange—which is by now usual for him, but this time even more strange than usual—makes coffee, cuts it with cola, crushed almonds, and cinnamon, then shakes out the contents of the basilisk eggshell amulet over the cup and gulps it without wincing.

I ask him what just happened.

Noble crunches the shell with his teeth and doesn't answer.

We can't help cringing, looking at the way he consumes his ghastly coffee and the stuff he's thrown into it.

"I leaned too close to the fire," he says finally. His grin is almost manic.

We wait for a while to see if he's going to expire right then and there, and then Smoker asks where he managed to find an open fire to sit next to.

Noble just smiles mysteriously. As if the House is lousy with open fires, each one surrounded by scores of people betting on who'd manage to lean the closest, and Smoker is somehow alone in not having noticed that.

If I were Noble I wouldn't be dressing up normal everyday stuff in so much romantic nonsense, annoying Smoker in the process, but he's in love. So what can you do? They're all a bit nuts. If he thinks that gobbling the basilisk eggshell, a unique specimen, by the way, would help him win Ginger's heart, he can gobble it all day long. My only concern here is Smoker. He's on edge as it is.

"Lary brought his girlfriend over," I say. "Knitting Needle."

"Really," Noble says. "How interesting."

Lies. He's not interested at all.

Sphinx sighs.

"Noble. Next time could you please not lean so close to the fire?" he says. "Fire really is a dangerous element."

"Oh god," Smoker moans. "I am so tired of you all."

I have a strange dream that night. A dead lake, grayish, calm as a mirror. Withered white stalks peeking out of the water. I sit by the edge and wait for some horrific creature that lives at the bottom to come out. There's a rusted sword on the sand next to me. The mist is drawing in, enveloping everything. Suddenly I'm in the water . . . and here I wake up.

The night is not too dark, even though the moon isn't visible. Noble is awake. He's sitting on the bed looking at me, absentmindedly gnawing at the collar of his pajamas. And petting Mona, the striped rug draped over his knees.

SORCERY

Mermaid crouches down by the desk drawer that she pulled out. There's a pile of junk in there, and mixed in it there's some really valuable stuff. Very little. Her textbooks and notes are in there too, along with the daily journal from two years back, taped over so that it's impossible to read without tearing it apart, certificates of achievement, and several bells rejected by Rat, the ones she refused to hang over her mattress. Mermaid sends her fingers to the back of the wooden cigar box (so old that the label is completely gone), and they find what she was looking for—a crocheted gym bag for the flats she wore at physical-therapy sessions. She pushes away the cat sniffing at her hands and spreads the bag on the floor. It's not exactly the way she remembered it. Grubbier, more mundane. There's a moth-eaten hole right in the middle. She imagined it to be much more attractive. She doesn't have to look closely at the pattern to remember how she knitted it. Row after row of tiny brown men, holding hands in a sort of silly dance. Each with its leg in the air at a different height, so they could all be different from each other. She loved them all, her ugly bubble-headed brown creatures. She was eight. She'd made a wish, and for it to come true she needed to do something extraordinary. Something that was hard. To knit a bag, for example, when everyone else was quite content with scarves. "Why would you want to take on something you don't have any idea how to do?" Hecuba had asked her then. Mermaid didn't answer. When the bag was done, and even Hecuba pronounced it "cute," but the miracle still wouldn't happen, that's when she thought of the little men. It is not easy to just abandon a dream. Much easier to complicate the road to it than to accept that it could never be achieved. Twelve little men. They took more time than the rest of the bag. The figure in the center was unlike the others. It looked a bit like a mop. That was Mermaid herself, wearing a fluffy crown made from her real hair. "Look at that," Hecuba said. "That's really good . . . You're going to knit amazing sweaters for your guy, mark my words." Mermaid did mark them, and weaved them into her enchantment—they sounded wonderful. She remembers as she runs her fingers over the little men. All of her wishes have come true. Except one. That last one. Her guy is not wearing her sweaters yet. In fact, he doesn't even know he's hers.

Mermaid folds the bag and secretes it under her shirt.

"What's that?" Catwoman asks from the mattress where she has been watching Mermaid. "Overcome by the childhood memories?"

"I guess you could say that," Mermaid says.

"I see," Catwoman sighs. "So the next thing would be Ginger digging up her favorite sling. Or Rat bringing in that baggie of arsenic, half of which she dumped into her dear grandpa's soup when she was four. I just can't wait. So sudden, so exciting!"

"That was mean," Mermaid says levelly, preoccupied with her own thoughts. "Want me to feed the cats?"

"No. Taken care of. You're all so courteous, so attentive. Catering to my every whim. Except you hightail it out of here when I so much as look away. But who am I to complain? I don't need much and I can spend a whole day here alone. It's not like I'm good company or anything. Of course, there are more interesting things in life than talking to a stump."

"Shhh," Mermaid says, closes her eyes, and puts a finger to her lips. "That's enough. Please."

She slips out of the room without giving Catwoman an opportunity to counter her words.

Lately, being with Catwoman has grown into something like torture. Incessant blackmail and their feeble attempts at countering it. Ginger is better equipped for it. Rat simply doesn't much care about anything. Mermaid envies them both.

She navigates the hallway strewn with mattresses and walks into the first classroom door she finds. Sits down on the freshly scrubbed floor, takes the backpack off her shoulder, and turns it out, emptying its contents. Then slowly and deliberately puts most of it back. What's left is a small pile of things that don't belong to her. Mermaid lies down, propping her chin on her hands, and looks at them: a suede pipe bag; a necklace, nutshells on a string; a coin with a hole through the middle; candied lemon peel; a shirt button; a crumpled diaper bearing traces of egg yolk; leather headband; guitar pick. Some of them she stole herself, others were brought in by Catwoman's sneaky children. For the necklace and the coin she traded fairly. Mermaid considers her hoard, bringing some of the items closer together, pushing them apart. Then she sits up and takes out the gym bag from under her shirt. She puts the items in it one by one, warming them up in her hands, breathing on them, whispering mutely, until all that's left on the floor is the crud that's been accumulating on the bottom of the backpack since time immemorial: hair, crumbs, twine. She blows on them, scattering them away. Then she stands up and walks to the window. There, with her back to the door, she takes out the most important piece—a small sewn-up bag on a string, a suede pouch decorated with beads. She stole it from a desk drawer in the Fourth. It is definitely the most magical object she's ever held in her hands. Out of the vest pocket she produces nail scissors and uses them to rip the seam. The pouch is now open, but Mermaid does not peek inside. From another pocket she takes a handkerchief and unfolds it, exposing a lock of her own hair. She twists the lock into a figure eight, binds it with twine, and lowers it into the pouch. Then slowly and carefully sews it back, still not having taken a look in it. The pouch goes back in her pocket, everything else in the gym bag. Mermaid cinches it and then stands there with her eyes shut tightly. She feels very tired. That might be a good sign. A confirmation that she has accomplished a really difficult task. She has to hold on to that thought if she wants to avoid crying.

The empty classroom shines. No one hauls mattresses in here, or dumps their clothes, or saunters in to rummage through the bookshelves. They warned that if the classrooms were to start filling up with junk they would start locking them, so the girls, with unexpected fastidiousness, stopped going in altogether. The hallway and the dorms are quite enough. The classrooms are for dusting, watering the plants, and airing out from time to time. Now that Mermaid is finished with the task she came here to do, she wants to leave as soon as she can. She slings the gym bag over her shoulder. It will now accompany her wherever she goes. She's not sure if it'll help anything, but it's safer this way. No one would be able to find it and look inside. And she still needs to put the amulet back.

She walks out of the classroom weighing in her head if she should return to Catwoman, but even as she's still thinking about it, her legs are already carrying her in the opposite direction. Catwoman is bitter. She needs to dump the long list of perceived slights and hurts on someone, and Mermaid tries to put off that moment. Until right before going to sleep. Or even until tomorrow.

The hallway isn't packed yet. Only two of the mattress piles are occupied, the rest are empty. The TV is not on. It looks like most girls are still in the boys' wing. When she walks by the staff room, Mermaid tries to make herself inconspicuous, the way she usually does, but it doesn't work this time. Long-necked Darling, sitting in the soft chair installed right in the doorway, calls out to her.

"Just a moment, child."

Mermaid freezes inside her cocoon of hair.

"Come here. I want to have a word with you."

Darling has climbed out of the chair and is pushing it back into the room, clearing the way. Mermaid goes in.

The coffeemaker sizzles and spits on the tiny table piled with packets of food. The staff room completely changes thrice each day. On Godmother's shift it is depressingly sterile. Not a speck of dust, not a piece of dirt, not a single item out of place. Godmother never eats here, or makes coffee or reads magazines. *And definitely never puts on makeup,* Mermaid thinks, noticing two eyeliners in a dish of peanuts. Two slender cylinders, one black and one brown, and a piece of cotton wool smeared with eye shadow. *She's going to eat those peanuts, too,* Mermaid thinks, overcome by a sudden swell of revulsion. In the hours of Darling's shift, the staff room becomes a total dump, and girls can only wonder how Godmother manages to wave it all away as soon as she passes through the door.

Darling yanks the coffeemaker cord out of the socket and sweeps a pile of magazines off the second chair.

"Have a seat. We have things to discuss."

Mermaid sits down on the edge of the chair obediently. Darling gets comfortable in the one opposite and takes out cigarettes. Mermaid glances at the gold-nosed shoes and hides her own battered sneakers under the chair.

"Now, you've taken to going over to the boys'," Darling says. "Don't even think of denying this, I know it for a fact."

Mermaid wasn't planning to deny anything. She's just tracing the smoke drifting up and melting under the sooty ceiling. Then she looks back at Darling.

"Yes," she says. "I do go there."

"Don't you think that maybe, just maybe, you shouldn't be doing that?"

Mermaid thinks about Catwoman. Could it be that she complained of being left alone too often?

"No. I don't."

"Many girls have friends there now. I gather you've heard about that."

"Yes, I know," Mermaid says. "Except it's not called having friends."

"Doesn't matter," Darling says, shooting her a disapproving look from under her silver bangs. "It doesn't matter what they call it. What matters is what they do over there. And, even more importantly, what it is inevitably going to lead to. You do understand what I'm talking about, don't you, darling? It is my opinion that one shouldn't behave in a certain way only because everybody else seems to be doing it, especially if a girl is not naturally disposed to that kind of behavior. Or because others would think her immature otherwise. Wouldn't you agree?"

Mermaid frowns.

"No. Who's that girl you're talking about? How would you know what I am naturally disposed or not disposed to?"

"Well, we'll just have to rely on my experience," Darling says, smiling sweetly. *I-am-your-counselor-don't-you-ever-dare-argue-you-pathetic-nobody!* "And on my considered opinion regarding who is disposed to what in this place, darling, I have worked here for many, many years. Do you have a sweetheart there? In the other wing?"

Mermaid laughs. *Sweetheart!* Now there's a great-grandma kind of word. *Suitor. Swain.* It's hilarious. *Sweetheart* is about the farthest thing from Sphinx that can possibly be. She imagines his face when someone tells him that he's her sweetheart and bursts out laughing again despite herself, even though she sees the irate look on Darling's face morphing into pure hatred.

"No, I don't have a lover," Mermaid says once she's able to stop laughing. "But I will. I am going to do my best to make sure that the person you have dubbed 'sweetheart' becomes my lover. He doesn't know about this, but he will find out soon."

"Why, you . . . !" Darling explodes, stubbing out her cigarette on the edge of the table. "Do you even understand what you're talking about, you stupid girl? Straight out of diapers, and here we go. A lover! You're not old enough. And that so-called future lover of yours needs his head adjusted with a good whack if he doesn't understand that! Which is exactly what I'm going to do right now! What's the idiot's name?"

Mermaid doesn't answer. *Has she heard a single word I said?* A sad feeling comes over her. She would have loved to sit here all day listening to Darling's abuse, if only it all had been true. Calmly and indifferently. It wouldn't be able to get to her, neither this, nor Catwoman's burbling. All right, so what if she imagined that it was true? After all, if she herself does not believe in her own sorcery, how could it work on others?

"Sphinx," she says, amazed at her boldness. "It's Sphinx. But he doesn't know yet that I've chosen him. So he'd be very surprised if you arrived with that good whack."

She gleefully observes the fight draining out of Darling, replaced by astonishment.

"Sphinx," Darling repeats, biting on the manicured fingernail. "Who would have thought . . . You sure have strange tastes, sweetie. Are you seriously considering making a move on him? If I were you I'd certainly look for a different target."

"What do you mean by that?" Mermaid says in a dangerous, faraway voice.

"Armless, bald," Darling counts off on her talon-like fingers. "That sickness that no one was able to diagnose . . . He looks like he's coming on twenty-five . . . Definitely, I'd have found myself a better catch."

"I don't think," Mermaid says slowly, "that you have the slightest idea about it."

"About what?"

"About love," Mermaid says. "That you even know what that is."

Darling's eyes narrow into slits.

"What kind of language is that to use with me, child? Isn't that a bit fresh?"

"No, it isn't. And I'm not your child."

Darling springs up aiming to slap her face, but Mermaid is faster. She darts behind the chair, positioning it between Darling and herself.

"Don't even think about it!"

"Or what?" Darling hisses, trying to wrestle away the chair. "You are asking for such a thrashing, you good-for-nothing ingrate!"

Mermaid shoves the chair at the counselor and runs out the door. She stops there, confident that Darling is not going to act on her threats in full view of everybody.

"Why?" she says. "Why me, and not Ginger? She goes over to the other side much more often, and she's only a month older. But you never say anything to her. Because with me it's easy. Because you despise me, don't you?"

Darling, still hemmed in by the chair, looks at her furiously, like a horse raring to bolt out of the stable.

"You bonehead," she says in a loud whisper. "Get out! Go, do whatever you want with whomever you want. I was just trying to care."

"You were trying to admire yourself!" Mermaid shouts back as she runs away. "That's the only thing you really care about!"

She flees down the corridor, feeling the counselor's fury as something hot and fiery, a wave lashing across her back. Someone greets her from the nearest mattress hut. She doesn't stop.

On the top landing, the merry gang of Logs in black leather race an electric toy car. Needle is with them. Round-faced Bubble sees Mermaid and cracks a smile.

"Hey!" he shouts. "Are you happy?"

"You mean right now?"

"I mean in general. Are you lucky or unlucky? That is, which happens more often?"

"I don't know," Mermaid says, downcast. "I'd like to find out myself."

"I doubt she would work as a lucky charm," Needle says, crouching on the floor with the rest, "if she doesn't know herself. Those who are happy are usually more or less aware of it."

"Maybe, but they would also never tell. Or it can get jinxed," Bubble argues, defeated but still hopeful.

Needle has on a leather jacket now, like all other Logs. Except instead of jeans she's wearing a cotton print dress, exposing her matchstick legs. She must have gotten over her hang-ups about them. She also looks loads happier than before, and Mermaid wonders why would counselors be so against girls being friends with boys. Look at Needle, turning into something reasonably cute and worry free.

Logs look away from Mermaid and turn their attention to the beat-up toy, whirring across the landing. Mermaid looks at it too. Short of the wall, the car veers into the railing, hits it, and overturns. Logs bolt up, shouting and whistling.

"Whose wager was that? And who was the dolt that aimed it? Termite, how about using your hands once in a while?"

Mermaid quietly leaves them to it.

She treads the boys' hallway, very slowly. Now she's level with the Fourth. She's going all the way to the Crossroads. There she'll sit on the sofa for a while and then go back. Pass by the Fourth again. Then maybe do the whole trip over. Or not. She needs to be sure that no one sees her when she goes inside, that she has enough time to replace the stolen amulet and sneak out undetected. Otherwise she may as well forget the whole thing. She is walking, becoming more and more flushed and beautiful with each step. The little bells woven into her hair tinkle softly. She is going to find out soon if she could work as a lucky charm.

BASILISKS

Rat is curled up in a gorgeous armchair. It looks like a hippo with glistening black skin. It's so cozy that she is able to relax completely in its embrace, almost dozing off. Only her leg, draped over the armrest, is in continuous motion, swinging back and forth. The foot is clad in a splendid black-leather boot, built like a tank, in perfect harmony with both the chair and Rat's cut-off jacket—shiny leather everywhere, exactly the way Nature intended.

The boot is infuriating to PRIP for some reason. He can't seem to look away from it. *I wonder why,* Rat thinks. *What's so irritating about it? The size? Or that it's swinging all the time?*

During his previous visits, PRIP kept ogling her tattoo the same way. You'd think he'd get used to it after all this time. The tattoo is more than two years old. Rat hadn't worn long sleeves ever since she got it, because how can you hide *that.* The rat looks almost alive. It even itches sometimes. Because of that, and to avoid confusion with her own nick, its owner named it Fleabag.

So now every time PRIP directs his full-of-loathing stare at his daughter he meets Fleabag's rictus instead. Which is only fair, since Rat herself never looks at him directly. Only through her badges, the little round mirrors slung around her neck. She's been seeing him in small fragments for so long now she can't even imagine him in any way other than a series of reflections. She can't perceive him as a whole. Not that she'd wish to.

"I am sick and tired of your continuous absenteeism," PRIP enunciates. "Your constant tardiness. Are you trying to get yourself expelled?"

Rat takes a sideways glance in the badges. She sees the jiggling pink spots of his cheeks and the piggy snout between them. Nothing else shows up anywhere. Then PRIP jumps up, freeing himself of the badges' attention, and proceeds to stomp and wail like an insane banshee.

"Put-that-disgusting-boot-out-of-my-sight-and-sit-straight-the-way-a-daughter-is-supposed-to!"

Rat takes the leg off the armrest.

"Stop yelling," she says. "Pull yourself together."

PRIP, short for Primary Progenitor, has a hard time controlling his runaway feelings. Rat closes her eyes and sighs. She needs to wait out the forty minutes allotted for parental visits. Good thing the chair is so comfy.

". . . no direction in life! You are completely passive! I'm surprised you even managed to learn how to talk. Must be only so that your mouth could spew forth all those vile abominations!"

"Would you please open your eyes, my girl, when your father is talking to you," Sheep bleats.

Rat opens them, reluctantly.

"Talking? To me?"

Sheep sighs pitifully.

Rat takes the largest badge and catches in it raging PRIP's reflection. Now his shiny red visage fits neatly between her thumb and forefinger. Is he ever going to shut up?

". . . procure those disgusting clothes and shoes and cover your body with sacrilegious graven images, contriving to look even more repulsive than you already are . . ."

Rat covers the paternal countenance with her thumb and presses on it, but the voice keeps wheedling.

". . . useless trinkets . . . Be so kind as to look at me when I am . . ."

She makes a fist around the badges, all four of them, but PRIP continues to squeak, tickling the palm of her hand, and then with surprising agility jumps on the buttons of her vest. Rat is mortified. She is covered with PRIPs, they crawl over rivets and buckles, they are on the steel toes of her boots, sliding on the shiny armrests—PRIPs everywhere, multiplying uncontrollably, screaming.

"The execrable foulness of your soul is reflected on your face! Out of every orifice you stink! Stink!"

She jumps up and tries to brush them off.

"Stink! Stink!" the PRIPs scream as she sheds them on the floor.

"Ow!" yelps the original PRIP, he who begat the rest of them, and he also darts away from her.

She can't see him do it, but she can definitely hear. The original PRIP is bulky, and his maneuverability is inferior.

Rat looks herself over, closely examining every button. Her hands are still shaking. At the other end of the room PRIP is trying to convince Sheep that his daughter is possessed by demons.

"Please calm down," Sheep says sweetly. "She is just upset. Nervous. Your girl has such a sensitive nature."

PRIP gulps the water he poured from the pitcher. He is aghast. Could Sheep really be as stupid as she seems? He starts to suspect that he's being played for a fool.

"That's enough!" he exclaims. "All the time I've wasted on her I could have spent on my other children. I have six of them, I'll have you know. Six!" he repeats significantly.

Sheep quickly gets to oohing and aahing.

PRIP likes that. Rat knows that he's lifted his eyes to the ceiling. Presumably because all of his six children dropped on him from above, without him being involved in any way.

"Why didn't you put on a condom if you couldn't hold it in," she remarks. "Might have helped with the children situation."

PRIP is speechless. Usually that only happens when he's asleep. He can't remain in that condition when he's awake; it's mortally dangerous, since he's so thoroughly unaccustomed to it.

"Now that was uncalled for," Sheep fumes. "For shame! Go on, leave now before your father gets upset."

PRIP finds his voice and starts screaming how upset he is. He's so upset that he can't possibly be any more upset. He'd be lucky to make it home safely, because he definitely can feel a stroke coming on.

Sheep pushes Rat out the door and rushes to assist stricken PRIP. In her flower-print dress Sheep resembles a pincushion. Very agitated, but completely harmless. Rat can afford not to even look back at her. She leaves.

Yes, the chair was very nice, but she'd prefer a bed of nails anywhere else. It's exactly a week until the next time PRIP comes here, and Rat knows that he is not going to miss it for the world. He adores visiting her. It must be his most favorite activity. Rat goes up the stairs, not taking her eyes off the boots, the target of repeated abuse. She always looks where she puts her feet, wherever she goes—this way she can be sure her feet won't carry her somewhere she wouldn't like to be. All kinds of people have all kinds of issues. This is hers. The other House maidens prefer lugging their mattresses around, like snails and their shells. They are extensions of the mattresses. Or is it the other way around? Anyway, they seem to like it that way, always being anchored to something familiar, something that smells of you. Lately several of these mattress-trailers have been parked at the Crossroads.

Rat sits down on the edge of one of the mattresses, squeezing between it and the sofa. It's a tight fit, so she has to shove her boots under the sofa.

"Make sure you don't break something when you stand back up," Owl from the Sixth advises. "The human body is a fragile mechanism."

The mattress is rather crowded. This is surprising. The mattress owners used to regard them as essentially their beds, never sharing them with just anybody. It's completely different now. There are five or six bodies on each one, and the owners are in a state of almost frenzied excitement—they giggle, they shift about, they roll their eyes. This is as close to group sex as they dare to get. The boys, even though not fully aware of what's going on, still can't avoid the nervous energy being radiated and also lose their heads.

Wedged between people rubbing against each other and breathing passionately, Rat imagines herself to be invisible. They are playing charades. Every time someone gets a word right, they all applaud with exaggerated enthusiasm, hug and kiss. Rat's badges begin to mist up.

Elephant, on the sofa with his face to her, is gumming the rubber giraffe. He takes it out of his mouth and then tries to applaud with the others. The giraffe falls in her lap. A very wet and chewed-up animal.

Rat hands the toy back without looking up. Elephant shrinks away. Hides his face in Horse's jacket and whines softly.

Horse takes the giraffe, thanks Rat, and says to Elephant, "There, there, what's this, you're a big boy."

Then he delightedly explains to all and sundry that Elephant is terrified of Rat.

"You are afraid, aren't you, Ellie? You shouldn't be. She's a nice lady."

"Scary," Elephant mumbles, digging his face deeper into Horse's shoulder and almost pushing him off the sofa.

The girls on the mattress giggle. Owl joins in the fun. They choose the next word.

"She has knives on her fingers . . . Sharp knives," Elephant whispers almost inaudibly. "Only you can't see them."

Rat stands up and offers her hands for Elephant's inspection.

"Look, no knives. Where would I hide them, those knives of yours?"

There's no one else reflecting in the badges except herself. Upside down. Hair over her left eye, lips distorted in a sad grin.

Elephant screws his eyes even tighter, determined not to look at the scary knives that are being thrust at him so persistently.

Rat is curious what it is that Elephant actually sees when looking at her. Pity Elephant can't explain it properly. Then again, if he could, he wouldn't be Elephant, and therefore would not see knives, or anything like that.

The left mattress failed to get the word. The right mattress is overjoyed. Owl and Bedouinne are snogging full-on. Rat watches them with great interest. Is this supposed to be pleasurable? Licking the insides of another person's mouth? What if one of them had a cold and a stuffy nose, could they do this? Or are you not supposed to kiss then? Bedouinne, out of breath, leans back on the jacket she rolled up, wipes her mouth, and takes a pack of cookies out of the inner pocket of her vest.

"Wanna bite?"

"Oh, yes," Owl responds passionately, not looking at the cookies at all.

Bedouinne sighs and tears open the pack.

Rat leaves.

The hallway is very quiet compared to the Crossroads, almost deserted. Only Red loiters near the door to the Second, as if waiting for someone.

"Hey," he says to Rat. "Where you going?"

"To my place." She shrugs. "Why?"

"Nothing. You don't look so good. Want to come in? I have this great liqueur. I think you could do with a drink."

And as Rat is trying to decide if she wants to have a drink in the company of Red, she's already being pulled into the Second. She immediately almost trips over the thing Rats call a table.

Red pushes apart the sleeping bags obscuring the view; slaps them, in fact, so they slide along the wire to which they're clipped, like drying skins. One is still on the floor, and its occupant is snoring. The stench of old socks is unbearable.

Rat sits down on the floor in front of the crate-table, leans against its surface, and gets stuck.

"Shit," she hisses, rubbing her now-sticky-sweet elbows. "How do you manage to live in all this?"

"That's just the way it is. It's not always this dirty. Wednesday is the cleanup day. And today is Tuesday, unfortunately. You have caught us at the very point of decadence. On the dirtiest day of the week."

"And how many Wednesdays have you skipped? I mean, truthfully."

Red takes a flask out of his backpack, pours out a capful, and transfers it directly to Rat's hands, bypassing the table.

"Tangerine-peel liqueur. Strong stuff."

"Your own creation?"

He laughs.

"Nah. Don't fret. Bought it off Little Pigs. Made to the highest standards of hygiene. Pheasant brew, imagine that."

There's a pair of bugged-out glasses reflecting in Rat's badges, and nothing else. Then the flask gets in the way.

"How's PRIP doing?" Red says, wiping off the liqueur mustache.

"Great. His two Persians and both of his mutts are also good. One of them, Millie, had a spot of diarrhea, but she recovered, thanks for asking."

"Oooh, you mean your daddy likes animals?" Red says.

"Adores them."

Rat's voice is so grave that it dawns on Red to stop exploring the topic. He's frantically searching for another one when Rat continues.

"He adores animals. He's crazy about them. They are pure and innocent creatures."

"Oops," Red says, grinning uncertainly.

"Exactly," Rat says, looking straight at Red, which she doesn't usually do to anyone, at least not for more than three seconds at a time. "What is it you know about him, huh? For your information, he's a writer. Wrote loads of books. All of them about animals. I'm pretty sure there are some in our library. Would you like to read a couple?"

"Probably not. Are they any good?"

"You'll drown in tears. But it's all going to be fine in the end. And if one of his books gets made into a movie then no animals are going to be harmed during production. He always puts a clause about that in the contract."

"Look, you didn't have to do that, OK?" Red says. "So everyone has their own skeleton in the closet. Why fly off the handle?"

Rat scratches the bridge of her nose.

"I don't know," she says glumly. "I guess this is how his visits work on me. I get ill. And then there's you with the questions."

"Sorry. I didn't know."

"Is there anything you do know?"

Red doesn't answer. He's also stuck to the table and is trying to pry away his elbows without attracting attention. The table doesn't want to let him off without a fight. It's easier for Rat with her bare arms.

"You might not believe me, but in summer it's great for catching flies," Red says.

Rat glances in the badges, appalled. Red sounds serious.

"Disgusting," she says. "If I were you I'd keep that to myself."

"Totally disgusting," Red agrees readily. "But also useful. In a limited fashion."

He fidgets, smiling at something only he understands, then slides the green shades up and morphs into a fairy-tale creature from another world. A very somber creature. One could use his eyes like a mirror, drown in them, stay there forever, stuck faster than a fly to a trap masquerading as a table. A reflection in them is always more beautiful than in an ordinary mirror. It's hard to look away from it.

Rat stares at the two images of herself. After a while she shakes her head, chasing off the enchantment.

"Why don't you take off your clothes too?" she says.

Red shrugs and lowers the glasses back. He then reaches out to her and slowly turns her badges backside-up, one by one. On the other side they are blank.

"Watch it," Rat says. "I don't let anyone do that. Those are my eyes."

Red snatches the hand away so quickly it's almost funny.

"And yours lie," she adds angrily. "They show an improved version."

Red shakes his head. "They show what is. You're the one with the lowered self-esteem after meeting with that parent of yours."

She wants to snap back, say something that would turn him off her forever. Make him regret his attempts at meddling in her soul and his cloying words of consolation. Make him stop showing her unreal reflections. But she can't bring herself to reject them. She does need them, at least occasionally, at least on days like this one. And Red is perfectly aware of that. She remembers herself in the chocolate pools that are his eyes. So beautiful.

"How is it?" he says once she takes a sip from the cap.

"Not bad. Considering it's the Pheasants—more or less brilliant. I had no idea they were into stuff like this."

Red, relieved that a scene seems to have been avoided, smiles.

"We know very little about them. They live in the House, but in a sense not quite."

"Yeah. They are not of this place. But not of the Outsides either."

They fall silent. Red pours out another capful for Rat.

"Listen," he says with inflated enthusiasm, "they say Noble is into Ginger now? Like really into her. Is that true?"

Rat's hand reaches for the badges by itself. She glances at them, but leaves them the wrong side up. She can see that Red is finally getting to his real point even without them.

"How would I know?" she snaps back. "I've just returned. Ask her, why don't you."

"She gets ticked off when I do," Red says glumly.

"Then don't bring it up with me either."

Rat's eyes become angry, but Red does not notice. He fiddles with the flask. Screws on the cap and lifts his head. Even the lenses of his shades betray apprehension.

"I worry about her," he says. "She's like a sister to me. I feel kinda responsible for her. To myself. She's been in love with Blind since forever, like, since she was ten. And Blind . . . you know . . . he doesn't give a crap. He wouldn't make an effort for any girl. If she jumps into bed with him—fine, her choice. That's the way he is. He doesn't care who he's doing it with. So if Noble lures her to the Fourth, they're going to be close together. Her and Blind. That's what I'm worried about. For Blind it's all fun and games, but not for her."

"All right," Rat sighs. "What's all that have to do with me? Where do I come in?"

Red smiles obsequiously.

"Well . . . you might . . . you know . . . work your way in there too. The Fourth, I mean. You're a girl, and a pretty one at that."

Rat's eyes narrow.

"And then what? Be Ginger's chaperone? Stop her from making the move on Blind?"

"No, that's not what I mean. It's just . . . If you made it look like you're in love with him . . . I mean, for real. Like seriously. Then she'd get him right out of her head, see? She'd never even go near him anymore."

Rat looks briefly at Fleabag, splayed over her shoulder, and stands up. Red shoots up too. He's wearing ridiculous purple pants with heart-shaped leather patches on the knees, a white shirt unbuttoned all the way down to his navel, and a bow tie. In short, he looks like a clown. With a very serious and somewhat frightened face.

"Please don't go! I didn't mean anything bad. All right, let's say that was a joke."

"Was it?"

Red doesn't answer.

Rat looks at him, biting her lip.

"You know what," she says finally. "I've seen creeps in my life, but never like you. So brazen, I mean. I'm going to play Blind's bimbo so that Ginger loses the hots for him, so that you can sleep easy knowing that your pretty little sister is not inconvenienced in any way. Did I get that right? Blind won't give a crap, he just needs somewhere to stick his dick, and I'm going to have the satisfaction of participating in this important endeavor. Saving Ginger from Blind's clutches. Now that we've established all that, sure, I guess we can say it was a joke."

Red, downcast, is rubbing the floorboards with his dirty sneaker.

"You're doing it all wrong," Rat says with a grin. "Matchmaker, my ass. You should've told me how Blind is this great guy and how he's crazy about me. How he weeps daily on your shoulder, moaning that he can't live without me. Then maybe you'd have a chance."

"Really?" Red says, perking up.

"No, not really!" Rat sniggers. "But at least it would have looked halfway decent."

Red wilts again.

"There's one thing I don't get, though," Rat says. "Wasn't this whole new Law your idea all along? It was you who got the thing rolling, right?"

"Yeah. I thought I covered all the bases pretty well. But now it's all gone south. Sphinx promised that if Gaby so much as gets her nose into that door again he'd personally have my scalp. But it almost worked . . ."

He's interrupted by the lunch buzzer. The body in the sleeping bag stirs.

"So now you need to replace her. And since we don't have another Gaby, Rat will have to do."

Red raises his head.

Her straight, glistening black hair diagonally bisects Rat's face, falling over her left eye. If not for those bangs you'd see that her eyebrows meet in the middle, forming one continuous line. They look even more bushy in contrast to her skin, soft as a baby's and almost transparent. Red swallows hard.

"I'm sorry," he says. "I didn't think it would sound that way. You can kick the snot out of me if you like. I'll understand."

"Lunch? It's lunch, right?" A head appears at the end of the sleeping bag, followed by the rest of its owner. It's Termite. Scrawny, clad in striped boxers, scratching his belly distractedly and staring at Rat with half-closed eyes.

"It all came out so lousy because I was speaking honestly," Red says, glancing over his shoulder at Termite. "Because I told it like it is, you know? But I never saw it the way you described it. I thought it would be easy for you to do . . . but if you take it that way, then sure . . . I mean, forget I even said anything . . . Actually, I didn't have much hope anyway, not with a girl as beautiful as you."

"Shut up, OK?"

"It's hot dogs today," says Termite, which for him counts as refined conversation. "And raspberry Jell-O."

"And by the way, Blind does like you," Red says. "Not that you're going to believe me now, of course."

"Well, maybe not Jell-O. Maybe I'm talking bull here," Termite continues.

"Believe you? Dream on. Do I look that crazy?"

Two Rat-Logs clatter inside.

"Lunch! What are you, asleep?"

They snatch backpacks off the stand and charge back out.

Termite hobbles around the room on one leg, trying to stuff the other one into his pants. Rat turns the badges over, mirror side up. One, two, three . . . four. The chains are all of different length, and they often get tangled.

Red hides the flask in his backpack. One of the badges catches a glimpse of his bow tie, red and white polka dot. Directly around the bare neck.

Rat looks around and notices to her surprise that it is, in a sense, beautiful in the Second, filth notwithstanding. Leopard's antelopes race across the walls, flowing into abstract stripy patterns as they run. Red puts his bowler hat on and offers Rat a handshake.

"No hard feelings?"

"Careful, or Fleabag is going to bite you to death," Rat warns him. "She can't stand it when someone tries to touch me."

The badges show three tiny doors. Three Termites are disappearing through them simultaneously. Red and Rat walk out after him, and the badges darken. The soles of their shoes cling to the floor with every step.

"I think it's too late for a cleanup," Rat says. "You won't be able to pry the brooms off the floor."

"So we won't," Red sighs. "So? The Hole is going to feature nice broom arrangements. And then—nice Rat arrangements. Like a wax museum, only with live people."

Rat shrugs and goes off in the direction of the girls' stairs. A slender figure in heavy boots too large for her. Red shouts "Bye!" but she doesn't look back. He purses his lips and turns toward the canteen. Giggling Birds run past him.

GHOST

Noble floats in a kind of sparkly black void. He has pulled the covers over his face and is now suffocating in the stifling heat, surrounded by apparitions. Her eyes. Her hair. The slender arm in the grasp of the woven strap of bracelet. Noble is barely breathing, afraid of spooking the phantom, but it grows more and more impatient, restless, melting like wax and soon disappearing. He pushes the blanket off and takes deep breaths. He's wet as a mouse that's just been fished out of a puddle.

The sounds return, now that the air is back. The sniffling and breathing of the sleepers. Black's snores, waves of aggression rising up to the ceiling. Closer by are the birdlike whistles of Tabaqui and the rustling of the bodies as they turn. Smoker, still fast asleep, pulls a pillow from under Tabaqui and aims to cover Noble with it. Noble manages to avoid it by shifting closer to the edge of the bed. There's a nightlight on in Lary's corner. Also in Alexander's, shielded by a piece of newspaper. Noble looks up into the ceiling, and it seems to pull him in. It grows closer, closer, and now he's almost level with the wheel, the birdcage, and the narrow eyes of the kite. It's strange, what's happening to Noble. He is lying on his back and at the same time standing up. The standing Noble is light as a feather. He sees the ceiling, Lary's mushroom-shaped nightlight, and the sleeping Bandar-Log with a pink halo around his hair. And also himself, down there, under the crumpled blanket. He sees it all from the height where he's never been before. His own height. As soon as he thinks about the window and the fresh breeze wafting through it, he's transported across to the windowsill. Night air soothes his burning face. The air also brings with it a blast of distant noise—the squealing laughter of Rats, having their raunchy fun. *Does this mean I can go wherever I want?* His shadow floats across the floor, insubstantial, passing through the door and into the darkness beyond. Noble closes his eyes to better see where there's a path for him and where there isn't. Darkened walls slide past, then he's through the yawning maw of an open door. The wintry moon glows in the windows of the Sepulcher, making it almost translucent. More steps, then a different corridor . . .

Noble stretches out his arm. It flows away into the black emptiness, probing, searching, sweeping through the doors on the way. He falls behind, and when his hand is feeling for *the* door, the only one he needs, he's still far away. The hand already glides over the face of the figure sleeping on the floor. Finally Noble catches up with her—no, with it, it's only his hand; its touch becomes his touch.

The red-haired girl, the strap of the tank top fallen off her shoulder, sits up on the mattress and peers into the darkness.

"What's that? Hey! Get out! Get out of here!"

Noble startles, back on the bed, gasping for breath.

There are groans, stirrings, and sighs around him. He lies perfectly still. *I was there. I was really there!* The palm of his hand still remembers the roughness of the fiery hair. He's melting above the waist and freezing below. *Could it be that in its wanderings about the midnight House my ghost froze its legs off?* It hurts. Noble's face is distorted in a grimace, and he's glad of the darkness enveloping him.

Black is snoring. Lary has a light on. Alexander has a light on. On the hotplate down on the floor, the kettle is preparing to boil. Someone seems intent on having tea.

"Fat chance! Choke on it!" Black enunciates clearly between two snores.

It's funny, but no one's there to hear it and laugh. Noble's sweaty back clings to the mattress. His face is on fire, his legs are pure ice. It's happened before, but tonight he knows that it is a payment being exacted for that strange something he has allowed himself to perpetrate. Someone is reminding him what he is. Half a man, with the legs of a corpse.

"No," Noble whispers. "I will not think about this."

And immediately imagines his legs actually dead, bluish-white, covered in spots of decay. He's running out of air.

Someone's quiet steps.

Alexander sits down on the bed next to him and inserts a hot bottle under the blanket.

"I was waiting for the water to boil."

Noble is silent while the hot bottle works to melt the ice and a faint warmth trickles to his feet. Warmth that would have burned his hands.

"Thanks," he says. "I'm a coward. It's simply blood moving too slowly there, like in a mermaid's tail."

"There's no need to be afraid," Alexander says and leaves. The green firefly of the lamp near the head of his bed switches off.

"Hey," comes Humpback's sleepy voice from the top bunk. "I thought I heard a song. Are you guys singing down there?"

Black stops in midsnore.

"No," Noble says. "No one's singing."

What I've done wasn't a song at all.

He lies quietly now. What he's celebrating with a fleeting smile on his lips and a hot bottle at his feet is a mystery even to himself. He won't be able to sleep tonight. He could leave this pointless prone position, escape to the hallways for real now, on wheels, and dull the ache in the squeakily tiled kingdom of the bathroom, in the company of other insomniacs like him, endlessly drawing and discarding card after card. The faces of the queens would acquire her features, and he'd be compelled to shield them with his hands, hide them before everyone could see what he sees: the fire of her hair under the regal diadems, the blackness of her eyes staring at him from the cardboard rectangles. "What's gotten into you, Noble?" they'd ask, and he wouldn't know how to answer. So he stays. Lying on his back looking at the ceiling. It's better to remain that way, bewitched, capable of spawning inquisitive specters. Mutely reliving the ghostly encounter.

A soft thing springs up, landing on his stomach, and sits down, wrapping its tail around its paws. A cat. Noble doesn't brush it off, even though he could see it isn't Mona. It's a strange cat. Noble's fingers sink into the fur, deep and luscious like a Maltese dog's.

"Where have you come from?" he asks.

The cat doesn't answer, as becomes a dumb animal. Instead, with a soft sniffle, Jackal awakens. His hair is standing on end, resembling porcupine quills. He looks like someone ran a jolt of electricity through him while he slept. He stares uncomprehendingly. Gradually his eyes fill up with reason and then with curiosity.

"Ah, so you're awake," he says. Then he looks in the direction of Noble's knees. "What's up with Mona? How come she's so fluffy all of a sudden?"

"That's not Mona," Noble says, smiling distractedly. "That's not Mona at all."

TABAQUI

DAY THE EIGHTH

He had forty-two boxes, all carefully packed,
With his name painted clearly on each

—Lewis Carroll, *The Hunting of the Snark*

In the morning we get a surprise. Flyer home from the Outsides, bearing the ordered goods. An exceedingly rare occurrence. Rat comes in before the first class with a black travel bag slung over her shoulder. She drops it on the teacher's table. The zipper whines. Rat—black lipstick, white makeup, a regular vampire—pulls packages from it one by one and arranges them on the table. Lary snatches the one that obviously contains a record from the general pile and makes off with it. I pick up the heavy box tied with a pink ribbon. After that I am lost to the world until I am able to dispose of both the ribbon and the wrapper and have a peek inside. Oh, the heavenly scent! The chocolate backs all glistening in neat rows. Each in its own crinkly nest, on its own little placemat, covered with delicate tissue. I lift it, touch one of the backs, and lick the finger. Then I count how many there are. Two layers, four chocolates in each row, and the rows are also four. That seems to make thirty-two. I close the box and hide it in my desk. The ribbon goes there as well. Now I'm ready to look at what everyone else got.

Black has fled to the windowsill with a stack of magazines. Before Blind's hungry, grasping tentacles Rat pitches three cans of coffee, four cartons of cigarettes, a pack of AA batteries, and dark glasses of an especially ghastly persuasion. Humpback has a set of combs and a meerschaum pipe. There are two more packets on the table, but we don't get to open them, as R One appears suddenly in the middle of the classroom inquiring what it is we think we're doing when the class has already started and the teacher is on the way. Rat somehow escapes his attention.

We quickly whisk away the items, the packaging, ribbons, string—in short, everything that smells of fun and can therefore upset the teachers, who are excluded from it. Rat zips up the bag and leaves.

"How're you feeling?" Ralph asks, stopping at Noble's desk.

"Good," he says with a shrug.

Ralph nods, walks away, and hovers over Smoker's head.

"What about you?"

Smoker blushes and blinks.

"All right, I guess."

Ralph gives him a look, as if he has deep suspicions concerning Smoker's all-right feelings, before scampering to his own chair.

During lunch break I keep pestering Sphinx until he relents and directs Alexander to take the map of New Zealand off the wall. We have two pictures stapled under it. Big ones, each almost the size of half the map.

One of them, done in black ink, is of a tree, gnarly and sprawling, almost denuded of leaves. On the bare branch there's a lonely frazzled raven, and underneath it, by the roots, what looks like a garbage pile. Even though the garbage is just regular human trash, it's still somehow obvious that it was the raven that's assembled it—the bottles, the bones, the concert tickets, the wall calendars. And the reason it's so sad appears to be that the whole of its life has turned into that waste. So the picture is actually about anyone and everyone, funny at first sight and somber at all the subsequent sights. Like every picture Leopard's ever drawn. The second is in color. A scrawny, sand-colored cat in the middle of a parched desert. It's got emerald-green eyes and looks a bit like Sphinx. Apart from it, there's only the cracked earth and ghostly brush populated by yellowish-white snails. On the ground near the cat's paws are broken snail shells. The shards are covered with scratches that are actually notes and Latin proverbs. Also on the ground, someone's footprints. Could be a bird, could be an animal. The prints straggle by where the cat's sitting, loop around the brush, and disappear somewhere in the distance.

We look at the pictures for a while. They make us a bit depressed. The first drawing belongs to me and the other one to Sphinx, but they are in fact communal property of the pack. So valuable that we never leave them out on display, to make sure we don't get used to them. We look and remember Leopard. They're his present to us. Blind usually takes part in the ritual as well. He has his own ways of reaching the right frame of mind, and we could only make wild guesses at what those are. But he never skips the picture-viewing sessions. The animals in the corridor are accessible to his fingers and he knows them as well as we do. Before filling them in, Leopard always scored the outline into the wall. But these he only knows from our descriptions.

So here we are, sitting and standing before our treasure. Looking at it and not looking, at the same time. Seeing it. Listening and thinking. Then we put the map back and return to the daily grind. Smoker isn't asking questions, which is a bit strange. Could it be that he too is finally growing up?

THE LONGEST
NIGHT

Smoker, on the floor, flips through old issues of *Blume*, slowly coming to the realization that the overwhelming majority of the articles had been written by Jackal. Noble is counting the hours until the card players' meeting in a secret location. Blind is also waiting. For the House to settle down. For the transition into the night. For the time when he can go out in search of the Forest. Humpback is inviting slumber by playing his flute. Sphinx listens. To him and to Smoker, who is arcing with irritation.

There are two toxic zones in the room. Around Smoker and around Black.

"I've got this hunch," Tabaqui says, finishing up the pre-repose batch of sandwiches, "that we're having the Longest tonight."

"Could very well be," Sphinx agrees. "I'd even say more likely than not."

He jostles Blind with his knee.

"Hey! What do you think?"

"Yes," Blind says. "Quite possible. It's a bit early this year, for some reason. Or maybe we're going to have more than one."

"That's a new one to me," Tabaqui says. "I've never heard of that happening before. So, why and wherefore did you get this idea?"

Smoker studies them warily, suspicious that they are deliberately talking nonsense to make him feel stupid and provoke him into asking questions. So he isn't asking them.

It's night. Only two wall lamps out of the dozen are on. Everyone who's left in the dorm is asleep. Except for Smoker. Smoker is on the floor next to the pile of magazines, deep in thought. He wants to do something he's never done before. Take a drive around the House after lights out, for example. This could be the old magazines talking. He's not sure. With bated breath he starts inching toward the door. He almost makes it when there's tossing and turning on the bed. A shaggy head leans down from it.

"What?"

"Going out," Smoker whispers back.

Tabaqui tumbles onto the floor.

"Horrible," he mumbles. "Instead of sleeping peacefully I've now got to look after this dunce lest something happens to him. He's going out, don't you know. In the dark. Possibly in the middle of the Longest. Enough to drive a man crazy."

"I'm not asking you to come with me. I want to go by myself."

"Yeah, and there are many things I want too. You're not going out alone. Either we go together or I wake up Sphinx and he knocks some sense into you. Your choice."

Before Smoker is able to crawl any farther, Tabaqui is already at the door, aboard Mustang. Still in pajamas. Clutching his socks and a handful of amulets. Despite the threatening voice, Smoker imagines that Tabaqui is looking forward to a ride with him.

"All right," Smoker says. "We go together."

Then he has to concentrate on trying to climb into the wheelchair, and when he's finally in he sees Tabaqui methodically stuffing his backpack. The backpack is already so bloated that it's impossible to close, but Jackal continues to add to its contents.

"What's all that for?"

"Sweaters, in case we get cold. Food, in case we get hungry. Weapons, in case we get attacked," Tabaqui explains. "You don't just drive out into the night unprepared, silly!"

Smoker doesn't argue. He follows Tabaqui into the anteroom and then into the pitch-dark hallway, where Tabaqui orders him to switch off the flashlight.

"Otherwise we are going to be seen by everyone who's already accustomed to the darkness, and at the same time we won't be able to see them."

Smoker obediently switches it off and darkness envelops them.

"Let's ride," Tabaqui whispers.

The house is spookily dark and seemingly asleep. Eyes do not get accustomed to darkness this deep. Walls loom suddenly ahead in places where they aren't supposed to be. Tabaqui and Smoker move slowly. Sometimes they think they hear steps, either ahead or behind them. They stop and listen. The steps immediately stop as well. Maybe they're just imagining it. Then they bump into something and switch the flashlights back on. It's an empty wheelchair. There's no trace of its owner, as if he's been abducted by the spirits of the night. Tabaqui fingers his amulet.

"It's like someone is trying to scare us on purpose, right?"

His voice is a mix of being terrified and reveling in it.

Smoker does not join him in the reveling part. He doesn't like this empty wheelchair a single bit. Tabaqui spends some time studying it but is unable to determine the identity of the owner.

"It's totally faceless," he says. "Abandoned."

They put on the sweaters, leave the wheelchair behind, and move on.

Barefoot Elephant in striped pajamas wanders past the Crossroads. His eyes are closed, his face upturned. His long pajama bottoms are collecting the hallway dust as he goes. Elephant is asleep, but his body slowly hobbles from one window to the next, stopping at each windowsill and feeling it with chubby palms before proceeding. The floorboards creak under his weight.

Blind floats along the corridors, not touching the walls. Even the wary rats don't feel him approaching until he's almost on top of them. He inhales the scent of damp plaster and the scent of the House denizens ingrained in the worn-out floorboards. When he hears steps he freezes until the night drifter passes by—a large animal in the thickets, crushing the ground underfoot and bumping into trash cans. Then he continues on his way, even more watchful and cautious than before, because those who wander at night drag dangerous secrets and fears after them. He approaches one of the dorms. Under the words carved with a knife, his all-seeing fingers feel for a crack. He presses his cheek against it. This way he can hear even the breathing of the sleepers and the groans of the bedsprings. Everyone's asleep inside. Blind passes through more empty rooms and comes to another wall. There's a place here where a large chunk of plaster fell down, and behind this wall nobody's sleeping. Blind listens for a long time, paying more attention to the voices themselves than to the words they're saying. He turns his head away at regular intervals, takes in the sounds around him, relaxes, and presses back against the wall.

Someone searching for a place to sleep sneaks down the ante-Crossroads stretch of the hallway. Someone pale and large-eyed, with patchy rust-colored hair.

Red is frightened. Asleep or awake, day or night. He's dreading and waiting. He gnaws down the caps of his pens and chews up the filter ends of his cigarettes. He thinks and considers. This has got to end at some point. Plump Solomon, and Squib with his face red from the burn. They keep scaring him with their meaningful sniggers. Their smirks, their glances and winks. Squib, Solomon, and Don. The rest of them are submerged in the electronic ocean of sound. They float in it, swaying on the spot when they stand and jerking to the beat when they lie down, and they don't care about anything that is not coming from the earphones plugged into the thundering emptiness.

They are always hostile, always hungry, always covered in spots from the sweets they consume to cheat hunger. They dye their hair and alter their pants with multicolored patches. Red is hopelessly older. Not in years, but in questions he asks himself. Young Rats are not concerned about tomorrow. Their life begins and ends today. It is today they need that extra piece of toast, it's today they need that new song, it's today they need to take the only thing that's on their mind and scrawl it in huge letters on the bathroom wall. Rats suffer from constipation but they'd still eat anything anytime. And fight over food. And over who sleeps where. And after the fight is over they'd listen to more music and eat again, with even more delight.

With all their complaints they come to Red. With the most painful zits and abscesses they come to Red. Busted Walkmans, drained batteries, lost possessions—they all come to Red. Except Squib, Solomon, and Don. Those three despise him. With each day their whispers become louder, laughs more insolent, conversations more hushed. They keep him constantly terrified, relishing the effect immensely. Red wanders at night, sleeps in uncomfortable places, and dreams of slitting the throats of all three, one after the other. Sometimes he twists open all faucets in the bathroom and plugs all drains. Then takes a shower in his clothes and leaves, the squelching sneakers parting the waters. He goes to the card players. He plays, dripping water on the cards. The players don't say anything, because he's a Leader.

The outfit Red has chosen for tonight's stroll is completely black. Only the white sneakers flash in the dark as he goes, two bright spots betraying his presence. A sleeping bag dangles off his shoulder. It's blue with yellow dots. Red is looking for a secluded corner where he could sleep, wrapped in the warm cocoon. He stops at the Crossroads. Elephant is moving through the space, barely illuminated by the moonlight, inspecting the windowsills. Red watches him. Then puts the sleeping bag down, sits on it, and lights a cigarette. And waits. Patiently waits.

Four card players are cooped up in Vulture's tent. It's cramped inside. Every awkward movement makes the canvas shudder and the multicolored lights sway under the triangular roof. Shuffle's collar is bristling with dull spikes. There's a trail of blood down his cheek from a scratched boil. He touches his finger to the spot and examines it.

"Not that damn thing again!"

"Got anything to drink?" Noble says, rubbing his eyes, tired of the lightbulb rainbows.

Dearest is swishing something hastily in a tin cup.

"Soon, very soon, dearest. In the meantime there's plain water, if you'd like."

He hands Noble a flask. Noble drinks and returns it. Dearest sighs mournfully. The cigarette in Vulture's teeth drops down a column of ash, showering the blanket in sparks. Crickets chirp in the speakers of the boombox.

Smoker and Tabaqui drive down the dark corridor. Suddenly a red cone flashes in front of them. It becomes blue the next moment. Then yellow. After cycling through six different colors, the cone blinks off, and it's dark again.

"What's that?" Smoker whispers.

"Vulture's tent," Tabaqui says.

They drive closer. Now the tent is shining and twinkling in every color at once, and it's possible to hear voices from inside it. The entrance flap is pushed open and someone crawls out on all fours.

"Hey," says the someone as he bumps into them. "I'm bailing out. Wanna play?"

"Hey, Shuffle," Tabaqui calls back, turning to Smoker and handing him the backpack. "Listen, my friend, could you manage hanging around here by yourself for a bit? I need to talk to the guys, if you don't mind."

He tumbles out of Mustang and speedily crawls inside the tent.

Shuffle's flashlight runs away, jumping from side to side. Smoker is alone. He listens to the voices coming from the tent and waits for Tabaqui until he runs out of patience. He drives closer, pulls out the brake, and slides down. Then he lifts the flap.

"Hey. Can I come in too?"

Beauty and Doll are kissing on the stairs. The trash can next to them and the cigarette butts strewn about concern them not at all. A pocket radio buzzes softly under

Doll's sweater. They devour each other with fevered mouths, opening wide like hungry chicks. Their kisses are passionate, interminable, and painful. From time to time they let go of each other and rest, touching their foreheads and furtively wiping their wet mouths. Their lips are swollen and sore. They only know how to kiss. Or maybe they don't even know that.

The squat cylinder in the shortened pajamas lays siege to the stairs to the third floor. He is searching. Searching for that miraculous, wondrous being—lithe and fair haired, so pleasant to be next to. Tubby knows that it's still here, inside the House. And that the place to search for it is where the stairs lead. He's never been up there, so it follows that it's exactly where the being could and should be located. Tubby's inner voice has never steered him wrong, and now it urges him forward. Wheezing softly, he conquers the steps one by one.

The feeble flame of an alcohol burner flares up in the teachers' bathroom. Shaking from both fear and cramps in his stomach, Butterfly is holding a spoon over it. Butterfly is all bones, sickly pale and covered in warts. A rubber mat protects his skinny buttocks from touching the freezing tiles. The open neck of his sweater reveals a meager chest hung with amulets and strings of garlic. Butterfly is nervous—about the dripping faucets, the imagined steps and whispers. He cringes from the damp and shields the burner from the drafts with his body. He has a cold. He also has diarrhea. Constantly shuttling to one of the stalls and back is too time-consuming, so he decides to move inside a stall with the entire setup, including the rubber mat, the burner, and a roll of toilet paper. He closes the door, throws on the hook, and feels safer, shielded from the dangers of this night.

It's stifling inside Vulture's tent. And as if it wasn't hot and cramped enough, there's also incense burning in two bowls. It makes Smoker's head spin. The strings of lights flash on and off. Smoker already regrets having joined the company inside the tent. It's too small to fit five. Tabaqui, on the other hand, is completely happy and content. He sips some indescribable swill from a coffee cup and regales Vulture with tales of people they've met on the way here, even though they haven't in fact met anyone. Smoker starts nodding off.

"Hey, wake up," Dearest whispers. "What are you having? Pretty Flower? Steps? Night Terrors?"

"Anything but Terrors," Smoker says. The proximity to Vulture is terrifying enough. They are separated by Jackal, but still, he could reach out and touch Great Bird should he wish to. "Do you have any coffee?"

"Alas, no coffee."

Smoker is handed a cup. He takes a gulp of something so bitter and astringent that his jaws immediately lock up. He chokes on saliva, unable to either swallow the vile liquid or spit it out. Tabaqui slaps him on the back. The rest are watching with interest. The lights keep blinking.

"There, there," Vulture says with concern. "You really shouldn't jump straight on everything you're being offered, kiddo. A little taste is often enough."

Smoker takes out a handkerchief and wipes off the tears.

"Horrible stuff," he says when he's able to pry apart his locked teeth.

For some reason Tabaqui puts on dark glasses.

Crookshank clambers out to the bank and sits down under the pole marking the largest cluster of underwater stones. The river was kind to him the previous several days, and he's expecting his good luck to continue. Yesterday it brought him a tire, three bottles with messages, and an empty gourd decorated with triangular markings. What's in store for today? Crookshank throws in the line and waits.

In the moonlit grass on the opposite bank a huge white elephant grazes, covered with a striped blanket. Must have run away from its masters. The elephant worries Crookshank because it can use its trunk to fish the floating treasure out of the river, and then he'd have to somehow get to the other side and claim it back. And it's a very big elephant. *What if I tamed it? It can reach a lot of stuff with that trunk. Would be very useful—to have my very own Elephant. That's even better than a live dog.* Excited by these thoughts, Crookshank puts the fishing gear aside. But the elephant is already trampling away, its wide back flashing in the brush. And the river is carrying something dark. It fetches against the largest stone and gets stuck there, bobbing in the current. Crookshank grabs the net. He's hoping fervently that it isn't a dead dog again. The dragonflies dart too low over the water, interfering with his aim. He swats several with a towel and eats them distractedly.

Saära lives in the swamp. He is alone there except for the frogs, the singers of clear songs. He sings too when the moon is out, and his songs are beautiful. That is all he knows about himself. Saära's pale skin is wrapped tightly around his bones, mosquitoes never alight on him, knowing him to be poisonous. His lips are ghostly white. When he sings, the song distorts the whole of his face and his eyes go almost blind. His fingers tease and tear the grass, he trembles, shaken by his own voice, and he waits. The song always brings him visitors. The smallest of them sink into the mud before they can reach him.

Sixteen Dogheads sit in the grotto in a circle around a crate, illuminated by three torches and three Chinese lanterns. The seventeenth is standing on the crate. He is addressing them, slowly rotating a snow-white bone above his head. The speech flows over the sharp-eared heads and out the hole in the ceiling, up toward the twinkling stars. Dogheads listen, yawning and loudly biting out fleas.

"We seem to be confusing meters and kilometers," one whispers to another. "Do you think this might have a global significance? What's your opinion?"

"I can only see the moon," his neighbor offers cryptically. "They say that the staff still had plenty of meat left on it before he snatched it."

The youngest, in a copper collar, suddenly breaks into a howl, head upraised.

"Death to the traitors! Death!"

They bite his flanks to quiet him down.

The white bone shines, mesmerizing them.

The changeling dances merrily on the pile of fallen leaves collected here by stomper birds for their mating fair. The pile is ruined. The changeling laughs. Unable to stand the suspense any longer, a mouse bolts from under the leaves and scampers away, but the changeling is upon it in two short leaps.

"Quick, quick, go bite a tick," he murmurs as he digs a shallow hole to bury the remains of the meal.

A sweet song reaches his ears. The changeling perks up and rushes toward the voice without hesitation. He bounds through the Forest like an arrow, but stops once his paws meet the sticky swamp mud. He shakes it off in disgust. The singing grows more urgent. It calls him into the swamp. To go or not to go? The changeling comes to a decision and rolls on the ground growling. One more turn, and one more. He rises up to a human height, yawns, and plunges into the heart of the swamp, treading carefully on the tussocks. The nocturnal dragonflies dart into his face. The singing keeps getting even more sweet, loud, and seductive.

The hunters grunt as they run. The loose ends of their headbands slap them on their backs. They run single file, one, two, three of them, noisily, scaring away the wildlife. The noise is deliberate. The one they're hunting will take fright and betray himself.

That's when the pursuit will commence. The real hunt, the one they've dreamed about for so long. So they run, huffing, pounding the dirt with their boots. In fact, they too are frightened. But their quarry is not supposed to know that.

Back in Vulture's tent, Smoker finally is able to stop coughing and choking on saliva, but doesn't have time to appreciate it because almost instantly something happens to his vision. The objects around him momentarily lose clarity and float out of focus, and when they return to their familiar shapes it turns out that they have been assembled from myriad tiny colorful shards, like a bright minute puzzle. The faces of those sitting next to him undergo the same transformation. Everything is now composed of shining dots. They blink in and out and even slough off in places, and where they do there's nothingness behind them. Smoker realizes that he's going to see them all extinguished and that he just had the true nature of the universe revealed to him, which means that his life is most likely about to end.

"World falling down," he manages to utter.

This remark has a bizarre effect on the others sitting in the tent. The fireflies constituting their faces begin to roil and swarm furiously, reflecting complex and strong emotions. And then Smoker's fears come true. Everything shatters. Tabaqui's face holds on the longest, but it too crumbles, leaving behind only two inky blots—the dark lenses of his sunglasses. The black spots hang in the void for a moment and then, just as Smoker is on the verge of losing his mind, become the center of another world as it assembles quickly around them.

A very bright, very sunny, very smelly one.

The sun strokes Smoker's back, pressing him down to the ground. It's a pleasant sensation. Except there's no ground visible. It's covered with a thick layer of trash, greasy and loose to the touch. Yet, somehow, incredibly alluring. Smoker longs to dive in it, take in more and more of its smell, separating the layers of new scents until there, in the midst of it, a truly astounding aroma opens. Something is preventing him from giving in to this temptation. Must be the black glasses floating in midair. The sun turned them into two blinding flashes, but when Smoker approaches them he sees himself reflected: a pair of black white-breasted cats, one in each lens. He opens his mouth in astonishment and lets out a loud yelp. His reflections cry back at him mutely.

"There he is!"

One of the hunters stumbles. From high up in a tree, where the branches are thickest, someone's fiery eyes are looking at them.

"There he is! Up there!"

The hunters, jostling each other, surround the tree.

"Burn it? Or chop it down? Or maybe . . ."

The creature hisses, feeling its way along the trunk. The hunters rattle the tree with the butts of their rifles. The tree groans. One of them passes his rifle to another and tries to climb up. The creature in the branches hisses even louder and then spits at him. The hunter crashes down, swearing. The creature giggles and coughs. Suddenly it cuts the laughter short and slithers down into the high grass.

The hunters dash after it, screaming. The hard carapace and the fiery hair of their quarry recede in the distance.

"After him!" the hunters yell, their boots thundering and splashing mud.

The grass snails tumble down as they run past.

"Get him! Tally-ho!"

The one who got the acid in the eye shouts the loudest. The entire Forest seems to shake from their screams.

Someone who has spent his whole life hiding in the hollow of a tree has been frightened by the commotion and the knocking. He digs in deeper into the rotted wood of his hideaway and uses the hook on the end of a stick to pull the food pouches closer, one by one. Each pouch, three layers of silky leaves cemented with his saliva, and the food in the middle, is priceless. It won't do to leave them to chance. He allows one of them, the smallest, to remain exposed and even nudges it toward the opening, hoping that the invader finds it easily and goes away, satisfied, without trying to sniff out the rest.

Crookshank jumps up and down excitedly, peering into the river. "Please don't let it be a dead dog, oh, please," he begs, casting the net. The object is heavy and unwieldy. Huffing and sniffling from the effort, Crookshank pulls and pulls, until he manages to haul it completely out. He studies the river's gift intently, then bounds up with a shout of joy. It's a sleeping bag. A splendid sleeping bag, completely intact! It's blue with yellow dots. Crookshank wrings the water out of it and hauls it away to dry in his safe place.

White-lipped Saära winds down his song and lies in wait. Bare legs squelching in the mud. Closer. Closer. He stretches his neck.

A human. Dirty white pants, dirty white sweater. Long hair the color of soot. Quite young. Not a youngling, but not an adult either. Saära crawls closer and jumps.

His own scream catches up with him in the air as he twists and flops limply before his prey. Prey? Ha!

Hoist with his own petard, how sad. Saära complains until the changeling interrupts.

"Now cut it out."

Then he stops scratching at the ground and sits down in the middle of the mandala he scored into the pliant dirt with his claws.

"Why," he says, "do you walk into the trap like some common prey?"

"Curious," the changeling explains. "And beautiful. Sing another one."

Saära fumes silently. Singing for nothing? Not luring, not yearning? Shame, shame for evermore!

"All right," he says finally. "But only if you come down with me. And give me something valuable in return."

"Deal."

The changeling rises. His hair is dripping mud on his shoulders and down the back, making it look painted. And he already stinks of the swamp.

"Let's go," Saära says, backing into the narrow opening of the burrow. "It's right here."

In the Dogheads' cave, with the condensation of their breath dripping from the ceiling, torches sputtering, and the Chinese lanterns melting from the heat, Spotted Face addresses the throng.

"Tighten the collar on him! Four more holes! Who's with me?"

They whine and shuffle their paws.

"Two more! Four! No, one! All of them!"

"Casting of lots!" someone shouts, springing up and knocking the torch out of the bracket with his head. "The lot shall decide!"

They put out the torch, spraying the burning crumbs around.

The tin can lands on the floor. They impatiently bump their heads trying to distinguish the number on top of it.

"Four," the youngest one giggles. He's no more than a puppy.

Dogheads exchange confused glances. The fat white-and-tan breathes loudly, tongue hanging out. His collar is already tightened so much that there is precious little breathing room. Four more holes will rob him of it completely. They look at him ravenously and start advancing. He drops in a faint, with very little effort. They bark at him with disdain.

In the cramped burrow encrusted lovingly with shells, Saära sleeps blissfully, having had his fill of the visitor's blood. The visitor gave it up voluntarily, so it cannot be said that Saära breached the code of hospitality. The guest sits next to him, drunk with the songs.

He touches sleeping Saära and says, "Hey, wake up . . ."

But the owner of the burrow sleeps. The guest gets on all fours and scrambles out. His frozen eyes reflect the light of the moon. He heads back through the swamp and through the Forest, he walks on and on until he's tired. Then he finds a hole dug up by someone and lies down in it, hiding from the prying eyes under some branches and leaves. Once inside he starts remembering the songs he bought with his blood. He needs to repeat them before he forgets. His back is caked in drying mud. He sits up and puts his arms around his knees. The long white stems of his fingers intertwine. He recalls all the songs, from the first words to the very last ones, and falls asleep, satisfied. The Forest waves its dark branches over him.

Shielded by the darkness, the lovers kiss with wounded mouths. They have their own songs. The Forest, invisible, rustles over them too.

The short, squat creature reaches the locked door and scratches at it, whining pitifully.

The cat that is Smoker screams. Loudly and hopelessly. The dark glasses hanging in the air tremble slightly from his yells.

"Oh, come on," a voice says testily. "Not another one. Is it ever going to end? I'm so tired of this!"

Smoker closes his mouth. At the edge of the trash bin he sees two large gray cats. They look dangerous, for some reason. He tries to say "Here, kitty, kitty," but doesn't seem to manage it. The cats look at him with obvious loathing. Smoker has never been able to discern cat emotions before, but now they are crystal clear to him. The trash smells more and more beguiling, but it appears that a good rummage in it is out of the question. Too many gawkers. He tries to put his thoughts into words once more.

"Help!"

"Quit shouting!" one of the cats snaps. "Pull yourself together. Get up here."

The cat's voice goes directly inside Smoker's head. He jumps up obediently, only to flop back down into the trash. He jumps again. Same result. On the third try he manages to find purchase on the bin's curving edge, pull himself up, and sit down uneasily, doing his best to prevent either his front paws or his bottom from slipping.

"Shameful," the cat nearest to him hisses. The other one flows fluidly down the front side of the bin and darts into the bushes. There is some commotion there. Smoker leans over the edge, trying to see what's going on, and nearly falls.

"Is he trying to catch something? Someone?"

"Of course he is, you stupid human," the cat who remained with him replies. "Your shadow. You weren't planning to die a cat, were you? Especially seeing as you make such a lousy one."

I do not, Smoker thinks, offended, and remembers his reflection in the dark glasses. *I'm a nice kitty.*

The gray one snorts. Then suddenly shoots up, spreading his paws awkwardly, and plunges down. *Come on, hurry up!* his thoughts reach up to Smoker. *Jump here, you goof!*

Smoker glances down and sees the cats splayed on the ground, kneading it with their paws. They are tearing up a small patch of shadow, unaccountably darker than their own shadows.

"Jump!" they shout in unison, so loud that Smoker's almost swept off the edge of the bin. "Jump into the shadow!"

He paces uneasily on the narrow strip of metal, not daring to make the jump that looks suicidal. The cats growl menacingly. It's only the thought of what they would do to him if he doesn't do as they say that makes Smoker jump. He yowls and tumbles down, aiming for the stretched dark spot of the shadow. The hard landing on all four paws knocks the breath out of him. Everything goes black.

Smoker opens his eyes. He is inside the stuffy tent. The blinking colorful lights are almost blinding. The flap is half-open, and his motionless legs stretch out through it. Smoker's head is propped up by Tabaqui's distended backpack. He feels sick. He moans, and Tabaqui and Noble, both holding the cards, turn their heads to look at him.

"I was a cat," he whispers, his lips barely moving.

"That's nice," Tabaqui says. "Now get some sleep."

Squib, Solomon, and Don pursue Red, illuminating their way with flashlights. Solomon is sweating and out of breath. Red, glancing cautiously about, knocks at Ralph's door. The door is locked and there seems to be no one inside. Red crouches down and freezes. The three hunters stop to discuss the situation. Red listens to the emptiness of the room behind the door and gnaws at his fingernails, paralyzed with terror.

Elephant is asleep back in the Nesting, sucking his thumb. He dreams of the strange phosphorescent violet, like a small blue flame. He found it by accident on the Crossroads windowsill.

Ralph opens the door to the counselors' hallway, illuminating the doleful eyes blinking in the sudden light.

"What are you doing here? Why aren't you in bed?"

Tubby tries to crawl past him, into the opened door. Ralph intercepts him and picks him up.

"No, you're coming with me."

He starts descending the steps. Tubby twitches and grunts in his arms.

"Quiet," Ralph says. "None of this nonsense. I'm going to have a word with your minders."

Solomon switches off the flashlight, looks at Squib, and nods at the door of the teachers' bathroom.

Red is trapped inside, between the sinks and the urinals, slipping on the wet tiles. He has nowhere to run. There are only stalls here, and they are unlikely to have locks. He tries one door, then another . . . Then he's blinded by bright light. He doesn't see who's behind it, but he doesn't have to. He knows. The light is getting closer.

Butterfly, on the seat in the sixth stall from the door, listens to the sounds. He was just about to flush, but then decided not to. He snuffs out the burner and sits there in the dark. He's afraid that he'll be betrayed by the smell.

Smoker and Tabaqui crawl out of Vulture's tent. Vulture himself follows them and assists Smoker with climbing into his wheelchair. Smoker is too weak to refuse his help.

"Good luck," Vulture says. "Do not get lost in the dark."

"Lost? Us?" Jackal says indignantly.

Bird waves them good-bye and dives back inside the tent. Smoker has only one thing on his mind—get back to the dorm as soon as possible.

"I was a cat," he whispers, steering his wheelchair in the wake of Tabaqui's flashlight. "Nice kitty . . ."

"Look, it's time you got unstuck from that," Jackal sighs. "So you were, so what? You're obviously not a cat anymore."

There's a bloodcurdling scream. Tabaqui drops the flashlight.

Red closes his eyes, shrinking away from the light hitting his face. Then flips open the knife. One thing he regrets is that he didn't think to put the green shades on. But then again, who knew? He forces himself to face the flashlights. A dark bulk hurtles at him. Red jumps away and thrusts with the knife at random. Someone grabs his arm. A razor slash burns his cheek. The next one opens a gash on his collarbone. Red shrieks. Two hands jerk his head back. He breaks free, kicking out with his feet but meeting only emptiness. He manages to shield his neck, and the razor splits open his hand. Red sinks his teeth into one of the hands holding him, wiggles out of his jacket, and flops down. The flashlight beams dance on the floor. He crawls inside the nearest stall, slams the door shut, and gropes for the latch. To his surprise, he finds it and manages to fasten the door before it starts shaking under the assault from the other side. He takes a step backward and trips over a leg. Someone is lying there, between the commode and the wall separating the stalls. Red yelps.

The prostrate figure raises its head.

"Stop screaming."

Red lowers himself down on the seat, shaking. His blood appears black in the light that trickles through the door.

Blind sits up.

"It's still night, isn't it?"

"It is," Red says, sniffling. "They're killing me. Three against one!"

As if in confirmation of his words, the door flies off the hinges. Blind rises unsteadily to meet Squib and Solomon. In the next stall the water rushes down noisily.

"Damn!" Squib says, taking a step back. "There's someone else over there! And here is Blind!"

"Where did Red get to, then?" Solomon says, shining the flashlight in from over Squib's shoulder.

"He's here too. What do we do now?"

The flashlight carriers pause. Red slides down on the floor and presses against the wall, trailing blood.

Don, on the lookout, emits a piercing whistle, warning of the coming danger.

"Run!"

Solomon grabs Squib's sleeve. They turn around and run into Ralph coming in the door.

Ralph is hampered by the flashlight, so he only manages to grab Squib. With a wave of the razor, Squib escapes. Ralph swears, picks up the flashlight that fell on the floor, and sweeps the beam around. The broken stall door. The tiles stained with blood.

First came the screams. Then, from out of nowhere, R One appeared with Tubby in his arms, put him down on the floor, told them to hold on to him, and ran back. Now Tabaqui and Smoker guard Tubby, who drones quietly, drools, and constantly attempts to crawl away.

"Something's happened," Tabaqui whispers. "We need to investigate. What did you think you were doing? Have you lost your mind?" He pinches Tubby and turns to Smoker. "Listen. We're going to put him on top of you and you're going to drive ahead with him. But you'll have to hold him tight, or he'll fall."

"What about you? I don't want to hold him."

"I can't. I'm too fragile."

They struggle to pull Tubby up to sit on Smoker's knees, and then Tabaqui quickly splits. Smoker attempts to wheel after him, but finds it impossible with Tubby in the way. He's so uncomfortable that when Tubby again begins to wiggle, Smoker pushes him off, turns on the flashlight, and observes him speedily crawling away into the darkness.

There's already a sizable throng by the doors to the teachers' bathroom. Everyone shines their flashlights away from their faces, so it's hard to tell who's here. They all mostly illuminate the doorframe. Finally R One appears. He's hauling someone who can't walk by himself, and that someone is dripping. A sickening sound.

"Someone with a light, to the hospital wing!" Ralph shouts, adjusting his burden.

One of the spectators steps forward, casting a hook-nosed shadow on the wall. Vulture leaves, lighting Ralph's way.

"Well, I'll be! That was Red," Tabaqui hisses, fiddling with Smoker's shirt. "Where's Tubby? Where did you drop him?"

Butterfly crawls out, shielding his eyes.

"Get your shiners away!" he says testily.

The beams point to the floor.

"My wheelchair was supposed to be here somewhere. Where is it?"

Butterfly scuttles in a circle, like a singed moth. Tabaqui bumps him with his backpack.

"Hey! What just happened?"

Butterfly mumbles something indistinctly. Tabaqui bumps harder. Butterfly hisses and tries to swat away the backpack.

"How would I know? I was taking a dump! I've got diarrhea! I haven't seen anything. I was sitting on the can the whole time. Could be that Red got cut. Or maybe it wasn't Red. I don't know nothing. Get me my wheelchair!"

Tabaqui leaves him to his troubles.

"Useless," he complains to Smoker. "He's playing dumb."

"Let's go," Smoker pleads. "I've had enough excitement for one night. Honest. I'm done."

Tabaqui looks around, aiding himself with the flashlight.

"Still, where's Tubby? I thought I told you to keep an eye on him!"

"I don't know. He crawled off somewhere. Let's go."

Tabaqui shines the light in Smoker's eyes accusingly.

"We were supposed to take care of him. And you failed. We have to find him."

"All right. Let's go find him."

Tabaqui is in no hurry. He directs the beam at the departing stragglers.

"Wait a minute," he mutters. "Now this is interesting. Look . . ."

Something heavy flies at them out of a dark corner. Tabaqui takes a hint and reluctantly switches off the flashlight.

"Have you seen that?"

"Tabaqui, what are you doing here?" says a familiar voice. "And why did you have to bring this . . ."

Tabaqui fidgets guiltily.

"Smoker and I just went out for a stroll. Couldn't sleep, for some reason. And then—shouting, Ralph, commotion. So we came to look. Who wouldn't?"

"All right, we'll talk later. Take him back to the dorm."

"We need to find Tubby first! Ralph told us. Tubby ran away. No wheelchair, no nothing. I mean, no anything."

"Go back. I'll look for him myself."

"All right. As you wish, Blind," Tabaqui says, turning around his wheelchair. "We're going."

They are not the only ones. Tires squeak somewhere in front of them. Those in front pick up speed from time to time, apparently confident that they are driving down the middle, and immediately crash into the wall. The noise they are making allows Tabaqui to correct his trajectory. Smoker, heartened by Blind's order, dutifully struggles to reach the dorm as quickly as possible. If Tabaqui could have his way he'd linger gladly, but he's not sure that Blind isn't following them. So he's in a hurry too. Butterfly, some distance ahead, wheezily brags that his diarrhea has just saved someone's life.

Ralph walks out of the hospital wing and sees Vulture waiting for him on the landing. He is amusing himself with painting zigzags on the ceiling with the flashlight.

"You didn't have to wait," Ralph says.

"I figured you wouldn't want to go back in the dark. I'll walk you over."

"Thanks."

Ralph heads for his office. Vulture limps by his side, shining light on the floorboards underfoot. They stop at the door. Vulture directs the beam at the keyhole.

"You may go," Ralph says, unlocking the door. "Thanks for your help."

"Take this, R One," Vulture says. He rummages in his pocket and hands Ralph something. "You're going to need it."

It's a joint. Ralph takes it without a word.

"Good night," Vulture says.

Ralph slams the door behind him and turns on the light. He studies his face in the wardrobe mirror. It features a strip of surgical tape, all the way down his cheek. The cut is superficial, but Ralph can't stop thinking that he's gotten away with something. Half an inch to the left and it would have been good-bye, eye.

"Sons of bitches," Ralph says to his reflection. He walks to the window, pulls up the blind, and looks out. Then looks at his watch. Then shakes it. By his reckoning it should be morning already. The darkness outside is still impenetrable. But that's not what's frightening. Winter nights have a habit of lingering. What's scary is the way the watch hands seem to be stuck permanently on one minute before two. And it's the same with the wall clock.

"Calm down," Ralph says. "There probably is a reasonable explanation."

Except he can't find it. He could swear that when he was leaving Sheriff's room— the Rat Shepherd had a birthday bash, and it was a proper one—he looked at the watch and it was quarter to two. A lot of time has passed since then. It couldn't have been less than half an hour for the hospital wing alone. Ralph stares at the long hand, hypnotizing it. The watch runs on batteries. Batteries run out. But . . . what about the clock, then? It keeps ticking, lulling him, enveloping in domestic comfort.

Ralph draws the blinds and takes a magazine off the desk. Thumbs through it standing up. Stumbles on an article about a popular singer, notes the time, and starts reading. The article about the singer, then three more—the world of algae, this winter's fashions, sheep husbandry. He skims through the sports section and flings the magazine on the floor. The clock deigned to move to two exactly. The watch still insists on one minute to. Ralph looks at it, for what seems like another eternity, and then finally decides, with a sigh of relief, that it must be broken. And the clock as well. Yes, simultaneously. Well, it could happen, and it clearly did.

Ralph carefully takes the watch off his wrist and lowers it into the desk drawer. Vulture's present sits untouched on the armrest of the sofa. Were he to smoke it, many things would become markedly less sinister.

"Something's wrong with the time," Ralph says loudly.

A faint scratching noise makes him spin around. He notices a slip of paper being pushed under the door. He reaches the door in a single bound and throws it open. Then curses himself and opens the outer one, but it's too late. The night visitor has vanished. Ralph stands there for a moment, peering into the darkness, then goes back and picks up the sheet marked with the ridged print of his own shoe. The letters, evidently scrawled in a rush, straggle up and down and barely fit on the scrap.

Blind snuffed Pompey. Everyone saw.

Back in the Fourth, Tabaqui takes careful aim, drops the backpack on the sleeping cat, waits out a short pause, and then screams at those who jumped up on the beds.

"You can't even imagine what just happened! Unbelievable!"

His shouting wakes up everyone who managed to sleep through the yowl of the cat.

Blind's clothes stink of outhouse, of Butterfly's sickness, of Red's blood and fear. He treads slowly. His face is untroubled, like that of someone sleeping peacefully. His fingers run ahead and then return when he remembers the way. Now is the time of the crack between the worlds. Between the House and the Forest. He prefers to cross it in his sleep. When he's inside it his memory stumbles over familiar obstacles, and the body stumbles with it. When he's inside it he doesn't have command over his hearing. He doesn't hear things that are there, or hears the ones that aren't. When in the crack he doubts whether he would be able to find those he's seeking, and then forgets whom he was seeking. He could enter the Forest and become a part of it—then he'd be able to find anyone. But the Forest twice in one night is dangerous, even more dangerous than the crack that consumes his memory and hearing. Blind moves slowly. His hands move faster. They dart through the holes in the sweater's sleeves—the sleeves were too long for him so he slit them with a knife all the way down from the elbows. His bare heels, black as soot, stick to the floorboards.

A beam of light hits him in the face. He walks right through it, oblivious. A hand catches his shoulder. Blind stops, surprised that he hasn't heard any steps.

"Come with me. We need to talk."

Blind recognizes the voice and submits to it. Ralph's hand doesn't let go of his shoulder until they are at the door.

The office is like the jaws of a trap for him. Blind hates it. The whole of the House is his domain, but the offices fall outside of it, those snare-rooms smelling of iron. Everything else he owns, but in them he doesn't even own himself. In the offices there are only voices and doors. He enters and hears the click. The trap has sprung. He's in a void now, alone with the counselor's breathing. There's no memory here at all. Only the hearing. He hears the window and the wind oozing through it. Also rustling, the way paper rustles. The paper in the three-fingered hand of Ralph.

"You were there. When Red was cut. I saw you."

"Yes," Blind says carefully. "I was there."

"You heard those who did it. You recognized them, obviously."

Ralph's voice, sharp as a knife's edge, floats back and forth, now near, now far. Battling the wind. There really is wind. It rings in Blind's ears, touches his hair. Something strange is happening to him. It's not supposed to be like that here. He hears the Forest in the stuffy office.

It's right outside.

It creeps closer.

It scratches at the door and groans with its roots.

It waits. It calls.

Run away, over the wet moors, under the white moon. Find . . . Who? Someone . . .

"What's going on? Did you hear me?"

"Yes." Blind tries to blot out all sounds except the voice. "Yes, I hear."

"You are going to leave them alone. Understand? We already got Red, and that's enough. Yes, I know the Law. Three against one and all that. But I don't care. This time the Law will have to be set aside. By you."

Blind listens. To this strange person who lives in the House and doesn't know what the House is. Doesn't know about the night and its own laws.

"The night brought them to me," Blind says. He feels like he's talking to a child too small to understand. "The night woke me up and made me hear. Hear the three hunting the one. Why? I don't know. No one knows."

"You are not to touch them. I forbid it. If anything happens to them you are going to be sorry."

Blind listens patiently. It's the only thing that's left. Listen when you can't explain. Thorns are springing up on the road to the Forest. The internal clock had chimed morning long ago. But the night doesn't end. Because it is the Longest Night, the one happening but once a year. And this conversation doesn't end. They both have their own truths, him and three-fingered Ralph.

"Do you hear?"

He does. He hears streams disappearing underground. Birds and frogs vanishing in the air. Trees walking away. The sadness of it.

"Not a single hair on their heads. Or you'll be out of the House before you can count to one. Got it? I'll make it my personal business."

Blind smiles. Ralph doesn't understand that there is nothing except the House. How is it possible to be out of it, then?

"I know you killed Pompey. The principal could find out, too."

So that must be what's on the paper that R One is clutching in his hand. The crumpled whisper of a snitch? *Red's scream that chased away his sleep . . . The smell of blood and the broken door.* He suddenly remembers who it was he was supposed to find. Tubby. The crack closes. The wind is storming the House, it's cold outside, and it's snowing.

"Stop smirking!"

Ralph's hands jostle him unexpectedly roughly. There must have been some words he was supposed to say. But he doesn't have them.

"I don't have the words you want, R One," Blind says. "Not tonight."

The breath of danger becomes closer. He can't explain anything. He follows the Law. He lives the way the House wants him to, divining its wishes. He hears what others can't. The way it was with Pompey.

"You're barking up the wrong tree, Ralph," he says. "It will be exactly the way it must be."

"You little brat!"

The air suddenly grows solid, becomes blobs of cotton wool. Blind's stomach fills up with glass. The glass breaks with a crash and stings him from inside.

"Shhh," Sphinx hisses at himself when he stumbles over a loose floorboard.

Humpback hurriedly aims the flashlight down. They are looking for Tubby, even though Blind actually promised to find him. That's according to Tabaqui, who woke them all up to relate the saga of his adventures. Sphinx is reasonably sure he knows where Tubby might be located, and pities him.

It's time for the morning to arrive, but the House doesn't know that, or doesn't care to know. The floorboards squeak disgustingly. A dog howls somewhere in the Outsides. It's noisy behind the doors of the dorms, and the pipes sing in the bathrooms.

"Not many are asleep," Humpback notes. "Practically no one."

"It's not every night that Leaders are being deposed," Sphinx says. "Each pack probably had its own prodigal Jackal."

They pass the teachers' bathroom. It stares at them menacingly, as befits a crime scene. They spook two shadows who shrink from the light, whispering.

"First tourists," Humpback sighs. "By morning it's going to get crowded here."

Sphinx is silent.

"Could it be that Blind has found him already?"

Humpback would like to keep the conversation going. It's soothing to him. He doesn't like being out at night.

"If he had, he'd have brought him. Half an hour is enough for him to find anyone, wherever they might be. More than enough," Sphinx says.

"Why isn't he back, then?"

"Ask another. I'm here with you, not there with him."

It stinks of cigarette smoke on the stairs. On the landing below them, someone sneezes sleepily. Someone who's listening to a portable radio.

"Going up?" Humpback says, surprised.

"There's one thing I want to check," Sphinx says. "I have a hunch."

Tubby is asleep, leaning against the door to the third floor. Shapeless and miserable. He sighs heavily and mutters in his sleep. Humpback lifts him up, revealing a half-dried puddle and two chewed-up guitar picks. Tubbs was probably using them to try and pry open the lock. Humpback, naturally attuned to the suffering of the Insensible, is almost in tears as he wraps Tubby in his coat, narrowly avoiding getting tangled in his own hair. Sphinx waits, banging his heel against the railing. The stairway drafts nip at his bare ankles. Tubbs grumbles and sniffles but doesn't wake up. The walk back takes longer. Humpback struggles to light their way because of bundled Tubby in his arms, and Sphinx can do nothing to help him without the prosthetics. The pocket-radioed someone sneezes again. The sky in the Crossroads windows is still pitch-black.

"Give me the flashlight," Noble says, rolling at them out of the darkness.

Humpback, startled, barely manages to hold on to Tubby but passes the flashlight over gratefully.

"What are you doing here?"

"Taking the air," Noble snaps. "What do you think?"

Two more, Sphinx says to himself, keeping count. *Now there's only Blind.*

Vulture, limping, hauls something bulky in the direction of the Nest. It trails behind him on the floor. He stops and greets them in his usual immaculately polite fashion.

"Nice weather," he says. "I hope you are faring well. Noble I already had the pleasure of encountering."

"What about Blind?" Sphinx says.

"Alas, no such luck," Vulture admits, visibly crestfallen. "Pity, I'm sure."

The five of them proceed together. Vulture doesn't let out a single word about Red. He talks exclusively of weather, and even when his flashlight illuminates Blind near the Third, he informs him only that "Oh, the weather outside is delightful." Blind's response is barely intelligible. Vulture bids them good-bye and disappears behind the door, carrying in front of him the bunched canvas of the tent and the poles crisscrossed with straps. The beam of Noble's flashlight jumps and shakes.

"Where've you been?" Sphinx says to Blind.

The anteroom meets them with bright lights, falling mops, and shaggy heads in the doorframe. Humpback brings sleeping Tubby inside.

"There he is, our dear tubbylicious maniac!" Tabaqui's voice enthuses. "Our beloved adventurer . . ."

Blind takes a detour into the bathroom. Sphinx follows him.

"Whose blood is that?"

Blind doesn't answer. But Sphinx isn't expecting him to. He lowers himself down on the edge of the low sink and observes. Blind, his face in the other sink, waits out a bout of nausea.

"The night has been going on for too long. Too long even for the Longest," Sphinx says, mostly to himself. "I don't like them in general, and this one in particular. I think that if everyone went to bed it would end sooner. So, whose blood?"

"Red's," Blind says darkly. "Later, OK? I feel really sick now. Our old friend Ralph just kicked the dinner out of me."

Sphinx sways impatiently on the edge of the sink, licking a bleeding spot on his lip.

"Because of Red? Was it you who cut him?"

Blind turns his face, with two red sores in place of eyelids, in Sphinx's direction.

"Don't be absurd. Because of Pompey. If I understood him correctly. He knows. Somebody snitched. He was rustling a scrap of paper all that time."

"Why now? I mean, tonight? Has he gone mad?"

"Could be. Certainly a possibility, if you listen to his blabbering." Blind bends down to the sink again. "Or if he hasn't cracked yet, he's going to soon. Bet you he's shaking all his watches right now, one by one, and changing the batteries in them. Trying to figure out who's punking him. Who bit the morning off and gobbled it up."

"Don't laugh, or you'll throw up again."

"I can't. He ordered me not to touch them. Bleeping Solomon and Squib along with Don. Couldn't see them himself, but considers it his duty to intervene. 'I know your Laws,' he says. *I* don't know our Laws. I don't, and he does. I should've asked what he meant when he said that."

Sphinx sighs.

"Now, correct me if I'm wrong. Solomon, Squib, and Don cut Red, and Ralph hit you because you wouldn't promise to leave them alone? Why do I get the impression there's more to it than that?"

"He punched me because he thinks I don't talk politely enough," Blind says, straightening up.

"Do you?"

"Depends." Blind adjusts the sweater drooping off his shoulder. "Damn, I'm going to fall out of this thing. Is this what they call cleavage?"

"It's what they call a sweater that's three sizes too big. So was it because of Solomon, or because of Pompey?"

"Because of nerves. He got cut too. So of course he's jumpy. And now those snitches . . . He made me wipe it all off before letting me go."

Blind frowns and goes silent. Sphinx doesn't like the expression on his face. He climbs down from the sink and comes closer.

"Something else?"

Blind shrugs. "I'm not sure. Maybe he didn't notice. I mean . . . people don't usually pay too much attention to the exact composition of someone else's vomit, do they? What do you think?"

"They usually don't. Why? Was there something to pay attention to?"

"Well . . . Honestly? The mice didn't have enough time to get digested. And there wasn't much in there besides. That could disguise them, I mean."

"Blind. Enough," Sphinx says, wincing. "Spare me the details. Let's just say I hope with all my heart that Ralph wasn't looking too closely at how you redecorated his office."

"Me too. But the silence that followed was a bit strange. I'd even say stunned."

"How is a stunned silence different from a regular one?"

"Different shade."

"I see," Sphinx says. "Well, if it's the shade, we're all screwed. It means he saw. And what his thoughts on that are we'll never know. Which is for the best."

Blind grins.

"He that increaseth knowledge?"

"Something like that," Sphinx says.

"This Ralph fellow sure is meddlesome. Gadding about at night . . . sticking his nose in other people's business. Bugging them with idiotic demands afterward. Irritating."

Blind takes a step away from the sink, jerks the towel off the hook, and wipes his face. Sphinx studies the footprints on the tiles. Bloodred.

"Your feet could do with a washing too. Where did you manage to cut them?"

Blind runs his hand over the soles.

"I did, huh. I don't remember where. That dump on the way, probably." He adjusts the sweater again. "Look, I'm really tired right now."

"Why do you always put on those rags?"

Sphinx is almost shouting. Blind doesn't answer.

"Why do you walk over glass barefoot?"

No answer. Sphinx's voice drops down to a whisper.

"And why the hell don't you even feel that you're bleeding until someone tells you!"

Blind is silent.

Sphinx sighs again and walks out quietly.

The light is still on in the dorm. Noble is smoking, wrapped in the blanket on the edge of the bed. Smoker, in a hushed whisper, recounts to Lary and Humpback the horrors of finding himself inside a cat's skin. Tabaqui, his face still bearing traces of total bliss, is asleep, clutching the backpack turned inside out.

SPHINX

THE LONGEST NIGHT

Tabaqui's tale, take four.

Afternoon tea, take three.

Jackal is alert and perky. He's already had time to doze off, wake up, provide additional details that he seems to have missed the first three times around, and start on the composition of a song worthy of the occasion. Lary and Humpback, in coats over pajamas, are crouching around the coffeemaker like trappers around a campfire.

"Some people have all the luck . . . Getting to see all that stuff," Lary sighs—and launches another half hour of Tabaqui's rapid-fire gibbering. Everyone's sick of it by now, except for him and the Bandar-Log.

Blind returns, a pale emissary from the world of shadows. From head to toe, exhibit one for Jackal's gruesome fantasies. The pack studies him and his stained sweater. Mostly the sweater. Naturally. It's not often you see something like that.

Tabaqui even pauses for a while, preening himself proudly, as if to say "See what I mean? The night is full of horrors!" Like it was he who personally dunked Blind in blood and vomit. Sinister visions loom before the pack, and I suddenly notice that Smoker is nowhere to be seen. I wonder if he's been drowned in the toilet. It's been constant vigilance with him recently. He's acquired this nasty habit of methodically getting on everyone's nerves.

"What a dirty . . . oh-oh-oh . . . sweater you have," Jackal's syrupy voice is chanting. "Where, oh, where did you manage to get it that way?"

Pale One ignores Jackal's entreaties and crashes down on the bed. Lary, shaking the remains of his sideburns, winks at Humpback. Humpback turns away.

"So," Black says in a disgusting tone of voice. "Yet another Leader bites the dust?" Who is he addressing, I wonder.

Tabaqui takes it to be him and immediately begins rehashing the gruesome narrative for the fifth time.

"We hear someone screaming. So I say, 'Something happened.' So we go looking, and you can't believe what we see . . ."

Black walks out.

"It's R One running from somewhere in the direction of the stairs," Humpback finishes the sentence. "How about enough, Tabaqui? How many more times are you going to go over this?"

Tabaqui takes offense. The way babies usually do when someone takes away their favorite toy.

Noble, still wrapped in a blanket, looks at me bright eyed.

"Want to play some chess?"

Hasn't had enough playing, obviously. Half the night spent over cards doesn't count. Apparently no one needs sleep in this room except me. I don't need it either, but it's all I can do not to yell at them. Pack them away to bed, turn off the lights, and in the darkness wait for the morning to come, pretending to slumber peacefully. I don't like this night. Or any of the other nights like this, starting from the very first. The morning after that first Longest was much, much worse than the night itself. I'm lucky not to remember almost any of it. With one exception. We all have our own well-worn nightmares. Mine is the white sail. Even now, when I can remember loads and loads of bad stuff to balance it, it still is without equal. It's not that it simply keeps me up at night, no, it shakes me up and fills my throat with tears. I love Jackal dearly, but I can neither understand nor accept his fervent passion for the Longest. He did live through that first one with me. With all of us. How can he still manage to enjoy them so much? Is it possible that he doesn't remember? I walk to the door, probing Tabaqui's suspiciously selective memory for the umpteenth time. I have to find Smoker. I need to assemble them all here, in the dorm.

"And what do you know, it's R One with Tubby. He tosses him over to us, bang! And those screams, screams everywhere . . ."

It's dark in the anteroom, but the light is on in the bathroom, and voices are coming from over there. I lean against the doorframe and listen. I don't have to see them to figure out who's bullying whom.

"It was me, but not exactly me," Smoker explains. "I was scared half to death, and at the same time it was kind of pleasant. I don't know how that works . . . Knowing that you look like that and not dying right then and there."

"What else did you expect, doing junk?"

I don't see them, but I know that Black's chin is suspended now over Smoker's head like a hammer over an anvil. And when it strikes we're going to see sparks.

"A cat, a kangaroo, a dinosaur . . . Whatever's your heart's desire, it can be arranged here. All you have to do is ask. Jeez! Crawling over to Vulture and guzzling crap in his hole! He hasn't eaten anything *but* dope for the last hundred years! If you need to kick the bucket quickly, then sure, come for a visit and help yourself to his goodies. Just don't whine afterward that something didn't go quite the way you figured. You're lucky to be alive. He was a cat, imagine that!"

"That's not what I mean!"

Poor Smoker. He's been boxed into a corner and tries to bite back, though timidly. He doesn't know whom he's dealing with.

"That's not my point . . . I'm talking about how it made me feel. I liked it, you see?"

"Yes, I see," Black echoes sourly. "Do you see where this is going, who it is you are trying to buddy up to?"

"But Tabaqui . . ."

"Don't tell me about Tabaqui. Better yet, don't say anything at all. Just think. Go back to the room, look at them all really hard, and think. What did Blind tell you?"

"Not to go out at night."

"Ha!"

Black tries to cram his entire stock of irony into that one syllable.

"But that's exactly what you're saying!"

"Except I was in the room the whole time. While he was—who knows where? Have you seen him? The way he looks?"

The door squeaks. I interrupt my listening session and take a step back, hiding under the coat rack. It's someone small and dark, tracking close to the wall.

"Who?" I call softly to the visitor.

"Me."

Ginger's voice.

"It's me, Sphinx." Her hand touches me and flees. "Are you hiding?"

"Not anymore."

I come out into the sliver of light on the floor seeping from under the bathroom door. We continue the conversation in whispers.

"What's wrong?"

"I have to know. Red. What's happened to him? People say all kinds of things . . ."

The Sepulcher is sprouting out of her words. Three kids in a trashed room. Girl's hair, bright as a flame. And the pillows flying from one bed to the other, spraying feathers.

"It's all right. He'll live. Just got cut a bit."

I'm saying what I think is the truth, not what I learned from Jackal. If Jackal is to be believed, Red's corpse is already cold.

"Thank you," the girl whispers in the dark, and starts crying.

All right, Sphinx, where's your shoulder? Come on, get it out. That's about the only thing you've got.

She finds it herself, by touch. We're standing there in the shadows, her face buried in my jacket. Water is rushing down in the bathroom, and Black's voice continues tormenting Smoker, pouring poison in his ears. In the dorm Tabaqui is composing a song about the night's events, and the one event he considers the most entertaining is that the guy that this girl crying into my shoulder thinks of as her brother got cut. A perfect subject for a nice song. I am fuming, even though I'm not sure who or what is more deserving of my anger. Probably this night that refuses to end.

"Let's go," I say to her. "We'll have some tea."

Now how to go about shutting up Jackal?

"No. I can't. I only wanted to find out about Red. I knew you guys would know . . ."

Lucky she can't hear either the song or Black's mutterings.

"Come on," I say. "You can spend the night with us. Tabaqui is going to tell you all about it. He was there, you know."

"But . . ."

"What is it?"

She takes a hesitant step back toward the door.

"Noble is going to take it the wrong way. We had a talk. Today. He came to see me. So if I came to your place now . . . That would look like an answer."

"Do you want to answer him?"

Silence. Of a more confused than an angry shade. At least that's what I read into it. Maybe I'm just fooling myself.

"Do you or don't you?"

She is still silent.

"Gingie?"

"Let's go." She grabs my sleeve. "I have no idea what I want now. But I know I don't want to go back."

We go together. Our arrival in the room cuts the song short and causes a state of general confusion in the pack. They come to relatively quickly.

Tabaqui delivers a welcome oration. Lary waves his hands invitingly from the cups to the coffeemaker and back. Humpback runs out, balancing a stack of ashtrays. Alexander steps into the saucer of milk for the cats and spills it all over. I lead Ginger to the quadruple bed. She sits next to Noble, and Goldenhead's eyes light up with a possessive flame. He bashfully extinguishes it with his lashes.

"Ginger is asking after Red," I explain.

It sounds like a bad pun.

"Oh, Red! What about Red?" Tabaqui switches gears, instantly reviving all of the corpses he has inventively piled up. "Nothing much happened to him, really. Ralph came in just in the nick of time and saved him. Here's how it all went down . . ."

BOOK THREE

THE ABANDONED NESTS

THE HOUSE MALE STUDENTS

FOURTH	THIRD	SECOND
	BIRDS	RATS
—	—	—
~~BLIND~~	∞ VULTURE	(RED)
SPHINX	LIZARD	VIKING
∞ TABAQUI	ANGEL	~~CORPSE~~
~~NOBLE~~	DODO	ZEBRA
HUMPBACK	(HORSE)	(HYBRID)
? ALEXANDER	BUTTERFLY	(MONKEY)
(LARY)	DEAREST	MICROBE
SMOKER	GUPPY	(TERMITE)
TUBBY	(BUBBLE)	SUMAC
	BEAUTY	PORCUPINE
	ELEPHANT	CARRION
	FICUS	RINGER
	SHRUB	WHITEBELLY
		TINY
		GREENERY
		DAWDLER
		> SQUIB

SOLOMON

AS OF THE END OF BOOK THREE

SIXTH HOUNDS	FIRST PHEASANTS	LEGEND
—	—	—
(BLACK)	<u>GIN</u>	~~STRIKETHROUGH:~~ WENT OVER COMPLETELY
OWL	<u>PROFESSOR</u>	**BOLD:** MOVED TO THE OTHER SIDE (THE SLEEPERS)
<u>CROOK</u>	<u>STRAW</u>	
(GNOME)	<u>STICKS</u>	
~~SHUFFLE~~	<u>BRICKS</u>	<u>UNDERLINED:</u> WENT INTO THE OUTSIDES
(WOOLLY)	**CRYBABY**	
>LAURUS	<u>BITER</u>	(PARENTHESES): LEFT WITH THE BUS
<u>RABBIT</u>	<u>GYPS</u>	
(ZIT)	<u>HAMSTER</u>	
~~SLEEPY~~	<u>KIT</u>	>: LEFT BEFORE FAIRY TALE NIGHT
(GENEPOOL)	>BOOGER	
>DEALWITHIT	>CUPCAKE	∞: MOVED TO ANOTHER LOOP
<u>SPLUTTER</u>	>SNIFFLE	
>HEADLIGHT	**PIDDLER**	?: UNKNOWN
<u>HASTEWASTE</u>		
>EARS		
>NUTTER		
(RICKSHAW)		
(BAGMAN)		
TRITON		
FLIPPER		

SPHINX

I am stretched out on the damp grass, feet up on the bench, face turned to the sky, which has just finished weeping. My feet in muddy sneakers are crossed up there on the seat of the bench, and the mud on them gradually lightens in color as it dries out, flaking off onto the rickety slats. Too fast. The summer sun is relentless. In another half hour there won't be any trace left of the short rain, and an hour later anyone who'd want to lounge here would do well to bring sunglasses. But I still can look at the sky with impunity for a while. It's bright blue behind the spiderweb of the oak branches. Below them is the gnarly trunk, a jumble of interwoven ropes turned to stone. The oak is the most beautiful tree in the whole yard. Also the oldest. My gaze slides down from its top, from the thinnest twigs all the way to the fat roots. I notice a thin, faded scrawl scratched into the rutted bark just above the back of the bench: "remember" something and also "lose." I raise my head to see better. I've learned to decipher writings much less legible than that.

Remember L. N. and never lose hope.

L. N. The Longest Night.
Apparently for some people it means hope.
I'd laugh if it weren't so sad. To flee from the House, where similar writings snake along the walls, intertwining and twisting themselves into spirals, biting their own tails, each of them a scream or a whisper, a song or an indistinct muttering, making me want to cover my ears as if they were really sounds and not simply words—flee them only to end up here admiring this very small but very scary sentence.

I am a tree. When I am cut down, make a fire with my branches.

Another one. Also cheerful.

Why do they have this effect on me? Maybe because they're out here, not in there on a wall, lost within the tangled web of other words. Here, unfettered, they sound more sinister.

And I really wanted to get some rest—from the House, from the words. From the exhortations to make merry—"WHILE YOU STILL HAVE TIME!" . . . From the hundred and four questions of the "Know Thyself" test (each one more vapid than the one before it, and don't even think of skipping subparagraphs). I ran away from it all. Out of the chaos and into the world of silence and of the old tree. But someone came here ahead of me, dragging along his fears and hopes, and mutilated the tree, forcing it to whisper now to anyone who comes close: "Make a fire with my branches."

The oak spreads those knobby branches majestically toward the sun. Ancient, beautiful, serene, like all its brethren ready to suffer the worst of the indignities inflicted on it by humans, without fear and without reproach. I suddenly get this picture very clearly in my head, of it standing amid the ruins of the demolished House, up to its knees in brick rubble. It stands there, still stretching upward. The letters scored into it still implore not to lose hope.

A cold shiver runs down my spine.

"Do you sometimes experience an irrational fear of the future?" This is question number sixty-one. They told us that all questions on the test were significant. That each added important detail to the psychological profile. In our case they could've very well started and ended the test with this one.

The crunch of gravel underfoot. I close one eye.

The sky . . . The branches . . . The legs in black trousers.

"You comfortable?"

Ralph, his jacket unbuttoned, the knot of his tie askew, sits down on the bench and lights a cigarette.

"Very."

I don't get up. I've already said I was comfortable, so now I have to look up at him from where I'm lying. Ralph is cool with that. He puts the lighter back in his pocket and takes out a folded piece of paper. Unfolds it and puts it under my nose. It's a list. Six names.

I know three of them well. Squib, Solomon, and Don—the Rats who split from the House, went to the Outsides. The first time they did it was back in the winter, after the Longest, but were caught quickly and brought back. They ran away again almost immediately. Over the next month they got returned twice more. For thirty days the inhabitants of the House gleefully ran a pool on how long they'd manage to hold out. Their names on "Wanted" posters became a fixture on the first floor. It was as if Shark finally cracked, went totally nuts and started to equate the first floor with the street, imploring the imaginary passersby from its walls: "Anyone with information regarding the whereabouts of the above-mentioned youths . . ."

Then they brought back Squib, alone. What happened to the other two "above-mentioned" no one had ever found out. Squib couldn't muster the courage to run away by himself and remained in the Den, a grotesque shadow of his former self, shrinking from even the youngest Ratlings.

"Yes?" I say. "The first three names are Squib, Solomon, and Don, and I've never seen the rest. Have they also run away?"

"Not exactly."

Ralph turns his list over and studies it carefully, apparently trying to make sure he's got it right.

"The rest are from the First," he says. "They haven't run away yet, but are rather keen to try, for some reason."

I sit up. Warm and toasty from the front, damp and freezing from the back. All covered in sand and ants. I brush them off, trying to get my spinning head under control.

"They call their parents," R One continues, eyes buried in the list. "They write letters to the principal. They demand to be released from the House immediately. One might assume that, were they not so . . . limited in terms of movement, they already would have followed the example of those first three. Almost like they are being terrorized. You wouldn't know anything about that?"

"No," I say. "First I'm hearing of it."

Ralph puts the list in his pocket and leans back. He is clearly not happy with my answer. But I really have no idea why all of a sudden three Pheasants simultaneously have decided to get as far from the House as possible. In fact, from what I know of the First, the question is what took them so long.

Ralph admires the view of the sky through the branches, enjoying the dappled sunlight on his face. He's got this face of a cartoon villain. No one who's really evil would have a face like that. Only in the old movies. And not even a trace of gray in his hair, not a hint of a bald patch, even though he's been working here for . . . what, thirteen years? At least. Iron Man.

"All right," he says. "Let's assume you don't know. Let's hear what you think. What is it they fear? What are they trying to run from?"

I shrug. "I don't think it's a question of fear. They're being squeezed out. The First is good at that. And not only the First . . ."

I can't stop myself in time because I remember Smoker. His name could have been right there on that piece of paper without even that much of an effort from us. But then, we're not Pheasants.

"Who are you thinking about?" Ralph perks up. He has this goofy look, like a bloodhound that finally has picked up the scent.

"Smoker. You can add him to your list if you'd like."

"Oh. I see . . ."

R One goes silent and pensive.

I probably shouldn't have told him about Smoker. Counselors are unpredictable creatures. You never know how they are going to interpret the information you give them. On the other hand, I doubt that my mentioning Smoker could do us any real harm.

"Do you remember much of the last graduation?"

I wince. There are things that just aren't mentioned. Rope in the hanged man's house and all that. Ralph knows this as well as I do.

"No," I say. "Very little. Only the night in the biology classroom. We were locked in it. Almost nothing of the morning. Bits of it. Here and there."

He flicks away the cigarette.

"Were you expecting something different?"

"Probably. I myself wasn't expecting anything at all."

To get up and leave now would be impolite. Even though it's the most logical thing to do. I'm very uncomfortable with the whole setup, my head being at the level of his knees. So I move onto the bench next to him.

"You are a Jumper, aren't you?"

I look Ralph in the face. He is completely out of all imaginable and even unimaginable bounds. What did I do to provoke this? Actually answered his questions? That might be it. Anyone else in my place would just tell him to get lost. There are countless ways of doing it without resorting to open insolence. Ralph wouldn't bat an eye if I were to say "What was that? A jumper? How do you mean? Do I look like a kangaroo to you?" He's most likely expecting exactly that. But as I run through the possible responses in my head, each feels more repulsive to me than the last. It's better to simply tell him to go to hell. But I can't do that, now can I. Because last winter when we sent Blind to him, asking him to find out at least something about Noble, he didn't tell us to go to hell. He didn't feign surprise. He didn't even tell us off for being impertinent. He went who knows where and did so much more there than we ever could have hoped. If I played dumb right now and started prattling about kangaroos I'd lose all respect for myself, however much I have left of it.

"Yes, I'm a Jumper. Why?"

Ralph is stunned. He looks at me with his mouth hanging open, searching for words.

"You sound very calm about it."

"I am not calm," I say. "I'm nervous. I'm just not showing it."

"But other . . . ," he stumbles and continues, "people like you never talk about it."

"Because I'm a bad Jumper. Defective."

Ralph freezes, his eyes glinting hungrily. He thinks he's found something incredibly valuable while rummaging in a dumpster, and can't quite believe his luck.

"Bad, what's that mean?"

That's when I realize that I probably need this conversation even more than he does. Because no one ever asks you about obvious things. Or things that seem obvious.

I lean back and close my eyes. The sun is directly in my face. A good excuse for not looking at the person you're talking to.

"I don't like it."

I don't need to look at him to see how surprised he is, and I answer his next question before he gets it out.

"I don't Jump. You don't have to do something only because you can. And you don't have to like doing it either."

I open my eyes and see him not even breathing, as if his breath might somehow spook me.

"It happened to me on that very morning," I say. "For the first time, and for six years. When I woke up and they brought me a mirror, it wasn't that I got scared of my bald head, as everyone assumed. I was scared to see a little boy there. Because I was no longer him. If you can imagine that, you'll understand why I haven't Jumped since then."

"Are you saying that ever since that time . . ."

"Yes, ever since that time. I haven't and I'm not planning to. Unless it happens by itself. A nervous shock, a sudden fright. That kind of thing leads to Jumping sometimes. Isn't it the same with you?"

"I've never . . . ," he begins.

"Of course you have. You just forgot. People forget it very quickly."

There we go. Now he's choking. And I'm not handy with the taps on the back. It's very hard to gauge the strength of a slap with prosthetics. This ruins many friendly gestures for me. I pull my legs up on the bench, put my chin on my knee, and watch him coughing spasmodically. A child playing with matches. Makes a fire, imitating his daddy lighting them, and then is honestly surprised when real firemen show up in a real fire truck. You'd think he had those books when he was a kid where this causal relationship was featured in big letters, short words, and colorful pictures.

"And now you'd like to go away," I say to him. "Or at least for me to stop talking. Everyone gets that, so don't worry."

Ralph is hunched over, fingers buried deep in his hair. I can't see his face, but the posture tells me that he's not feeling too good.

"I'm not going anywhere," he says. "And I would like you to continue."

Resilient, isn't he?

"Too bad," I say. "I like this conversation less and less the longer it goes on. Besides, I'm waiting for my date."

He doesn't believe me. I lean back again and close my eyes.

We banged the hell out of that door. We almost smashed it to splinters. If they hadn't let us out I'm sure we would have. Because by morning nothing was holding us back anymore. We had sat there through the night, docile and patient, respecting the will of the seniors and their big reasons. We knew we were too little to be taking part in the proceedings. The snub made us want to cry, but we held on. That night wasn't the last for us, but it was for the seniors. It belonged to them. We spent it on two mattresses on the floor of the biology classroom. They had remembered to bring in the mattresses. And a bucket.

"There were fourteen, fifteen of us," I say to Ralph. "They hadn't given us time to dress or put on shoes. Siamese, Stinker, and Wolf they took away separately. Must have figured that a mere locked door never would have stopped those guys. And no one had been able to locate Blind. He'd disappeared before they came. The only one of us who hadn't been locked up that night. The pajamas we were in, Magician's crutch, and a pack of candies were all we had. We'd gone through the entire pack in the first half hour, and the crutch we used in the morning to bash the door. We threw everything at that door trying to break it, because by then it was obvious that they'd forgotten about us being there, and that we could only rely on ourselves if we ever wanted to get out."

The unpleasant memories make Ralph cringe. He was there too. Most likely he was among those who did come to let us out. They tried to corral us, but it would have been easier to hold on to fourteen streaking meteors. We swept away our saviors and tore down the hallway, screaming hoarsely. Some of us were already bawling, even as we ran. Simply because we were scared. We did not yet know what had happened. Where it was we were in such a hurry to get to, I still cannot understand. But I remember well what did manage to stop us. The puddle. A small pool, richly crimson, right at the Crossroads. And in the middle of it, a half-submerged white sail. A handkerchief. It still comes to me in my dreams. Was that puddle really as boundless as it seemed to us then? Anyway, it made one thing absolutely clear: no one could lose that much blood and live. I looked at it, transfixed, and all the time I was being jostled from behind by those who kept arriving. They shoved me in the back, forcing me to take tiny steps in its direction. A step, then another, and another. Until I realized that my socks were soaked through. I don't remember anything after that.

After six long years I returned and finally learned what had come to pass that night. But it forever remained for me something remote, out of the distant past. I hadn't lived through it with the others. One of the most horrible nights of the House begins and ends for me with the crimson puddle, the half-submerged sail of the handkerchief, and my own cold and sticky socks.

When I awoke, after six years by my time and a month for everyone else, I saw a strange creature in the mirror. Bald, scrawny, much too young, staring wildly . . . I realized that I was going to have to start my life all over again. And cried. Because I was tired, not because I had no hair. "An unknown virus," they explained. "You are most likely no longer contagious, but we'd like to keep you quarantined for just a while." The days spent in the quarantine saved me. Gave me time to adapt. To get rid of some of my grown-up habits, to get used to the new skin. The Sepulcher staff dubbed me Prince Tut. The transformation from Prince Tut to Sphinx took me another six months.

Ralph is silent. An eternity passes.

"Curious," he says. "There was blood everywhere. The floor, the walls. Even the ceiling, I think. But your memory only managed to hold one single puddle."

"Oh, it was enough," I assure him. "More than enough. My puddle contains the whole of that Night, and all of the days that followed."

"And then . . ."

"And then nothing. I'm not telling. It's irrelevant."

He sighs and pulls out the cigarettes again.

"All right. Anyway, thank you. You are the first to talk to me about these things at all. The first in thirteen years. I probably shouldn't be asking you any further?"

"You shouldn't. The less talking about . . . these things, the better."

"Are you trying to scare me?"

"I am," I say. "Trying, that is. But you are too headstrong to get properly scared. That's not good. The House demands a reverent attitude. A sense of mystery. Respect and awe. It can accept you or not, shower you with gifts or rob you of everything you have, immerse you in a fairy tale or a nightmare. Kill you, make you old, give you wings . . . It's a powerful and fickle deity, and if there's one thing it can't stand, it's being reduced to mere words. For that it exacts payment. Now, with you duly cautioned, we can continue."

"Risking . . . what?" he asks carefully.

"Your guess is as good as mine. Probably better than mine. You know much more than you think."

That seems to annoy him.

"Would you stop playing with words!"

Silly man.

"Oh, I don't think you've ever heard real wordplay," I say. "There are grand masters in the House. I am not worthy of being in the same room with them."

That's when Mermaid finally appears. Comes down from the girls' porch and shuffles across the yard toward us. Flared jeans, crocheted vest, and impossible hair, almost down to her knees.

Ralph squints. Looks at her. Then at me. It's an odd look. One I'm very familiar with. Mermaid is sixteen, but she looks all of twelve. With her looks you'd expect her to still play with dolls and believe in Santa Claus. Which is why any adult who sees me and her together looks at me as if I'm a pervert. It rubs Mermaid the wrong way. It doesn't bother me.

She stops a fair distance from us, not wanting to interrupt. Just stands there looking at us. Those aren't the eyes of a child at all. They're too big for her small triangular face.

Ralph gets up. Gives his pockets a few slaps, checking that everything's still in place. Has the good sense not to say "So, that's your date, huh?" Mermaid lip-reads phrases like that from very far away.

"I guess that's it, then," he says. "Thanks again. I'll go and digest what you said."

"Good luck," I say. "And be careful. We can walk in circles around those mysteries, write poems and sing songs, call ourselves Jumpers or Striders, but we're not the ones who decide here. It's all being decided for us, however scary that sounds."

Ralph is reluctant to go, aware that we are unlikely to ever return to this conversation.

"You be careful too," he says finally, and walks away.

When he passes Mermaid he nods to her and says something. Then cuts straight across the grass, and the hunched crows jump away, grumbling about the violation of their personal space. Humans made the pavement, they should keep to it.

Mermaid runs over and plops down on the bench next to me.

"Wow. Why is it I'm so afraid of him? He's harmless!"

"Really?"

"Don't laugh." She frowns. "Yes, I know it sounds silly, but you should have heard the stories they tell about him."

Mermaid dives into her thoughts, then shakes her head resolutely.

"Yes, it is silly. He's nice."

I laugh.

"He said hello to me and didn't call me baby, imagine that."

My imaginary hat is off to Ralph.

"What were you discussing for so long? I thought he'd never leave."

"It's a secret," I say. "A sinister mystery. Go, tell that to those who were spying on us from the windows."

"Sure, I'm so gone," she snorts. "They can't wait. Already waving messages to me in code and preparing the recording equipment."

She shifts closer to me, completely unconcerned that she won't be learning the details of my conversation with Ralph, and begins wrapping my leg in her hair. Wrapping and tying each strand with knots.

"That's new. Some kind of sorcery?" I say. "It's not like I was going anywhere."

"Tabaqui gave me this book," Mermaid explains. "Very interesting. It's called *Kama Sutra*."

"Oh boy," I sigh.

"Says there that to attract your beloved you need to bind him with fragrant hair, adorn him with flower garlands, and wreathe him in clouds of incense. It's all described very convincingly. Oh, right, and also anoint him with aromatic oils."

"You don't say. What does it recommend to do with the oily bodies of the suffocated beloveds, still wrapped in hair and garlands? Put them out on the porch to serve as a warning to passersby?"

"Nothing." Mermaid shakes her head as she ties the knot on another loop under my knee. "It does not mention those weaklings at all."

Then we just sit on the bench, or rather lie on it. Quite likely in accordance with the wisdom of ancient texts regarding the appropriate behavior for lovers. The oak shuffles from root to root and shifts so that we end up in its shadow. Of course, it might just be the sun moving in the sky. But I prefer to think it's the oak.

I fall asleep, for real this time. Mermaid's presence, her hugging my knee—it acts like a sleeping pill. She has this catlike ability to induce calm and drowsiness, and also to sleep herself in the most uncomfortable places. If only I had fingers I could have conjured sparks out of her hair, the kind cats give off when someone strokes their fur. I sleep and not sleep at the same time. I am on the bench here and now but everything else moves away—the writing on the bark, the conversation with Ralph. Everything except me, asleep, and my girl. The girl who wears my old shirts, sleeps curled up on my legs as if they were an easy chair, wraps herself in the sleeves of my jacket, disappears at the first rumble of a thunderstorm and reappears again once the sun is back out. It's her most incredible feature, that limitless capacity for empathy, for picking up someone else's mood, for dissolving into thin air when that's what is needed.

Someone's voice on the wind. I startle and open my eyes. My leg is free of hair, and Mermaid's face is looking down at me, very somber and intense. She's only like that when she's sure no one can see her.

"Every little thing wakes you up," she says. "The tiniest peep. I don't like that. You should sleep calmly and soundly."

"Snoring and heaving my broad hairy chest," I say. "Except I wouldn't call those Hound howls tiny peeps. I wonder what's gotten into them. Probably the freshly minted Leader flexing his muscles?"

"Not freshly at all. You just can't get used to it."

It's true, I'm having a hard time accepting the fact of Black becoming the Sixth's Leader. Even though upon reflection that's exactly the place for him. Pompey's throne didn't even need adjusting for size, and Hounds received what they constantly crave—a strong, steady hand on the collar.

"You know what's funny?" Mermaid says. "The way your voice changes when you talk about Black. It's not even yours anymore. I can't understand why you hate him so much."

"Didn't I explain about a dozen times already?"

"You did. But I don't believe your explanations. You aren't that vindictive, to keep hating someone just because he bullied you a long time ago. It's not like you at all."

She sounds so sure of what she's saying that it makes me uneasy. I am not the flawless, ideal Sphinx she fell in love with. And that's not the worst part. The worst part is that I would very much like to be him. That just, kind, magnanimous guy she likes so much. If I were like that I'd probably have acquired a halo by now. Shined with divine light and trailed heavenly fragrance, like a saint.

"It is too like me. It *is* me. My true evil nature!"

Mermaid doesn't even argue, just bites on her finger and goes pensive. She detests arguments. Having to prove and defend her point of view. Which does not make her position any weaker. Not in the slightest.

I bump her lightly with my forehead.

"Hey. Don't go too far. I can't see you all the way over there."

"Tell me something interesting," she says immediately. "Then I'll stay."

"What about?"

Mermaid's face lights up. It's amazing how she loves stories. All kinds, it doesn't matter. Lary's tedious laments, stumbling over each syllable, Jackal's epics, convoluted and branching in all directions—nothing fazes her. She's ready to spend hours listening to anyone who'd have an urge to unburden themselves in her company. This to me is her most unusual quality, one the least common in her gender.

"So, what kind of story?" I ask, unable to resist her infectious eagerness.

"Tell me how Black became Leader."

"Not Black again! What's so special about him?"

"You offered a story and asked what kind. I'm interested to hear about him because to me he's interesting. As someone you dislike."

"Dislike, now there's an understatement."

"You see? How can that be not interesting?"

I can only sigh in response.

"So you don't want to tell me a story anymore?" she asks, or rather clarifies. "Just as I thought."

"No, that's not it. I'm afraid you'll be disappointed. I don't really know how it happened. I think I can guess. He and Blind were stuck in the Cage. Nothing to do. Blind got this bright idea to send Black to the Sixth as Leader. That wouldn't be the most bizarre thing that someone came up with while in there. So he suggested it, and miracle of miracles, Black agreed, even though it's completely against his principles to agree when he can refuse. And that's how it came about. It might not have been exactly this way, but I wasn't there, and no one was, apart from the two of them, which means that only they can know for sure what really happened."

"How come they were stuck there together?"

"That's a different story altogether. One I don't much like to recall. It started back on the Longest, and I don't particularly . . ."

"Wow, the Longest!"

Mermaid tugs at my shirt imploringly.

"Please tell me, please? The Longest—that's so exciting! All those tales . . ."

"That you've heard a thousand times already. Ask Tabaqui. He'll read you the two-hundred-line poem he composed in honor of that night. And sing you any of the ten songs on the subject. Ginger was with us that night too. Let her tell you all about it. Why should I repeat something that you know by heart? That everybody knows?"

"Ginger is Ginger, and you are you. I'm not asking you for a retelling of Tabaqui's songs and poems. But if you're so uncomfortable with this, don't say anything at all, of course. I just don't understand. They all like to remember that night . . ."

"Ginger included?" I say, sure of the answer.

"No, not her. She cringes and changes the subject. Like you."

"All right. Come up here. Listen, and maybe you'll understand why it is that I don't like to recall that night when everyone else does."

Mermaid quickly clambers up on the bench and makes herself comfortable against my side. Her long, loose vest is crocheted so that the rows of fluffy knots running across the whole width of it can move freely, with the openings then exposing any writings on the shirt underneath that Mermaid feels like sharing with the world. She has more than a dozen different shirts with scribbles on them, fit for any occasion. When she sits the way she does now the only message that's visible is on her left shoulder: *I remember everything!* What this *everything* includes is not clear. It could be that other messages help clarify the situation, but I can't see them.

She wraps the stained sleeve of my sweater around her neck and hangs her tiny backpack on the back of the bench.

"Now you may begin."

I sigh and dive into the vortex of blood that is the Longest, into its impenetrable darkness, the stuff of House legends. I dive in and swim through its muck and gore, invariably the favorite subject of those legends.

I begin where the Longest began for me. Anticipating the gasps from the audience along the lines of "Are you saying that you were simply asleep before that?" I even pause dutifully to give Mermaid the necessary space for expressing her indignation, but she does not avail herself of it, and so I stumble forward—after Humpback, who is lighting my way as we search for Tubby.

Truly "The Hunting of the Snark" has nothing on "The Hunting of Tubbs," especially the way Jackal performs it. "Tenderly passionate lover, lover who conquers darkness, scratching through walls of stone, gnawing through doors of iron . . ." And so on, in the same breathless key. With slight variations, where, on the narrator's whim, Tubby morphs from a tender lover into a libidinous maniac and back, while the finding of him by Sphinx, "he who at length discovered," changes by degrees from one stanza to the next so that I perform progressively impressive feats, ranging from digging Tubby out from an avalanche of bricks, the remains of the wall he destroyed (listening to this version I picture myself as a huge shaggy Saint Bernard, complete with the Red Cross bag across my chest), to extracting him (using my teeth) from the boudoir of the innocently sleeping stark-naked tutoress. My teeth generally play a decisive part in the proceedings while Humpback's participation is mostly glossed over, so it is I, with Tubby hanging down from my jaws, who crosses the interminable hallways, somehow capable at the same time of holding an extended conversation with him, chiding him gently while he whines contritely. The reality is so colorless and dull, so paltry compared to that elaborate nightmare, that I race through it in double time, through my entire stumbling night journey, up the stairs with Humpback, down the same stairs with him and Tubby . . . Noble, Vulture, Blind . . . And here we are, back in the dorm, where Tabaqui is already rehearsing the early drafts of the tales and songs he is going to dedicate to this L. N.

"Now you see, this stripling was hell-bent on going for a stroll in the dark. You realize, don't you, what would have inevitably transpired were I not by his side? We moved in pitch-darkness, but nevertheless we moved, and I turned to him and said, 'Be it as it may, my friend, but you're definitely crazy!' 'If only I could have known!' he replied."

Electric light assaulting the senses, faces in sleepy torpor. Lary clucks excitedly, kindling into the fire of Jackal's imagination. The House is tightly wrapped in the blackest blanket up to its roof, making me wonder how much air we still have left here, inside it, and what is going to happen when it runs out.

The pajama-clad, crazy-eyed pack, the dying embers of the feast in honor of Ginger, who is sitting between Noble and me, I count the minutes, the hours, and even allow myself to hope that maybe, just maybe there is enough air for all, enough night straight on till morning, but here comes the gaunt, doleful silhouette, Vulture holding a coconut, nothing but mourning in his clothes, his eyes, and his voice, he looks like a somber Hamlet with Yorick's skull all withered from a long stint in the grave. With his arrival, all hopes of time finally getting unstuck are on hold, at least until we get to hear the dismal news he's about to impart.

Vulture rolls the woolly orb around in his hand.

"I am loath to have to tell this to you, I really am, but there is no one else I can turn to at this juncture, so . . . Long story short, there's a stiff in our bathroom. I have just discovered him there."

Jackal's harmonica squeaks forlornly.

"My sincere apologies," Vulture sighs. "I am truly sorry about this."

Crab, whom we are carrying to the first floor an hour later, in life was a greedy but discreet creature, with but two fingers on each hand. Then he, who knows why, quietly found himself within the realm of the Nesting and quietly met his death there from who knows what. And became the mystery of the Longest, one that was never unraveled.

We would carry him, wrapped in the Crossroads window curtain (the off-white train ostentatiously dragging on the floor behind the procession), to the lecture hall and leave him there, surrounded by lighted candles in tin cans, very festive and very alone, and on the way back Black would feign insanity. Or maybe really go nuts. Yes, I know how it feels to play a patient observer and wait, wait until that singular moment when you can finally act. Anyway, he'd loudly and unequivocally proclaim his opinion of the situation. The impossible night would be ripped in two, and into that gash in the blackness would pour the swarm of fireflies, the flashlights in the trembling hands, and the raging creature in the middle of the hallway would crouch and scream, his squeals penetrating through walls and ceilings, up and down and in all directions, piercing the immovable Time itself. I thought then, and remain sure now, that it was this clamor that started the seconds flowing, as if someone, jostled by it, woke up in a world that has domain over this one, stretched sleepily, banged on the clock that was stuck and got it going again.

It is possible that Black should be thanked, for that if for nothing else, but I somehow don't have the slightest inclination to do so. It would become a matter of habit for many, when remembering the Longest, to mention the frayed nerves of poor little Black. What exactly happened to his nerves to make them so much more frayed than anyone else's, including my own, I do not quite understand. As for his lost marbles . . . I've never before chanced to see the marbles that, having been lost, were then found so quickly and restored to their proper place without any visible detriment to the owner. It might even be argued that by pitching that suspiciously convenient fit he made the first step in the direction of the throne vacated by Pompey, though at the time it looked more like a quick saunter toward the tender embrace of a straitjacket. I understand, it's comforting to shake one's head sadly and point out the tough guys, like, say, Black, snapping under pressure—implying, of course, your own mental toughness that's quietly superior to his. "We've seen things worse than that. Yeah, rough night, that one was. Poor Black . . ." Luckily, I don't have an elevated opinion of my own toughness, so I'm naturally doubtful when I see Black's nerves snap, especially when it happens so unexpectedly and so dramatically, but all that would come later. Back then, when I heard his squeals, I felt only numbness and an overwhelming desire to extinguish that sound. Many would share it at that moment. The human mass, clinging to Black like ants to a caterpillar—"Murderers! Enablers of murderers!"—would roll down the hallway, muffling the screams. By our doors he'd manage to shake us off and even stomp on some, increasing the amount of loud cursing in the dark even more.

As I make my way toward Black (to disrupt, to seal, to stamp out forever and ever that screeching orifice!) I would stumble, knock out someone's tooth with my shoulder, and bite my own lip clean through. By the time I reach the door to our dorm there would be no Black, or his victims. They'd all have filtered inside, and there, on the territory that's been out of bounds for strangers since the beginning of time, the Night would unspool another loop of its interminable tail while Black and Blind entertain the assembled public by staging a "delectable rumble," kicking dust and blood out of each other. The spectacle that would inspire certain Logs, Jackals, and other sundry historians to reach unsurpassed levels of excellence. Tabaqui, to pick a name at random, would in all seriousness claim that the most damaging blow Black delivered was with the words "Love me, love my dog!" To which Blind, though busy parting the floorboards with the back of his head, still managed to yell "Dream on!"—prompting Black to thump his chest, roar, bend the iron bars of the headboard, and bark, "In that case, prepare to die!" Fascinating, isn't it. The bending of the bars especially. No one bothers to inquire to what possible end Black might have wanted to do that, they just open their mouths and take it all in rapturously. And so do I. I don't recall Black specifically banging Blind's head against the walls, but it is possible that when Blind fell a couple of times he might have bumped his head. I emphatically do not recall Blind tearing Black's jaws (that scene is obviously borrowed from Greek myths). And I am pretty sure Black did not tumble down with a cry of "I'm finished," and Blind did not then place his foot on the fallen body before wearily lighting a cigarette.

I too feature in those stories, quite prominently. I'm always somewhere close, beside myself with rage (that's actually a realistic touch) and "waiting for the most opportune moment." I wonder which moment that was. I guess I expected Blind to quickly lay him out (or the other way around, though far less likely), and then I'd jump in and throw them all out of the room, all those scowling, drooling gawkers, most of whom at any other time would not even dare dream about entering our place, but once there immediately felt themselves at home, covered the floor in spit, and even started rummaging in the back cabinets under the radar. This made me break out in horrible nervous hives right then and there. We never could find some of the tapes, cups, and ashtrays after, to say nothing about cigarettes—those were swept clean. I anticipated that, and wasn't much surprised. I also anticipated the outcome of the fight. No one has ever managed to lay out Blind one-on-one, so I wasn't too worried until it became obvious that he was ending up on the floor more often than Black was, and was taking more time to get up, too. That's when I remembered he'd already taken damage from Ralph that night, and became really nervous. Time after time Black pounded his leaden fists into Blind, and Blind doubled over, and Black waited until he straightened up to pound again. The third time around, Blind crashed to the floor. There wasn't much more noise from him falling than there would be if a bar stool fell, but the spectators gave out an almighty yell that continued all through Pale One's attempts to restore the supply of oxygen to his system. I tried to picture in my head the nightmare that living under the Leadership of Black would be, failing utterly, which convinced me that if I couldn't even imagine it, then it couldn't exist in this universe. I flogged my imagination, scratching myself with my chin in all places I could reach, while all around me handkerchiefs and beer-bottle caps went flying, tossed by the ecstatic audience. I've never seen anything more disgusting. Blind got his breath back and stumbled a bit while getting up, grabbing the headboard of the bed near where I was sitting.

"Horror and shame, isn't it?" he whispered in my ear.

"Wake up," I pleaded. "Fight, or he'll break you."

"I guess you're right," he said. "I seem to be a bit out of practice lately."

While we were thus conversing Black decided to finish the job. He took a step toward Blind and aimed a swing at him so hard that, had it landed, we'd have had to haul Blind down to the first and put him next to Crab. Blind ducked and appeared to lightly touch Black in return. Black gasped and fought for breath for at least a minute, and after that it was all over. I didn't even have to look to know how it would end.

I see . . .

Blind tiptoeing away from Black, hunched, eyes half-closed, lips fixed in a grin. He's not circling, he's not stepping. It's more of a dance. A soft, silent dance of Death. There is an exceedingly beautiful and fascinating quality about it, which I've observed dozens of times and never could figure out where it came from. It's that leap into a different world, a world without pain, without blindness, where he stretches time, making each second last an eternity, where everything is just a game, even though it's the kind of game where he could flay someone alive or turn him inside out with a flick of a finger. I know that for a fact even though I've never seen him actually do it. I feel the scent of madness on him in those moments, too pronounced not to scare me half to death. In that strange world of his he turns into something that is not human, something that creeps closer, slinks away, flies on rustling wings, spits poison, seeps through the floor. And it laughs. It's the only game Blind knows how to play with someone else. Black has no hope of catching him. Black has been left on this side. His time is too slow.

I see . . .

Black crumpling. Falling down on his back, like a big doll on a string. Pale One materializes next to him and yanks the string, jerking him upright, then dropping him, again and again. He's playing. Having fun. Except it's too creepy to be funny. He doesn't even seem to touch Black, and at the same time smears him across the floor, from the door to the window. Everything is covered in Black. In his teeth, in his skin. Laughter glints from under Blind's hair. Humpback and I jump into action simultaneously, he off the bed, I off my perch above it. The rest of our guys were seemingly waiting for the signal and now join us. While we're busy scraping Black and Blind off each other, Tabaqui notices the opened cabinets and the beer puddles on the floor.

"What the? I count to three, then I start shooting!" he screams, frantically searching for something in the pillow mound. The guests bolt for the door, tripping over each other, and I almost expect Tabaqui to snatch a machine gun from under the covers and make mincemeat out of a couple of straggler Logs, but by the time he emerges from there, with only a harmonica in his hands, there is no one left in the room but us. He grumbles and stuffs the harmonica back, postponing the dark revenge until a more convenient time.

I sit down on the floor. Someone pushes Blind in my direction. He crawls over, shaking and coughing, buries his face in my shoulder, and freezes. His sweater stinks of a garbage dump, with whiffs of a sewer. I am immovable, like a statue. Alexander and Ginger artfully decorate Black's body with surgical tape. Lary shuffles around the room, scraping a broom across the floor. It's quiet. Dead quiet, if you don't count Jackal's fevered muttering. Mona decides for some reason that Sphinx is the only safe place left in the room and jumps on my knees. Saunters back and forth, twice, brushing my shirt with her tail, kneads me gently with her paws, and lies down. I still haven't moved. Smoker, his hands shaking, puffs on a cigarette over my ear. My shoulder is propping up Blind, my knees are a cat's bedroom. Now I only need Nanette to land on my head, and it's a perfect shot for *Blume*: "Sphinx at rest."

Alexander and Ginger finish tending to Black and look at Blind uncertainly. Tabaqui crawls closer and also gawks.

"Horrible," he whispers. "Look at him. Vampire, pure and simple."

I look out of the corner of my eye. Blind is asleep, his face calm and peaceful. He never has a face like that when he's awake.

Lary drops the broom and stares at Blind in shock.

"He's right, you know. Why would he be so blissful all of a sudden? He shouldn't be blissful. And he shouldn't be sleeping. I don't like this."

Tabaqui revels in it.

"That's exactly how they are, Lary my friend. Lying in their caskets, happy and rose cheeked, grinning from ear to ear. That's how you tell their ilk. A stake through the heart!"

From the corner of the room where Black is located suddenly comes a sound, half moan and half roar. Noble is fussing over the swollen, eyeless head with alcohol pads, while Nanette peeks at his hands from behind the pillow.

"A stake," Tabaqui keeps muttering. "This, you know, sharpened thing . . ."

Black groans again and pushes away Noble's hand.

"We should drive one through your tongue," Noble snaps. "Can't you give it a rest, Tabaqui? Aren't you tired at all?"

"Right. Where was I? I seem to have lost the thrust of the narrative . . ."

"Look," Ginger cries all of a sudden, pointing at the window. "There, look!"

Humpback and Alexander run to the window. We turn around and look there too. Into the blue-black sky where a feeble sliver of the morning is trying to part the darkness.

"Morning!" Lary exclaims majestically, waving the broom. "The sun!"

There is, of course, no sign of the sun. Lary straightens up and salutes with the broom in the direction of the window. Smoker and I receive a shower of slowly falling gray clumps of dust mixed with cigarette butts.

And that was how that disgusting night ended. Not at the exact moment when we noticed the first glimpse of the coming morning, of course. And not even when the morning finally came. I mean, we realized that what surrounded us wasn't the night anymore, but it was hardly possible to call that gray substance "morning." A transition between one night and the next, that would be more accurate. Especially considering that none of us managed to either go to sleep or wake up properly. I don't even remember if we had any breakfast that day. I don't remember much at all, really.

Myself, at certain moments. Blind with the guitar next to me, and it's dusk in the room again, must have been evening. Rows of empty bottles on the nightstand, even though I can't recall anyone drinking. Lary's angry yelp, as he lifts a bottle: "So that's what they've been doing here, while we worry about them and stock up on provisions there." By "there" he most likely meant the canteen, but was that lunch or breakfast? And "they" must have included me as well, because I don't remember leaving the room or eating anything, which means I was among the drinkers.

Noble, pulling the blanket over sleeping Ginger. Black, in a cloud of smoke on his bed. Not much of him visible, just one eye and the cigarette, everything else covered by the crisscrossing white stripes of tape. Blind nodding to his own song. He's grayish blue, the color of faded jeans. This must be how Lazarus looked right after having been told to rise up and walk. Still in the remains of the white sweater, reeking of wine and alcohol pads. Hunched over the guitar, twanging the strings, mumbling indistinctly. Something about a forest, empty paths, and the streams made bitter by the grass growing along them.

Ginger, sleeping with her hands tucked between her knees, curled up in the pillows. Hair like the scarlet feathers of a woodpecker shot through the heart, and everything else mundane and commonplace in comparison. Her lying there also feels routine, like something that's always been thus, no one gives her a second look except for one person, who's wrapping her in the blanket, like a miser hiding his treasure from prying eyes.

Lary picks up a bottle and shakes it indignantly.

"So that's what they've been doing here, while we worry about them and stock up on provisions there!"

"Don't waste your breath," Black says. "It's not worth it."

I listen. I listen very carefully to the tone of his voice, almost gloating, and I wonder what could he, beaten, tired, and hungry, be gloating about. Then I look at Blind and understand what it is that's making him gleeful there under the bandages. His happiness looks like Blind's face with a swollen eye and a split lip. That on the day when they found a corpse. On the day when any scratch is a mark of involvement. Involvement and guilt. He doesn't care that he's completely covered with those marks, the important thing is that Blind's got them.

Forest . . . Dark and fragrant, smelling of mint . . . Sweet songs, lures for the strangers . . .

Black stubs out his cigarette against the six-pack abs of the bodybuilder on a poster above his bed.

"What do I say to Ralph when he asks about the shiners?"

Beaten, tired, he earnestly solicits his packmates' opinion regarding correct behavior in a tight spot. Not a reason at all for someone to break out in hives from the cheeks all the way down to the navel, the kind that are going to still itch a week later, yet I feel them coming, the tiny burning gnats spreading like wildfire, bitey and sticky-footed, as if someone has thrown a handful of them under my collar.

"Say whatever you were planning to when you kicked off the hysterics," I suggest. "Or don't say anything at all. Both of those choices work fine for your purposes."

The sparks of rage directed my way seep through the strata of tape.

"What's that supposed to mean?"

"Nothing. Just that I wouldn't be in such a rush to return to normal after a bout of insanity, if I were you. Didn't you go nuts, Black? As recently as yesterday, if the memory serves. So hold on a bit with the reasonable questions. That would definitely look more natural."

I talk and talk, can't stop talking, my speech sounds more and more like a sermon, and I even remember it being eloquent and not simply protracted. But then again, maybe that's just wishful thinking, because I also vividly recall a finger that I waved in front of Black's Band-Aided nose, and where would I have found a thing like a finger on my body? I presented a broad outline of the classic descriptions of madness, from Ophelia to Captain Ahab, discoursed on pig tails peeking from under the skirts and on lovers jumping out of windows to escape jealous husbands while leaving their pants behind. I expounded extemporaneously and convincingly, interrupted only by Tabaqui's rapturous applause and the attacks of my biting gnats, and when I was finished Black asked, "What was that crap supposed to mean?"

Tabaqui advises Black to "let the sleeping dogs lie," because "it's obvious he's extremely, and I mean extremely, tense, isn't that enough for you?"

"Listen to the voice of the people," I say to Black. "You, Ophelia who somehow stopped just short of the river."

Upon hearing the mention of a river, the actual candidate for the madhouse, our beat-up Leader and Forest pilgrim, nods and imparts, "Rivers are a tricky substance . . . You never know if you can drink out of them. Best bet is to lie down and listen for a while, until you're sure that there are frogs in it. Then drink all you want, it's not going to be poisonous."

"Thank you," I say to Blind. And then to Black, "There. Learn from the masters."

Then, without listening to his aggressively barking repartee, I leave, the scratchy bugs having almost finished eating me alive. I bump into Ralph on the way out, also grayish in color from the sleepless night, and also wearing surgical tape on his face.

What happens next is easy to predict, and I do predict it. The Cage for Blind and Black, where they quite probably are going to tear each other to pieces from boredom and mutual antipathy; interrogations and investigations into the circumstances of Crab's death; state of confusion among Rats temporarily left without their Leader; and many other things, both related and unrelated to those mentioned above. What I totally fail to predict is that, after a long time spent in the Cage, Black and Blind are going to come to an agreement regarding the Sixth. I can't imagine either how bored they were for Blind to come up with an idea like that, or how much Black loathed returning to the pack to accept it. It's possible that if they had spent a little more time in there, Blind would have thought of something even better. The Cages are conducive to introspection, unless you're stuck there for too long. The longer you sit in them, the harder it becomes not to give in to fear, and that kicks all the thoughtfulness right out of your head. But that's if you're alone; for two it wasn't unheard of to last a week. The detention of Black and Blind smashed all Cage records—eleven days and change. Good thing I'm bald, or my head would have acquired that exact number of snowy-white hairs, one for each day of their absence. We have Ralph to thank for it, or rather his concern for the Rat runaways. He got it into his head that Blind was going to squash them as soon as he had a chance, so he did his best to make sure Blind didn't get that chance, leaving Blind with plenty of time for all kinds of novel ideas. He'd discuss them with Black, and the rest of the time they spent playing chess and peeling the upholstery off the walls, looking for the secret cigarette stash. That was a traditional endeavor for visitors to the Cage ever since that time when Wolf had announced publicly that he'd sewn a carton's worth into its walls somewhere. It was most likely a joke and treated as such by everyone. Except that after two days in the Cage, the sense of humor is usually the first thing to go, and then people start looking. That's why the chintz featured rips and gashes, marking the places where the prisoners' fingernails and razors had gone to work. There already wasn't an untouched patch more than four inches square. It was customary to sew back up the checked-out places, for which purpose there was always a threaded needle left stuck right above the door. Black and Blind didn't need it, because they went past the upholstery, past the foam, and even past the plasterboard, all the way to the brickwork.

Shark sincerely suspected them of trying to tunnel into the Outsides. After Squib, Solomon, and Don, he became very jumpy in that regard and spent a lot of time questioning Black about where they would have gone if they had managed to get out. He must have imagined that this way he'd be able to track those three, as if the Grayhouse folk, like spawning salmon, were only capable of moving in one direction. I haven't personally witnessed the devastation the merry couple wreaked, but judging by how long the repairs took, the Cage sustained some serious damage.

I realize with a start that I've been talking for a while now without hearing any response, and look suspiciously at Mermaid's head, which has slipped down from my shoulder.

"Hey. You didn't doze off, by any chance, great lover of stories? I've been full of sound and fury especially for you, you know . . ."

"Of course not," a pointedly alert voice replies, slightly muffled by the sweater sleeve. "I've been listening all this time. And thinking."

"What exactly were you thinking about, sleepyhead?"

She gently pushes away, and I again see that she "remembers everything" in the gaps of her vest.

"I'm thinking how the same story comes out completely differently depending on who's telling it. And for all that, none of you is really lying."

"Because whoever's telling the story creates the story. No single story can describe reality exactly the way it was. I told you that I personally prefer Tabaqui's version."

"And I prefer to listen and compare."

Groaning, she straightens her legs. The sneakers, in service for so long that they're now uniformly gray, have been darned with thread where the canvas meets the rubber. Baby shoes. So touching I can't look at them without misting up. When Mermaid shifts, the knots on the vest shift too, exposing a different slogan. *Hate to the grave!*

"What's with the hate?" I ask.

"I don't know. Just in case. I thought I needed something sinister too."

"And I don't think you do. At all."

The *Hate to the grave* slides back under the knots, and my mood lightens. I know it's all child's play, but I take these things seriously. Maybe because I happen to know that the games are never just games in the House.

Mermaid pulls up her knees and hugs them. No slogans, no shape anymore, just a flowing mass of hair.

"You think that I'm not cut out for strong feelings. That they don't really suit me, right?"

I've trodden on the favorite toe. I keep forgetting the Gray Mouse Complex.

"You see, I don't have a personality. I'm so dull inside. Faded . . ." It's no use fighting it, and it drives me mad with the unassailability of its tenets. "Take Ginger, for example . . ." That is, take someone for whom controlling her emotions is a daily losing battle, who bursts into fireworks at the slightest touch or even without it, jumps from laughter to tears and back with nothing in between, wears all her loves and hatreds on her sleeve: now that's beautiful, that's feminine, that's attractive, like bright patterns of a butterfly's wing, it's a whirlwind, a torrent, a trap; but very few people can stand Ginger's flamboyant personality for more than a couple of hours at a time, even when her feelings are directed not at them but elsewhere. Long live Noble, Noble's patience and everything else that he has and I don't, I guess this is something that he knows and understands, because he used to be that way too, until he went in for a stint where the real crazies live, and yes, they do look great together, this couple always at the point of combustion, fire-haired Isolde and sapphire-eyed Tristan, both on the edge, both wide open, breathe in deeply and hide the breakables, but one thing I don't understand in all of this is why should anyone envy it and agonize about it, I could never understand this and in my attempts to convince Mermaid rose almost to the Noble-Gingerish heights of passion, except it always ended up the same. "It's nerves, simply nerves, and in this case they hang out like live wires, so anyone passing by trips them; it's got nothing—nothing—to do with personality and its richness, you silly little girl!" But instead of a reply I get only pursed lips, and all my gnashing of teeth and banging of head against the wall do nothing, the matter is closed and not subject to negotiation.

And then there's Rat, a predator, as like Blind as a twin sister, except less friendly, no comparison with Mermaid, thank God, except that my sincere "thank God" is a cold comfort for Her Mousy-Walking Grayness.

I look at her, hidden under hair all the way down to her shoes, then close my eyes
and embrace her tightly with my nonexistent arms. Mermaid readily leans on me as if
I really did that, and I am struck again by her sensitivity. She always responds to the
touch of my ghostly hands, even when she's upset and has other things on her mind.
Like now.

"We're not going to discuss exceptional personalities, right? Remembering them
one by one, marveling at how beautiful and special they are?" I whisper to her. "If you
don't mind, of course. Do you mind?"

"Of course not."

She shifts, throwing back her head to better read the expression on my face, but
I move my chin to block her view, again and again, until she abandons her attempts
and curls up in a tender catlike knot, so familiar to my touch. "You must hate me
for constantly bringing this up. You had such a miserable voice just now. I'm talking
about it too often."

"No. Often is not the problem here. It's just that I detest this entire subject:
'Wouldn't you like it if I were more like . . .' No, I wouldn't like it. And I never will. It's
possible that sometime, on a beautiful day filled with divine wisdom, you'll understand
this. Then I'll go to Tabaqui and ask him to commemorate it by adorning me with
festive ribbons and colorful tattoos."

She pulls a long cord out of her vest, or maybe it's a thread, and brings it to her
mouth. Now she's going to gnaw on it until it almost dissolves into a sloppy mess.

"I guess I'll have to give this shirt to you now. You've got people to hate until the
grave, so it should be yours by rights."

"Who are you talking about?" I say suspiciously, lightly tapping my chin against
her part. "It's not Black again, is it? Would you like to tell me something I don't know,
or is it just that his manly charm has you in its grasp? I don't remember us ever spending so much time discussing him."

"What if I do want to tell you something? About him?"

Now it's my turn to crane my neck, trying to look her in the eye.

"Just promise me you're not going to say you're madly in love with him. Everything
else I think I can handle."

She pushes away, shaking her hair.

"Picture him in your head. It shouldn't be too hard."

"Why?"

"No reason. Just get the picture of him as you remember."

I straighten up and dutifully imagine Black. In all the shiny glory of his splendid
muscles. It really is not hard.

"All right. Now what?"

"Now tell me, who is he trying to look like?"

"He's trying to look like an idiot. Who else?"

"No, that's not it. Someone you are very familiar with. You're going to be surprised when you get it."

I am already surprised by what she's saying, so I carefully study the image of Black in my head. My imaginary Black is a carbon copy of the real one. I've lived side by side with him long enough to get full measure of the man.

"I don't understand," I have to admit. "He looks like only one man, himself. There are no others like him."

"I'm not talking about his looks. It's about his style. Like, for example, the way he started dressing after becoming a Leader. Did you notice any changes in that?"

Black did change his style since assuming the responsibilities of the Alpha Hound. He abandoned tank tops, shaved his head, and stopped wearing suspenders over baggy pants. Those made me want to throw up for many long years. You could even say that his taste in clothes underwent a marked improvement. It didn't help to make him look like anyone other than himself, of course. All that I relate to Mermaid.

"All right, then tell me who else, among those now living in the House, shaves his head, drapes jackets over his shoulders, wears bandanas, and wraps the ends of shoelaces around the ankles?"

"Jackets—only me. As for the shaved head . . ." I suddenly get what she's driving at. "You're crazy! I do not shave my head! And I only started wearing a bandana because you gave it to me! You can't be serious. He hates me with a passion! He's made it a point never to go in the shower after me!"

"Maybe so." Mermaid shrugs. "It's just that all this jumps out at anyone who cares to give an unbiased look. He imitates your walk, your attire, he even started talking like you. And all of that began when he moved to the Sixth. That is, to where you can't see how he looks and what he does every day."

"And what does that prove?" I ask dumbly.

Mermaid is silent. Eyes like two green grapes with the pips showing through the semitranslucent skin. Very somber and serious eyes.

"Oh god, that's horrible!"

I cringe and glance up at the windows of the Sixth, shining silver in the reflected sun. Almost fearing that behind each of them hides Black, a grotesque facsimile of me, shaven headed and frowning, in a pirate-like head scarf covered with skulls and bones. It's a nightmare.

"And besides, my bandana is unquestionably more beautiful, tending as it does more to floral motifs. But it's a matter of taste, naturally."

"You should be ashamed, Sphinx." Mermaid laughs. "Next thing, you're going to be saying your legs are longer . . ."

"And they are! You mean they aren't? And my head is of a much more dignified shape. He can't even dream . . ."

"Stop being such a baby! Or I'll have to get you a bib and a onesie. You'd think he's doing something bad to you."

We go silent and study the surrounding landscape for a while. No, that's not a fight at all, we never fight, just a sensible time-out for processing of new information. Usually people smoke in pauses like this one, but Mermaid is a nonsmoker and I don't have any on me, so I bravely do without, only allowing myself to sweep the ground with my eyes, because it's in places like this where the good cigarette ends like to hide.

"Should we go now? I think I'm getting sunburned on my nose," Mermaid says. "Was it very upsetting, what I just said?"

"No. But I need some time to adjust. Let's go find cigarettes and something for your nose before it starts peeling."

We get up. Mermaid looks at me, squinting a bit. How long was I here, on this bench? Not too long. Why does it seem like hours, then? Could be that it's bewitched, this innocuous-looking bench. Someone has placed an enchantment on it, and now it provokes anyone who sits on it to speak their mind.

We shuffle back to the House, pushing our shadows in front of us, headless and almost round at this hour.

"At least now I know why you dislike the Longest so much," Mermaid says.

The porch meets us with the suffocating scent of geraniums. Pots with those flowers, which I can't stand, have been placed all along the length of the railing.

"Curious. Not a single face in the windows. Something must have distracted all those people from spying on us. I wonder what," I say. "By the way, your *Hate until the grave* is of the exact same color as this geranium."

"I'm going to throw away that shirt," Mermaid says thoughtfully, mounting the stairs. "You are obviously against it."

"Could you bleach it out or paint over it or something?"

The stairs are completely empty, not a soul, neither on the landing above nor below. I have no idea where everyone is, but it explains why they weren't ogling us from the windows. There's an all-hands going on somewhere in the bowels of the House. Mermaid listens intently and comes to a decision.

"Kiss me while no one's around."

We get comfortable on the landing, leaning against the railing, and seize our moment amid the lull of the House. Quite short, or maybe it only seems that way. When we resume walking, my head is spinning slightly, and my stride is less self-assured than usual.

The hallway is empty. If they all did gather somewhere, it's not on this floor. Then at the other end we see two lonely, straggling silhouettes and make our way toward them. Blind and Rat. Such a beautiful couple, it makes your heart skip a bit. Both pale like corpses, shading to bluish under the eyes, identically emaciated, bordering on dystrophy. Blind also seems to be split open from the neck down to his navel. His shirt hangs in strips, exposing skin covered in long scratches. A sinister sight, especially considering that Rat's fingernails have traces of blood on them.

"There you go," I say to Mermaid. "Something like your *Kama Sutra*, only with selected chapters from Marquis de Sade thrown in. Doesn't look too nice, does it?"

Mermaid looks at me reproachfully (translation: "You didn't have to do that") but I'm already wound up, so on the way to the dorm I expound on sexual deviations, with Rat and Pale One listening politely and in silence. That makes me a dozen times madder than if one of them just told me to shut up.

The four of us barge into the dorm, finding no one there except Jackal, totally absorbed in purring into a tangle of colored wires. The wires grow out of the wall and disappear back in it, most of them dangle idly, not going anywhere and not connecting anything, but about a dozen or so form the trunk snaking all the way to the walls of the girls' dorms, and some of them even as far as rather specific sets of ears. This is Jackal's generous gift to all the lovers out there who are "separated by the circumstances," to quote Jackal himself, except the gift is absolutely useless without his active participation, he being the only one who can make heads or tails of the jumbled mess.

We walk in on him in the middle of a direct contact with someone from "over there," and he's just communicated that "Well then, I guess you're even dumber than you look!" Upon seeing us he nods excitedly, shielding the mic, and rolls his eyes, miming terminal exhaustion.

"Where's everybody?" I ask.

He doesn't hear me, of course, and continues to bow and smile.

Mermaid goes through the contents of the nightstand to find a first-aid kit for Blind. Rat sits down on the floor and freezes, head in hands, bloodied nails buried in her hair. She has on a leather vest, leaving arms and shoulders bare, and badges hang around her neck. An outrageously skinny girl, the kind you don't often meet, thankfully. It could be that she really can get satisfaction only when kissing is accompanied by disemboweling, that she needs strong emotions that are not accessible to her except through refined methods. Who the hell knows, but the thought that Blind is encouraging her in this gives me the creeps.

Pale One slowly divests himself of the remains of the shirt. Mermaid passes the vial of something mediciney to him and looks compassionately at the process of anointing the wounds.

"Why don't you go there yourself, darling, and don't stop until you've reached the Outsides," Jackal recommends to someone and pulls out the earbud. "Is it ever hard to hold a conversation with certain personalities! Labors of Hercules! And where have you all been hiding, if I may be allowed to ask?"

Tabaqui then takes a look at our appearance, nods to himself, apparently having come to some sort of conclusion, and says, "They're all downstairs, by the way. Shark's preaching again, aren't you interested to find out what that's about?"

Tabaqui has been in his Button Period ever since the last masked ball. He's covered in them, as iridescent and multicolored as an acid trip. The permanent collection of the button museum has as its backdrop a scarlet tailcoat with wide lapels (that way there's more space for them), but the jeans are relatively undecorated (or it would interfere with crawling), which vexes Tabaqui so much that, once ensconced in place, he flips the coattails to the front and starts fidgeting, trying to catch the reflection of the electric lamps in the countless pieces of shiny metal, and he's not content until he resembles an eye-watering imitation of an oversized Christmas-tree decoration.

"Who was that you were just squabbling with? Not Catwoman, by any chance?" Mermaid asks Tabaqui as she pulls the wet, mud-encrusted sweater off me.

"Of course not. With Catwoman it's never that trivial. And who said I was squabbling? I am simply keeping up the fighting spirit in some people. Providing both human contact and an occasional shake-up to those in need of it. It wouldn't do to sink into benign complacency and lose the edge only because you couldn't find anyone to tick you off at the right moment."

"So who were you ticking off?"

"Doesn't matter." Tabaqui sticks the earpiece back in and chooses a wire from the bundle. "You do agree with the principle, though, don't you? Calling the party, over." He scowls into the mic. "Feral Wolfdog here. Talk to me, my mysterious and lonely friend!"

The buttons shine next to the rainbow tangle of the wires. I glance past them to the open doors of the cabinet, to the carefully folded sweaters, shirts, and vests. I can't complain of a particular paucity with regards to my wardrobe, but to find something in there that would be uncommon enough to be inaccessible to someone with a desire to imitate it suddenly seems a challenge. Almost enough to consider becoming a human display case, in the manner of Lary or Jackal. Then at least I can be sure of being unique in my ugliness.

Mermaid reads my thought again.

"I can make you a vest out of colored rope. I have this huge skein, grass-green. Unless Catwoman's kids got to it."

Tabaqui seems to be listening in, even through the earbuds. He turns sharply around and stares.

"Keep it down," I say to Mermaid. "Or you'll end up doing ten of them, and then sewing a hundred buttons on each. And that would be child labor."

Tabaqui leans precariously in our direction and cocks one ear. Mermaid grabs the closest shirt and drapes it over my shoulders.

"I think I better go to our side and see if there's anyone lying there prostrate with a heart attack," she says with concern. "Some people have really peculiar notions of charity."

"Sure, go ahead. I'll go down to the first, find out what's the buzz. I've been separated from society ever since this morning. Also from food and cigarettes."

Blind, already in a fresh tee, stuffs a pack of Camels into my breast pocket.

"What was all that long talk with Ralph about?" he asks. "Inquiring minds want to know."

"Potential runaways. People being slowly squeezed out of the House. He's got them all on a list, those who'd like to bolt as soon as they can."

"Those counselors sure like their pieces of paper," Sightless One says, astonished. "Could it be that they all suffer from memory problems?"

He picks up his backpack, also emaciated.

"Let's go listen to Shark. He's been at it for half an hour already, must be just about getting to the point by now. And he's got a whole mound of paper."

"Could you take that thing off my head, please," I say. "It's starting to get on my nerves."

Blind sweeps the bandana off me. Mermaid is waiting for us outside the door, peeking in when she thinks we're not looking. Rat is still on the floor, face buried in her hands. She doesn't seem in any hurry to leave.

"Oh, hello," Jackal breathes beguilingly, hugging the mic. "Could this be number fourteen oh-one? It has been a while. How are you doing, oh-one? I've missed you. Hope the feeling is mutual?"

Blind and I appear in the lecture hall and immediately find ourselves in the thick of action. Shark, sweating from heat and indignation, shouts into the mic that periodically cuts out, the audience is partly listening, partly dozing off, and the aisles between the rows closest to the lectern are strewn with paper, as if someone clumsy was trying to film a snowstorm.

I crouch down and slip into the center row. Blind copies my movements step for step, even pinching the bottom of my shirt to steady himself. Shark notes our being late but is too busy to comment. He's about to move to "documentary evidence of the above-mentioned," in the form of a pile of paper delivered by obsequious Pilotfish. Blind and I position ourselves on the ugly metal chairs and join the listeners. There aren't many of us—those who really are listening. Mainly the first rows, occupied by the teachers.

"The results of the mandatory testing . . ."

The pack is in a state of drowsy apathy. The perkiest around here are Tubby, gnawing on a carrot, and Needle, counting the stitches of her next knitted master-piece. Humpback is nodding halfheartedly to the song playing through his earphones. Alexander is using a safety pin to extract a splinter out of his finger. I look a bit farther out, into the Hound rows, where Black's pink shaved head looms. Four Hounds next to him mimic his pose exactly—arms crossed, one foot on the seat of the chair in front. In their desire to be like their Leader they put even Logs to shame, but if what Mermaid said is true, I shouldn't be the one laughing. Especially considering that I almost shoved my own foot on the next seat in the same fashion, and now can only sit like a statue and stew silently. Because, after all, who's supposed to be copying whom?

"Almost no one managed to score even a fifty! Which is the bare minimum for an average numbskull!"

Shark furiously tosses a pack of the pernicious "yes-no" sheets into the air. They flutter and settle down, forming another layer of the fake snow. So that's how it got there.

"Let me explain to you what this means! It means that the vast majority of you are not qualified to fill any position that requires a functioning brain! You are outside the boundaries defined by your peers!"

The teachers' row, second from the podium, turns around as one, to look at us reproachfully. The counselors don't bat an eye. We have long ceased to be capable of surprising them. The mic cuts out again. Shark continues his harangue, not noticing it, then pauses and starts screaming even louder than before.

"You're basically imbeciles! Explain to me, will you, who do you think you've dealt this devastating blow by your stupid tricks? Me? You think I'm going to cry over it? Try to convince someone up there that you're smarter than this? You maybe think I care where you end up when you get out of here? Or what you're going to do there? It's your own lives you flushed down the toilet, you halfwits!"

I realize that I did sneak the foot onto the next seat. I let it stay there. I refuse to sacrifice the basic necessities of life only because I don't want to be copied.

Blind yawns and hides inside his palm. The lemur-like fingers easily swallow his entire face, including both his forehead and chin. A simple gesture, sure, but one that can't be copied by anyone present. I sit there, consumed by dumb envy. All right, enough. Time to shake off the paranoia. I suddenly realize that it's not Blind's hands I envy, not his independently alive fingers, but merely the gesture that I can't appropri-ate. Am I really as stupid as I often appear to myself to be?

Shark's latest "maybe you think" is unexpectedly picked up and amplified a hundredfold. The soundest sleepers wake up with a start. Tubby drops his carrot.

Humpback winces and stuffs his earbuds farther in. Even Shark himself cringes up there at the lectern.

"Therefore," he continues more calmly, "all the exams that were to take place this month have been canceled, along with the general evaluation, even though you're supposed to have been preparing for it since the end of last semester. Both have now lost any modicum of significance. The results of your testing are not going to allow you to enter any institution of higher learning. Not that you had any chance of that before."

Noble turns his face, curtained by the silver-colored dark shades, to me and stretches his lips in a wide grin. I smile back and then see, to my horror, that he's surrounded by sloppily made copies as well. I shake my head but the ghosts refuse to disappear. A couple of Logs on both sides of Noble, the High Keepers of Noble's crutches, one per person. Both are wearing mirrored glasses and Noble-style goatees. With no time off for chewing, gossiping, or Shark's speeches, Zit and Termite polish the crutches with their handkerchiefs and scrape dirt off the rubber tips. A ridiculous, risible sight. I can't help but smile. Noble lifts his eyebrows quizzically. I nod at his retinue. He shrugs—"What are you going to do?" Ginger's colorful crest is flaming by his elbow, her translucent chin sunk into the hands is positioned a little lower, and then the slanted front teeth and devoted eyes of the crutch-bearers, proud of their assignment. I again note with surprise how much Noble grew up during his trip to the Outsides. It only took him six months to learn to accept stoically the things that still push me over the edge.

"I shall now announce the names of those few who passed the tests with reasonably high scores . . ."

Into Shark's expectantly snapping fingers Pilot inserts another file. Shark grabs it and grumbles threateningly.

"So . . . In the First . . ."

The teachers' row hums and whispers. Humpback produces an ashtray from his pocket, flicks it open, and puts it down on the floor. There isn't anyone actually seen to be smoking, but the telltale gray cloud hangs thick overhead. Shark reads the first batch of names. I whisper them after him, recollecting vaguely that I seem to already have encountered them recently.

"Strange," I say. "I would have thought there'd be more Pheasants. But it's their own business, of course."

"Of course," Blind confirms right over my ear, laughing softly, his maddening insane laugh.

His Adam's apple performs a dance on the bare neck, his eyes are mirrors, each containing a Sphinx, just like the puddles of Noble's glasses.

"They were on the list that Ralph had," I explain. "The list of students wishing to bolt as soon as possible."

"Now we shall see," Blind says, overjoyed for some reason, "how well they are going to manage that. And who else besides them."

"You mean you knew about them?" I ask suspiciously.

"You crazy?" Blind says, aghast. "You just told me yourself."

I did, didn't I? But he wasn't very surprised when I did. Or he hid the surprise very convincingly. At least he didn't ask any questions, or demand clarification.

Shark, in the meantime, has moved to the geniuses of the Second. That doesn't take too much time, because the Second boasts just a single outcast—poor unfortunate Squib.

"Take that! Yeah . . . that's the way," Rats drone two rows ahead of us, after the "interpreter," forcibly divested of the earphones, attracts their attention by gesticulating wildly and then relates the news to them. "Keep on it, listen, you'll tell us all later," they encourage the interpreter before the entire pack plugs the phones back in. Well, not the entire pack, rather a dozen of its imprisoned representatives, but for Rats that's a lot when we're talking about a function as dull as an all-hands meeting.

Red loudly cracks a nut with his teeth and spits out the shell. Ringer, the interpreter, sighs and turns back toward the lectern. Squib, the immediate beneficiary of the whole business, does not react, doesn't even move at all, indifferent and self-absorbed, the bill of his cap lowered all the way to his nostrils.

Having skipped over the Third, who flunked the tests in their entirety, Shark declares, "The Fourth . . . ahem. Congratulations! It's Zimmerman!"

Smoker's death sentence flies up and flutters between the rows like a small graffiti-covered kite, and in the counselors' row R One's sharp-beaked head turns around and stares at me.

"One way or another," I whisper. "Somehow we do rid ourselves of them."

"Were you discussing Smoker with Ralph?" Blind wonders. "Why would you do a thing like that?"

Ten rows ahead of us, Ralph grimaces as if he heard what Blind just said, and turns away. He slightly resembles Smoker at that moment. They seem to have temporarily swapped their eyes, to better confuse me. Shark is done with the Sixth, all of three names, and is now talking about the girls.

"Whatever gave you that idea?" I ask Blind.

"Oh, that's just my bright, logical mind," Blind says proudly. "It's come to this conclusion."

"Your bright mind appears to be malfunctioning lately."

This is my freshest and most persistent nightmare—Blind, lost forever in the ghostly forests and swamps of the Other Side of the House, a vegetable here, a person who-knows-where. Blind, who's abandoned me to deal with all those faces and nicks alone, all their fears and hopes, the most horrendous outcome I can possibly imagine—and also the only one, as far as I know, that would satisfy Blind himself. My fear should be evident to an ear much less fine-tuned than his, but he just laughs, even though this isn't funny at all.

"Must be from overwork," he says, meaning the bright mind. "All things need rest."

"Not at my expense," I say. "Please."

Blind immediately assumes a solemn expression.

"Of course not," he says. "Who do you think I am? I will never leave you here alone. Neither you nor the others."

I close my eyes, trying to get a handle on the spinning head that's making the objects around me elongate, flow, and merge into colorful stripes. He will never leave us, wouldn't you know! I am familiar with that smug self-assuredness in his voice all too well. But will he allow us to leave him? I doubt it, at least not those of us who have already been touched by the House.

"Hey, what's that?" Blind grabs me by the collar and jostles lightly. "What's going on?"

"Go to hell!" I whisper back.

"Tomorrow!" Shark thunders, shaking the lectern like King Kong on a rampage. "Tomorrow we are saying good-bye to our esteemed teachers, departing on their well-earned break. Since the exams have been canceled, it is going to begin a full month earlier than was planned."

The entire teachers' row stands up and turns around to face us. A sustained ovation. They earnestly put on a display of being touched, but the elation in their faces shines clean through even from afar. Conversely, the counselors' row sinks further into depression as they are coming to the realization that soon they alone are going to be left with us face to face. The audience applauds, the teachers bow, Shark melts with delight. Through all this Blind keeps a firm hold on the back of my neck, seemingly concerned that as soon as he lets go I'm going to faint right there and then. He's not far off in that, and he'd get even closer should he attempt to soothe me in the manner that he's already tried just now.

"Now we are going to hear from those of our teachers who wish to say a word to all of you," Shark says, blotting the sweat behind his ears with a tissue. "I would only like to add, in closing, that on this Saturday as well as the next one, the parents of students who have completed the testing successfully are invited to visit, and if they'd like to take their children away at that time in order to provide an opportunity for them to apply to various colleges and universities, they are certainly welcome to do so."

The audience claps lazily, celebrating the end of Shark's oration. One of the more ebullient Hounds even shouts "Bravo!" and whistles, but is quickly suppressed, so Shark departs the podium amid scattered feeble applause, and his place is taken by the biology teacher, a slight old man burdened by the massive scroll of his prepared remarks.

"Your nervous system," Blind remarks, "seems to be rather shaky."

"Thanks in part to you," I snap back. "And get your hand off my scruff, I'm not planning to fall down."

"Sorry," he says, removing his hand obediently. "It's just that I got this impression that you were."

His smile is missing a tooth and lacking kindness, but he's intent on bestowing it on me. I look at him closer and notice certain changes. Sightless One used to walk around in a black jacket, so long that it resembled a turn-of-the-century frock coat, directly over his bare skin. Today he's got a tee under it, and also something ringlike hanging on a string around his neck, catching on the buttons.

"What's that?" I ask. "On your neck."

"This?" he says, showing me a steel ring. "Oh, I keep forgetting to tell you. I'm engaged."

"Oh boy. Who to?"

"Rat. Last night."

"Congratulations," I sigh. "I realize there's no use in trying to debate this after the fact, but could you maybe have considered someone more . . . sane?"

"Yeah, right," Blind sneers. "Like I was going to consult you about it. After you've torn my first love away from me. In a cold-hearted manner, I might add."

"You can't mean that maypole Gaby? For goodness' sake, Blind, you don't even come up to her shoulder."

"On the bright side, Rat and I are the same height."

He slips the ring under his shirt, but immediately winces and pulls it back out. It must have scratched at his wounds.

"So the decorations on your hide are kind of an engagement present?"

Blind's face hardens.

"Enough," he says. "This matter is closed for discussion."

"Yes, sir!" I bark and turn my attention back to the podium, where the biologist already has been supplanted by surly Chipmunk, reading his own farewell sermon. I can't make out a single word of it because neither Shark nor Ralph is present, having retired temporarily from the hall to have a smoke, and the discipline is deteriorating rapidly. Many are already puffing out in the open, the din of voices grows in intensity, certain individuals run between the rows to converse with the neighbors. Rats turn up the volume on their music.

"With all our hearts . . . blaze the trail . . . bright future . . . in spite of . . . the honor of our school . . . in high esteem . . . ," Chipmunk drones unenthusiastically, stopping only to take a hopeful sniff at the empty water carafe.

I shove my other foot on the chair in front of me and assume an almost horizontal position, even though the chairs here seem to be designed specifically to prevent people from getting comfortable. Humpback clicks off the Walkman, sighs, and puts it into his backpack.

"What just happened?" he says.

"Our dear teachers are saying their good-byes. They're taking off, tomorrow or maybe the next day."

"Really?" Humpback goggles at Chipmunk in surprise. "You serious? We're not going to see them anymore?"

"Guess not. So if you feel the need to hug any of them and burst into tears, you better hurry. Oh, and by the way, our Leader is engaged. You can hug him too."

Blind makes a vicious face. Humpback clears his throat. We're prevented from a further exchange of information by Red, cigarette in his mouth, filtering to us from the front row and sidling next to Blind. Our row is suddenly teeming with visitors, crowding and shoving each other.

"What do you say we move?" Humpback says. "It's getting a bit busy here."

I nod. He grabs his stuff, throws his backpack on his shoulder, and we migrate three rows back to put some distance between ourselves and the pack that is acquiring guests and hangers-on at an alarming rate.

"Who's Blind engaged to?" Humpback asks.

"Rat, who else."

"Could have been anybody," Humpback says. "He's like that, you know. Unpredictable."

Very true. Only the people who rarely voice their opinions are capable of doing it in such a deadly straightforward way. It still doesn't cheer me, though.

"Rat's better than Gaby," Humpback insists.

"Depends," I say, remembering the gashes on Blind's chest.

My mood crashes even further. Humpback lights a cigarette and stretches out on the chair. From the general direction of Birds a radio cuts in suddenly, so loud as to drown out everything else, but is hurriedly hushed.

"Good luck to you on your journey, my dear children, the journey into your adult life and the pursuit of your dreams! I wish you all the best!"

Chipmunk scurries off the podium, replaced by Mastodon. His appearance is met with unhealthy excitement. Also Shark and Ralph return. The last defectors, in the rush to take advantage of the pause created while they cross the aisle, are stomping loudly and moving chairs around. I look at Mastodon and miss the moment when someone sits next to me. Humpback's greeting makes me turn to the side and notice that someone is in fact Black.

He doesn't look half as imposing without his customary retinue of Hounds. You might even say he looks harmless and familiar. Still I tense up. Of course, a courteous greeting is a matter of habit, and then I turn back to look at Mastodon. Otherwise I'd be brazenly ogling Black.

"Well, what can I say . . ."

Mastodon, the checker-coated rectangle with the flattened boxer's nose and the lips to match, stares at us over the scrap of paper with his notes.

"A good machine gun in your hands," prompts someone in the audience, rather loudly. "And for the first two rows to hit the floor!"

Mastodon turns livid and tries to move his neck, seeking out the offender.

"You down there," he rasps, "shut up!"

The assembly goes quiet. But not for long.

"Like the other teachers talking here, for me it's been blood and sweat and . . ."

Black is telling Humpback of Nanette visiting him this morning.

"And then I see her trying to climb through the crack in the window. All by herself, I didn't call her or anything. I didn't even realize at first how unlike her that was. You should know, she never came to me before, not even when she was a chick, but there you go."

Black is staring at Mastodon while saying that, and Humpback does as well. They barely move their lips, but I still hear everything. This makes me uncomfortable for some reason, as if I've been eavesdropping. Except that I absolutely have not. It's not my fault they are sitting so close to me. And if Black didn't want me to listen it'd be easy for him to catch Humpback any other place.

"Tried to get you a little bit stronger," Mastodon's voice muscles its way into my head. "Can't say it worked too well."

"Sure would be handier with that machine gun," comes the voice again.

Mastodon holds a pregnant pause. The audience giggles.

"But as I told you time and time again . . ."

"The only good cripple is a dead cripple!" an entire chorus sings in unison.

Of course. Mastodon's maxims are classic. Quoting them from memory is something even Elephant can do.

"You bloody bastards!" Mastodon roars, slamming both of his fists against the top of the lectern. "Waste of genetic material! Human debris!"

A cloud of dust floats up in the air. The audience howls and applauds furiously.

"I wish I had a hand grenade, screw the gun . . ."

He is being dragged off the podium. The entire counselors' row pitches in. Shark, out of range in the back, flaps his fins miserably.

Black turns to me and asks, "What's going to happen to Smoker now?"

"Same as the others, I guess. His parents will come and take him."

He nods, thoughtfully rubbing the chin.

"I've got two of those in my pack, too. And still I worry more about him than about them. Strange, huh. I guess that's what's best for them, but I still feel like a traitor. Wonder why that is."

"Because it's true. We have betrayed them."

Black glowers at me. The tiny skulls on the scarf wrapped around his head do their black-and-white dance.

"How so?"

"By failing to change them."

Black takes a pack of cigarettes from his backpack, shakes out one, and stashes it in the front pocket of his shirt.

"Too bad. He's a nice guy. You just got to him with your tricks, no wonder he's flipped. I know how that works."

"Yes, you would, wouldn't you," I say politely.

Humpback steps on my foot while continuing to study the ceiling nonchalantly. But strange as it seems, Black doesn't take offense. Leadership certainly has effected some positive changes in his demeanor as well.

"You're a meanie, Sphinx," he says.

And that's it. I wait for the follow-up, but it never comes.

Shark announces that "one of our students expressed a desire to address us" and a proud Pheasant is being wheeled out to the podium, indistinguishable in his black-and-white fatigues from any other representative of the species.

"Every pack," Black says, "has its own black sheep. Even Pheasants. We only notice them if one gets kicked out and lands on our territory, the way they did it with Smoker. Hounds are no different. Snapping at each other until they concentrate their attention on one person. Then for him it's curtains."

I open my mouth, catch Humpback's eloquent look, and shut it back up. Black, however, manages to read a lot in my expression.

"You were going to say something about me again? Go ahead, say it. Except it's not exactly the same. I wanted to be a black sheep. I was goading you. Maybe I did become it, though not to the extent I wished."

"Whose degree of blackness concerns you at this moment, yours or someone else's?" I say. "What is it exactly we're discussing here?"

"Everything concerns me." Black takes out the stashed cigarette and starts rolling it between his fingers. "The Sixth has its own rules. It's in the Sixth that I understood how the nonconformist, the 'other,' is bullied. Whatever was going on in the Fourth is child's play compared to that. Once you see what real hazing looks like you recognize it anywhere. It's not a pretty sight."

"I'm so happy," I say, "that you finally saw something like that. As for me, I lived through it when I was ten. As I remember, with your help. And enthusiastic participation."

"Hey!" Humpback throws up his hands. "Sphinx, don't . . ."

"No, wait." I'm angry now, and it's hard to stop. "He says he's never seen anything like it until he ended up in the Sixth. So I'd like to know what exactly was it he saw when his gang was chasing me all over the House like a plague-ridden rat!"

Black torments the still-unlit cigarette without looking at me. I am slowly cooling off and beginning to regret my outburst. This is probably the first time ever that we've had a normal conversation. Or at least tried to.

Black tosses the gutted cigarette.

"All right, I'll tell you what I saw. If you want. You're not going to like it, mind you. But it's probably better that way. Because I'd really like you to understand. It was not about you. Absolutely not. It was about Elk." Black takes the bandana off and stuffs it in his pocket. "You see, I ended up in the Sixth, and then it took me a while living there to finally understand what was going on with me in the Fourth. I was even asking myself afterward how I could be so stupid and not see it right there. But then I figured that if I didn't make that step away, didn't look from a distance . . . I mean . . . Try to do the same thing. Picture all of us back then. The House. Elk. Imagine that you're that squirt, ankle biter, and there are all those grown-ups around, and they never have any time for you, none of them, except one. And that one you can't just share among everybody. So we're all jumping out of our skins to be special, to be noticed, to have him say something only to you, to ask something only of you. But all of that is on the inside, you never show that, because it's embarrassing when you're a big guy, ten years old already and so on. Blind wasn't bothered about that and tagged after him like a mutt, but he was the only one. And Elk never fussed around over him more than with anyone else. He never played favorites. Until you. Yes, laugh all you want, it may sound funny now, but just imagine yourself in our place!"

"I'm sorry, Black," I say, fighting the giggles, "please understand, but it's been such a long time since I've last heard that. 'Elk's pet.' And to think how much grief that nick caused me. Honestly, I would never have thought I was his favorite. Or that it would look like I was."

"Yeah, I guess you wouldn't."

Black is very red, and it looks dangerous, though much more familiar than his newfound serenity. I'm bracing for the explosion, so it's hard for me to concentrate on what he's saying.

". . . as soon as we stepped off the bus. He was waiting for us in the yard, in the corner. He assembled us around him and then told us about you. And that we shouldn't touch you. And that we had to help you."

"What? That's a lie!" I scream, springing up from the chair as if someone hooked it up to an electric socket. "That never happened! It couldn't have!"

Humpback pulls at my sleeve.

"Hey, what's gotten into you? Shark's looking."

I crouch down next to his chair, and Humpback whispers in my ear, looking sideways at the podium, "That's how it was. The way Black's telling it. It's true. I was there too when he said that."

"You never told me!"

"In the back row!" Shark thunders. "Stop that commotion!"

I lower myself back on the chair, trying my best to look calm. Humpback stares ten rows ahead, all rapturous attention.

"What for?" he whispers. "What difference would it have made?"

"You were the first newbie we had to help," Black presses on. "We were helping each other anyway, with anything we could. Some more, some less. But before you came in no one had ever told us we *had* to do it."

"Damn," I say. "Was he that much of an idiot?"

At the word "idiot" Humpback and Black both wince.

Humpback says, "Watch it, Sphinx." Black doesn't say anything, but his silence is so expressive that I understand: not only am I a favorite, I'm a favorite who doesn't appreciate his privilege. Who treads on the most sacred. Now I need some time to come to grips with the Joseph complex that these two have managed to force on me, with being that one guy who always rubs his brothers the wrong way. And to accept that the disgusting blond youth whom I remember being tall as a tower, muscle-bound, and completely, utterly free of the need to be loved by anybody could have been tormented by jealousy. Him and the others. Him and Humpback, the proud loner. Him and possibly even Solomon née Muffin, who is no longer with us. All of them.

I need time to look at them from a distance. To understand and to forgive. I am stretching out that time, slowing it down, erasing their faces from the album of childhood memories and allowing the photographs to develop anew. I realize that there still won't be enough time for me to do it here and now, that the work is too involved to fit into a few minutes. I also understand that I've just hurt both Black and Humpback, and that I'm lucky it's them sitting next to me and not Blind.

"That was some favor Elk did for his favorite," I say, trying to smile. "Wouldn't wish it on my worst enemy."

"Drop it, please," Humpback hisses. "Leave it alone. It was long ago, and it ended long ago. Silly to still be talking about it now."

"We wouldn't be talking about it now if it really had ended," Black says glumly. "Look at Sphinx. You see something that's ended? I see something that's only beginning.

He's pissed off like it was yesterday he got beat up. Any one of us would have given an arm to be in his place even for a moment. But he's the one pissed!"

At this moment the mental dusting off of the childhood pictures arrives at Blind, and I freeze uncertainly. I have a reasonably good idea what Blind's jealousy looks like. Why didn't I see any traces of it back then? Why Black, why Humpback even, but not him?

"Was Blind present at that event?"

"Oh jeez." Black leans back in the chair and bares his teeth. "Blind! You can rest easy as far as he's concerned. Gods and jealousy don't mix. It's a completely separate disorder."

"What was it you just said?"

"Look, we're going to come to blows over this," Humpback says desperately. "It's all right for you, you're used to it, but how's that my fault? I'm going to sit somewhere else."

I shake my head.

"No, you're right. We should drop it. I have made my few steps away and looked at it from there. Thank you, Black. It was indeed useful, albeit a tad painful."

After that we're silent.

Black is darker than a storm cloud, his meat hooks folded over his chest. Humpback is ruffled and miserable, like a raven that's been ambushed by a bird catcher. I shudder to think how I look.

Counselor Godmother recites some sort of schedule. Minutes pass before I'm able to figure out what it's about, and all that time I'm fleeing the image of Elk that keeps catching up with me. Twice every year, at these all-hands meetings, he stood approximately where Godmother is now standing and made short announcements, smiling with his eyes. The same kinds of announcements she's making. Someone's achievements or setbacks, someone's health progressing or not. The physicals calendar. Except unlike with Godmother, everyone listened to him no matter what he was saying. Every single one of us in the audience. With bated breath. Because he was born the Catcher of Little Souls. You could grow up, free yourself, but even those who had gone into the Outsides long ago carried traces of his glances, his touches, may still be carrying them for all I know. Did a man like that have a right to be wrong? He least of all, not with all the hungry, yearning eyes on him. He had no right to make mistakes, to have favorites, or to die.

Godmother reads the list of those who have been prescribed vitamin shots. Then another list, much longer, of those whose body-mass index is not simply low, but shamelessly so. That marks the end of the ceremonies. The departing throngs file past us, walking and riding, rattling the chairs as they go. Up on the podium they cover the lectern and the portable screen that they'd hauled out for some reason. Then we're alone.

Humpback, Black, and I. We seem to have already said everything that needed to be said, and it's not entirely clear what we're waiting for and why none of us left with the others. I mean, I understand why Humpback hasn't, he's busy being a lightning rod, but why do Black and I keep sitting here like we're stuck? Humpback waits, frets, tries to pretend he's dozed off. Black and I are still silent. Finally Humpback's patience snaps.

"How about we get going?" he asks plaintively. "Everyone's left already."

Tacking between the upended chairs and avoiding the shoals of spit and cigarette butts, we reach the hallway. Huge blue letters stretch along the wall: GOOD NIGHT SWEET TEACHERS! The dot on the exclamation mark drips like a tear.

"Was it really painful? What I told you about Elk?" Black says, keeping pace.

"Not too much. It certainly explained a lot. I could have guessed myself, if only I'd given it enough thought. When you're little you imagine the grown-ups to be these flawless beings. And then you learn that it isn't so."

"Sometimes you learn it not only about the grown-ups," Black mumbles to himself, without elaborating who or what he means. "I guess you took my bodybuilders off the wall?" he asks suddenly, changing the subject abruptly, and I remember that it used to drive me nuts, this habit of his—jumping suddenly from one subject to the next, as if someone switched him off and then back on, but tuned to a different station.

"No, why?" Humpback says, surprised. "Still there, where you left them. Why would we want to take them off?"

"Revenge, Humpback. Revenge," I cut in eagerly. "Not only take them off, but also stomp on them and rip them to little pieces. Like you need such simple things explained?"

"Sphinx, sometimes I really want to smack you one," Black says. "So much that I have to grab myself by the arms."

We go around a chair that someone sneaked out of the lecture hall but abandoned on the way. Black stops.

"There's one thing I need to tell you. If you promise not to laugh. It's about getting out."

Humpback shrinks and hunches down, tightly gripping his backpack, as if preparing to fight someone who is about to push him into the Outsides.

Black bites his lip, trying to muster the courage. Looks at the walls, then up, then down at the floor, and finally at me.

"Whatever," he says. "I guess you can laugh if you want. I happen to know where to get a van. Used, but in decent shape. And also I know how to drive. Learned it recently. Because I had an opportunity."

We gape at him silently.

"Yes, I know it's bullshit," he says quickly. "You don't have to tell me. I'm not a baby. What I just said sounds funny to me too, but I had to say it. I don't care if you die laughing now. I'm only asking you to keep it in mind, OK? That's all."

He turns around and walks away, more runs away, eager to put as much distance between us as he can, as if pushed by the imagined tide of our laughter at his back.

"Black, we're not laughing," I call after him.

He waves his hand without turning around and disappears up the stairs. A panicked retreat, there are no other words for it. Humpback and I exchange puzzled glances.

"Now this is something," Humpback says. "There was this one guy in the entire House who dreamed about getting to the Outsides, and look what happened to him."

"Good-bye, bull terriers in checkered vests," I sigh. "There won't be much space in the van, even without them."

"Stop it," Humpback says. "It's not funny. That's why he ran away, because he didn't want to hear the lame jokes."

"I would never tell them with him around. I'm not laughing, Humpback. How can I laugh at things like that? It's Tabaqui's kite, the one that he says the seniors used to fly away, except Black seems to have mastered the art of driving it."

Humpback shakes his head.

"Don't do it with me around either. Don't laugh. Don't say anything. At all."

He kicks away the chair, even though it would have been easier to step around it, and plows ahead, shoving his hands into his pockets with such force that I imagine hearing the sound of the lining being ripped. Terminally upset, either by Black's words or by my reaction to them.

I follow him, turning this sad fairy tale over and over in my head. The one Black is trying so hard to believe. The magical mystery van. The children of the House rushing toward dawn, in a stolen car with Black at the helm, tearing down the highway, exuberantly belting out road songs. In the real world this trip is going to last for about an hour, tops. Pity. Because this fantasy is even more beautiful than having the seniors depart to the hidden world beyond the clouds by means of a kite. More beautiful and more touching exactly for the fact that it was invented by Black, the staunchest realist.

When we return to the dorm, only Ginger and Smoker are left there, sitting at the opposite corners of the bed and annoying each other. The tension is palpable enough for Humpback to immediately get out of the way and hide on his top bunk. I go to sit between those two, doing my best to disrupt their line of sight. Oh well, that's fair, now it's my turn to be the lightning rod. Even though Tabaqui is so much better at it than I am.

Ginger smokes, studying the smoldering end of her cigarette intently. Smoker peers now at her dirty sneakers, now at the ash she's shaking all over the place—a Pheasant to the core, all but writing notes about it in a diary. Ginger's irritation barely registers, but Smoker's is throwing sparks all the way across the room. My presence interferes with his indignation, so he shifts on the bed to better see her— dirty-uncouth-repellent, but something else too, more personal, I can't quite put my finger on it. Did she tell him off or pour soda in his precious sneakers while we were out? He's blushing every time he looks at her, gazes away but then looks again, almost forcing himself, and I become more and more curious. What was it she managed to do? I am clearly not cut out for the role of the lightning rod, so I rejoice when Jackal returns, whistling something cheerful and out of tune.

"There we go," he says after climbing up to join us. "Gaby is shouting to the four winds that she's pregnant, can you imagine that?"

"By Blind, of course," Ginger says. She doesn't seem too excited.

"Not at all! She never said that. None of the 'Long live the young dauphin,' not even a peep. Supposedly by Red or by Viking. Something indeterminate with a pronounced Rattish slant."

"She's lying," Ginger concludes, throws away the cigarette, and walks over to Tubby's box. Fishes him, still sleepy, out of there, puts him on her back, bending double under the weight, and walks out. Tubby burbles something incoherent but looks generally content.

"Hey, where are you taking the Insensible?" Jackal asks, astonished.

"For a walk," comes Ginger's voice from the anteroom, then the outer door slams, and it's quiet again.

"Aww," Jackal sighs. "And we were doing so well."

We weren't doing well at all, but Tabaqui's optimism stores are inexhaustible, and no one takes the bait.

"What an incongruous person," Smoker says.

He probably needs someone to argue with him. Or maybe he said it just to say something.

"Who is? Ginger?" Tabaqui wonders. "Why?"

"No reason. There's just something missing in her. Many things, actually."

Tabaqui fiddles with the tuning knob on the boombox and says, "If only you knew how many things you yourself are missing, you'd be a lot more reticent, but since you are not of that kind, do us a favor and elaborate."

Smoker jumps at the opportunity.

"She's abrupt," he says. "Coarse. Unfeminine. The way she behaves would be appropriate for a twelve-year-old, but she's not twelve, not by a long shot."

"Oh wow!" Humpback exclaims, leaning down from his bunk.

Seemingly encouraged by his interest, Smoker adds, "She's also messy. Hopelessly so."

"Ooh, ooh." Tabaqui sways, puckering his lips like a nervous chimp. "You're talking such nonsense, Smoker. Can't you hear it yourself?"

"She spends her nights in a room with six guys. Walks around the bathroom naked and doesn't even bother to close the door. And supposedly she sleeps with Noble, except I wouldn't be surprised if she does it with Blind as well, and I don't know who else . . ."

Humpback tosses a pillow at Smoker, and Tabaqui immediately jumps on top of it, pushing it down as if he wants to squash Smoker flat. Tamps it thoroughly, lifts it for a bit, making sure Smoker is still breathing, and quickly covers him again. As they are shutting up Smoker in this unorthodox fashion I catch the image of Ginger that has so stunned and infuriated him. A flash—the spare boyish figure. Dark nipples on pink skin over protruding ribs, red tuft of pubic hair. Arms, legs, and almost nothing between them. She's looking at me, or rather at Smoker, a faraway, completely impassive look. One arm is twisted, and there's a reddish sore below her elbow. She licks it. Then lowers her arm, not even attempting to cover herself, and walks inside the shower stall. That walk is imprinted on Smoker's retinas in a sequence of narrow snapshots, one sliding over the next. That's what was making him blush so painfully. I understand. It's not what he's seen that hurt him, but the reaction to his appearance. Or rather the absence of a reaction. It is indeed unpleasant, to be looked at like you're not even there, like you're an empty space. This would be discomfiting even to someone much more balanced.

"She's like an animal," Smoker says, pushing off the pillow. "Completely shameless."

"Horror of horrors," Tabaqui fumes. "Humpback, all our efforts were for naught. He is irredeemable. He can only be exterminated."

"They're taking him away this Saturday," Humpback reminds him from above. "You keep forgetting."

"I do not. This thought is the only thing that keeps me sane. This one and a handful of others, similarly cheerful." Tabaqui looks up and inquires plaintively, "Tell me, how is it any of his damn business who she does and doesn't sleep with? When even Noble keeps out of it?"

"That's the kind of cantankerous creature he is," Humpback says as his head disappears over the edge.

Smoker is hugging Humpback's pillow. The narrow frames with the naked girl walking away unspool before him rapidly, replacing each other as they fall. The last one is the slammed door of the shower stall.

I go out to the yard, to look for Ginger.

There's this place where the walls of two buildings meet, a nook overgrown with weeds. The beginning of summer usually means stinging nettles up to the knees, but on the other hand they cover up the trash, making it temporarily invisible. Presumably the most private place in the whole House, because neither of the walls has any windows.

They're there. Sitting in front of a small fire. Ginger made it in the old spot, the blackened, charred scrap of earth marked with a stone circle. This is where seniors always had their fires. It used to be much cozier back then, with chaises and old crates for chairs. No trace of them now. Could be they burned them all.

Tubby sits on top of Ginger's coat, staring into the fire and droning softly. When the burning branches crackle he startles and grabs his cheeks. Such a cute girlish gesture, half fright, half delight. Ginger is whispering something to him. I can't make it out. I come up to them and sit down. She just continues her monologue as if I'm not there.

"The important thing was to grab a space somewhere in the back, so they wouldn't shoo you off, and look. Only look, without listening. That's important. Because they would sing, play the guitar, bake potatoes in the fire, and so on, and it was very distracting, all that romantic stuff people do when they get together and want to prove to themselves that they're having a blast. I liked to look at the fire, that's all. This one time someone snatched a burning stick out of it and wrote something on the wall with the blazing end. I was almost blinded. A word that's shedding fire. The burning letters of God. All that was left of them the next day was the black outline of a common swearword and a sooty smear, but still it had been a miracle, and I witnessed it."

She throws a sizable chunk of dry wood on the fire. Sparks fly in the air, reflecting in Tubby's bugged-out beady eyes.

"Also I would come here to have a good cry," Ginger says. "Once a week, like clockwork."

"So would I," I say. "Until I found out that just about every other inhabitant of the House came here too for the exact same purpose."

She smiles. The smile transforms her into a completely different person, unfamiliar now, but one that I seem to have known a long, long time ago.

"Yeah," she says. "I always bumped into one or another of them and had to close my eyes and pretend it didn't happen. The most freaking private place in the whole House!"

"There are no private places in the House."

"There sure weren't back then."

She opens the backpack and takes out a pack of sandwiches—"Oh, by the way, I've got . . ."—and freezes, watching Tubby. He crawls closer to the fire, eyeing it intently, and there's a wood chip gripped tightly in his clumsy paw. He's angling to throw it in, a very complicated matter requiring a great deal of effort and concentration. We observe him swaying as he stretches his arm and even his lips forward and carefully drops the chip. And immediately shrinks away in fear, as if the tiny chip would cause the fire to flare up to the skies. It doesn't flare. Tubby looks sideways at me, then at Ginger, and resumes his monotonous droning, now signifying joy and complete agreement with the world.

The wind is blowing smoke straight at me. I shut my eyes tightly and roll over closer to Tubby. Sit down on the edge of the coat and put my rake over his pudgy shoulders. Then we watch the fire dying down. Ginger settles on Tubby's other side.

"I'm not giving him the sandwich," she says.

I voice agreement. Of course we shouldn't give Tubby any sandwiches. Nothing exists for him now except the fire. Anything we can give to him will immediately end up in it, because no dinner can possibly approach the happiness of feeding another, especially if that other is Fire, a powerful deity of whose actual power Tubby is only dimly aware.

So that he wouldn't get upset because of the fire dying, Ginger tells him about the embers. How they're beautiful too—"like little red stars," she says, and Tubby nods, affirming the similarity.

"I'll make you another fire tomorrow, just like this one," Ginger promises.

"Why are you doing this?" I ask. "He might get used to it."

Ginger doesn't answer. *So let him,* I hear in her silence. *I will bring him here every night, and make fires for him. Let him feed wood chips to them and sing. It's no use thinking about the time when I won't be able to, when there won't be any "here." That's the last thing I want to think about right now.*

"Haven't you tamed enough people, Gingie?" I say.

There's nothing but tenderness in my question, I understand her too well. I understand how it must be impossible—not taming when you love being loved, when you acquire little brothers for whom you are then responsible to the end of your days, when you turn into a seagull, when you write love letters on the walls addressed to someone who never would be able to see them. When, despite your complete certainty that you're ugly, someone still manages to fall in love with you, when you pick up stray dogs and cats and chicks who fell out of their nests, and make fires for those who didn't ask you to do that.

She gives me a quick glance and looks away. Because I too am one of those who was tamed long ago. I'm lucky that I didn't end up helplessly and hopelessly in love, needing constant care. That the responsibility for me has been partially shifted to

Mermaid, who in a certain sense has managed to outgrow Ginger. But still I'm one of us, of those who are forever under her tattered seagull's wing.

She leans toward me and we embrace, touching foreheads over Tubby's head. Just for a moment, then she shifts away.

"You're mad because of Noble," she says. "But I can't . . ."

"I'm not mad."

"And Smoker . . ."

"Oh, forget it." I laugh.

She doesn't care how many people witness her fights with Noble, doesn't care who Blind is with if he's not with her. It's all the same to her whether she's clothed or naked, a girl or a boy, she's a social animal, the kind that is best adapted to life in the House. Smoker is right at least in that—Ginger is a monster, like many of us. Like the best of us. I'll be damned if I'm ever going to hold it against her.

She nods and gets up. It's almost dark, and the embers are barely smoldering. Tubby must be cold. He fidgets in his romper, grunting quizzically.

"We're going," I say. "We're almost gone."

Ginger puts him on my shoulders. We don't have to tie him down, he's used to riding on someone's back and usually holds on very tight. She picks up the coat and the backpack and stamps out the last remaining embers.

Tubby coughs significantly.

"Yes," Ginger says. "I remember what I promised you about tomorrow. But this place needs to rest now. To cool down."

We walk in the dusk, keeping to the strip of pavement that looks lighter than the surrounding trash. Keys and coins jangle in Ginger's pockets. Now that the fire is gone I can see that it's not completely dark yet.

Tubby gently paws my face, mumbles something, and then, uncertainly, launches into a song. Must be the song of this evening. But unlike Tabaqui's songs on similar occasions, no one will ever understand this one.

On this Saturday the physicals are mandatory for all, so the line to the Spiders' office stretches all the way back to the Sepulchral landing, and even spills out onto the stairs. We spend so much time in it that Logs manage to haul in blankets and hotplates from the first floor, pitch a camp on the landing, and make at least two rounds of tea before the tail end of the throng slithers inside the Sepulcher.

Once inside, life immediately becomes boring. Can't smoke, can't boil water, can't even talk loudly. Many doze off. Birds lose themselves in a poker tournament, Elephant parades his toys on the linoleum, Noble and Ginger fight and make up, Jackal picks apart a bread roll and stuffs the pieces under the cabinets—for the Sepulchral sprites.

"It's a mystery how, with an attitude like that, people here are afraid of graduation," Smoker says. Feeling my stare, he turns and adds, "You are conditioned to make do with so little, wherever you may end up."

It's a confrontational statement, but no one thinks to argue.

We've been depressingly nice to Smoker ever since this morning.

The line keeps shortening. The white plastic chairs, on which no one ever sits on general principle, mark the stations of our journey. When we're one chair away from the office it is suddenly announced that Smoker is staying in the Sepulcher.

No explanations, which is the way it is customary with Spiders. They just send for his things and we're left wondering what could have happened to him in the time since the last physical, that all of us have overlooked. If it were anyone else but Smoker we would have left a scouting party in the Sepulcher to wait for information, but Smoker was going to be taken away by parents in any case, so we don't protest or make a scene, and return to the dorm.

At lunch we have this stupid argument about wheelers and their abilities. Tabaqui considers those abilities limitless and attempts to persuade us that legs are, if you think about it, a completely extraneous part of the body. That allegedly the only people who need them are soccer players and runway models, and everyone else only makes use of them out of habit. And that once humanity finally comes around to augmenting itself through complete motorization of the lower extremities, this bad habit is going to die off by itself.

Humpback and I mount a halfhearted defense. We like legs, we're fond of them, we don't wish to have them motorized. Lary mutters something that mentions sour grapes.

Tabaqui, scandalized, challenges all present leg chauvinists to a contest of speed, tightness of turns, and forward thrust.

Noble says that after a contest like that we're all going to end up in the Cage. Those of us, that is, who aren't going to end up in the Sepulcher.

"*Et tu, Brute?*" Tabaqui whispers, defeated.

After lunch we witness what Jackal terms "The Great Exodus." There's nothing great about it. All that happens is that some successful test takers, most of them Pheasants, are released to their parents. The House, however, is good with imbuing any event, however insignificant, with pomp and grandeur.

The first floor is cordoned off beyond the reception area. The role of the sentry falls to R One. Logs immediately crowd in front of the barrier with the intent of storming it and getting to the other side. Black Ralph holds the gate. The other counselors are busy shuttling their charges, along with the luggage.

A skinny girl named Lenses arouses an almost universal admiration. Her worldly possessions take up three huge suitcases, two duffels, and a plastic bag. Jackal declares that he finally found a true soul mate within these walls, but ah! too late, too late, and his heart is now broken forever.

After her burdensome luggage has been delivered, Lenses starts squeaking that she forgot to pack her favorite jacket. Three Reptiles, girl counselors, are sent to retrieve it, and each of the three bears an expression that unequivocally promises Lenses bad news. There's no trace of the jacket. Lenses screams that she's not going anywhere without it. Logs burst into applause. Finally the "sweet girl" is hauled bodily, by Shark personally, to reception, and after that nothing more interesting happens, apart from young Pheasant Sniffle crying hysterically and Hound Laurus delivering a farewell speech where he calls all of us shitholes.

We don't get to see any of the parents of those being taken away. Stands to reason: if we saw them, that would mean that they, in turn, would see us, and Shark still has enough sense not to allow that under any circumstances.

At length the favorably tested are packed and sent out of the House. The barriers are coming down, Reptiles drift off for a soothing cup of herbal tea, and we return to our room.

"It's a good thing we didn't have to say good-bye to Smoker in these idiotic circumstances," Humpback offers.

"Do you think he would have called all of us shitholes too?" Jackal says.

"It's a possibility," Humpback says.

SPHINX

I'm climbing up to the attic the only way I know how. From the backside of the fire-escape ladder with my back pressed against the wall. The higher I go, the more unpleasant this way becomes. In theory there shouldn't be anything particularly hard about it. In practice it quickly turns out that I've failed to account for some things. Like nails sticking out of the wall. The first one gets me in the back about fifteen feet up, the second immediately follows the first, and by halfway I'm already bleeding like Saint Sebastian, so I forget about the speed of ascent and concentrate on not meeting with another nail.

Noble—with whom I made a bet about who'd be able to get to the attic faster—evaporates at about the same time without so much as a "See you later." Tabaqui, our referee, whose cheerful shouts are only marginally less annoying than the nails, remains at his post.

"Hold on, old man! You're almost there! Just forget you've ever had a back, and you'll see how easy it becomes!"

"Thanks for that!" I shout, dragging my leg over the next rung, pushing myself farther up the wall, scraping a bit more skin off the shoulder blades. "Your advice is, as always, filled with wisdom. And where did Noble get to?"

I look down at Jackal, who's now casting about forlornly, and can't stop myself from laughing. Giggles are the last thing a man in my position should be attempting, so I clench my jaw, avert my gaze, and for the umpteenth time count the remaining rungs on the ladder.

"Exactly. Where is he?" Jackal says indignantly. "Could it be his nerves snapped? I despair of this generation. Weaklings all, may I be forgiven. Can't stand the heat."

Seven rungs left. Here, two walls of the House come together. This corner used to be an outer wall, but then it was covered and glazed and now it's just a rectangular space, housing the fire escape and the emergency exit. The wall I'm leaning against is painted baby blue, the opposite wall is exposed bricks, and the one facing the yard is glass, but you can't see anything through it because of all the grime, so the view is not distracting me.

On the fourth rung from the top my calves start cramping up. I slide up as far as I can, trying to straighten against the ladder so that I barely touch the previous rung with the toes of my sneakers, but instead of putting my heel on the next one I catch my instep on it and hurl myself forward. There's no way anyone could make me repeat this trick. I stand now without leaning against anything, the way a person with real arms would be standing on a stepladder, doing my best to believe that I have them too. From here on it's easy. Straighten up again and imagine that there's a soft pillow a couple of feet down from where I'm standing, which would cushion my fall nicely. I picture it in my head, make a step, and here I am, up in the attic. Or rather my head is. Not forgetting about the pillow, that's the important thing. I don't. One more step, and my upper half is in there; another one, and the rest of me follows.

I climb out of the hatch, stretching on the floor, but don't have time to congratulate myself on the successful arrival before the leg cramp twists me around, making me roll on the floor hissing, risking a fall back through the hatch. I can neither rub nor squeeze my poor appendage, there's only one remedy available to me, and that's biting my own calf, and I'm just about to resort to it when it becomes clear that there are two of us up here in the attic.

In the far corner, on a blanket spread under the pitched roof, there's a ghostlike girl in a long dress. The dress is fiery red, the girl's hair is green. I recognize that hair, but can't quite remember the nick, and when I do I'm not sure I have it right until she twists the thin-lipped mouth in a disgusted grimace. Then I say to her, "Hello, Chimera."

I'm sure I resemble an Ouroboros, but I'd like to see someone get a good grip on their calf with his teeth while looking dignified. True, I don't think I've ever looked more idiotic, but the ridiculousness of my pose is not enough to explain the loathing with which Chimera is looking at me. Her look conveys to me that I'm the most revolting sight she's ever encountered in her life. Under Chimera's stare even the cramp begins to subside. I slowly uncoil and make another attempt at establishing contact.

"I wasn't expecting to meet anyone here."

"And I wasn't expecting anyone to drag himself all the way up here to have an epileptic fit."

There's enough poison in her words to make each and every one of them deadly.

"I also didn't know we were such good enemies" is all I can say.

To put at least some distance between us, I walk back to the hatch and assess the situation below. I'm not surprised to find Noble there, confidently heaving himself up the fire escape. Noble is a very persistent guy, far from the touchy and unstable image he likes to project sometimes.

Tabaqui wheels back and forth at the bottom of the ladder, looking up intently. The blue wall bears the bloody trail of my attempt. As I look at it I can feel my back burning and itching again, and I also get another feeling, telling me to step away from the edge. When in dangerous places, one shouldn't be standing with one's back to people who look at one in a certain way. I make a half turn. Chimera's smirk tells me that she's well aware what made me do that.

"Hey!" Tabaqui shouts. "There you are! I thought you'd fainted up there! Where've you been?"

I nod at him.

Noble's patterned shirt makes him look like a butterfly when seen from up here. A very purposeful and stubborn butterfly, shorn of its wings by some nasty person. He's successfully navigated the spot where I stumbled because of the first nail and is making nice progress, but even looking at his admirable turn of speed I am still uneasy. I step away from the hatch, as if my not looking is going to make his endeavor less dangerous.

"What's your deal?" Chimera asks. "What are you doing here?"

"What about you?"

No answer.

High cheekbones, narrow eyes, hair dyed emerald green. A living doll. She's got a plaster collar around her neck, green eye shadow extends all the way to her temples, lips are the same bright red as the dress, and there's so much powder that it completely conceals her eyebrows. I recall that as she walks something is always clanking under her clothes and her gait is somewhat stilted, making the image of a broken toy even more apt.

"We had a bet. Who could climb up faster."

There's only disdain in her fixed gaze.

"You're both idiots."

I happen to agree. That's exactly the case. I go back to the hatch despite my firm resolution, only a minute ago, not to do that.

Noble is closer than I thought he'd be, but his tempo has slowed markedly and he pauses on each step, recuperating. I feel slightly sick and go to stand as far away from the hatch as I can to prevent myself from peeking in accidentally, counting the seconds in my head. About half a dozen rungs left. I slow down the count. Chimera in the meantime sullenly goes through colorful epithets that are equally applicable to both Noble and me, and can't seem to choose one and go with that. Apparently none of them fully reflects her opinion.

A short while later, Noble drags himself through the hatch and stretches out near the edge, breathing heavily. Chimera's voice strengthens. Without paying her any attention and even before he gets his breath back, Noble starts turning out his backpack.

"Self-absorbed morons! Infantile halfwits! Brain-dead steeplejacks!"

Noble lines up a bottle of medical alcohol, cotton wool, a pack of surgical tape, and a flask of water on the floor. Now I understand where he's disappeared to. He went to fetch the first-aid kit, and then lugged it up here on his back.

"Macho offspring of a middle finger! Snobs with heads up your asses!"

Noble treats the holes on my back. Chimera slowly winds down, and finally the attic is bathed in blessed silence. Goldenhead looks around, puzzled, as if he's just realized that it was much more noisy up here until now.

"Hello, Chimera," he says. "Why did you stop all of a sudden?"

Chimera freezes, mouth agape. Not for long.

"God, I'm excited," she hisses. "I have been benevolently noticed! And by whom! Why, it's Noble, the most beautiful of the House males!"

"Now that's an exaggeration, sister," Noble says, bestowing a smile upon her. "It's not entirely correct. I mean, of course I'm far from being ugly, but the most beautiful, that's a bit much. Makes me uneasy listening to that, however close to the truth it might be."

Chimera gasps for air.

Only someone closely acquainted with Noble can discern, appreciate, and enjoy all the nuances of this game, him playing a vainglorious dreamboat. The alcohol stings like seven hells, Chimera's fury is flooding the cramped space, splashing through the hatch down to Jackal, and I'm still giggling—because Noble is deadly in this role of Prince Charming, deadly and also completely insufferable.

He casts a condescending look about and says, "It would appear that you're hiding here to be alone with yourself. Such a familiar feeling."

"Oh, really," Chimera snarls. "Who would have thought that you of all people would be familiar with it? And now that we have all admired your perspicacity, get the hell out of here. Leave me alone with myself!"

"Can't," Goldenhead says. "The descent for a man in my condition is significantly harder than the ascent. And by the way"—he turns to me—"my time was better, so the bet is decided in my favor. Arms beat legs, it has now been established beyond any doubt."

There's horror in Chimera's glance directed at me.

"How is it possible you haven't killed him yet?" she asks.

I look around the attic: gray lumber walls, dilapidated cabinets in the corners, broken furniture. Everything is covered with a thick layer of dust—that is, except the blanket on which Chimera is sitting. That looks almost new, as does the coffeemaker on it, even if it has seen some heavy use. Noble notices the coffeemaker too.

"Oh! Would you treat us to some coffee?" he says.

"Get lost."

I go back to the hatch. All the way down there, Jackal wheels back and forth fretfully on his Mustang. When he sees me he slams into the wall and almost overturns.

"Go bring someone who can help us get down!"

"Who is that there with you?" Jackal asks suspiciously. "Who are you talking to? I am not deaf, I'll have you know. I hear everything. Sphinx, what's going on? You're having a date with someone, aren't you? By the way, if you're still interested, you lost."

"Go get help," I say and walk away from the hatch, to stanch the stream of questions. I can hear him swearing generously and bumping the wheels against the base of the ladder.

"Who was that?" Chimera asks.

"Little Tabaqui," Noble imparts majestically. "He was keeping score."

"He's not going to barge in here too, is he?"

"It is safe to say that he indeed will not be doing that." Noble clamps the water flask into my rake. "He has not advanced his abilities far enough."

Chimera rolls her eyes.

"You're overdoing it," I say to Noble. "She's already on edge, I wouldn't provoke her further."

"As you wish," Noble agrees. "It's just that I'm slightly at a loss concerning the correct mode of conversation with someone who swears at me blue before I even had a chance to look at her."

Chimera looks at him, then at me, then bites her lip. It appears to be dawning on her that she's been behaving somewhat oddly all this time. She shrugs—her dress doesn't have any straps, it's a mystery how she manages not to fall out of it—and produces a packet of ground coffee from behind the coffeemaker. Grabs a handful and tosses it in.

"Coffee coming right up," she says, doing her best to appear gracious.

The graciousness grates.

Noble clears his throat and looks at me askance, in the sense of *What did you do to her? Own up.*

"Nothing," I reply aloud. "On my honor."

Chimera gets up, hobbles to the furniture cemetery in the corner, and switches on the television that's standing there. In front of the television there's a procession of empty plastic bottles. She kicks one, sending them scattering.

"Almost out of water," she says. "We might be a bit tight."

Her bright dress looks screamingly out of place among all this detritus, while its hem allows a peek at the brutal boots underneath when she walks. A Cinderella who's not quite completely transformed.

I sit next to the blanket, but not on it. Noble crawls closer. On the screen some bearded guy in an orange safety vest explains something, bobbing up and down on an inflatable raft. It's impossible to tell what he's talking about.

"I couldn't get the sound working," Chimera says darkly. "I did tap the antenna feed, but there's no sound. Could be why it got tossed."

Noble and I exchange glances.

There's nothing special about the coffeemaker, there's lots of people lugging them around the House in their backpacks. But attempting to fix an old television is something entirely different. It says that Chimera has spent a considerable amount of time up here.

"Did you have a fight with somebody?" Noble inquires carefully.

"With your ass," comes the rapid-fire answer. "Keep your nose out of other people's business, OK?"

"OK."

We get about half a dose of coffee for the both of us. Chimera gleefully passes a plastic cup with some liquid on the bottom to Noble and says that she's giving us her share. We each take two sips, and then the cup is pointedly crumpled and thrown away.

Goldenhead is irritated, but you wouldn't know it looking at him. He lies down, propped by the backpack, and begins advancing conjectures.

"Well, it's clear that she's here not because of a quarrel," he says thoughtfully. "A girl like this would sooner smash the offender's brains out than run away to the attic to mope."

"Don't forget the dress," I add. "Could it be she has a date up here? That would explain the cheerful reception."

"A date? That would mean that someone is not in a great hurry to arrive to it," Noble says, nodding at the bottles. "I'd say, late by a couple of days?"

Chimera has turned to stone. Her hands, seemingly dark in contrast with her face, are clasped on top of her knees. Noble and I don't even have to look at each other to continue this game. We've spent enough time paired up in poker.

"And about that dress, I can't imagine how she climbed all the way up here in it," Noble says. "A completely wrong equipment for climbing."

He does not mention his own legs, also completely wrong equipment for climbing. And good for him.

"She came down from the roof," I chip in. "You can get there by regular stairs if you obtain the key. Which is not that hard if you really need it."

"Could she be hiding here?"

"In that dress?"

"Didn't have time to change."

"You mean that's regular daily wear?"

"And someone has been bringing up food."

"Yup."

"So at least one other girl would know."

"We should ask them."

"Right. Start with Ginger . . ."

"Enough!" Chimera screams, putting fingers in her ears. "Stop this right now!" We stop and wait silently.

"You're even worse than I thought," she says, looking confused. "You are so full of shit. Why can't you just leave it alone?"

There are plaintive notes in her voice. For Chimera this is tantamount to admitting total defeat, so I am not surprised when she breaks down crying. Noble, however, is shocked, contrite, and ready to yield immediately. I shake my head, and he turns away with a pained look on his face.

Chimera doesn't notice any of that. She's busy drowning in tears. The green eye shadow turns out to be of a waterproof kind, it doesn't run or even smear, but Chimera is a sorry sight anyway.

"What happened?" I ask. So gently that my own voice scares me a little.

Chimera wipes her nose.

"All right," she says with disgust. "I'll tell you. You were going to drag it out anyway sooner or later."

She turns away.

"From our windows you can see the counselors' floor. And also the roof," she says, not looking at us. "Some time ago this guy wanted to jump off. He even slid down and hung there, holding with his hands. But he couldn't let go. I know how that works. Believe me, I know. Then I saw him again. Same place. Standing there and looking down. Just looking down. I managed to get the key, and so when I saw him next time I climbed up here too. And we talked about stuff. He even told me why he wanted to jump . . ."

As I listen to this otherwise ordinary story it rings somehow very familiar. I swear I'm hearing about this for the first time, but the feeling of familiarity is unusually strong. And I don't understand where it's coming from.

Chimera's trembling fingers tease out a cigarette from the pack that's been sitting on the blanket. The long fingernails are covered in green polish.

"And that's it," she says. "We started coming up here. Meeting here. It was our secret. For quite a while. Since before the Law. And then I had this dream. A bad one. So I dragged myself up. And now I sit here feeling like an idiot. Funny, isn't it. The dress. Me keeping the watch for three days straight, and he still doesn't come. And I mean, it's just a dream, right, but I couldn't stay still, I kept thinking what if this one was really prophetic, and then I might be too late. Now you can laugh all you want."

Humpback pops up through the hatch. He's got on his tattered shirt made from strips of cloth and also a miner's hard hat mounted with a flashlight. The hump, the bare feet, and the shaggy mane peeking from under the hat give him a slightly other-worldly look.

"Don't forget to tell him everything," Chimera says, pointing the cigarette at Humpback. "About this painted moron taking residence in the attic. He'll die laughing."

"Who is he?" I ask.

"None of your business."

"Hey, are you coming down or what?" Humpback says. "Because Tabaqui said you wanted to . . ."

I look into the eyes rimmed with green shadow and see in them a rainbow-colored pathway, a corridor leading to . . . But even before I step into that corridor of unsaid words coming at me in a low whisper, I can tell that it ends at a door. A locked door, and behind it, someone whom I know very well. I feel his scent, even without opening that door. I take a step forward . . .

"Don't you dare sneak into me," Chimera squeals, and I barely manage to shrink back, avoiding the emerald fingernails flashing not half an inch in front of my face.

"Hey, cool it!" Noble catches her arm. "One Blind is quite enough."

"Then he shouldn't be sneaking inside me!" Chimera thrashes, trying to free her hand. "Tell him not to do that! And get out of here!"

"Sphinx, you'd better go," Noble says, wrestling with Chimera. "While I'm still holding her. Got it?"

I get up and sleepwalk to the hatch, where Humpback is waiting for me in his ridiculous outfit, swinging his bare legs over the drop.

"Going down?" he says, jumping up. Then takes a length of rope out of his pocket and passes it through the belt loops around my waist. "Just insurance. In case I can't hold on to you."

I stumble down the hallway, eyes staring fixedly ahead. Something is interfering with my progress. I finally realize what it is and stop, and at the same moment Humpback crashes into me from behind.

"Sphinx! I've been calling to you all this time, didn't you hear? Or are you planning to walk on a leash from now on?"

He takes off the safety rope, loops it around his hand, and stuffs it back into his pocket.

"What happened?"

"Nothing," I say. "Just thinking."

"That's some thinking! All right, I'm going back up to get Noble down before he's devoured. That Chimera seems a bit unstable. It would be better not to leave them alone for long."

He disappears and I forge on, all the way to our room, where I sit on the floor just inside the door and observe Tubby wander under the bed, humming and getting covered in dust.

I look at him for such a long time that he manages to traverse the space under the bed, crawl to the center of the room, flip over a chair, and gum everything that fell off it.

Then Noble and Humpback return.

Humpback is just in time to take someone's sock away before Tubby puts it in his mouth. Noble throws a towel on the table and says that water is out in the whole House.

"Why were you doing that?" he asks. "What did you need her confession for?"

"I have this feeling that it concerns me too," I say. "I don't quite understand why or how, but it concerns me. And I don't like it."

Noble sidles up on the bed and pulls off the colored smock.

"Forget it," he says. "Forget the whole thing. Disgusting business."

"He can't," Humpback says. "I have no idea what you're talking about, but whatever it is, Sphinx is not letting go of it. I can see it in his eyes."

Nanette angles to drop on his head but slips on the hard hat and flops down on the floor, deeply offended.

"How do you do it?" Noble asks. "I had this impression that she was going to spill it all, whatever you needed to know."

I close my eyes.

"It was back in the summer," I say.

Chimera didn't say that, it's my own insight. Why is it important that I shouldn't know who it was? Is it because he too is afraid of me? I've almost caught him. I think I can figure it out now even without diving into Chimera's eyes.

"I'll go find Blind," I say, getting up.

"Wait. I'll go with you." Noble pulls a knot of shirts out of the dresser. "Except I need to change first. Still, I don't understand why it's suddenly so important to you."

"Neither do I," I say, and an unpleasant chill down my spine makes me cringe.

Half an hour later, in Black's giant red-and-white jersey with a number on its back, my back crisscrossed with surgical tape, I scour the House in search of Blind. Noble also has on one of Black's jerseys, in white and blue. His number is twenty-two. People we meet on the way ogle us in shock, apparently suspecting that this is an advance notice of the new fashion about to be established. The progressive-sporty style. These stares seem to unnerve Noble, but he's handsome even in a jersey hanging down below his knees. It gives him this edgy hobo flavor with a dash of the dump. Combined with his looks, the effect is simply stunning.

I have to wait for him and adapt to his pace, because he's much slower on crutches than in the wheelchair. After the second circuit of the hallway, complete with peeking in every door, nook, and cranny, Noble asks for a breather.

"He's not going anywhere. And my armpits are killing me. And hell's bells, they're all staring at us, like we're a trained monkey show. I'm sick of that."

"Deal with it," I say. "You volunteered to tag along. Or have you forgotten?"

"Because I worry. About you, about your wanderings, and about this whole business. I have to be close. By the way, what makes you think Blind knows anything about this?"

"Nothing makes me think that. He either knows or he doesn't. But if there's anyone at all who does, it would be him." I stop for a moment. "Coffeepot! We haven't checked there!"

I make a beeline for the Coffeepot. Noble shuffles after me, swearing under his breath.

Coffeepot is all dusk and billowing smoke, as usual. The table lamps throw green palm fronds of light on the walls. The curtains are drawn on the windows, but the sun still finds its way in through the cracks here and there, ruining the attempts at coziness.

Blind is there. Perched on a mushroom-shaped stool, in his epauletted black frock coat. Young Dracula hiding from the deadly rays. There are three cups of coffee on the counter in front of him. The next mushroom is occupied by benignly scowling Vulture, except in place of coffee he has a pot with a cactus in it.

I crash on the nearest toadstool, and my body responds with a full-throated wail in a hundred different places.

"Heavens," Vulture says, emerging from his personal smoke cloud. "What happened to you, boys? You both look . . . er . . . somewhat unusual."

"The water's out," I say. "These are Black's rags. Blind, I've been looking for you. I need to ask you something."

"I am at your service."

Blind peers vacantly into emptiness, hands folded on the counter, like a dutiful student in the presence of a teacher.

"Who tried to kill himself last summer by jumping off the roof?"

Vulture whistles and shields the cactus with his hand, protecting it from the unpleasantness. Noble, having climbed onto the counter to give himself a rest from bipedal locomotion, drags his finger along the smear of spilled sugar. Blind is rigid like a marble frieze.

"So, how about it?"

I understand that no answer will be forthcoming, but it's still worth it to try and drag at least something out of him.

"Come on, Blind. Speak."

He reanimates and turns his face to me.

"I take it back. I am not at your service, Sphinx. Sorry."

Short and to the point. And about as disgusting as Chimera's fear. If not worse.

"It wasn't you, though?"

"No comment."

Noble, hunched over, watches us anxiously, clawing at his chin.

"I'm going to find out anyway."

Blind shrugs. "I have no doubt. But not from me. I think you should go now, Sphinx. You're starting to get on my nerves."

I climb down from the plastic mushroom.

"You said enough by not saying anything."

Blind turns to one of his cups. The conversation is over. I walk out without waiting for Noble and cross the hallway, bumping into people and wheelchairs. Beaten and humiliated.

What is it to Blind that there was this unsuccessful suicide last year? That someone likes walking around roofs? Whoever he is, whatever it is that drives him to the edge, how can I be dangerous to him? There isn't anything ever in Blind's empty eyes, there aren't any corridors or closed doors in his words, but I can read the answer to my question in the solid wall he's built in front of me. And that answer causes me pain.

I enter the dorm. Tubby stops chewing on the blanket and looks up at me.

"Carry on, old man," I say to him. "Who knows, by trying to eat everything you can get to, you may one day make an important discovery. Find a new category of food and cover your name in glory forever."

Tubby doesn't understand the meaning of the words but recognizes the tone. My voice calms him down, and he stuffs the blanket farther into his mouth. I crouch down before him.

"Have you noticed how we've taken to wandering around the House, and there's never anyone in the room? That we've been leaving you here alone more and more often? Life has moved to the hallways, and you've been left behind, poor guy. But maybe that's what's better for you? The entire room is yours. So many things in it. But you see, the problem here is that it was one of us up there on the roof. Someone who can walk. But not Blind . . . not Humpback . . . and not Lary. Black? Alexander?"

Tubby spits out a loose thread and makes a face.

"It could very well have been Black. After what happened to Wolf, it even could have been me. But it was someone else. Let's say Black. And this green-haired girl was ready to claw my eyes so that I wouldn't find out who it was. Curious, no? She was afraid of me. Oh, she wanted to chase Noble away too, but of him she wasn't afraid. Now riddle me this, Tubby. Who's afraid of little old Sphinx? And why? What could I have done to cause this? Something very, very bad. That's the last question I have. And it seems I know the answer to that one. Or maybe I'm just imagining it. Am I lying here in wait for someone who'd answer me?"

Tubby sighs, staring at me with his beady eyes.

"Now I am afraid, Tubby. You see? I'm deadly afraid. Of looking into his eyes and understanding. Why he was stuck up on the roof then and why he keeps going there still. What his guilt is and what his fear is."

Tubby is clearly waiting for me to tell him the tale about the blue sea and white sand. The threads are hanging down from his puffed lips here and there, like whiskers on a catfish, and he's trying to groom himself as best he can, but he still listens intently. He looks at me and then at him, who is sitting next to me, or rather also crouching. There are three of us here, in a circle around the chewed-up blanket, and the third is listening closely, because my words are really directed at him, as are my questions, and he knows that.

"What have you done, Alexander?" I ask.

"I think I've killed him," the soft, toneless voice answers.

"Why?"

"I was afraid. My fear could have done it without my knowledge. I never would try to hurt you, you know that. He was horrible inside. I am glad that I said this to you, Sphinx, and that you thought to ask. You can do what you will with me now. If you tell me to go away, I'll go away."

Tubby tears open a pack of cigarettes and hoots excitedly at them tumbling out. He grabs two and stuffs them in his mouth, then immediately spits them out in disgust.

I get up and walk out. I have no idea where I'm going. I know only that I must move. Doesn't matter in which direction.

"Hey, Sphinx, by any chance are those my clothes you're wearing?"

A figure looming ahead. Must go around. It's Black, hugging a huge speaker.

"Yes. They are yours. Noble and I had a day of reminiscences."

I step to the side, but he follows, still blocking my way.

"Sphinx, what's wrong? You look like hell."

I just stand there, waiting for him to tire of loitering in front of me. I look at his chin pressed against the speaker. Then the speaker drops away, deposited on the floor. The chin disappears along with it. Black assumes a crooked pose, like his spine is somehow damaged.

"I see," he says. "You're a scary sight to behold, but I think I'll manage. Is there any way I can help?"

"Sure. Stuff me in a crack somewhere and plaster it over."

"Understood," Black says, straightening up. "Let's go. I've got what you need. The crack, the plaster, and the gravestone. Just hang on until we reach the first floor."

He leaves the speaker in the middle of the hallway, as a monument to our momentous meeting. I follow him obediently. We come out to the landing. Go down, continue on. In the lecture hall someone is tormenting the piano rapturously, as usual, and the waves of exuberance crest over the entire first floor. Black leads me to a half-empty room. It seems to be some kind of storage space, with cardboard boxes stacked against the walls. One is ripped slightly, and inside it I can discern a commode in plastic foam. We're in the graveyard of commodes.

Black grapples inside one of the boxes, mumbling indistinctly. Produces a bottle, and another one.

"It is my opinion," he says, "that you need a drink. Can you hold this? I don't have any crystal goblets around."

"I'll try," I say. "What's in it?"

"Grain alcohol cut with apple-juice concentrate."

I laugh. Black upends an empty box and arranges the bottles on top of it.

"Your introduction to the Hound tastes. This is their favorite tipple. It's not that bad once you get used to it. It all depends on the ratio."

"For all I care," I say, "this could be pure alcohol."

"I can see that." Black sits down on the floor and unscrews the cap off one of the bottles. "Now what's happened? Want to tell me about it?"

I shake my head.

He passes the other bottle to me.

"As you wish. I'm not going to insist, of course."

The doggy mix is unlike anything I've ever tasted. It's vile stuff, but after three or four gulps that no longer matters.

"Lay off a bit," Black cautions. "It really goes to the head."

"Hounds are strange," I say. "As are their tastes."

"Our tastes," Black notes. "I'm a Hound now too, don't forget."

"That's right," I say. "Brown. Shaggy. Very big. Have you ever noticed what color eyes Alexander has? *Feuille morte*. Fallen leaves. Dappled."

"Never thought to look."

"Your loss. There's a lot hidden inside there. Do you know what my deepest secret is, Black? I mean, everyone has their own secret here in the House. And mine is that I can bail out of here anytime. Anytime I want."

Black chokes and lowers the bottle.

"Where would you go?"

"Also here. But not exactly. The here that's a little out of here. But it's a secret, understand?"

"Got it," Black says. "Inside the bottle with alcohol and apple juice. Looks like you've had enough."

I spread myself across the wall and put up my legs on the box. The clamp on the rake is stuck closed, so I'm now doomed to be holding the bottle of Hound Delight until the day I die.

"Count the fingers for me, Black. I'm going to name for you the parallel universes suitable for hiding."

"Go ahead," Black says. "Be my guest."

The door opens, revealing Noble, swaying elegantly between the crutches.

"Found you!" he says.

"Another one wearing my clothes," Black says in surprise. "What's with you today? Noble, come here. Looks like he's already sozzled. Just started talking about parallel universes."

"A fascinating topic."

Noble floats toward us, flops down on an unoccupied box, and drops the crutches with a clatter.

I close my eyes, and open them again.

And find myself in everything at once. The walls, the ceiling, Black, Noble, even Noble's crutches. I am a vortex into which the world is emptying. The part of me that's the most intact is alarmed by what I'm doing. It's alarmed that it revealed the bottle stash to the other me and allowed him, the bald and crazy-eyed one sitting across with his feet up on the box, to partake of its contents.

This part is also the most convenient to operate, and it says, "Damn. I didn't know he was going to go to pieces like that. What do you think we should do, Noble?"

Yet another part of me, the one slowly crushing the cardboard box (the poor thing contained a bathroom sink once, and is holding on for its dear life), is also irritated and a bit scared, and says, "Why are you asking me? What was it you gave him?"

I am sloshing inside the bottle, clinging somewhat to the sides, because one of my ingredients is a thick viscous syrup. I am not entirely colorless, and that's syrup again. There aren't any others like me, this kind of Me is only made here and exists here and nowhere else. I was stored among the commodes and I seem to remember that this

Me is related to dogs in some fashion, as is the Me sitting across, while the other Me, the one looming over, thinks that I am poison.

My armpits are on fire, sending shooting pains down the rib cage, and my neck is stiff and it takes an effort to turn, and the box under me keeps sagging. I should probably get up before it goes completely flat.

I don't want to become the box too, the feeling of it is too unpleasant.

The Me slumped against the wall says, "The entire world is part of me now, do you understand that?"

I answer to myself, having jumped over to the buckling box, "Honestly, I would prefer not to."

And immediately soar up and crash back down, expand in all directions and solidify, peek through thousands of tiny apertures with a billion eyes. I like this Me most of all, it's so peaceful and so enormous, a cube that contains all others. It's rather more like Us, and we are the foundation of the House, we carry and support it. It takes an effort to keep myself within the confines of this single room, because it is more natural for walls to be joined up with other walls, but for some reason I feel that this would be dangerous, even if I don't remember why exactly. I lose the sense of hearing. The little scurrying We, restless and much too emotional, move and squeak so fast that I can't pick up the high-pitched sound they produce. I am closer to being asleep than awake, this state is familiar to me, and only the apprehension of joining up with other walls keeps me from giving in to it entirely. But it becomes harder and harder. I am feeling more strain than the unfortunate box, but the Me perseveres as long as it can, and when its strength starts to fail I concentrate on the point where I am coming in contact with the hairless, metal-handed Me. I flow into him and hear Black say, "What do you say we go find Blind?" and Noble responds, "We can't leave him here like that."

I sit slumped against the wall, feeling its smooth, cold surface with my shoulders and with the tape that's binding them, and recognizing in it an almost kindred spirit.

What I've just done is forbidden: dissolving in the environment is too addictive and too dangerous. Dissolving in people is safer, but inanimate objects tend to bind to the dreams and it's easy to get bogged down for years and not even notice. The trick with the walls saved me once, when I was a kid and life had served up a particularly scary episode. I had barely made it out that time, and gave myself a promise never to do it again. But promises are made to be broken, eventually, the way Alexander has broken his. I still can't bring myself to think of his words, of what he said about Wolf, but his broken promise I can already start to mull over. The short stint inside the walls calmed me enough for that.

I look back at Black and Noble.

"One of the variations of the Game," I tell them, "is being in everything. You are in everything and everything is in you. It's dangerous, though."

Black and Noble exchange glances.

"Never tried," Noble says. "You're an extreme guy, Sphinx. That's not good."

"He looks a bit more sober," Black says hesitantly, pointedly addressing Noble, like a Spider within earshot of a patient.

I nod. A bit, yes. But not completely, because I'm still in the Game. Both Black and Noble look slightly unusual. Black must be forty-something. An imposing figure of a man, naked above the waist, with an axe tucked into his waistband for some reason. Handsome. Head balding in the front, face more lined than might be expected, but still. A Conan the Barbarian in his middle age.

Noble is younger, and not that impressive. A sharp, severe face without any trace of his usual beauty. A slight overbite. The eyelashes white as if powdered with dandruff. He's clad in disgusting rags that come apart at the seams every time he moves.

The rules of the Game are not the same for everyone. Black is the way he wants himself to be. Noble is the way he feels himself to be.

This might be interesting.

Black gets up, crowding half the room.

"Let's get out of here," he says to me. "We'll take you out for a little spin. Now let go of that bottle, will you?"

I unclasp my long and very human fingers, and the bottle falls down and rolls on the floor. I'd be interested to know what I look like, I mean the whole of me, but there are no mirrors here. Black bends down, bathing me in dog reek, grabs me under the armpits, and hoists up.

"There we go. Easy does it. One step at a time."

I shuffle to the door obediently. You don't argue with Conans, now do you? I feel his breath on the back of my head. The Alpha Hound. The door is mossy, overgrown with mold and lichens, armies of ants traverse it, and in place of a handle there's a splintery branch.

Black's paw framed by the spiky bracelet grabs it and breaks it clean off. The door flies open and we march out to the abandoned highway under the inhospitable gray sky.

Fields stuck with telephone poles, cracked asphalt, the white dividing line barely visible, half-buried in blowing sand. The wind twists Black's jersey, which I'm still wearing, tickling my belly with its icy fingers. Noble tries to put up the collar of his coat, but it immediately tears off and remains in his hands. He flings it away in disgust.

"Ready to go?"

Black rushes forward purposefully, shouting, "The speaker! I left it in the middle of the hallway. Better go pick it up before someone swipes it!"

I look back at the door, but it has already disappeared. Of course. Noble hobbles ahead, catching the crutches in the cracks of the pavement and digging them back

out, cursing and swearing. Through the rips in his pants I can discern something green
and leafy springing up.

The clouds loom threateningly. It's going to rain soon. Black is already far away.
This endless highway for him is just a few feet of wooden floor. That's the reason he's
moving with such an astounding speed, throwing surprised looks back at Noble
and me.

"Where are we going?" I ask Noble.

"How would I know?" he says indifferently. "It's your Jump, you figure it out."

He notices something in the grass, stops and pokes it with his crutch. There's a
cigarette end stuck to the rubber tip when he brings it back. Noble peels it off and
carefully stashes it in his pocket.

"That's nice," he says. "Forgot my backpack. A couple more like that, and there's a
whole smoke right there. You be on the lookout for them too, so that we don't miss any."

I peer into the withered grass.

"You're catching on fast, Noble," I say. "Like it's an everyday thing for you."

Noble laughs, exposing sharp teeth.

"Not every day. But not rare either. Wasn't it you who explained that there was
nothing special about me doing it?"

"It was," I agree. "But it looks like I've bungled the explanation if you keep shuttling back and forth. I should have scared you more thoroughly."

"Oh, you have," Noble says. "Don't worry. But we're on the boundary, not inside.
We can go back anytime we want."

"Boundary has its own dangers," I keep pressing.

He looks at me in surprise.

"What dangers? It's only our own guys here, isn't it?"

I choose not to argue further.

A purplish bolt of lightning suddenly splits the sky above us.

"We're going to get wet," Noble says, looking up and shivering under his rags.
"Black must have found his precious speaker by now. Not falling through has its
benefits."

"I'm sorry," I say.

"I'm not blaming you. It was my idea to follow you here."

Five or six crumbled milestones later we finally get a bearing. The sugar cube of
the roadside diner, still far away. Surprisingly, there's no rain yet. But it starts to get
dark unnaturally fast.

The closer we get to the diner, the more attractive it looks. The white building
with a steep-pitched roof and striped awning. There are a lot of cars in front of it, one
more ancient than the next. A parade from the dawn of the automobile era. I used to
collect cards with cars like that. Here they look decrepit. The most rickety rust-bucket

convertible is occupied by two half-naked girls who start to squeal and wave as soon as they see us.

"Hey, big boys, wanna ride? Wind in your hair! We can jump off a cliff, groovy, man!"

One of them has Marilyn's face, and her breasts under the skimpy faded bikini top bring to mind soccer balls. She parts her pouting lips and licks them expectantly. "How 'bout it? A ride?"

We make our way around them and enter the diner, diving into the noise, commotion, and beguiling meaty scents. The small square room amazingly manages to fit an entire throng of people. They sit at the wooden tables, but they sit under and on top of them as well.

The tables haven't been sanded and they are full of splinters; some of them still have patches of bark. The faces around me look unfamiliar. In reality I know all of them, of course. Colorful slogans blaze on the walls. As soon as I concentrate on one of them, it starts swelling, growing in size and obscuring its neighbors.

Noble and I grab a miraculously free table against the wall, under the unchanging woodblock print of a seascape. Someone in a chef's toque and a golden carnival mask with a long beak drops a couple of plates off the tray as he rushes past.

I look closer. Finely minced meat over something grainy and yellow, like corn mush. Noble unzips his tattered coat and tucks in. He has a huge, glowing heart pendant around his neck, enclosing a flaming lock of hair of truly frightening proportions. I gulp the food in the same greedy fashion as everyone else. There's a display attached to the wall underneath the print, its screen flashing green numbers, 2 and 2. Two times two. That's the number of our table.

My plate is almost empty. The next table gets swarmed by a raucous gang of old farts in black leather, with unkempt beards. Their snorting and laughter drowns out everything else. Still, even over the din they're causing I can clearly hear something angrily banging at the window.

Its insistent knocking finally attracts attention. The window is opened and in flutters a big-eared creature, resembling a half-baked hyena with faceted wings made out of flower petals. It flaps futilely under the ceiling and crashes down on our table, overturning Noble's plate and sending up a cloud of pollen that makes my nose itch.

"Look at them," the hyena says indignantly. "I've been searching all over for you. Where have you been, you bastards?"

"Nowhere special," I say. "We're having a lunch, as you can see."

"A lunch, huh," the winged hyena drawls menacingly and breaks into a coughing fit. His open maw drips saliva that crystallizes and cascades down with a glassy tinkle.

"Where's my grub?" the flyer demands hoarsely. "And after that I'll deal with you, and it's not going to be pleasant."

Noble drums his fingers on the table.

"Hey, Sphinx. You think it's time we got out of here? Before the rest of them arrive?"

The hyena transforms into a frail, pensive, middle-aged Sikh. No sign of wings. Black suit, snow-white turban. He unfolds the napkin and takes a plate off the tray.

"I am very sorry if I seem intrusive," he says politely. "But if I were you I would refrain from sudden movements at this time."

"We will," I assure him. "I'm waiting for someone. And if that someone isn't here in the next half an hour we'll try to scramble out. I just need some time."

Noble sighs and takes out the cigarette butt he salvaged. The pendant around his neck is pulsating in sync with his breathing. The Sikh, humming softly, produces a gold-plated hookah out of thin air.

Blind's soft hands rest on my shoulders, giving me a substantial electric jolt. I startle.

"How are you?" he asks considerately.

"Lousy."

Sightless One sits across from us. He looks exactly the way he always does, no image changes for him. Maybe a little more transparent, that's all.

"That's not good," he says. "Pull yourself together. You've got responsibilities."

"Keep your leadership lectures for another time, will you," I say. "I'm not in the mood."

Blind agrees with surprising amiability.

"As you wish. Except there might not be another time."

The lights blink and switch back on. Twice. The beards in the corner whistle disapprovingly.

"Wow," Noble says, aghast. "Will you look at that . . ."

I turn around. There's a strange creature making its way toward us between the tables. It's naked and skeletally thin, with stubs of wings over its shoulders, covered in sores and welts from head to toe. A rusty iron collar encircles its neck, trailing an equally rusty chain all the way to the floor.

"What kind of sick thing is that?" Noble whispers. "Night of the living dead?"

"Of course it's not dead," the Sikh says reproachfully, taking a break from the hookah. "This is our dear Alexander."

The mangled angel stops in front of us, holding his chains gingerly, and waits. The white feathers that he has on his head instead of hair are hanging down over his face, the remains of the wings expose the bones. It would be better not to look too closely. Every wound is crawling with something that would be better not to notice. The face bears an expression that would be better not to remember. Noble turns away and fumbles for his crutches, taking sharp indrawn breaths.

"Alexander," I say. "Enough with the crazy."

He raises his eyes at me. Wine-red eyes on the white face. I see that it's in fact Ancient. Or that he looks like Ancient.

"Stop this, please," I beg him. "I've already forgiven you. There is no blame on you."

"Really?" he says in a cracked voice. "You're not just lying to me out of pity?"

"I never lie out of pity."

The lights go out again. Screams in the darkness.

I close my eyes, and when I open them I'm back in the canteen. A boombox is blaring under the Rat table, a continuation of the screams that ended my visit to the Not-Here. Lary nods in sync with the music, wiping a plate with a piece of bread. Tubby is dozing next to him, face down in a stained bib. Alexander is busy with his soup, bent low over it so that no one can see he's crying.

Tabaqui shoots me a withering look.

"Sphinx, what's going on here? I demand to know what's going on!"

"Nothing," I say. "What possibly could have happened *here*?"

"You hurt Alexander, didn't you?" Jackal presses on. "Because I'm going to kick the crap out of you if you did!"

"Everything's fine," I hiss through clenched teeth, getting slowly steamed by his nosiness. "Calm down and leave me alone."

"If everything's fine, why is he crying?"

"And why are you asking Sphinx?" Blind inquires, throwing a crumpled napkin on the plate. "Can't a member of this pack have a cry in peace without you butting in?"

"Sphinx has promised something to him," Tabaqui persists. "And now Alexander's crying."

I get up and leave the canteen before he has a chance to really get to me.

Right outside the door, I walk into Noble sitting on the floor with a look of someone just condemned to death, hugging his crutch. I sit down next to him.

Noble blows his nose loudly into a handkerchief and says, "You need nerves of steel with this crowd."

He goes back to cuddling the crutch. I look up at the ceiling, at a snaking line of letters barely distinguishable from down here, and think: *There we go, the need for expression has driven them to the ceiling, it's only a matter of time before ceilings start looking like walls with all the writings and drawings, and whoever would want to read them would need a stepladder, so we're going to have an infestation of stepladders in the House.*

I sit in silence and think about all of this.

RED

They throw a bucket of soapy water on the floor. Clanking, splashing, sudsy rivers flowing. Colored green, for me. For everyone else they're probably gray. Those who didn't scamper out in time now besiege the windowsills and peer down, terrified.

The second bucket. The rivers receive reinforcement, and there's a veritable lake on the floor. I wouldn't want to swim in it. Just the accumulated spit alone would be enough, though it can't be seen, actually, having merged with the suds. But the cigarette butts and assorted floating half-eaten dreck melts and congeals unpleasantly.

"I wish I had a boat," Whitebelly squeaks from the windowsill, leaning precariously. "Sail away, sail away! A rowboat!"

Someone pushes him off, and we have one more Ratling-worth of general wetness.

Microbe and Monkey, both sour-faced, push ahead brooms wrapped in rags. Water splatters everywhere. They look at their shiny boots in horror, as if they haven't been walking over this same crap for the last month, only sans water. The brooms reach the wall and turn the other way. Honestly, it's all just spreading around the dirt. Not much effect at all. Still, if this isn't done once a month, I shudder to think what would happen to all of us here.

Gaby, Echidna, and Treponema mill at the doors, pretending like they're all dressed up to pitch in. Echidna is even clutching a brush, with two painted talons, as if she's holding a delicate flower arrangement.

I look around the dorm. It's almost empty, apart from the spectators. Everything that could be hauled out has been. I grab a sleeping bag that's drifting nearby and drag it to the bathroom. It spews forth torrents of water. The maidens scatter. Figures. This is the communal screwing bag, better not to imagine what's inside. Personally, I wouldn't venture to climb in on the pain of death.

I lower the leaky monster in the bathtub, open both taps wide, and pull on the zipper. It's stuck, naturally. I yank on it harder. Then I leave the bag to bleed out and beat a retreat.

There's a mini-assembly in the dorm, in the middle of the remains of the lake. They mourn the disappearance of the hallowed bag. "O brethren, where shall we copulate?" The looks directed at me are not exactly friendly.

"You've thrown it away! How's we supposed to do it now?"

Whitebelly rinses his sneakers in the bucket. He couldn't care less about the bag.

"We'll take yours, then," Hybrid says, businesslike. "Yours is even roomier. Because you went and got the old one wet. And it'll take a while to dry out."

I demonstrate to him how, where, and under what circumstances he's going to so much as lay a finger on my sleeping bag.

"I'm gonna cut you," Hybrid screeches. "Tonight! Cut you up like a sausage! It's coming, you hear?"

I hear. I hear all kinds of stuff from him. All he ever cuts is furniture. Sometimes the walls. No one has been paying any attention to his screams for ages.

"The room isn't going to clean itself," I say.

Hybrid rummages in his pockets, looking miserable. Dropped his razor somewhere, I'll bet. Again. Always the same story.

Surly Rat-Logs wring out the washing rags. Viking, shirtless, is hard at work on the table, spitting on its surface from time to time in lieu of other cleaning liquids.

I close my eyes and . . .

A vision. This very dorm, except squeaky clean, like on the first day we entered it. Snow-white walls, sparkling windows. No sleeping bags. No Rats. Not even a single Walkman. In short, Sepulcher. The dear old home. Only without Spiders.

I shake myself out of it, grab the nearest mop, and run to the farthest corner. I scrub and scrub until my head spins. A tiny little light spot appears on the floor. That's all I get for my trouble. And my back is already howling in protest. Got to sit down.

Whitebelly splashes closer, in cutie-baby mode.

"You need help? May I?"

"Sure," I rasp. "Knock yourself out. I don't seem to be producing much of an effect."

"There's this clean spot over here," he assures me and grabs the mop.

Its handle is not much thinner than he is. I look at him laboring, then at the Logs, who quickly assume a busy look, then at the condom floating by. Someone added more water, even though I told them two buckets is the limit, otherwise it would trickle down to the first. It would be one thing if they dried it out quickly, but they just slosh the water from one wall to the other.

Also someone gnawed on the aloe plant again. A minuscule nub is all that's left. I take the pot and look at it, and immediately Hybrid starts cleaning his nails, whistling tunelessly. It's not often you meet a person who can gobble absolutely anything, and only get healthier for it. Hybrid is one. I have this suspicion that he even takes an occasional bite out of us when we're asleep. Carefully, so that we won't notice. The disappearing stocks of toothpaste are definitely him. There aren't any others who'd eat it.

I make it look like I am preparing to toss the pot at him. He shrinks and screeches. Microbe and Monkey whine, "But Red, but Red! We're cleaning!"

So sincerely that one might even believe it's actually the case. Unless the one is me.

"Right," I say. "Carry on."

And go out to grab some fresh air, a quick smoke, and something to eat. Maybe also have a rest somewhere. I know I shouldn't. Even before the door closes behind me they're going to drop everything and dash to the bathroom to check on their priceless bag, if it's still holding together.

Four homeless Ratlings sitting right outside. Poor orphans on a winter night.

"When is it going to be over?"

"Can we go back now?"

"Why is it taking so long?"

"Patience, Red. Patience," I say under my breath, but loud enough.

That should shut them up for a while. I take advantage of the pause in the action and leg it to the Coffeepot. No guarantees, though. If they have a mind to they can barge in there too. Good thing I'm not their father, or I'd have throttled the whole gang long ago. Nothing but whining and zits. Enough to drive anyone nuts.

It's girls' night in the Coffeepot. Six walkers, crowding the counter, deep in conversation. Three of the maidens are fresh off the cleaning shift. Still bearing the traces of honest working sweat. Judging by the hushed exclamations, the subject is serious business. The shorts-clad bottoms sway like the tails on fretful cats. Apart from them it's a thin crowd. Corpse with his book and Sleepy dozing in his wheelchair.

"Over here!" Corpse screams. "Move your flippers! I'm holding a place for you."

Places are abundant, so his screaming is more in the nature of a habit. I go over and sit down, and all the girlies immediately turn around and stop talking. I don't like the glint in their eyes. It's as if they've been waiting for my arrival.

Corpse turns his head from side to side, trying to figure out what the deal is. There's a chilly pause, and then the gunshot of a glass slammed against the counter.

"So that's it," Gaby says loudly. "I'm now damaged forever. Because of that lowlife."

I was planning to go get a drink, but their stares make me reconsider. There's a real danger of choking on the first sip.

"What's wrong?" I say, because it's somehow clear that the lowlife is in fact me.

"And he's the one asking," the supporting cast drones helpfully as Long drops down from her stool and hobbles in my direction, miraculously not toppling off her heels.

"You bastard," she spits through the strata of lipstick. "I'm pregnant, that's what!"

Three-ring circus, that's what it is. Even Sleepy wakes up. And I've got enough of empty hysterics without cause back in the Rat-hole.

"All right, I get it. What's that to do with me?"

"With you?" Gaby repeats sharply. "You maybe mean it wasn't you and your damn Rats that's done it?"

"That's enough. Get lost," I say, at the same time realizing that it should be me getting lost, and fast. So I start getting up. It's either that, or fighting with her.

"Oh, nooo! You're not getting off that easy!" Gaby screams, jumps closer, and slaps me one across the face.

Heavy as hell, my head almost flies off. I just manage to grab the camouflage glasses. The girls at the counter cheer. I return the smack an instant before it dawns on me that it's that very reaction she wanted.

Gaby throws her head back and squeals, more gratingly than an electric drill biting into a cement wall. The maidens pick up the infernal squealing and unstick themselves from the counter, one after the other, falling off like overripe toadstools. Except the toadstools wouldn't then turn on me.

I jump up and shield myself with the table. A couple of pointy heels crash into it. The girls, huffing and puffing excitedly, try to conquer the obstacle, constantly getting in each other's way.

Sleepy, in the background, quickly steers toward the exit, trying his best to appear invisible. Tongue hanging out from the effort. Echidna climbs up on the table. The rest are pulling her down. And all of this is accompanied by the unceasing squeal bordering on ultrasound. Crazy. Enough to make me feel like an honest-to-goodness rat. One that's about to have its spine crushed by the sharp heels. And then smeared across the floor. Why? No reason. And the worst part is that before it ends, it's going to hurt. A lot.

The table slams into my stomach and drives me backward in the direction of the wall. I'm boxed into the corner. By pushing my back against the wall I manage to stop the advance, but at the same moment my hair is grabbed so viciously that it has a hard time staying attached. Now it's my turn to squeal.

"Are you mental?"

That was Corpse. What an inopportune moment to be joining the discussion. I'm shielded by the table, and he's not. He's immediately shown the error of his ways. I save my scalp at the expense of a handful of hair, while Corpse ineffectually fights back against the kicking feet and the piercing talons until he ends up on the floor.

I jump out of my pen and run to him. In any other circumstances I wouldn't have, because Corpse is not someone who requires outside assistance. His other nick is Scorpio, as his see-through complexion is matched by his overall fuzzy harmlessness, but I'm not sure about anything anymore. And it appears that the girls will more likely kill him than not. There's already a sizable crowd in the Coffeepot, and someone gets to them before me. Which is good, because Echidna sinking her nails into my face hampers my progress.

After that it's no longer clear who's slugging who and for what. A writhing knot of bodies, wheelchairs and tables being overturned, the squeals climbing higher yet, and at the most dramatic moment, Sheriff and Black Ralph come bursting in.

That is to be expected. What's unexpected is that their arrival fails to stop the melee. Probably because the maidens don't give a hoot, to put it mildly, about our counselors. They are afraid somewhat of their own hags, but they've learned that our geezers, one, never would lay a finger on them and, two, have no way of raising a stink later. So the ballet exercises continue. Not for too long, though, because the girl-tamers are not far behind.

I haven't been taking an active part in the proceedings for a couple of minutes now. I'm busy sitting under the counter trying to ascertain the source of that unpleasant crunching sound I heard when someone stomped on my hand. Also of the ringing in my ears and the double vision.

"Hey, Red. You all right?"

I'm being jostled gently. It's Ginger. I look at her until the two very pink faces float closer and combine into one, and then tell her that yes, I am all right, but not really.

The Coffeepot is strewn with bodies and debris. The bodies seem to be alive, or at least stirring, and the world around me is unusually bright and pretty. Takes me some time to figure out that it's because I'm not looking at it through green lenses. It's useless to even think about finding them now.

Microbe whines pitifully in the middle of the room, clutching his jaw. Horse is attempting to get him to stand up. He succeeds after two more tries, and the two black-jacketed figures lead out the third ceremoniously. The brotherhood of Logs. Such a moving spectacle.

"They are all bastards! Animals!"

Reptile Godmother is wheeling out the chair with Bedouinne, who is drowning in tears and tightly clutching something flail-like in her puny hands. Where does Bedouinne figure in this at all, I wonder. What could possibly be her problem?

"What happened?" Ginger persists. "Are you going to tell me or what?"

"I wish someone would tell *me*. If such a sage could be found, I'd personally present him with my favorite table fan."

I get up, checking my brace for cracks with the hand that's still functional. But it's not there. At all. I only now remember that I stopped wearing it two weeks ago. Which means that all this time I was hopping around with my spine left completely unprotected. The thought makes me deeply sick.

"Hey, you!" Ginger says, alarmed. "You're not going to faint on me, are you?"

"No. It's just my heart sinking. Visibly."

Tabaqui the Jackal is busy arranging the variegated hair samples around himself, like a wizened old shaman who's just received a fresh consignment of scalps. Humming softly. Spooky stuff.

My hand is swollen and hurts like nobody's business. I try to wiggle the fingers and immediately regret it. Also, someone was sick at some point in all that ruckus. On me, it seems.

"Come on. I'll help you wash up."

Ginger takes me by the clean sleeve and makes for the door.

We negotiate the piles of overturned tables and chairs, sprinkled with the shards of the broken lampshades. Noble, sitting on the bar, nods at me sullenly. The whole gang's here. And they're *not green*! That freaks me out, it really does.

In the shower stall (I seem to have acquired a strong aversion to them lately) I try to explain to Ginger what has transpired. Not having much success, because I actually have no idea. She lathers my hair as she listens, so I can see neither her nor her reaction to my ramblings.

"You think Gaby made it up about being pregnant?" she says.

"How would I know? If pregnant girls behave like brainless berserkers, I guess she didn't."

The blackberries of her eyes seem to be tearing up, because I look at them through the curtain of water.

"What about the others?"

"They jumped right in. Like it was the plan all along."

She shoves my shirt into the stream, and the razor case falls down on the tiles. Ginger picks it up and looks at it intently.

"Tell me. If it were guys going at you, would you have taken this out?"

"I guess. I'm not sure. I always carry it around, and then always forget to get it out in a tight spot. Corpse, now he doesn't need to even think about it. The razor finds its way into his hand by itself. I don't know how he does it."

"Why didn't you use it? Either of you?"

I push the hair away from my eyes so that I can see her when she says that.

"You mean to scare them? I don't think it would've worked."

Somewhere outside, Sheriff howls for all the "clowns" to present themselves for Sepulchral ministrations.

Ginger rinses off my shirt under the shower. Her own is almost as wet. Shorts too.

"You have to understand. They could have killed you. Easily." Having said that, she looks me straight in the eye for the first time. "It wasn't mercy that made them stop when they did."

"Oh, I got that. I just don't understand why."

"Yeah, you don't."

I continue to hold up the damaged hand, away from the walls and from my body. Because of the constant worry that I might bump it against something, it's hard for me to concentrate on the conversation. That, and Sheriff banging on the stall doors.

Ginger is right, but not entirely. I did understand something back there in the Coffeepot, except I can't quite pin it down. That happens a lot. The knowledge sits inside you somewhere, and you don't notice it until something shakes you up, and then you understand it's exactly what you've been waiting for. But you still won't know why that is.

This annoying thought keeps chasing itself around my head, that if not for me there might never have been this new Law. Even though it doesn't much matter now.

The door slides to the side, admitting Viking's head.

"Everyone went to the Sepulcher," he reports, then cracks a dirty smirk. "I'm not interrupting anything?"

Ginger decides to walk me over. It's peace and quiet in the hallway. We stumble on, leaving puddles in our wake. Big ones and small ones. Ginger wrung out my shirt before slapping it on me, but the hem is raining water again, both pant legs are streaming, and my sneakers squelch lustily. This is the first time I've looked like that in the full light of day. A regular water sprite. Ginger isn't much better.

"What do you think is going on right now in the Sepulcher?" I say, imagining our triumphal entrance.

"If you think I'm going in there, forget it."

I'm grabbed and squeezed at the edges to wring off some more water.

"I hate public displays of all kinds," Ginger says, getting up from her knees.

"Then you should've changed my clothes. And if you're really serious about this, how can you live alongside Jackal? Did you see his ripped-out-hair collection? Now don't tell me it's not him you're living with. He is there wherever any of them is."

No answer. She doesn't like talking about the Fourth with me. I don't know why. She just doesn't.

My purple shirt not only drips, but also stains. I am covered in spots the color of dawn. Or of baboon's butt. I've never had problems with associative thinking, so looking at them I picture myself bleeding out, and then Solomon. These images always go together.

Solomon, my very own illicit basement-dwelling Rat. The pudgy wobbling cheeks, the haunted look, and his damn asthma. One and a half candles until the day after tomorrow, a flashlight, and a stack of newspapers. Good thing I hauled some grub down to him last night. He's probably OK for today. I am not going to the basement with my hand in this condition, no way. And don't tell me about rats and their behavior. I used to keep a real rat. Not one of those white ones, no, I mean a genuine authentic gray. You can go to sleep with it. Just feed it out of your hand, that's all. No tricks. But a human—that's entirely different. Feed him or not, but never come close, especially when not healthy.

What was I thinking when I agreed to that? Is it that I'm compassionate, or simply stupid? It's a great feeling when your worst enemy is dependent upon you for absolutely everything. When he lives the life of a lowly rodent, never seeing the light of day. There's the answer, I guess. I'm enjoying it.

"Why the long face?" Ginger says. "You were looking much happier just now."

"Thinking about my moral fiber."

She nods. Not a single word to make me feel better. Is it because she agrees that there's a reason for the face elongating? I guess. I should keep quiet, because whatever else, she's going to give it to me straight if I ask. "Having your respect is all that matters." I'm never telling her that. You just don't say things like that out loud. Even to someone who's a dozen times closer to you than a sister. I'm talking to her too much as it is. She knows everything about me, and I know almost nothing about her. Because she never discusses her business with anyone. Ever since the time that she was teaching me not to whine when it hurt. She is the older half of our tandem, and the older sisters do, of course, wipe the noses of the younger brothers, but when it's time to cry on someone's shoulder they run to others. It rankles immensely, but there's nothing that can be done about that. She looked after me, so I am forever a baby to her, only grown up a little. The month in my favor that separates our birthdays is a silly joke of the calendar. Tyranny, if you think about it. I will probably never know if she cries on Noble's shoulder or not. I'd like her to have a shoulder like that, for crying, and I'd like to know that Noble is not just another infant for her to care about, but whatever's going on between them is none of my concern. Or I might start stomping my little feet in a jealous pique, pawing at her shorts, whining. Or whatever she imagines me doing. Heaven forbid I'd find out what that is.

"I'm off. Don't sit in the Sepulcher chairs unless you want your backside kicked by the Spiders."

She turns around and leaves. Wet like a squirrel out of water.

I shout after her, "Yes, chief!"

And rush in the Sepulchral door.

Spiders detest Rats, especially when the latter are wet and numerous. Which is why we get treated out of turn, and expeditiously.

Sheriff stomps and swears, "He golden teeth aflame." I leave with my hand in a cast and a handful of pills in my pocket. I can feel them doing me good already, even before I've taken any. I'm the only such freak in the whole House, getting a cheerful boost out of the Sepulcher. Yes, I know I'm perverted, but what can I do? Not that I want to. My life, almost all of it, has been spent inside it. I sometimes even feel like I was born there. So all that high-minded stuff about blessed home and hearth—for me it's always been more about the Sepulcher, not the House itself. I don't exactly make it a point to come here often, but when it happens, it happens. I also heal quickly, so I have no fear of this place, unlike some who go to pieces every time they're anywhere near it. It probably should have been the other way around, because there isn't anyone who's been split open and stitched back up more times than me, but human nature is a strange beast and logic doesn't figure into it.

I'm not sure who's staying for observations from the other packs, but we lose only Hybrid. Corpse and I are the first out the door. Must be our fame, that of the cheerful undead who are ready to party even in their graves, preceding us. Being an exceptional individual has its privileges.

We take a detour into the common crapper and compare the loot. His haul of pills is almost as big as mine. It's not every day you get this many, even after a major surgery.

"Cheer up, man," I tell him. "There's an entire fortune here, if you spend it wisely."

"But I've got nothing that hurts," he says. "Strange, huh?"

I'm full of envy. Because I do have things that hurt, and how. I'm not sure I'll be able to hold out.

"I'm surprised you haven't stolen more," Corpse says. "Oh, right, the hand."

I don't answer, because I've just noticed something really troubling. It's lying in wait under one of the sinks. The Phoenix plastic bag. Sneaked behind the pipe and probably imagines itself well hidden. As if that acid-blue color could ever blend into the background. Those ghastly wadded bags hunt me constantly and everywhere. There is no more disgusting sound than the rustling of a bag that's creeping after you. Supposedly it's the wind pushing them. Yeah, right. Wind has nothing to do with it. I mean, if there is wind they behave even more brazenly, but they can ambush you even when it's totally still. Ever since that time when a particularly dusty and sticky member of the species attacked me from above, parachuting onto my face and clinging to it in the manner of a carnival mask, I've been very touchy on the subject.

Their favorite gathering spot is under the porch. That's where they usually chase each other around like tumbleweeds, crackling merrily, and that's where they prepare the ambushes, because the last thing a person coming out on the porch expects is a bag flying out from behind the banisters, ready to latch on to any exposed body part.

They don't quit, even when swatted down. The only sure way of fighting them is to nail them to the ground with a stone, no easy task since they're very quick to flee and repulsive to the touch.

And the white-and-blue Phoenixes that have taken over the House and its environs, because that chain is the principal source of toothpaste, creams, deodorant, and shit like that, are the most insidious. I recognize them by their rustle. It's somehow louder than any other kind. And that's why, upon noticing one of them hiding under the sink, I stop listening to Corpse's mutterings and prepare for battle.

"Damn," Corpse says, apparently tracing my gaze. "Enemy at the gate?"

I nod silently. The bag chooses this very moment to attempt a furtive feint, but freezes when it realizes it overestimated its chances. Corpse and I shrink back.

"Wait here," Corpse whispers, reaching for the mop by the door. "Don't worry, I've got this."

Hunched, on his tiptoes, he hobbles toward the sink.

The bag stays put. Corpse sneaks at it like a warrior with a lance, he sneaks, sneaks some more, then lurches forward and pins the bag to the floor with the mop. It emits a desperate crunching crackle.

I turn away.

"Done," Corpse says, raising the mop with the speared Phoenix. "It's finished!"

We put it to the torch, dump the ashes in the toilet, and flush thrice. Time for the victory smoke.

"Thanks," I say. "I'm forever in your debt."

"Don't mention it," Corpse says, waving away my gratitude. "I hate them too. Especially the ones that go flying at night."

He French-kisses the cigarette and slides down the wall, turning greener and greener. No, it's not the glasses, since I don't have them on. It's just that Corpse has this delicate tint to his skin, and every little thing changes it for the worse. Smoking, for one. They told him long ago that his first drag was going to be his last. So every day he keeps experimenting, getting more and more pissed at those liars.

But we have a deal, me and him. On the day that I appear to him in his dreams, he quits smoking. Except when that happens it would most likely be too late, so it's just empty words to calm my nerves. You see, I have a peculiar habit of visiting the soon-to-be-dead in their sleep. I seem to come to them and not really do anything except sit silently on the edge of the bed. And soon after that, they die. I don't really like talking about it, to save myself from the assorted crazies. It took a real effort to get rid of my old nick. I console myself by thinking that as nasty habits go, this one isn't the worst I know.

"Where you heading?" Corpse says drowsily.

"Vulture's place. Going to wheedle something green off him. For Hybrid. So he can eat it in peace. You're supposed to bring gifts when visiting the afflicted."

"Oh," Corpse bleats. "Good deeds. Sweet, sweet, sweet. And Spiders are like, 'Of course, babe, eat all you want, you need the vitamins.' Perfect!"

He shakes his blue dreadlocks, quaking with laughter. I bet he's going to fall asleep right there on the tiles as soon as I'm gone. It's bad for him too, so he never misses an opportunity.

So I go out into the world, carrying the cast in front of me like a tray of my own bones. A handsome specimen of a man, getting handsomer by the day. The zit on my right cheek will have to be scratched by the left hand for a while. The drying soles of the sneakers have developed these unpleasant ridges, biting into my feet.

On my way I take a peek in the Den. And regret it. I completely forgot about the cleanup, and here it is, or rather its aftermath. The entire floor is covered in slimy gunk, and the trash piles are still where they've always been, except now they're damp right through and even more revolting. The crate-table is in the middle, upside down, stuck to the above-mentioned unmentionables, and the prevailing scent is that of puke, even though the bulk of the puking has been performed elsewhere.

No Rats in sight except for Whitebelly, rubbing a sponge over a spot the size of a football. He's almost all the way through to the floorboards.

"Good boy," I say to him, by way of encouraging his diligence, but immediately realize that he's got earphones on, so he can't hear a damn thing.

What was the idea with that cleanup anyway? They're nothing but trouble, that at least is obvious.

RALPH

Once every six years, the wall separating the House from the world sprang a leak. Ralph had observed it three times already, and still he couldn't make himself think of graduation as a natural occurrence in the order of things. That the Outsides could suddenly permeate the House—that the House could bleed its creatures, who until then appeared joined inseparably with it, into the Outsides—was not something you could accept and get used to. The more experienced counselors passionately loathed the pregraduation term, and their newly hired colleagues had to spend a couple of years listening to their horror stories. "If you haven't been there for a graduation, you haven't seen anything." Ralph had been lucky (or unlucky, take your pick) to have arrived in the House shortly before a graduation, and so wasn't a target for such remarks. He was one of those who "had been there" from the start. A fresh conscript finding himself immediately on the front lines and in the thick of battle. Even though all he could later recall from that, his first graduation, was an indeterminate feeling, mostly a result of the parents' all-out assault.

Just as there weren't two students who were alike, there weren't any parents who were alike. But still counselors placed most of them in two broad categories: Managers and Contacters. Managers maintained active communication with their children, made regular visits on assigned days, and pestered counselors with phone calls. Contacters appeared only in the days before graduation. The rest fell somewhere between the two extremes, and were unworthy of a separate classification.

Contacters' visits coincided with the arrival of supervisory committees, fire and sanitary inspectors, and all and sundry child-welfare agencies (it was always a surprise how many of those there actually were in existence). Every six years the counselors were reminded that there was an authority above them, and that the authority was very interested in what they had been up to. Their work was checked and rechecked. They had to produce reports and reviews, duty-shift timesheets and exhaustive evaluations of each and every student. All of that was then collated, examined, and cross-referenced. The fire inspectors tested the extinguishers and quizzed the counselors on proper procedures. Those who could not quickly rattle off the sequence of steps to be undertaken in case of a fire were sent to remedial training. The medical inspectors took over the hospital wing and turned it inside out. The sanitary inspectors went through the kitchens with a fine-tooth comb. The Contacters demanded advice, immediate attention, and, often, first aid. The Managers demanded respect. Some inspectors, after going away, returned for the second and even third go-around. By the end of the month the principal was a human wreck.

Then summer break came, allowing the counselors some time to recuperate, and then they were immediately thrown into the pool of freshly admitted six-year-olds. Ralph considered the system of handling admissions and graduations that had been adopted in the House completely idiotic. He could not understand why the juniors, in the graduation year, were not being sent away from the House earlier. Even by itself, the House losing half of its inhabitants was a shock to them, and that they were allowed to witness it happening Ralph considered inexcusable. Also that in the summer camps they received an unlimited license to discuss what had happened, with no classes to distract them and almost no counselors to supervise them. And that, upon return, they were faced with the new batch of students, their successors, a constant reminder that soon they too would share the fate of the seniors, because the seniors were now them. It was no surprise they didn't have any love for the juniors, never cared about them or helped them with anything. It was also no surprise that they never forgave the counselors their betrayal and never trusted them again. What was surprising was the abject adoration that the juniors had for those disgusting youths. Seniors could ignore them or treat them like dirt, the squirts didn't mind at all. They absorbed everything seniors had, including the dread before the graduation, and that dread by degrees became a part of the fabric of their lives. A sign of the coming maturity.

This time Ralph was alone among the counselors in having been through a graduation, and it struck him as curious that the pregraduation month had passed quietly, almost peacefully. A single visit from the supervisory committee. No parents except those explicitly invited. Several docile Managers, no Contacters at all, no inspectors, no reams of reports. The committee arrived and departed without a single comment. All that despite the House being completely, comprehensively in tatters. Shark was singularly inept at being a principal, and the state of records and accounts could only be described as disastrous.

Ralph had thought about that and soon figured out the reason for the unexpectedly forgiving attitude. The House was on its last legs. No one cared anymore about its overall dilapidation, the falling chunks of plaster and the condition of the fire extinguishers. The fire and sanitary inspectors could not be bothered about a building slated for demolition. It would have been silly to insist on repairs and check the safety procedures. Ralph, with a sadness that surprised even him, realized that in the Outsides world, the House already had been struck from the registers. All that remained was for it to die.

On the day of departure of the last successful test takers, he managed to push out the troubling thoughts. That day even resembled the previous graduations somewhat. The parents of the four smarty-pants had arrived simultaneously and before the announced time. The active Manager among them, Booger's father, caused a gorgeous scene that lasted a good half of the morning. Bedouinne's parents weren't into scenes, but their daughter did everything in her power to make this day memorable for them and succeeded brilliantly. Chickenpox's mother fainted when she discovered that her daughter's body had been adorned with no fewer than three separate tattoos, a parting gift from her loving friends.

Tradition dictated that the counselors see off the students from their groups, so Ralph was free to be engaged in the role of a guard. For two hours straight he chased away from the reception area the gawkers who desperately desired to join the fun, listening to the screams behind the door until the crowds finally dispersed. Not two minutes after the hallway cleared, Homer emerged from the reception, and two Pheasants wheeled after him. Homer was a wreck, Pheasants beamed.

Ralph waited for Shark to come out, reported that his hallway shift had been uneventful, and inquired why the farewells took so long.

"Good thing they happened at all," Shark said. He had a guilty look.

From the reception came the sound of breaking crockery and someone bawling. Ralph guessed that this was Darling unwinding after her encounter with the parents and decided to leave it at that. A counselor who's just gone through the ordeal of spending time with the departing students and their parents was, to one who hasn't, as a soldier who has returned from a skirmish to one who's stayed back in the trenches. Seeing Ralph in the room could push them over the edge.

He wasn't visiting Smoker but did inquire after his well-being every day. Not because he felt concerned about his health, but because of a guilty conscience. Besides, he was afraid Smoker might sink into an even deeper funk. Spiders respected Ralph's wishes and hadn't invented any mysterious disorders to explain Smoker's stint in the hospital wing, saying to him instead that they were simply concerned with his blood work, but the hypochondriac boy had freaked out anyway. This needed to be resolved soon, one way or another. Ralph couldn't insist on keeping him for more than ten days, but on the other hand he didn't want to return Smoker to the group from which he was clearly being squeezed out.

He went into the staff room, to make the requisite call about Smoker, and ran into Godmother. She was one of the few who really used her desk there as a work space.

She was behind that desk now, sorting some papers, nodded curtly in response to his greeting, and then asked if he could spare her a few moments. That didn't surprise Ralph. As the graduation crept closer, the counselors started asking him about his experience with the previous ones. By now he was used to the questions, which were always the same, and they kept asking them over and over again, as if they didn't hear his answers, or couldn't understand them.

Godmother collected the loose sheets into a file and only looked at Ralph after making sure the surface of the table was clean. She folded her hands on top of it, neatly, palm to palm.

"I remember you saying once that at the time of the last graduation the situation in the House was less stable. If I'm not mistaken, you were referring to the ongoing confrontation between two belligerent groups."

"Yes," Ralph said. "It had been much worse then."

He sat down, feeling somewhat uneasy, as he always did in Godmother's presence. This woman had an ambiguous effect on him. Yes, she was undoubtedly good at what she did, effortlessly handling the problems that would reduce Darling to a sniveling mess, she was smart, responsible, and rational, and the girls respected her. At the same time, her aloofness was off-putting. No one in the House liked her. To Ralph it looked like she had no feelings at all for her charges, that she was comprehensively impersonal. He tried to convince himself that this was just a professional deftly hiding her emotions, but it did nothing to dispel his prejudice. Godmother was too icy for her job. Or too old. Trim and straight, like a retired ballet dancer, invariably in the same gray pantsuit, white cuffs gleaming, she appeared fifty while in reality pushing seventy.

"I would be interested to know if that remark hasn't been simply an attempt to calm down the principal," Godmother said.

Her eyes behind the glasses glinted severely and accusingly. The cold, round, staring eyes, the hooked nose, the long neck—they all combined to make her look like a bird of prey. But despite all that, anyone talking to her got the impression that she had been a great beauty once.

"No," Ralph said after a pause. "I don't remember exactly the conversation you're referring to, so it is possible that I was trying to calm him down, but the last time the situation really was much less stable."

"Are you concerned at all that as of today there are again two belligerent groups in the House?"

It took some time for Ralph to understand what she meant, and when he did he almost laughed out loud.

"No," he said. "I am not concerned. I do not consider this conflict to be serious."

Godmother's fixed stare became unblinking.

"Why?" she said.

"You see," he said, feeling awkward for intruding on her turf with his musings, "this so-called war is entirely the girls' invention. I think it's their way of coping. They are aware that graduation is coming whether they like it or not, and with it the separation from the boys with whom they have established relationships. They also see no chance of those relationships continuing beyond the gates of the House. So, what's easier: accepting the separation or convincing themselves that those who they're being torn from are the enemy? They chose the latter. On balance, it would mean less pain for them overall. The war may look silly, but it appears to be an effective technique."

"Do you consider yourself an expert on female psychology?" Godmother said.

What infuriated Ralph wasn't the question itself but that it made him blush.

"No," he said drily. "I do not. I was merely expressing an opinion."

"An opinion that deserves the highest praise," Godmother said even more impersonally. "I salute you."

Ralph again tried not to let his annoyance show.

"Would that be all?"

"Apparently," Godmother said. "I would like you to keep one thing in mind, however. The principal does not share your optimism."

"I would imagine," Ralph muttered.

"And he is prepared to use all options available to him to ensure safety at the time of graduation. What would your attitude be toward that?"

"One of understanding," Ralph said, getting up. "If you'll excuse me, I still have some unfinished business to attend to before the meeting."

Godmother nodded. "Of course. Should we be expecting any suggestions from you?"

"Possibly."

As he left, she remained in her place, looking ahead at the wall, like a robot that's been switched off. Sitting very straight, with hands folded in front of her.

A round-faced, big-eared boy in a black skull-and-crossbones T-shirt peeled leisurely away from the door. Ralph closed it behind himself.

"What were you doing?" he whispered.

"Listening in," the boy said earnestly. "I am well aware that I shouldn't," he added, preempting Ralph's reaction.

Ralph lightly massaged his eyelids.

"Why do you do it, then?"

"Sometimes my curiosity gets the better of my ethical values," the boy admitted. "Has that ever happened to you?"

Ralph leaned against the door.

"Please leave," he said. "Get out of my sight."

Whitebelly nodded eagerly and retreated.

"Did you hear that?" Ralph mumbled, making his way toward the stairs. "And this one isn't even a Log."

But in all truth, he was glad of the encounter. Charmingly insolent Whitebelly chased the image of the unmoving mannequin in the staff room from his mind's eye. A frightening image, even if he wasn't quite ready to admit it.

Ralph climbed up to the third floor, to the break room where the meeting was scheduled for three o'clock. Originally this was supposed to be a home away from home for counselors, but the drab institutional furnishings and rickety tables piled with dog-eared magazines invited the ghosts of a dentist's waiting room, so there never had been any volunteers to spend their free time here. Finally the administration hauled in three desks and a slide projector, put up a dry-erase board, and designated it a meeting room. This breathed new life into the space, and soon counselors claimed parts of it for storage, divided up the chairs, and declared the tiny balcony to be the smoking area, and Sheriff even brought his favorite boombox. Now at any time of day or night someone would be in, even if most often that someone was Homer, dozing on the sofa.

Today the room reeked of menthol and medical alcohol, again reminding Ralph of the dentist.

Homer and Raptor, slumped in chairs, had all the appearance of victims of a natural disaster. Homer's balding dome was crowned by an enormous cold pack. Raptor stared fixedly at the ceiling. Their ties looked like they'd been used recently in vigorous attempts to strangle their owners. Their jackets were nowhere to be seen.

One desk was occupied by Darling, applying a fresh coat of paint to her face; another, by downcast Sheep, preparing a new cold pack. Sheriff crowded the door to the balcony. The smoke from his cigar wafted into the room, and that concerned him not a bit: his body was safely in the smoking zone, and where the smoke chose to go was its own business. Sheriff wasn't about to miss a single detail of what was going on in the room.

Ralph sat on the sofa between the two chair dwellers, moaning Homer and ominously silent Raptor. Sheep tiptoed over to Homer, changed the cold pack, and shot Ralph a reproachful glance. "Where have you been hiding while we were in agony here, desperately in need of your help?" was the approximate message of that glance. Or maybe she was just chiding him for staying silent. Or for lack of compassion. Or maybe neither. Sheep's watery stare seemed always on the verge of tears and always accusing of something. The playful curls of her hair and the girlish ruffs of her dresses clashed with the permanently sour expression on her face.

"Thankfully I was able to refrain from throttling anyone today," Darling muttered through clenched teeth, studying her reflection in the compact's mirror. "An amazing feat of self-control . . ."

"Ha, ha," Raptor said grimly, as a reminder that he was still alive.

"And to think, I assumed Lenses had set the bar impossibly high," Darling continued. "But that oversexed cow Bedouinne managed to top even her."

"How can you say things like that about a child?" Sheep exclaimed indignantly.

"A child?" Darling almost dropped the compact in surprise. "A child? The dumb little slut looks older than her mother!"

"Language," Sheep squeaked.

This was obviously far from the worst language that had been uttered in the room recently, and Sheep's indignation somehow lacked conviction. Ralph again congratulated himself on not coming up here earlier. The hysterics seemed to have died down, and he wasn't enough of a sympathetic listener to precipitate another round. He had no doubt, however, that all the sordid details of the indignities suffered by each of them would be rehashed anew before the meeting started.

"What is it you're trying to see there?" Homer said caustically. "New lines that appeared since morning?"

"No!" Darling snapped the compact shut. "New gray hairs in my nose!"

They exchanged looks full of deep mutual loathing. Homer self-consciously probed his own nose. There was plenty of hair in it, gray as well as other colors, projecting happily far beyond its confines, so he could only take Darling's remark as a personal jab.

"Look who's talking! Like he's the one aggrieved," Darling sneered. "After everything that we had to listen to on his account!"

Homer moaned, jerking his legs in untied shoes, and hoisted the cold pack higher.

"He has the temerity to portray himself a victim!"

Sheep, seemingly to cool down the room's overheated atmosphere, switched on the fan standing in the corner. Sheriff stomped to the windowsill and mounted it.

Darling, unexpectedly pretty in anger, her eyes shining and even her nose appearing somewhat shorter, addressed Ralph directly.

"Now you tell me, whatever has he been thinking, dragging three Pheasants to meet with the parents of one of them? I wish someone would explain that to me!"

Nobody was planning to explain to her anything about Pheasants, Ralph least of all, but Darling wasn't really in need of explanations. She wanted to spill out her frustration. A silent listener was perfectly acceptable. But she got some unexpected competition.

"Damn Shark couldn't be pried off the phone," Raptor said to Ralph as if taking him into confidence. "Forty minutes! Booger's daddy is eating me alive, and the old codger keeps babbling nonsense into the dead receiver. Ain't that a riot?"

"What did he want?" Ralph said, accepting that one way or the other he'd have to listen to the whole story.

"Who?"

"Booger's father."

"A graduation certificate, what else! What do all of them want when they start that whole song and dance about quality of education? 'I don't care where you get it from, that's your problem, you should have warned us that you were running a school for retards here,' all that crap."

Raptor rubbed his forehead.

"Boogy brought his old man a copy of the question booklet. So this buffalo keeps waving the goddamned sheet in front of my face, roaring so loud you could hear him two blocks away. Wants to know how come most of our students botched the answers to those questions. And what am I supposed to tell him? When the hardest one in there is 'Austria is located in a. Europe, b. Asia'? And to top it off, those disgusting little Pheasants of his"—he nodded at Homer, who blinked guiltily—"are right there next to us, tossing out Latin proverbs and happily citing philosophers of antiquity."

Homer moaned, loudly and defiantly, sending Sheep scrambling.

"Then," Raptor went on, winding himself up, "Cupcake's mom takes that splotchy little scrap from Booger's daddy, acquaints herself with its contents, and starts an inquest, for what possible reason these boys here"—Raptor switched to a high-pitched voice—"these two gentlemen, who have just displayed an astonishingly high level of intellect, could have failed this, the most straightforward of tests."

Ralph couldn't help himself and smiled.

"So, how did they wiggle out of it?"

"Wiggle out?" Raptor said. "Pheasants? They didn't! They just sat there ogling us and smirking! I was the one who had to do all the wiggling. For everyone, because Alf here decided to keel over and play dead!"

"It was a heart attack," Homer protested. "I really could have died. There was not an ounce of deceit!"

"Yeah, right." Raptor nodded. "Of course not. One's clutching his chest, the other his phone. Guess who's left to deal with the mess?"

"If you ask me," Sheriff growled from his perch, pointing at Homer, "it's all his fault. There's no call to be pushing his Pheasants everywhere. They'd give anyone the willies. Now take my Ratlings, they make sense whenever they open their mouths."

"I see, so that's why their mouths are always hanging open," Darling interjected. "And their eyes are closed. And their heads are twitching."

"Right, that's what I'm talking about," Sheriff said, unfazed. "Just the ticket."

Homer, wearing a deeply haunted look, swallowed a couple of pills and took a swig out of the mug brought over by Sheep.

"Coffee? Tea?" Sheep addressed the assembly.

Before anyone could answer, Shark came in. His suit was rumpled, the tie hung askew, but overall he was unusually bright and businesslike. Godmother followed right behind him.

Shark went to the table, poured himself some water, drank it up, looked around the room with the air of a commander before the final battle, and announced, "The topic of today's discussion is graduation."

Ralph thought that Shark couldn't be anything but disheartened by what he saw. His hastily assembled putative army was in disarray. Homer, even after having pulled the cold pack off his head, cut a pitiful figure. Raptor, with his twisted tie and vacant stare, wasn't much better. Sheriff, perched on the windowsill, brought to mind Humpty-Dumpty just before that great fall. Flustered Sheep imitated a pincushion. Darling, as always, overdid it while applying her makeup; the result was a teenager on her first trip to a nightclub.

And still this motley gang, as idiotic-looking as it is, is my pack, Ralph thought. *Or whatever can be called my pack. I am one of them.*

Godmother was alone among those in the break room in having a presentable appearance. Trim, collected, resembling an aging French actress, she took position behind Shark, arms crossed, and the shoulder pads of her gray suit seemed tailor-made for military patches.

"So. Graduation," Shark repeated meaningfully. "At our last meeting I called upon all of you to give this issue some serious thought and prepare suggestions." Shark thrust his hands in the pockets, rocked on his heels, and added, "I shall now hear those suggestions."

He fell silent, and it took the counselors a couple of minutes to realize that the introductory speech was over. They exchanged puzzled glances. Whatever else, Shark was never known to be succinct. For him to come to the point was usually the labor of the better part of an hour, giving everyone else enough time to finish their coffee, exchange some whispered gossip, and even catch a couple of winks. They'd acquired a knack for appearing to be listening to Shark's speeches while engaged in their own little distractions, and now, deprived by him of their customary ration of forced boredom, felt almost cheated out of it.

"I'm waiting," Shark reminded them after the brief pause and fell silent again, to everyone's consternation.

Sheriff was first to get his bearings back. He yanked at his suspenders a couple of times before droning, "So, my suggestion is gonna be like this. On the night before the graduation we all go to our groups, right, and we stay there in the dorms and maintain order. Until morning."

He cast a proud look around.

It was obvious that this was going to be rejected out of hand, but it allowed him to project the aura of a tough guy.

"If I may be allowed an observation." Godmother stepped forward and planted herself in front of Shark. "To make your plan a reality, some of us would have to become twins." She rested her gaze on Ralph. "And that is to say nothing of the situation in our quarters. Where we have thirteen dorms and four counselors. I am afraid you have not taken that into account."

Judging by Sheriff's grimace, he'd never even heard about this until today.

"Um . . . I mean, how many have you got?" he said.

Darling giggled.

"We are caring for fifty-six young women," Godmother articulated. "Housed between nine four-bed rooms and four six-bed ones. If I were you I would not be so ready to admit ignorance of such basic facts about the place where you've been working for years."

Sheriff was not to be intimidated that easily.

"Come on," he scoffed. "Like I would ever go there. I've got enough trouble as it is. All right, if'n that's so, let's knock our heads together some more. We can get all the girlies in one place. When it's just for one night it's not gonna be a big deal."

"Speak for yourself!" Darling exploded. "And what, pray tell, is that place you're talking about? The lecture hall? I for one am not too thrilled to be cooped up on graduation night with dozens of deranged girls in a place that doesn't even have adequate sanitation. How do you propose we take them to the bathroom? Under armed guard? Or will you provide each with a personal chamber pot?"

Sheriff broke out into his infamous convulsive laughter. Swaying back and forth on the windowsill, he slapped his thighs, gurgled, and snorted, and his checkered polo shirt seemed ready to split apart under the assault of this much mirth.

Godmother finally took a seat. At the very edge of the chair near the door, still facing the counselors; more like a stern teacher in the classroom than one of them.

While waiting for Sheriff's exuberance to ebb, Shark pointedly stared at his watch.

"That's a winner!" Sheriff wiped his livid face with a battered handkerchief. "I'd pay to see that . . . Your stuck-up heifers . . . all in a row . . . holding the potties!"

A more conscientious person would have been skewered to the spot by the look Godmother was sending him, but not Sheriff.

"Now if your fertile imagination has fully enjoyed this picture, can we, perhaps, move on?"

Shark's sarcasm also missed wide. Sheriff's thick skin made him almost invincible.

"Sure, why not. Let's hear it," he agreed. "So my idea didn't fly, I get it. Let's have others give it a shot."

"Thank you," Shark said icily.

And now if he says "Anytime" Shark is going to throw him out, Ralph thought. *No one ever gets fired during the last term, but Shark will make an exception.*

Luckily for him, Sheriff said nothing. Shark gave him another minute of the silent treatment and then, satisfied that there were going to be no more remarks coming from the windowsill, went on.

"Anything else?"

Darling rose up. She gracefully smoothed out her skirt and puffed her silver bangs to the side.

"I have a very simple suggestion," she said earnestly. "We lock ourselves up on the third and let the night take its course. It's not like we have any idea what they're planning anyway. They could sleep quietly through the next morning, for all we know. Or they could throw a farewell bash. After all, don't they have a right to celebrate the occasion? It's the same in every school." Darling batted her lashes and smiled obsequiously at Shark. "Wouldn't you agree?"

"This isn't a plan, it's a surrender," Shark snarled. "I am not entertaining any more 'run and hide' proposals, or their variations, at this point."

"Well, then." Darling shrugged, doing her best not to show how hurt she was. "I have nothing further."

Shark stared at Ralph. Transferred his gaze to Raptor, waited a moment, then waved a hand in invitation. Godmother stood up. Observing Shark's pointed courteousness as she took his place, Ralph realized that those two were in collusion over this. He didn't like it.

Godmother nodded to the assembly. Reset her spectacles. Cleared her throat.

"I cannot conceive of supporting the last proposal, even though it would be preferable to some others we have heard today. In my turn I would like to offer two ways to approach the current predicament. Please be assured that both of them were exhaustively researched to encompass all eventualities."

Godmother spoke so softly that it seemed any noise, no matter how insignificant, would make her inaudible. Everyone strained their hearing in order not to miss a single word. A well-worn speaker's trick, but you had to admit—she really could make it shine.

Sheriff was leaning precariously off the windowsill, cupping an ear with his hand. Advertising his hearing problems. One could almost believe that the requisite earphone wires snaking into the ears of each Rat, deafening them, all somehow had ended up in his ears as well. At least, this was the impression he was trying to convey. That it was a workplace disability.

Ralph felt the rising tension. Something was about to happen, and happen very soon. Godmother was nodding at Shark and he leered at her in return. They behaved like two conspirators who didn't care to conceal their conspiracy.

"As all of you must be aware, the graduation is officially scheduled for the seventeenth of June," Godmother went on. "I recommend moving it up. If the graduation happens earlier than anticipated, we may reasonably expect the pregraduation night to remain free of incidents. It goes without saying that under no circumstances should any students be apprised of this. The whole enterprise hinges on maintaining the utmost secrecy."

There was a well-placed pause.

The counselors exchanged glances. Sheep's eyes filled with tears. Homer applauded quietly. Raptor shifted excitedly.

"Well, I'll be! That could just work," he blurted. "It really could! What a nice idea."

"It could work," Darling admitted sourly. "Unless *they* get wind of it."

Ralph didn't say anything. The thought of doing this to them didn't sit well with him. Declaring the graduation at the moment of graduation? It was low, it was unfair, it was cowardly. Very Shark-like, in short. But . . . Raptor was right—it could work. Had he any right to take away something that would guarantee them a month of peace? Especially when not offering anything in return?

So—silence, which also could be taken for acquiescence.

"In the interest of avoiding disclosure it will be necessary to institute restrictions on the communication between the students and their parents." Godmother gave the counselors a severe look. "All calls to parents must take place exclusively on the third floor, and only with one of us present throughout. All visits to be approved on a case-by-case basis by the principal, with all visiting parents briefed in advance. Under no circumstance should we be mentioning the date being changed either in personal conversations or in written form when finding ourselves beyond the third floor. My strong preference would be for that rule to be observed even here. The telephone currently located in the staff room, I propose to eliminate. There is a suspicion that students do avail themselves of it."

"Yeah," Raptor whispered. "Suspicion my eye. They've been using it for ages. Who's this hag think she is?"

"And in conclusion." Godmother's voice became louder as she shot a disapproving look at Raptor. "In conclusion. The true date of the graduation shall be known to two persons only, our esteemed principal and myself."

Ralph imagined hearing the thud of Raptor's jaw hitting the floor.

Homer shot up, waving his hands madly. "This . . . It's an outrage! What do you mean—we don't know the graduation date?"

Sheep surprised everyone by piping up, in a reedy squeak, "I object! This is disgraceful!"

The explosions from the two most cowed counselors made Sheriff's menacing growls seem insignificant by comparison. Raptor peered ahead fixedly, gripping the arms of his chair. Ralph desperately hoped that he himself did not look stunned quite to that degree. Godmother, composed and self-assured, calmly weathered the barrage of hostile stares. Ralph couldn't but admire her composure.

"Allow me to explain," Darling said when the excitement died down.

Clearly impressed by Godmother's grace under fire, she did her best to appear equally dignified. It was painful to watch.

"What you've just suggested is impossible, for several reasons. One," she said, flashing a purplish-pink fingernail, "one, they need to gather and pack their belongings. It takes time. Two, parents! Even assuming that you do not reveal your secret date to us, you'll have to tell them, right? Why do you assume they would keep silent? And when the day comes, some of them are going to show up early, the others late, and then there will be those who will simply inform us that they can't quite make it on that day but anytime else is fine with them, and so on. Imagine the mess! More than a hundred students suddenly finding out they're being taken away before having time to pack, say good-byes, put on makeup, write farewell notes, or whatever it is they would want to do . . . and add to that the parents—and us, also completely frantic, because . . . because we, imagine that, had no warning that the graduation was going to happen on that particular day! It's ridiculous! Just four of them leaving today has reduced us to ruins, and now you're expecting—"

"Please. Calm down," Godmother interrupted Darling's effusive oration. "This is not the end of the world, as you seem to be imagining. Especially if we can keep our wits about us and refrain from inflating the issue to apocalyptic proportions."

"Right." Shark, visibly downcast, perked up. "It's not that bad. We went over the procedure in great detail, secured the assistance of certain third parties, and expect that with their help unrest can be prevented."

"And who would those parties be?" Darling inquired.

No reply was forthcoming.

Godmother paced the room, arms folded firmly.

"I have an impression that you do not fully appreciate the need for maintaining complete confidentiality," she chided, stopping by Homer, cowering in his chair. "Our pupils are nothing if not perceptive. The least misstep, from any one of us here, and the secret will be out. It is not even necessary to actually mention the date being shifted. An unusual burst of activity. A concerned expression. We could be sending signals and not realizing it. I am not talking about preparations." Godmother glanced in Darling's direction. "But if for no apparent reason our belongings started disappearing from the staff room, it would attract attention. I want to stress that it is possible to slip unintentionally, thus endangering the entire initiative."

"I'm not arguing with you." Homer waved his hand feebly, obviously imagining that the harangue had been directed at him. "You have been quite clear. I apologize for my outburst."

Godmother was smiling, looking over his head at Ralph.

He smiled back.

I get it, Iron Lady. Running around in panic—that's Homer. Darling has a packing fetish. Sheriff is a windbag. Raptor can betray himself by the triumphant look on his face. Sheep, by the long-suffering one. But what about me? What is it you suspect me of? Are you imagining I'm going to run straight to them and blabber about those precious plans of yours?

He caught that "yours" in his own thoughts, cringed, and half closed his eyes.

Is that really how I've put it? "Yours" and not "ours"? Maybe she really does have a point there, the old bitch.

"I am waiting for confirmation," Shark demanded. "From everyone. No exceptions. Now. Because I do not intend to return to this after we vote."

"I mean, I agree it's a clever plan," Homer said hurriedly. "Even though I am annoyed at the lack of trust the administration has demonstrated."

Darling snorted, "Oh! Lack of trust. That's what this is called now? Nice!"

"Do you agree or not?" Shark demanded.

"I agree."

"I don't," Sheriff grumbled from the windowsill. "Precisely for that reason. Making me into some kind of old gossip who can't be trusted with keeping a secret? I'd sooner resign than put up with this kind of attitude!"

"Perfect." Godmother nodded. "No one is keeping you in the House by force. If your decision is final, prepare your resignation letter. The principal will sign off on it."

The silence that fell on the room was disturbed only by the blades of the ceiling fan slicing through the air. Godmother, speaking for the principal in front of him, made everyone uneasy, and Sheriff doubly so.

"Now this is going too far!" he blurted. "Where d'you get off jerking people around? Who gave you that authority?"

"Everything our esteemed colleague expressed here has been discussed with me," Shark said gleefully. "Discussed and approved."

The expression on Sheriff's face was hard to describe. Ralph never imagined that he could be that shocked.

Where have you been for the last thirty minutes, you silly little man? How come you're only now getting what we all have already understood and accepted?

"And unless you decide to reconsider, please make sure that the letter reaches the principal's desk within twenty-four hours," Godmother demanded. "We need to know definitively whether you are leaving or staying."

"I am not about to resign this close to the end of the year!" Sheriff roared.

But he couldn't quite put his usual bluster in it.

"In that case I will thank you to refrain from more empty threats in the future."

Sheriff slumped sullenly on the windowsill. He looked like an irritated gargoyle that's put on weight. Looking at him, Ralph even felt a twinge of compassion. He thought that if now Godmother were to tell Sheriff to get off the window and sit down on a chair properly, he would most likely capitulate.

Luckily Godmother was above petty gloating. It was obvious to everyone that Sheriff had been comprehensively defeated and his humiliation was to serve as a warning for anyone foolish enough to contemplate insubordination.

Godmother was now circling around Ralph.

"Let's move on with the voting," Shark prompted.

They moved on with the voting.

When Godmother's suggestion secured a majority, Shark applauded briefly (Homer decided to join in but stumbled when he saw that no one else did) and then requested for the second suggestion to be revealed.

"I am trembling with anticipation," he announced, rubbing his hands together.

"Look at him trembling," Raptor muttered under his breath but perfectly audibly to Ralph. "I wonder how many times you two have rehearsed this."

"Yes, the second part of the plan." Godmother looked squarely at Ralph. "I propose that we remove from the House some or all persons whom we, after careful consideration, deem dangerous. Persons who are psychologically unstable, behaviorally maladjusted, and at the same time capable of influencing the rest of the student body."

Ralph leaned back in the chair and closed his eyes. There it was. Now it was his turn to protest and be cut down to size. Godmother was in for an unpleasant surprise.

"Ah!" Darling perked up slightly. "That's interesting. So who are they, these dangerous, influential crazies? I am looking forward to the naming of names."

Raptor, on the other hand, darkened.

"I vote no!" he said, jumping up. "This will only provoke them. We'll get exactly what we're trying to avoid, only earlier."

"I vote yes," Homer said. "A very reasonable and timely action."

"I have a question." Sheep dutifully raised her hand, like a student in class. "Are you planning to include girls on that list?"

"Certainly if you can think of a specific candidate," Godmother said, fighting back a smile. "We would be happy to consider her."

"God forbid," Sheep squeaked. "I would never!"

"So we're talking about boys, mostly?" Darling pressed on.

"Yes. The so-called Leaders."

Raptor grabbed his head.

"I suggest we discuss Sphinx, from the Fourth," Darling said. "Popular, influential, and clearly a disgusting character. A real pervert, if you ask me."

"There are no unstable persons in my group," Homer pronounced proudly. "I ask for the First to be excluded from this conversation."

"Well . . ." Shark tried to make it look like he was weighing a decision. "This is against the rules, you understand. But the First really is an exemplary group. I am open to making an exception. So ordered. As for Sphinx . . ."

"He is not one of the Leaders," Godmother prompted softly. "So he is not the object of the present discussion."

"Precisely," Shark rushed to agree. "He is far from the most influential figure, let's not waste our time. Denied."

Darling went into a pout.

"We are not debating the actual candidates yet, but the proposal itself," Godmother said to her by way of consolation. "Two of us for it, one against . . ."

"Emphatically against," Raptor put in.

"Two abstained," Godmother went on without so much as a glance at Sheep and Sheriff. "And one more is . . ."

There was a pause.

"Against," Ralph said.

Godmother nodded, satisfied, as if this was exactly what she had expected him to do. She then made another pause and when he failed to make use of it, continued.

"Two ayes, two nays, two abstentions. I am, naturally, voting yes, and our esteemed principal . . ."

She turned to Shark, and that's when Ralph decided he'd had enough. He was tired of looking at Godmother, tired of listening to her, and disinclined to perform the rest of the lines she'd written for him in this play.

"Excuse me," he said, getting up. "I still have some important things to do."

Shark's expression promised a coming storm.

"What's that supposed to mean?" he said. "What things could be more important than this meeting?"

"What things?" Ralph stopped at the door. "Oh, you know, of an urgent and unavoidable nature. Compose a resignation letter, type it up in duplicate. Pack, tidy up around the office a little. It's amazing the way the dust just seems to stick to it. Return the linens to the laundry and some books to the library."

"Oh god!" Raptor gasped. "Just what we needed . . ."

"Wait a minute!" Shark said. "I'm not signing that."

"Don't." Ralph shrugged. "Honestly, I don't care if your signature is on it or not."

"Aren't you the least interested in the results of the discussion?" Godmother said in a surprised voice. "In finding out who we are going to choose? Are you concerned about the welfare of your charges at all? Your childish behavior seems to suggest otherwise."

Ralph smiled.

"I am reasonably sure that it will be my charges you are about to single out, and this is exactly why I am refusing to participate in this charade. As a counselor I am responsible for every single person in my groups. When someone pushes me aside and starts running their lives for them, the only thing that's left for me is to say good-bye. I'm done here."

Godmother grimaced.

"How easily you abandon your post. And how quick you are in forcing your responsibilities on others. It amazes me, frankly."

"You just won't believe"—Ralph glanced briefly at Shark, frozen in place—"the extent to which it amazes myself."

He tidied the office, took a shower, and packed his black duffel bag. Used the old typewriter to type the resignation letter, signed it, and left it on the desk. Then, to his own surprise, he realized he was whistling a tune. *So, is this really it? I am leaving forever? Just like that?* Now that Shark and Godmother had revealed their plan, there was in this a justice of a sort. He wasn't allowed to say his farewells properly to this place, to let the departure sink in, just as they wouldn't be. Feeling ridiculously light and empty, he went out without even bothering to lock up. There wasn't anything left in the office worth worrying about.

Ralph nodded to the on-duty Log (who undoubtedly took notice of the bag), crossed the hallway, and went up to the third floor.

The staff canteen was open until eight. It was cozy and quiet here, especially in the evenings. Round tables, on each one a wicker basket with bread, a massive wooden napkin holder, and an amusing salt-and-pepper set shaped like mice. Flower-patterned curtains. A neatly handwritten menu to the side of the serving window.

Ralph got two slices of meat pie and a tea, and went to sit at the corner table.

He was eating and looking at the photograph on the wall, under glass in an elaborately decorated frame. There were six of them in the canteen, all six utterly bewildering. Street shots. No people, no dogs, and none of the buildings caught in them could be considered of any interest. It was a mystery why these featureless images had to be printed in this large format, framed, and hung on the wall. Certainly not for aesthetic reasons.

Ralph studied the one closest to him and thought that, after he left, both it and the rest of them would forever remain an enigma, because without him no one would remember that these had been made by Flyers. They were of the Outsides. Flyers had photographed it haphazardly. The important thing had been to simply capture it. They returned to the House with their trophies, enlarged and printed them, framed them, and put them up in the windowless Horror Chamber on the first floor. The Chamber had existed specifically to cause discomfort. The children of the House liked scary stuff. There were other items in the horror storage, but the photographs of the Outsides were the undisputed highlight of the collection.

Then those who had created the Chamber of Horrors left, and the juniors who replaced them came to hate the exposition they'd inherited, so much that it had to be dismantled. The photographs ended up on the third floor. None of the current students had ever seen them; the entire thing happened before they had come here. Ralph often wondered what they'd feel if faced with them. Astonishment? Curiosity?

The shots might as well have been taken by Martians. A comprehensive detachment. Outsides distilled. That's how it looked from *their* point of view. Not beautiful, not ugly, not anything at all. Even total strangers who happened to see the pictures couldn't help being vaguely disturbed.

As Ralph looked at them, he realized that if, upon exiting the House, he really would be met with this faceless, scrubbed world of empty black-and-white streets, he would have felt much worse than he did now, and how lucky it was that for him the Outsides was not like that, and how unfortunate that he could not share that knowledge, that certainty with any of them.

Raptor and Shark came bursting into the canteen together, hooting and hollering as they saw Ralph there. Godmother entered quietly and unassumingly, and took her place at the next table.

"You bastard, making me sit and wait for your notice! Do you care at all?"

Shark dragged a chair over, plopped on it, moaned, and loosened his tie.

"Then we run to your damn office and see that damn notice on the desk! You couldn't even be bothered to bring it over for me to sign! Planning to split on the sly, weren't you?"

"You said you weren't signing it."

Shark noted Ralph's duffel under the table, made a face, and told Raptor to get some pie for him too.

"Two slices. No, one slice and some scrambled eggs. And a coffee. I urgently need sustenance."

Raptor went over to the serving window.

Godmother pulled her chair closer to their table.

"You have surprised and disappointed us. Couldn't this public display of disapproval have been avoided?"

Ralph shrugged.

"It could. I'm just not used to being manipulated."

She sighed.

"No one was manipulating you. Your perception of the situation is prejudiced."

They were silent when Raptor returned with a tray. They were silent while Shark shoveled food in his mouth. Godmother's hands rested on the table, palm to palm, the pristine cuffs setting off the grubbiness of the tablecloth, which had looked perfectly clean until she appeared. Ralph knew that Godmother wasn't going to move until he finished his tea, until Shark was satiated, until Raptor stopped fidgeting. Like a statue. She didn't need to engage her hands, to shift her pose, to busy her mouth with idle conversation. She could simply wait. It was unbearable.

"You would make an excellent sniper," Ralph said.

"Pardon?"

Shark pointed his fork at Ralph.

"Let it be noted that you haven't proposed anything. Anything! And when the people who were desperately seeking a solution made suggestions, you went on a crusade against them and then washed your hands of the whole thing! How's that fair? What is your problem with the decision to move up the date? Because I seem to have noticed it wasn't to your liking either."

"Then you probably also noticed that I wasn't arguing with that one. I don't like it, true, but it certainly has a chance."

"Aha!" Shark said. "So what you didn't like was not being among the elect, right?"

"Wrong. I don't care about the exact date. Especially considering that it would be fairly easy to calculate."

"Then what precisely do you object to with regards to that proposal?"

"Its cruelty."

He was unprepared for the indignation that flashed in Godmother's expression.

"Cruelty?" she repeated, and her voice trembled with suppressed emotion. "Do you mean to suggest that this is more cruel than what happened six years ago?"

"No. Which is why I didn't argue."

Godmother pursed her lips. Ralph again was overwhelmed by a suspicion that this was all a performance. At this particular moment she was playing the indignation that she wasn't feeling. He didn't understand why she would need to do that, just as he didn't understand why she'd come here to persuade him to stay, now that she'd done everything in her power to make him leave. He didn't understand too much of what this woman was doing, and the sheer volume of that ignorance was starting to affect him. Shark and Raptor were so engrossed in their exchange that they forgot all about the coffee. They looked like a pair of Bandar-Logs, only older—the same naked, shameless, prying curiosity.

"The first suggestion is simply dishonest. But the second is abusive. I will not tolerate my students being abused."

Godmother's face was a mask of equal parts weariness and disgust.

She blushes from the neck up, Ralph thought. *And it makes her look older. What is she after? Power? A position on top of the pecking order? In a place where there's soon going to be no one left to peck? Or is she in such a panic over the graduation that she's honestly searching for ways out of the tight corner she's been placed in, and the methods she's employing are simply what come naturally to her?*

He didn't believe any of that. Not her panic, not her sudden desire to rule the roost, and least of all her selfless, breathless service to the principal. Godmother wasn't cowardly, servile, or stupid. He did not understand her motives, and that made him vulnerable. He didn't know what he was fighting against.

"Ultimately," Godmother said, "we shall have to rely on your judgment. If you are certain that none of your charges represent a threat to the others at the time of graduation, it is incumbent upon us to try and share your conviction, and refrain from undertaking any additional measures."

"I have no such certainty," Ralph said.

"Just as I expected."

"But I am also not certain that your so-called considered measures won't make the situation worse."

"Neither are we. We just prefer action to inaction."

"Sometimes action is worse than inaction."

Shark turned his head from side to side, as if tracking a tennis ball in play. Godmother lowered her glasses to the tip of her nose and pierced Ralph with a schoolmarm glance.

"Is it your position that a graduating student is irreparably harmed by the very fact of the graduation happening a few days earlier than planned?"

"Depends on the student," Ralph said and stumbled, realizing that he'd just walked into a carefully prepared trap.

"Are you implying"—Godmother's nostrils flared in anticipation—"that there are those who will be harmed by it and those who might not?"

"You could say that."

"But wouldn't you agree that it is precisely the person who is so ill-adapted to life outside the House that a mere change in the manner of his graduation could prove disastrous for him, that it is this person who represents a clear danger to his peers?"

Ralph was silent.

Shark smirked. Raptor avoided Ralph's gaze. Godmother reached across the table and placed her hand on Ralph's arm.

"There will be no voting," she said firmly. "You will reach your own decision, and we will all abide by it. Who is the most dangerous? Only you, their counselor, are familiar with them well enough to answer that, to make that choice. And it therefore falls on you to guard them, to the extent possible, against grievous harm."

That night Ralph attempted to get drunk. He was drinking alone, locked up in his office, and almost succeeded, but the desired oblivion eluded him, leaving behind only a dull headache and a sullen apathy.

Deciding to leave was simple. As he was packing and typing up the notice, he'd felt uneasy because of the suddenness of it all, but at the same time never doubted that what he was doing was right. That under the circumstances it was the only available option. Talking to Godmother had robbed him of that sureness. Deep in his heart Ralph realized that agreeing to participate in Shark and Godmother's scheme was a sellout. Betrayal of one for the benefit of many was still a betrayal.

That right to choose, so graciously bestowed on him, was pure torture, all the more unbearable because in reality there was only one choice. He had no doubt that Blind was indeed dangerous, and would become extremely so at the moment of graduation. He also had no doubt that removing him from the House would only make matters worse. Someone would have to pay. He had a pretty good idea who that someone was, and it definitely wasn't Godmother. Could that be the reason she was trying to make him stay? They needed a scapegoat, and Ralph was perfect for the assignment.

"A goat," he whispered to himself. "You are so useful, my friend, you'll make a nice goat . . . or maybe a lamb. A stupid sacrificial lamb."

He cringed, realizing that he was behaving like a drunk, when he wasn't drunk at all. A little, maybe. But mentally running through the conversation with Sphinx once Blind had been removed from the House was sobering him up quicker than a cold shower.

Getting comprehensively sloshed and meeting Sphinx with inane, drunk blabbering wasn't going to cut it. Maybe he should listen to Darling and remove Sphinx as well? Ralph counted off the hierarchical structure of the Fourth on his fingers. Next step down from Sphinx they had—no, not Noble, but Tabaqui, strange as it may have seemed. As Ralph imagined Jackal in the position of the Master of the House he smiled, but the smile quickly became a fixed scowl. If that happened, drinking or not drinking would not make the slightest difference. Might as well really barricade themselves up on the third and wait. Tabaqui would disassemble the House brick by brick and only then agree to negotiate the terms of their surrender—if they were lucky.

By that time everyone would be clamoring for Blind's return. Did this mean he had to remove Jackal too?

Ralph went to the bathroom, stuck his head under the faucet, and then furiously rubbed his face with a towel.

Going over the list was completely pointless. Every single one of them was dangerous. Including that tacit mute, Alexander. It was not a good idea to push them. He had to make Shark understand that, and then let him duke it out with Godmother.

Ralph remembered that there had been cases of students who, having been sent out of the House, were then hastily returned, for varying reasons. Those had to be recorded somewhere. The former principal was a stickler for protocol and also liked to look for similarities and patterns in everything, so he surely had a file somewhere detailing all of those cases. Ralph should go and find it.

His headache subsided a little and Ralph knew he wouldn't be able to sleep anyway. Why not go to the library, then, and look for that precious file? The more he thought about this, the more logical it seemed to him.

He put on a coat, to have a good pocket for the flashlight, checked the batteries in it, and went out into the night.

The old night guard, always short of breath, opened the door to the third floor for him and shuffled back to his glass-walled nest to continue napping, or watching TV, or both.

On the third the lights in the hallways did not go out at night. Ralph followed the threadbare carpet to the library. It was very different from the common library down on the first—in its compactness, its wide selection of specialized tomes, and the decent condition of the books.

Ralph turned on the lights between the stacks one by one as he moved to the last aisle. There, against the wall, stood a tall steel cabinet, its drawers flashing stickers denoting their content. On the bottom drawers the writing was clearly readable, by halfway up the paper was already graying and the letters became barely legible, and closer to the top the stickers gave way to random scraps until they disappeared completely near the ceiling. The contents of those were to remain forever a mystery. Fortunately Ralph had no use for them now.

He pulled out one of the lower drawers and shuddered at the sight of the files massed tightly together. He dragged the drawer to the little table in the corner and started taking out the files. He briefly thumbed through the stapled sheaves and put them aside, file after file, until he was satisfied that this drawer did not contain what he was looking for. He replaced it and pulled out another. Then another. The stack of files that he wasn't able to stuff back in their drawers was growing, and Ralph hoped that at some point he was going to stumble on a half-empty one and dump them all in there, so as not to leave behind on the table a pile of paper.

At some point he looked up momentarily and noticed that the night guard was now sitting in the chair between the stacks. The guard, under his customary uniform cap with a green bill, looked asleep, but was in fact watching him closely.

"I wasn't going to smoke here, if you came to warn me about that," Ralph said.

The guard shook his head.

"I was wondering what is it you're so diligently seeking."

"That doesn't really concern you."

Ralph turned back to the files but soon realized that he was exhausted. The presence of a stranger interfered with his concentration. As he kept turning over the sheets he struggled to take in their meaning. Ralph stuffed the remaining files in the drawer in front of him and decided to stop punishing himself—and allow the guard to go and slumber in peace, which was probably what he was hinting at by coming here.

"You're wrong if you think it doesn't concern me," the guard said suddenly.

Ralph slowly turned around.

"What? What did you say?"

"I said that you were wrong to think it doesn't concern me," the guard repeated. "You're going through the archives of the former principal, if I'm not mistaken?"

Ralph walked over to the guard and stared at him closely.

"You're not," he said.

The guard produced from his breast pocket a white smoking pipe with a battered stem, put it between his teeth, straightened up, and took off his cap.

"I might be useful to you in this endeavor."

Oh god, Ralph thought. *He's always had a flair for the dramatic. I guess I'm supposed to faint now from all the excitement. And I didn't even gasp. How rude.*

"Yes," he said. "It appears that you're just the man I was looking for."

The guard looked offended.

"You could have at least acknowledged your sudden luck," he said, pointing at the rows of drawers with his pipe. "This is far from one night's work."

"It's shock," Ralph explained. "I'm shocked. I am at a complete loss for words."

Those were actually exactly the right words that he'd found. The guard sprung up and squeezed him in a tight hug. Ralph stoically accepted the outpouring and, in turn, patted the former principal on the back.

The man stepped away and looked him over.

"Well, well! How are you, my boy?"

He hugged Ralph again.

Fatherly, he probably imagined himself. *Dwarfishly,* Ralph thought as his chin rested on top of the old man's head. Old Man, that was what everyone called him.

Old Man jostled, squeezed, and probed him, then let him go and went to sit in the chair and get his breath back.

Ralph replaced the last drawer he'd taken out.

"I was looking for mentions of those expelled from the House," he said. "Whose parents took them away shortly before the graduation. Some of them seemed to have developed this strange disorder, the Lost Syndrome, they called it. Do you remember?"

Old Man knitted his brow.

"Lost Syndrome . . ." he muttered. "That wouldn't be here. You'll have to go dig in the sick-bay archives. Rare thing, that, but yes, sometimes . . ."

"Were there any cases similar, but not exactly like that?"

Old Man sank even deeper in thought.

"There were lots of things," he said finally. "All sorts . . . Can't say for sure."

Ralph felt acute disappointment. When you start hoping for a miracle you sometimes get it, and then it turns out completely hollow. What did he expect from this old clown? Even in his better times he couldn't see past his own nose.

As if confirming his suspicions, Old Man waved his hand dismissively at the cabinets.

"What you're looking for isn't there," he said again, tapping his forehead. "It's all in here, collected and stored. The fount of memory is inside, and all that is just dumb paper."

With that he grabbed Ralph by the hand and pulled him to the door.

"Let's go! I will tell you everything I remember, and I remember everything!"

Alarmed by this promise, Ralph shuffled after Old Man while he, not letting his mouth close even for a moment, clicked the switches that gradually restored the library to darkness.

"You see . . . As soon as I saw you today, I immediately thought: Time to come out! It was like lightning! I simply had to come out, that's what I thought . . ."

The night-guard quarters, the first room from the stairs, turned out to be a tiny nook stuffed to the brim with mismatched furniture, old magazines, and clocks. The clocks filled all available space on the walls. Ralph's first impression was that the walls were encrusted with glass plaques in lieu of wallpaper, and he had to look closer to realize his mistake. It was indeed mostly clocks, with a few watches here and there, and even some alarm clocks thrown in. He froze in stunned amazement, studying the dials that surrounded him. None of them worked. Their hands pointed at different angles, some had no hands at all. For some reason Ralph's memory brought up that endless winter night when his watch and the time itself refused to move, an experience he didn't much like to recall.

Old Man obviously relished his reaction.

"Impressive, isn't it? Took me fifteen years to collect. Not everything was salvage-able, of course, and then I have some I couldn't fit here. I've got two more boxes under the bed, both chock full."

He hung the cap on the nail in the door, squeezed sideways between the table and the bed, went to the far corner, crouched down, and started rummaging there.

It occurred to Ralph that he was going to be presented with the undisplayed part of the collection, but when Old Man straightened up he was holding a bottle.

"Someone mentioned that the life expectancy of a clock in the House, doesn't mat-ter what kind, was surprisingly small," he said, wiping off the bottle with a suspicious-looking piece of cloth. "That was what had set it in motion. I was only collecting the wall clocks at first. The ones in the canteen and the classrooms. I expect others in my position would just give in and stop putting them up, but I was intrigued. It was a challenge of sorts."

He proudly placed the bottle on the table and admired it.

"Usually we couldn't find any evidence of them being tampered with, you see. Then it came to me that watches should be out there somewhere too, and I put a word out for the janitors to be on the lookout and bring me any that they found in the trash. Now those were being broken on purpose. Crushed down to dust, almost. The collection got a big boost. After a while I had to stop accepting the ones that were completely destroyed."

Ralph attempted to read the label on the bottle, but Old Man switched off the light and turned on a feeble desk lamp.

"That better? The collection does make people a tad uncomfortable sometimes."

"It is better," Ralph agreed. "And it is uncomfortable. Too sparkly."

"I'm used to it. It's all a matter of habit. I would miss them if they went away."

Old Man presented Ralph with a glass and pulled up a stool, then made himself comfortable on the quilt-covered couch. The glass appeared to be holding wine.

"What is it that you do here, exactly?" Ralph said.

The question sounded somewhat impolite, but Old Man clearly had been wait-ing for it to be asked and wasn't too particular about the precise wording. He leaned forward, clutching the unlit pipe in his hand.

"I observe. I track the situation as it develops. Truth be told, I seem to have missed some things in my time."

Practically all of them, Ralph thought. *And you missed them while sitting in the principal's office. What do you hope to see now from the night guard's post?*

"I had some theories I wanted to check." Old Man downed almost an entire glass in one gulp. "That old story kept tormenting me. A couple of years ago I finally real-ized that I had to go back. And so—here I am!"

It sounded so pompous that Ralph winced. He knew he should try to be tolerant, but Old Man was grating on his nerves. His self-righteous complacency, that idiotic clock collection—Ralph's day hadn't been going too great even without all this.

"I suppose you enjoy full access to a lot of things now?" he said. "From this room, I mean. In your position as a guard."

"More than you can imagine," the former principal said importantly, leaving a significant pause.

Ralph at this point had neither energy nor desire to feign interest. The pause lingered.

"Ask!" Old Man prompted, leaning back on a stack of magazines that gave way under the weight. The magazines cascaded down on the floor. Old Man pretended not to notice.

"What about?" Ralph said glumly.

"Anything! Don't you have any questions at all?"

The wine was sweet to the point of stickiness and almost impossible to drink. Ralph felt the encounter moving inexorably to Old Man taking offense and Ralph feeling guilty for having offended him. Old Man desperately required an enraptured listener, and Ralph was crushingly bad at it. He rolled the syrupy liquid in his mouth and managed to force it down.

"I am afraid," he began cautiously, "that the questions I have are not the kind you might have answers to."

"Try me! What have you got to lose?"

Old Man frowned.

"Oh, all right. I get it. That's fine, you don't have to. I'm not going to push you. I just thought that you might be interested in learning some things. You looked like you were stumped." He filled his glass again and emptied it in two gulps. Fighting the belch coming up, he added, "I'm telling you, Rex's grandma is something else. She isn't the goody-two-shoes she's playing. I figured you'd appreciate my help, now that you've locked horns with her."

Ralph straightened up.

"What?" he said, not quite believing his ears. "Who are you talking about?"

"That granny of Rex's, who else?" Old Man looked at him quizzically. "Wasn't it her that you crossed at the meeting today?"

Ralph took a huge swig of the wine.

"Once more from the beginning," he said. "Are we talking about the same person? Godmother? Is she somehow related to Vulture?"

Old Man nodded.

"Sure. His own dear granny. You mean you didn't know?"

"Where did you get that?"

"For crying out loud!" Old Man said hotly. "Where! Same place you'd get it, if only you made an effort and utilized your head once in a while. I used to have this habit, you know, of checking out people before hiring them. And she was the only one who looked halfway professional among the riffraff that your new principal dragged in. Of course, that piqued my interest. People like her don't all of a sudden come to work for people like him. I conducted my usual due diligence. All of her credentials turned out to be fake. Then I just sneaked a peek at her driver's license, registered under her real last name."

He gave Ralph an incensed look.

"Don't tell me you didn't even suspect it!"

Ralph poured himself more wine. "Except that's the truth. It has never crossed my mind. I guess I was surprised when she came in, but that was the extent of it. I wouldn't dream of checking someone's papers. Who knows what her reasons were for coming here."

Old Man looked crestfallen, and Ralph rushed to console him.

"Please understand. Here I've always been surrounded by decent people. Like you said, professionals. I probably got too used to it. Her arrival came unexpectedly for you, because it wasn't you who hired her. And I just thought—great, now there's someone on that side who looks like she knows what she's doing."

Old Man shook his head again, but not as ruefully this time. The well-placed flattery was having an effect.

"Well, all right," he said. "I guess I shouldn't be surprised. You young people just haven't the knack for paperwork, 'cause we always tried to shield you from it. Another one of my mistakes, now that I think about it."

"Don't blame yourself for everything," Ralph demanded in a fit of self-loathing. "I'm not that young. You're entirely correct, I should've used my head."

Old Man patted him on the shoulder, put away the empty bottle, and immediately extracted another one from behind the couch.

Ralph broke out in nervous laughter and said, "I would appreciate it if you'd explain to me one more time what a dunce I am. Tell me what she is trying to accomplish with her suggestions. I can't imagine why she would all of a sudden need to show everyone who was the boss here with only a few days remaining until graduation."

Old Man perked up.

"Yes. Exactly. Few days remaining. And she's scared witless that her grandson is going to do any of that graduating. Because then, by the terms of his late grandfather's will, the family mansion passes on to him. So, she would either have to live with him under one roof, or go find herself another place, which isn't that easy at her age."

He scratched his chin thoughtfully.

"I guess those two didn't get along too well. Or maybe they did at first and then they didn't anymore. Anyway, Grandpa played a nice dirty trick on his dearly beloved. I've seen quite a few people do that. How it's supposed to make them feel better when they're dead, I have no idea."

Ralph poured himself more wine.

"What about the parents?"

"The parents? That's a sad story right there. Mother killed herself at nineteen. Father—now you see him, now you don't, no one even knows who he was. Grandma and Grandpa shipped the boys to an orphanage with the mother still alive, right after they were born, and haven't given a hoot about them since. At least they never tried to find out anything about them once they were here. I mean, I don't think Grandpa ever did care, except he couldn't think of another way to get at her."

"You are a genius," Ralph said earnestly.

Old Man waved him away. His eyes were shining.

"Everything is actually very simple if you get the right information. And I still have ways of getting it, thankfully."

They drank some more. Ralph had the sensation of his stomach congealing into a sticky blob. The syrup also messed with his head.

We're having a Fairy Tale Night, Ralph thought. *Drinking and telling each other scary stories about the Outsides. Me and the former principal. Or rather he's telling and I'm listening. And I'm already plastered.*

Suddenly a thought occurred to him that made him jump.

"Now wait a minute! I still don't understand . . . She wants to remove Vulture from the House, right? Hoping that it's going to break him down. All right. But. They told me that they expected *me* to make that choice. That I was the one to decide who it's going to be. Which means . . ."

"Which means you got snookered." Old Man shrugged. "Or did they guess right?"

"No. They didn't."

"They'll talk you into it, then. Dressing it up like that's what you wanted."

Ralph felt cold fury flooding him. Trying to stanch this sudden shivering, he hugged his own shoulders, but the cold was spreading from inside. Even a fur coat would not have been enough.

So all this time, while he was fighting his conscience and mulling over the inevitable standoff with Sphinx, the damn hag was angling to throw out Vulture. And he would be her able assistant in that tomorrow, trotting out every last argument against removing Blind that he'd spend the night digging up. All she had to do was agree with him and then put out a counterproposal that he would have no choice but to accept. Because unlike the Fourth, the Third had no one who could take Vulture's place. The entire pack would just freeze. It was quite possible that in Shark's mind that would

count as a huge victory in his battle to ensure safety at all costs. And the most disgusting part of it all was how well she'd managed to get into his head while sitting on the
other side of the House, seemingly absorbed in her own duties and responsibilities.
Ralph shuddered at the thought that the old crone had been watching him closely
for the last four years and he simply didn't notice. Him, Vulture, and everyone else
for that matter. She'd predicted Ralph's reactions to a tee, including the show he'd put
up of quitting, and had woven them into her plans. There was only one wrinkle she
didn't count on: an equally shrewd old-timer hiding in plain sight right under her nose.

Old Man was insistently pushing a restorative glass of wine at Ralph, getting more
and more anxious.

"Don't get so upset, my boy! Buck up! You look pale. You'll need all the resolve
you've got to fight the enemy. Do you hear?"

Ralph realized that he'd better take the glass before he got drenched. He drained
it in one gulp and resolutely set it aside.

"I think that's enough for me for tonight. Or I might just go and bump off
someone."

This statement horrified the former principal.

"No! Never! Violence is never the answer! That would be your undoing!"

"No, you don't understand. I was not planning to kill her. No way. Revenge is a
dish best served surreptitiously." Ralph got up, realized that his legs weren't equal to
the task, and lowered himself back on the stool. "Did you make this wine yourself?"

Old Man was kicking up such a fuss around him that Ralph felt slightly uneasy.

"My dear old gnome," he said. "Don't worry. I'm perfectly all right."

This somehow failed to calm Old Man. He tripped over the kettle's electric cord
and crashed down on the pile of magazines.

"Enough of that," Ralph said, helping him up. "I told you, everything's fine. We're
going to sit down now and have a nice long chat. You're going to share your wisdom
and experience and provide advice. And I'm going to listen. And so on and so forth."

"Perfect!" Old Man exclaimed hotly, steadying himself. "What a great idea! That's
exactly what we'll do!"

For the next hour, Ralph pretended to be listening to Old Man. To his stories of
the tangled webs of intrigue from the old days. He even voiced agreement from time
to time. The stories became more and more complicated as Old Man's speech became
less and less coherent. After the fourth bottle, the headache returned and the sense of
time vanished.

*That's good . . . that's nice . . . just the way it should be. I need to get really far over the
edge to be doing what I'm planning to do. Really, really far . . .*

Suddenly the lamp went off.

Ralph peeked out into the hallway and discovered that it was completely dark there too.

"Lights out," Old Man grumbled. "Just what we needed. And in the most interesting place, too. I have some candles in the desk over there."

Ralph pulled out the drawer, felt there for a bundle of thick tapers, and lit one of them.

"I had a flashlight," he remembered. "But I don't anymore. I left it. In the library. In the coat. With the coat. Sloppy, sloppy."

Old Man proffered him a saucer. As Ralph started dripping wax on it, he discovered with amazement that it was incredibly hard to make the drips land in the same place. The wax seemed to want to splash all over the desk. Defeated, he returned the candle and the saucer to Old Man and said that he had to go.

Old Man was already sleeping on his feet, and didn't protest.

"You sure? All right. Take a candle. Another candle. And I need to walk you over. Lock the door behind you and all that. Because the keys. I have the keys. I am the guard here, I'll have you know!"

Ralph assured Old Man that he would on no account forget that.

Swaying, they went out into the hallway together. Ralph was holding the former principal under the arm, while the principal waved the candle around, splattering them both with hot wax, and discoursed on the topic of revenge. According to him, the best kind was to sit at the bottom of the river and wait for the bodies of your enemies to float by.

"Are you sure it's the bottom?" Ralph said. "Like algae?"

"Precisely," Old Man said. "Those ancient Chinese, they knew their stuff. Did I mention it was a typically Chinese way of revenge?"

When they reached the door, Ralph took the candle from Old Man and tried to use it to light the second one, but Old Man's excited breathing as he hung limply off Ralph's shoulder kept blowing it out, until finally he extinguished both of them. Ralph decided that it was for the best. He wouldn't have been comfortable leaving Old Man here with an open flame. He somehow managed to haul him to the guard's post, remembered about the cigarette lighter, and with its help found the second copy of the key on the nail in the wall. He dumped Old Man, already snoring happily, on the battered chair in the corner and set off on the return journey.

After locking the door behind him and coming to the landing, he lit the candle. He was taking the stairs very carefully, step by step, to maintain balance and to keep the candle from going out, feeling like a character from a gothic novel.

His entrance in the corridor on the second floor was quite spectacular. He shuffled forward slowly, dimly aware of the appreciative whispers from the unseen audience, holding the candle in front of him—white shirt, sunken eyes, hair sticking out. He desperately wished for a candlestick. A graceful antique affair, with a winding stem, he'd look so much more dashing if he had that. Also he wished for some more steadiness. And for the rustling around him to stop.

The corridor was supposed to lead Ralph straight to the door of his office, but it was playing tricks tonight. It branched three times instead, demanding that Ralph choose which turn to take, and every time he had grave suspicions that he'd chosen incorrectly.

Finally, in a filthy, garbage-strewn corner—the House had never had such places before tonight, Ralph was absolutely sure of that—an unfamiliar-looking young boy courteously touched him on the arm and offered his assistance.

"Yes, thank you," Ralph said. "I seem to be slightly lost."

"Where would you like to go?"

Ralph studied the boy closely. At least he lacked visible wings.

"I need someone to help me exact a terrible vengeance," he explained. "But not the Chinese kind. For the Chinese kind I'm not quite ready yet. Would you happen to know anyone of that persuasion?"

The polite boy said nothing but nodded matter-of-factly and went ahead. Ralph, bone tired, tagged along behind. The candle was half-gone. His fingers no longer felt the burns.

At length he was brought to a surprisingly cozy room and put in a high-backed chair. There he was provided with a splendid candlestick, a pill for the headache, and a glass of water. Afraid that he might fall asleep, Ralph rushed to explain the purpose of his visit.

"I am a stoolie," he said, peeling the flows of dried wax from his fingers. "A snitch. And I am tattling. Betraying my own. Exposing the evil plots of the Outsides."

This revelation was received with sympathy.

Ralph, inspired by the reception, told everything he knew about Godmother.

"Vulture needs to be warned," he said, concluding the confession. "Tell him he's in danger."

The hospitable owners of the cozy room promised Ralph that they would do just that.

Ralph remembered nothing about his way back.

When he woke up he was on his own couch. His insides were burning and his bladder threatened to burst, but there was, surprisingly, no trace of a headache. He shuffled to the bathroom and relieved himself, staring in horror at the wax-encrusted trousers. The shirt wasn't much better. He washed his face, did his best to scrape the wax off the glove and the shoes, then changed and went out. He needed to get to Shark first, before Godmother had her way with him.

Shark was in a state of total stupefaction. Godmother was nowhere to be seen.

"I came to make a statement," Ralph said.

"Your statement is just the thing I need right now. Have a look at this," Shark said, passing Ralph a sheet of paper. "Like it?"

It was Godmother's resignation letter, citing "family circumstances." Ralph stared at the looping signature under today's date and shuddered, like from a sudden burst of cold wind.

"When did she bring it?"

"She didn't!" Shark roared, jumping up. "No one in this whole damn dump can be bothered to actually bring me something in person! At least she had the decency to take it as far as my office. And staple it to the door! How sweet of her, don't you agree? Because I know some people who couldn't manage even that!"

Shark dashed about the office, frantically kicking the furniture.

"Who do you all take me for? Your elderly deaf granny? Family circumstances, all right, great! But coming in and explaining what the hell happened—oh, no, that's not how we do things! We're in such a hurry we barely have the time to write this!"

The door opened a crack and Raptor peeked in. He read the situation correctly and realized that the best strategy for him at this time would be to vanish. Ralph waited it out while Shark's ire peaked and then he said, "Has anyone seen her today?"

"Not me," Shark grunted. "And I don't give a damn about what anyone else saw!"

He stopped and finally had a better look at Ralph's appearance.

"What's this, a tropical safari? I've had it up to here with Sheriff and his polos, and now you come strolling in here in sneakers? We have a dress code, you know. A suit! Trousers, button-down shirt, jacket! And a tie! All right, I'm not going to insist on the jacket when it's this hot, but jeans and a tee—that's too much. You're going to be the death of me, all of you!"

"My trousers are slightly ruined at the moment. With wax," Ralph admitted. "And the shoes too."

Shark shot a mad look at him and crashed in the armchair.

"The death!" he repeated and closed his eyes.

Ralph decided that he'd better go.

He saw that Shark was in the throes of panic. Godmother's exit he interpreted as her running away in fear, and the fact that she chose this particular moment for it—that what she feared was the graduation. Shark himself dreaded the graduation so much that no other possible explanation would even occur to him.

Ralph didn't believe in the urgent departure either, but his doubts were of a different nature. *What did they do to her* was the principal question on his mind. That it was something *they* did he had no doubt, but what was it? What could make Godmother abandon the House?

In the duty room it was Sheep's shift. She was sitting there alone, thumbing through a magazine instead of her customary knitting. Ralph's question about Godmother set her eyes blinking.

"A letter of resignation? Can't be! Well, no, I haven't seen her today, but her shift is not until two and she never comes down before that. The letter must be someone's idea of a silly joke."

By three o'clock Ralph had established that no one in the House had seen Godmother that day.

Not on the third floor, not on the second, and not in the yard. Her room was cleaned out, her car disappeared from its place in the garage, and there was not a single thing left in the duty room that could have belonged to her.

Exactly when, in the course of the few hours, she managed to wipe every trace of her presence from the House and leave without anyone noticing remained a mystery.

The old guard swore to Ralph on his honor that he hadn't unlocked the door for Godmother, neither at night nor in the morning. Ralph believed him. When he'd left last night, Old Man could have slept through an artillery attack. But the spare set of keys, usually available for the use of the counselors, Ralph had taken.

Ralph knew that the children of the House could get in and out of the tiniest cracks, but he could not imagine the same arcane paths being taken by an elderly lady. As much as he tried to chase it away, his imagination kept unfolding this surreal picture before him: the boys, resembling at the same time a group of busy black ants and a detachment of sinister ninjas, dragging a listless woman, bound tightly like a mummy, swiftly along the rainwater pipe. Variations on this theme included the body being delivered ceremoniously to the basement or stuffed down the storm drain. Then the ant ninjas soared on their invisible strings to the third-floor windows and went to work on the counselor's room, filling their capacious backpacks with her personal effects.

The vision of Vulture thoughtfully putting down the signature at the bottom of Godmother's resignation letter, carefully checking it against her real autograph on some paper or other, was much less bizarre and much more frightening. In a peculiar coincidence, Bird Leader was known for his advanced ability to forge any handwriting. It was a point of pride for him on par with, if not more than, his talent at picking locks. And the one thing that Ralph could not picture, no matter how he tried, was Godmother stapling an important document to the door of the principal's office. She'd never do that. It was against her style.

Ralph made sure to personally examine the basement, the attic, and every empty room on the first floor in both wings. The closer inspection of the storm drain he decided to postpone until dark. He took a break in his investigations to pay another visit to Shark and convince him not to declare an emergency assembly and not to remove anyone from the House unilaterally, since Godmother's flight clearly indicated that she herself had grave doubts about the success of such actions. Shark made a brief display of reluctance and then quickly surrendered—almost eagerly, Ralph thought.

On his way out of Shark's office, Ralph bumped into Raptor, who shook his hand.

"The victory is ours," he whispered.

Sheriff was more direct.

"Way to go, man, throwing out that harridan," he said, bathing Ralph in a gentle wave of alcohol reek. "Keep it up!"

Sheriff had been celebrating the happy riddance of Godmother since morning, and by this time could hardly be called lucid, but it still made Ralph pause. What did the counselors think he'd done when congratulating him? After running through several possibilities of what they might have been imagining, he decided to cancel the dive in the storm drain altogether.

Ralph hadn't been back to his office through the day, but when he finally reached it around ten at night, there was a surprise waiting for him inside.

On the floor in the middle of the room stood a massive bronze candlestick. One of its two cups was empty, but the second contained the lopsided runny stub of the taper.

SMOKER

The hallway is flooded with the bluish dusk and that familiar scent—of what, I wonder. Plaster? Damp? Rain puddles? I clutch tighter at my skinny bag, containing a change of underwear, a drawing pad, and a box of paints. Also the diary. It is only two days old, but the first entry is backdated by a week. I am going to use this notebook to let R One know of my impressions. Which means I'm a snitch. I am having a hard time coming to grips with that thought. I will write what I see and hear, and he will read my scribblings after fishing the diary out of the trash bin in the common bathroom. And put it back there once he's done.

He's probably feeling uneasy right now as well, even if he doesn't show it. Not that I can see his face. He hasn't let a single word slip about our agreement, and that's for the best, because I'd hate it if he started talking about it now.

I am looking very closely at my bag.

We roll past someone's legs and they jump back to the wall quickly, out of our way. The Crossroads floats by. Monkey the Bandar-Log flies out of the door of the Second and rolls on the floor, screeching indignantly. Then he sees us, springs up, says "Oh wow!" and dashes back in the room. I'm only seeing this out of the corner of my eye, since my gaze is firmly planted on the bag.

Finally we stop. Ralph wheels me around and bangs on the door. The sound makes me flinch.

"'S not locked!" the familiar testy voice answers.

I take a deep breath, but don't have time to let it out before Ralph uses me to swing the door open. He does in fact use his hand to push it, but I still get an impression that it is me.

The first three days in the Sepulcher flew by quickly. First I was sharing the room with Lizard and Monkey, then with Monkey and Genepool. In the end it was Viking from the Second and his dislocated finger. And then I was the only one left, and that made me realize that having roommates is better than not having them. Even when they're noisy, play cards around the clock, spit all over the place, and constantly clog the only toilet around.

Once I was left alone I had no defense against sinister thoughts. When, after a routine physical, you're suddenly told that you'll be staying in the Sepulcher, "no arguments," not even allowed to drive over and get your things, it's not that scary by itself. But when, in a week's time, still no one is in the mood to explain anything, you start suspecting that your days are really numbered, that you won't be getting out of here alive. So I was preparing for the worst.

Then I got a visit from R One. That wasn't a surprise; after all, he was now my counselor. If anything, he could have considered coming earlier.

He sat in the only chair in the room, the "doctor" chair, and crossed his legs. He was holding some kind of package in his hands.

"Well, how're you feeling?" he said.

"All right," I said. "Can't complain."

"That's good," he said. "Anyone visit you here?"

"Black," I said. "Also Noble, twice."

R One perked up.

"Noble? That's interesting."

"Not really," I said.

Noble would present me with a packet of gummy bears, say "How's it going," and go over to my neighbors' beds to play blackjack with them. I always thought that if you came to visit someone who's sick it would be nice to at least have a conversation with them, but apparently Noble had a different opinion. I think the fact of my existence went right out of his head as soon as he handed me the candy.

Now Black, he behaved like a human being was supposed to. Gave me the rundown on the latest news, told me to hold on, and even tried to pump the Spiders for any information regarding my condition. Not that he managed to find out anything, but I was grateful even for the thought. And one time he brought me some tomato salad that he'd made himself, reducing me almost to tears.

I certainly wasn't about to explain any of that to Ralph. All I said was that Noble's visits were not really interesting. Which was the truth.

"You would probably like to know why you're stuck here?" R One asked.

"Of course. Everyone keeps telling me about blood work, but they never did any tests other than the one after which they made me stay. And why couldn't they go back and recheck that first one? That's what I don't understand."

I suddenly grew very agitated. Because it dawned on me that R One, being my counselor, might have gotten an insight, been told something that no one was telling me.

"There's nothing wrong with you," he said. "You're perfectly healthy."
I gawked at him.

"You're here on my orders," he said. "I asked them to hold you in for a while."

I still didn't ask anything. I guess I was too surprised. By the way he was saying that. He was very calm when admitting to these things. To making me think who knows what. I'd been preparing to die because of what he did.

"I had a call from your father," R One said. "He said that you'd asked not to be taken away. That you wanted to stay until graduation. When did you talk to him?"

"The night after the meeting. I used the phone in the staff room. Someone showed me how to get inside."

He just nodded, as if he knew that already without my explanations.

"So, you're curious about the graduation?" he said. "You'd like to see it for yourself?"

I didn't answer. I try not to answer stupid questions. If I didn't want to stay, I wouldn't be calling home asking not to be taken away.

Ralph turned the left side of his face to me for the first time in this visit, and I saw that he had a huge shiner there. It cheered me up that somebody had given him a good one. A sincere one. Broke the skin on the cheekbone, even.

"I am also curious about the graduation," he said. "I'd like to have some more information about what's going on in the House. At this particular moment." '

It finally dawned on me what he was driving at. I didn't let on, though. I made a quizzical face, as if I didn't understand.

He was looking straight at me, and he had these eyes like it wasn't him who had said what he'd just said. Honest and earnest. You'd never guess that a man with eyes like that would be trying to make you into a snitch.

"Stop the charade," he said. "You got my meaning."

"Was it the previous snitching candidate who scratched you?"

He felt the shiner with his finger and said that he didn't want to quarrel with me. That was how he put it.

"I also don't want to quarrel with anyone. So why don't you tell me up front what's going to happen to me if I refuse? So that I know."

I was sure he'd tell me that I was going to be stuck here in the Sepulcher until graduation. That really was worse than being sent home, because it was much more dull. But apart from that, he didn't have anything else with which to threaten me.

He stood up. Took a thick notebook out of his package, put it on my bed, and went over to the window. Looked out, then came back.

"Nothing is going to happen to you," he said. "Either way you'll be discharged tomorrow."

I couldn't understand what the catch was. That didn't sound threatening at all.

"What would be the point of me agreeing to snitch, then?" I said. "For the sheer joy of it?"

He was silent for a while. Then sat back on the chair. Took the notebook and thumbed through it. It was completely blank.

"I'm not very good at stories," he said. "But I'd like to tell you the story of the last graduation. And the one before that. If, after hearing them, you still refuse to help me, I'm not going to insist. You'll go back to the Fourth and try to forget we ever had this conversation."

He didn't ask if I agreed to listen. Simply started to talk. Without going into detail, pointedly detached and tedious, but it made what he was talking about even scarier. Like an article in the paper—no emotions, just facts.

"Is that true?" I said when he finished.

I already knew that it was. It was all true. I saw Blind kill Pompey. I saw Red on the night when they tried to kill him. And I saw how everyone reacted, or rather did not react, in both cases. I knew that no one in the House called Blind a murderer, because no one thought of him that way. Except me. No one stopped talking to him, no one felt uneasy being next to him. I made myself look like an idiot when I refused to put on his shirt the night of the murder. A lot of things that were beyond the pale for me, they took completely in stride. So yes, I believed that those who had been here before them, who were a bit like them, really could massacre each other in the grand finale of their Great Game. I haven't abandoned that word, just acknowledged that the Game is not a game, that it is for real, and a "for real" ending for it would probably look something like what Ralph described.

"It is true," he said.

And then asked if I kept a diary.

Everyone kept a diary in the First. Reading them must have been even more of a chore than writing in them.

I said that I still had my old diary, but I only used it for drawing.

"You can draw in this," he said. "Except you'll have to write some too. No one would be surprised when they see that you picked up the diary again in the Sepulcher. It can be pretty boring in here."

"But I haven't agreed yet," I said.

"No?" He felt his cheekbone again. "And here's me thinking that I was reasonably persuasive."

I took his notebook.

I am sitting in my old place, between Tabaqui and Noble. The lights are out, the boombox is moaning on the other end of the bed, and everyone's silent. That's how it's been for two hours already. Maybe that's a silent Fairy Tale Night. How would I know? Or are they all simply enjoying the music? It's better not to ask questions, because either you're one with the pack and know everything about everything, or you aren't and you don't, in which case you're just getting on everyone's nerves.

So I am dutifully listening to the music, admiring the blinking red lights of the boombox, and smoking. I've already smoked more this evening than in all of my days in the Sepulcher combined.

One of the indistinct shadows slinking around the bed sits down next to me.

"How are you feeling, Smoker?"

It's Blind. Unusually courteous.

"All right. I mean, pretty good," I say.

"What happened to you, exactly? If you don't mind, of course."

I do, that's the problem.

"My parents asked them to run a full checkup on me," I say. "Since classes are over and there's going to be no exams. And I had this low blood count, so . . ."

At that moment someone switches on the lights. When I open my eyes, everything I was planning to say goes right out of my head.

Because this is my first good look at Blind after my return from the Sepulcher and he looks like someone enthusiastically took a sander to him. To his cheeks, his chin, his neck. In short, it's me who should be asking how he's feeling, not the other way around. Which I don't, of course. I collect the tattered remains of my thoughts and pick up the story about the blood count, but Blind gets up in the middle of the sentence and leaves. As in leaves the room. If he didn't care about getting an answer, why ask at all? Or is it that he suddenly remembered he was contagious? I light up again, to calm the nerves.

Noble closes his eyes as he yawns and doesn't open them again. The yawn bounces off him and goes around the room, alighting on the faces. When it reaches me it multiplies, spawning an entire clutch. Must be the nerves. I yawn and I yawn, until my eyes start to water. Through the curtain of tears I look at Sphinx. He's down on the floor, sitting propped up against the door of the wardrobe. For him to inquire about my health would be too much of a bother. But he is, in fact, looking back at me. With that faraway look that Humpback calls "fuzzy." When you're the target of the "fuzzy" there's always the feeling of a draft somewhere. You're just lying there, smoking, and there's all this cold air streaming over you mercilessly.

I decide that I've had enough of the yawning and shivering, and ask, "What happened to Blind? Allergy?"

Tabaqui lazily puts away the knitting needle he's been using to excavate his ear.

"Actually, it's the Lost Syndrome," he says. "But you can call it allergy if you'd like."

I wait.

He also waits. For my questions.

He doesn't get them, so he picks up the needle again.

"LS is this thing that only we can get. The House people. If we suddenly find ourselves in the Outsides and get lost there. They say it's a mark the House puts on its own. On those who have no business being in the Outsides."

I fall for it hook, line, and sinker, and open my mouth to beg him for the details, but Noble is quicker.

"That's new," he says, frowning. He had to open his eyes for this, and he's not happy about it. "You never told me about this."

"You never asked." Jackal shrugs. "Or you'd get the same answer."

Noble furrows his brow, assembling a spider's web of creases on his forehead. An ominous sign for anyone familiar with his habits. But not for Tabaqui.

"I personally witnessed LS only twice. One time was when Bison went chasing some Outsides kid who was teasing him and then couldn't find his way back, and the other when Wolf sleepwalked out of the House and something out there woke him up suddenly. All other cases I know are hearsay. Spiders have their own opinion about it, and if anyone's interested they can drive over and ask them, but I wouldn't bother. They'll just present you with a booklet saying, 'If you have a cat allergy stay away from cats,' and what do cats have to do with it, or where have they seen an allergy that looks like that, it's useless even to ask, they're not going to answer anyway."

"Wait," I interrupt Tabaqui's soliloquy. "How did Blind end up in the Outsides? Does he sleepwalk too? What happened to him?"

"Ralph happened to him," Tabaqui sniggers. "This is the most heartrending story of the last six months, believe you me. I couldn't even bring myself to make a song about it, I was so scared."

He holds a cruel pause before continuing.

"Imagine, if you will, Smoker, one fine day, or rather night, good old Ralph, whom we all held to be a person of certain decency and composure, bursts in, grabs our Leader, and whisks him out of the House. And then, somewhere in the depths of the Outsides, conducts a cruel interrogation. I'd even say torture. Because LS is a very scratchy thing. And when you give in and start scratching it, it's a very bloody thing."

I look back at Sphinx. Should I believe Tabaqui or not? Sphinx shrugs. *Signs point to yes* is how I read it, so I turn back to Jackal, who can't be stopped now, even by a direct shotgun blast.

"You are going to ask, what could have prompted this barbarity, this inhuman violation of the human rights of our Leader? And I am going to answer: I don't know. Because Ralph's true motives have remained a mystery to us. The stated reason was the resignation of counselor Godmother. The girls had her for a while. So she resigned and left, and R One imagined for some reason that we were somehow involved in this, risible as it may seem. We didn't even know her that well."

"Then why would he think . . ."

"Exactly," Tabaqui says. "Why would he?"

"If she only worked with the girls . . ."

"Exactly. That's what I've been saying!"

"But could it . . ."

"It couldn't!"

I finally blow up.

"Are you going to let me finish the question?"

"No! I mean, of course."

"Her car was found a couple of blocks from here," Sphinx joins in. "Then it turned out that no one has seen her since she left the House. So now she's officially listed as missing."

"Where does Blind figure in all that?"

"Go ask Ralph."

"Once a nutter, always a nutter," Tabaqui summarizes. "I guess he just needed an excuse to torment someone. That's what nutters do."

I stealthily pull my bag closer. My snitching diary is in there. Could it be I'm working for a madman now? Or did they really do something to that woman? But hard as I try, I can't think of a reason why they would. Tabaqui's right, Blind and the girlie counselor don't mix. Maybe it was the girls who did something to her?

I lower my head so that no one can see my face and hunt for the cigarette pack in my pocket. When I light up I immediately break out coughing. Should have quit long ago.

That's the House for you. In all its splendor. You sit staring at the wall. Or the ceiling. Listening to music, or not listening. Going crazy with boredom and chain-smoking to have at least something to distract you. While at the same time Leaders roam around covered in bloody scales, the House puts or doesn't put its mark on you, the only normal-looking counselor suddenly turns out to be crazy, the air is full of viruses unknown to medical science, and all this could very well be Jackal's fevered imagination, since he's well known to enjoy scaring people with his stories.

"Was it Blind who prettified Ralph's face?" I say.

Noble nods reluctantly.

"What did you expect?" Tabaqui jumps in. "You are kidnapped. Subjected to interrogations and torture. It's only natural to fight back. And it's only natural that someone can get hurt as a result. By the way, Ralph has opened himself up for liability in court, for unlawful imprisonment. And for premeditated interference with a Leader on the eve of graduation. Because what kind of life is that, when the Leader sleeps and sleeps, like a groundhog or something, and when he's not asleep all he does is scratch at himself, and can't even put two words together."

"Or won't," Blind corrects Tabaqui from behind the door that's slightly open. "Maybe he prefers to leave it to someone who's better equipped for it."

"Thank you," Tabaqui says, not in the least concerned about Blind's presence in the conversation, and then asks why is it that the voice of his beloved Leader seems to be coming from somewhere below.

"Because I'm lying on the floor. I have this bath towel here and I'm lying on it. Carry on, don't mind me. Just imagine I'm not here at all."

Alexander offers me a glass. There's something dark sloshing in it. Definitely not tea.

"Mountain Pine," he whispers. "Drink carefully."

That's when I remember the diary again. Isn't it time to start filling it, beginning with Jackal's stories? I thumbed through some diaries of famous people while in the Sepulcher (Ralph hauled in an entire stack of those from the library for me), and one thing I noticed was that they often skipped days and sometimes even weeks. I don't have that luxury, because the day after tomorrow I am supposed to present my first report. Which means it's time to accustom the pack to the sight of me writing in it. The sooner, the better.

Despite Blind's invitation to continue, everyone's silent. I put the glass with the brown liquid smelling of pine needles on one of Tabaqui's plates and take out the hallowed notebook. I open it, write today's date—and freeze. *So here I am, back in the Fourth* sounds unbelievably corny, but I can't think of anything else. I turn it this way and that in my mind and finally write it down, my ears burning with shame. Then I add: *The reception was less than enthusiastic.*

Tabaqui is reading as I write, snuffling and breathing into my ear.

"Ah, you've started a diary! Was it that boring in there?"

"Actually it's pretty useful," I say. "In a couple of years I'm going to open it, read the things I wrote today, and remember everything that happened. I mean, not everything, but at least the important events of the day."

"Like the reception being less than enthusiastic." Tabaqui nods. "A major event, and what's more important, one that's pleasant to remember."

"It's a diary, so it's supposed to be honest. If there's no enthusiasm, then that's what you write."

"What if there were, but hidden deep inside the heart?" Tabaqui persists.

"I write what I see, not what someone's hiding from me somewhere."

"Got it. Were you planning to write up my theory? About the Syndrome?"

"I'll try."

"You're going to bungle it. Definitely. You're going to twist it the way it suits you. Scribblers always do that. Not a single word of what was, only what they thought they saw."

I shrug.

"I'll do my best."

"Nonsense!" Tabaqui grabs the notebook. "You can't. I'll do it myself. That's the only way I can be sure the wisdom survives intact."

"Hey! Wait! At least let me finish the introduction!"

"What for? You think you won't be able to figure out that it was me who took it? Were you planning not to open it until you go totally senile?"

The snitching diary is dragged to the other side of the bed, where Tabaqui is free to properly expound on his creepy theories, but not before hiding from me behind a pillow.

That's surprise number one for Ralph.

I take a swig from the glass and choke. The liquid burns my lips, it's bitter as wormwood, and it does indeed stink of mutilated pine. It takes me a while to get my breath back.

Noble is swilling the piney concoction like it's water, with a placid look on his face. Sphinx sips his through a straw the size of a fire hose. Either their Mountain Pines are diluted, or they're already habituated to the effect.

"Where's Humpback?" I say.

"He took residence up in the oak," Noble says. "It's been a week that he's living there with Nanette. They call him Druid now, and there's an established pilgrimage."

"They leave offerings under the oak," Jackal adds. "Some of them tasty. Baskets of seeds and stuff."

"Seeds?" I say. "He lives on seeds now?"

"Of course not, silly, it's for Nanette. Even though she prefers sausage. So the top two bunks are free now, and we have girls sleeping there."

This saddens me. I have nothing against Mermaid, but the second night guest is most likely Ginger, and her I can barely tolerate. I take another sip—the Pine really does become less offensive as you go—and add another stroke to the insane pastiche that is the House. Humpback, cast as Tarzan.

There's a scratching at the door, then knocking, and in comes Ginger with a gray cat under her arm. One of the three that are completely indistinguishable from each other.

"Hi," she says to me. "Welcome back."

She drops the cat on the floor with a thud and sits down next to Sphinx.

"What was Blind doing outside the door?"

"Listening in," Noble explains. "It occurred to him that all the interesting conversations happen while he's absent. So now he's kind of here and not here at the same time."

"Oh, I see. So I probably shouldn't have noticed him."

"True," Noble agrees.

Cat strides back and forth on the blanket, thick tail up in the air, sniffing at our legs. A huge tomcat, the color of ash. Or of backs of mice. The Pine makes the outline of Noble sitting across from me blur suspiciously, while the cat begins to resemble a giant rat. Those cats, all three of them, give me the creeps. I always feel uneasy in their presence.

The door slams again and Vulture stumbles in, with Beauty in tow.

Vulture is holding a pot with a cactus in it. Beauty is armed with a pole, its top swaddled in rags. Blind comes next, carrying his towel.

"Here we are!" Vulture declares coyly. "Four of us this time."

Noble tosses two pillows down on the floor. Vulture takes one of them. Beauty leans his pole against the wardrobe and remains standing. Vulture has pulled his hair back in a ponytail so hard that his eyes take on an elongated shape. To emphasize that shape he's put on eyeliner highlights all the way to his temples. It makes him look unfamiliar, like he's dressed up for a masked ball. Beauty, on the contrary, is wearing slippers.

As soon as everyone settles down and Alexander turns off the lights, Tabaqui screeches that he can't see squat and that it interferes with his writing. A wall light is switched on for him. I've already forgotten that he's still hard at work over my diary. Pity R One. Crazy or not, deciphering Tabaqui's chickenscratch is no easy task.

Ginger complains to Sphinx about Catwoman, the owner of the three haughty cats. Vulture lets Blind in on the plans for his funeral.

"I am to be displayed in a glass sarcophagus, and the mourning period is not to exceed twenty-four hours."

"What about the poor Birdies?"

"You may immure them nearby. Them, and my entire cactus collection. But I'll expound on the exact procedure in my will, so you don't have to worry about getting it wrong."

"How are you doing, Smoker?" Beauty asks bashfully.

He puts out his hand and flips over the glass of Pine. And becomes upset. Terribly so. A brownish line trickles down the blanket.

Alexander hands me a towel.

"You seem to have spilled something."

I towel myself off, shake Beauty's hand, say, "Hi, nice to see you, don't worry about this, it's just alcohol," and try to crawl away from the pine-scented puddle slowly seeping into the covers—but there's nowhere for me to go. I am hemmed in by Noble on one side and Jackal's boundary pillow on the other.

"They had it good in the old times, being buried together with their horses and the entire household," Vulture says dreamily. "So that's my request too, to be interred among my cacti. Close my eyes, put two small silver keys on them, and cross two lockpicks on the chest . . ."

"I am so, so sorry, Smoker!" Beauty wails. "It is all my fault! Everything is always my fault! Everything!"

"Don't be ridiculous," I protest, digging in my shirt pocket for a handkerchief, but grab the smoldering cigarette instead, and it hurts. Very much.

"While we're on the subject, how is my dear relative doing?" Vulture says to Blind. "Is she well? Has everything she requires?"

I can't hear Blind's answer, but as he speaks he shows Vulture the palm of his hand for some reason.

"Tsk, tsk." Vulture shakes his head. "What an utterly vicious creature."

I decide that Vulture probably gave Blind a cactus as a present, and now they're discussing it, so I switch my attention to Ginger.

"I don't think she's got much left," she's saying to Sphinx. "Sleeps almost all the time, and doesn't recognize us anymore. Even the cats are avoiding her."

Sphinx says that this is sad.

"Or not." Ginger shrugs. "I guess everything's for the best."

I knew that the girl was a monster, and so did Sphinx, apparently, which is why he's not appalled by those words.

The monster extracts a ragged teddy bear from the backpack and puts it on her knee. Playing up the innocent child. I get almost physically sick from her routines and all that talk stuck on death and burials. I lie down and turn my face to the boombox's speakers, so I can avoid hearing any of them.

But even here I'm ambushed by Lary, jumping out from who knows where.

"Even if Spiders found something really bad with you, it's still not the end, man, it's not the end," he says, handing me my own pack of cigarettes.

"Thanks," I say. "That's very comforting to know."

It is Tabaqui who wakes me up.

There are only two of us in the dorm. It's very sunny and very hot. One half of the bed is made, exactly up to the place where I am. Tabaqui is wearing three T-shirts of different lengths, with no buttons in sight. None. I remember that yesterday I didn't see any on him either. I guess that period of his life has come and gone.

I rub my face, scratch my head, and yawn.

"Let's ride!" Tabaqui demands impatiently. "It's the perfect time for paying visits! Come on, get dressed! Quick!"

An untidy bundle is aimed at my head. I unwrap it. It's my shirt, crumpled, covered in brown stains and with the burn mark on the breast pocket. I put my finger through the hole; it's black when I pull it out. I decide not to change out of my sleeping T-shirt. It also isn't fresh, but at least I'm not going to look like I killed someone.

Tabaqui crawls to the edge of the bed and noisily tumbles down to the floor. Had he tried that trick in the Sepulcher he'd be put in plaster casts for a week. Arms and legs, both. To wean him off that nasty habit.

The paying of visits begins in the Coffeepot. We take the table by the window, and Tabaqui orders two coffees and some rolls. It's a sparse crowd today. Four Hounds, yawning, work on scrambled eggs.

"Do they serve stuff like that here? I thought it was only rolls," I say, not entirely sure because I've never been a regular.

"They do now. Almost no one goes to the canteen for breakfast anymore, so Shark has authorized some stuff to be redirected here. It gets reheated, and the result is truly atrocious. I emphatically advise against it."

"Where is everybody? Why is it so empty?"

Tabaqui extracts a cigarette from behind his ear, sniffs at it, and pulls the ashtray closer.

"Who's everybody?" he asks suspiciously.

"I mean, our guys."

"I don't know. Look, we'll sit here for a while, have a talk, and then go visit Humpback. Then we'll be three of our guys."

We drink the coffee in deathly silence. This is so unlike Tabaqui that I feel more and more awkward.

Hounds finish their reheated eggs and leave. I suddenly remember what it was I wanted to ask Tabaqui.

"Listen, where's my diary? Where did you put it yesterday?"

"Your what?" he says, looking puzzled. "Oh, the diary. Must be in the room somewhere, I guess. I didn't put it in with my stuff."

He slaps the side of the fat backpack strapped to the back of his Mustang. The backpack is so overstuffed that it would have tipped him over if he hadn't balanced it with small weights attached to the footboards. They jangle and rattle as he goes, and must be getting in the way, but Tabaqui is ecstatic at his own ingenuity and is not planning to get rid of them. One might even think he likes the clamor.

For some reason I start talking about the Sepulcher, how bored and alone I felt there, and how I couldn't even get down from the bed and crawl around to keep myself in shape. Crawling is frowned upon in the Sepulcher. As is smoking. Or reading at night.

Tabaqui listens with apparent interest.

"Horrors," he says when I exhaust my complaints. "I don't know if I can eat properly, now that I know all this. Or at least if I can enjoy food anymore. A scary place, that Sepulcher, I've always said that."

I say that it's not that bad really, that it's more comfortable than a Cage, that you only get prodded and bothered during the rounds, and the rest of the day is yours to enjoy peace and quiet, but Tabaqui just repeats that he's never heard anything more horrible.

"Rounds," he mutters. "Imagine that. Horror, pure and simple."

"You mean you've never been in the Sepulcher?"

"No, I haven't. And now it's unlikely I'd end up there before the end. Which is the only thing that comforts me when I think of graduation."

Someone slaps me on the back and says that he's happy to see me. Black. Carrying a pack of milk with a straw sticking out. He sits down on the edge of our table and asks me how I'm doing.

"Great," I say.

"Horrible!" Tabaqui counters, swaying back and forth in his Mustang. "Don't listen to him, Black. He's just been telling me about all the ghastly things happening in the Sepulcher, so ghastly I wouldn't even venture to repeat them."

Black winks at me, with the eye that Tabaqui can't see.

"And what does Sphinx say about it?"

"Sphinx didn't hear that. He wasn't here at the time."

"No, I mean what does he say about him returning, not about the Sepulcher."

"About Smoker returning he has so far said nothing," Tabaqui explains readily, "which means he probably won't be saying anything about it. If he has something to say, he either says it right away or doesn't say it at all. Anyway, whatever you say or don't say, he's been returned, and that's the end of it."

Black finishes the milk in one gulp, crumples the pack, long-tosses it in the trash bin, and says, "What I mean is, if he decides to say something after all, I'm ready to take Smoker. Anytime. Tell him that when you see him."

He gets up from the table, smooths out the tablecloth, says "See you around," and leaves.

"How incredibly kind of him," Tabaqui fumes. "He's always ready to add another Hound to the eighteen he already has, but only if Sphinx starts behaving like a crotchety old maid and says something untoward. I'm so touched I'm going to cry!"

"Listen, you promised to take me to Humpback," I remind him. "Could we go already?"

"We could," Tabaqui mutters darkly. "Unless you are of the opinion that I am now required to pass Chief Hound's message to Sphinx while it's still steaming."

"I am not. The message can wait."

"Let's ride, then."

Tabaqui takes a battered acid-green baseball cap out of his backpack, shakes it out, and shoves it down on top of his shock of unruly curls.

"I'm ready. Don't leave the cigarettes, they'd be gone before we get two feet away."

It's warmer out in the yard than inside the House. A group of fully clothed Bandar-Logs are sunning themselves, splayed theatrically against the wall. They quietly acknowledge us from under their drawn-down caps as we drive by.

"Like a firing squad's just been," Tabaqui notes. "Except there's no blood."

The oak gives a dense, almost purple shadow. The dappled sun plays on the gnarly trunk. Tabaqui turns off the path into the grass, stops, and rummages in his backpack.

"He's got a whole system set up," he explains. "With every visitor having a distinct call, and a way to communicate the reason for coming over. As a hint that we shouldn't bother him too much. Because you know how it is, there's this rumor now that he can see into the future, so they started coming here in droves. Ruined the lawn. It's strange, really. All it takes is climbing up a tree, and suddenly you're a prophet."

Not pausing for a second, Tabaqui takes out his harmonica, wipes it off, puts it to his mouth, and starts tootling the Rain Song.

I look up at the oak. From here it's hard to tell where Humpback's tent is, let alone Humpback himself. It's all vaguely canvas-y, half-hidden in the canopy. I peer at one flap, shielding my eyes from the rays piercing the mass of leaves, and imagine that those are Humpback's underpants drying on the clothesline, and somewhere higher up he has pots and pans hanging off the branches, and strings of dried acorns, and maybe right now he's working on some mysterious concoction of oak leaves, June bugs, and crow guano. While I'm picturing all that, here he comes, in the flesh, tanned almost black, shaggy and half-naked, looking very much the hermit, the whites of his eyes flashing and some trinket on a string around his neck jingling.

He sits down in a fork of two thick branches and crosses his bare legs. Not high and not low. Too high for us. A walker could probably reach him.

"Hi!" Tabaqui waves the harmonica. "See? Smoker's back. And he's staying until graduation. Who would've thought, huh?"

"Who indeed," Humpback says.

He's only got his boxers on. The hair is cinched on the forehead by a grubby-looking cord. I don't think he'd be able to see anything otherwise. He isn't surprised by what Jackal has just told him. No wonder, since he surely spotted me before coming down.

As Tabaqui rattles off the latest news, he keeps looking over the oak and its inhabitant in a proprietary sort of way, like a native guide showing off a famous landmark to a chance tourist. I am the tourist and Humpback is the landmark, so we're both silent. Humpback keeps his eyes on the lawn and the Logs in the distance. I'm watching the lower branches of the oak and his bare legs.

"So, what do you have to say about all this?" Tabaqui demands, having disposed of the news.

"Say?" Humpback looks up distractedly. "I'd say that it's all probably for the best. What else can I say? Excuse me, this is not a very comfortable place for sitting."

He nods at us, with not a hint of a smile, gets up, and disappears in the branches. We hear the rustle as he climbs up, and quickly lose sight of him.

"Hear that? The oracles of antiquity got nothing on him," Tabaqui says admiringly. "That's why he's so popular. Because he can toss off tired truisms and sound good doing it."

We make a couple of rounds of the yard, looking at the oak now and then, at the canopy where Humpback is hiding from the world. Suddenly Tabaqui stops dead.

"There's one other thing I think you need have a look at," he says. "Give me five minutes and then come to the classroom. That should be enough for me to prepare it."

"Prepare what?"

Jackal smiles mysteriously and drives off.

I watch with apprehension as he's approaching the ramp. The weights are not going to be enough to hold the wheelchair upright when he's on the incline. The backpack will tip the whole thing over.

Without slowing down, Tabaqui reaches over, extracts from the pocket on the back of Mustang a length of rope with a grappling hook on one end, unspools it, and makes a deft throw, catching it on the railing on the first try. He even neglects to give it a tug to check if it is lodged securely, simply flies up the ramp hand over hand on the rope. On the porch he can't help himself and looks back at me. Have I seen that? Have I admired that?

I have, and I have. Tabaqui, looking very pleased, stows his siege weapon and disappears inside.

On the stairs between the first and the second floor I bump into Lary. He's also plenty tanned and managed to grow a patchy beard. I didn't get a good look at him yesterday.

"Hey, Smoker," he says. "So you're, like, healthy now? Nothing hurts?"

I tell him I'm fine and ask if by any chance he knows what that wondrous thing is that Tabaqui is planning to show me in the classroom.

"Oh. His collection." Lary waves his hand dismissively. "It's nothing. A pile of junk, if you ask me. But don't even think of calling it that. Tabaqui's going to kill you if you do."

"Thanks for the warning," I say.

"Anytime, man."

He continues down, for his sunbathing session, and I go up to look at the collection.

Which turns out to be a pile of junk. Literally. Dumped in the middle of the classroom. The desks have been pushed against the walls, probably to give it more space. Mermaid has chosen one of them to sit on, completely cocooned inside her hair so that only the very tips of her sneakers peek out. Tabaqui, frozen in anticipation at the bottom of Mount Rubbish, almost seems like a part of the collection himself. A living exhibit.

"Well?" he says. "What do you think about all this?"

I make my face reflect deep cogitation and circle the collection. It is not exactly overwhelming. A garage sale. A couple of paintings, two huge photographs of the Crossroads glued to wooden frames, a rusted birdcage, an enormous high boot, a battered ottoman, a dusty box of cassettes, and assorted knickknacks spread on chairs: small boxes, books, pendants, trinkets.

I make another go-round.

Further driving seems pointless, so I tell Tabaqui, "Looks nice. What's it supposed to mean?"

"What? You don't remember? You were there when I started assembling it! Those are all nobody's. Completely, totally no one's. No one admits to owning them. No one remembers anyone else ever owning them. They just appear in odd places all by themselves, under mysterious circumstances."

"Oh. I understand now."

I don't understand anything, of course. How could things be nobody's? So those who had used them are no longer in the House, so what? The House has gone through so many people and things that it's impossible to claim to know who owned what.

"All right," Jackal grumbles. "Out with it. I can see the direction your thought process is taking."

"Good for you," I say. "I hope your collection happily grows and multiplies."

Mermaid jumps off the desk and runs to me, the bells in her hair tinkling.

"You don't believe us? But it really is nobody's, all of it."

I like Mermaid. She reminds me of a kitten. Not those postcard-ready fuzzballs, but a homeless, scrawny one, with hauntingly beautiful eyes. It's impossible not to pick one up even if it isn't asking you for it.

So I say that of course I believe them, I believe that everything they've assembled here really and truly does not belong to anyone, and that it must be amazing and odd, finding things like those, except I don't understand why they need to do it.

Tabaqui's eyes fill with disdain.

"You see," he says, "life does not go in a straight line. It is like circles on the surface of the water. Every circle, every loop is composed of the same stories, with very few changes, but no one notices that. No one recognizes those stories. It is customary to think that the time in which you find yourself is brand new, freshly made and freshly painted. But the world only ever draws repeated patterns. And there aren't that many of them."

"But what does this old junk have to do with that?"

He sighs, visibly hurt.

"It has to do with the sea, for example, always bringing up the same things that are nevertheless always different. If this time you got a twig, it doesn't mean that the last time it wasn't a seashell. A wise man brings all of it together, puts it with what's been collected by those who came before him, and then adds to it the stories of what came up in the olden days. And this way he would know what the sea brings."

Tabaqui isn't mocking me. He's deadly earnest. Even though what he's just said sounds like he's delirious. Mermaid is hanging on his every word, eyes open wide, almost glowing from the inside. I think about how she's still just a child, really, and so is Tabaqui.

"These things are nobody's things," Tabaqui insists. "They don't have an owner. But there must have been a purpose to them lying forgotten and lost in some corner all this time, right? And then being found suddenly? They might contain some sort of magic. The answers to all our questions are right around us, all we have to do is find them. And then the seeker becomes the hunter."

The sun forces its way in through the glass panes. I look out the window. It would have been easier were Tabaqui alone here, but they, the cracked hunters of junk, are two, and the other one is a girl who likes stories.

"Very interesting," I say. "I'm not sure I understood everything, but it is all very likely just the way you described."

Two tiny furrows appear on Mermaid's forehead. Very light, almost insubstantial. Tabaqui cringes.

"You know, there's no need to pity us," Mermaid says. "We didn't call you here so you could pity us."

I take one last look at Tabaqui's hunting trophies and drive out of the classroom. Looks like we just had a falling-out.

I spend the next thirty minutes looking for my diary. The notebook is nowhere to be seen. I check the desk drawers and the bookshelves, I open and close nightstands, I crawl down on the floor peeking under the beds. It's not there. Finally I ask Alexander.

"Is it a thick brown notebook?" he says. "I think I've seen it somewhere around." He goes to Tubby's pen, leans over it, and says, "There you go. He's been stockpiling fuel again. Give this back, you hear? Hey! It belongs to someone else."

Tubby responds with indistinct cooing. Alexander turns back to me, holding the diary, wipes it off and says contritely, "Looks like he tore it up a bit. Is that all right? I should have watched him better. I'm sorry. I didn't check what all that rustling was in there."

I accept the mangled diary. The cover has been chewed, and it's missing half of the pages. Empty ones, fortunately. Tubby started from the back.

"Thanks," I say. "I think it's still usable."

Alexander just shrugs.

I thumb through the filled pages. There seem to be entirely too many of them. I read a random paragraph: *The stems of cacti are susceptible to rot, viral infections, and infestations of the cactus moth and various aphids. The proper care for those is pruning the affected areas and spraying them with preparations containing cupric ions.* Did Tabaqui unconsciously switch from Blind to cacti?

"I don't understand," I say. "What's a viral cactus doing here?"

Alexander takes a look.

"That's Vulture's handwriting," he explains. "I guess he chanced upon your diary yesterday and decided to put in something to remember him by. Does this upset you?"

I flip the pages, horrified. One, two, three . . .

Summarizing the above-mentioned circumstances, it is fair to assert that the highly targeted nature of the said disorder does not lend itself to any explanation within the framework of conventional medical science, affecting as it does almost exclusively those who are the least suitable for integration within the society that for the purposes of this discussion may be, within certain limitations, broadly described by the controversial term "Outsides."

Dear Smoker, Tabaqui told me to write a message for you in this notebook so that you can read it and remember me. I don't really know what to write . . .

*The glochids of the Opuntioideae easily detach from the plant and lodge in
the skin, causing irritation. The tender white prickles of some Mammillaria
and the silvery threads of the Cephalocereus, the Old-Man Cactus . . .*

"I think they've all had a hand," I say. "It's not a diary anymore, it's a yearbook."

I flip to the empty pages and notice some strange marks, tiny holes punched
through and arranged in rows.

"And someone bit on it here," I say. "Or maybe not. At least the back portion was
definitely gnawed by Tubby."

Alexander looks closer and then feels the holes with his finger.

"This is Braille," he explains. "Blind wrote you something. He has this tool, like
a thing with a nail in it . . ."

"Oh," I say. "A remembrance. I'm going to read it in my old age, when I lose my
sight and learn to read Braille. Cool."

"Listen," Alexander sighs. "Can I just give you another notebook? Almost like this
one. Tubby spoiled the cover too."

"I don't need another one. I'll manage," I say. "I'm sorry for all the grumbling. It's
not like you had anything to do with it."

He shrugs.

"As you wish. We could place it under a stack of books, then. Straighten out the
pages a little."

Alexander brings some glue and we mend the bedraggled cover the best we can.
Then we put all the books we could find in the room on top of the notebook. Then
Alexander makes some tea. Tea is not the best thing to be drinking when it's so hot
out. In the Sepulcher I was getting it cold-brewed and with ice, but it's time I forgot
about life in the Sepulcher.

Alexander shows me Tubby's bag. It's a toddler backpack, and it overflows with
little balls of chewed paper.

"Food for the fire," Alexander says. "He's been saving them for a while."

Then he says that I should tear out the page with Blind's message.

"Why?" I say. "How is it better or worse than Tabaqui's?"

"But you have no idea what he's written there," Alexander persists. "And for
whom."

"What do you mean, for whom?"

Alexander's gaze goes right through me. It's directed somewhere above the bridge
of my nose. He shrugs.

"You know . . ."

I break into a cold sweat from the hints he seems to be dropping.

"Nobody reads Braille here in the House, do they?"

He shrugs again.

"Some people do. Ralph, for one."

He looks away tactfully.

I'm silent. It's stifling in the room. The sun is melting the glass in the windows. Alexander is not looking at me and I am not looking at him. I know what I am ashamed of, but I don't understand why he should be ashamed as well. Why he should look guilty.

"Thanks," I say. "You're right. That's what I'll do. Tear it out."

He nods.

Smoker's diary (excerpts)

It might seem that nothing much changed in the House. The lights-out and morning bells keep getting ignored just as before. The pack spent half the night feverishly discussing the subject of "Jerichonies," whatever they are, that are supposed to "presage the end," and then shortly before dawn Tabaqui woke up everyone with a scream: "Here he is, I've got him!" When they switched on the lamp he was sitting under the table, flashlight in hand, surrounded by the shards of a smashed flowerpot.

Mermaid is knitting a rug, or something similar. It looks like a chessboard. Every night before going to bed she puts it up on the wall and then sleeps under it. According to her, this kind of netting protects from bad dreams. According to Sphinx, it steals the dreams and makes intractable tangles out of them.

Humpback is still living up in the oak. Lary spends his nights on the first floor. Logs created something like a tent city down there and are "keeping watch." That is, they discuss their pocketknives all day and paint on the nearby walls all night.

No one talks about graduation, except to mention some kind of bus. "When we are on the bus," "When the bus comes for us," or something about life on four wheels. I could never get out of them any details about this bus, or whether it even exists. Could be just a figure of speech, to avoid saying the word "Outsides."

Since the day I failed to give Tabaqui's collection its due he only refers to me as "child" or "that youth."

Jerichonies are these tiny creatures that are invisible under artificial light and at the same time afraid of the sun, so spotting them is an almost impossible task. There are more and more of them in the House every day, and right before graduation they will assemble in multitudes and start shouting with a great shout. And that's going to be the end of us, since the walls of the House, naturally, will fall down flat.

—Tabaqui, "Common Wisdom for the Inquisitive Youth."

Today in the Coffeepot I asked Red, draped over the counter, what his tattoo meant. He didn't have a shirt on, and I saw this man with a dog's head on his chest. I was only looking for what Tabaqui terms "a friendly chat," but got way more than I bargained for. He said it was Anubis, the god of the dead. "In short, the protector of all stiffs."

Then Red lowered his head into the crook of his elbow and went all gloomy for some reason. I suspect that he wasn't quite sober. On the other hand, he only had a cup of coffee in front of him. Everyone turned to look at us. That was unpleasant, and I tried to wheel away. But Red suddenly perked up, peeled himself off the counter, and grabbed my sleeve.

"And I am his angel in the Upper World! His freaking emissary, get it?" he screamed, tugging at my clothes. Gawkers started gathering around, and then he let go of me and ran out. I think he's depressed from the overdose of green. From not taking his green glasses off.

Found on the walls:
"Brothers and Sisters, stop fooling around. IT is near." Know-it-all.
"Cleansing campaign tonight. Presence mandatory, except for those on the third loop and above." The Inside Man.

Alexander stashed a pile of cups and pans under his bed. But not before spending a whole hour scrubbing and washing them.

"Might be useful," he said when I peeked under the bed for the third time.

"Useful where?" I said.

"Anywhere, I think," Alexander said and pulled the cover lower to hide his treasure.

Even though graduation is never discussed (apart from the bus and those Jerichonies), the inevitability of it is in the air. Girls, for example, cry often. Their eyes are red and swollen, at least from what I notice on the three girls I see every day. Mermaid lives in our room and Ginger sometimes spends the night. Needle comes in the evenings to borrow the coffeemaker for Logs. And they're all really touchy, so that I'm afraid to say even one word to them. Ginger especially. Everywhere she goes she drags this ancient teddy bear with her, with one glass eye and a shirt button in place of the other. If you jostle it you'll get a cloud of brownish dust, and it smells so old that it is immediately clear that this must have been her great-grandmother's favorite toy, and even back then it was already the way it is now. This nightmarish teddy always ends up lying next to me, and if I ask her to put it somewhere else she gets this miserable look, like I've just deeply offended her.

The House is in mourning, on the occasion of the repairs that they were threatening us with for as long as I can remember. Stepladders everywhere, and the plasterers are hard at work scraping the drawings and the messages off the walls. People apparently can't stand such a blatant violation of their living space and have retreated to the rooms. The wave started from the hospital wing and is slowly rolling toward the Crossroads. I ventured out to have a look. Don't know what it looks like, but definitely not like our corridor. The walls are all dirty and feel somehow injured, covered in great gouges. If they thought this would make the atmosphere brighter, it didn't. It's even more depressing than before.

"Blood! Revenge and blood!" Tabaqui screams at regular intervals. Just as I finally calm down and start thinking about something.

Everyone's busy packing. They drag the backpacks out into the hallways and back to the rooms, take everything out and put it back in. Whoever it is, you can be sure that they're packing. The weather is hotter and hotter.

"The War with the Girls" means Jackal wheeling in shouting "It's them! Again!" Everyone jumps up and then sits down and returns to whatever they've been doing. In the meantime a group of surly maidens storms the Coffeepot and occupies it for the next two hours, only to vacate it afterward in the same belligerent fashion. It's not entirely clear why they call it "war," and why the guys insist on hiding in the dorms and ceding the hallways to the girls, and then sulk that the hallways have been forcibly taken from them. I have a strong suspicion that this is yet another invention of those who don't know how to amuse themselves. Like Lary and Jackal, who seem to require nonstop excitement of the scary variety.

The plasterers have scrubbed and smoothed the walls and moved to the first floor. The stepladders and the protective plastic remain, though. They say that the painters arrive tomorrow.

Logs struck their camp temporarily. Lary's back in the dorm. Logs spend their days out in the yard now, because the new hallways creep them out, and they're already out of habit of being inside a room.

"I'm out to hunt," Tabaqui says, maneuvering his way out of the room in the morning. Every day the footboard of Mustang acquires one more weight, but the backpack is gaining bulk faster. Tabaqui clanks and rattles as he drives, like a hardware shop on wheels.

"He's like the White Knight," Noble says. "Tumbling down every couple of feet. It's only a question of time before he hurts himself."

"His luck seems to be holding so far," Sphinx counters. "You're not suggesting we take that backpack off him? That would be equal to at least two invasions of Jerichonies."

"Of course not," Noble says in a frightened voice. "Better to go on the bus than that."

"What is that bus?" I ask Lary after breakfast. "You know, the one they keep talking about."

He yawns widely, like a crocodile, and stares at me dumbly.

"What bus? There is no bus, what's gotten into you? Where would they find it? It's just people talking stuff. Someone's joke. And now here you are spreading it around."

"But you're spreading it around too. You talk about it all the time."

"Me?" He takes offense for some reason. "I never did. Why would I? I've got enough problems as it is."

"You mean you don't care. Whatever happens, you're content."

Lary darkens.

"Of course I am. I mean, why not. If they tell me 'Here's the bus, get in,' I will."

"Get in the imaginary bus?" I attempt to clarify.

"If that's what they tell me, yeah."

Lary looks around stealthily and leans over to me. The squint in his left eye is really horrible.

"The questions you're asking, Smoker . . . Strange questions," he says in a low whisper. "I don't like them, all right? Why don't you just go on your way. I've got some business here. I have no time for you now, all right?"

Found on the walls:

"Through unrelenting meditation discovered the Law of Non-action. Inquiries welcome, the Sixth from 3:00 to 3:05." Big Brother.

Ratling Whitebelly comes up to me and timidly asks that I write about him "in that notebook you have."

"Why?" I wonder.

"So that I'm there too."

A beseeching look, chocolate smears on his cheeks. He looks at least five years younger than everyone else.

"Listen, how old are you, anyway?" I say.

"Sixteen," Whitebelly says, darkening. "So?"

"Why do you need to be in my diary? The truth, please."

"This is my first loop," he says in a flat voice. "I need to anchor myself everywhere I can, or I'll get thrown out."

"Where?" I am almost wailing now. "Thrown out where?"

Whitebelly looks at me in abject horror and backs away. I drive at him, but I don't think he understands that my intention is to apologize, so he turns around and legs it away without looking back, ignoring all my shouts of "Wait!" and "Hey!"

Sphinx says that if I continue driving around scaring the kids I'm going to get it from him personally.

"It was he who scared me, not the other way around."

In the morning there's some unusual activity by the window, and it wakes me up. I open my eyes and see them all crowding there, discussing something. Arguing loudly.

"I'm telling you, it's Solomon and Don! They have returned!" Jackal screams. "With a posse of like-minded avengers! You'll see!"

"And I think they are from the nearby houses," Lary suggests. "Came to demand the House be demolished right now. Because they're tired of waiting."

"It might be someone's parents," Ginger frets. "Only parents can pull something like this."

"You think our grandmothers could be down there too?" Blind says, visibly worried. He is also there at the window, but isn't peeking out, of course.

"Why grandmothers?" Ginger says.

"What is it?" I call to them. "What happened?"

The only one to turn to me is Sphinx.

"Tents. Right next to the House," he says. "Four of them."

"It's a camp!" Tabaqui screams, hanging onto the window bars. "A camp of revenge!"

I start dressing. In a great hurry, for some reason. I wouldn't be able to climb to the windowsill even if all the rest of them climb down from it, but I still behave like I'm going to get up right now, muscle my way through, and have a look for myself.

Noble is the only one besides me who stayed back on the bed. Smoking and pretending like he doesn't give a hoot.

"It's unlikely grandmothers would want to live in tents," Ginger says. "At least that's what I think."

Ginger is standing with her feet on the windowsill, in a cut-off spaghetti-strap top and briefs. The top does not even come down to her navel. The undies are bright red, the color of her hair. The moldy bear is in its usual place, under her arm. I realize that Noble must hate what he sees. That the reason for him sitting glumly on the bed is Ginger parading herself half-naked in the window. If I were him I'd be grateful she at least has something on. She could have just as easily climbed up there topless. I happen to know that for a fact.

"Blind is just paranoid." Tabaqui giggles. "Imagining grandmothers lurking behind every corner. They have robbed him of his peace of mind."

"Why not grandfathers?" Mermaid says.

"I wonder when they're coming out," Lary says.

I am already dressed, so I crawl closer to the edge of the bed. If I can't see it, at least I can listen to them talk. Alexander notices my movements and comes over to the bed.

"Would you like to have a look? Come to the window, I'll lift you up."

"Never mind," I say.

As I crawl toward the window, Mermaid slides down from it. She is wearing men's pajamas, about three sizes too big for her. She turned up the sleeves but the pants legs still flop around. Ginger gives me a hand and hoists me up on the windowsill, almost without any help from Alexander, who's pushing me from below.

I see them now. Four tents. Two camouflage green, one orange, and one dusty blue. They really are right against the fence, as if the House has sprouted them overnight out of itself, like mushrooms.

"I wonder if it's not the survivalists from the Sixth," Sphinx says uncertainly. "Could be that Black decided to train them for the rigors of the Outsides. In stages."

"Who's coming down to the yard?" Ginger calls. "To look at them up close?"

"What about breakfast?" Jackal says indignantly. "You have all been neglecting it! It's boring, going to the canteen by myself."

I end up looking at the tents longer than anyone else, because I was the last to see them and because I can't climb down. Gradually they tire of discussing this event, and soon I am alone on the windowsill. When Alexander comes to help me, I notice that he is very careful to avert his face.

"What's wrong?" I say.

He shrugs.

"Nothing. I'm just not interested."

It doesn't sound very convincing, not at all.

Once in the hallway everyone darkens, and some put on sunglasses. The walls are not scary anymore. They are uniformly the color of malted milk, smooth and squeaky clean. The stench of paint is overwhelming.

"We are a continuation of the Sepulcher now," Lary says ruefully. "You call this life?"

No one else says anything.

A good half of the House is already down in the yard. Many are still in pajamas. At least it's clear that Sphinx was wrong. Hounds of the Sixth have nothing to do with this. They are as eager as everyone else to find out who's been hiding in the tents. Even the Brothers Pigs are here, all in a row, wheel to wheel. Identical stares and identically opened mouths. No one has risked approaching the wire fence yet.

Finally the flap on one of the tents is thrown open, disgorging three inhabitants. Bulky camo overalls. Cleanly shaven heads. Empty eyes, staring exactly like Ginger's bear. It doesn't look like anyone is eager to make their acquaintance. On the contrary, those closest to the fence take several steps back. When I look around a couple of minutes later, I feel that there are significantly fewer of us here.

One of the tent people presses against the fence, contorting his face in a smile. I zoom backwards toward the porch. Only when the wheels bump into the lower step do I realize that never before in my life have I driven backward at such speed. Lary overtakes me and flies up the stairs.

"An empty skin," he mumbles as he runs. "An empty skin!"

Logs quickly disappear inside.

The tent man puts his fingers through the netting and says something. Still smiling. I wish he'd stop doing that. I'd prefer it if Ginger's bear smiled suddenly instead of him.

The Brothers Pigs drive by me, each jostling my wheelchair, because I'm right there in the way at the bottom of the stairs. Then Zebra and Corpse run past, pushing crying Elephant before them, and almost flip him over. One of the last to evacuate is Jackal.

"What do they want?" I ask him. "Who are they?"

"Empty skins," he answers, busily unspooling his hook on a rope. "They are looking for someone who they think would fill them."

"I don't understand!" I cry after him, but he's already up on the porch, hotly arguing with Red.

He doesn't hear me.

BLIND

Blind crosses the yard that's been imbibing the heat all day. The asphalt is warm under his bare soles, and the stubble of the lawn prickles them gently. The grass is thicker under the oak, thicker and softer. He comes up to the tree and allows his hands to enter it. The bark leaves wrinkled indentations on his palms. He climbs slowly, even though he could fly up like a cat. But it's not his tree. Today he is merely a guest. To the right of the entrance extends a wide corridor, leading to the place where the swing was once attached, until Elephant tore it off with the yelp of "I'm flying!"—and to the left, a narrow passageway that only the thin and small-bodied could use. That branch is cooler to the touch than the others, because they all keep the traces of every ascent and descent, and Blind likes it best. He whistles as he climbs, sending up a warning.

Humpback says hi and rustles the twigs. The greeting is not welcoming, but Blind didn't expect it to be. Humpback settled up here in the hopes of being left alone, not to entertain guests. But Nanette, rushing through the leafy thickets to meet Blind, is ecstatic. The wings brush his cheek and his shoulder is bestowed with a blob of gelatinous guano. She's become heavier, and she smells of a fully adult bird now, that is, not exactly nice. While he and Nanette exchange pleasantries, Humpback asks what Blind is doing up in the tree.

"Nothing much, really," Blind says. "Would you play for me?"

Humpback doesn't answer.

Nanette flies a little way off, attacks the canopy, sings with abandon, dances above their heads, making noise and pretending she's three birds at once. Blind wipes off his shirt. His hand becomes sticky.

"Why?" Humpback says.

His voice is different here than in the room. A confident voice, even when he's speaking softly.

Blind takes a step forward. His face is a frozen mask, his hands bear the traces of the tree's undulations.

"No reason," he says, and sits down in the goblet-like junction, the only place here that's suitable for comfortable sitting.

He always chose that place, preferring it to all others. Anyone sitting here cannot be seen either from the ground or from the windows. This is the very heart of the tree.

Blind sees that Humpback's seclusion is a burden to him. Being alone is hard when you're accustomed to living among many, and that which he thought would bring him peace is not helping. The moon shines brightly through the night, and the air is full of tension. Humpback is part of that tension he tried to flee, he brought it with him and placed it in the branches, hoping that the silence and the tree's vitality could do something to it. Something that he himself couldn't. Everybody's the same. Running around trying to hide everything deeper inside, then hiding themselves and their birds. Stepping back, always stepping back and smelling of fear, but keeping up appearances, smiling, joking, quarreling, eating, and procreating. And Humpback is not like them, he's bad at it, he only gets as far as the very first, overt part of any action, and that makes him even more unhappy.

The mingling aromas of vanilla and unwashed hair. The first of those he carries in a pouch of smoking tobacco around his neck.

They are silent. Humpback searches for the words to say to Blind, Blind waits for him to find them, and then Humpback walks away on a shaky branch, returns, sits down across from Blind, and starts playing. Very softly. It's almost a lullaby, but the wrong kind, there is no calm in it, no caress. Through its ostentatious tenderness Blind feels the cold breath of Humpback's loneliness. Blind waits for it to subside, to dissolve as Humpback gets carried away and forgets about his presence, but he never does.

"Happy?"

Blind reaches out.

"May I? I would like you to remember something."

His hand accepts the flute. It's not merely warm—it's hot, like the places on the walls where someone has just written something important. The handprints are always hot, visible to the touch. The flute trembles and meanders in Blind's hand, the dead wood follows the traces left by the live wood. Blind plays the song he had heard once, the one with the wind, the spiraling leaves, and the boy in the middle of the whirlwind, protected and vulnerable at the same time. Blind plays well, this is not the first time he has played this song. He re-creates all the nuances faithfully, and he can be proud of his performance.

"What was that?" Humpback says.

"You used to play this down in the yard. Remember?"

Humpback shakes his head. They often respond like that to Blind, and only then check themselves and put their movements into words, but by that time it's already unnecessary.

"No, I don't."

Blind plays another snippet, and Humpback's aloof silence tells him that Humpback really does not recognize his own song.

"Too many repetitions."

Blind doesn't tell him that the repetitions are his, that they helped him weave the protective net, that it's what the magic of monotony is about, completing the circle, doubling on itself until the end becomes the beginning, building an impenetrable wall around the player. The words remain unsaid as he hands back the flute. Other people's songs have damaged Humpback, he can no longer do magic even when he lives in a tree. What he used to do so well is now but a trivial melody for him.

"The tree is not good for you," Blind says. "And the loneliness. Come down and look for what you've lost there. You might find more than you expect to find while sitting here."

"How would you know what I want to find sitting here? What I've already found? What makes you think you know what's going on in my head?"

Nanette crashes down on Blind's shoulder like a sack of feathers and passionately pecks him on the earlobe.

"How about you come down yourself and stop bugging me?" Humpback says, taking the bird off Blind. "Leave me alone."

Blind distances himself from Humpback's words, his voice, Nanette's crowing, stops seeing their movements by the noise they're making, and brings up the memory of the big fish flapping its fins in a deep basin, immersing himself in that sound. Someone had done that long ago. Took a fish, put it in a basin, and placed it in the room where Blind lived. Blind spent so many hours sitting next to that basin that he can now restore those sounds inside him even in the noisiest of places, restore them and lull himself to sleep. He brings his big fish and lets it roam among the branches of the oak like a giant scaly bird, lets it splash and float in the leaves. The longer it does that, the calmer he becomes. When he touches his fingers to the bark, it is not warmer than his skin anymore, he washed it of its memory, the tree will stand untouched now for some time, like a primeval oak in the primeval forest.

Humpback quiets down also, listening to what he wrought.

Dozens of paths above them, growing thinner and thinner and breaking off into nothingness, dozens of ways, some wide, some narrow, all ending identically, but not for those who can see. The highest of them soar above the canopy, if you follow them you can feel them buckling under your weight, and if it's windy you may hear the squeaking of the invisible door as you swing on the branch over the void, inhaling the scent of the closed-off path. Blind climbs the oak when he needs to feel the Forest. When his arms and legs are restless and his head is full of words he seeks solace in sending his body up the waterspouts to the roof, up the wire fence, up the trees to the highest branches. He likes himself when he does these things. He hasn't visited the oak for a long time. He's content here, he's home, and even if Humpback turned him out now he'd still carry away something valuable. Humpback's fear and apprehension. The old song, the smell of tobacco, Nanette's excitement, and the splashing of the giant fins. And the image of the little girl, crouching, sucking on her thumb. The girl with a surprisingly heavy gaze, wearing a battered short dress stained with egg yolk and blood. Humpback is scared of her. Blind will take her with him.

"Why is it you don't ask before taking something from us?" Humpback says sharply. "Why do you never ask us?"

Blind is astonished by Humpback's perceptiveness, almost frightened by it. He leans against the gnarly branch. *Always? From us?* What does he always take from them, from Humpback, without asking? And why would Humpback tell him about it now, just as he realizes something is indeed being taken? He scatters Humpback's words and puts them together again, listening to the sound they make, and sees that Humpback did not mean what he assumed. He was not talking about that which Blind has taken a moment ago.

"Everyone grabs what they need wherever they can," he says. "You included. We all take something from each other."

Humpback's branch jerks, mirroring his move. Or maybe he thumped it angrily.

"Yes, we all do. But you, especially so. You are greedy, Blind. You take like a thief, and it's so obvious. I sometimes think that you feed on our thoughts. That there is no you, only what you've taken from us, stolen from us. And that . . . loot—it walks among us, it talks to us, sniffs at us, pretending that it's one of us. I feel myself emptying in your presence. I hear you saying my own words—words that I never said when you were near. Logs call you a changeling. They say you steal other people's dreams. It's supposed to be a joke, you're supposed to laugh like it's another one of their silly ideas, except I know it's true, have known it for a long time. I know you're a fake. You're tiny shards of us glued together."

"That grew into your Leader," Blind prompts. He's not being sarcastic or cruel. He doesn't hear conviction in Humpback's voice, only desire to hurt him. "I can assure you, Humpback, that I did once exist outside the House, without any assistance from any of you."

Does Humpback smile?

Blind knows where this superstition comes from. A big part of it is his habit of quietly assuming the inflections of anyone he's talking to. It happens by itself, almost unconsciously. By doing that he reduces the distance, makes the words easier to understand. Sometimes it makes even the thoughts easier to guess. But this habit by itself wouldn't make Humpback want to hurt him now.

"I had my dreams," Humpback says. "They were my own. My secret place. No one knew about it. And then you barged in and ruined it. Forced that horrible child on me. She hides all the time and then jumps out when I least expect it, and starts biting and scratching like a wolverine. You turned my dreams into nightmares. I can't even be in a room at night anymore, I'm always expecting her to sneak in on me and tear at my face. I'm not even talking about being able to sleep. Only here, in the tree, and only for minutes at a time. I know why you did it. Because you can't stand it when someone escapes from you! Escapes to where you have no power!"

Blind laughs.

"What makes you think that you're the only one to have that dream? That it's a dream at all?"

Humpback suddenly reeks of danger. The scent is so strong that Blind grabs the nearest branch, even though it's not nearly thick enough to support him.

"If I were to push you off right now, are you going to reach the ground? Or will you evaporate on the way down?"

Humpback's voice echoes with the sound of Blind's fall and the twigs cracking. Or maybe it's bones.

"I'll grab you, and we'll fall together."

"That's not an answer."

"I didn't like the question."

Humpback sighs heavily.

"Those aren't dreams, Humpback. Believe me," Blind says. "But you must have already figured that out."

Nanette pounds the trunk with her beak, imitating a woodpecker. Blind tears off a leaf that's been tickling his cheek and crushes it in his fingers. They become slightly sticky and bring in the smell of the Forest. It helps Blind regain his composure. You should always smell of things that surround you, that's one of the Forest survival tricks. Becoming a part of it reduces the danger. It's a bit like copying the inflections. Blind has long been a believer in this technique, ever since the time he devoured the walls of the House when he was little.

"If not dreams, what is it, then?" Humpback says.

"You know yourself," Blind says indifferently.

Humpback is silent. Only his fingers move, rubbing the flute. The dappled rays of the sun are hotter now, they burn Blind's skin where they touch it, these solar bites wandering back and forth in the feeble breeze that ruffles the leaves.

Once, long ago, on this very junction where Blind now sits, he was hit by a crossbow bolt. It didn't pierce him, only hit and bounced off. He remembers how frightened he was. Not of the blow itself and not of the pain that followed, but because the one who did it remained invisible. He could not guess who it was, standing below with the makeshift weapon that was in vogue among the juniors, he could not even be sure it was one of his classmates and not a senior, and it's the thought that it could have been *anyone* that was scarier than meeting a barrage of arrows from a noisy, arrogant, obvious adversary. Why was he remembering it now? What makes one relive an event that does not, on the surface, have anything to do with the conversation he's having? Blind's hand slips under his shirt, the fingers caressing the stomach in the spot where the bruise used to be.

"How much time does it take to reload a crossbow?" he says.

Humpback's silence is more telling than would be his scream. Blind is amazed at his discovery. So it really was Humpback. Honorable and generous even at six years old. Protector of strays and bullied newbies. Blind had all the reasons to be frightened back then. The one standing under the tree with a crossbow turned out to be the one who could not have been standing there and doing what he had done. That's where the silence comes from. Humpback is ashamed, like a grown-up would be ashamed of an evil deed.

"How much time does it take to vanish?" Humpback says stiffly. "To fade away into thin air, like you never existed?"

"You didn't answer my question."

"Nor you, mine."

Blind spits out a strand of hair that somehow found its way into his mouth.

How can you explain something that is in the nature of things for you, and at the same time impossible and fantastic for everyone else? How can you express the knowledge, the experience that took you years to accumulate, in mere words? Yes, of late Blind finds that he is being called to do just that more and more often, but it doesn't make the task any easier.

"When I came here I was five," he begins. "Everything was simple then. The House was Elk's House, and the miracles were of his making. As soon as I entered I realized that I knew more about this place than should have been possible, and that I was different here. The House opened itself before me, opened all of its dreams, its doors, its endless paths, all but the tiniest objects in it sang loudly to me when I approached. It was Elk's House, so how could it be otherwise? At night I ate pieces of its walls, believing that this brought me closer to Elk. He was the god of this place, the god of its forests, swamps, and mysterious ways. He used to tell me, 'The world is boundless, it opens up outside the door, and there will come a time when you'll understand it, my boy.' What could I have thought of those words except that we were not allowed to talk, other than in riddles, of what only the two of us knew about?"

Humpback is silent. Only his breathing betrays his presence.

"Years passed," Blind continues, "and I realized that all that had nothing to do with him. That he was not the creator of this place, or its god, that it existed separately from him, that the secret I thought we shared belonged to me alone. Then it turned out that there were others, but it made no difference anymore. Because for me it was always about him. And he simply didn't know. He lived his life on the Day Side, lived there and died there, and the House did not protect him. It would have protected me, because I was a part of it, but Elk wasn't. The House is not responsible for those it didn't let in. It isn't responsible even for those it did, if they get lost, or get scared at the wrong moment, or don't get scared at the right moment, and especially if they think that what they see are just dreams. Dreams where you can die and then wake up. Those like you. Thinking that the Night Side is a fairy tale. The Night Side is strewn with their skulls and bones, with the tattered remains of their clothes. Every dreamer thinks this place is his. That since he created it, nothing bad could happen to him while he's there. Sooner or later it does happen. And one morning he doesn't wake up."

Humpback swallows.

"What about you?" he says. "Did you know right away that it wasn't a dream?"

"I never had dreams before I came here," Blind says drily. "I am not sighted, if you recall."

Humpback shifts on his branch, sits differently. Clicks the lighter. He clicks and clicks, again and again, until there appears a cloyingly sweet, vanilla-scented cloud.

"So I'm a Jumper?" Humpback says indistinctly. The pipe gets in the way of words. He takes it out and adds, "That word always sounded funny to me."

Blind shrugs.

"You can call yourself something else if you wish. The word is irrelevant."

"And that little monster . . ."

"Is Godmother," Blind says. "I had no choice but to drag her over, and it's not my fault she turned into what she did. I've left her with you to wake you up."

Humpback's silence is so long and deep that Blind begins to suspect he'll never talk again. There's no more smoke, the pipe must have gone out.

"Damn," Humpback says finally. "I know you're not lying, but I still can't believe it. Is it true, what they say about her and Vulture?"

"For the most part," Blind says, getting up.

"She bites really hard."

"I know."

Humpback gets up too.

"You climbed up here only to tell me all this?" he says suspiciously.

"No. I climbed up here to ask you to play for me. I need a piper on the graduation night. Someone who is a Jumper and can play the flute."

"What for?"

Judging by the tone of his voice, Humpback can guess at the answer and doesn't like it at all.

"To lead away the Insensible."

Blind feels the horror in Humpback's gaze directed at him.

"A dozen of them," he says. "I need someone they would follow. Run and drive after. Someone who is capable of walking them over. The Pied Piper. He must love children and animals. He must be one of those who always have homeless puppies and hungry kittens tagging after them. His playing needs to assure them that a warm home and tasty food await where he's taking them."

Humpback sits back down.

"This is crazy," he mumbles. "Complete nonsense! Do you even understand what it is you're babbling, Blind? I'm not the Pied Piper. He only exists in fairy tales! And I am not him! I don't believe in all this, anyway!"

"Believing is not a requirement."

Nanette drops some debris on Humpback's head and caws coyly. Humpback shakes the adornments out of his hair.

"Go away," he says. "Please."

Blind steps down onto the next branch, but before he is able to slide down the trunk, Humpback grabs his sleeve.

"You can't know these things about me," he says. "You just imagine that I am the one you need."

Blind takes the sleeve away.

"I do sometimes become a changeling," he says. "And it's a lot like being a dog. I'm sorry, but I happen to know for sure whom I'd follow if I were a pup. That's about the only difference between us: I'm a little bit more of a dog than you are."

"You're a little bit more of a whole bunch of things," Humpback mutters. "And a little less of a human. No space for him, with so much other stuff in there."

"But you like dogs."

"They're better than humans."

"Then I am better, too."

"I don't like you."

"That's only because I don't eat out of your hand or wag my tail."

Humpback is silent. Blind feels that he's chewing on something. An oak leaf, too?

"I was not going to shoot again," Humpback says reluctantly. "I almost threw up after the first shot anyway. They said you'd eaten the rabbit. You know, the one that disappeared from the cage. The one we looked for all over the House. Rex showed me its bones and skin. They said that you'd eaten it raw. At first I just wanted to beat you up, but then I took the crossbow and made a hunt out of it. Like in the movies . . . the dark avenger . . . all because of a rabbit!" Humpback giggles nervously. "Defender of Nature . . ."

"I didn't eat it. Do you really think I would kill a rabbit and then keep its bones under my bed?"

"How do you know where they were?"

"I found them. I thought they were rat bones and threw them away."

"You could be telling the truth," Humpback sighs. "I have no way of knowing. I'm sorry I said all those things. And I lied about the song. Of course I remember it. I just hate it when people listen in on my playing. I hate it when they listen in, period. Read my poems. See my dreams. I need to have something that's mine, where no one else can sneak in."

He sighs again.

"How is it, when you see other people's dreams?"

How is it? Sad. Agonizing. The dreams never speak of anything you need to know. Nothing is really the way it looks in someone's dream. There everything is too shaky, the transitions are too fast, and if you try looking closer at a face it immediately disappears. Only by picking the tiny pieces, by noticing the barely noticeable similarities, by threading familiar paths through many, many dreams can you assemble the picture of someone's world. You could even try looking for yourself in it. You will start spotting your own face, or rather your white mask, more and more often, until one day you look into your own eyes and see how limpid they are. *I am beautiful!* will be your rapturous thought, your smugness will bleed through and become visible to everyone, and they will all turn away from you, but you won't care anymore. Your happiness will last for a spell, you'll even begin brushing your hair. Until your next encounter with yourself, where you'll have the deathly-white eyes of a boiled fish, and your face will be covered in disgusting pustules. You'll shrink back in horror, and from that day you'll hide your eyes behind long hair and dark glasses, become an outcast, believing yourself too ugly to be close to other people. Until the next dream encounter. This time you'll have no eyes at all. You will grow resentful of those who have been seeing you as that eyeless monster, and stop visiting their dreams. Only later will you realize that everything is deceitful in the dreams of others, including your own face, and the only thing that matters is that you understand now how the dreamers look when you're not looking at them.

Blind attempts to explain all this to Humpback but fails. Humpback doesn't hear him. He still thinks that it must be fascinating—to see someone else's dream. Blind says to himself that it doesn't matter. That he didn't climb up here to ask forgiveness. Or to persuade. Why is it important what you see when watching someone's dream? Why would Humpback refuse to share pieces of his dreams?

"All right," Blind says. "I'm going."

"Wait!" There's panic in Humpback's voice. "I need to ask you . . . lots of things."

Blind sits down. But not on that comfortable, chair-like branch. This one is rather like a bifurcated threshold, a place to linger awhile for those who are already halfway out the door.

Humpback's breath is labored. He's chasing the questions that refuse to be caught. He already knows those lots of things, all that's been embedded in the songs, poems, sayings, and nursery rhymes. All the miracles of the House have been distilled into them, and he swallowed them whole at the age when miracles mundanely coexist with the rest of reality, so he already has the answers to most of the questions he could ask now. The longer he searches for them, the better he understands that this is so. Blind waits, stepping over the unasked questions together with Humpback. A step . . . and another . . . and another.

"What's going to happen to her now?" Humpback asks finally. "This . . . Godmother. Will she stay there forever?"

Blind nods.

"She will. And what becomes of her there is not our concern. Not mine and not yours."

"She's so little!"

Blind searches his pockets for cigarettes but doesn't find any.

"She's tenacious," he says.

Humpback is silent for a few seconds, evaluating this argument.

"Where is she hidden?" he asks, revulsion dripping from his words. "You know . . . The grown-up her."

Blind sees what Humpback has just imagined. How Godmother's chrysalis is extracted from a gym locker, and how much commotion that causes among the rest of the counselors.

"She isn't anywhere except the Forest," he says. "I've dragged her over completely."

He cringes, already anticipating the next question. Because this is never talked about. It's not mentioned in any poems, songs, or nursery rhymes.

"Is that possible?" comes the question.

"Yes," Blind admits. "But it's very hard. You can't really do that. The House doesn't like it and makes you pay."

With fear, he adds silently. *With the possibility of losing everything. With helplessness, banishment, and sometimes even death.*

"When Ralph took me away," he says with a shudder, "I thought that was the end of me. He said that he wasn't returning me to the House until I told him where she'd disappeared to. Where we have hidden her. And you know . . . If I hadn't dragged her over completely, I would have told him anything he demanded. Never in my life have I been more scared than at that moment. I ceased to exist. Turned into a nonentity."

Blind is shaking and not noticing it. He brings the lapels of his buttonless jacket closer together over his chest. He doesn't realize how pitiful a figure he's cutting, and is surprised by Humpback's hand outstretched to him.

"Don't say it." Humpback grips his shoulder. "I understand. I am not going to ask you to bring me over completely."

"No," Blind says. "There's only one person for whom I will do that. For him I am prepared to pay the price. But no one else."

"Try not to think about it, all right?" Humpback says.

Blind nods.

"I will find you there. And then I will bring you over. I'm allowed to do that to those who are already halfway gone. I think. I hope. But it might take time."

"You don't have to," Humpback says firmly. "Not for me."

Blind nods again and slides down the trunk. The closer he is to the ground, the cooler the air around him, as if it's not the asphalt exhaling the heat of the day that's waiting for him there but a sea of tall grass. When he reaches the last branch he jumps off. His fingers touch the ground and encounter small squares of cardboard. A lot of them, like someone has spilled pieces of a child's jigsaw puzzle. It's the questions for the Oracle. Blind picks one up and puts it in his pocket.

"Hey," he hears a dejected voice say from above. "What do you think the Pied Piper would be playing?"

"Madrigal of Henry the VIII," Blind answers immediately.

TABAQUI

The days are wound tightly, like strings. Each tighter and higher than the one before it. I feel like I'm sitting on a string waiting for it to snap. When it finally happens I'll be thrown far, far away, farther than can be imagined, while at the same time staying exactly where I am.

Waiting is unpleasant business, especially when compounded by this heat.

The sky is piercingly blue, and all day I suffer from its presence, longing for the night to come and deliver me from it. Sometimes I imagine dead birds tumbling down from this sky. Broken and drained of color. I even seem to smell them. I bet if we looked hard enough we'd find a pile of rotting sparrows.

I fight the heat by collecting no one's things and sending out letters.

Sixty-four letters have now been sent to various celebrities, letters offering them the opportunity to take over the maintenance of the House, together with all of us in it. The first one to take the plunge will be provided with unlimited advice from me, in any field and at any time. I am also offering myself in a role of fortune-teller, astrologer, secretary, tamer of domestic animals, jack and master of all trades, shaman, talisman, and novelty desk ornament. So far no takers. I wasn't expecting any, of course. It's only sixty-four letters, after all. Not that many. But the fact that no one has responded at all, not even in jest, is troubling. It could be I haven't been persuasive enough. My advanced age must be showing.

Before exiting the room I let everyone in front go ahead and drive into the hallway after them, looking down unassumingly. Even though I'm dying to see how what we've worked on through the night looks in the light of day.

The appreciative hollering of the pack makes me blush.

"Wow!" they yelp. "Oh wow! Look at that!"

I so like giving surprise gifts. It is deeply gratifying, and it's a great pity that I only very rarely get the opportunity.

The blank walls the color of malted milk are no more. We labored at the very boundaries of human endurance to remake them the way they're supposed to be. Everything—yes, we did tend more toward monumental than detailed, but none of it was done haphazardly—every letter is decorated with great care. It probably could do with more drawings, but that would mean sacrificing quality in pursuit of quantity. Everyone has limits.

"Yay!" Mermaid shouts and runs ahead, swinging her tiny backpack.

Smoker is busy copying some deep thought or other off the walls into his diary. The bloated three-foot-high letters glisten like wet lozenges. Even I am struck by how imposing all of it looks. It's not entirely clear what everything means, but that's unimportant. Others will come to work on the empty spaces between the drawings and the letters, and in a couple of days—no, scratch that, in a couple of hours—we're going to have important announcements, news, negotiations, poems, basically everything without which neither we nor our walls can function properly. We just gave it the first nudge.

Mermaid runs back and reports breathlessly that it gets even better.

"There are these six elephants trampling across, one after the other . . . and one of them is checkered. What's that mean, do you think?"

Smoker doesn't think it means anything. Sphinx suggests that it had been done simply to fill the space.

"Someone must have cut out a stencil."

"Wait, is there by any chance this teeny-tiny aphid next to them?" Smoker says. "Next to the elephants, I mean. It should be green."

Of course there isn't. There is, however, a cute slumbering *Lanthanosuchus* with its little legs up in the air, but I don't want to spoil it.

Mermaid dutifully sets off looking for the aphid. We're moving along, already past the elephants, and everyone's still searching for that aphid.

"Aw. A dead crocodile," Mermaid says sadly.

And they all agree. It appears that no one among them is capable of telling a sleeping *Lanthanosuchus* from a dead crocodile.

"Now I understand why we couldn't wake up Noble," Ginger says. "And why he stinks of paint thinner."

She adjusts Tubby's panama hat and wheels him ahead.

We catch up with them near the Third, where there's a significant crowd assembled. They're all silent, staring at the wall. I push myself through—and get the same knock to my senses that all of them have just received. This area was too far away from mine, and I didn't visit it last night.

They have left only rectangles outlined in black, with notes in the middle: *Here was* Antelope, *by Leopard. Chalk, ochre, bronze paint. Surviving fragment of the diptych* The Hunt.

Big letters snaking along the lower border of the empty frames say: **STRANGER, BARE YOUR HEAD.**

Ginger slowly pulls off Tubby's panama.

I put on dark glasses and drive away. Mustang clangs, sending the passersby scattering, both those in a hurry to get to the canteen and those not in a hurry to get anywhere: they all readily jump away, because as Mustang is becoming heavier and less maneuverable every day I'm having a harder and harder time steering it, while the dark glasses interfere with my ability to recognize obstacles. I can't take them off, the sunny weather ruins my mood, and they help mask all this sunniness. With them I can even pretend that the sky is overcast instead of bright blue, so I have been wearing them continuously for the last week, eager to deceive myself, and getting into accidents, but better a couple of accidents than the depression that will inevitably follow if I'm forced to live under the cloudless sky.

Someone with the same case of bad nerves as me has destroyed the master bell, probably figuring that it is not needed for ringing the classes anymore, and people wouldn't miss meals. In that he was mistaken. Many do. They come late, or early. Breakfasts are the hardest hit. In the morning it's almost exclusively Pheasants in the canteen, chomping on their grass, that is, salads. A sorry sight. I've never much cared about that bell—I don't like any indicators of time passing. But while it was working it at least made the atmosphere in the canteen a bit more lively.

I drive up to the table and put on the napkin.

Smoker, across from me, is sipping his tea like it's a cup of hemlock. Lary, next to him, is busy mangling a roll with a dull knife. That's it. Four at the Rats' table, three for the Birds, a solitary Hound shoveling food into a backpack. Only Pheasants are all duly present and accounted for, and the crunch of their morning carrots can be clearly heard across the room.

I make myself a sandwich to demonstrate to Lary how it's done, but he doesn't even look in my direction. Huffing and puffing and torturing the bread.

After my second sandwich Alexander comes running, wheeling Tubby in before him. Tubby's miserable look tells me he's not exactly thrilled with being here. Alexander parks the wheelchair at the table and starts loading food into the poor guy. Tubby's suffering, and Alexander, usually so very attentive, seems not to notice. If the bell were still operational it would have been ringing by now, but it isn't, so what's the rush? I take a camp pot out of the backpack and roll it over to Alexander.

"Dump it all in there, leave the kid alone."

Alexander is just in time to catch the pot, but drops the spoon.

"See," I say. "You're asleep on your feet, you shouldn't be feeding people. And, by the way, he's already helped himself to a roll this morning. I wouldn't put it past him to choke now, what with this treatment. People croak left and right from that, you know."

Tubby slurps mayo off his chin and hiccups softly, as if in support of my speech. Alexander turns the pot this way and that, apparently amazed at its capaciousness. He clearly wants to drop everything and run back under the shower. He's spent the last three days in there. Hoping to wash the Alexanderness off himself?

"Move it," I say. "Time's a-wasting."

Lary grumbles something to the effect that there's too much noise coming from me. That I generally produce too much noise, and in the mornings especially.

"Put that in your notebook," I tell Smoker. "He was always boisterous, and in the mornings especially."

I observe Alexander filling up the pot, fold my napkin, and drive off. These boring breakfasts you can keep.

I'm barely out into the hallway when I realize that I do indeed produce too much noise. And the reason for that is the removal of a fairly bulky item, namely the camp pot, from the backpack. Something has shifted inside and clanks insistently now, something that it was safely pressing against. And besides, old Mustang also started creaking, unpleasantly resembling the phantom cart that always passes by the House around dawn, closer to the night that's just ended than to the morning that's about to start.

I'm at my wits' end with that cart. Could be a hobo returning with the nightly haul of empties. Could be a wheeler risen from the grave where his wheelchair had been buried alongside him and is now rusted to hell from being underground for so long. Or maybe it's a runaway wheelchair all by its lonesome, passing by the House like the *Flying Dutchman*, rattling the decaying bones of its former master.

Establishing which of these theories best describes the reality is impossible. In this narrow slot between night and morning the dreams are too sweet for me to climb out of bed, and even if I were to climb out I still wouldn't see anything, because *it* drives by when it's still dark. I decided to make a recording of the mysterious squeaking object and then listen to it when I'm awake. But no matter how many times I've left the recorder in the open window, I've never caught that obnoxious noise. The cassettes with the failed attempts I've stashed in a box and secreted in the pile of no one's things.

And now it's me who's squeaking like that elusive object, be it a cart, the ghost of a wheeler, or the wheelchair sans ghost. And this means that Mustang is due for an oil change and a check of the fasteners. A tedious, dreary, wearisome business.

Anything interesting that's happening in the House sooner or later gravitates either to the Crossroads or to the Coffeepot. If you're not looking for something specific, the best strategy is to sit there and wait until whatever you need finds you. I'm not the only one to set up such ambushes. During the hours of the hunt, the territory of the Coffeepot is strictly divided among the people tracking this and that. We try not to infringe on each other's turf, but stuff happens, so we're mostly aware of what everyone else is collecting. From time to time the Coffeepot suffers from the plague of girls in search of confrontation, and then we have to depart swiftly lest we become the trophies.

We stake out the corner table by the wall, Mermaid and I, and wait. The banner on the Mustang is acid-yellow and smells of decaying sparrows. I have on the T-shirt emblazoned with pirates, as a warning, and I'm wearing sunglasses. They're helping me cope with the sunny weather. Mermaid's hair ensconces her and her chair in a kind of tent, cascading down to within a couple of inches of the floor. It mingles with ribbons, cords, and chains of tiny bells, and in the gaps of her vest I can see question marks. Only question marks, two dozen Whys all in a row. She is waiting too, patiently and silently, her hair drips beads of silver, and the question marks seem to flow like upturned droplets.

I very much wish myself luck now, while Mermaid is here. For her sake, not mine. My own good fortune has abandoned me lately, not surprisingly, since I've already caught a lot of things. It's possible that every lucky day brought me closer to some kind of limit and now I'm bumping against it. This makes me nervous, and to calm myself down I take out the ream of paper and launch into the sixty-fifth variation on the theme of "*A la recherche du* Crazy Benefactor." After the first dozen or so I stopped using the form letter, because I didn't need to anymore, but also because something that's been copied out is always less sincere, even when it's exactly identical to something that's been transcribed from memory.

Mermaid drinks her coffee and watches the door. As I fold my missive, she frowns suspiciously.

"Do you really believe something's going to come out of this?"

"Well, to be completely honest," I say as I put the file back into the backpack and take out an envelope, "no, not really. Things like that only happen once, if at all. The probability of history repeating itself is vanishingly small. But even the tiniest probability should not be ignored."

"You mean it already has happened? When?"

I sigh. No one seems to be aware of the history of their own abode. And no one seems to care that they aren't. It's all moldy rubbish to them, they can't spare a single minute to take a good sniff at it. Truly, not a single one among them has the capacity of becoming an archeologist, of deriving pleasure from digging and of rejoicing at the results.

"Once upon a time there lived a man," I say. "And he was extremely rich and extremely ugly. Or maybe not exactly ugly, but afflicted with a disfiguring disease. We'll never know now because he never posed for any pictures, and if somebody took one of him in secret he immediately would drag them into court. He lived holed up in his house, assembled a collection of antique musical instruments, and didn't give a damn about anyone. He did write articles and send them to various magazines, signing them with the pen name 'Tarantula,' but they were almost never printed, because in them he mainly vented at the government and all the institutions and organizations he ever had to deal with, or, as he himself put it, 'spit venom.' And who'd want to print that, right? I think in ten years he only had one article accepted, and that about the antique musical instruments. All of his relatives couldn't wait for him to croak to finally get their hands on his money. He knew that, of course, and that's why he dug up this orphanage that was about to be shuttered because the building it was occupying was falling apart. He bought that building, financed the repairs, and endowed a trust that was supposed to maintain the orphanage after his death."

I make a pause and with the end of my spoon trace an invisible spider on the tablecloth. As I was telling the story our table had acquired several more listeners. I don't mind, anyone can listen if they wish.

"And he compiled a list of rules and regulations for those who were going to live in his house and receive his money. Except that it happened so long ago that many of those rules aren't being observed anymore."

"What were the rules?" Mermaid says impatiently. "Come on, you have to know. Tell us!"

"Well, there was one about having the building repaired at least every three years. And also cripples having a priority in admission; that started with him. They didn't admit anyone who was unfit mentally, because he designed the program of studies himself, and it was very hard, you had to be smart to follow it. He even ran into some opposition there, they accused him of throwing such a lot of money at one crumbling orphanage, when he could have used it to build twenty more like it, and then barring the entrance to it for those who were the most disadvantaged."

"Tabaqui!" Lizard says hotly. "How could you know stuff like that, and in such detail? You invented all this, admit it!"

"I admit. I was sitting here and inventing. Because I had nothing better to do than exercise my imagination."

Lizard grabs my cup and unceremoniously takes a big swig.

"It's too romantic," he grumbles. "It never happens like this in real life. Even if there was something, you still wrapped all kinds of fluff around it."

"But at least I've managed to touch you. See, you're even gulping other people's coffee, you're so touched."

Lizard returns the cup, looking at me accusingly.

"So it was all bullshit?"

He's got incredibly bushy eyebrows, his forehead is hidden behind thick growth, and even his ears sport big tufts of coarse hair. He resembles a minor folkloric demon. You can almost spot the little horns. Angel, ever the effete pervert, keeps rolling his eyes behind Lizard's back at his every word. Another chair has been occupied by Guppy, he of the interminably leaky nose and big ears, the biggest in the whole House, after mine, of course. I think it would have done old man Tarantula good to see all of us here.

"It must be the truth," Mermaid says earnestly. "When Tabaqui's making up something he always defends it to the last. He'd never confess that he's invented something."

Lizard turns his shaggy head this way and that.

"So what am I supposed to think now? He says he's made it all up, you say he hasn't."

"Archives are for reading, children," I say. "And history is for knowing, to the extent possible."

Lizard frowns and falls silent. As do the rest of them. Pensive Mermaid drips question marks, they slide off one after the other and dissolve in the floorboards. My cup is empty, so I surreptitiously pull Mermaid's closer, even though she never adds enough sugar.

Angel repositions the eyes that he kept rolled all the way up.

"I propose we install a totem pole at the Crossroads in honor of our patron saint," he intones in his crystal-clear little voice. "Shame on us that the memory of the person to whom we owe so much is languishing forgotten."

"You'd be honoring everyone all day and all night if you get the chance," Lizard snarls, still looking suspiciously in my direction. "No archives could possibly have told him all the crap he just fed us."

"But it did happen!" Angel exclaims. "And you have to agree, the cult of the spider is well established in the House since times immemorial. Take, for example, these widely known lines . . ."

Lizard's irate howls drown out the widely known lines. Mermaid sticks fingers in her ears, and Guppy closes his eyes for some reason. I guess because two fingers are nowhere near enough to plug his ears. I follow his example and close mine too. When I open them again I'm looking at Horse.

He seems to be saying something, but I can't hear a single word until Lizard stops howling and drives away from our table.

". . . and he was kind to birds and beasts!" Angel finishes lovingly.

". . . he said you were into useless trash." Horse places a string of something indeterminate on the table before me. "You think you might need this?"

I snatch it, and there it is, the miracle. Rat skulls attached to a thin, bridle-like
strap. I sweep off the shades to better see the long-awaited prize.

"Horse. Whose is it?"

"Heck if I know," he says. "I found it in the shoe locker. I went there for the shoe
polish, and it was right there, so I thought, what's that crap?"

My hands are shaking as I untangle the strap. The skulls are seven, and only one
of them has a fang broken, otherwise they're in mint condition. The strap is decorated
with dull copper studs and spikes, it's rather beautiful even by itself. If this is not a
magical object, I don't know what is.

"What a monstrosity!" Angel exclaims. "What poor creatures had to suffer for this?"

"They're rat skulls," I grumble. "What were you doing in biology class, that's what
I'd like to know?"

Horse beams.

"So, if you need this, it's yours. I've got no use for it."

"Disgusting," Angel whines. "So many rats dead, and for what? Ooh, could it be
someone casting a hex on the Second?"

"Hey!" Horse crosses his fingers and looks around suspiciously. "Angel, you'd
better, you know, watch it. I found this in our box, you know. So you mean it was us
casting the hex, that what you saying?"

I bang my hand on the table, slightly splashing Mermaid's coffee.

"Enough! Out, all of you. I need some time alone with the loot. Horse, thank you,
I'm in your debt. Angel, thank you too. For keeping company."

Angel, deeply offended, rolls his eyes so hard they're pointing at the back of his
head. Horse smirks, salutes me, and rolls the wheelchair with Angel, temporarily
blinded, to the far side of the Coffeepot. Guppy stays in place, frozen, desperately
hoping we're going to forget he's there.

I take out the box with the scale models of my collection and position them on
the table. Mermaid drags her chair closer and we proceed to shift the models this way
and that, trying to incorporate the rat skulls. It takes us a while. Guppy gets tired of
the show and dozes off.

"No," Mermaid says finally. "Doesn't work. We need to figure out what it is first."

I drape the strap over my neck. Then wrap it around my head. Then sling it
around my waist.

"Definitely not around the neck. And not as a belt. And it's supposed to latch to
something right here, see this spot?"

"What if it really is a hex?" Mermaid says. "Then it's not no one's, but the owner
is never going to admit it's theirs."

"Wherever did you see a hex like this? They're not pierced, they're not cracked, they're perfectly whole little skulls in great condition!"

"How would I know what a proper hex is supposed to look like? I've never used them on anybody."

"Then listen to those who do know, and you'll never go wrong."

Mermaid puts her head on her hands and stares at the models scattered across the table.

"There's only one thing I'd like to know. Where do they come from, these experts on all things? Those who know everything about everything."

"Not everything," I say modestly. "'A lot' would be more correct. And they are in fact forged in the crucible of experience."

"I see," Mermaid says, nodding. "Except to acquire this much experience it would be necessary to live for a hundred years and make some pretty impossible acquaintances. So that's what I'm trying to find out, where does it grow, this experience?"

"You'll know when you're older. Or not. Depending on your luck."

"That's the song I've been hearing all my life from all sides," she scowls. "And surprisingly, the ones singing it to me are uniformly way older than I am. Not."

I gather the cardboard toys and return them to the backpack.

"Let's go. Nothing more is happening here. Lightning never strikes twice in one day. We can go check how it fits with the rest."

Mermaid collects the cups and takes them to the counter. I fiddle with the ties on the backpack.

Time doesn't flow the same way in the House as in the Outsides. This isn't talked about, but there are those who manage to live to a ripe old age twice in what for others would feel like one measly month. The more often you fall through timeless holes the more you've lived, but only those who've lived here for a while know how to do that. That's why the difference in age between old-timers and newbies is so drastic here. It doesn't take a great feat of perceptiveness to see that. The greediest can Jump several times a month, and then trail several versions of their past after them. There probably isn't anyone in the whole House greedier than I am, which means there's no one here who's lived through more loops than I have. It's not something to be proud of, but still I'm proud. Greed this extraordinary is an accomplishment of sorts.

Mermaid returns and looks at me expectantly. I say that I'm ready, and we depart the Coffeepot leaving Guppy snoozing at the now-empty table.

Every time I pack and unpack the things I realize that this is a completely pointless endeavor. The actual contents of the backpack play almost no role in it, the important thing is the process itself. Take something out, smell it, put it aside. Take out, feel, put aside. And then when you try to stuff everything back it won't fit. That's an interesting but separate conundrum. And so on. It acquires an almost meditative quality.

It used to be called "One Bag Syndrome." A very serious disease. As I observe its symptoms in myself, I don't quite understand what could have caused it. There are no luggage restrictions, either by weight or by size, for the graduation. And still I fret immensely that the backpack obstinately refuses to accommodate the kite. I guess that's the mind playing games. A distracting tactic. You huff and puff and count the loot, and gradually forget what it was you started the whole repacking over. Instead a lot of other things bubble up to the surface, because each item means time, events, and people compressed into a solid form and requiring a proper place among its own kin.

My backpack must be at least forty years old. No one makes them this sturdy anymore. Real leather patches, heavy brass buckles, ten pockets on the inside, five on the outside, and a dedicated knife holster. It's not a backpack anymore, it's a cave from "Ali Baba and the Forty Thieves." Twice I had it stolen, and both times I managed to return it, and I myself stole it so long ago there isn't anyone left who remembers that it hasn't always been mine.

I'm relating all that to Noble as the backpack disgorges its contents and I slap the deflated sides affectionately.

"See this pocket? There's a safety-razor blade inside, coiled and ready. As soon as you pull on the zipper, out it jumps, and then it's good-bye."

"Good-bye what?"

"Good-bye, fingers. That's how I got it back both times after the thefts. You look around the canteen, spot whoever has a bandaged arm, wheel over and tell them nicely, 'Give it back, you dirty bastard.' And they do. Because they know it would be worse for them if they didn't."

Noble peeks inside, intrigued.

"It's a mystery to me how come you haven't soaked it in poison. It doesn't sound like you, giving a thief an even break."

"Nah," I say, putting back the woolen blanket and the mug with my initials on it. "One of the burglars was Lary. You realize, of course, how much whining ensued, now imagine what would've happened if it had been poisoned."

The archival album with the cuttings and stickers goes on the bottom. The clay whistles nestle in the mug. The camp pot, the binoculars, the purple vest, the box of glass beads . . .

Noble drags the pillow closer to the pile, flops on it with his belly, and observes. For about a minute and a half. The next time I raise my head he's already out cold. Feels like a door that's been slammed in your face. You are talking to someone, and suddenly he's gone.

I sigh and pull off his mirror glasses. The envelope with the stickers hasn't gone inside the backpack yet. I go through the specimens. Pick out the two most appropriate for the occasion and peel them off. A large strawberry goes on one of the mirror lenses, and the other gets a cartoon boy with his pants down. I thread the glasses over his ears and lower the lenses back on his nose. Noble's look takes a definite turn toward festiveness.

"My soul longs for music," I say to Smoker. "But we don't have anything that hasn't been listened to hundreds of times. So, that calls for bright colors to liven up things."

"You can decorate me," Smoker suggests glumly. "Or start a fire."

He's flat on his back, staring at the ceiling and only occasionally gazing down at the world below. And that reluctantly, as if there's something extremely important just about to happen up there. He probably dreamed of being a pilot when he was little. At least that's the impression I'm getting.

"You know," he says after a pause, "I would never in my life even dream of opening your backpack. Never."

And falls silent. Sounds like a very definitive and somewhat threatening statement. Like I've spent the past several years imploring him to get a good rummage in there, and today is finally the day when he conveys to me his firm and unyielding refusal.

"Why's that?" I ask.

Silence. Of a very meaningful kind. Likely in stern disapproval of my tamper-detecting devices. There isn't anyone else I know who can be silent as meaningfully as Smoker. As exhaustively covering the entire issue.

I continue to pack, reverently listening to the ominous silence. Noble is still sleeping.

A deck of cards, spare bulbs for flashlights, compass, saltshaker, earplugs, feather for the hat, suspenders.

Yes, yes, I'm a philistine, I'm bloodthirsty and somewhat paranoid, and generally far from perfect. But I have my good moments when I'm nice and caring, and Smoker's prosecutorial silence does not allow for that at all. Having had my fill of it I finally snap and declare that he's being ridiculously unfair and prejudiced.

Smoker lifts his head lazily.

"Oh, really? I don't think so."

I open my mouth to present him with the authoritative proof of my point, and this is where Alexander enters. Seeing him sends my thoughts and words scattering, screaming.

Alexander sits down on the bed and smiles at us. He's wearing the whitest pants and a white T-shirt. His freshly washed hair is brushed back. This is the first time since the day I've first seen him that he put on anything brighter than the color of a dirty mop. Or bared his forehead.

"What? Why are you staring like that?" he asks, shifting nervously back and forth on the edge of the bed.

"You're a vision in white, Alexander," I say. "Like a snowflake. What's happening to you? Talk to me."

He doesn't really look like a snowflake. Rather a white knitting needle. Because today's clothes fit him normally, while everything else until now hung like a sack. This fact is no less strange than the others. Like here's someone who's been hiding in a dark corner somewhere all his life, and suddenly shot out of there howling, dressed to the nines. On the other hand, if he's shooting out it means he really needs to, and that's that.

"Looks nice, actually," I say, "just unusual. I promise I'll get right on getting used to it."

Noble's already awake. He's endured the shock stoically, as he has both the strawberry and the pantsless youth..

"Play something on the harmonica," he says.

I can take a hint. He's trying to get me to stop talking. But that's part of being a true friend to your friends, not refusing a request even when it's directed at shutting you up. So I take out the harmonica and play. Noble crawls closer to the bed rail, spreads himself across it, pulls out the guitar, and positions it on his belly.

It is easier for the harmonica to follow the guitar than the other way around. So at first we keep bungling it, unable to get in sync, hissing and swearing, but then it starts to take shape, and we're happy with that, even though the sound is nothing special. In these matters the process itself is what's important, just as in the packing, so we sink deeper and deeper into it and get thoroughly stuck. It's not long before I feel a Howl coming up. I'm guessing Noble does too. He starts to hum and whistle. Things like that wind me up enormously, me and my Howl voices.

I tamp them down until I can't anymore, and when that moment comes I drop the soaking-wet harmonica, screw up my eyes tightly, and screech, "Gangway down to the water! Circle the wagons! Artillery ready! Fire!"

Thus bringing our cooperative music making to an abrupt end. In the ringing silence that follows the Howl, I open my eyes and see Sphinx sitting on the nightstand.

"Again," he says.

"Again," I agree sadly.

Screams of all sorts have taken residence inside me lately. Some days, after an exhausting whirl around the House observing this and that, I'm overwhelmed by the desire to bark in a manly voice, "Women and children to the shelters!" What women? What children? The subconscious would not be pushed and is silent. It just wants to herd everyone into a shelter, and that's it. I think it's the first response area of the genetic memory. Or take the "artillery," for example. Every time I hear it I immediately imagine these ancient catapults. With a depressing regularity. Generally when I need to scream I scream, I don't bottle it in. Better to have a nice scream or two and be done with it than to be constantly on the edge. Except my screams make the pack nervous. They can't seem to get accustomed to it.

"Whoever heard of a gangway being lowered to the water?" Noble asks in a dying whisper. He's slightly on the greenish side, due to him being too close when I blew up.

"Exactly!" I say indignantly. "The subconscious really went rogue. And really needed to lower it in that fashion. And to circle all the wagons. Or we'd all be screwed."

"And did you lower it?" Sphinx inquires.

"I did."

"Wagons duly circled?"

"They are."

"Thank goodness. We can relax until the next time."

I wipe off the harmonica. An exceptionally stifling day. No air at all. Noble is prostrate under the guitar. He peeled off the lewd boy but left the strawberry, a scarlet patch over his eye. Smoker is still waiting for news from the ceiling. Alexander has split.

"Hey," I say to Sphinx. "Have you seen Alexander and his amazing snow-white coat? Clean as a whistle and white as a daisy?"

He nods.

"And how do you like it?"

"I think he looks nice."

"He even slicked back his hair. He's behaving in an unusual manner. To say nothing of the fact that he always hated white. Pointedly so. So quit pretending that you don't understand what I mean."

"Could it be he's trying to convey the message that he's sick of cleaning up everybody's messes?" Smoker offers without taking his eyes off the ceiling.

There's that prosecutorial voice again. Implying an entire sea of issues that he chooses to leave untouched for the time being. Fortunately for us.

"No one's making him do that," I say. "Never has."

Smoker smirks, without even a glance in my direction.

So I did lie on the second point, of course, but that was out of simple forgetfulness, not malice. This is not the first time today that I want to throttle Smoker. If this keeps up it'll become a recurring theme.

"I had made him do that," Sphinx says. "And I had made Noble, too. And Lary, when it comes to that. Only you got skipped over. For some reason."

"I wonder why," Smoker says smoothly.

"Me too. And Alexander's image refresh does give us an opportunity to remedy that. How about today's your turn to clean?"

Smoker finally deigns to turn over, bestowing his surly visage on us. On Sphinx, more accurately. Looks at him with a sort of perverted longing.

"Sure. If you can make me," Smoker says. "The same way you made all of them back then. So that even Tabaqui would say that it never happened."

A breathtakingly rude remark, so much so that my nose starts itching, and the areas of the brain responsible for talking and acting are telegraphing up new Howls, along the lines of "Traitors against the wall!" and "Take no prisoners!" I barely manage to subdue them.

Sphinx is looking straight at Smoker, and it's unclear if he's going to kill him right now or simply laugh. Just looking. He at Smoker, and Smoker back at him. The silence seems to drip in huge heavy drops.

"Goodness," Noble says reverentially. "So much drama."

I can't hold on to an inappropriate and somewhat oily snigger, and it escapes.

Sphinx switches off the headlights and then puts them back on, directed at us. That's the way the man blinks, what of it? The eyes are cheerful and a bit on the impish side. He would have laughed. Most likely. But on a day as hot as this one you can't be sure of anything.

Alexander reappears and sits on his bed this time.

"Hello, polar explorer," I say to him. "You've almost caused a conflict here. If there's one thing we hate, it's for things to be left unsaid. So if this is some sort of protest, just say so. Otherwise we have Smoker here speaking for you, and we've already learned by and by that he has a dust allergy."

Alexander always looks terminally earnest. You almost start believing everything he says even before he's said it. It is therefore a blessing that he says so little, because listening to really honest words is somewhat tiring.

"I hate the color white," he says.

This tires me instantly and very deeply. The mental effort of it, I mean.

Alexander looks at us, obviously expecting that we've already understood everything, but since our faces display a profound lack of understanding, he adds, "I dreamed I was a dragon. I hovered above a city and singed its streets with the fire of my breathing. The city was empty, because of me there. And I . . . it scared me."

I pull at the earring hard. It hurts, but also clears the mind. Both when I'm drunk and in cases like this, when I see things. Things like scarlet-winged lizards flitting between charred houses. Lizards that look like bonfires. Alexander said nothing about the color red, but I know. And I also know that when your true color is ripping you apart from the inside you can swathe yourself in a dozen layers of white, or black, and it won't help a single bit. It's like trying to mop a waterfall with a tissue.

"The white shirt isn't going to save you," Sphinx says, putting my thoughts into words.

Alexander's stare is unblinking. I imagine that in another moment all the bones in his face are going to be exposed, and then the only thing for me to do would be to count them and go kill myself quietly. They're almost out already. The bones, the gray skin, and the swampy puddles of the eyes, with tadpoles for pupils.

"But it wouldn't hurt either," he says uncertainly. "Besides, who knows?"

Sphinx doesn't argue. Neither do I. Noble dives behind a magazine. Smoker yawns ostentatiously.

"It's time, Sphinx. Time for you to bust the glass for us. Can't you see what's going on? Time to fly. This one's already taking wing"—I nod at Alexander—"and the others are champing at the bit."

"Bust it yourself," Sphinx says. "I am not ten anymore. I forgot how it's done."

These words are the last straw. It's as if this was the only hope I was holding on to. Even though it started as an old, half-forgotten in-joke.

"When I had a nightmare once and told about it, Sphinx said he was going to bite me if I didn't shut up," Smoker says casually. "I remember it very well."

"I do too." Sphinx nods. "I also remember that I promised it to Noble, not to you. You have a very selective memory, Smoker. It skews the events. Presents them in an unflattering light."

"What if I dreamed I was a flying hippo?"

"It would mean you ate something nasty at dinner."

"Why then for Alexander it has to mean that he needs to dress in white?"

"I don't know," Sphinx says. He climbs down from the nightstand and sits on the floor, leaning his bald pate against the bed. "And I've never said it had to mean that, if you noticed."

Smoker laughs.

"Now this was a beautiful explanation. Exhaustive and succinct. I finally understand everything."

His laugh is not exactly sane, but not completely mad either. Equal parts of both. He's got a lot of laughing to do if he hopes to catch Noble in his best years, but it still grates. We all of us urgently need a breath of fresh air. While it's still around. Because it's quite possible that it won't be around for long.

I put on the dark glasses, plunging the world into shadow, and ask Alexander to help me with strapping my backpack to Mustang.

As I drive up to the Crossroads I remember:

The Amadán-na-Breena changes his shape every two days. Sometimes he comes like a youngster, and then he'll come like the worst of beasts, trying to give the touch he used to be. I heard it said of late he was shot, but I think myself it would be hard to shoot him.

I cross the Crossroads, mumbling this canonical nonsense, and come to a stop at the back wall. Between the stand with the busted television and the wall there's a tall mirror, so dusty that many think it's facing the wrong side out. Girls do divination with it sometimes. Rub small areas with their fingers and look at what's reflected in them. In a tiny spot of the mirror even a fragment of your own face seems portentous.

I clear a small patch too. It's been a long, long time since I looked myself in the eye. You'd think that experiments like this should not be attempted when depressed. But I suddenly realized that the days have been flying by too fast, so fast I might not get another chance to see myself in the divination mirror.

First I make a small circle above my eyes, from there trace a line down toward the nose, and finally my double is peeking out from the neat window like from a hole in the wall. Hasn't aged a day. The same fourteen-year-old mug. I'm sure I'll still have it on the day they bury me. I rub out the side spaces for the ears, and push the hair off them so they come out better. The double resembles Mickey Mouse now. A very sinister Mickey Mouse. It hits me square on: I'm old. The mirror still reflects the same me as five years ago, but something's missing on the inside. And it shows. The familiar prankster isn't there. If you think about it, it's been bloody ages since I did something amusing. Brought pox on all houses. I can't even remember the last time I got beat up.

"Hey, you," I say to my double. "What's this? You're not growing up, by any chance? Drop it, or it's over between us."

The reflected Tabaqui bugs out his eyes. Scared, or mocking me. One or the other.

"What is it that's written on their mugs? It says there: *Graduation's nigh! The sky is falling! We're all gonna die!*" I whisper. "And what does yours say? The exact same thing. Who the heck are you and what have you done to the guy who was there before?"

He blinks. Meaning: what do you mean, who am I?

"You are the Horror Creeping in the Night! The Predator Gnawing at the Enemy's Entrails! The Sharpshooter! The Pox and Perdition!"

It doesn't work. The double dutifully scowls and strikes an even scarier pose, but still it's obvious how insignificant, hollow, and rotted he is.

"I wish I had a good dumbbell with me. Yeah, you heard that right. And stop ogling me."

I take the marker from behind my ear and draw a toothy smile right on the mirror. And roll back quickly so I don't see the double jumping out of it. And he doesn't. He's too late.

As I drive along I get to thinking how many things are too late for me now.

I still can't play the flute or do card tricks. Or make the chili infusion properly. I've never been up on the roof, never sat on a chimney, and never dropped anything in it so it rattled all the way down. I've never climbed the oak. I've never picked up a swallow's nest and eaten it. Never flew the biggest, scariest kite at dawn under the Pheasants' windows. I couldn't even read the message from the olden times by collecting all the no one's things that exist in the House.

Burdened with these thoughts, I roll into the Coffeepot. With my shades on, of course.

A couple of Rats, a triple of Hounds, and Mermaid with Ginger in the far corner. They've got three cups on the table, which means they're waiting for someone but the someone isn't here yet. So it would not be unreasonable to assume that it's me who they're waiting for. I head directly for them, say, "Why, thank you," and grab the cup.

Coffee with milk. So, not Sphinx but Noble. I push the shades up my forehead and drink. One more thing I still can't do: avoid gulping, even when the ladies are present.

"Tabaqui, did you just have a fight with somebody?" Ginger asks, looking at me intently.

"A vicious one. Scary even to talk about. I can say only that I've ripped him another smile, but that's all I can reveal without devolving into the grisly details."

They exchange glances. Ginger has on the paisley shirt, my own find at the last week's Change Tuesday. Mermaid's wearing the gray vest, still exposing the question marks in its gaps. Two dozen Whys, eerily in sync with the general mood and atmosphere.

"Poor guy," Mermaid says, probably meaning the victim.

Very warm and caring.

"Exactly," I say, touched. "Poor, unfortunate, unenlightened, and dusty."

"Is it the ficus tree at the Crossroads he's talking about?" Ginger muses.

"I know! It's your bear!" Mermaid gasps.

Ginger feels in the backpack that's hanging off the back of her chair.

"The bear is right here with me. And since you mentioned it, it's not dusty at all. Just old."

I look at the window. Is it me, or did the sun really go away? The windows are always draped in the Coffeepot, and it's already twilight outside, but I still imagine that the weather's changing.

"Come on, come on," I whisper. "Bring in the clouds, drop down the rain, water the trees, bathe the crows . . ."

"Magic," Mermaid sighs respectfully. "I wish I could do that. Bring the storm."

"The entire House has been trying for the past month," Ginger scoffs. "If even one of them could really do it we'd already be flooded up to the roof."

"Speaking of, where've you been lately? It's doom and gloom in the dorm. As soon as you take your eyes off someone, bang, he's asleep. No one to talk to. Humpback is up in the oak, Lary is down on the first, and now you have disappeared too." I wipe off my nose and chin and tease the coffee puddle over the placemat. "Boring."

"Needle's been sewing the wedding dress," Mermaid says, springing a surprise on me. "In our room, so that no one could see her. She and Lary are getting married as soon as . . . well, you know. As soon as they can. And I'm in charge of decorations. White beads all over, imagine that."

"All over Lary?" I say, horrified.

Ginger snorts, spraying coffee, and bangs her feet against the floor.

"Of course not. All over the dress. She wants everything to be proper."

I picture Lary at the altar, in his customary black leather, spearing the wedding band with his long pinkie fingernail, and almost faint.

"Yuck! Disgusting petty properism, that's all I can say about this. Still, I'm going to give them my blessing. And a present. I think I'll get them a richly illustrated edition of the *Kama Sutra*."

Suddenly I feel desperately sad. As if Alexander and his realization of the inner self weren't enough, now it's Lary and his wedding. I come to the conclusion that I should be drinking something stronger than coffee, drinking and drowning my sorrows in that something. But the Coffeepot is the Coffeepot, it never stocks anything nerve-calming. However, I remember that Ginger used to carry a flask.

"This calls for a drink," I say. "It's not every day Lary makes a decision this momentous."

"Today is not the day he's made it," Ginger demurs.

I give her a reproachful look and say, "Don't tell me you'd begrudge me!"

The flask is passed over, accompanied by a look of deep offense. I pour out a little into the coffee cup. It's Doom, just as I expected. I invented this pick-me-up myself. It's unlikely that a dose as small as what I've managed to beg is going to have any effect, but better a little something than a big nothing. I raise the cup and, to my own surprise, my voice is trembling from all the tribulations.

"My friends! Time, our principal and primary enemy, is implacable. The years take their toll as they roll by. The old grow older, the young grow stronger. Little dragons leave the ancestral shells and cast their misty sights at the sky! Improvident Bandar-Logs enter into matrimony with no regard to the consequences! Cute little boys turn into mean surly youths with a pronounced tendency to snitching! Our own reflections disrespect our advanced age!"

"Oh wow," Ginger says. "All this, and he hasn't even had a drop yet."

I feel Noble's hand on my shoulder, and his crutch clangs against Mustang's weights.

"That's my coffee talking. Those of a thieving nature always get a high when acquiring something that isn't theirs."

"All right, but not to that extent!"

"The creaky bones ache, feeling the chilly breath of the grave," I insist. "Recently proud men now permit the assorted riffraff to blatantly trample their self-respect. It pains me, pains me and frightens me, my friends! As does the fact of my nonparticipation in all these happenings . . . But Jackal is Jackal, he never grows up, And marry never will he! He'll say good-bye to all of his friends, and forever nowhere he'll be!"

I'm being patted from three different sides. Ginger is cradling my tear-stained head, saying, "Come on, Tabaqui, what's with you, don't cry . . ."

Noble says, "Stop soothing him, or he'll never shut up."

At the next table Viking is trying to wrestle the razor from Hybrid, while Hybrid's bellowing, "No! No! Give it back! He's right about everything! Everything, I tell you!"

In short, it's quite a hubbub, but my own time has frozen in a little lump. And while a part of me is hamming up the unquenchable sorrow, this devious and cunning lump senses through the shirt the two warm bumps, positioned so frighteningly close to each other. Soft and firm at the same time. And if a man in the throes of agony would draw spasmodic gasps, no one would suspect that he is in fact desperately sniffing something. Because it's quite likely that never again in my life will I have an opportunity to smell a girl this close, in direct contact, and it would be a crying shame that my nose is full of snot, except that if it weren't for the snot she wouldn't be pressing me to her breasts.

But I must have shifted wrong at some point, because Ginger pulls away abruptly and looks down at me like I've just bitten her. And goes red. Terribly red, the way gingers do, when you expect them to burst into flames at any moment. I must have gone red too. Ginger narrows her eyes. I close mine, waiting for the well-earned slap across the face, but before I do I have time to notice that our little pantomime didn't escape Noble's attention, while completely escaping Mermaid's, who's too busy being upset.

Still there's no slap coming. This is a bit insulting. She can't be pitying me, can she? I open my eyes. Ginger has traveled to faraway places. She's fingering the wet shirt and looking in my direction, but not seeing me at all. Mermaid pushes a handkerchief at me.

I blow my nose loudly.

Ginger snaps out of her trance and says, "Tabaqui. It's OK."

And goes back to her chair. That's it. Still, it would've been satisfying to receive the well-deserved thrashing. That would put me on the same level as all other full-blown smart alecks sniffing at other people's girls.

Mermaid keeps petting my head and whispering that I am not at all old and that no one is planning to say good-bye to me and be forever nowhere.

"You silly child. You little naïf. That's their destiny. And my destiny is to look at them receding in the distance and wave the wet hanky. It's life, baby."

Viking has disarmed Hybrid. Now all Hybrid can do is to stare at me with puffy eyes and transmit secretive signs and winks. Probably inviting me to join him in the hallway so we can hang ourselves together or something.

The Hound table is deep in a heated argument concerning whether it's possible to get drunk from one sip, and if it is, what should be in the cup. Another minute, and they're going to be driving over to check, so I take a hasty gulp of the Doom. Their inspections are always bad news.

Hound Rickshaw, having split right at the beginning of my attack of melancholy, now returns with Sphinx, Alexander, and Smoker in tow. If that's how he's been planning to intercede and save me, he's way too late.

Alexander, still white as a polar mouse, dives behind the counter straight off. Sphinx joins us, grabbing a free chair on the way with his foot and plopping it down next to Mustang.

"There," Noble says. "If I'm not mistaken, that's one of the proud men who's been permitting us to trample their self-respect. Sphinx, please stop permitting it, it interferes with Jackal's nervous system."

"Wait, what was that? Trample what now?"

"It's not my quote. Self-respect. Assorted riffraff trampling it blatantly, and you tolerate it."

"You snitch!" I fume. "Dirty stoolie!"

Noble smiles beatifically. It's Mermaid who goes red instead of him. Smoker, ensconced in the corner, takes out his diary, maintaining his customary sour grimace.

"Time affects different people differently," Gnome shrieks at the Hound table. "Just look around, and you'll see . . . some grow up and change, and the others don't. Why's that? Tell me!"

"Crazy stuff," Noble says and takes a nonchalant swig out of my cup.

"I found this strange tape in your nightstand," Smoker informs me, bent over his daily toil. "With crunching sounds and some kind of snorting. And nothing else. Is that supposed to mean something?"

So he stumbled on one of those six tapes ruined by the pursuit of the elusive ghost cart. The last one that I didn't bring over to the classroom. I try explaining it to Smoker. He keeps looking at me with the same "you can't convince me and don't even try" expression that's really started to grate on me lately.

"Time is not a solid substance and can't therefore act on some and not others," Owl expounds in an edifying voice. "It's fluid, one-directional, and not subject to outside influence."

"Not subject to your influence, maybe," Gnome says, pointing in our direction. "And those who do have influence over it would never say anything, and that's why we think it doesn't happen."

"Wow, people sure hold entertaining opinions about us, don't they," I say in surprise. "Did you hear that? I'm blushing."

"It's your own fault." Noble scowls. "That's what you get for publicly hinting at exclusive abilities."

"I was in mourning!"

"It didn't have to be that ostentatious!"

I spy with my little eye that Sphinx, who's been affecting boredom all this time, is suddenly no longer bored. He's frozen, coiled like a spring, pupils dilated. Anyone else wouldn't have noticed, but I do. I prick up my ears and sniff at the air intently, trying to determine if something's changed in it.

Not obviously. It's a bit less stifling than before, or maybe it only seems that way because I've simply gotten inured to it. The window drapes sway and snap back. And Alexander, having dropped off the cups, suddenly grabs the edge of the table, as if someone's trying to pull him away.

"You missed the best bit," Noble says to Sphinx.

"I've already gathered that."

"And it's you who's at the bottom of his complexes, if you dig deep enough."

"Tabaqui doesn't grow up, because he knows the secret," Owl says to Gnome, but loud enough so that everyone else can hear it too. "He's just said so. 'But Jackal is Jackal' and so on."

Alexander is staring at the window, all strung out under his white vestments, like an arrow that's already chosen its target. Like something winged, cooped up uncomfortably in a closed jar. The gnawed fingers, now clenched on his own shoulders, elongate and darken before my very eyes, turning into talons. The sand-colored clouds of the Outsides cross his face, flashing the unfallen rain when they reach his eyes.

"Ow. Ow. Ow," I mumble, not able to look away.

Tired, cross, and not a little scared, Smoker asks if he understood it correctly that my cassettes contain recordings of various night noises.

"They contain evidence of an otherworldly phenomenon," I tell him patiently.

"You mean they don't."

"Which is the same thing. Ghosts cannot be captured on tape."

And no Howls in my subconscious, not one. Leached out. Only a helpless grunt. The stuffy Coffeepot air, viscous with smoke, begins to luminesce faintly, setting the silhouettes of its inhabitants trembling. Mermaid retreats behind her hair, like a fright-ened bird. Ginger turns to stand up. The universe around us floats outward in spi-rals, like invisible waves from a stone thrown in water. Hound Rickshaw crosses the Coffeepot hobbling lamely, trying to outrun them.

"So the fact that there's nothing there proves the existence of ghosts?"

Smoker's voice is desperate and betrays his almost final conviction in my mental incompetence. When a person talks in this fashion he is definitely in need of being rescued, except I can't decide who needs saving more: Smoker, who's on the verge of desperate wailing, or Alexander, who's on the verge of flying out the window, break-ing both the glass and the bars outside. Because I definitely can't get to both of them in time.

"I've had it! You are just trying to drive me insane, all of you!" Smoker shrieks, his pallid eyes bugging out.

He drives right at me, clearly intent on running me over. But at the same moment there's another shriek, and something fiery-scarlet singes the ceiling, flying across the room with a blinding flash. All sounds fall away.

"Avast!" I yell, pushing away from the table, and to the disjointed accompaniment of the fading echo of my own "vast-vast-vast," I keel over.

Disgustingly slowly. Judging by the clatter, Smoker's wheelchair crashed into Mustang, weights and all. I am on my back, observing the curious crystal rain fan-ning out across the floor. The small beads hang in the air, suspended over the faster, bigger shards. I reach out with my hand, mesmerized, trying to catch one of them, but miss. Obviously, I comprehensively squandered my chance to get to Alexander, and obviously it was him I needed to rescue first and foremost while Smoker could wait, because it's one thing when someone is cracking because of loneliness and it's quite another thing when someone else turns into a dragon and scoots off. Having realized this, I attempt to climb out of the wheelchair and do at least something, which puts me straight under Smoker's wheels. My universe is temporarily dark, boring, and stinking of soot.

When I come to, I'm under the table. How I arrived here is a mystery. Next to me is Owl, and there's a muddy coffee rain dripping peacefully off our common roof. There's also an ample goose egg on my forehead, spreading down over the eye. I feel it, remembering the glass rain, and gasp.

"You know what," Owl says irritably, glasses flashing, "your pack is completely out of bounds. It's an outrage what you've been up to lately."

"Right. The guy had a fit. What were we supposed to do? It is a sometimes occur-rence with epileptics."

"A fit? Epileptics?" Owl cackles unpleasantly. "So that's what you call it in the Fourth!"

I endeavor to explain to Owl where exactly he can stuff his indignation, preferably in written form and wrapped with razor wire.

"Screw you," Owl mumbles as he extricates himself from under the table.

The coffee drops, now less frequent, plop on his scruff.

I wait for him to crawl away and then peek out myself. Legs, shards, water, clumps of foam. A couple of people are trying to tidy up, while the rest just prance around ogling the scenery. Hounds, Rats, even the girls. Must have forgotten that we're in a state of war. The surviving part of the windowpane seems to be frosted over. The slightest touch, and it'll come tumbling down too. There's a gaping hole in the middle. Resembling a starfish. I stare at it, and then feel myself being lifted up by Black. He picks me up and carries me away, briskly striding through the throng of people and shoving those who don't step aside. It's good to be purposefully carried. You can just relax and go with the flow. At the Coffeepot entrance, a gaggle of gawkers serenades us with whistles and murmurs.

"Don't cry," Black keeps repeating to me.

"I'm trying."

There's no viscous luminescence anymore. The world is back to its regular shape, the sounds carry clearly and loudly, but something did change. Here and there the windows creak and slap, and the wind strolls down the hallways. The door to our room snaps to behind us with such force that even Black startles and my teeth clank.

The room is taken over by the pre-storm dusk and, when seen from the lofty height of Hound Daddy, looks surprisingly small. Sphinx, Blind, and Mermaid sit in a neat row, backs against the wardrobe. The dusty whirlwind rattles the windows and throws flying debris at them.

Black lowers me to the floor. I crawl over to our guys, trying and discarding on the way successive faces that may be relevant to the situation. The problem is, I don't quite understand the situation. Was today the day we've been orphaned forevermore? Have we just lost the last of the dragons that don't exist in nature? Does the glum expression on the faces of those assembled here imply silent mourning, and if so, should I kick the boisterousness up a bit to shake them out of that?

Blind shuffles aside, freeing some space between Sphinx and himself. Big enough to fit a rabbit. Miraculously, I manage to squeeze in, and immediately decide to abandon the boisterousness. I've already been plenty boisterous today. Let it be calm here now, and let the wind howl and tear up the Outsides. I'm tired, and my head hurts.

Black crouches down by the door. There's something long, wrapped in a towel, on Sphinx's knees, and it stinks of burned plastic. I peek under the towel, but even before I do I already know that it must be the rakes in there. And it is indeed them.

Unattached, with fingers melted off, flashing the nakedness of the steel frame. Ugly. Very ugly.

"Leave it," Sphinx says. "It's trash now, nothing more."

I lower the corner of the towel back. It's an unpleasant feeling—touching something that's died so recently.

"Did it hurt?" I ask, feeling stupid.

"Like you wouldn't believe."

"What about Alexander?"

"Alexander is upstairs. Sleeping."

The words come fast and clipped, and I understand that I shouldn't be asking for clarification. Upstairs means on Humpback's bunk, and why exactly he's there and in what condition—insignificant details I'm not going to delve into. The important thing is he hasn't flown away completely. I close my eyes and go limp, squeezed between the rib cages of Sphinx and Blind, trying to convince myself that sleeping in this fashion, like a piece of cheese between two graters, is exactly what I've always wanted. I don't exactly fall asleep, of course, but crash into some kind of slumber. I have enough thoughts that need thinking, and the thinking of them is best done in this semiconscious state. So I think them.

With gold-braided rope, I have encircled the space that's taken up by the collection. It looks like a small stage. The photographs of the Crossroads in the ancient times serve as a backdrop. In the gap between them I have this large white-and-blue plate, shining like the Moon. I'm not sure it was the right place to put it, but the arrangement holds a special attraction for me, combining as it were the Moon and the House, two of my favoritest natural phenomena.

In front of the boards with Crossroads landscapes I put stools of varying heights. The tallest of them supports the birdcage. It is also tall and very narrow, and frankly would feel cramped even for a budgie. A shorter stool holds some kind of crooked thing that no one could guess what it is. What it most resembles is a malignant tree growth that got cut off the tree, squashed flat, and fashioned into a tray. Who knows what for? It would be hard to call this dried knobbiness beautiful. If anything, it's unsightly. When I was a kid it used to lie around the room the seniors called "bar." I don't know where this story came from, but among the squirts there was a persistent rumor that if it were ever pierced, the resulting hole would spew forth a torrent of foul, squelching slime that would engulf everything around it. The world would turn into a swamp. So even though we were mortally curious to find out what was inside the knobbiness, no one had dared to be the one to check. We just caressed the rough skin, listening to the swamp within, trying to determine if it threatened to gush out, excited by our touch. We did it when the seniors weren't around, and even though we never dreamed of piercing it, just touching the swamp was terrifying enough. It could have been only pretending to be solid to throw us off guard while waiting for an opportune moment, for that one incautious poke of the clumsy finger.

The swamp is now part of my collection. It looks smaller and somehow darker than it did once, but it's still waiting. In case any careless visitors get any bright ideas, I've stapled a piece of paper above it, saying *Do not touch!*

In fact the entire collection is bristling with exhortations, directional arrows, and road signs. Crossroads boards in particular. In the middle of the left board I've also hung a magnifying glass on a toilet chain. It can be used to study the photographs more closely. Next to it is the mailbox on a wooden leg. Painted pink, green, and red. The leg bears traces of rat teeth, but the top part is still quite presentable.

The boards, the mailbox, the cage, the swamp, the moon plate, the blue lantern with a hinged flap, also on a wooden leg like the mailbox, the chair with the stuffed crow glued to its back and nails pounded into the seat (and there's a note hanging on the crow saying *Hitchcock says hello!*), the dog collar with bells (what's that supposed to do, drive the dog crazy?), the box of assorted dried beetles, the bottle with a mysterious letter inside and sealed with red wax, the leaky boot of a gargantuan size, the sack of divining beans, the stop sign, mangled as if it's been run over by a truck, the wide-brimmed black hat, three horseshoes, the twisted root that has *common mandrake, male* scratched into it, and the straw parasol, shedding profusely at any attempt to open it.

The objects can be broadly classified into ephemeral, magical, and natural. In the ephemeral I include the plate, the parasol, and the birdcage. In the magical, the chair with the crow, the beetles, the "common mandrake," and the sack of beans. Everything else is natural, except maybe the swamp. Once I was driving around the collection playing the harmonica and discovered that near the stop sign the tune tended to become plaintive, while near the mailbox, jaunty and chirpy. Which obviously means that the mailbox had once been used as a birdhouse, and that the sign had encountered some rather sad circumstances.

It all started with the plate, the one playing the Moon. That was the day when an embassy of girls arrived and cut the cable, thus severing the communication channels between our side and theirs. When they left there were bundles of colored wires strewn on the floor. Everyone kept stumbling over them, so I was forced to hang them on the wall, because there was no other way to use them and I couldn't very well throw them away.

While hanging the wires I climbed up on the wardrobe and found this cracked serving plate on top of it. Also a rusty sponge and a mummified cockroach. This upset me. I got to thinking about all the old junk that nobody needs, the completely useless stuff that doesn't get tossed only because at first no one could be bothered to and then it kind of fades away, about all the things that people attract to themselves at a frightening rate wherever they appear. The longer you spend somewhere, the more there are things around you that need to be thrown out, but when you move to a new place you never take all that trash with you, which means that it belongs more to the place than to the people, because it never moves, and in each new place a person finds scraps of someone else, while transferring the possession of his own scraps to whoever moves into his previous place, and this goes on everywhere and all the time.

The longer I thought, the more it scared me, so in the end I lost my will to move and stayed there on the top of the wardrobe, in the company of the deceased cockroach and the dirty sponge, infinitely dear to my heart precisely because of their utter uselessness.

When Sphinx asked me what was the matter and I explained to him the horror of the situation, he called me a material fetishist.

"Sphinx, think about it," I said. "They are more of this place than you and I could ever hope to be. No one will take them away from here. They have this huge advantage."

"Would you like to become an old sponge, little human?"

Sphinx leaned against the wardrobe, offering his shoulders as a climbing-down aid, and I scrambled over them, bringing the cracked plate with me.

Noble asked me, in an evenly malicious voice, whatever it was I thought I needed with that busted dish.

"I'm going to share my bed with it," I said. "Or put my earring in it every night."

Noble said that my fetishism had long morphed into breathtaking egotism, and that it needed to be brought under control, even though he personally had no idea how that could be accomplished. That I preferred things to people and spent my days plotting to shovel crap on top of him and all the rest of them until they surrendered and stopped moving.

While he was speaking I wiped the dust off the plate, shined it, and placed it on the nightstand. It was even more beautiful than I'd thought. White with light-blue flowers and berries.

All the time I was busying myself with it, Sphinx was staring at it and frowning, as if he was also dead set against the unfortunate thing.

"What?" I snapped. "Yes, so it's symbolic to me. Is that so hard to understand?"

"No, it's not that. The thing I don't understand," Sphinx drawled thoughtfully, "is where did it come from. Has anyone seen this dish before? I haven't. I can't imagine how it ended up on top of our wardrobe. Now you, Tabaqui, do you remember it?"

I didn't. Neither did Noble, Humpback, Lary, nor Blind. I spent the next two days driving around the House pushing the cracked white-and-blue plate into people's faces, and not a single one of them recognized it. And then it turned out that the House was full of unexpectedly unrecognizable objects. That was the start of my personal quest and of the Hunt that the pack happily dismissed as insanity. After three days of the Hunt, I was chased off the common bed with all my loot. On the sixth day the collection was transferred to the empty classroom.

I wake up in a dark and stuffy place, racked by the Howls that have taken me over and shaking from oxygen deprivation. Someone not very bright has fashioned a sleep nest and shoved me inside. I'm sure they had only the best intentions in mind. You have to have a knack for building nests, it is even a science of sorts, because if you get it wrong it's liable to collapse or smother you accidentally. But whoever's built this poor imitation wasn't bothered about details like that. So I emerge out of it sweaty and half-asphyxiated, and it folds in on itself even before I'm fully out, sending a couple of pillows tumbling on top of me.

Smoker is studying the ceiling. If it were him imprisoned in the nest instead of me, he'd have expired right there, quietly and peacefully.

Lary is making tea. Ginger is scraping off some stuff that got stuck to her bear. I ask where Alexander is.

"He went out," Ginger says, turning her button-eyed beast to face me. "Feeling embarrassed, I guess."

I see. A bashful type, our Alexander. Except when he isn't. Then it's advisable to be as far away from him as possible. Actually, I don't think that way. I wouldn't have missed my own role as an active participant in what has happened for anything. I climb back over the ruins of the nest. This way I can see Noble, sitting on the floor. A proud owner of a beautiful new shiner, he's cradling Ginger's flask and quietly getting piss drunk.

"They say you threw a homemade bomb that blew away half the Coffeepot," Lary informs me. "Like, said a farewell speech and tossed it. I told them you never had any bombs, but they don't believe me. They say I'm covering up for my own kind."

"That's nice, Lary. You should always cover up for your own kind. We're one pack, after all. That's serious business."

He blinks.

"But there wasn't any bomb, right?"

I feel the lump on my head. "Are you sure?"

Of course he's not sure. He sniffles and scratches his chin. Or rather the place where chins are supposed to be located on people. His meditative state does not bode well for the prospects of us having tea in the foreseeable future, but it certainly improves his overall appearance.

"And Alexander got spooked and had a fit," Lary says, visibly downcast.

"Was that a question or a statement?" I say.

He just sulks silently.

I lie on my belly and squint. The squares of the comforter stretch before me like a wavy chessboard. Like a runway for the stuff strewn on top. The glasses case is an armored car without doors or windows, the comb is a peeling, listing fence, my cap is a flying saucer with pins for portholes. A hauntingly beautiful and uninhabited little world. Well, not completely, as I set my fingers running across to liven it up. As they do, a primitive white contraption lowers itself to the surface, belching steam.

Ginger's voice inquires if I'm all right.

"You seem to be unusually prostrate."

I sit up and pull the cup closer.

"I just came back from the Blanket Country. A very peaceful place. It's inhabited by a race of snakelike sentient beings. They're pink, blind, and rather nimble. And there's one collective conscience for every ten of them. The Snakers have this myth that their world has a lower counterpart, and on that lower level each Snaker has a double, only shorter and less mobile. Naturally, not everyone believes this nonsense. But there's an even more extreme sect. Its members are convinced that a common conscience unifies not ten Snakers, but twenty, of which ten are from the netherworld. That's widely considered heretical. The sect members also like to use forbidden stimulants in order to expand the boundaries of their universe, and have been mostly hunted down and eradicated by now, one way or another."

Noble's head emerges from the other side of the bed and positions its chin on the edge.

"I wonder why it is that your tales are always creepy, Tabaqui?"

"Because I'm a creep. And the sleep of my reason produces monsters. By the way, if you're interested in serving as the Voice of God for the poor Twentiers, you can try addressing them. Bear in mind they're deaf as well, though."

Noble shudders and peers closely at his own fingers, which he's brought together under his nose.

"How am I supposed to address them, then?"

"Tapping in Morse code. They'll understand."

"Listen to you," Lary says indignantly. "You're doing this to confuse me again, aren't you?"

Noble's eyes widen suddenly, Doom billowing up in them.

"You're a bastard, Tabaqui, you know that? How can I tap anything for them unless I'm the conscience of the twenty? That would be against their religion."

"So you'll be a false Voice. It's been known to happen."

"You! It's you who's false! You just enjoy tormenting those poor . . ."

"Oh man," Ginger moans. "I'm so sick of you! How can you stand it, being out of your heads most of the time?"

"It's Tabaqui." Noble tries to shift the blame, pointing at my fingers splayed over the blanket. "He's a liar. He's made himself into an idol for those . . . those . . ."

"Twentiers," I prompt.

"Exactly."

"It's just them trying to confuse me," Lary insists. "Always the same story. I don't know why they have it in for me. I haven't been here for ages. But as soon as I show up, there it is again."

"Right! Let Lary address them," Noble suggests, brightening up. "He would be quite consistent with their dogma. Lary, my friend, be a good man, tap out a message. Tell them that they have got it pretty close, if you don't count the half-baked freaks like Tabaqui and me here, and that we fully support their thirst for knowledge."

"You know, I almost believe in the bomb now," Lary complains to aloof Smoker. "Or should I say I believe in it more and more."

"So? You can believe in whatever you want," Smoker says, looking at the unfortunate Log out of the corner of one annoyed eye. "Do you even know Morse code?"

"What the hell are you talking about?"

"Then why don't you just say so to Noble? He'd stop pestering you."

"Slaving for them, making them tea . . . And this is what I get . . ."

"They are ungrateful beasts," Smoker agrees. "Ungrateful, unintelligible, and unpleasant."

"That would be us," Noble translates for me. "Everything he's just said was about us. You heard the words he said, didn't you, Tabaqui?"

"No, unintelligible—that was about you personally. And unpleasant too. Look at that shiner. It definitely interferes with the pleasantness of your visage. Very much. Where'd you get it?"

"A shock wave from the blast," Noble leers drunkenly.

"Liars," Smoker continues, going down his dispassionate list. "Windbags . . ."

"And where, if I may ask, is Sphinx?" I say quickly. "Where's he been gallivanting while I am forced to suffer this indignity and abuse?"

"We both are, Tabaqui, we both are," Noble points out. "Sphinx is at the funeral. I think he'll be some time. If they are doing everything properly . . . They've put them in a box wrapped in black velvet . . ."

I realize that he's talking about the burned rakes, and feel embarrassed for my initial scare. Then I feel wronged for not having been invited.

"Encased them in wax . . ."

"What for?"

"To make sure," Noble says. "Don't you get it? Blind didn't want them to be scavenged for souvenirs."

"And also they are all absolutely mad," Smoker says, bringing to a close the full account of our distinctive features.

Smoker fairly reeks of watches. He's been hiding one somewhere on his person ever since returning from the Sepulcher. I'll get to it. Sooner or later I always do. When he's out taking a shower, for example. That thought calms me down a little. But only a little, because at present the watch is perfectly intact and leaches the life out of me slowly by the mere fact of its existence. I can't live in the proximity of watches, they are killing me, but just try and explain this simple fact to Smoker. He is convinced I'm faking it. Faking! Me! I look at him meaningfully and reproachfully, but he keeps sipping his tea without a care in the world. I guess the cup is in the way, shielding him from my reproach.

Noble scratches forlornly at the blanket with his finger. His soul clearly hungers for the dialogue with the deaf-and-mute Twentiers.

"Tried it every which way for them," Lary mumbles. "Bring this in, take that out . . ."

Enter the dragon, quietly and unassumingly. No eyes of flame, no burbling as it came, none of that. Tiptoes in, keeping close to the wall like the least mouse in the whole world. And he comes bearing us a huge egg. Must be a tribute, for all the tumult he made us undergo. Passes it on to me and holes up in his bed.

I unwrap the egg-shaped pack. It contains unevenly cut slices of cabbage pie.

"Cool! Is that from the wake?"

Alexander startles.

"Relax," I say to him. "It was really fun, actually. Look at Noble. He tumbled down from his crutches and is drinking himself silly now, under the guise of his disability. If you hadn't provided him with an excuse he'd be ashamed. So, breathe easier."

"I'm not drinking," Noble counters. "It's medicine."

"My point exactly."

Alexander is still miserable and concealed. Horrible thing, moral scruples.

"So it was Alexander who did it, then?" Lary says hopefully, clutching the can of tea leaves to his chest. His lips move with a newfound purpose. "Threw the bomb, or whatever it was back there in the Coffeepot."

"No," I say. "He didn't throw anything. All he did was try to fly away."

The wind howls between the double panes. Ginger dons blue glasses.

"The weather's changing," she says.

The wind moans and bangs at the windows for the rest of the day. I change cold packs at regular intervals and generally take care of my lump. Sphinx's eyelashes are gone and his cheeks are seared, so he's walking around slathered with burn cream. The overall impression is unusually bright. Noble continues his journey into the bottle. The girls have left, to protect Needle and her wedding dress from the evil eyes of malicious loiterers.

Instead of them we receive a visit from Black. He's exchanging banter with Smoker about their favorite painters. Even without listening closely, it's obvious that this topic is a struggle for Black. He's suffering, but soldiering on. Must be imagining that as soon as he's out the door we'd all fall apart, done in by assorted vicious ailments. Or, conversely, worrying about Smoker's psychological state in our continued presence.

Blind is doing his best to play Alexander's replacement. The water boils over, the cold packs get lost, and when he does find them they've been thoroughly trampled—by him. When he tries to repair Mustang his finger gets caught in the works, and I end up lovingly tucked in with Tubby's much-pissed-on blankie. To quote Sphinx, "Where would we be without you?"

I'm the only one to drive out to dinner, after Smoker's feeble protestations that he's going to join me.

The Coffeepot is still besieged by the curious throngs. I stop by to listen to the scuttlebutt and find out that apparently Alexander doused himself with kerosene, protesting the graduation, lit himself, and jumped out of the window. I liked it better when it was a bomb.

At the doors to the canteen, Monkey catches up with me.

"Hey! Did you know Lary went into the Outsides with the Flyers? Said he needed something out there urgently."

The frightening news makes me put on the brakes. Lary in the Outsides! Apocalypse! He's going to get whacked before he goes around the nearest corner. Or lost, admiring his own shadow. And if he manages to return, he'd be covered in Syndrome from head to toe.

I say to Monkey, "Sure. Of course we know. Thanks."

And drive on.

In the canteen, under probing stares, I prepare mounds and mounds of sandwiches that I need to bring back. I spread this and that, shake some salt on them, and fold the pieces together. Continuously fretting about that idiot Lary. In a leather getup like his, an inhabitant of the Outsides is supposed to roar past on a Harley, not perambulate with his mouth agape. As he is, Lary would provoke an irresistible desire to beat him up in any sane male under the age of forty. And I'd just bet that the whole risky business is about something like a ghastly-colored tie for the wedding.

Smoker arrives, towing Tubby after him. I am busy for a while spooning oatmeal into Tubby's mouth, and then it's suddenly the end of dinner. I leave Tubby unfilled and try to satiate myself with whatever I can before it's all carted away. I can feel for Blind, in a way. It's hard being Alexander if you've never been him before. Tubby blinks pathetically over his bib, opening and closing the empty mouth in hopeless expectation of more food. I slap the fork down and inquire of Smoker if his vacation is quite over while I'm struggling here with pangs of both hunger and guilt, and if it is, would he be so kind as to maybe help me out? Smoker doesn't argue, to my surprise, and takes Tubby's spoon. His style of feeding is exceedingly slow. The oatmeal is delivered in minuscule portions, but it is at least something, and I can return to unhurried mastication.

One by one the entire canteen crew assembles around us. Hovering and throwing meaningful glances in the direction of the clock. I shove the sandwiches into the bag, pat Tubby, filled to the brim with the oatmeal he hasn't swallowed yet, say "Step on it!" to Smoker, and make a dash for the exit. I am probably the least stable when there is an increasing number of unseen watch dials crowding around.

When we arrive at the door Smoker hesitates, as if undecided whether he wants to enter or not. I can see he's not really thrilled about it, but on the other hand it's not like he has any choice.

He puts his hand on the knob and says, looking away, "You know, I've been there too. In the Coffeepot, with you. It was the first time I've actually seen something extraordinary happen, instead of listening to you tell a story."

"Oh. So, how was it?" I say, intrigued. "Are you still bored?"

"No." He lowers his eyelashes, so it's impossible to tell what his eyes reflect now. "Not anymore. But tell me this. What I saw . . . Did it really happen?"

"That depends on what you saw."

"I don't want to talk about it. For some reason. I haven't figured it out for myself yet."

I sigh.

"None of us wants to talk about it. I thought that's what was driving you nuts."

"No," he says, sounding surprised. "Quite the contrary. I'd be mad if you started debating it. I think. I'm not sure. But even you haven't said anything."

"And good for me," I say. "Alexander wishes to sink through the floor as it is."

Smoker nods and opens the door.

Sometimes I get this curious impression that he's one of us. Rarely, though.

I wonder what would you do if your roommate, bedmate, tablemate, and mate of every other kind suddenly woke you up in the middle of the night with a hoarse cry of "There you are! Finally I've found you!"

In the Outsides it's customary to call for paramedics in cases like that, but we're not in the Outsides, so I speedily crawl away from him, put a pillow between us, and start deliberating whether it's time to cry "Help!" yet or if it could wait for a little while longer.

"I found you," Noble insists, tugging at the pillow. "You're not going to wiggle out this time. I know who you are."

He looks like he's totally round the bend.

I tell him that I had no intention of wiggling, and that luckily for both of us I also happen to know who I am.

"And now that we've established who both of us are, and know everything about each other that's possible to know, what say you we get some sleep? It's dark. Everyone's sleeping. Look. So, hush-a-bye . . ."

"I want to go back," Noble says. "Back here, but earlier, and I want everything to be different. I mean, the same, but with me in it."

"And it is very stupid of you."

"I've made my choice."

Amazing how they all consider these words to be a final argument. Like it's a spell against which I'm helpless. I'd have laughed if I didn't want to cry.

"Think," I say with a sigh. "Think carefully, and come another time."

His fingers clamp on my wrist with such force that I'm afraid it'll break.

"No! Please!" he says. "I might not find you another time. Even once was hard enough."

The guy's crazy, I tell you.

"Hold it!" I say. "Wake up, baby. I'm here all day, every day. There's no need to go searching."

I push the pillow aside, sit up, and give him a slight fillip on the bridge of his nose between the eyebrows. Very lightly, in fact I barely touch him, but Noble reels back as if I whacked him with one of the weights from Mustang's footboard, and almost falls on his back. He closes his eyes. Opens them. Stares at me like he's never seen me before.

"Damn you," he says. "You hurt me."

"And you woke me up. Now we're even, and can go back to sleep satisfied. Sweet dreams."

I fluff the pillow and close my eyes, painfully aware that peaceful sleep is not likely in the cards.

And I'm right. Noble doesn't back down.

"You are him," he says. "You can't fool me."

I sit up again.

"Of course I can fool you. Easily. Anytime I want."

The lights of the two tiny wall lamps make his eyes look like black vortices. Windows into a bottomless blackness.

"You can't do this. I found you. I asked you. You must help me now."

What wonderful arrogance!

For the next half hour I am busy assembling everything that's necessary into the spare backpack.

Then we crawl. Slowly, because of the need for stealth. Finally we're in the anteroom, wheelchairs and flashlights at the ready. I free Mustang of the weights, to save on clang and clatter. I don't have the master backpack with me, so there's no chance of it overturning. I'm not sleepy anymore. I'm alert and perky, and wouldn't say no to a nice snack, because the first thing that catches up with me when I'm perky is hunger, with everything else switching on later.

Noble is quiet and exceedingly polite. Very helpful and not at all annoying. And good on him, because I'm not in the mood for explanations.

The journey is short, since our destination is the classroom. A midnight visit to the beloved collection, you might say. Once inside I open the spare backpack and take out the three items I'm going to require. The chain with watch gears hanging off it. Those that live in old watches, not the modern ones with batteries inside. It goes over the neck. Also I hold a notepad in my hands and a pencil in my teeth. Now I'm ready.

Noble gnaws at his fingernails, studying the collection with a haunted look on his face, like it was me luring him out here and not the other way around. Fingers the strap with rat skulls that I have hanging on the birdcage, takes it off, and turns it this way and that.

"A delicate specimen," I warn him, extracting the pencil from my mouth. "Possibly a hex. I wouldn't touch it if I were you."

He hangs the skulls back. With a fleeting smile that immediately trips my hunting instincts.

"All right, what is it? What did you just understand about them? I saw it, 'fess up!"

Noble shrugs. Leans to the side, fishes the wide-brimmed black hat out of the pile of no one's things, and winds the strap around its crown. The skulls line up in a circle. Noble clicks the copper buckles that obviously were designed to be latched to this very hat and carefully places it on the seat of the chair with the stuffed crow.

There is nothing left for me to do but to gasp slowly.

What's been simply a hat has now become the most meaningful item in the entire collection.

"Wow! Thank you," I say. "You know, I had this impression for a moment that you were going to put it on."

Noble looks at me blankly.

"It's not my hat," he says after a long silence.

I look at the hat. Then at him.

"Of course not," I say.

Then open up the notepad and clear my throat.

"So. You have made your stupid choice and you don't want to think it over." He nods.

"You are aware that your memory is a part of you? And not an insignificant part. Those who return could become somebody quite different from who they were before. And not experience some of the things they have experienced on the previous loop. Which would make the next loop itself different as well."

"I know," Noble says. "You're wasting your time. I will not reconsider."

"You are of the Forest," I say. "It's in your blood. You shall not find rest until you join with it."

"I know," he says. "But she is not there."

"Your love has consumed you. And the first thing it devours is reason, mind you. Speaking of love . . . Are you sure that when you become a different you, you'll still love the same person that you love today? Absolutely sure?"

"Of course."

And he smiles. The smile of a maniac. Or of someone in love. Which is the same thing, come to think of it. His love has eaten him alive, stripped him to the bones, and still he smiles at me. This smile overpowers all. To hell with tradition, with the rituals, and everything else, including the questionnaire. I've never neglected to go through it before. Ten questions must be asked and answered, and I've asked them of everyone, but Noble will get not a single question more. He is the Little Mermaid who came to exchange her tail for the useless legs, and gave up her voice too, and if the Sea Witch asked her for something else, anything else, she would've given it to her as well. Lovers and maniacs are all the same, they rush in where anyone else would fear to tread, and arguing with them is a fool's errand.

He has no idea what it is he's just asked for. That's his problem. He believes that his love is so strong that it'll catch up with him on every loop. Let him believe. Who am I to tell him otherwise?

"All right," I say. "You have convinced me."

I unclasp one gear from the chain and place it into his open palm.

He looks at me "fuzzy," then takes my hand and kisses it. And this, horrible as it is, transforms me into Master of Time for a moment. Standing at death's door, standing there for so long now that it's become something of a habit, because the he-me is ridiculously old. It's impossible to live for that long, only to exist. And I hate doing that, which is why the damn old man is so inaccessible—he's almost always in hibernation that's stretched into eternity. A curt nod—he doesn't waste time on words, a nod is usually more attention than we allow ourselves to bestow on anyone—and I return into the dear old precious adorable sweetie me, who's unable to hide a disgusting giggle.

Noble staggers like I've just slapped him.

"Come on," I say. "No reason to be embarrassed. I promise not to remind you of what we did tonight. At least not too often."

SPHINX

Sphinx dreams of the House breaking out in cracks, raining down pieces, bigger and bigger, until they're the size of entire rooms. The fragments disappear together with people, cats, the writing on the walls, the fire extinguishers, the commodes, and the clandestine hotplates. He knows that many share these dreams with him now. It's not hard to figure out who. They sleep in their clothes with bulging backpacks for pillows, and they try not to enter empty rooms and not to walk around the House alone.

Which is why, when Sphinx wakes up and discovers the fat cables woven into the bars on the window, with their ends extending in both directions, to the windows of the Third on the right and of the Sixth on the left, he's not surprised. It just means that someone's dream mirrored his own. He reverentially studies the knots, as big as his fist, and tries to decide if this can be considered a sign of full-blown panic or if it is still at the level of fear. Alexander is watching the tents of the shaved heads from behind Sphinx's back and thinking about something sad.

He's no longer as white as the day before. He has on Humpback's old hoodie, striped gray and orange, with the hood over his head. A sort of compromise between his usual curtain of hair and yesterday's opened face.

"This is the first time I've looked at them." He addresses Sphinx, who's sitting on the windowsill.

"I know," Sphinx says without turning around. "You have been avoiding windows ever since they came. Afraid?"

"No. Their presence changes me, that's all."

Sphinx turns around, trying to catch Alexander's eyes.

"It sure does," he says. "Radically so."

Alexander smiles a haunted smile.

It is hot and stuffy in the dorm. The day is cloudy, and the sky has a curiously yellowish tint. The color of a desert waiting for the coming sandstorm. Sphinx leans his head against the bars. There's only a solitary figure on a camp stool down by the tents, with a hood drawn tightly.

Mermaid stumbles around the room, in the dusk that filters through the curtains, collecting her clothes. From the chairs, from the bedsteads. The clothes and the six bells. She clutches them in one hand and climbs up on the table. It is going to take her no less than an hour to brush her hair and braid the bells into it, even though she never takes out all of them at once, only six out of the dozen. Ensconced on the bed, head in hands, Smoker is staring at her. The pack likes to watch Mermaid brush her hair. This spectacle never gets old for them.

Down in the yard it's windy, but not a bit less hot than inside the House. Sphinx sits on the stump in the middle of the parched lawn and looks at the tents. After a visit from Shark, its inhabitants moved back. Not much, just several feet. It still allows them to congregate by the fence and even hang on it, holding on to the wire mesh. And it still allows them to try and attract the attention of anyone who steps out of the House, imploring them to arrange a meeting with the Angel, who "dwells here among you, we know . . ."

"He was this close to not dwelling anymore," Sphinx says to the young shaved head whom they usually send forward for parleys, more often than any others. The shaved head waves his hand at him cheerfully and invitingly. Sphinx doesn't move.

The night snowed in the yard under a mound of trash. Among the plastic bags, bottles, and scraps, Sphinx notices a couple of garish booklets printed on cheap paper. They feature a winged angel on the cover, his hands outstretched to the readers, informing them that *Sharing in the divine grace is attainable in this life, my brother (sister)!* Alexander is the last person whom this creature resembles. Ruddy cheeks, golden curls, and a moronic smile. It reminds Sphinx only of Solomon when a child, and a more disgusting child Sphinx had never seen in his life. And hopes never to see again. He studies the booklet while holding it down with the toe of his sneaker.

Humpback comes over, with a huge backpack slung over his shoulder. He looks like a pilgrim returning from faraway lands. Bronzed and dirty. His hair, sticking up and in all other directions, is full of leaves and twigs.

"I'm moving," he says darkly. "What kind of life is it when those guys loiter here constantly? I've seen them in my dreams tonight, so I've just about had enough."

Humpback sits down next to Sphinx, propping his elbows on the backpack, and peers owlishly at the windows of the House.

"What's with the ropes?"

"They're not ropes, they're cables," Sphinx says. "You're not the only one to have bad dreams."

Humpback frowns, trying to discern the relationship between bad dreams and cables wrapped around the window bars.

"And over there?" he says, pointing at the window of the Coffeepot. To the empty frame with soot spread around it like a palm frond.

Sphinx looks at Humpback in surprise.

"That's from the fire," he says. "Where were you yesterday evening? You mean you didn't see anything?"

Humpback doesn't answer. Instead he takes out his pipe and silently fills it.

"Tell me, who does this winged youth remind you of?" Sphinx says, kicking the battered booklet.

"Solomon," Humpback says after the briefest of looks. "Who else? When he was still Muffin, I mean."

"Me too. And they," Sphinx says, nodding at the tents, "are sure that it looks like Alexander."

"It's not funny," Humpback says.

"No, it's not. And the one who thinks so most is Alexander himself."

Humpback turns to look at the gate, where by now four shaved heads are nodding and leering obsequiously.

"You mean they dragged themselves over here for him?"

"They think so. But at the same time they carry the image of Muffin with them, so I'm afraid they're not entirely clear on who it is they need."

Humpback falls silent. Puffs on his pipe, sneaking sideways glances at Sphinx.

"Why aren't you wearing rakes?" he finally asks.

"Rakes got damaged in the fire. We buried them yesterday, right under your oak. Don't tell me you missed that too."

"I was in the Not-Here."

"You know, I figured as much."

They are both silent for the next ten minutes. The shaved heads crowded around the gates are desperately trying to attract their attention. The air smells of the coming storm. The sky is almost orange now, and the swifts are flying low. Sphinx takes his foot off the booklet, and it is immediately whisked away by a gust of wind. He starts whistling the Rain Song. The missing eyelashes and the red burns on the cheeks and forehead make him look almost festive. Like a country lad kissed by the sun. Humpback, on the other hand, is sullen.

"What are you going to do without them? They're not going to bother ordering a new pair for you now."

Sphinx nods, his eyes still closed.

"No, they're not. But I'm managing so far. It's even easier in some sense. Like I'm little and helpless again, and not responsible for anything. And no one is allowed to hurt me when I'm that way. I was absolutely convinced of that before I ended up here, imagine. That no one was going to hurt me. Ever."

Humpback coughs and looks at Sphinx askance.

"You mean you returned to your Outsides childhood?"

Sphinx laughs.

"Almost. Or it's rather like senility. A person can only be saying farewell to everything around him for so long. Waking up, going to sleep, and even in his dreams. To every face, every object, every smell. You just can't do it. The day comes when it gets so exhausting that you simply stop feeling. Anything, at all. And then on top of everything else you lose your prosthetics. Say the solemn farewell to them too, and realize that this was the last straw. That it's time to start saying hello to at least something. And since you can't actually do anything, you say hello to your own self. The long-ago, helpless self. Whom everyone helped and no one dared to hurt. Cool, isn't it?"

Humpback shakes his head.

"I don't think I like your attitude. It smells of the nuthouse, it really does. The way I see it, it's better to just grieve inside, quietly, than laugh over things that aren't funny at all. More normal, I mean."

Sphinx laughs.

"There's no such thing as normal here anymore. But don't worry, it'll pass. By the way, why are your fingers bandaged? Were you banging in nails, from Here to Not-Here?"

Humpback looks at his hands. The left thumb and the right index finger are bandaged. Thickly and sloppily. The bandages are black with dirt and barely holding together. Humpback, slightly embarrassed, begins to unwrap them.

"Oh, that . . . It's nothing. Just bites. There's this little tot . . ."

He tears off the bandages and studies the wounds. Sphinx leans in to look as well, and when he straightens up the look in his eyes makes Humpback shrink back.

"You are going straight to the Sepulcher," Sphinx says icily. "Or rather running. No shower, no changing. No visiting the guys. The backpack you can leave right inside the door. Go."

Humpback springs up and stuffs the pipe back in his pocket, swearing when it burns him. Straightens out the straps of the backpack clumsily and heaves it over his shoulder.

"You mean like this? Barefoot?" he says, but meets Sphinx's stare coming the other way again, nods and departs hastily, muttering under his breath.

Sphinx continues to sit motionlessly for a while longer, then gets up and slowly shuffles toward the House. The first drop of rain pecks him on the forehead when he's already on the steps. He turns to look at the shaved heads, to see if they are leaving yet, and to his surprise sees Red in front of them, on this side of the fence. Rat Leader is talking them up, smiling from ear to ear, all effortless charm. In cutaway jeans, barefoot, and shirtless, but with the bow tie around his neck and a bowler on his head.

According to his, that is, Rats', standards, he is dressed for the occasion. The shaved heads are apparently of a different opinion. It is possible they take the Alpha Rat for a village idiot. Sphinx cannot distinguish the expressions on their faces from this distance, but he's learned in the past three days that those expressions never change. They listen to Red, clinging to each other tightly, and no one is hanging on the fence anymore. Are they confused? Astonished?

Without a pause in his smiling and blabbering, Red pulls off his glasses. The enchanted zombies immediately take a step forward and get stuck to the fence. Sphinx, filled with contradictory emotions, rushes inside. No, he's not second-guessing Blind's decision to send down to them an angel that's so different from the one they were looking for. He himself was ready to do anything he could to make them go away. Still, he pities them a little. The poor, deluded, poisoned strangers.

There's a cat huddle by the trash can on the landing between the first and second floors. Smoker is also there. On the wall next to him, a charcoal portrait. A grotesquely scowling, ugly face that nevertheless looks very much like Vulture. Sphinx stops to look at it, and a gaggle of Logs thunders by on the way down, motivated by Jackal barking commands at their backs.

"Atten-tion! Squad A, search the yard. Squad B, reinforce the door defenses!"

Tabaqui notices Vulture's portrait and puts on the brakes.

"Yechh!" he says. "Sickening!"

Logs, pushing, shoving, and clattering, throng around for a look. Smoker, scandalized, smears the drawing with the palm of his hand, but even in the resulting blob, Great Bird is still easily recognizable.

"Tut, tut," Tabaqui sighs. "Total disregard for the exalted stature of a Leader, imagine that! Sphinx, I sincerely hope that you shall explain it all to him thoroughly, because I have a much more important task ahead of me at the moment." He points at Logs. "There. Volunteers. We're going to reinforce the approaches to the House. Lock 'em down so tight not even a mouse could sneak in!"

The volunteers stand to attention. Horse has a huge padlock in his hands. Monkey is carrying a bunch of wires, probably the remains of the alarm system.

"At ease," Sphinx says. "It's just that there's rain about to start out there."

Logs exchange excited glances and cascade down the steps, hooting and hollering.

"Quiet! Distance at two paces!" Tabaqui shrieks, rolling down the ramp.

It does become quiet for a spell. Then the door is thunderously thrown open and slammed shut again. Mona, dawdling around the trash can, instantly sprints down and catches the plastic bag blown in by the gust of wind. While she's busy disemboweling it, as if it were alive and could be therefore killed, Red saunters past Sphinx and

Smoker, whistling, but not before saying to her, "Thanks, babe!" There's so much genuine gratitude in his voice that Smoker's eyes open wide, and they become almost round
when Red, not slowing down and not even taking a good look at the wall, sweeps off
the bowler and pays a bow to the dirty spot that had recently been Vulture's portrait.

"I thought this was a secluded spot," Smoker says glumly. "I thought I could just
sit here in peace."

"Just sit and just draw," Sphinx clarifies. "Never draw anyone's portraits on the
walls, Smoker," he continues sternly. "This is not done. Or were you aiming to start a
rumor that you're putting a hex on Vulture?"

Smoker, deathly pale, shakes his head vigorously.

"Then don't do this again. And if you are looking for seclusion, keep away from
the stairs."

Sphinx climbs up to the second floor to the accompaniment of the rustling that
signifies the hurried and thorough destruction of the portrait.

The model for that portrait is sitting in the flesh in their dorm, playing solitaire. He
has on a gorgeous brocade vest with golden buttons, there's a gold earring in his ear,
and so many rings on his fingers that they barely bend. Next to him on the pillow
are two chocolate bars. Great Bird always endeavors to make any visit an occasion by
means of small offerings. For him, leaving the Nest for the twenty-step voyage down
the hallway is reason enough to decorate himself and come bearing gifts.

"The weather, apparently, promises to be stunning," Vulture says, sweeping the
cards off the blanket.

His sour face sorely clashes with the festive attire.

Sphinx sits across from him.

"Where's everybody? Was it empty here when you came in?"

"Almost," Vulture says tactfully.

Sphinx realizes that the "almost" is in fact Smoker, so discombobulated by the
encounter with Great Bird that he needed to flush it out by covering the walls of the
House with nasty caricatures. It saddens him that without the rakes he can no longer
make coffee for the two of them, and also that Vulture is nervous and seems to be
preparing to ask him for something but can't muster enough courage, but most of all
that Vulture has dressed up and brought chocolate, trying to conceal the purpose of
his visit.

"I wanted to pass a warning to Blind," Vulture says. "My Birdies, numbering two,
say they saw Solomon last night. I thought Blind might want to be apprised of that."

"He returned? In secret?" Sphinx says, surprised.

Vulture's shoulders twitch.

"I do not know. Perhaps. Birdies' tales are generally not to be trusted. However, they did see him independently and their descriptions seem to match. They say he looks fairly bedraggled."

The news of the raggedy runaway Rat sneaking around the House at night does nothing to cheer up Sphinx, but nothing to scare him either.

"Sad story, if you think about it," he says. "Thanks for the heads-up."

The patter of the raindrops against the ledge quickens. The room is darkened. Sphinx gets up and goes to the window. Where the clouds haven't consumed the sky yet, it is still orange. The yard is flooded with otherworldly light, and Logs, ecstatic at this sudden gift of nature, jump about in the rain. Mustang with Jackal aboard does loops around and between them. Sphinx knows that Tabaqui's expression is incredibly smug now, making Logs suspect that he was somehow involved in the weather changing.

"Now tell me what it is you really came here for," Sphinx says, turning around.

Bird has closed his eyes and turned to stone, the way only true birds of prey can. His amber-colored raiment seems to glow in the dusk.

"Sphinx, you are my only hope," he says calmly and evenly.

The disconnect between his words and the way they have been said is disturbing. "What happened?" Sphinx says.

"What happened, happened long ago. Only yesterday for me, but long ago for everyone else. We all need miracles, Sphinx. Some of them are possible and some are not, so we choose to pursue the possible. But then, after you've chosen, it turns out that you are not strong enough to achieve even that. Do you understand what I am talking about?"

Sphinx does. He would have preferred not to.

"Jackal is a close friend to you," Vulture says softly. His words are almost drowned in the rustling of rain and the clamor from below. "Ask him for me. He will not refuse if you are the one asking."

Sphinx comes back to the bed and sits down next to Vulture, to avoid looking in his face.

"He will," Sphinx says. "Trust me, a thing like that he will refuse. He'll pretend to not understand what I'm asking. He'll just be Jackal. The thing is, he wouldn't even be pretending, not really, because that which distributes return tickets is not Tabaqui at all. And he—it—is an expert in handling situations like that, has been since way before you and I were born. And . . . I swear, there's no way of reaching it from here. Only from the Other Side."

Vulture sags, resting his chin on his hand. He has already accepted defeat, but still says, "You are not that easy to refuse when you ask for something." What he wants the most at this moment is to end this unpleasant conversation, leave Sphinx, and grieve alone, privately. That's what he wants. But he perseveres.

"Neither are you," Sphinx says sadly. "Which is why I'll do what you asked."

"But he will refuse."

"But he will refuse."

Vulture's devilish yellow eyes stare at Sphinx.

"In that case," he forces himself to say. "If you are so sure about that . . . Do not concern yourself. I believe you. If it were this easy, it wouldn't be a miracle. But, you know . . . Sometimes I feel, or rather I used to feel, that it was me who it was supposed to have happened to. Max and I . . ."

Noble chooses this moment to wheel into the dorm, and Sphinx is almost ready to kill him for the unfortunate timing, but Vulture continues as if nothing had happened.

"We were too much of a single person for one of us to remain alive after the other went away. We were not simply close, we were one. After what happened to him, I figured that since one half of me stayed on, and kept staying on, then at least the life I was leading should have some meaning. Which it would, except for my utter worthlessness. I remain a mere Jumper even after all the poison I have forced into myself. On the Other Side the events control me, not I them."

Noble is frozen near the door. He is looking down at the floor as he listens to Vulture. Sphinx glances in his direction and is filled with compassion. Judging by Noble's expression, he is unlikely to fully appreciate the fact that Vulture has just accepted him into the closest circle, made him one of those worthy of listening to his innermost secrets. Likely as not he thinks that Vulture simply didn't notice him.

"And the worst thing is," Vulture says. "The worst thing is, if it were him instead of me, he would have succeeded where I have failed. He was so much stronger."

The rain picks up, drowning the screams in the yard below. Beyond the window it's a uniformly gray curtain. Drops ricochet off the ledge, the windowsill is already soaking wet, and there's soon going to be a puddle on the floor. Sphinx wishes to simply watch all of this unfold. Or stick halfway out of the window, under the streaking, streaming wetness, and breathe it in. Washing off the pain that's not his own.

"So I keep thinking," Vulture sighs. "How did it happen that the one who died was the wrong one?"

The canteen is in a festive mood. The atmosphere is cheerful, noisy, and squelching. The floor is covered in dirt and crisscrossed by the trails of rubber wheels. Those who got a dose of the rain showed up either wrapped in towels or, if they came up directly from the yard, simply soaking wet. Rats have their boombox blaring at full blast, and their table features a likeness of Iggy Pop cut out from a magazine and glued onto cardboard, at the place of honor in the middle. A patron saint, as it were. It is also his voice that's screaming from the speakers. Birds strut with black towels on their heads and warm themselves by means of sipping from mysterious bottles that they pass around under the table.

The table of the Fourth is more soulful than merry. Lary, in a striped turban fashioned from towels, slurps his soup with the pinkie of the hand holding the spoon sticking daintily out. Smoker scratches industriously in the infamous notebook, shielding it from prying eyes. Tubby is busy chewing on the napkin. Tabaqui, swaddled in a bath sheet from head to toe, occupies a chair while Mustang is drying next to him, and judging by its look it has a lot of drying still ahead of it.

Sphinx is barely able to sit down before Tabaqui already sidles up to him along the edge of the table.

"The love potion for Mermaid came out great," he announces above the din. "One hundred percent guaranteed results."

"What would she want with it?"

"What do you mean?" Tabaqui says incredulously. "For the parrot!"

Sphinx recalls that someone in the girls' wing keeps an aggressive bird, a female, that's learned to open its cage from inside. A big chunk of their hallway is now out of bounds as a result, and the inhabitants of the rooms near the parrot's den do not venture out except with opened umbrellas at the ready. Sphinx lately hasn't heard anything about the exploits of the old macaw and assumed that the problem had been dealt with one way or another.

"You'll see," Tabaqui assures him. "One whiff of the potion, and the birdie is going to trail Mermaid everywhere, moaning passionately."

"I do not approve of anyone or anything trailing my girl with passionate moans!"

"Your approval is immaterial. Too late, the machinery has been put in motion. The only thing left to do now is wait for the results."

"Are you trying to lure her away from me?" Sphinx says. "Massaging brush for the cats, that light-up umbrella, the alarm bracelet, now this. To say nothing about your joint hunting trips."

The music suddenly cuts out, and feisty Rats stop punching each other.

R One has stopped at the door and is looking over the canteen sullenly. A counselor at lunchtime is always bad news, and the room goes almost completely quiet, with only the Insensible continuing to munch happily.

"Please stay where you are."

Ralph slams the door closed behind him and leans against it, arms crossed.

"The dorms and classrooms are being searched as we speak. Once the search is over you will be allowed to leave the canteen."

Rats explode with noise. Bespectacled Pheasant Leader is forced to shout to be heard.

"Excuse me! On behalf of the First I would like clarification, please. The search being conducted, does it encompass all of the dorms?"

"Yes, it does," Ralph says coldly.

The look of deep affront on the faces of Pheasants somewhat raises the spirits of everyone else. Almost everyone. Except for those who clearly have something to worry about. Lary, for example. Looking at his rapidly graying face it's easy to imagine that the search of his bunk would yield a bloody scalp at the very least.

"Lary, what's wrong?" Sphinx says. "What have you been hiding?"

Lary is silent, apart from heavy sighs. Then he plugs his mouth with the good-luck bolt he has hanging on a cord around his neck and screws up his eyes tightly. Sphinx and Tabaqui exchange glances. Tabaqui shrugs.

"Hey!" he shouts out to Ralph. "How about some extra food, then? To help while away the hours pleasantly?"

Ralph does not acknowledge the suggestion. He has turned his back to those in the canteen and is holding a muted conversation with someone through a crack in the door. Then he steps aside, allowing Humpback in. Humpback enters, looking around suspiciously, and startles when he hears jubilant shouts directed his way.

"And the hermit home from the hill!"

"The Druid has left the hedge! Yay!"

Tabaqui valiantly crashes down on the floor and crawls to Humpback through the muck. Humpback snatches him up, and they come to the table together, Jackal wrapped around his neck, cooing tenderly.

"What's going on here?" Humpback says.

"Search," Sphinx says. "Rain. You?"

Humpback displays the freshly bandaged fingers.

"Everything's fine. The thumb was starting to ooze a bit, but only a bit. Nothing serious. No reason to go nuts over it."

"Yes. There. Was. Reason," Sphinx enunciates.

"All right, there was." Humpback unloads Tabaqui on the table and pulls a plate toward himself. "I did everything like you said. Calm down, all right?"

Smoker collects whatever's left of the food on Humpback's plate. Lary, still plugged up with the bolt, waves his hand in a feeble salute.

Sitting idly in front of empty plates soon loses its attraction. Rats drift off into the corners with their Walkmans. Birds clear the table and start a round of poker. Tabaqui tosses a white cloth on the floor, sits on top of it, and declares that he's ready to tell fortunes by casting glass beads for anyone who asks. A modest queue forms in front of him.

Ralph steps away from the door, and in come two Cases, each lugging a sleepy Hound. Red dashes over and tries to pump them for news. Hounds yawn and shrug.

Sphinx leans back in his chair.

The dorm searches are nothing new. They've also never yielded anything. This time the counselors are most probably after the knives. Or the drugs pilfered from the Sepulcher. It doesn't matter, really. They are going to find nothing, apart from maybe Solomon, the erstwhile runaway now hiding in the House, if he really is hiding and if they happen to stumble upon him. The only thing that makes Sphinx slightly uneasy is Lary sitting there petrified with the magic bolt in his mouth. He looks like an idiot.

"I have this feeling," Tabaqui says, shaking the cup with the beads, "that they are not looking for what we think they're looking for."

"Meaning?"

Tabaqui purses his lips importantly.

"The details are better left unsaid. That would be more appropriate, in my opinion."

Lary moans softly.

"Damn it, Lary!" Sphinx erupts. "Are you going to tell us what's wrong or are you going to sit here with that thing between your teeth?"

Lary shakes his head and looks at Sphinx accusingly.

Cases reappear. This time they bring Noble and Alexander. Red reprises his dash in hopes of acquiring important information and has to retreat again, defeated.

"So what do I do now?" Hybrid asks Tabaqui glumly.

He's crouching in front of the divination cloth, waiting for some words that would make sense, because he couldn't find any in what Jackal has just told him.

"It would be best to do absolutely nothing," Tabaqui says. "The way it came out, I'd hold my breath if I were you, old man."

Upon hearing this pronouncement, three of those waiting in line for their fortunes quickly disperse. Hybrid remains seated in front of the menacingly glittering pattern, dutifully holding his breath.

The next to be brought to the canteen is Blind. Who appears to have been sleeping and taking a shower at the same time.

"Left . . . Straight . . . There," Sphinx says as Blind approaches the table. "What's going on? Are they going to let us out anytime soon?"

Blind carefully positions the chair at some very specific angle, the importance of which is known only to him, sits down, and says that unfortunately the counselors are not in a habit of sharing their plans with him.

"I do not constitute an authority for them."

"Any prisoners marched down before you? Anyone who smelled like Solomon?" Blind takes a sniff at the empty plates and shakes his head sadly.

"You have an elevated opinion of me, Sphinx, if you think I can distinguish Solomon by smell from any other Rat. Why don't you ask Noble?"

Noble, pointedly shielding himself from the world behind a book, doesn't look like a person in the mood to share information. When suddenly woken up, he is better left alone. Especially if it's Cases doing the waking up.

"Why would anyone smell like Solomon?" Tabaqui asks. "What is this about, Sphinx? What are you hiding from us?"

Sphinx relates Vulture's message. Tabaqui reddens threateningly. Lary silently upraises his hands. Blind, in the meantime, homes in on the food that Humpback secreted away for Nanette, relieves him of one of the packets, and contentedly devours it.

"Yep," he says indistinctly. "Sol has been living in the basement and Red brings him food down there. I didn't know he ventured out, though. Must have gotten bolder."

Sphinx is surprised and heartened at Blind's awareness. Tabaqui is aghast at Red's behavior.

"The damn murderer!" he fumes. "And there's Red feeding him! You guys are completely mental! This, after everything that happened between them! It's a miracle Solomon hasn't finished the job yet. On the other hand, who'd feed him then? On the other other hand, depends on what the feed is. If it's the scraps like what Blind's been gobbling, might as well cut him. Nothing to lose either way."

Blind puts the empty packet aside, unbuttons his frock coat, extracts the bedraggled crow from its recesses, and places her on the table.

"Almost forgot that I brought her along," he says. "I thought I'd better. Those Cases don't exactly inspire confidence."

Humpback snatches his pet and straightens out her feathers.

"What were you thinking, Blind? Keeping the bird under your clothes all this time! She can barely stand, poor thing!"

"I'm sorry. I told you, I forgot."

The pack solemnly regards the Leader who is capable of forgetting about a crow hidden on his person.

"He's not a completely lost cause yet, tempting though to think he is," Tabaqui says to Sphinx soothingly. "Believe me, he's still full of surprises."

"Of that I have no doubt." Sphinx stands up. "I'll go ask Red why he's so jumpy all of a sudden. I hope he isn't holding a horseshoe in his mouth that would interfere with his ability to speak."

Sphinx starts in the direction of the windowsill occupied by Red, but is intercepted by Black, rising up from the Sixth's table; his desire to have a private conversation is so

obvious that every Hound in the vicinity immediately makes himself scarce to allow
him the opportunity. To the extent it's possible in a room crammed with people.

"Sphinx, can I have a minute?"

Sphinx waits resignedly for Hound Leader—decked to the gills in the regalia of his
position, including the collar that for him is not a required accessory—to approach.

"I need to tell you something . . ." Black's chin thrusts forward, his pale eyebrows
bunch together over the bridge of the nose. "I have finally done it!"

This sounds so ominous that Sphinx is reluctant to clarify what he's talking about.
He's overwhelmed by the desire to cry out "Why, oh why have you done it, Black"—so
strong that he's barely able to stop himself.

"You are probably going to laugh . . ."

"No," Sphinx says firmly. "I'm not. Whatever else, this I can promise."

Black's eyes glaze over.

"I found a bus. A small one."

Sphinx nods, says "I see," and uses his shoulder to wipe the sweat off his face.
Then he says "Why?" in exactly the plaintive voice that he successfully fought off not
a minute ago.

Black looks around and begins to whisper confidentially.

"I had to distract them with something, don't you see? Buck them up a little.
I couldn't just sit on my hands looking at how they were all running scared half to
death. And then there was all this talk about a bus. So I figured I'll get them their bus.
I'm their Leader, after all, right? Remember how I told you that I knew where to find
one? Well, I didn't get it from there exactly, there was this other place. Doesn't matter,
anyway. The important thing is, it exists."

Sphinx nods.

"Right. That's the important thing. I get it, Black. It's great, it's wonderful. But
what are you going to do if they take it into their heads to actually use it?"

"That's exactly what I wanted to talk to you about," Black says pensively. "Because,
you see, I can't just go and tell them that it was all for show, so that they wouldn't go
stir crazy on me. I parked the bus near the dump and tossed some trash over it. You
wouldn't believe it, but they used to visit it three times a day, every day, until those
guys with the tents showed up. So now they don't anymore, of course, but the fact of
it being there is what's keeping them together, you see?"

Sphinx looks at Black like it's the first time he sees him. The blue icicles of the
eyes framed by the pale eyelashes. The dancing skeletons on the black pirate bandana.

"What I see is that you're screwed," Sphinx says. "That's what I see."

Black sighs.

"I know that. So, what do you think I should do?"

Sphinx itches to give him Jackal-like advice. To live holding his breath. To sing noiseless songs. To wash his face with softer water. But Black is a Leader, and this is not the kind of tone to assume with Leaders.

"Tell them that the bus is useless without a driver, and a driver is useless without a license. This they have to understand. It's common knowledge."

Black shakes his head and sighs again. Takes off the bandana, scratches his head. His unhurried movements make Sphinx break out in an itch between his shoulder blades.

"Remember how I said I learned to drive? I mean, not that I'm an expert, but I'm pretty decent. And now I have the license too. Fake, of course. Rat got it for me. But the point is, I have it."

"Black?" Sphinx says, looking into his eyes. "You've already decided, haven't you? What else do you need? Everything's in place, all that remains is to load whoever takes you up on the offer in that bus and drive into the sunset. What is it you want from me?"

Black shuffles his feet. Wipes the face with the scrunched-up bandana and says without lifting his eyes, "Nothing. I just had to tell you. That there's another way, you know. In case any of you guys would like to use it. I've already talked to Lary, he and Needle are definitely going. But maybe someone else?"

Sphinx looks at Black and thinks that this man in front of him is undoubtedly the same old Black that he's known for years, and at the same time someone completely different. That his Leadership has pushed him to the edge of inspired madness, beyond which even familiar people turn into strangers. He considers whether that's good or bad, and cannot decide definitively. It's probably bad for Black himself, but Sphinx likes this new unpredictable stranger much more.

"Thanks, Black," he says.

Black shrugs.

"Not at all. I just wanted you to know. OK . . . I'll see you."

Black walks away in his swaying, bearlike gait. Clutching the bandana with the skeletons in his hand, wearing a quietly heroic expression. As Sphinx looks at Black's receding back, Noble drives up to him.

"What was it he wanted?"

"You know what," Sphinx says, ignoring the question, "I seem to be acquiring a philosophical attitude."

The search is apparently over. Counselors and Shark mill around the entrance to the canteen, arguing hotly. They come to some sort of agreement, haul Pheasants' table to the door, barring it, and Shark announces that since many of the things known missing haven't been discovered, the backpacks of everyone currently in the canteen will have to be searched as well. No one can hear anything after that. Shark's speech is drowned out by indignant howls and whistles. Even Pheasants join in, discipline be damned. Shark makes a couple of futile attempts to finish his thought, then shrugs and goes back to the counselors. They are huddled together at the table, waiting for the outrage to subside, but if anything, it keeps growing. Rats start throwing crockery. Plates and cups explode on the floor a couple of feet from the counselors, so it can be argued that Rats aren't aiming directly at them, but it still looks threatening, and Sheriff's nerves are the first to snap. He snatches the starter pistol from his pocket and empties the clip at the ceiling. He fires until everyone's ears start ringing.

Rats pipe down a little, especially since they ran out of things to throw. Pheasants, tableless, decide they've had enough and line up for the inspection, backpacks open and ready.

Smoker whips out the notebook again and feverishly scribbles in it like an obsessed reporter who suddenly stumbled upon a sensational scoop. Nanette, shaken by the gunshots, flutters away, but not before decorating the tablecloth with greenish squiggles of guano.

"They are especially vicious today, aren't they," Noble says. "I wonder what it is they're missing, apart from all the things we know about?"

Sphinx looks at Tabaqui, who has been saying the same thing, but he is half-stunned with his own screams and neither hears Noble nor notices Sphinx's look.

One after the other, Pheasants' backpacks spill their frighteningly uniform contents on the table before the counselors. Packs of tissues, first-aid kits, daily organizers. Every backpack is then turned inside out and shaken repeatedly. The pockets are turned out separately, yielding only handkerchiefs and combs, neatly numbered.

"The way this is going, might as well settle in for the night," Noble says. "Not that I relish the opportunity. How about letting Tabaqui go first? He's got that evil backpack."

"Don't do that. That'll just make them mad," Humpback says.

Sphinx looks around the canteen. It brings to mind the aftermath of an explosion in a pigpen even more than usual. The shards are still glinting by the door. The oilcloth snatched off Rats' table lies crumpled on the dirty floor. Curtains have been stripped off the windows, and several people pretend to be sleeping now wrapped in them. One corner is occupied by anxious Logs holding an emergency war council, in the other Birds are constructing a screen for a makeshift latrine, harried by Elephant squeaking miserably, "Want pee-pee! Want pee-pee!" at regular intervals. When Sphinx imagines the stench of urine added to the overall conditions in the room, he flinches disgustedly. And all the while the Leader of this entire joint is dozing off contentedly under the serving window, with his frock coat for a bed. As Sphinx observes the peaceful scene he imagines himself screaming, shaking Blind, kicking and trampling him. He starts walking, overflowing with these emotions.

He walks past Tabaqui, busily forcing something into his backpack that would make it even more deadly. Past the flowerpot containing an acid-green plant, made of plastic but still visibly gnawed on. Past the conspiratorial Logs watching the door warily. He's almost there when Blind speaks without opening his eyes.

"Sphinx. You're stalking me like a hungry tiger stalks a lamb. If you want to catch people unawares you'll need to make your walk less expressive."

Sphinx pushes the urge to scream and kick deeper down and sits next to him.

"Let's talk. I have a lot of questions."

"Let's. Where do we start?"

Blind's unruffled attitude should be infuriating to Sphinx, but instead it saps the fight out of him. The fight and the desire to discuss anything at all.

"Black's bus. I don't like this business with the fake license. He can't be any good at driving. Even if he did take a couple of lessons, that still isn't enough. He has no experience. He's going to kill himself and everyone else stupid enough to join him."

"I don't think so. He's a very responsible person. Besides, it's not like I can stop him from doing something after graduation. I can't even stop Lary after graduation."

"But you wouldn't even if you could."

Blind shrugs.

"That's right. I wouldn't. It's his decision. He's a Leader. Why in the world would I want to stop him?"

"I see. I had the feeling that this was going to be useless."

Blind opens his eyes, sends his arm under his shirt, and scratches himself furiously.

"I thought you said you also had a lot of questions," he reminds Sphinx.

Sphinx looks at him probingly.

"I did. It's just that I'm not sure anymore if I should be asking them."

"Try me," Blind suggests.

"Do you know why they are being so thorough with the searches?"

Blind straightens up.

"I do."

"And?"

"They're afraid of the graduation. They are making sure no one's assembled a stash of explosives, poisons, and so on."

"Then why today? The graduation is not until . . ."

"Tomorrow. All we have left is this evening and this night. And also a bit of the morning, but I wouldn't count on it."

It is now Rats' turn at the inspection table. The Pheasants have been checked and cleared, along with Elephant. It is likely that he managed to reach the toilet before it was too late.

"Where . . . ," Sphinx begins, but has to clear his throat. "Where did you get that information?"

He speaks very softly, his outward appearance is completely serene, he does not make a single sudden movement, but the heads of those sitting at the table slowly turn in his direction. Tabaqui. Noble. Humpback.

Counselors extract condom packets by the fistful from Red's backpack. It appears to hold an inexhaustible supply of them. The melancholy smirk of Rat Leader quivers and floats in Sphinx's eyes, as if he were looking at it through a thick layer of water.

"Tomorrow morning they will call another all-hands," Blind says. "Assemble everyone in the lecture hall and declare it. And about ten minutes after that the parents will start arriving."

Sphinx is silent. He is counting the days that have been stolen from them, from him . . . from all of them. Seven. No, six and a half. A pittance. They would've flown past quickly. But now, robbed of them, he is so shocked that he's unable to speak or react to what Blind is saying.

A lamp inside a pink shade switches on above them. The shade has the form of a glass flower, and there is a crack across the translucent bell. There's something dark attached to the winding stem. Sphinx looks closer and realizes it's a switchblade, hidden there to avoid the search. It's an ingenious spot. He sees the knife, and also something on top of the frame around the locked serving window, something that's been left there. He suspects that were he to stand up and look around he'd be able to see everything that's been concealed around the canteen, all the invisible objects, dangerous and not, valuable and worthless, everything that counselors are trying and failing to discover. He is doing his best to avoid looking at people. Looking at them the way he used to, the way Ancient taught him to. Now is not the time. But when did he stop doing that? Simply looking. Simply seeing. Simply living in the present day. Not yesterday and not tomorrow. When did his hours and days grow diminished with the fears and regrets?

"How long have you known?"

"Since they settled on the date. Last Monday."

The pink reflections of the lamp in Blind's eyes, two tiny pink flowerlets. Under them, the somber grin. His fingernails tease and scratch the palm of the other hand. The hands are as restless as the face is calm. He used to know to look at Blind's hands first, and only then at his face. There are a lot of things he used to do right, and doesn't anymore.

"We have a Fairy Tale Night ahead of us," Blind says. "It will also be Long. And then it will be morning. All things come to an end."

Sphinx slumps against the wall and closes his eyes. He's out of practice of seeing everything at once, and it's tiring for him. Anyone who looks at him now would assume he's dozed off, but even through the closed eyes he still feels the alarmed glances of the pack. Even Smoker's, seemingly.

"I wonder if they are ever going to leave me alone," Sphinx whispers.

As he opens his eyes he sees the canteen wobble in and out of focus. The wind is howling through the fence he's sitting next to, as if playing on the harp with strings of rebar. The battered road overgrown with weeds, the telephone poles stretching out to the horizon, the sunset sky splashed purple—all of that combines into a semitransparent hologram through which he still distinguishes the shape of the canteen and the spectral figures ambling aimlessly around it. This overlapping of the two worlds, the real one and the ghostly one, makes Sphinx nauseated. He knows that if he concentrated on seeing one of them, the second would immediately blink out of existence, but something is not letting him choose between them, so he tries to keep both pictures going, even as the nausea and the vertigo grow more intense.

"Sphinx! Stop it right now! What do you think you're doing? This is not a game!"

The habit of obeying Blind works at the level of reflex. A very old habit. The canteen fills out with color and volume, the road and the fields on both sides of it disappear.

"Sorry," Sphinx says. "It happened kind of by itself. I didn't want to."

"Exactly," Blind sighs. "You either want or you don't. Choose the direction before you start running."

Sphinx is amazed at how precisely Blind read his actions. That what he really wanted was to run. But not where the House wanted him to.

"I am so sick of being cooped up here."

"Why didn't you just say so? Easily accomplished."

Blind stands up resolutely and pulls Sphinx after him, striding toward the inspection table almost at a run and sending the conspiratorial Logs scattering, frightened by the abruptness of his movement. Sphinx runs after him. He's afraid that Blind is going to crash into one of the counselors and then they will regard it as the beginning of the assault. Fortunately Blind stops a couple of paces short of Sheriff's blubbery belly.

"Could we please be excused?" he asks politely, earnestly staring into the empty space above the counselor's head. "We do not have any backpacks with us."

The queue does not raise any complaints, and neither does Sheriff, already beyond nervous. They are perfunctorily searched and pushed out.

"The entire House is yours," Blind whispers as soon as the door closes behind them. "Except for the First, but you're not exactly eager to go there, are you?"

"I'm not," Sphinx says sullenly. "I'm not eager to go anywhere except my bed. I need to grab some sleep and get my head together. It's going to be a long night."

Blind slows his pace. "I'm sorry," he says, "but there are some questions that I need to ask you too. The bed will have to wait. We can go to the Coffeepot. Or we can go to another place, where you'll have enough time to sleep, watch the sun rise, have a breakfast, and collect your thoughts before we have our talk. Your call. The second choice would save us a lot of trouble."

Sphinx stops and looks at Blind intently.

"No," he says firmly. "I prefer the Coffeepot."

"As you wish."

There isn't a single soul inside the Coffeepot. Blind goes behind the counter and rummages there, searching for coffee. Sphinx directs his actions. After having obtained two cups of black coffee, they independently choose the same table, under the window that no one's bothered to reglaze. Somebody has put a rag under it, but didn't think to push away the table, and now the oilcloth features an elaborate puddle of grayish rainwater. Blind plops an ashtray in the middle of it and is surprised when he has to shake the droplets off himself.

Sphinx looks out, at the cloudy sky.

"Looks like there's going to be more rain tonight," he says.

Blind sits next to him, lights a cigarette, positions it on the edge of the ashtray, and immediately lights a second one. He leaves it in his left hand, picks up the first one with his right and holds it in the air with the filter pointing away. Sphinx doesn't have to bend or even turn his neck, the cigarette is hanging directly in front of his lips. To take a sip of coffee, Blind lowers both cigarettes into the ashtray and lifts his cup with one hand while simultaneously holding Sphinx's cup in the other. All of this he does reflexively, without giving it a single thought, and just as reflexively Sphinx drinks the coffee and smokes in sync with him.

"Well?" Sphinx says when there's less than half remaining in the cup. "Ask. Let's get it over with."

"You already know what I'm going to ask."

"I do," Sphinx says. "Am I staying or leaving?"

Blind nods.

"I am leaving. I'm sorry, Blind."

His hands. Look at the hands, not the face, Sphinx says to himself. Then he looks up and sees the puzzled grimace. It dawns on Sphinx that what he said could have sounded to Blind as exactly the opposite of what he meant. If he'd said, "I am staying," Blind would have understood right away. He still understood, but not because of the words, purely by the tone and the apology, he needs a couple of seconds to square it with the meaning of Sphinx's "mistake," and when he does his face turns to stone.

Sphinx wants to apologize again but stops himself. It would be worse than silence. He realizes that the way he misspoke, purely by chance, told Blind more than any explanation he could come up with. Maybe it's for the best.

"Is this final?"

"Yes. And I don't want to talk about it."

Blind frowns.

"But I do. It's because of them, isn't it? Those who can't leave?"

"No, not because of them. All right, maybe it is. But I wouldn't have stayed even if everyone else did."

He probably shouldn't have said that. But he's trying his best to be honest. Just as Blind is trying his best to remain calm.

"Why?" Blind says.

"It's my life," Sphinx says. "I want to live it. It's no one's fault that for you the real world is there, and for me it's here. That's just the way it is."

"Does Mermaid know yet?"

"No."

Sphinx turns away, to avoid looking at Blind's face suddenly lit up with hope.

"But it doesn't matter," he says. "She will choose what I choose."

"Happily, I suppose?"

Blind's subtle clarification remains unanswered, to his delight.

"You sound very sure of yourself," he says. "I get it, it's love . . . for better, for worse, for richer, for poorer and all that. But what if she doesn't have the same choice?"

"That can't be."

"It can. Believe me, it can."

Sphinx feels a fleeting prickle of fear. Of a cold, hungry void. But then he sees the trace of a triumphant smile on Blind's lips and realizes he's toying with him.

"Blind, stop it," he says. "I am not staying. And you are very bad with threats."

"She can't remain here," Blind persists. "She is of another world, there is no place for her in this one."

Sphinx looks at him, heavily and darkly, trying to gauge the degree of his sincerity, and can't decide if Blind is lying or telling the truth. As usual.

"So be it," Sphinx says. "If that is true, then we weren't meant to be together. But admit it, you invented that a moment ago."

Blind's face remains unclouded. It's his breath that sounds suddenly ragged, as if someone has just hit him.

"Yes," he says after a pause. "I invented that a moment ago. To scare you. Of course she's just a common girl. There are thousands more like her. The Outsides is lousy with them."

The vengeful notes in his voice make Sphinx sit up.

"Do you know something about her? About where she came from?"

"From her parents, where else?" Blind feigns surprise. "Otherwise you'd have to assume she hatched out of an egg, right?"

Sphinx closes his eyes resignedly.

"I asked you once, and I'm asking you again. Stop this," he says. "Enough. I am tired of living in the shadow of the House. I don't need any more of its gifts, of its worlds that turn out to be traps. I don't want to belong to it. I don't want anything from it. No more lives that unfold before you as if they were real, and then you find out that you're old, your muscles have atrophied, people look at you like you're a reanimated corpse and celebrate your ability to tell the right hand from the left. I hate this, I'm afraid of it, and I wouldn't wish it on anyone, even you, but you don't see me pleading with you to stay here!"

It's almost completely dark now. The wan strip of light in the sky has been extinguished. Wind is walking freely in and out through the empty frame. Blind is hunched over, clutching his head.

"Why did you refuse to go there with me just now? Were you afraid I'd drag you somewhere you can't crawl out of? Leave you there and run away?"

Sphinx nods. "Something like that. You got it. Do you mean to say you wouldn't?"

Blind raises his head.

"I don't know," he says fiercely. "I might have. Except it's not that easy. You are stronger than you think. You'd get out. There are no doors there that wouldn't open before you. But you are choosing to stay here and live out the rest of your stupid life as an armless cripple."

The last sentence convinces Sphinx that Blind is teetering on the edge. He's never used those words before. Never said them out loud. Blind is having a harder and harder time holding himself together. Sphinx is having a harder and harder time observing him in this state.

"People live with this," he says.

"Of course they do," Blind says. "Go ahead, live with it. I hope you don't have an occasion to regret the choice you've made. I could have brought you over completely. You know that. Even Noble could have done it. Think about it."

"Noble has others to take care of."

Sphinx stands up.

The House is looking at him through Blind's empty, translucent eyes. The House does not want to let go of him. For a fleeting moment Sphinx imagines that there's no

Blind in the room. Only someone, something, that would stop at nothing to keep him in. He feels a cold knot in his stomach. It passes as quickly as it came, and he again sees Blind, who'd never do anything to hurt him.

"Go away," Blind says. "I don't want to hear you again."

If Sphinx had arms he would have pounded his fist into the table now. Maybe it would've helped a little. But there are no arms. The only thing he can do is leave. Everything that needed to be said, was.

He walks out into the hallway and stops as he hears a crashing noise from behind the closed door. Blind has done what he himself couldn't, smashed his hand against the table. Sphinx closes his eyes and stands quietly for a while, listening intently, but there are no more sounds coming from inside the Coffeepot.

SMOKER

Tabaqui told me to write in the diary that "Fairy Tale Night is coming." We've just returned from the canteen, having spent more than four hours there, all told. I've never felt more drained in my life.

It's not that the dorm looked especially ransacked. If anything, it was even cleaner than usual. But the probing hands had obviously rifled wherever they could, so everyone dashed to check on their secret places. I didn't have any, which is why I unloaded myself on the bed and lay there while they ran around counting the losses. The biggest of the losses was the hotplate. That definitely got taken away. But most of the things that were then said to also have been lost were found afterward. And even though Lary kept whining that some incredibly valuable object had been stolen from him, no one believed him, because as soon as he checked his bed he perked up markedly and even spat out the metal thing he'd been sucking on all that time.

I was so tired that I thought I was going to switch off as soon as I touched the bed. But after lying there for a while I realized that I wasn't sleepy at all. My tiredness was of the canteen, not of anything that was inside me, and our room cured me of it. Still, I couldn't imagine that they would insist on arranging a Fairy Tale Night after a day as hard as this one. I was sure everyone could appreciate some rest.

"Go on, write," Tabaqui said. "You'll get to rest during the breaks."

"What do you mean, breaks?" I said.

"This Night is going to have breaks in it. Everyone knows it's the last one, so most probably it'll go on till morning. Besides, we are expecting guests, so make an effort and behave yourself."

I didn't understand what that was about. When was the last time I didn't behave myself with guests present?

It was an exceedingly bizarre evening. Very much resembling those evenings after which happened the nights I didn't like to recall. When Pompey was killed, and the other one, when they cut Red and Crab was found dead.

Everyone was so bubbly, everywhere you looked there were bright eyes and broad smiles, but as soon as they started speaking you noticed that their voices were shaking and their hands were trembling. Like they were all slightly drunk.

Humpback said he was going to perform an Irish jig for us.

"Just you wait. I'll do it," he said in a kind of voice people use to threaten suicide.

Then he tore apart the notebook with his poems, fashioned paper airplanes out of the pages, and tossed them out the window. Dropping one on the way. I picked it up, turned this way and that attempting to figure out what was written on it, and then rushed down to the yard to try and salvage the rest, but in the time it took me to drive down, half of them had been snatched up, and the other half landed in the muck and got dirty and soggy, rendering the letters completely illegible.

Tabaqui was singing nonstop. He must have done four dozen songs in a row, each one more depressing than the one before it. All funerals and broken hearts, all the time. Noble, the only one of us who had at least some success in the past in getting him to shut up, inexplicably decided to practice patience and just smiled.

Blind appeared about an hour and a half after our return from the canteen. He had one of his hands swaddled in a towel, and his complexion was so gray that Tabaqui took one look at him and fell silent. Blind looked like all the protagonists of his songs at once. Those about the funerals, and broken hearts, and abandoned wreaths. He said that he wasn't feeling too good, climbed up to Lary's bed, and lay there without a sound.

Tabaqui darkened. Wheeled around the room a couple of times and then also clambered up to join Blind. A little while later he peeked out, called to Alexander, requested to be taken down, examined one of his top-secret hiding places, and disappeared back into Lary's bed with a bottle of brandy at the ready. Tabaqui had exactly one way of treating any ailments. The only variation came in the brand and alcohol content.

I don't remember when exactly it was that I started to suspect that the graduation was happening earlier than the next week, and quite probably even tomorrow. I guess it was shortly before Blind's arrival. It was definitely clear as soon as he appeared. When Ginger came in wearing the same cheerful expression as Blind and began hugging people left and right, my suspicion grew into certainty. She even hugged me. Like it wasn't even a thing, like we hugged each other anytime we felt like it. That was the moment when I understood everything about tomorrow. And about today. Why the search, why Noble was willing to sit through the interminable funeral laments, why Blind looked like a corpse, and why Humpback was threatening to dance. And about the smiles, I understood them too. I mean, why everyone around was smiling like an idiot. I had this lump in my throat that stood in the way of words, so I too could only smile now, just smile and nothing else.

"Please look after my bear for a while," Ginger said. "I'll be right back."

I took the bear from her.

"Oh, look, one more paranoid grin," Sphinx said, entering the dorm. "Another one joins the fun."

He looked at me intently, then at Ginger's bear, which I was clutching tightly, because I did promise to take care of it even if I hadn't quite put it in words, and then turned away.

"There's all this bread in the Coffeepot," he said. "From the canteen. No one's turned up for dinner at all. Shark ordered everything to be brought into the Coffeepot. If we want to claim our share we should hurry. Hounds already started sneaking it away."

Tabaqui got ready in a flash and wheeled away to get the bread, taking Lary with him. Before he left, he felt it his duty to smack me on the back. Cheering me up, I guess.

"Did you figure it out yourself?" Sphinx said.

I nodded. Then wheezed that it wasn't that hard. We both looked up at Lary's bunk. I noticed there was a paper airplane peeking out of Sphinx's shirt pocket. The burns on his cheeks were still fairly bright, making him seem ruddily healthy.

Then came Black, who asked if we were in need of brute force. He was dressed like he was going out into the wilderness. Heavy boots coming up almost to the knee, cargo pants with a dozen pockets, a shirt on top of another shirt. All of it on the greenish-brown side of the spectrum. And a hat on a string behind the shoulders.

Sphinx said that the brute force would be needed in about half an hour. Black said in that case, he would return in about half an hour, and walked out, leaving behind a jar of olives.

Alexander hauled out the box of cups, all of them different sizes, and started arranging them on the table. Tabaqui and Lary came back laden with packages. In addition to bread, they turned out to contain two jars of sandwich spread, a wheel of cheese, a stick of salami, and a bunch of scallions.

"I shall call this dinner 'The Last Flight of the Flyer,'" Tabaqui explained and added Black's olives to the loot on the table.

Ginger returned and took the bear off me.

Then all was incredible hustle and bustle. They dumped the clothes out of the wardrobe and piled unfamiliar bags in the anteroom. There was a line to use the showers. I looked at this for a while and then decided to take a stroll. I didn't have anything to change into anyway, and sitting there idly in the middle of it was quickly getting old. So I wheeled out.

The hallway was empty. Not a soul, not even at the Crossroads. Doors slammed, from time to time someone would sprint from one room to another, but mostly the commotion was confined to the dorms. I went to sit by the Crossroads window. The rain had stopped a while back. Sun even made an appearance, albeit a short one. It was setting now, and the puddles in the yard glowed gold. I decided that I had to do a painting like that. Later sometime. An evening, in the bluest of blue, and the yellow puddles, and a thin line of yellow in the sky. I didn't have my notepad with me to sketch it, so I did a quick one right in the diary, to make sure I didn't forget, even though I knew I wouldn't forget anyway. I saw this painting in my mind so vividly it got me doubting that it was going to happen. Everything that I imagined in such detail before I started drawing ended up worthless, or looked nothing like what I was imagining.

I took another couple of laps around the hallway and returned to the dorm.

They were in the process of moving furniture, trying to free up the space for the guests. The master bed had been disassembled into regular, narrow ones. They pushed one against the wall, the other against the wardrobe, and the third got squeezed somehow between the bunk and the table. It was now impossible to reach the window or to open the wardrobe, but there was this big empty space in the middle of the room. Covered with dust and debris. Lary attacked it with a broom, Alexander went over it with a mop, and then they let Tubby, in his festive red overalls, crawl around it to his heart's content.

Tubby was crawling, Tabaqui was slicing bread on the table, Sphinx and Black were discussing something, sitting on Black's bed, Noble was offloading the medicine bottles from the wobbly nightstand that invariably got knocked over anytime we had guests. I noticed that he was throwing them into a garbage bag, and then I noticed the backpacks, in neat rows under the bed, all closed and ready. And more backpacks in the anteroom. Also coats folded on top of some of them. It dawned on me that everyone had already packed. Except me. I had this creepy feeling that they were all going to vanish any moment now, and I'd be left here alone in the empty dorm to wait for the morning. It passed, but left such a bad aftertaste that I hurriedly stuffed my things into the bag. I didn't have much. Sketchpads, notepads, paints. The sweater that Humpback knitted for me and the cup, Jackal's present.

Tabaqui shouted to me to climb up on the table and help him with the sandwiches.

The next hour I was very busy. Busy putting spread on all the bread he'd sliced, and since he'd sliced a sizable mound of it, the work promised to never end. The buttered pieces Tabaqui ingeniously decorated with this and that, and as a result managed to create enough sandwiches out of the limited amount of ingredients to feed an army.

Looking at them, I even started to doubt if we'd be able to eat them all in one night. The finished sandwiches we arranged in layers on serving plates, but not before sticking a toothpick in each.

"There!" Tabaqui said. "I'm done with working for today. It's party time!"

With this, he and Noble holed up in the corner with bottles of homemade hooch, tasting and mixing. I wasn't going to be of any help in that.

While I was contemplating what else useful I could be doing, two Bird-Logs came in carrying mattresses, plopped them in the middle of the room, and went away again.

Then came Lary, in Noble's white shirt. It was the kind of shirt the lead singer in *Tosca* usually wears for his big number. I keep forgetting what his name is. Anyway, it was a very operatic shirt. Lace on the collar, billowing sleeves, that sort of thing. Lary looked stunning in it. It went especially well with high boots. Actually, they had all spiffed themselves up, it's just that on Lary it seemed especially jarring.

I was still sitting on the table. Shooing Nanette from the sandwiches quietly going stale, and drawing anything and everything around me right in the diary. Bits and pieces of them.

Bird-Logs came back. Dragging in Vulture's stepladder. Mermaid and Needle came with a round tray. There was a pie on it. They put it next to me and set to cutting it up. I grabbed the knife and joined in. The aroma of the pie made me realize how beastly hungry I was. It was a meat pie, still warm. I had no idea how they'd made it and with what, but they certainly weren't using a hotplate. We arranged the slices on the same tray.

"I think we should try it," Mermaid said. "If it came out all right, I mean. It's getting cold."

So the three of us took a piece each, and we gave one to Tubby as well. He was slurping it with such gusto that everyone immediately gravitated to us, eager to participate in the tasting. We only managed enough willpower to get the pie away, on top of the wardrobe, when there was about half of it left. Humpback climbed on the table to place the tin pan over it, to keep it from Nanette, and when he stepped down again he was in a kind of a swoon. He said that he'd marry the one who made this pie. Mermaid and Needle exchanged glances and giggled.

"It was a joint project," Mermaid said. "You'd have to become a polygamist."

Humpback confirmed that he would gladly do that. He was absolutely serious when he said it. Deadly serious. Like this thought just hit him, that the one thing that had been missing from his life up to this point was polygamy. I couldn't believe it was really him saying that. Always so reticent, so quiet, and suddenly—promises of dancing, paper airplanes, joking with the girls . . . It sure was strange, the effect that the upcoming graduation was having on him.

"Oh! I have to go get changed!" Needle said and ran off.

"What about you?" I said to Mermaid. "Are you getting changed?"

"I did," she said, reddening. "Changed, I mean."

"Ah. Of course. Right. How stupid of me not to notice! You look great."

I was desperately casting for something I could point out and praise, something that I didn't see on her every day. In vain.

Mermaid nodded. Then she teased out a long strand of hair and showed me the fish. It was tiny, whittled out of a striped seed that didn't look like it came from any fruit I knew. She shook it, and something inside the fish rattled. Not exactly ringing and not exactly knocking, something in between.

"There is this one single seed inside, very resonant, so it's a fish and a bell at the same time," Mermaid explained.

"Cool!" I said. "What's it made from?"

She shrugged.

"Blind's present."

I assumed that guests meant Vulture with Beauty, Shuffle, Black, and maybe a couple more of those who usually turned up some nights. I was completely off.

Vulture came with Lizard, Angel, Beauty, and Horse. Red brought Viking, Corpse, Zebra, and Whitebelly. Along with Black came Owl, who'd never been in our room before, and then also Shuffle and Rabbit. They were carrying musical instruments. Two guitars, two flutes, and a lute. Vulture delivered two bottles of tequila, his own creation. Red hauled in a jug of mulled wine. An unfamiliar girl with green hair, wearing a long red evening dress, brought a packet of cakes.

It was getting crowded on the table, so I climbed down, first to the nearest bed, the one by the window, and from it to Black's bed.

All the wheelchairs they had lined up in the hallway, there was no place for them inside. Blind must have left Lary's bed at some point, because I saw Zebra and Corpse climb up there along with their backpacks.

Red was hectoring everyone to hurry up and take a seat, because the mulled wine was getting cold.

Then Mermaid sat next to me, thankfully. Then Lary, and finally Needle, flushed and out of breath. I nearly tumbled down from the bed when I saw her. She had on a real wedding dress. The train, the veil, everything a proper bride is supposed to have. The works. She was also holding a small round bouquet bound with shiny ribbon. Mermaid struggled to help her fit the expansive white skirt on the bed between Lary and me. He squeezed into the far corner and I had to press myself to the wall to make enough space for the chiffon creation. After it had been duly positioned and straightened, Mermaid was able to sit and wrap it over herself, or rather burrow into it like it was a snowbank.

I could imagine that our merry gang was pretty silly to look at. Snow-white in bridal finery and three dwarves peeking bashfully from under it. Everyone felt it their duty to approach and compliment Needle's dress. She was sitting there beet red from embarrassment but uncommonly pretty, nodding and thanking them, and I thought how it was strange that a simple wedding dress can turn even a homely girl into a beauty.

I had barely enough time to collect my thoughts after seeing Needle's outfit before an even more stunning thing happened. Two people from the tent camp showed up. A man, lanky, unshaven, and undernourished, and a woman, big boned, with broad shoulders and massive arms. They came with Alexander. He invited them to sit on his bed and gave each a cup of coffee, like it was something natural and expected. Like they were in the habit of popping in nightly for a coffee.

They themselves obviously weren't feeling it the same way Alexander did. They looked shy and nervous, sitting close to each other, very straight, quiet and tense, keeping their eyes down. There was something strange about their bearing. I would even say weird. I wasn't alone in wondering why they were here. But no one said anything either—guests are guests, whoever they are, and you're supposed to be polite with guests.

About five minutes after they appeared, Tabaqui mounted the stepladder, which I assumed had been brought for Vulture, and shouted that he was delighted to welcome all assembled, and happy to announce that he was going to emcee this Fairy Tale Night, "because there seems to be quite a lot of us here, and this requires a degree of coordination."

Everyone applauded.

"We are waiting for just a couple more guests, and after that we shall begin! I would like to ask those sitting in proximity to candles to be ready to light them on my command."

Mermaid laughed softly, and her bells tinkled.

"Who else is coming?" Needle asked.

But the last guests were already there. After the tent people I guess I shouldn't have been surprised by anything, but I still was when R One showed up, and with him a bandy-legged old man in a peaked cap.

"That's the night guard from the third floor," Lary whispered, leaning down from the bunk to get a better look. "I'll be damned. Whatever does he need here?"

R One and the old man sat on the bed by the wardrobe.

"Please give a hand for our guests!" Tabaqui squeaked.

Everyone applauded again.

The old man sprang up, swept the cap off, and took a formal bow.

Lary made a curious sound, like something was stuck in his throat, and sat up very straight. He had a look like something really shocking had just happened to him, but I didn't have time to ask what it was, because Tabaqui declared that everyone was here now and we could start.

They switched off the lights. Red lit the candle nearest to us. He was sitting on the floor in front of me, hugging Tubby.

As soon as it became dark Tabaqui stopped screaming and said in a normal calm voice, "We have plenty of time ahead of us tonight, but still, let us begin."

NOBLE'S TALE

He found himself in the middle of the road, a place where it was impossible for him to be. Strangely, this fact did not alarm him. Also, something odd happened to his memory. He remembered nothing at all, but he knew somehow that he had ended up here of his own accord, and that it was very important for him to find something.

He was dressed all in black, and in his backpack there was a book in a language unfamiliar to him, a change of clothes, a camera, and a notepad. The notes in the notepad had been clearly made by him, but he didn't remember when or where. Walking turned out to be very tiring, as did even standing still, so he was mostly sitting on the shoulder and only getting up when he saw a car approaching. Most of the cars weren't in what you'd call decent shape. At least on the outside. As he sat there he was thumbing idly through the notebook, trying to decipher his own notes. They were mostly illegible, accompanied by drawings with a profusion of arrows pointing in all directions and confusing him even more.

Finally one of the drivers took pity on him and agreed to give him a lift, "but only to the crossroads." At the crossroads he found a bus stop and a tiny store with two tables inside, making it into a kind of roadside café. The store owner, a kind woman, called him "you poor forgetful little Jumper" and fed him potatoes fried in bacon fat. The smell of the sizzling bacon made him nauseated, but he was hungry and also didn't want to upset her by refusing her kindness. From her he learned that the buses that stopped here went in three different directions, and one of the names rang a bell, faintly.

"A useless place," the café owner said. "No work there, don't even think about it."

He smiled politely. Blackwood. The name of the "useless place" was calling out to him.

The place did indeed turn out to be useless. But there was something in it. Something unusual, mysterious, existing outside of reality. He stayed. Took a bed in the guesthouse, doing odd jobs and waiting. He knew something was going to happen.

He spent six months there, making acquaintances with the local hobos, chatting up old crones at the market, and befriending stray cats infesting the guesthouse. The residents of the Roach Motel were of two sorts: temporary and permanent. The first kind they called tumbleweeds, the second, transients. All of them lived in the present day, never mentioning the past and never planning for the future. To have enough food on the plate for the night, that was the one and only goal worthy of their attention.

He worked odd jobs all over the place. It was easier in the summer. He helped the photographer install the bulky cardboard backdrops, depicting sailboats and dolphins, on the river beach. Made bracelets from colored wire for the two sisters who then sold them among other trinkets on the same beach. In the mornings he raked the sand in front of the riverside diner before it opened.

Autumn came, and the first downpours turned the river murky and wild. Trash overwhelmed the beach, the cafés and diners closed. There still were the gas station and the car wash, but they had enough help without him. He went there only rarely. They never let him into the repair shop. Neither him nor the other transients. Car parts were worth their weight in gold in Blackwood, so even the most run-down repair shops hired armed guards.

He was surprised when one day these two guys from the repair shop turned up at the Roach Motel and asked for someone to help with a car. He was even more surprised by the reaction of the tenants. Some immediately made themselves scarce, others pretended they couldn't hear or understand a single word. They marched him away before he could figure out what was going on.

There was a black car in the yard behind the shop. The first decent-looking car he'd seen in the last six months. The first not appearing to be ready to fall apart right that moment. No dings, no dents, no stickers covering the rusty patches, no flaking paint. They said he was to wash it. Nothing more. The hose was right there on the ground. Also a bucket and two sponges.

He knew he was in trouble even before he took a peek inside. The car wash was right around the corner. It was useless to ask why they couldn't just drive the car over there. Useless straight off, and even more so after he saw what he saw. They helped him detach and haul out the seats. That was it. When he found a severed finger under one of the rubber mats, he didn't try to hide it, just threw it in the bucket full of dirty water. For four hours straight he washed blood out of the car. He was sure they were going to kill him as soon as he finished.

Later that night, back in the Roach Motel, Filthywings told him that his troubles were only beginning. And that he needed to disappear. He knew it himself.

"Would you like me to darn your shirt?" Mockturtle asked. She was always kind to him.

He gave away all of his belongings—the hotplate, the kettle, the warm coat he had won in a raffle. Picked up his backpack and left the Roach Motel. Its denizens, it seemed, breathed easier. Now they wouldn't have to witness his death and be upset by it.

When he put enough distance between himself and the guesthouse he sat on the low railing in front of some house and thought about what he was going to do next. His legs hurt. In fact, they were getting worse. He wasn't going to get far on foot. Hitchhiking meant endangering other people who didn't have anything to do with what happened. Buses were out for the same reason. Besides, their usefulness was very limited. They moved at a speed barely above that of a trotting horse. He could only wait. They had promised to pay him the next morning for washing the car. When he didn't show up for his money they'd start looking for him, and the search wouldn't take long.

He knew that if he managed to survive this, he was going to remember it as an exciting adventure. Even though there wasn't anything particularly exciting about his stay at the Roach Motel, and his daily quest for a paying gig wasn't very adventurous either. Or was it? He tried to remember everything that seemed amazing to him here. Everything that was unusual.

The talk of the Forest, for one. The first he heard about it was from a chatty drunken tumbleweed who spent one night at their place, wouldn't shut up the whole time, and in the morning left him the hotplate and a compass before moving on.

"You'll need that, mate," he said. "You could find yourself in the Forest at any time, and what are you gonna do then, huh? At least this way you'll know which way is north."

The hotplate was now with the girl who had mended his shirt, but the compass was still in the backpack somewhere.

The jokes about the Forest became commonplace for him after about a week at the Roach Motel. He had learned to ignore them. He had learned to ignore many things. The mushrooms that seemed to sprout in the dark corners overnight. The local rats, whistling as they ran by. The wondrously multicolored feathers that the somber guesthouse kids played with. "Who knows when you might end up in the Forest?"

He closed his eyes and tried to end up there. The smell of the strange mushrooms, when they pried them off the walls, enveloped him. Was that how the Forest smelled? Black Forest. Blackwood.

"If you are here, please come," he said.

"That's not the way to call it," someone said.

He opened his eyes and sprang up in panic.

It was pitch-dark. No streetlight, no illuminated windows of the house. Only the leaves, rustling and whispering. And also coolness. The air felt different, no city could have air like this, no town or village. The fear that took hold of him turned it chilly. How could he have wished to end up here? He hugged the backpack, thinking only of the coat that he'd so stupidly left back in the Roach Motel. So warm. To take the compass and leave the coat. What an idiot. What good would knowing which way was north do him now?

He rummaged in the backpack, even though he knew that there was no coat there, no flashlight, not even a book of matches. He was doing it just to give himself something to do, to push away the panic. His fingers stumbled on the compass. He took it out, brought it closer to his eyes, and realized that he could see it. Not just the glowing needle, all of it, every last mark. He flipped open the notepad. In a way that was different than under sunlight, he could still somehow see the writing and, what's more, read it. The Forest glowed. Not for everyone, only for those who could see in the dark. It appeared that he could.

A giggle nearby spooked him. He turned around and then, unexpectedly for himself, tumbled into the grass and came back up three paces from where he had been standing, under the eaves of the nearest tree. He did it smoothly and instantaneously, in one fluid motion. Unconsciously. As soon as he leaned against the tree he forgot everything. It wasn't just a warm safe place, more like an embrace. The tree embraced him like only a tree could, soothing, protecting, sharing its strength with him. He forgot to think about the invisible danger, giving himself fully to this feeling of oneness. As he pressed his face against the scratchy bark, he started crying.

"Welcome home," someone said.

That someone came out from behind the next tree and stopped. He was wearing a T-shirt with *Yellowstone Park* written on it and smiling. Or maybe scowling. And he wasn't entirely human. His eyes glinted green in the dark, like a dog's.

"Hello, Blind," Noble said, recalling everything he had not been able to remember for the past six months. "How did you find me?"

Blind laughed.

"I didn't. It was you who found me, you forgetful Jumper."

GINGER'S TALE

She lived there too. In Blackwood. But she wasn't staying at the Roach Motel all the time, oh no, you could keep that filthy hovel. Only forgetful Jumpers and total losers lived there, and she was neither, thank you very much. Blackwood was a dump, for sure, but it was clearly close to the border, otherwise she'd never have even shown her face there.

She needed a guide. Someone to tag after. Someone who'd help her cut the loose ends and go over completely, the proper way. She knew it was possible, and she also knew she couldn't do it by herself. She wasn't a complete flop, but she wasn't quite at that level either.

She worked at the eatery. At least she had enough food, and it was fairly decent. She washed dishes because she could swear at the dishes all day long and they wouldn't mind. Objects are better than people that way. So she washed dishes, and the rest of the time she prowled around looking for a guide. Except she didn't quite know what he was supposed to look like. Unfortunately.

Which was how she stumbled upon the Grayfaces.

That's what everybody called them. Total creeps. They bleached their hair, wore mascara, and painted leaf-like patterns on their cheeks. The patterns were supposed to be green. Or maybe blue. Whatever, their creations looked like filth from a distance, so the name stuck. They dressed in the whitest shirts, black leather jackets, and blue jeans, horribly expensive, with buckles of their belts made, as some said, of platinum, but at the same time went around barefoot, and their feet were always dirty. They called themselves Forest Folk. Imagine that, those goblins and the Forest!

But she shouldn't have laughed at them. Grayfaces never forgave. They caught her, beat her up, and took her with them. They lived in one of the old mansions on the outskirts of town. The basement they made into a bowling alley. There was supposed to be billiards somewhere higher up too, and above that probably living space, but they never let her see it. Only the other girls were allowed there. Their own. The fake platinum blondes with prickly leaves on their cheeks.

She didn't like to recall the days she'd spent there. Very soon she started to doubt that she'd ever been brave or foolish enough to scoff at one of them to his face. Grayfaces made her forget how to scoff, how to swear. How to talk at all. But the most horrible thing they did was make her forget how to Jump. She was no longer a Jumper. She was robbed of the only thing she was ever proud of in her life, because a Jumper who retains memories is a rare beast indeed, and she was that beast until she ended up with the Grayfaces, who broke something inside her. It had been known to happen before. She'd heard the stories when she was still very little, scary tales of those who did not return, not because they didn't want to but because they couldn't, but once she herself became a Jumper she stopped believing in them. It was simply too easy when you knew how. Might as well believe that you could forget how to talk. Grayfaces made her wiser. She saw now that it was at any rate possible, either of those things and both of them. All she could do now was wait. Wait and clean up their puke for them. They threw up constantly, because the dope they were doing made their stomachs reject normal food. She would have most probably died there, because they didn't give her much food either, but it so happened that one of their painted girlfriends decided to torch the house along with everyone in it. There was no damage to the basement, but the whole thing was distracting and Grayfaces let down their guard that night, so she was able to give them the slip.

She went into hiding for ten days, until her face healed up. Then she stole some clothes. In a sheepskin vest, a flower-patterned skirt, and an idiotic wide-brimmed sun hat she looked like her grandmother. It was just what she needed, to look like someone else. She dyed her hair and went around in huge sunglasses, rounding out the disguise. Now all she required was money, and then she could get out of town.

And that's when she saw him. He was raking the sand on the beach in front of the diner. At seven in the morning. When she saw him she was speechless for a while. Not because he was so unbelievably beautiful; it's just that he reminded her of Grayfaces. Or rather, the other way around. In that instant she understood who it was they were trying to emulate. And also how lousy they were at it. It came as a shock. The fact that they would use eye shadow and makeup pencils in hopes of becoming *this*. It was a point of particular glee for her that his hair wasn't even white. And, of course, no leaves or flowers on his cheeks. But she did understand what they so desperately wanted when bleaching their hair and drawing the patterns. For the first time she did understand. When she saw a live elf.

She was sitting on the jetty, her skirt fanned around her, feet in the water. He walked by, picking up debris left on the sand by the bathers. He only looked at her once. Violet eyes. They weren't human. She knew then that those eyes could change color, from light gray to deep indigo.

She froze, afraid that she might spook him, and her heart was beating like crazy until he moved far enough away to not feel her burning stare anymore. He had this strange walk. It was as if walking was unfamiliar or uncomfortable for him. Or maybe it even hurt his feet. He was wearing flip-flops and dragging the trash bag after him along the sand.

Here he is. The guide, she thought. And trailed after him at a distance, afraid to lose sight of him.

After a week of living in the Roach Motel next to him she learned that he didn't remember who he was, wasn't aware of any secret passages, and generally knew nothing about anything. He didn't even notice that people were shunning him. She kept a tireless watch, but nothing came of it.

His room smelled of forest. His mattress was stained by blobs of squashed berries. There was no dust in the corners, only dried leaves. Where he washed his face in the morning edible mushrooms sprouted by the afternoon, his windowsill was encrusted in a thick layer of guano. The entire Roach Motel sustained itself on mushroom soup, and still he didn't notice.

She would smile at him when they met. He would greet her politely. Sometimes he smiled back. His teeth were on the sharpish side, but that didn't make him any less beautiful. She wasn't exactly pretty even before donning the rags that made her look like an old hag, so she never tried to talk to him. People like him did not talk to people like her. That would be unnatural.

One time she came to him while he was asleep. He slept alone, even though the Roach Motel usually packed them six to the room. She tried not to make any sound as she entered, and sat for a long time looking at the fireflies hovering over the edges of his mattress in a luminous rectangle. That night she decided that she had had enough. She was almost ready to kill him. She fought with herself and, exhausted by the fight, fell asleep right there in the corner. When she woke up she was in the Forest. He helped her go there without even realizing it. Because wherever he was, the Forest was always nearby. Oh, how she hated him for that.

In the Forest she spent no more than ten minutes, but that was enough. She knew she was going to dream of going back there for the rest of her life. But she still remained just a Jumper. And an unstable, touchy Jumper at that. In the time since all of this happened, she learned that she'd gotten incredibly, fantastically lucky. To actually find a guide was an almost impossible task. Especially a guide like this. Unless he himself wanted it, that is. But there was still one thing she was proud of: she never asked him for anything. Not then, and not since. And she never would.

SMOKER

Vulture's story was the first. It was about a witch. An old and disgusting witch, and all she dreamed of was dancing on the graves of all her relatives. Only a brief dance like this, performed once every few years at best, would make her happy. Nothing else ever brought joy to her life. But in order to be able to do her dance and be joyful even for a moment the witch needed to take great pains, because people didn't just drop dead all by themselves, and unless they were helped along she herself might not live long enough to celebrate the dance she yearned for. With time, the witch accumulated so many exquisite ways of sending her closest relatives to a better world that she easily could have published a bestselling book on the subject. As the years went by and the witch grew older there were fewer and fewer relatives left, until finally it all came down to one single grandson. With him she had to work really hard. He was hiding underground, in the caves of the dwarves, and it was a very dangerous place, so dangerous that even witches never risked going there. But this one did, so strong was her desire to do one last dance on a fresh grave. And so she followed her grandson into the dwarf caves, but got lost there. Dwarves lured her under the magic hill, where time flowed backward, and the evil hag turned into a small girl.

Here Vulture got distracted describing the various properties of magic hills and spent a lot of time telling us about what happened to those unfortunate enough to end up under them. Those who got lost like that could become old in an instant, or crumble to dust, or get back their youth and good looks, could turn into an animal, a plant, or even something that didn't exist in nature, but whatever it was, the process was irreversible. Even if they were to cast off the spells of the magic hill, they'd never be able to return to their former selves.

Vulture's tale was interrupted by R One. For some reason he urgently needed to know what the old hag looked like.

Vulture said she was hideously ugly.

"And then?" R One said. "I mean, now?"

Vulture said he had no idea. "But they say she looks about four years old, at most."

"Who is 'they'?" R One shot up.

"The dwarves," Vulture said, and the tone of his voice was so icy that it was clear he wasn't in the mood to answer any more questions.

R One got the message and went silent. But the old man who Lary said was the guard perked up instead. He giggled and inquired if there were any dwarves in the audience.

No one answered him.

That was the end of the tale. Either Vulture took offense at being interrupted, or there really wasn't anything else he wanted to say.

The next speaker turned out to be Black. I was surprised, because as far as I knew he'd never participated in Fairy Tale Nights. I was even more surprised at the tale itself. It didn't sound very fairy, and I suspected that it wasn't a tale at all. Black talked about the Outsides. About his adventures there. He told us how he, assisted by Rat, or rather Rat with his assistance, because he was more of a silent member of their partnership, swiped an old crumbling bus from the back of the garage of a nearby school. And that right now the bus was standing in the vacant lot next to the House, hidden under the trash, and waiting. What exactly it was waiting for, Black did not elaborate, but it wasn't hard to guess.

While I was wrapping my head around this information, R One went to the stepladder and asked Black if he knew that to drive anything anywhere in the Outsides required a driver's license. And that a bus full of underage hoodlums without a single piece of identification among them would be stopped in very short order.

Black said that he was aware of it.

Would he be aware, then, R One continued, that a stolen vehicle had most likely been reported as such to the police, and that even if it were to be repainted, someone would still be bound to recognize it.

Black said that he was aware of that also.

"Then what the hell are you trying to pull?" R One screamed. "Or do you think that the slammer is a nice place for getting acquainted with the Outsides?"

Needle hugged Mermaid and started to sniffle quietly. I couldn't see in the dark who it was crowding R One, but apparently they were asking him to sit back down. Black said that he was just telling a tale.

R One said that he was tired of people screwing with his head.

Tabaqui again asked him to sit down and behave himself.

I couldn't quite see if Ralph did sit down or remained standing.

"So . . . ," Black said and paused, as if afraid he'd get interrupted again. "In the fairy tales it is customary to have fairies and things like that. My tale may not be very interesting and stuff, but it does have a fairy. Two of them, actually, and also two more . . . What do you call guy fairies? I mean, they all have driver's licenses and they offered to help . . ."

Everyone applauded. I got to thinking who those four fairies were and why would they want to help Black, and the longer I thought about it the less I liked it. Because there wasn't anywhere they could've appeared except from the Outsides, and I had it on good authority that even if selfless fairies had ever existed there, they'd long gone extinct.

I wanted to discuss this with Black, but it had to wait until the break. In the meantime Tabaqui mounted the stepladder for an announcement.

"Not everyone may be fully aware of the rules," he shouted. "Which is why I would like to reiterate them, just in case. Anyone present is allowed to ask the narrator a question. One question! Preferably at the end, without interrupting the tale. Statements are also acceptable, but not encouraged. Speaking out of turn is completely prohibited! As is moving about! There will be breaks for that. Anyone found in violation of these rules will be henceforth shown the door, without regard to the laws of hospitality! Am I clear?"

As his monologue progressed, Tabaqui was screaming louder and louder, and swinging back and forth on the stepladder wider and wider, so at the end of it he barely managed to hold on. He was making much more noise than Ralph had, but no one thought of it as a violation of rules.

I couldn't keep my thoughts away from the bus and how all those jokes about it turned out to not be jokes. And also about how furious R One was. He could easily get it into his head that I'd known the truth all along and purposely wrote gibberish in the diary to keep him guessing. I was so occupied by this that I missed the beginning of Noble's tale.

It too was not a fairytale. Noble was telling us about living in some small town, what he did there and how he was trying to make some money. It was clear that he'd invented this out of whole cloth, but at the same time I had this gnawing feeling that he was in fact relating something that really happened. It was only the ending that did turn magical, and that suddenly and way over the top, as if Noble got tired of straining his imagination deciding how he was going to get his character out of the bind he'd put him into. There even was an appearance by Blind there, contrived and inappropriate, in my opinion.

Next was Shuffle's turn. He played more than he talked, and his tale was along the same lines as Noble's. There was also a small town and small gigs for money. It sounded quite a bit more lively, but that simply could be because he got to perform his entire catalogue. Spliced it into the narrative.

After Shuffle's tale, Tabaqui finally declared a break. I thought that it would mean turning on the wall lamps, but no such luck. Everyone remained seated in the dark, so I didn't dare leave the bed. Black moved somewhere, I couldn't see him anymore from where I was. Tabaqui switched on the boombox. All around me people droned and whispered, discussing what they'd heard. We had a plate of sandwiches passed from below; I took one and passed it to Lary.

"Wicked. Just wicked," Lary muttered. "Did you hear that, huh? I mean, I get it, but I mean, just straight out like that . . ."

I said I didn't know about how straight that was, but I personally preferred the stories from the last Fairy Tale Night. They were more fairy.

"Exactly," Lary mumbled, chomping on the sandwich. "That's exactly what I'm talking about."

"So how is tonight wicked, then?" I said.

"Right, that's how. For this very reason."

I decided not to waste any more time with him and asked Mermaid and Needle what they thought about all this.

"Nothing," Needle squeaked. And in case I didn't get it the first time, repeated: "Nothing, nothing, nothing . . ."

"I liked Noble's tale," Mermaid said dreamily. "So beautiful."

I could not see the expression on her face, but I could imagine it in detail.

"Blackwood . . ."

"What was that?" I said.

"Blackwood. That was the name of the town. Did you forget already?"

It could be that Noble had mentioned it. Probably at the beginning, when I wasn't paying attention. In any case, there wasn't anything beautiful about the place the way he described it, apart from that name.

"Los Angeles would be even cooler!" Lary chimed in.

"How did you like Black's tale?"

I did it on purpose, calling it a tale when it wasn't that at all. I wanted one of them to say it. But Mermaid just sighed, Needle mumbled that it was very nice, and Lary got to chomping even louder.

"Nice? You call that nice?"

Needle snuggled up to Lary, and instead of an answer they started kissing, even though Lary's mouth most likely was still full of sandwich.

"Don't worry about it," Mermaid whispered. "It's not that bad, really."

I tried to explain to her what it was I didn't like in this whole bus business. Mermaid listened very attentively and nodded in the right places, but I got the impression she was doing it only to humor me.

Tabaqui declared the break to be over, and all the thoughts about the bus went right out of my head, because the next to speak was the woman from the tent camp.

She must have been really uncomfortable to be doing this. She was barely audible, and she remained where she was instead of climbing the stepladder. Her story couldn't be called a fairy tale even by someone who's never heard a single fairy tale ever.

She told us about herself—fifty-seven, not married, no kids, no bad habits. She was a veterinarian by trade, working with cattle. She also rattled off a list of her various ailments. I didn't catch all the names. She looked stout and healthy, so it was strange that she had so many things wrong with her. Then she told us how she became a member of this sect that coalesced around the Angel, and how happy she was there, how she realized that she had finally found her place in life, and how the Angel, who had the appearance of a tender youth, had cured her of all infirmities "with a single touch of his heavenly palm."

Then she started talking about their weekly prayer meetings and all the other great things they got to do, and here her story started to grate on me, because she was now talking in a sonorous, not-quite-human voice, preaching almost, and stuff like that makes me gag, to be honest.

There was also this Holy Elder who was supposedly taking care of the Angel, and also, as I understood, of divesting the "blessed devout" of their money. Then he croaked, and that was the end of the good life. The Angel had been taken away by some "evil people" who claimed to be his parents, and the commune fell apart. But not completely, because some of them desired the continued communion so badly that they resolved to seek the Angel and free him from the evil clutches. It wasn't easy. They were being persecuted, called "fanatics," even arrested and involuntarily committed.

Her voice began trembling and gave out in some places, and I vividly imagined the man in fatigues clutching her shoulder, and her putting a hand over his and patting it comfortingly, like "it's all right, I can handle it." Sometimes my imagination runs out of control, but in this case I wasn't even ashamed of it, they were so fake. It was as if they had invented themselves. Badly.

Long story short, they had found their Angel. Those who were the most fanatical. And as a reward for their fortitude and perseverance the two of them had been allowed to witness the Angel ascending to Heaven.

"Testify!" the man interrupted in a resonant baritone, making Mermaid startle.

"Wreathed in fire and light, the divine sword pierced the Heavens and returned as a falling star," the woman explained. "Does this not prove that he was being sent to us, to those who followed him faithfully, so that he could lead us forth?"

She fell silent.

And everyone else kept silence too.

"Creepy," Needle whispered.

I said nothing. Because it was. Creepy and scary. I finally put two and two together and got four. Understood who the angel was they were talking about. And why they'd pitched their camp against the fence of the House, and were now sitting on Alexander's bed.

He worked as an Angel, and he got really fed up with it, Sphinx's voice repeated in my head.

I realized that I was shaking. Because I'd been there, right there with him when he "ascended wreathed in fire and light." If I'd known back then that this was the "divine sword piercing the Heavens," I'd have probably shaved my head too and joined the Devout. I was pretty close to something like that anyway. It's strange how quickly and easily this all had faded away from memory. Well, not really, just got hidden somewhere. Where normal people hide things they can't explain, to try and preserve their sanity.

And one more thing I understood. That some people in here had it much harder than I. Because if it were me after whom the Devout came to make me lead them forth, I would've hanged myself straight off. Even if I were an angel.

I had a hard time getting into the next tales. I was listening, sure, but did not follow the plots. I tried. There was a lot hidden in those stories, they all had some kind of secret, even the most fantastic of them, I got that, but still I couldn't listen to them with the same attention as the others did. It wasn't just because of the shaved heads. I was too tired, and the darkness, stuffiness, and the smell of wax all combined to mold the tiredness into a kind of torpor. Some stories shared certain details, some involved the same characters, some seemed to happen in the same places. I guess it would have been exciting to trace all of those intricate connections, except for the drowsy lethargy that overtook me.

During the next break I decided to go sit somewhere else where it would be easier to breathe and harder to fall asleep, and made a stupid move—slipped down from the bed. Someone immediately squeezed into the space I had vacated, and I immediately regretted having done that. Crawling on the floor was impossibly difficult. In the places where no one was lying down someone would be sitting, and where no one was sitting there would be backpacks and more backpacks. The candles had burned down to almost nothing and gave out more smoke than light. I didn't go two walker's paces before landing in a plate of sandwiches, bumping my head into the bed leg, and bowling over Whitebelly, who was just climbing down from that same bed. Then someone stepped on me. I figured I'd better get up on the nearest bed before they trampled me, but there was no space on the nearest bed. It was occupied by Shuffle, his guitar, Owl (I think), and someone hiding behind a backpack.

That someone said, "Hey, what are you doing? It's packed here."

So I crawled on.

In the next three minutes I got stepped on about two dozen times, so by the time the break ended I was hurting all over. Thankfully, when Tabaqui declared the end of the break and everyone took their seats, someone lit the Chinese lantern. Just one, but that was enough to save me. I saw a place for me. It turned out that place was next to Vulture. No one ever chose to sit next to him, but I didn't care anymore.

Angel told about an enchanted house that could move about. Ginger told another one about the same town Noble had been in, and about Noble himself in it.

Then for a while I wasn't listening at all, because Noble squeezed in between me and Vulture and started whispering something in his ear, and then took off some bauble that was hanging around his neck and gave it to Vulture. And then Vulture, I wouldn't have believed it if I didn't see it with my own eyes, Vulture burst out crying. I mean, if it were only my eyes I wouldn't have believed them anyway, but I was sitting so close to him, and he sobbed so hard, that there could be no mistake. I didn't know where to put myself. Then it got even worse, because he suddenly hugged Noble, still crying. And he was crying as if he couldn't breathe. It was painful to listen to. Noble hugged him too, and held tight until Vulture calmed down, and he looked like he didn't give a damn what anyone would think about them, because there was only one thing they could think if they saw something like this. I didn't think anything of the sort, of course, but it upset me greatly that others certainly would. Lizard, and everyone else sitting close enough. I think I was so upset because I realized right away that what had just happened between Noble and Vulture was important, sad and joyful at the same time, something that couldn't be expressed in words, that you could only laugh or cry about. The way Vulture was crying.

RED'S TALE

In that world Death came to people wearing one of the two disguises, that of a young man or a young woman.

The woman was pale with black hair. The man's hair was red. The woman was sad, the man merry. That's how it's always been in that world, since the beginning of time.

Some people were afraid of them. Others awaited them eagerly. They were mentioned in prayers, asked to postpone or hasten the end. Their images were on playing cards and old engravings. Very few thought about how many of them there were. It was agreed that Death was one, just in two different personifications. Night and day. Light and shadow.

In fact, there were many of them. They were almost godlike, possessing innumerable wondrous abilities, and unbearably lonely. Sometimes they would flee to other worlds, to meet their own deaths. Some of them would even be born in other worlds. They were always born dead there, coming to life only later. Those of them that could. These refugees from different worlds were no longer true emissaries of Death. Their abilities were not as sharp. In time they became almost harmless, and could only bring death in a dream.

Here is how you can tell them. They have beautiful voices, they dance well, and they know everyone's secrets. They are also lazy, never losing themselves in the pursuit of a single goal. The women don't know how to laugh, and the men don't know how to cry. They hide their eyes, sleep a lot, and never eat eggs, because in their world they hatched from one.

TABAQUI'S TALE

Once upon a time and ever since then there lives a curious little old man. He lives in a secret place. This place is very hard to find, and to find the old man in it is even harder. He has many houses, or maybe it's the same house that only looks different for anyone entering it. Sometimes it stands in the middle of an orchard, sometimes it is in an empty field, sometimes on the bank of a river, and it almost never looks the same, only very rarely. It could even be that there is no house at all, that the old man is holed up in a single room of a huge project. And there were times when he chose to live in the hollow of a dead tree.

That's why finding him is so difficult. No one who visited him can describe his dwelling to anyone else, or point out the way and explain how to reach it. There are many who would like to meet him, but only those who seek tirelessly and have the knowledge of invisible ways and passages, of secret signs and prophetic dreams, can ever hope to come to the right place. But even when they reach it they often have to leave empty-handed, because the old man is grumpy, obstinate, and does not like giving out presents.

The old man's houses all look different from the outside, but very similar on the inside. They are crammed with things. Sometimes there are so many that the old man can barely find a place for himself among them. But this way everything he needs is always close to hand. It would be impossible to imagine something that he does not have.

He keeps music inside conchs, skulls of small animals, and fruit seeds. He puts smells in the bean pods and nutshells. Dreams, in empty gourds. Memories, in cabinets and perfume bottles. He also has hooks of every shape and ropes of every thickness, clay pots of any size, except large ones, and jugs, also small but very elaborate. Whistles, flutes and fifes, buttons and buckles, jack-in-the-boxes, precious jewels and stones that only he knows the value of, spices, seeds and roots, old maps marked with locations of sunken treasure, flasks, earrings, horse-shoes, playing cards and tarot cards, figurines made out of wood, gold and ivory, crumbly pieces of meteorites, bird feathers, baubles, bangles and beads, bells, eggs being kept warm, insects encased in amber, and also some toys. And most of these objects are usually more than what they seem.

But those who come to the old man do not want spices, jewels, myrrh, or frankincense. They all want gears from busted watches. The old man loathes parting with those.

Some of the guests get snared by the inventive traps the old man keeps around the house. Others he lets through and refuses himself, for varying reasons. He has a list of questions, and if you do not answer each and every one of them you will not get your present, this he ensures firmly and gleefully.

The unluckiest guests of the house find only the old man's mummified corpse. It lies in the cardboard box that the stereo system came in, in the company of withered flowers, carved nutshells, and faded postcards. Some bury him before leaving, others dump him out of the box and beat up the body, venting their disappointment, and then there are those who remain in the house, waiting for who knows what—another old man instead of this one, a replacement, so to speak, since this one seems to be dead? Sooner or later they too leave empty-handed. The old man can be a mummy for however long he wants. It doesn't bother him at all.

There are plenty of legends and rumors about him. People tell tales of him in places near, far, and very, very far. The oldest of those depict him as sitting on top of a mountain with two skeins of wool, black and white. He winds up one of them and unspools the other, turning day into night and night back into day. The later tales say that he eternally spins an enormous wheel, divided into a summer half and a winter half, and the summer side of it is red while the winter side is white as snow. There are other stories. But all of them end the same way, in bestowing of gifts. Everyone who meets the old man receives a present from him, and it's those gifts that people desire when they go out in search of him.

The lucky visitors receive gears from broken watches. The luckiest of all, an egret feather. The first gift means one thing while the second means quite another. Everyone asks for the first and no one asks for the second, because no one knows that this gift even exists. It is not mentioned in any tales or legends. The watch gear can be lost, exchanged, or given away. The feather disappears if it ever leaves the possession of its owner, so it cannot belong to anyone else.

It is not easy to get the old man to part with a watch gear, the feathers he gives out extremely rarely, and no one ever receives anything else. Almost never. There was only one time when he was asked for a dream. A very peculiar dream, one that explained how to see other people's dreams. A small boy asked for it, and took with him a gourd stoppered with henbane. Some years later the same boy, now grown, came again with an even stranger request. The old man was intrigued. Out of the eggs he had, he chose the most beautiful, green with white speckles.

"They are very delicate," he warned. "Be careful. Keep it warm near your heart, and when she hatches, let her out into a stream, but make sure there aren't any predatory fish around. In forty days she will be grown."

"What will she be in twenty days?" the boy asked.

He was an odd boy, and the old man was slightly apprehensive about the fate of the creature inside the egg, but he liked giving unusual gifts, and the boy was the only one in many, many years to want something other than what everyone always wanted. With him the old man wasn't bored.

And boredom is the one thing that the old man hates. From time to time, tired of the monotony of the gifts he gives to others, he makes a present to himself. The simplest things, really. Nothing valuable or extraordinary, but it's always nice to receive an unexpected, unusual present. Especially if you then forget that you received it from yourself.

SMOKER

Humpback retold the old familiar tale of the Pied Piper. Changed some details, that's all. I didn't remember it all too well, but I am pretty sure it didn't used to say there that he only led away the smallest children, three and younger. "Pure of mind and desires." It sounded rather strange. Because it's not clear how it would be possible to lead away kids who, for example, can't even walk yet.

Humpback never explained that, so I imagined away, coming up with some truly amusing images. Like babies cooing and kicking their little legs, floating up from their cribs, circling around the rooms, flitting out of opened windows, and flying to the tootling piper in his red tunic.

That wasn't even the half of it. To imagine a one-year-old that the parents wouldn't be able to hold on to was even harder. Then I realized that in the original tale this wasn't explained either. It just said that the Piper led away all children, period. So the littlest ones had to be included in that, too. I don't think I'd ever thought about that before.

Lary told about an enchanted princess. Obviously meaning Needle. Red told about fugitive deaths. Likely meaning himself.

Tabaqui told about a little old man who so disliked making presents, while at the same time being somehow obligated to do exactly that, that he even faked his own death to make them leave him alone.

Owl and Corpse dovetailed their stories with Tabaqui's, telling about their own encounters with this old man.

Vulture and Noble continued whispering to each other, and Lizard fell asleep. I thought it wouldn't be a big deal if I tried to get some sleep as well, but it didn't work out that way.

Because the next person to climb the stepladder was Blind, and the ringing silence that followed knocked the sleepiness right off me.

Blind remained silent too for a while. The candles went out, the lanterns didn't give off much light, but I could see that he was barefoot, dressed in his regular clothes, and that his hand was now wrapped with a bandage instead of a towel.

Finally he spoke. He said that he wished all of us luck, whether we were leaving or staying. Or leaving thinking we're staying, or staying thinking we're leaving. Or, finally, returning. Blind said that whatever we chose, every one of us would have to begin our lives anew, because the life that's waiting for us would have nothing in common with the one that was ending. Many would remember nothing of this life, but that shouldn't frighten us. "Those who live believing in the possibility of a miracle will find it." Then Blind said that he was not saying good-bye to those who were leaving, only to those who were staying and returning.

By this time I was thoroughly confused, and couldn't figure out which of them I was.

But it got even more mysterious.

Blind declared that he needed two volunteers—an experienced guide for the inexperienced guide, and a caretaker.

"This latter position is permanent," he concluded, and jumped down.

As soon as he did they switched on the wall lamps and everyone started getting ready to go.

I didn't realize that the Fairy Tale Night was over, it happened so suddenly.

The lights exposed piles of dirty plates and half-eaten food, candle drippings, and overstuffed ashtrays. It was no longer cozy, as if we all found ourselves in a train station, and just like people do when coming to a station, everyone everywhere hugged, said good-byes, and gave each other trinkets to remember them by.

Black sat next to me, slapped me on the shoulder, and said, "Take care, man . . . See you around." And then left. Then I was being kissed by Needle, her face tearstained and puffy. Horse gave me a tiny broom, for luck. Lary hugged me and burst into tears, so passionately that it was all I could do not to start sniffling too.

I didn't have time to wallow in misery and get steeped in the farewell spirit. They quickly hoisted the backpacks on their shoulders and went out, with a sizable crowd trailing along to see them off.

Alexander helped me climb up on the windowsill, and together we looked at them crossing the yard.

It was still dark out, but Needle's wedding dress seemed to be glowing, and I could clearly see her in the crowd. Her, and Lary in his operatic white shirt. For some reason, out of all the happenings of that night, this stood out in my memory, how they all walked across the yard to the gates, bride and groom leading the procession. Someone was holding Needle's train. Black was certainly striding along purposefully, lugging his enormous backpack, lips pursed severely, but him I couldn't distinguish from above, I just knew that he must have been there. Him, Horse, Bubble, and Zit, and Genepool . . . and also Red, as it turned out later. And those two from the tent camp.

There actually weren't that many of them leaving, but the darkness made it seem like it was a large crowd, so I even started fretting if they all would fit in their bus, because I remembered Black saying that it was quite a small one.

Then they closed the gates, those who were seeing them off returned, and we tried to re-create the cozy night in the candlelight, but it just wasn't the same anymore. People still cried, talked in whispers, said good-byes and gave out remembrance gifts, though more subdued now. Less tragic.

I discovered that I'd been holding armfuls of presents, and more were scattered around on the bed, but I didn't remember whom most of them came from.

Humpback climbed on the top bunk and was playing the flute. Beauty and Doll discussed Needle's bridal attire in excited whispers.

The old night guard disappeared somewhere. I didn't know then that he had also left with the bus, so I assumed he just went away like the two from the tent camp. R One was the only unusual guest still remaining. He was sitting on the bed that was pushed against the wardrobe, drinking Vulture's tequila straight from the bottle.

Blind sat next to him and asked something. Ralph choked, and Blind slapped him on the back. I was curious what it was they were talking about, so I crawled closer.

"As you wish," Blind said, getting up. "But it is entirely up to you."

R One grabbed his arm and made him sit back down. "That was a joke, right?"

Blind said that he had no intention of joking. Then he extracted a grubby brown envelope from his pocket and handed it to Ralph.

"If you change your mind, open this. When you are done with all the rest of it."

Ralph immediately stood up and looked around. He looked like Blind had just reminded him of a bunch of urgent and important things he had to do.

"All right," he said. "How much longer is this night going to last?"

Blind shrugged.

When Ralph left, Blind took his place on the bed and grabbed the guitar left by Shuffle. The bandage on his hand interfered with playing, so he took it off.

Sphinx sat down on the floor next to the bed. Tabaqui stopped driving around the room and also crawled closer. A little while later, Alexander joined them too.

Blind twanged the strings, very softly, Tabaqui whistled, Sphinx and Alexander just sat there silently. The morning refused to come.

I got tired of waiting for it and fell asleep, so I don't know how long the others were able to endure this.

Shortly before dawn I awoke to the sounds of the flute coming from the hallway. Plaintive and repetitive. I opened my eyes, registered the deepening blueness of the sky, and went back to sleep. Right around that time someone also stroked my hair. Tousled it and went away. I would never know who it was.

Those who had left at the end of the night tried to do it quietly.

I was woken up by Sphinx.

"Get up," he said. "Or you'll miss graduation."

It would have been less jarring if he'd set off an alarm clock by my ear. I sprang up.

"What? Already?"

The room was thoroughly trashed. It looked like that after every exciting night, though, so the mess was entirely expectable, but no less disgusting for that. And not a single soul in sight save for Sphinx and me.

"Have they all left?"

"They have," Sphinx said, wearing a crooked smile. "And know what? You'll have to help me, because there isn't anyone else."

He had these huge shadows under his eyes. They took up half of his face. He obviously hadn't slept a single wink, otherwise his clothes would have been as rumpled as mine were. I'd fallen asleep on one of the mattresses they tossed on the floor, amidst my presents. Horse's broom had left an imprint on my cheek, and I appeared to have crushed the flashlight that Humpback gave me. This made me very upset.

"You'll glue it back later," Sphinx said. "Just toss it in your bag, they're going to take this place apart brick by brick."

"Why?" I said.

I had trouble with coherent thinking that morning.

"Because," Sphinx said.

I collected all the gifts and put them in my bag. The crushed flashlight I wrapped separately, hoping to mend it afterward somehow. Then I had to make coffee and do the tidying up, because Sphinx couldn't do any of that without his prosthetics, and Alexander never showed up. Of course, it was not a proper cleaning, the way Alexander would have done it. I just stuffed the bulk of the trash in black plastic bags, smoothed out the crumpled blankets, and emptied the ashtrays. Only when we finished the coffee did I ask where all the others had gone. I had been reluctant to ask before, because there was something not quite right about us being completely alone.

"You'll know soon enough," he said.

And I did. Relatively soon. This knowledge still haunts me, often keeping me up at night. That, and also that I'll never find out who tousled my hair before leaving. Every time I think about it I imagine different people doing it, so it was almost as if they all did it. Well, maybe Tubby wouldn't be able to. Anyway, I only learned in the morning that there was another big group that had gone away. Who knows where? They had both left and stayed back. Neither dead nor alive. People would get to calling them Sleepers, but that would be a couple of years later, back then no one called them anything at all. There just wasn't a word for what they were. They had all assembled in the Third for some reason.

"Probably because there were so many of them from the Third," Sphinx said. "Six in all."

I didn't pay close attention to his words then.

There was no graduation that day. The parents did come, but no one was released. Some of the parents stayed, for support and also to keep an eye on the way we were interrogated. Thanks to them, and to Spider Ron, or we'd be in trouble. Sphinx was right about the House being taken apart brick by brick. They did almost exactly that. I don't think there was a single object left that wasn't probed, sniffed at, or disassembled. All drugs in the Sepulcher had been checked and rechecked, down to the last pill. On the second day a K-9 unit conducted a sweep of the House, with two German shepherds and a bloodhound. From the basement they extracted unfortunate Solomon. I only caught a glimpse of him, from a distance. Someone pudgy and filthy was marched down the first-floor corridor in handcuffs, loaded into a police van, and driven away. Then they unearthed human bones in the basement. I thought we'd be eaten alive, but luckily for us it soon turned out that the bones were more than a century old, and everyone promptly calmed down.

The interrogations went on. Two, three hours each day, sometimes more. Different people each time. Some were more interested in those who had disappeared, others in those who had turned into chrysalises. But it made no difference, we could not help them because we didn't know much, and what we did know we could never say.

We all became very close during that time. I guess nothing pushes people closer together than a shared secret. Lizard, Guppy, Dearest, and Dodo moved in with Sphinx and me. After us, the Third had the biggest loss, and they looked even more confused than we did. The Sleepers were moved to the hospital wing right away, but it was obvious that for Lizard and the rest of them the Third felt creepy. They only ever went there to water the plants and then came right back. Also we had two fathers, mine and Guppy's, spending the nights with us, and once out of the four nights, Ralph.

Dearest was the first to be taken away. I don't think he was right in the head. Other Birds assured me that this was normal for him, but clearly his presence bugged the hell out of them as well, and Dearest had gone home two days before everyone else.

At some point, I don't remember exactly but I think it was on the third day, I realized that no one had asked a single question about Tabaqui. And no one came for him. Then I noticed other strange things. I hadn't seen the Sleepers, and had no desire to gawk at them, as it were, the interminable discussions were quite enough for me. But the entire town seemed to know that there were twenty-six of them. We also knew that all the Insensible of the House were there. I counted our Insensible, added the girls, and got twelve. Which was too many. There couldn't have been only fourteen others, because if you took us and the Third that would already make thirteen. I turned this over in my head for a while and then tried to forget about it. Anyone to whom I could point out this incongruence would simply tell me to go to the Sleepers and count them myself. We weren't prohibited from visiting them, provided we had an escort. But my curiosity hadn't yet reached the level where I'd actually drive over to have a look at something like that.

Eventually I couldn't keep it in anymore.

"You know," I said to Sphinx, "it seems that more people have disappeared from the House than we think. Blind, for example. And Noble. Everyone counts them among those who disappeared. Which means they are not there among . . . them, you know. But they did not leave with the bus, we both know that."

Sphinx sighed and gave me a reproachful look. Almost like all this time he'd desperately hoped that I would refrain from asking him this very question.

"Striders go over completely," he said.

After he had said that, he didn't need to worry anymore that I would pester him with questions. There are sentences that cause the brain to activate its defensive mechanisms, and the first thing it does is stop asking. I came to the conclusion that they went and drove away not in two groups, but in three, and moreover, the third group, the smallest of them, was itself made of two parts—those whom everyone knew had disappeared, and others who were forgotten as soon as they had vanished. Tabaqui clearly belonged to that last one. And that wasn't the weirdest thing about it.

A lot of stuff got left in the room that used to belong to those who had gone away, sunk into the unending sleep, or disappeared. Many of the things were painful to see, at least for Sphinx and me. But nothing, and I mean not a single thing of Tabaqui's remained. Not even a button. I searched for them specifically. Turned over everything. Not a sock, not a worn slipper, not a pin, not a stale bread roll. Nothing. At all. I stopped looking for the traces of Tabaqui when I noticed that his drawings and writings had disappeared from the walls. There weren't even empty spaces where they used to be. There was something there, just not what had been there before. And then it came to me that I'd forgotten his face. I could re-create him in my mind in general, the frizzled hair, the outrageous outfits, where he liked to sit, how he liked to chomp loudly, but his features eluded me. What color were his eyes? What about the nose—aquiline or snubbed? I thumbed through my sketches. I'd drawn Jackal a million times, in pencil, in ink, in crayon. I couldn't find a single one. It was as if someone went methodically through my drawings and stole every one that depicted Jackal. Instead I found a bunch of sketches I'd never done. That is, I didn't remember doing them, though they certainly were in my hand.

I told Guppy about this. I didn't want to bother Sphinx.

"Tabaqui?" Guppy asked, frowning.

I swear, it took him two full minutes of racking his brain to figure out who I was talking about. So I was a little surprised when I found that my diary still contained Jackal's musings, and the little figurine he made from a walnut and gave to me was still in my bag.

"A present stays back," Sphinx said. "And if he considered what he wrote in the diary to be a present, it would also stay."

I went through the diary and saw that only Vulture's cactus notes had disappeared. In their place there was nothing. Clean paper. It became a little clearer what had reduced Dearest to the state he was in, and why Guppy would periodically call Lizard "Leader."

My insights, doubts, and fears were spread over the four days of our vigil, dulled by the discussions and the waiting. I felt like a fish in a tank that hadn't been cleaned for a while. Everything was murky, uncertain, and unexplained, and it seemed that the ability to be shocked had been lost somehow.

The weather was beautiful. Not hot, not cold, no rain, no wind, no withering heat. The air remained clean and clear. Lizard whiled away the hours playing solitaire, mumbling under his breath, or else incessantly pumping the weights he'd hauled in. Guppy and Dodo played cards. Dearest, before he was taken away, just sat in the corner scowling angrily.

When I said that we who remained in the House became closer, I didn't include Sphinx. With him it was the other way around, like he was fading in the distance with each passing day, becoming even more withdrawn and emaciated. I was afraid that if this kept on he too would simply disappear. He slept in his clothes, and I never noticed him eating, drinking, or going to the bathroom. It was better when Mermaid was around, but in her absence I tried not to look in his direction. Because when I did I always ended up trying to help somehow, and then he would tense up, thank me, and leave. He behaved the same way with Guppy and Dodo, to say nothing of Lizard, but they unexpectedly hit it off with my father. Held long discussions through the night. My dad, whom I'd always known to have a single mode of behavior with anyone younger than twenty, and that is hooting and slapping them on the back, suddenly opened up as a great listener, a philosopher even, demonstrated a sharp sense of humor and generally amazed me to no end. He also managed to force Sphinx to take a shower, and afterward put clean clothes on him, so neatly you'd think he'd spent all of his life practicing. Pity that he could only come in the evenings, after work.

Then they announced the new graduation date, and our life in suspended animation came to an end.

It was Sunday, so my father didn't have to go anywhere. We had a peaceful breakfast in the canteen, freshened up, and went down to the first with our bags. The lecture hall was packed with the departing students and their parents, the parents being somber and businesslike, in a rush to leave, and compared to them, those who had stayed with us for the four-day vigil looked almost like slackers and layabouts, I didn't know why. Viking's mother kept pushing hair out of his eyes, giggling moronically; the glasses on Rabbit's mother appeared absurdly large, making her nose stick out from under them like a button in an elevator: Guppy's father was wearing a suit that didn't fit, like he took it off someone; and my dad inexplicably turned into an aging hippie, and even started talking in an absurd drawl. Women threw him sideways glances, like he was a bum who had sneaked in somehow. I wanted to sink through the floor, I was so ashamed—for him, and for myself for being ashamed.

I don't know who came for Sphinx, except that it wasn't one of his parents. Could be his personal driver. Or maybe a distant relative. Sphinx regarded him as no more than a porter for his suitcase. He himself wasn't letting Mermaid out of sight even for a second. Her parents turned out to be quite elderly. Small, dressed all in black, as if plucked out of some remote village and brought to the House by a magical twister. I noticed them writing diligently on the sheets of paper they tore out of a notebook, or rather the father was writing what the mother dictated. They passed the sheets over to Mermaid, and she folded them and stuffed them in Sphinx's breast pocket. I knew then that he wouldn't have any trouble finding Mermaid in the Outsides. He hadn't asked for my address, but my father stalked the driver (or the relative who looked like one) until he managed to obtain some kind of information from him, and only then said we could go.

And we went. With no farewell hugs or kisses, because we had already said our good-byes more than once.

EPILOGUE

TALES FROM THE OTHER SIDE

The Man with the Crow

No one could say he had it easy. In the bed of his pickup truck there were twelve little mattresses, a box with clean baby clothes, a bag with the dirty ones, another bag, this one with disposable utensils, a boombox lashed to the side with wire, and eleven kids, aged one to three. At least he got lucky with Rat Fairy. She drove while he busied himself in the back with the children, and sometimes spelled him for a short time in this capacity, so he could get some sleep. Not too often, because it meant that the truck wasn't moving. She looked more like an evil enchantress than a good fairy, but she was neither evil nor good, she was just fulfilling the task she had been charged with.

With the children he was also lucky. They were all smarter than their age, and almost all of them endured the trip quietly and patiently. But they still would get carsick from time to time, they needed to eat and drink, many were not toilet-trained yet, those who were still couldn't do it sometimes in the shaking truck bed, and no matter how he tried, each day it became harder and harder for him.

People who saw this strange family were surprised that many of the children were of the same age while not being twins, and that none of them looked like their father. Also suspicious was the father's relative youthfulness, the crow ensconced on his shoulder, and the wide-brimmed black hat adorned with a ring of the yellowed skulls of some small animal.

"Gypsies, I'll bet," they said, glowering. "And the kids are stolen."

"They are not all mine," he would explain self-consciously, when the questions became particularly probing. "Half of them are my sister's."

And he pointed at the raven-haired girl behind the wheel. She chain-smoked, resting her sharp elbow on the edge of the window, and her shoulder featured an unusual tattoo: a scowling rat. As soon as people had a good look at it, even the most inquisitive of them thought it best to walk away, and the questions tended to end abruptly.

The truck rolled around seemingly without purpose, but Rat Fairy did, in fact, constantly check the map. Some houses were marked on it with a red cross. They tried to reach them at dawn and without disturbing the neighbors. Each time they were met there, usually by a man and a woman, but sometimes only by women and once by a single man. A brief hushed conversation ensued, one of the children would be transferred from the truck to the house, and they left as quietly as they came. Other houses were marked with green crosses. These they visited openly, at any time of day or night, and picked up boxes of baby food.

And even though there were fewer and fewer children, they grew more and more tired, and their journey became more arduous. They started forgetting days and dates, talked less and less, confused the kids they'd already fed with the ones who were still hungry. Twice Rat Fairy lost her way, making the quest longer by many hours.

Still, when it came the time to part with the last child, he started crying. Rat Fairy slapped him on the back.

"Oh, come on. You'll have your own someday."

She wasn't really evil, it was just that there were things she had no way of understanding.

The Waitress

Every night when her shift ended, about half past eight, she would go out into the backyard of the café carrying the scraps for the cats. She distributed them between two paper plates, leaned with her back against the deck railing and simply stood there, resting or maybe dreaming, until it became dark. The cats strolled around. Gray cats did it invisibly, of course, black-and-whites were half-visible. She stood there, also almost invisible except for the apron and the lace cap, hands tucked under her armpits, and waited. "The twilight is the crack between the worlds." She'd picked up this phrase in some book, back when she still had time to read. She no longer remembered what happened in that book or who wrote it, but this phrase alone stuck in her mind. *The crack between the worlds,* she kept thinking, staring into the deepening blue dusk. *Here. Now.* When it became too dark to distinguish the shape of the lilac bush near the fence, five feet from the deck, she went back. Feeling rested and full of energy, as if the half hour she spent doing nothing cleansed her of the tiredness, the kitchen reek, and the kitchen gossip.

Because of that strange habit, the other kitchen girls started calling her Princess. Some days, when she returned to the kitchen for her bag before leaving, she heard them talking about her.

"You'd think she would run back to the child, right? But no, first she needs to nip out back for an hour, day in and day out. Some mother, is what I'm saying. If you ask me, I wouldn't let people like her within a mile of children."

"She must be doing this because she doesn't like taking care of the baby. I have no idea who she dumps the poor thing on while she's here."

Sometimes the woman who was relieving her shift would chime in.

"Ah, but have you looked at that baby? I'd like to see you rushing back to something like that. He's got this huge head, and a mouth full of teeth. Eight months, my eye! He gives me the willies, he does. And she wouldn't even call him by name. Tubby this and Tubby that. And he's not that fat, really."

"Maybe his daddy was tubby."

"Whatever he was, must've been a scary sight if the kid's taking after him."

"Not after her, surely. She might be all speckled like a quail's egg, but she is kinda cute for that."

She didn't pay attention to any of that talk. She couldn't afford to make a scene and lose the job. And it didn't hurt her that much anyway. Tubby was a perfect child. Not a beauty, maybe, but very clever, and he could already say at least half a dozen words. He patiently waited for her to come back from the afternoon shift, gnawing on the biscuits she'd leave him for lunch and playing with the stuffed dinosaur. The neighbors never once complained about him crying. He didn't need a nurse. He knew how to wait. They both knew, because that was the only thing they did. Together and separately, while playing, working, making dinner and eating it, in the crib, and around the back of the café, even in their dreams.

Their father, also the Beautiful Prince from the Not-Here, looking at the same time like the faded dinosaur with button eyes (the way Tubby imagined him) and like the small sprig of jasmine growing in a pot on her windowsill, was going to find them sooner or later, if not today then tomorrow, they only had to wait for him. And when he did, they wouldn't have to worry anymore about the price of diapers, or the vicious gossip, or any of the small inconveniences of life, because he would take them with him to his fairy land, where everything would be different. So they waited.

The Three-Fingered Man in Black

He took residence in the abandoned three-story house, the one that spawned insistent rumors of being haunted. It was some time before people noticed. The house was out of the way, and the new tenant did not turn the lights on, did not advertise his presence in any way. At first they took him for a drifter. But drifters aren't usually clean shaven, dressed in suits, or in the habit of buying a week's worth of groceries. When it became clear that the man was in the house to stay, they sent a committee made of residents of the nearby houses to clarify the situation. It was a small town, and foreigners here were usually met with suspicion.

The man amiably received the committee and politely refused to answer most of their questions. Some things they did manage to find out, though.

The owner of the house—yes, it turned out that he did exist—had hired this man to look after the property. The man showed them the papers, and the papers were all in order, even though no one could remember a time when the haunted house had been owned by anybody, and the owner's signature looked strange indeed, resembling as it did a fat spider. One of the neighbors, a retired lawyer, assured them that there appeared to have been nothing unlawful here. The man in the black suit said that he was going to remain in the house until he received further instructions from the owner. There wasn't anything they could say against that, and the committee departed, unsatisfied but with the general feeling of having done their duty.

The house had always been a strange place, so it surprised no one that its owner signed papers with a spider and sent people to guard his property when there wasn't much left of it that hadn't crumbled to dust.

The new occupant of the old house lay low for some time, and then one day this surly young woman in leather came to visit him astride a motorcycle, scaring the neighborhood cats half to death. She brought a small fair-haired girl, offloaded her, and roared away immediately. This event turned the people completely against the man. Even his single-father status could do nothing to endear him to the neighbors. Besides, the girl was an exceptionally unpleasant child.

BETWEEN THE
WORLDS

Sphinx would take a room in the college dorm, tiny but private. He would spend the winter there, studying for the exams, and the winter would be the coldest in the last fifteen years. He would never find Mermaid. The address given by her parents would turn out to be nonexistent. Sphinx would visit everyone having the same last name as that strange family, then everyone with similar last names, and after two months of searching and asking would start to doubt if they hadn't been a hallucination.

From time to time he would receive letters from his mother. He'd read the first two. The others, unopened, would go to the bottom of his suitcase. The reams of newspapers he'd buy and scan hastily would go into a pile outside his door, growing day by day. Some of them, with articles he found interesting, would join the letters in the suitcase. The neighbors would be polite and courteous to him. At some point he'd realize that he was leading the life of a hermit and try to become more outgoing. He'd start attending student parties.

After one of them, instead of returning to his freezing room, he'd go straight to the bus stop and board the first bus of the morning, the only passenger in it. Changing buses twice, he'd arrive at the edge of town.

The House wouldn't be there, or rather it wouldn't be the House. Three walls, still standing amid mountains of bricks and rubble. Blanketed with snow. He'd walk along the fence surrounding this future building site, find a place where the boards did not come together, and sneak into the former domain of the House. One of the remaining walls would be covered in writings, from top to bottom. Names, addresses, phone numbers, short notes. He'd read all of them, and wouldn't find that which he wasn't hoping to find anyway.

He'd complete the circle around the wall and sit down on the pile of rubble dusted with snow, feeling warmer each minute, against all the laws of nature that dictated he should be freezing.

"I'm sorry," he'd say. "You seemed to me a monster that devoured all of my friends. I was sure that you'd never let me go. That you needed me for something known only to you. That I would never be free until I left you, even though I lied to Smoker about the freedom being inside of a person wherever he happens to be. I was afraid that you changed me, made me into your toy. I needed to prove to myself that I could live without you. I blamed you for Elk, and for Wolf. Elk was killed by accident and Wolf was killed by Alexander, but it was easier to think that it was your fault than to admit that the fault was with Wolf. That he was neither kind nor wise, the way I imagined him to be. That he wasn't perfect. That Elk wasn't perfect. Easier to blame you than admit that. Easier to say that you killed thirty-odd people than to see that they were cowardly fools or little children who had lost their way. Easier to think that it was you demanding Pompey's death than to imagine that it gave Blind pleasure to kill him. Easier to be sure that you forced me to remake Noble than to know that I liked doing it . . . Easier to hope that Blind lied about Mermaid than to concede that she really does not exist in this world, neither she nor her strange parents, nor their addresses that they gave to me so eagerly. So much easier just to believe in all of that than to realize that she was your gift, given to me in the hopes of holding on to me when the time came, only with that, not by force or deceit."

Sphinx would be talking until he was exhausted, until the words dissolved in the frigid air with the little white clouds of his breath. Then he'd get up and climb down from the pile of icy debris, slipping awkwardly. When he'd turn the corner of the wall with the addresses he would see that they were no longer there, and neither were the phone numbers. It would be dirty white, with multicolored spirals, triangles, suns, and moons . . . And the wondrous ugly beasts roaming underneath. Crude, sharp toothed, their legs of different length, their tails sticking straight up rigidly.

Sphinx would approach them carefully. He'd know better than anyone else where *that* wall had been, but now it would be right here. With all the creatures that inhabited it, great and small. The wolf with the sawlike teeth crowding his jaws, the yellow giraffe resembling a tower crane, the zebra looking more like a stripy camel, the spotted goblin, the green dinosaur, the faded outline of a seagull. As he looks closer, he'd see that in among the familiar drawings there would be others, also familiar but that never were next to them—the white bull swaying uncertainly on spindly legs, the dragon with the blue stone for an eye . . . and moreover, those that were familiar but actually had never been drawn—one more dragon, fiery scarlet, and a fish with a small bell tied to its tail. The bell would be real.

Sphinx would pluck it off the fish's tail and hide it in the pocket of his coat. Then press his forehead against the wall. He'd stand like that for a while, listening to the silence surrounding him, until the silence became absolute, because it would start snowing. Coming down in an avalanche of enormous flakes, and Sphinx, blinded by them, would stumble around the ruins in search of the crack in the fence that would lead him out.

On his way back to the dorm, jostled by the bus ride, striding along the snowy street, he would think about the bell secreted in his pocket, fighting the urge to take it out and confirm that it really exists. Then he'd feel a prickly sensation in the other pocket, stop and pull out a white feather, so long that it would be impossible to put back without breaking it. He'd have to stick it in his hat, hoping against hope that it didn't look too outrageous.

He'd meet his neighbor on the stairs, a morose bespectacled girl. She would say that someone was waiting for him.

"This tiny slip of a girl, with gorgeous hair," the neighbor would add, eyeing the feather suspiciously. And of course, she would be immensely surprised when the untamed loner, the standoffish recluse in prosthetics, jumps at her and kisses her right there on the stairs, like a drunken reveler.

"And a feather in his hat!" she'd stress every time she tells the story. "Red nose, crazy eyes, and this huge feather!"

She would never admit that her neighbor seemed to her at that moment the most beautiful man in the world.

VOICES FROM THE OUTSIDES

Smoker

I still get asked about those events from time to time. Less frequently now compared to twenty or even fifteen years ago. But many do remember. It's amazing how many. They remember that I had something to do with that story and imagine that it somehow influenced my soul and my paintings.

I have met with quite a few of the former occupants of the House since graduation. Some have done pretty well for themselves and others barely scrape by. There are probably also those who are in pretty dire straits, but since they are not in the habit of attending my personal shows, I can't vouch for their existence. Of those who remained in the town, I know six. They meet regularly to wallow in memories, but I've never felt the need to join their company. There are none among them whom I'd really like to see. I actually see very few people, apart from Black.

I collected news clippings about the Sleepers for a while, but then abandoned the whole thing. It was too painful, thinking about them, imagining them. Easier to deal with the living or with the truly dead.

Horse

No, we none of us went to visit them. What's the point? Not even Red. First it was because we were lying low, and then there was too much to do. But I never wanted to anyway. We knew about them, I mean, who was where and stuff, but going there—no, that didn't happen.

Black

Honestly? I don't care about the Sleepers. I'm not even going to pretend that I'm griev-ing for them. It was their own choice, their decision, and the last thing I would do is drag myself over there clutching a bunch of carnations, drowning in snot around the corpses. Because let's face it, corpses is what they are. Living corpses who don't give a damn about any emotions coming from me. What would I be busting my tail for, then?

Red

I do visit them from time to time. No flowers, of course. Why shouldn't I? I even got myself a special permit. I didn't do it before because I didn't want to blow the cover on our guys, because naturally the "dormice" were under constant surveillance. Now that no one cares, I can do it. And I don't consider it to be perverted or anything. There's nothing scary about them. They don't wither, they don't waste away, they don't look like corpses at all. Besides, it's always fun to visit with old friends. I don't tell the guys about this. They might think themselves obliged to accompany me and start hating themselves for not wanting to. Nobody needs that.

Smoker

Lary and Needle moved to the suburbs. He is now a part owner of the repair shop where he started back then as a grease monkey. She's keeping the house. They have two kids, the eldest daughter got married recently. I was at the wedding, gave the newlyweds a picture. Not one of mine, though. Mine are not everyone's cup of tea. It was amusing to follow the expression on the bride's little face as the present was being unwrapped, and to note the look of relief when they could finally see it.

Lary and I never talk about the Sleepers or the vanished. We keep a knowing, competent, friendly silence about the subject if we happen to meet. But we do discuss other Outsides-mates, and he always has some exciting new piece of information for me because he tries to keep up with what's happening as much as he can. Horse and he are still very close, even though Horse is still living with the commune (the sect, let's be honest here) founded by the passengers of the bus and the Devout. It's a royal pain to drive all the way there, but Lary performs the pilgrimage at least every month. "In honor of past friendships," he says.

Needle

I've never said anything against old friends. Never told my husband he couldn't see someone he wanted to. But those trips are very hard on him. He's not himself for days afterward, almost as if he's ill, or something bad happens to him there. I am a mother. It's my duty to think about the children first. I surely don't want people blabbing around them that their father lived in that place, you know what I mean? I come from there myself, and I'm not ashamed to admit it, but it doesn't mean such things should be discussed with strangers. Nobody could say that I am not like everyone else. I am a normal woman, and that's exactly what the children need—normal, regular parents. And as for that commune . . . excuse me, but it is not a place where I would ever go myself, not that my opinion matters, of course. And they are not the people with whom I would want to have anything in common.

Hybrid

Oh for Pete's sake, we didn't do nothing! It's just that Red took it into his head that we should support the Sleepers. Those who were going completely unclaimed, at least. With no relatives. Because who knows, right? So we passed a plate around. We weren't doing too bad at the time, so we could've swung it ourselves, but we thought that maybe some of the guys would like to chip in. Nothing sinister. And then Needle made it look like we came to rob them. Of their last shirt, like. They're pretty well off, you know. And we helped them with everything we had in the very beginning, when they didn't know squat about how the Outsides worked. Two stupid kids in love! Right, whatever. Lary came afterward, with all kinds of excuses, brought a couple of coins. We never took anything from them. Imagine if she barged in right after him and demanded we give all of it back!

Smoker

I saw Red at the opening night of my latest exhibition. He lives in the same commune as Horse, and is considered a person of authority. Kind of like a respected elder. At first the whole affair was being run by the old night guard who had joined the fugitives after the graduation, but he's been long dead, leaving behind only his collection of broken clocks, so now Red is the big man there.

He looks like an aging rock star, fairly washed out but still deadly. Hair halfway down his back, a tattoo on his forehead, a necklace of dangerous-looking claws. He generated way more interest than my paintings ever could. All the photos from the exhibition featured Red, from different angles, and the paintings only ended up in a shot because he happened to be staring at them. The poor photographers just couldn't keep their lenses off him, and I totally understand them.

Red's got eight children (he swears that they're all from his wife), four dogs, two horses, and a flock of sheep. He showed me pictures of all of them except the latter, and it would have been a nicely satisfying day had he not picked a fight with my manager. It was a messy, juicy scandal, and there were too many reporters hanging around to let it go to waste. Red was raring to go, calling Black a traitor and a renegade, and it took no small effort to shut him down, and an even bigger one to explain to the curious what these two possibly could have had in common with each other.

Black

I know many people consider me a traitor. So what? I couldn't just stand by and watch that shyster pull for his side at our expense day after day. I should have smelled it from the start. Two former Leaders in one place. But I thought I had it under control. I had the numbers, six of mine against three Rats. But then some of them went away, some things changed, and before I knew it Red was already on top, and it was too late to roll it back. He's made a neat little profit for himself, I'm sure. It wasn't an easy time for the commune, but we would've gotten our stuff together even without his financial shenanigans. Hard work and a steady hand, that's all we needed.

Smoker

Red was the only one to try and talk to me about the Sleepers. After the fight we holed up in the bar across from the exhibition hall. Holding an ice pack to his shiner, he told me with a significant smirk that there were fewer Sleepers now. A lot fewer.

"How's that?" I said. "They woke up?"

"No. They vanished. The first couple of cases they wrote about, but since then mum's the word. Don't you read the papers?"

I don't read papers and I don't watch TV, but I decided not to elaborate on that. It wasn't a pleasant topic even by itself, and Red's smugness only added to it. The whole thing reminded me of that time when I asked a lot of questions and received no answers, until it almost drove me crazy. So I didn't ask. Not about who vanished, not about where they went. Red was obviously expecting my questions, and when he realized he wasn't getting any, he soured and quickly left. I haven't seen him since.

Red

If you ask me, he's gotten too bigheaded. All those exhibitions, reporters. I mean, he's a nice guy, but a bit too jumpy for my taste. "Devoted to his Art," Old Man would've said.

I like him, I respect him, I value him and so on, but he's not getting out in the fresh air enough. And there's no air in his pictures either.

Smoker

I see Sphinx only rarely. He's a child psychologist now, working in a boarding school for the blind and legally blind. Or maybe not anymore. An exceedingly strange person. Never misses my exhibitions. Visits the Sleepers. Tags along with my father when he goes fishing.

He can show up tanned in the middle of the winter and bring a yellow-blue butterfly in a glass case as a present. His wife is a bit of a mystery—one day she's there with him, the next day she isn't anywhere, and her disappearances can last for months. He's got the most unusual dog in the world—a German shepherd guide dog that is trained to train other German shepherd guide dogs. I have inquired specifically with people who know about these things and they all say that it simply cannot exist. He also keeps an owl. And collects antique musical instruments.

In the last ten years he twice received inheritances from some murky sources. For some reason he doesn't think it at all strange. He didn't even try to find out who those people were. I have no idea how he spent all that money, all I know is that it didn't make him a penny richer.

They are very tight with my father. I suspect it's at his prompting Sphinx comes to visit me at the low points in my life, to frolic in the fields of compassionate psychology. I dutifully pretend that it's helping me. Except when I don't.

Smoker's Father

I decided then that I was going to stick with the guy until he gets his feet under him. When we first met he was going through a very rough patch. I don't know how many years it took me to figure out that I needed him way more than he needed me. We'd just go fishing. Or to the movies. Listen to the music of my youth, look at the photographs of my girlfriends, talk about my son. Only later did it dawn on me who was humoring whom. I don't know how he did it. That's just the way he is, always giving more than he receives. He understood that I desperately wanted to take care of someone, and did the one thing that Eric never had—gave me the permission. With him I feel like a real father. And a friend. I quit drinking, I'm a vegetarian now, I dropped thirty pounds and twenty years. Now you tell me, which one of us was saving the other?

Horse

Sphinx came exactly three times. First when they'd just sniffed us out, you know, "established the whereabouts of a group of the former boarding-school students who had disappeared without a trace" and so on. Like it wasn't us who allowed them to. We decided to legalize our status, that's all. We finally were of age and no longer afraid of parents swooping in. We had just one house for all of us, and one barn. We ate whatever came our way, slept in our clothes to save on heating, and worked. Day and night, like we were obsessed. He was here for a couple of hours. Said hello to everyone, sat down to dinner with us, and left. Some were imagining he came to stay, but not me. I saw that he only needed to make sure we were all right. And he didn't want to upset Black. Because Black was panicked, even if he didn't show it. The second visit was six, maybe seven years later, I can't say for sure. That time he was with us a while. Maybe because Black was no longer here. But it was still clear he wasn't staying. I asked him, joking like, when he was moving in. "To do what? Farm with prosthetics or mooch off your work?" he said. And the third time that thing happened.

Red

I always knew Sphinx had one good turn in him. That he didn't stay back just because. I remembered that he'd received something from Jackal that no one else had, before or since. If anyone were to get Tabaqui to hand him something that none of us common folk could even dream of, it was Sphinx, no doubt about that. It was also clear that he was going to use that present sooner or later, and I thought that's when I'd get to know what it was. But it took so long to finally happen that by that time, I'd almost forgotten how much I wanted to find out.

Smoker

It was my second show that made me famous. So much fuss, I've never been able to replicate it since. On the one hand, it hurts that the later works remain underappreciated, but on the other it's more important that I know them to be stronger. I'm not ashamed of the earlier paintings, but when you're twenty-two you tend to bare your soul a little too eagerly, and also amateurishly at times. It makes you somehow uneasy, looking at them afterward. Uneasy at yourself, and at the fact that it's exactly the amateurishness that gets people so excited. I am wiser now, and so are my paintings. The only detail that keeps reappearing again and again, dragging over from the old times, is the stuffed bear. I still can't get rid of it. It just learned to hide better, that's all. On the latest canvases it's been painted over. It's not visible. But it is still there, lurking under the layers of paint. Probably one day I may be able to leave it behind, even though for me it has long become something of a spooky talisman, an insurance policy, guaranteeing long life for the paintings.

Smoker's Father

He liked those of Eric's paintings that I didn't understand at all. For example, the works of his stripy period, as I call it. Circles within circles with triangles encroaching on them, all that geometry. All in black and white. Even the infamous teddy bear morphed into a pile of triangles. Sphinx stood in front of one of them for forty minutes, I'm not kidding.

It was on the day after the opening. We always went when the crowds thinned out. I walked around the collection once, twice. When after the third loop I found him still stuck in front of the same picture, he turned to me and said, "You know, Smoker took more of the House with him than he thinks."

The painting was of those same tired black-and-white circles. Edge to edge. It looked like nothing so much as a dartboard, complete with a dart stuck in it.

"I'm sorry," I said. "I guess I just don't get modern art. Especially of this kind."

"Time does not flow like a river. A river that you can't enter twice," Sphinx said. "It is more like circles on the surface of the water. That's a quote, I didn't invent that."

He raised his gloved artificial hand and pointed at the dart in the middle of the target.

"And if into those circles you drop something, say, a feather, like it is here, it would generate its own circles, you see? Small, weak ones, almost invisible . . . But they will expand and intersect with the large ones."

I tried to visualize what he was talking about. I felt like Winnie-the-Pooh, a Bear of Very Little Brain. I probably even started to smell of moldy stuffing.

"So you think that is what it is?" I said, staring at what stubbornly refused to become anything but a dartboard.

He nodded. His face was lit up by inspiration, like some insane prophet's. At times like that I always get a sneaking suspicion I'm being hypnotized.

"If you were this feather, where in the past would you have wanted to drop? What would you change?"

This got me depressed. What would I change in my own past if I could? Everything, for a start. But I doubt that anything good could come out of it anyway.

"I'd have to be dropping nonstop," I said. "There are too many places."

"You've got one shot," he insisted. "One single shot."

"Then I wouldn't bother. My life can't be changed in one shot."

He switched off the mesmerism.

"You don't understand," he said, turning away. "Your life can't be changed, period. It's already half-lived. The only thing you could do is go to a different loop. Where you would not be the exact same you."

"Why would I want to change something there?" I said. "If it wouldn't mean a change here."

The damned tie was biting into my neck. All I wanted to do at that point was to go away from this place. I guess Sphinx noticed the state I was in.

"Let's go," he said. "You're turning red."

And we left. Eric wasn't at the show that day. Or I would have asked him a couple of things.

Horse

When we saw him we didn't put two and two together at first. I mean, sure, we realized that the boy was the spitting image of Blind. But we couldn't imagine it was really him. I mean, think about it. Would you if you were in our place? Would anyone?

Hybrid

So this one time Sphinx shows up, and he's not alone. Climbs out of the car, cracks open the rear door, and pulls out this scarecrow. Thin as a rail, and all covered in some kind of nasty rash. All of ours already had the chickenpox and all that, so we don't sweat it, make it look like we don't notice even. And it's clear as day who he looks like. Makes you feel uneasy, like you saw someone carrying a photograph of his late wife with him everywhere. You don't exactly come out and say it, right? So we don't. But the kids get to him right away, because he looks such a city slicker in his white sneakers and his stickered shirt, they can't help themselves. So they gather around and start discussing his clothes, his rash, how he can't even move he's so scared. Teasing him.

But not that hard, you know. I decide to knock some sense into them, because he's a guest and that's not the way to treat guests, and I take a step toward them, and then someone, I guess it was Red's youngest, pulls at his sleeve. And that's when it hit the fan.

Horse

He lost his dark glasses in the melee, and then it was obvious. To anyone. I mean, anyone who'd ever seen Blind. At least that's what I thought. I was wrong. Termite, for example, did not get it.

"Oh, look!" he said. "Blind's little boy! Would you look at that, a perfect likeness!"

I wasn't going to argue with him. Heredity is now one of his favorite topics. How nurture's got nothing on nature.

The kids were so upset when they saw they were picking on an unsighted that we didn't even need to tell them off.

But Sphinx took his boy behind the barn and gave him a good scolding. To tell you the truth, I couldn't help it and peeked a bit, to see what was up. And I wasn't alone. Red got there first. So we see Sphinx blabbing his head off, and the kid just stands there, calm as could be. Maybe listening, maybe not, no way to tell.

"Poor Sphinx," I whisper to Red.

"Depends on the point of view," Red shoots back. "Didn't you get lectured about the proper way to behave when you were a kid? Didn't that make you want to throw up?"

"What would you have done in Sphinx's place?"

"Told him that it was a brave thing to do," Red says without pausing even for a second. "And to keep standing up for himself."

"What? You mean, him?" I say, aghast. "Tell *him* to keep it up? This guy here?"

Red stares at me strange like. And asks if I am really as stupid as I look.

What do you say when someone insults you to your face? I turned around and left.

Red

After we packed the goons off to bed, Horse got off the phone and I stopped fretting about the size of the long-distance bill that was bound to arrive after his intimate chat with Lary, that is, after things calmed down a bit and Sphinx and I were the only ones left out on the deck, I asked him where he'd dug up that boy.

"Where he no longer is," he said, in the best tradition of the Fourth.

"Thank you for that informative answer," I said. "What are you trying to prove by this, and to whom? That's what I'd like to know."

We were drinking hard cider, legs up on the railing. We didn't turn the lights on, so that the nightlife wouldn't get any ideas.

"All I want is to undo some mistakes made by one good man," he said.

It sounded . . . normal. Like something that happens. Something that we all should be doing from time to time. Then he said that I would've done the same thing. If I'd had that chance.

When he said that, I had to work hard to bring my imagination to heel. Because why not? I've got four daughters, three of them gingers, and I know which one I love just a little bit more, and why. Even though the resemblance is mostly in my head.

"Maybe," I said. "But this is different."

He shrugged. I couldn't say for certain in the dark, but I think he was smiling.

"To each his own," he said.

"Yeah," I said. "But to each not the same acquaintances."

He flinched and spilled his cider.

"Shhh," I said. "I didn't say I blamed you. That was just envy, pure and simple. A very common phenomenon."

We sat there silently for a while, finished what was left in the bottles, and I felt a sinister prophecy coming up.

"You're going to catch a lot of grief with this guy."

"I know," he said. "I know that. It's just that I wanted him to learn to love this world. Even a little. As much as I could teach him to."

I guess it was cruel of me, because now he couldn't have changed anything even if he wanted to.

"He will learn to love you," I said. "And for him you are going to be the whole damn world."

He didn't say anything for so long that I realized he was afraid of the same thing. But he's a stubborn guy, and it was clear he wasn't going to back down. He'll prove his point, to someone who would never know about it, or die trying. Funny, isn't it.

I didn't even ask about the rash on the boy. I got it. The House put its mark on him. In advance, in anticipation of losing him and before he could end up there. I didn't tell Sphinx that.

"Right. Well, good luck," I said instead. "If you ever change your mind, you're welcome to stay. We've got loads of kids, all of them crazy. A little changeling would blend right in."

In the morning they left. I watched them walk to the car, and I swear I couldn't decide which one I pitied more. Sphinx, I guess. He has a history of attempting the impossible. And it doesn't always work out in the end for him, not by a long shot.

Black

That's all bullshit, and I'm sick of hearing it. I'm a grown man, not a baby who day-dreams about hopping into a time machine and bringing back a small dinosaur for a pet. And if someone's half-cocked brain is coupled with a sick sense of humor, I don't see why the rest of us should sing along. I have no clue where Sphinx got that boy, and I don't give a damn. Like there's a shortage of undernourished blind orphans in the world, even if they also have black hair and white eyes. Yes, he could even be Blind's, so? No one knows where he is or what he's been up to. He could have rattled off a dozen mole rats like that. What he could never do is become a decent father.

As for Sphinx, he's just the kind of man to turn any little thing into a planetary event. Into something mysterious and idiotic. He's always been like that, since he was little. Drag in some piece of slime and go, "Ooh, look, the aliens left this!" I wouldn't be at all surprised if it turned out he stole that kid. That's his style. He even managed to steal someone else's father, and that's got to be harder to pull off.

Smoker's Father

Of course I've heard the talk. And of course it's all made up. They are rather mystically oriented, those guys from the commune. Sphinx starting those rumors himself? He never did. The kid's parents put the boy in his care for the summer, and then either the boy got used to him, or the parents decided it would be more useful to not take him back right away. It's always advisable for children like that to have as much access to a specialist as possible. Adoption? Nonsense, have you any idea how much of an effort it is now to adopt? Especially for someone like Sphinx. And I am sorry, I'm not even going to discuss kidnapping.

Eric says the boy doesn't really look like who everyone says he does. "Nothing in common." Those were his exact words. And I believe him.

Smoker

I'm seeing very few people. I have many questions, but I'm not asking them. Never. There are times when I think Black knows the answers, but just as I'm about to ask he gives me this miserable look and changes the subject so abruptly that I can't bring up the courage to say it. He's so vulnerable then, it's scary. I don't want to blow holes in the protective shell he's spent so much time and effort to build and maintain.

I have even less desire to go asking Sphinx. In his case it's the very real possibility of receiving the answers that's frightening. It's too iffy between us as it is. I like him, but I can't get over the fact that he has been given a choice. A choice I have been denied. And no matter how friendly he tries to be, his world will always be different. Not the same as Black's and mine. We can never forgive him for that.

THE HAPPY BOY

In the room they call Stuffage, a seven-year-old boy woke up one early morning. At first he thought that it was a bad dream that made him wake up. He lay there with his eyes shut tight, trying to remember what was so disturbing that he saw, but the dream kept slipping away, not letting him catch it, until the boy got tired of chasing it.

When he opened his eyes he was astonished at the sudden change in his mood. He was usually gloomy and irritable in the mornings. But not today. This morning felt wonderful. He looked around the room with an unexpected and unfamiliar delight. Looked at the roommates, their heads buried in the pillows, at the clumsy drawings on the walls, at the pink blot of the sky in the windows thrown wide open, and finally, with a strange longing in the pit of his stomach—at the head of his brother on the other edge of the pillow. The head that was an almost exact copy of his own. The boy knew that this wondrous feeling was going to disappear soon, and in the hopes of making it linger just a while longer he shook his brother awake.

The brother opened his eyes. Round and bugging, they didn't close completely even in his sleep. That glinting sliver between the lashes, making it look as if he wasn't really asleep but just faking it, annoyed everyone. Except his twin, who had the exact same peculiarity.

"What?" the brother who just woke up whispered.

"I'm not sure," the boy said, also in a whisper. "I'm feeling kinda strange. Kinda liking everything, very much, so much I want to cry. Do you have it too?"

The brother searched inside himself.

"No," he said, yawning. "Not yet. Could be because I'm still sleeping."

And he closed his eyes hurriedly.

The boy lowered his head onto his end of the pillow and tried to go back to sleep. The joy that had been overflowing inside him was not going away. He pressed his palm against his heart, as if probing it through the skin. Cradling it.

He did not know yet that this feeling would stay with him for a very long time. It would become less sharp, almost mundane, but at times would strike him again with the same unexpected force, like a soft blow, making him gasp in wonderment, filling his eyes with tears and his soul with delight. He also didn't know that he and his twin were now and forever different from each other. That he would always look older. "More corrupt," Black Ralph would say. When the boy overheard that, he wouldn't be offended. That would be another new feature of his character—nothing much would be able to offend him anymore.

THE
ENCOUNTER

Room number twenty-four is under a reign of terror since early morning. It is not the cheeriest of rooms even under normal circumstances. All the wheelers who did not leave for the summer have been living in it, the seniors and the juniors together. There aren't that many of them, only six, but the two nurses who remained in the House have been running ragged taking care of this bunch.

The seniors are beset with the ailments that prevented them from going, racked with envy of those who did go, and tormented by their own petty needs, by the fact that they have been deprived of the familiar dorms and sent to the room that was considered cursed because its windows were looking out into the street instead of the yard, the way they were supposed to in decent dorms. And also by the necessity to share this room, unpleasant as it is by itself, with the juniors. The presence of juniors is what irks them the worst. Especially one of the juniors.

The juniors suffer from all of that too, but unlike the seniors they don't have anyone at whom they can vent their frustration.

All six of them are terror professionals in their own right, but none can compare to Stinker, can't even come close. Stinker is in a category of one. His aptitude for terror is otherworldly. He is a peerless prodigy, capable of dealing death for a mere sideways glance, in lieu of a smack upside the head. Moreover, the death would leave him above any suspicion, and be visited upon the victim by means of cutting-edge technology, utilizing the latest inventions, including his own, implemented meticulously and lovingly, by weapons such as the world has never seen, based on his unique research in the fields of physics, chemistry, and mathematics, with side trips into history and biology. Stinker is an expert in all these fields, but his grades are still poor, because he has no time to parade his knowledge before the teachers. There are things infinitely more important that demand his attention. The seniors never pick on Stinker. They never say anything bad about him at all, even in private. Listening devices are Stinker's specialty, and he is constantly at work refining and perfecting them.

Scolding and punishing him is something that's reserved exclusively for the nurses. "There is something motherly about it," Stinker likes to say. "Something warm, fuzzy, and creepily nostalgic." It's been noticed that the older and homelier the nurse, the more he is prone to using this phrase.

Such is Stinker, a living horror all of nine years old.

Which is why, when one unfortunate morning he shakes everyone awake before dawn and proceeds to tear apart the room, preparing for the Event, no one dares to say a word.

Stinker does not deign to explain himself. He constructs a watchtower. The table, pushed against the window, serves as its base. On the table he mounts several pillows and the tripod for the spyglass, then installs himself, surrounded by cookies, binoculars, party poppers, and tissues. The two juniors dutifully paint letters on the white canvas stitched together from a cut-up sheet. Stinker leans down from his post at regular intervals, evaluates their progress, and exhorts them to work faster. The seniors flee the room in an attempt to get some rest.

Breakfast is served to Stinker directly at his post. The nurses, spooked by his increasing nervousness, attach the finished *Welcome!* sign to the window and wheel the juniors away to scrub the paint off them.

Stinker frets, more and more as the time passes. By midday he becomes dangerously sullen. The nurses bring out the smelling salts and disappear in the bowels of the House with the terrified juniors in tow. Seniors return and watch Stinker with increasing curiosity. He distributes the party poppers and orders them to be shot out of the window at his command. The seniors prepare. Judging by Stinker's defeated look the Event has not happened, and is increasingly unlikely to happen, so when they suddenly hear his hysterical "Fire!" two of them simply drop the poppers, and only one reflexively pulls on the string.

Stinker, waving the spyglass, performs the triple "Hooray!" wiping off the tears streaming down his face, and snarls at the seniors, "What are you staring at? Never seen happiness before?" Then he detonates the reserve cracker, showering the senior who climbed up on the window in confetti.

They walk slowly. The boy shuffling a little behind, the woman bent under the weight of the suitcase. They are both wearing white, both are fair-haired, tinting almost to red, both seem slightly taller than one would expect: the boy, incongruous with his age, the woman, with her femininity. The boy drags his feet, catching the sneakers against each other, and keeps his eyes half-closed so that he can see only the gray pavement bubbling in the heat and the marks being left on it by his mother's heels.

He also sees the scattered confetti. Bright, shiny dots on the gray background. He walks around, taking care not to step on them, not to dull their luster. In doing so he bumps into his mother and stops.

"This must be the place."

The woman lowers the suitcase to the ground. The squat gray bulk of the House looms in front of them, a breach, a rotted tooth in the dazzling row of the snow-white houses on both sides of it. The woman takes off the sunglasses and studies the sign on the door.

"Yes, this is it. You see? We got here in no time at all. No need to take a taxi for such a trifle, right?"

The boy nods indifferently. The building looks grim to him.

"Look, Mom . . . ," he begins, but then there is a muffled explosion and a snow of confetti. The boy takes a step back, looking in surprise at the fresh portion of the rainbow-colored dots on the asphalt. They are also on his clothes and in his hair. He runs back so he can peek into the windows of the House, and imagines that he can hear someone inside it, someone whom he cannot see from below, hoarsely shout "Hooray!"

ABOUT THE AUTHOR

Photo © Artashes Stamboltsyan

Mariam Petrosyan was born in 1969 in Yerevan, Armenia. In 1989 she graduated with a degree in applied arts and worked in the animation department of Armenfilm movie studio. In 1992 she moved to Moscow to work at Soyuzmultfilm studio, then returned to Yerevan in 1995.

The Gray House is Petrosyan's debut novel. After working on it for eighteen years, she published it in Russia in 2009, and it became an instant bestseller, winning several of the year's top literary awards, including the Russian Prize for the best book in Russian by an author living abroad. The book has been translated into French, Spanish, Italian, Polish, Czech, Hungarian, and Lithuanian.

In interviews Petrosyan frequently says that readers should not expect another book from her, since, for her, *The Gray House* is not merely a book but a world she knew and could visit, and she doesn't know another one.

Petrosyan is married to Armenian artist Artashes Stamboltsyan. They have two children.

ABOUT THE TRANSLATOR

Born in Moscow, Yuri Machkasov studied for a career as a theoretical physicist before moving to the United States in 1991. He lives in the Boston area and works as a software developer. Yuri has translated several books into Russian for Livebook Publishing, among them the Carnegie Medal winner *Maggot Moon* by Sally Gardner. He has also translated poetry from Russian into English, including the work of the Moscow poet Vera Polozkova.